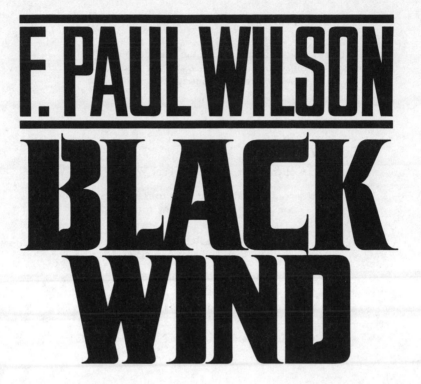

F. PAUL WILSON

BLACK WIND

A TOM DOHERTY ASSOCIATES BOOK
NEW YORK

BLACK WIND
Copyright © 1988 by F. Paul Wilson

A TOR BOOK
Published by Tom Doherty Associates, Inc.
49 West 24 Street
New York, NY 10010

ISBN: 0-312-93064-X

Library of Congress Catalog Card Number: 87-51401

First edition: September 1988

0 9 8 7 6 5 4 3 2 1

ACKNOWLEDGMENTS

This novel could not have been completed without the generous assistance of the following people:

Sue Burkhart
E. Scott Royce
Derrell Smith
Chelsea Quinn Yarbro

AUTHOR'S NOTE

Captain Ellis M. Zacharias, General Leslie R. Groves, General Curtis LeMay, and Admiral Isoroku Yamamoto are historical figures who appear as characters here. To varying degrees (least of all with Captain Zacharias, who is on record as having issued the warnings he gives in this novel, more so with Generals Groves and LeMay) I have taken dramatic license with their participation in some of the events described in this novel. However, every possible effort has been made to keep the work historically accurate.

In Japan, the surname is customarily given first. For the sake of clarity, I have reversed the order in *Black Wind*.

Finally, no remnant of the Kakureta Kao is known to exist in modern-day Japan.

FOREWORD

SLATER-SAN PLANTATION
MAUI

This is a posthumous memoir. Long ago I gave my word not to utter a word of this story for as long as I lived. Strange to be sitting here writing this now and knowing that if someone is reading it, I'm dead.

So be it: Here's the story of the late Frank Slater—me. It's not going to be easy to tell.

Mostly it's about the War. Not those skirmishes in Korea and Vietnam. The Big One. WWII.

It concerns the Kakureta Kao, a mystical order of monks who were instrumental in fueling the war and committing some ghastly atrocities during its course.

It also concerns two Japanese—a man and a woman. The woman I have loved more than life itself. The man I grew up with, loved like a brother, and then deserted when he most needed me.

I told you this wasn't going to be easy.

But it will be true. It will be the truest damn thing you've ever read. Whatever else you've heard or read that contradicts what I say here is a lie. People have said otherwise but they were telling lies—maybe not deliberate lies, but repeating lies created by others who needed to safeguard their reputations or their places in history.

This is the *real* truth.

I know because I was there. And if I wasn't on the spot every moment, I got it straight from someone who was, or from documents that once belonged to the Kakureta Kao.

This is my testament. I'm writing it to set the record straight once and for all. And I'm arranging for it to be released immediately after my death when I'm finally beyond their reach, when they can't threaten or cajole or coerce me into retracting a single word.

They . . .

Even as I dictate this, I hear that word, *they*, and I think to myself: *You sound paranoid, Frank.*

Maybe so. Read on. Decide for yourself. It's about war and peace, about honor and betrayal, about searching for and finding your place in the world. It's about me. It's about my boyhood friend, Matsuo Okumo, and about the woman we both loved.

It's all true.

I swear it.

(signed) Francis Xavier Slater, Jr.

It begins with Matsuo who, as a teenager, had many troubled nights . . .

PART ONE

1926

1926

THE YEAR OF THE TIGER

A slithering sound awoke him.

Matsuo shot up to a crouch on the *futon* and strained to see through the room's inky blackness.

Not again! Please, not again!

Out of the darkness the voices began their whispering.

"Are you the one? The one who bears the seeds? Are you the one to die?"

And then he saw them, limned by the faint light from the hallway, wizened, near-naked forms with bare, glistening scalps. Their faces were dark blanks except for an occasional shining pair of eyes. They all carried knives that gleamed in the darkness.

All except one. A tall, gaunt, hooded figure stood in the bedroom door. Its face too was entirely in shadow except for a pair of glowing eyes, burning softly as the creatures inched toward him along the floor.

Some crawled, some crept, some dragged themselves along, and one writhed along the floor toward Matsuo with a knife blade clamped between his teeth in an obscene parody of a snake. They slithered closer, their voices rising.

"Yes! He's the one who bears the seeds! He dies! He dies now! Kill him!"

One reared up and thrust his dagger unerringly toward Matsuo's throat—

—and he woke up gasping, trembling, drenched with sweat.

The dream again! For a few months it had stopped, but now it was back. *Only a dream,* he kept telling himself, but he could not escape the terror or stop his trembling. He did not want to be alone but he could not tell Nagata. He had described the dream to him once and had been told never to mention it again. It was the first time he had ever seen the old *samurai* afraid.

Only one thing ever helped. Matsuo crept out of his room to the small Shinto shrine where Nagata kept his *daisho*—his pair of samurai swords. Daisho—it meant "Big-Little," a perfect name for the blades. He placed his hand on the bigger sword, the *katana,* and felt his trembling cease and the terror fade away. Now he felt safe. He did not know what it was about these swords, but they never failed to give him comfort. He lifted the katana—it was heavy, almost ten pounds—and carried the sword back to his room where he laid it on the futon next to him.

Sleep was slow in returning, but with his hand resting on the pearl inlay of the black enameled scabbard, he knew if he was patient it would come. And when it did, it would be peaceful.

■   ■   ■

My folks called me Frankie. The kids called me Spot.

On the morning of July 10, my sixteenth birthday, I stood in front of the bathroom mirror and stared at the source of my nickname. I'd done this countless times. I didn't see my ears, nose, mouth—none of which were remarkable. Nor did I see my blue eyes or sandy brown hair.

Only that awful purple mark.

It's known in my family as the Slater Stain. All Slater males carry it on their faces to varying degrees. The medical books call it a capillary hemangioma, which tells you nothing. Granma Slater always called it a "port wine stain," which pretty much captures the look of it. Imagine spilling a glass of burgundy onto a white linen tablecloth and letting it sit there overnight. That's a good picture of the Slater Stain.

My father and my uncles had little ones, barely visible at their hairlines. I had all the luck. Mine was as wide as my hand and it ran up from my left upper eyelid, through my hairline, to the top of my scalp.

No words can convey the loathing I felt for that mark. I tried combing my hair over it, but my hair would never quite reach. I even went so far once as to borrow my mother's makeup powder to cover it, but the result was hideous. I would have peeled that purple skin right off my face if I hadn't known that the resulting scar would have left me even more disfigured.

There were times when I cried over that mark. And over the nickname it brought me. It was the thing that kept me from being a regular chum, one of the boys. It was the only thing keeping me out of Mick McGarrigle's gang. He'd like me if not for that. And so would the girls.

And so I stood there, dreaming someone would come along and offer me a birthday wish. Anything I wanted: gold, jewels, power, fame. My heart's desire. There wouldn't be a moment's hesitation. I knew exactly what I'd wish for.

"Frankie!"

I recognized the voice: Matsuo, calling from outside. Matsuo never called me Spot.

I stuck my head out the bathroom window. I was on the second floor. Matsuo was standing on the grass over to the left below my bedroom window.

"Hello, below!"

"Want to come over?" he said, his amber Japanese face tilting up. He was smiling, but his eyes looked a little hollow, like he hadn't been sleeping too well. He was dressed like me, in a short-sleeve shirt and knee-length pants.

I had few friends. In fact, to be honest, I had only one. And most likely I would not have been friends with Matsuo if he hadn't lived here on the grounds of my family home. I was that shy.

"I can't today. My father's taking me sailing." The new Lightning had arrived last week and Dad was going to start teaching me how to sail.

"Come out till he gets back."

"Back?" I had a sinking feeling. "Where'd he go?"

Matsuo shrugged. "I just saw him driving out."

I ran downstairs. Mom was in the dining room where everything was mahogany and crystal, talking to Oba-san. Mom's hair was twisted up in countless tight little curlers. Her face looked tight and pinched without her hair around it. She was sitting at the long table under the chandelier, smoking a cigarette in a little ivory holder and going over a list with Oba-san.

"Happy birthday, Master Frankie!" Oba-san said in her thickly accented English. She smiled and bowed.

I bowed back. *"Arigato."*

"Yes, darling," Mom said, wrapping an arm around my waist and giving me a quick hug. "Happy sixteenth."

"Arigato," I said again.

"Speak English, dear."

"I like speaking Japanese."

"You do Oba-san no service by speaking Japanese to her. She's in America now and wants to learn to speak English. Isn't that right, Oba-san?"

Oba-san said, "Yes, ma'am," to Mom but winked at me.

Oba-san was an ever-cheerful woman. The normally slimming effect of a *kimono* was lost on her portly frame. She was our cook as well as Matsuo's aunt. Her real name was Kimura, but Matsuo had called her Oba-san—*oba* being the Japanese word for "aunt"—as long as anyone could remember and that was now her name around our house.

"Where's Dad?"

"He had to meet with Commander Foster."

I felt a lump swelling in my throat. "But we were supposed to go sailing!"

"Oh, darling, he didn't forget. It's just that there were some last minute problems with this new contract and he had to iron them out. I hate it when they bother him with business matters on the weekend but he had to go."

I hated it, too. Dad was always getting called away.

"Maybe this afternoon," I said.

"I'm afraid it will be too late then, dear. You know we've got all these people coming for cocktails and dinner at five. There won't be time. But he'll make it up to you. You know that."

Trouble was, I didn't know any such thing.

"And as soon as he comes back, we'll have your birthday cake. Okay?"

"Okay." I didn't have much choice.

"Swell. Now you just go out and play for a while. I've got to plan tonight's menu with Oba-san."

I waved and ran outside, determined to hide my disappointment. I had been waiting all week for today: my birthday, sailing with my dad, just the two of us on the water with no phones and no telegrams.

I walked to the ocean edge of the yard and looked down to where the brand-new Lightning sat on rollers on the thin strip of beach fifty feet below. There was a sob hiding somewhere within me. I didn't look for it. I had learned from Matsuo and Nagata that the face within is not the face for the world.

Matsuo came running up. "You're not going sailing at all?" he said when he stopped beside me.

I guess I still needed practice keeping my two faces separate. I shook my head, not yet ready to trust myself to speak.

"I think you made a good decision," Matsuo said, shading his eyes as he looked out over the Pacific. "It looks choppy. Too much wind to learn sailing. Wise to wait until tomorrow when it will be calmer."

I looked north past the deep brown stone of the Presidio to where the morning sun lit the fog flowing through the Golden Gate, then out to the misty Pacific that was calm and gently rolling toward shore under an easterly breeze that couldn't have topped five knots.

I glanced at Matsuo and had to smile. This was the truest friend a fellow could ever have.

He had a lean face and body, dark brown eyes, and short black hair. He was my age and almost as tall. Only in the past year had I begun to stretch past him in height, and only by half an inch at that. But while I clomped along, Matsuo moved like a cat. His mind was as agile as his body and he spoke English as well as any American. And why not? He may have been born in Japan, but he grew up here. He had been speaking English almost as long as I had.

I threw my arm over his shoulder. "What does Nagata-san have in store for us today, chum?"

"*Ikebana.*"

"Again?"

I disliked the lessons in flower arranging. They seemed sissyish. So did the *origami* lessons in paper folding, but at least they were fun. I say *seemed* sissyish because nothing Nagata did could by any stretch be called sissyish. If he wanted to teach us flower arranging and the tea ceremony and anything else, I would go along just to be in his presence and hear the tales he told.

As we climbed the outside stairs to the rooms over the two-car garage, I peeked into the window to see if Dad had taken the Franklin. Yes, it was gone. Dad loved his new Series 11 sedan and never missed a chance to show it off to his customers. After all, it cost almost three thousand dollars.

We reached the second floor and stopped on the landing to take off our shoes. The garage used to be a stable and on hot days like this you could still catch a whiff of horse odors drifting up from the ground floor like restless ghosts from the past. Nagata's *furin* hung from the eave over the stairs and tinkled delicately in the breeze. Instead of the usual three, I noticed a fourth wind chime.

"A new furin?"

"Yes." Matsuo reached up and removed it from its hook. "For you," he said, extending it toward me. "For your birthday."

A brass bell, hammered into a shape that roughly resembled a fish, hung by a fine wire from the center of a free-floating pagoda roof; suspended from the bell's clapper by another wire was an elaborate brass ideogram that caught the breeze and swung the clapper: music.

"I made it myself," Matsuo said. "Nagata-san taught me how."

I took it and clapped him on the shoulder with my other hand. I was touched. "Arigato," I said. "I know just where to hang it." It would go right outside my bedroom window where the breeze off the Pacific would keep it ringing.

I followed Matsuo into the servant quarters where he lived with his aunt, Oba-san, and his uncle, the family gardener, Takijiro Nagata. Those rooms were another reality, a spacious, spartan world of bare white walls, spare, low-slung tables, and floor cushions; a world full of light and air where shoes were left behind and bare feet trod the creaking, rush-covered straw *tatami* from one wall to the other; a world I had come to know and love far more than the streets of San Francisco outside.

Nagata rose and bowed from behind the low table where he had collected a group of potted gladiolas from the nursery, an assortment of leafy plants, some twigs, a mound of earth, and three empty vases. He spoke in Japanese, slowly, to be sure I could understand.

"I am honored you should come here on your birthday," he said. "May it be a most happy one."

I returned the bow as he had taught me many years ago and thanked him in Japanese.

We all knelt at the table and Matsuo and I began to follow Nagata's lead in the arrangements. We filled the vases with moist earth, for ikebana is not an art of death, but of life. We worked with living plants in their budding stage, listening to Nagata as he spoke of letting the essentials of the art flow through our eyes and arms and fingers to the vase, to the arrangement, to see the meaning in the point of a leaf, in the curve of a branch, in the open spaces left between, to achieve harmony in the juxtaposition of color and texture and emptiness.

As we worked, I kept glancing at Nagata who was a constant source of fascination for me. Such contrasts. His short thick fingers could work so delicately with the flowers and were a positive marvel with paper which he could fold into fragile birds and animals of infinite variety. Yet they could also lift huge chunks of lava stone in Dad's garden and twist and wire the trunks and branches of small trees into exotic weathered forms. He could weep at the beauty of a falling leaf, spend hours staring into the sunset over the Pacific or contemplating the surface of a stone.

But there was another side to him, one he kept hidden. One morning last spring, I was up early and spotted him in the dim light of dawn as he strode down the path to the beach at the bottom of the bluff. There, naked but for the brief white *fundoshi* girding his loins, his big belly protruding like a copper bowl, his face and balding scalp glistening with sweat, his arm and chest muscles bulging, he would wield his engraved katana in a dance of death. The gleaming sword would flash like lightning. He would fill the air with guttural cries as he defended himself against invisible enemies or attacked them with two-handed strokes of brutal grace that would surely have cut any flesh and blood opponent in half.

I had never imagined that a single human being could be so fierce and so deadly.

My father's gardener, the soft-spoken man who taught me paper folding and the tea ceremony and the Japanese language, was also a kind of killing machine. This stirred my imagination endlessly. I imagined that my father had secretly hired him to protect us, that by day he was a humble gardener but by the light of the moon he was a fierce samurai warrior who tirelessly prowled the grounds, keeping the household safe from whatever might threaten us. Since then I had spied on him many times.

"Tell us about the war again," Matsuo said as we arranged our blossoms.

"Again?" Nagata said. "Don't you ever tire of those stories?"

"Never!" we chorused.

He laughed and began the now-familiar tale of his part in the Japanese Third Army's assault on Port Arthur during the Russo-Japanese War in 1904. As usual he began with the sneak attack on the Russian fleet by Japanese torpedo boats that opened the hostilities, then proceeded to recount the bayonet charge that finally won the day at enormous cost. Nagata spoke feelingly of his disdain for the rifle and how he had joined the charge armed only with his two swords.

I glanced over at the small Shinto shrine—little more than a raised platform before a small painted screen in the corner—where his *daisho* sat on the black lacquered rack, the big katana mounted over the shorter *wakizashi*. To think that those swords had actually killed someone—many someones, according to Nagata, who claimed the blades were hundreds of years old.

Our flower arrangements were finally finished. Nagata's was beautiful, a perfect balance of budding gladiolas with leaves and arching twigs winding over and through the design. Next to his, Matsuo's and mine looked like wild brambles.

We all shared some cold rice balls and vegetables Oba-san had left behind. I cleaned my plate, especially my rice, remembering Oba-san's persistent warning that every wasted grain became a wart on a loved one's face.

When the meal was over, we stood and I bowed, offering my host the humblest of thank-yous. "*Katajikenai*, Nagata-san."

He bowed in return.

Then Matsuo said to me, "I have to go to work."

"So early?"

"Izumi-san wants me to give the store a good sweeping before it gets too crowded this afternoon."

I was disappointed. Now I'd have to spend the day alone. In the summer Matsuo worked in Japantown most mornings and every Saturday afternoon, but usually he didn't have to go in this early.

"Come with me."

"Oh, I don't know . . ." I got bored hanging around the store while Matsuo worked. I liked to practice my Japanese on the *issei* who bought vegetables at Izumi's *yao-ya,* but that got tiring after a while.

"Come *with* me, Frankie," Matsuo said with an intense expression.

"Sure," I said.

I hung my furin on the hook outside the door until later, got my shoes on, and followed Matsuo down the driveway. It was a fair distance to the sixteen or so square blocks on the southern slope of Pacific Heights known as Nihonmachi to its residents, Japantown to the rest of us.

We walked over toward California Street. The houses up here in Seacliff where I lived were big and new with lawns and gardens. They got smaller and closer together as we neared California Street where we stole aboard a passing cable car, clinging to the brass rail and squatting low on the back steps until the conductor spotted us and kicked us off. It was mostly downhill from Seacliff to Nihonmachi, but forty blocks is forty blocks.

We walked down the long slope for a while, eyes ahead to the long upward slope waiting for us. The sun was bright and hot, glaring off the sidewalks and the curved glass windows of the turrets of the Victorian houses lined side by side along our way. These were old, some falling apart, some in excellent repair. They had been old before we were born, survivors of the great quake and fire back in '03.

We were clinging to our third California Street cable car when we reached Japantown. I readied myself to jump off at Fillmore, but Matsuo grabbed my arm and shook his head. So we hung on all the way up the near-vertical slope of Nob Hill where the imposing bulks of Grace Cathedral and the Union Pacific Club and the ritzy hotels ruled. I could see the bay glittering behind the tower of the Ferry Building far below as we crested the hill and began the giddy descent. Matsuo nudged me off when we reached Powell Street.

"Where're we going?"

He smiled. "Follow me."

As usual, I did.

We hopped a southbound cable car for the steep ride down to Market Street where we jumped off again. I now had a pretty good idea what Matsuo had in mind. The guy was crazy about movies, and Market Street had most of the city's theaters—the President, the Imperial, the Capitol, the St. Francis, the Granada, the California, and the Golden Gate, all within a few blocks.

We were both immediately attracted by the posters at the St. Francis for *The Flaming Frontier*, all about Custer's last stand. The poster of Olive Borden in a sarong for *Yellow Fingers* at the California was tempting, but we kept looking.

The city was pancake flat down here and the walking was easy. We strolled up and down Market perusing the posters, and passed a small shop with a smashed front window. I could still read Nakamura

Laundry on the upper part of the glass. A board had been nailed up to cover the break, and someone had stuck a poster to the board. We stopped to read it:

JAPS

You came to care for lawns,
    we stood for it
You came to work in truck gardens,
    we stood for it
You sent your children to our public schools,
    we stood for it
You moved a few families in our midst,
    we stood for it
You try to open businesses in all our neighborhoods

BUT

WE WON'T STAND FOR IT
You impose more on us each day
until you have gone your limit
WE DON'T WANT YOU WITH US
SO GET BUSY JAPS, AND
GET OUT OF SAN FRANCISCO

I looked at Matsuo but his face was impassive. He glanced at me with a wry smile and shrugged.

"Some of Mr. Hearst's friends, I imagine."

I forced a laugh. This sort of thing embarrassed me. The Anti-Japanese Laundry League had been quieter since the Immigration Act reduced the Japanese quota to zero two years ago, but its nastiness still popped up once in a while. I supposed they were angry that the government hadn't kicked out the Japanese who were already here.

We walked on and, because of its suggestive poster, finally settled on Pola Negri in *Good and Naughty* at the Granada. There was a major problem, however.

"I'm broke," I said, checking my pockets. "How about you?"

"Me too," he said, but gave me a sly smile as he pulled a paper clip out of his pocket. "That never stopped us before."

Obviously, Matsuo had been planning on a matinee for a while. But he had to be sneaky about it—Nagata disapproved of movies.

"What about work?"

"I can be late."

I couldn't help laughing. "Let's go!"

We ran through the alley to the rear of the building where a warped old delivery door led to the basement. Matsuo straightened the paper clip, rebent it his own way, then began to play it in and out of the lock, twisting it this way and that with his eyes closed. Suddenly there came a soft click. The door swung open, and we were in. There hadn't been a live performance at the Granada for years so we were alone backstage with the dark and the dust. When the show started, we sneaked up into the ghost-lit area behind the screen and belly-crawled down from the stage to the seats. No one saw us.

We sat in the third row and watched Charlie Chaplin dunk a man's beard in soup. Matsuo laughed so hard I thought he would choke. His uncontrolled laughter got me going, too, until I was afraid the ushers would come by and ask us for our tickets. Chaplin always did that to him. I think the little man's complete lack of reserve and total disregard for common decorum outraged Matsuo's Japanese sensibilities to the point where he had to laugh hysterically or flee the theater.

Then came the feature. During the credits, Matsuo nudged me out of my seat and we trotted up a side aisle to the balcony stairs. Up in the loge, he reached into his shirt and pulled out a familiar green pack: Lucky Strikes. We lit one of the rumpled cigarettes and passed it back and forth between us. I practiced my smoke rings and Matsuo made no sound from then on. Pola Negri was on the screen and he was mesmerized. We finished a second cigarette by the time "THE END" appeared.

"Good movie," Matsuo said as we wandered out toward daylight.

"It was okay." I hadn't found it particularly interesting. In fact, I was disappointed. The poster had been far more risque than the movie itself. But I was feeling good, even a little lightheaded from that second cigarette.

Then I spotted a familiar figure outside and everything changed.

"Let's wait here for a while," I said, stopping at the top of the front ramp that led to the street.

"What's wrong?" Matsuo said.

I pointed to a group of boys leaning on a car outside the theater. "Look."

Mick McGarrigle and his gang were hanging around out front. He was a year older and at least an inch taller than either of us, although he was still in our grade level at school. He was beefy and round-faced with red hair sprouting at all angles from under the dirty plaid cloth cap he always wore.

Mick terrified me. I had only to catch sight of him, even from this far away, and I felt like I had to pee. Mick—my nemesis from first grade. He had taken one look at my port wine stain and that was it—I became "Spot," his favorite target.

Maybe if I had been a different sort, I could have changed things before they ever got this bad. Maybe if I had taken a swing at his nose every time he called me Spot back when we were six years old, he might have found another target. But I had only cried and turned tail. Maybe because I *felt* like someone named Spot. It was too late to change matters now. Our roles were set: Mick was the bully; I was the victim.

God, how I hated it! I dreamed of striking back, vowing to launch myself at his throat the next time he called me Spot. But I never did. Just seeing him made me feel like a whipped pup.

Matsuo was his other favorite target. At times it seemed as if we were both born to be picked on by Mick McGarrigle. Lots of kids picked on Matsuo, though, just because he was Japanese. Dad once explained that to me in his usual style by saying, "The country's going through a particularly virulent period of xenophobia, especially here in California." I eventually got him to explain that he meant that people hated foreigners just because they were foreign.

Maybe that was why Matsuo never fought back. He probably knew he would catch the blame for any fight, no matter what the provocation against him. So Mick pushed him around, just like me.

But somehow, Matsuo never seemed like a victim.

We waited and waited. I was about to suggest sneaking out the back way when Mick and his four pack dogs finally moved on. We came out blinking in the sunlight, ready to make our way uphill to Nihonmachi, when I heard the nasty, grating voice that never failed to form spicules of ice in my stomach.

"Well, well! If it ain't Chinky-boy and his pet dog, Spot!"

I turned and there was Mick, stepping out from where he and his boys had been leaning against the wall. He blocked our way. The blue eyes that peered out from the mass of freckles under the peak of his cap held the unmistakable vicious glint that bullies always seem to develop.

■ ■ ■

Mick watched Spot Slater's face pale to a sick white when he turned and saw him. He called it the White Look—white with fear. There were only a few kids he could count on every time for the White Look, and Slater was one. He used to hate them for being such pantywaists, but now he felt mostly contempt and something akin to affection. The White Look was like a kind of dope. Every so often Mick needed a dose to make him feel good, needed to know that all he had to do was appear on a street or a playground and certain kids would want to be sick. It also meant that he had to do something to the kid to keep him ripe. Let him pass too often without something to remember ol' Mick McGarrigle by and pretty soon the White Look would die out.

He had seen Slater duck back into the Granada and had decided to wait. It was a dull Saturday and he needed a dose.

"Hey!" he shouted and gave Slater and the Jap kid each a shove hefty enough to send them sprawling. "You was gettin' yer shadows on me!"

Jack, Jerry, Vinny, and Al all got a laugh out of that. Good old Spot Slater looked like he was going to pee in his pants. His eyes were down on the ground, staring at everybody's shoes. The Jap kid pulled on Spot's arm.

"Come on," he said in a low voice. "We'll go this way."

They turned and started to walk off the other way, but not before the Jap kid flashed Mick his own look, the one he always flashed, as if to say Mick McGarrigle was a piece of shit.

God, how he hated Japs! *All* Japs, but especially this one, this Matsuo Okumo or whatever his name was. Mick called him Chinky-boy because Matsuo seemed to hate being taken for Chinese. Mick didn't know why. According to his father, Japs were a thousand times worse than Chinks. Chinks at least knew their place, but Japs—Japs were why Pop was out of work so much. At least that was what he said. And when he was out of work, he drank more. And when Pop was on a bender, everyone knew—Mom and all the kids—to walk on eggshells. Sometimes he could make Pop laugh and get him in a good mood by telling him how he had made some Jap kid or a rich sissy like Spot Slater crawl. And then Pop might take him down to O'Boyle's pool hall and show him some shots. But sometimes nothing would get him in a good mood.

Mick felt a sudden burst of rage watching Spot and Chinky-boy move off. He ran up and wrapped an arm across Spot's throat and whipped him around so he was facing the guys.

"Lookit here!" he shouted, using his free hand to pull Spot's hair up off his forehead. "I had a dog once with a spot like this, only the dog's was brown. He was kinda cute. But this is *ugly!*"

The guys roared. Mick glanced around at Spot's face and saw how red it was. A little bit tighter and maybe he'd start blubbering like a girl. Mick held him securely around the neck, but took no special precautions against him. Some other kid, held this way, might kick backward or drive an elbow into Mick's belly, but not Spot. Spot was too well trained. Spot knew Mick would beat him bloody if he tried anything stupid.

Then Mick heard a voice, close to his ear, cutting through the guys' laughter.

"Hey, Mick! How about it? You and me behind the theater."

That little Jap bastard. The voice chilled him. So calm, so cool, like nothing in this world scared him.

Mick let Spot go and faced him. He could see dark fires alight in the Jap's eyes.

"You lookin' for a fight, Chinky-boy?"

"Just you and me, alone, behind the theater. Just the two of us. We'll see who walks back out."

Mick's mind raced. He hadn't expected this. The Jap had never pulled anything like this before. At least he wasn't doing nothing but talking so far. Usually the Jap didn't even talk.

That day last winter in the boys' room at school when the Jap had come in while Mick was sneaking a smoke, he hadn't talked much then, either. He took one look at Mick and walked by like Mick wasn't even there. Just like Pop always said—these Japs don't know their place. It had got Mick mad. They were alone so Mick decided to stick Chinky-boy's head in one of the toilets—that would give Pop a laugh for sure.

He had gone over to start things off by giving the little yellowface a casual shove as a kind of warm-up. But as soon as his hand touched the Jap, he felt himself twisted around and slammed against the wall. He thought he must have slipped so he charged right back. But this time he felt his arm grabbed and his feet coming up off the tiles as the Jap rolled him over his hip and somehow threw him. He landed flat on his back on the floor. With all the wind knocked out of him, he fought for breath while the Jap kid looked down at him with that expressionless slanty-eyed face of his and walked out, not saying a word.

Mick knew he couldn't face anything like that behind the Granada, and especially not out here in front of the guys. They would help him out for sure, but he hated the thought of them knowing he needed help handling *anyone*.

"Don't make me laugh!" he said good and loud, slapping his thigh. "I'd be afraid I'd kill you! And besides, my dad'd kill *me* for getting Chink blood on my hands!" As the guys laughed at this, he shoved Spot toward the Jap. "Take your pet back to Japtown while you can still walk, Chinky-boy!"

Mick signaled to the gang to follow and they all trotted up behind him. But as he crossed Market Street, he glanced back at the Jap and the rich kid. He saw Spot sneak a backward look of his own, but the Jap kept on walking like nothing had happened.

God, how he hated Japs!

■   ■   ■

It took me a block or two to overcome my shame. I finally spoke to Matsuo as we turned a corner.

"Why is he afraid of you?"

"All bullies are cowards inside. Surely you know that, Frankie."

"I've been *told* that, but I've never seen it."

"It's true. Nagata says so."

Matsuo's eyes were guileless as he spoke, but I had a definite feeling he was holding something back.

"I honor Nagata-san's words," I said, "but I know that if *I* had invited Mick behind the theater, he'd have been there in a flash."

Matsuo shrugged. "Maybe."

Something wasn't adding up. After Mick had let me go at Matsuo's challenge, I saw something flit across his pudgy, bully face, something I never thought I'd see there: fear. Mick was afraid to face Matsuo alone. Why? He had used Matsuo as a public punching bag for half of his life. It didn't make sense. I wondered what I'd learn if I kept a closer eye on my friend.

■ ■ ■

Matsuo swept the floor of Izumi-san's store and thought about the nightmare. It had left him alone since the spring, and now it was back. Those hideous, crawling, creeping forms—why should they want to kill him? What did it all mean? It made him afraid to go to sleep. Only the katana seemed to protect him from the dream. That was eerie. Almost as eerie as the dream itself.

He would have preferred to dream of Japan. Although born there, he had lived in America since infancy and had no memory of Japan. But he knew from Nagata's stories that it was a wonderful, magical place, close to the hearts of the gods, where the land trembled and the mountains spewed forth smoke and fire. And Nagata should know. He had lived there all his life before coming to America to raise Matsuo according to Father's wishes.

Besides all that, Japan was where Father lived: Baron Okumo, who existed only in photos and in the stories Nagata told about him. His brother, Hiroki, four years his senior, was there, too. All he knew about his brother he had learned from Nagata who had last seen him as a small boy.

Japan sounded like paradise. But then, anywhere would be better than living here among these mean-spirited Westerners.

"Haku! Haku!" Izumi said, gesturing to Matsuo's immobile broom. He waved a skeletal hand before Matsuo's eyes as he passed. White-haired, reed-thin in his tattered, stained work kimono, Izumi the greengrocer hustled back and forth through his shop, his wooden *geta* clacking on the floor as he greeted customers, helped them make their selections, checked the bins and dumps to see that they remained filled to overflowing with their proper fruits and vegetables, with the best on top—always the best on top.

Despite Nagata's concerted effort to instill into Matsuo a contempt for all members of the merchant class—who, according to tradition, were one step above the outcasts and untouchables—Matsuo felt a genuine affection for old Izumi-san. He was as generous as he was gruff, a hard taskmaster who worked harder than any of his employees. And every year, on the fifth day of the fifth month, Boy's Day, he hoisted a stout bamboo pole before his shop and flew *koinobori*, brightly colored carp-shaped streamers, one for every boy who worked for him.

But though Nagata despised merchants, he made Matsuo come to Japantown to work here regularly, for it was in accordance with Father's wishes that he be exposed to as many issei as possible while he lived here.

Let him come to know America like an American, but keep him Japanese!

Nagata had repeated the baron's words to him times beyond number. And so Matsuo worked in Izumi's yao-ya.

"Matsuo!"

He looked up and saw Sachi urgently motioning him toward the front of the store. Sachi was Izumi's grandson, a year younger than Matsuo and more than a bit on the chunky side. He was standing next to an impatient-looking middle-aged woman.

"See if you can figure out what she wants," he said as Matsuo came up. "I can't."

"Sure, boss."

Matsuo listened to the woman. Her Japanese accent was unfamiliar to him, but still it was clear that all she wanted was some *wasabi* root. He found some for her and she thanked him profusely.

"She's in America now," Sachi said when the woman had gone. "She should learn English."

"Maybe you should learn some Japanese, boss," Matsuo said with a wink. Sachi understood a smattering, but could speak virtually nothing of it. He and Sachi had been having this conversation for years. Each knew the other's responses by heart, but that didn't stop them from replaying it time and again.

"No thanks."

"It's your heritage. You shouldn't forsake it."

"Why not? I'm an American. You won't catch me pining away for Japan. I was born here and I'm staying. Learning Japanese is nothing but a big waste of time."

"Anything you say, boss."

Matsuo went back to sweeping while Sachi returned to the front counter. He called Sachi boss because he was the legal owner of Izumi's store. Matsuo also used the term as a barb against the anti-Japanese laws of Sachi's beloved America. The 1920 Alien Land Law forbade any alien from owning land. Two years later, the Supreme Court supported a decision that declared all Japanese aliens "ineligible for naturalization," thereby permanently excluding them from citizenship. As a result, no issei—those born in Japan like Nagata and Matsuo and Izumi—could own a home or a farm or a store. But an American-born nisei like Sachi was automatically a citizen, so some years ago the store had been put in his name.

The unfairness of it all made Matsuo grind his teeth every time he thought about it, but Sachi took it all in stride. He turned a deaf ear to Matsuo's railings against the United States and powerful California Jap-haters like William Randolph Hearst and his San Francisco *Examiner*. The bigotry that made Matsuo long to return to Japan seemed only to harden Sachi's resolve to carve out a place for himself in a land that hated him.

Frankie helped him stack the new shipment of oranges in the front trays under the awning over the sidewalk. Matsuo wished all Americans were like Frankie. Maybe then he could walk the streets without feeling the weight of all those stares, all those eyes watching him with suspicion, waiting for him to make a wrong move, ready to pounce on him. Maybe then he could buy a piece of candy at the newsstand without being elbowed aside by the white customers and ignored by the proprietor until he was the only one left.

Yet even without the thousand daily slights of life as a *gaijin* in America, he would still long for Japan.

As he and Frankie carried the empty crates toward the back, an all-too-familiar voice called out behind them.

"Hey, Chinky-boy!"

Mick and his gang. The five of them were standing at the front of the store, each with an orange in his hand. As Matsuo watched, Mick tore open his orange and took a big, sloppy bite out of the middle. His chums followed suit.

"Real good, Chinky-boy," he said with the juice dripping down his chin. "Good fruit. *American* fruit. You ain't good enough to sell this. You should be selling little shriveled up Chink apples."

Izumi suddenly appeared from the back, brandishing a broom handle. "You boy pay for orange now!" he cried.

Mick laughed. "Not from your store, yellowface!" He threw the orange at the old man.

As usual, the gang followed Mick's lead and began pelting Izumi with their fruit. But they slowed the old shopkeeper's charge only momentarily. As he neared them, wielding his broom handle like a *bo*, they turned and ran off, jeering.

On his way down the sidewalk, Mick kicked a corner support out from under one of the standing fruit trays. It collapsed, sending cantaloupes and oranges rolling in all directions along the sidewalk. Izumi began chasing the fruit instead of the boys.

Matsuo and Sachi helped; so did Frankie, although Matsuo noted that his friend waited until Mick was well gone. Poor Frankie. His terror of Mick was a palpable thing. He wished he could relieve his one white friend of his paralyzing fear.

"You should call the police!" Sachi said, visibly angry.

"Shikatoganai," Izumi said, as he always did when harassed. *"Shikatoganai."*

But it *could* be helped, Matsuo knew as he righted the tray and reset the support. *He* could help. But he was not allowed to.

For the thousandth time he wished he was free to give Mick what he deserved. This afternoon when Mick took Frankie in that stranglehold, Matsuo had almost lost control. One swift jab to the left or right of the bully's spine, where Nagata said the kidneys lived, would have ended the scene in an instant. But Matsuo yearned for a slower reckoning. He wished to reduce the bigger boy to blubbering tears, pleas for mercy, to a lump of battered flesh, to humiliate him in front of his friends the way he humiliated Frankie, the way he tried to humiliate Matsuo. But that was a dream. One he would never see.

Nagata forbade it.

He taught Matsuo the arts of combat on the strict condition that he never use them in America. Matsuo's expertise at *jujutsu* and his growing proficiency with the sword, the staff, and the bow and arrow were skills that he had sworn to keep hidden in this land. Nagata never seemed concerned with Matsuo's tales of the batterings and indignities he suffered at the hands of Mick and his gang. He simply kept repeating his warning never to draw attention to himself. *Never!*

And so Matsuo played the coward. His *shi-no-on*—his obligation to his teacher, Nagata—restrained him from breaking every bone in Mick McGarrigle's body. But today he had almost lost control, just as he had lost it in the boys' room last winter. The look in Mick's eyes as he had lain gasping on the tile floor was that of someone who thought he had picked up a harmless garter snake only to find that he held a poisonous pit viper.

But for all the satisfaction of that moment, Matsuo knew now that he had made a mistake. He had allowed Mick to see his inner face. He had shown him the fire within and now Mick wanted to extinguish it. Mick had doubled and redoubled his insults and petty attacks, but had never again confronted Matsuo alone. Mick's bully sense had grasped, though, that Matsuo would not fight back in public and Mick took full advantage of that.

It was a war, but one in which Matsuo was not allowed to fight. There seemed no way out—

—except to return to Japan.

Nagata had promised him that he would return to meet his father and brother before he began college. Two more years to go. Two more years of war.

He sighed and began restacking the cantaloupes.

■ ■ ■

That night, I had to bounce three pebbles off his bedroom window before Matsuo finally heard one. I waved my free hand in wide arcs, hoping he would spot me in the fog.

"Come on down!" I whispered as he lifted the sash. "And bring the Luckies!"

He came out a few minutes later, barefoot and wearing a light kimono. "What is it?"

I held up the quart jar I had spirited out of my folks' kitchen. "Here. Have a taste."

He took it, unscrewed the top, and sniffed. "Orange juice . . . and something else."

"The 'something else' is vodka."

"Vodka? Isn't that a liquor?"

"Yeah. Like gin, only not as smelly. Put vodka in orange juice and it's called a screwdriver." At least that was what they were calling the mix at my folks' dinner party.

Matsuo made a face. "They named a drink after a tool?"

"Just take a swig, will you? It's good."

"It's safe?"

"Of course. You know my father only buys the best bootleg. Imported only. No basement stuff."

Matsuo took a drink, and nodded appreciatively. "It's good." He drank again. "It's *very* good."

■ ■ ■

"We must find a way to bring Mick to justice," Matsuo said. He spoke slowly and carefully, but still could not overcome the slur in his voice.

We sat in the bushes between the Japanese garden and the patio and watched the party through the arched windows of my white stucco-walled Spanish-style house. Dad had had everybody out to see his Zen garden before dinner, and now they were all in the living room. Dinner was over. At first the Navy men had stayed in a group with my father, drinking and talking at one end of the room while the women put on the record player and danced the Charleston at the other. But now they all were gathered around the piano singing "I Found A Million Dollar Baby in the Five-and-Ten-Cent Store" and "Bye, Bye, Blackbird." They all seemed to be feeling pretty good.

Matsuo and I weren't feeling too bad ourselves. We had finished off the screwdrivers and were sharing a Lucky Strike. Matsuo had had less than I but seemed to be feeling it more. Even in the faint light from the house I could see that his face was flushed a deep red. Suddenly, he had started talking about Mick.

"Who will bell the cat?" I said.

Matsuo didn't seem to hear me. He seemed to be in his own world. "We must bide our time like the Forty-seven *Ronin*, and wait until the moment is right. And then, when Mick least expects it, we must strike."

I knew that story by heart. Nagata had told it to us many times. It was my favorite Japanese epic, but I didn't see how it applied here. I reviewed it in my mind:

In 1703 Lord Asano was deceived by Lord Kira into violating his *chu*, his duty to the shogunate; Lord Asano committed *seppuku* to right the wrong. His fief was confiscated, leaving his samurai retainers masterless, and thereafter called ronin. Forty-seven of these ronin entered into a blood pact to avenge their lord. But to throw the powerful Lord Kira off guard, they played the part of wastrels and drunkards; they became despised by all because they neither committed seppuku like their lord, nor did they strike against the man who had engineered their master's death. But when the time was right, when Lord Kira and his retainers were lulled into a false sense of security, they rose up as one and avenged their fallen master by taking Lord Kira's head.

"The lesson," Nagata would always say, "lies not in the bloodshed and deceit; it lies in *giri*—the obligation, the debt—to one's master. The forty-seven put giri to their master above all. Consequently, they violated chu—the unrepayable debt to the Emperor, the law of Japan—by slaying a lord without the Shogun's permission. Lord Kira's death satisfied their giri to their master; only their own deaths would satisfy chu. So all forty-seven committed seppuku in the Sengaku-ji temple."

The story always fascinated me for its melodrama, but I also saw it as a primer for the twists and turns of the Japanese concept of *on*—one's accumulation of debts and obligations. Matsuo had been exposed to the patterns of on since birth, and even he wasn't completely clear on them. I was a Johnny-come-lately playing catch-up and felt I had almost no chance of grasping the full meaning.

But I understood some of the levels of on. The highest were chu—to the Emperor—and *oya*—to one's parents—neither of which could ever be fully repaid. Others were various forms of incurred debt—giri—which had to be repaid tit for tat, such as giri to one's name and one's master and one's teacher and so on.

"I don't get the connection," I said to Matsuo.

"We must satisfy the giri to our names," he said.

"How?"

Instead of answering me, he said, "I have to go now." His voice sounded strained.

"Why?"

"Because I am going to be sick." He got up and staggered off toward the garage.

As I watched him go, I mulled what he had said about the Forty-seven Ronin. Did he mean we should pretend to be cowardly wastrels afraid to fight back? I didn't have to do any pretending for that.

Or had he been talking about himself? Was Matsuo some sort of secret samurai, waiting to satisfy our giri? What an exciting thought! It kept me awake most of the night.

■   ■   ■

Matsuo knelt before Nagata's daisho and made an offering of his breakfast fish and rice at the shrine. He could not bring himself to eat this morning. He could not remember ever feeling this sick in his entire life. His stomach quivered and his head throbbed as if the giant bell in Grace Cathedral were clanging inside it. He swore never again to touch another screwdriver, or any other form of Western liquor. Only *sake* or plum wine for him from now on, and even those in small amounts.

Matsuo reached up and lifted Nagata's katana from its resting place. He pulled the scabbard halfway back and studied the intricate carvings on the blade. A Masamune blade. The only ones that could rival it were those made by Masamune's rival swordsmith, Murasama. It was said that when a Murasama blade was plunged into a running stream, the floating leaves and twigs that brushed against its edge were cut in two; but it was said that when the same was done with a Masamune blade, its edge was so keen that floating leaves and twigs avoided it and passed on either side. There was a power in a Masamune blade that went beyond sharpness, strength, and flexibility. Matsuo swore to save all his money and buy such a blade for himself when he returned to Japan.

But he knew there was no other blade in the world like this one. According to Nagata, Masamune had fashioned this particular blade from another sword given him centuries ago by a wandering gaijin. The original had been a very special sword that Masamune had hammered and folded and reshaped into its present form.

It must have been a magic sword, Matsuo thought, for he sensed a hidden power in Nagata's daisho. He could feel it shimmer through his nerve endings when he held the blade.

"Dreaming of beheading your enemies?" said a voice behind him.

Matsuo quickly thrust the blade back to rest within its scabbard and replaced it on the *katana-kake*, then turned to face Nagata, fresh from his morning bath.

"No, *sensei*. I would need only my hands to defeat my enemy. But I cannot use them." He gave Nagata a sidelong look. "Although giri to my name might demand that I use my hands just once."

"Giri demands no such thing. Oya and shi-no-on—your duties to your father and your teacher—demand that you play the part of an ordinary poor issei boy and draw no attention to yourself. You stand out enough merely by being Japanese. If you use the jujutsu and *bujutsu* I have taught you, you will injure an American, perhaps severely. You might then become a focus for the hatred of Orientals in this city. What if someone like Hearst-san decided to attack you in the *Examiner?* What if this brought to light the identity of your father? Such incident could cause the baron great embarrassment. And I would be disgraced because I am responsible for you. I would have no recourse but to bring you home and commit seppuku."

Matsuo felt as if he had been doused with ice water. To be the cause of Nagata's death—the thought left him speechless.

"Besides," Nagata continued, "there are ways other than brute force to satisfy giri. You would do well to follow the wisdom I learned when I studied at the Tenshin Shoden Katori Shinto Ryu as a boy. I learned bujutsu—all the martial arts—just as you are learning. These arts are designed for one purpose: to kill. But to rely on brute force alone is the way of animals. We learn to kill, yes, but we must also learn that it is not necessary to reveal our strength. We must reach for and grasp a higher form of wisdom and keep our brute power hidden. Those were the thoughts of Choisai Sensei, founder of Katori Shinto Ryu. They are words we must both live by.

"So look upon your trials here as tests of your *shuyo*," Nagata said, thumping his ample belly. "But enough of this. It is time to work in the garden." He turned and strode toward the door.

Shuyo . . . self-discipline . . . Matsuo wished he had more. Everyone knew that shuyo built up the belly, the seat of control. Matsuo rubbed a hand over his flat abdomen, then followed Nagata out to the garden.

■　■　■

"Your rake is asleep," Nagata said. "Wake it up."

The morning air had done nothing to improve the way Matsuo felt. The light of the rising sun was a knife blade through his eyes and into his brain. The soft, steady strokes of Nagata's rake through the fine stones was a thunderous rumble in his head.

Matsuo forced himself to follow his sensei's lead, dragging his

wide-toothed rake to form parallel lines in the small stones: arrow
straight in the open spaces; gently curving around the bases of the lava
stones and twisted trees.

When the raking was done, Nagata squatted and slowly made his
way around the perimeter of the garden, walking like a crab. When he
completed the circuit, he stood with hands on hips and smiled.

"It is done," he said. "It is good."

Matsuo had watched him spend weeks arranging the varied lava
rocks, moving this one three inches to the left, that one an inch to the
right.

"Why is it good?" Matsuo said. What was so special about the
placement of the rocks that Nagata had to spend a whole month at it?

"Sit," Nagata said, and Matsuo sat. "Look out across my sea of
raked stones. Feel the tranquillity of the surface while you sense the
currents below. Count the large stones."

Matsuo counted. "Eight."

"Move somewhere else. Anywhere." When Matsuo chose another spot, Nagata said, "Count the large stones again."

Matsuo shrugged and counted. "Eight."

"Are they the same stones?"

"Of course . . ." Matsuo said, then caught himself. No, they
weren't the same eight lava stones. "Wait." He stood. "The stone at
the far edge there—I could see it before, but now it is hidden behind
this big one here. And that crooked one over there on the left is visible
now but I didn't see it the first time."

Nagata nodded with pleasure. "Move around. Sit anywhere along
the edge. Tell me what you see."

Matsuo tried viewing the rocks from every conceivable angle.
There were nine rocks in the stony sea, but no matter where he sat,
only eight were visible. Each of the nine had its turn in view as he
changed position, but never more than eight were visible at any one
time, no matter where he sat.

"What does this tell you, son of the baron?"

Matsuo thought a moment, then, "That wherever one goes in life,
no matter how hard one searches and how clear one imagines the view,
something is always hidden."

"Excellent! I am truly proud of you!"

Matsuo watched Nagata as he stood with his arms folded atop his
potbelly and surveyed his latest addition to the Slater property. *And I
am proud of you, sensei.*

"Nagata-san," he said after a moment. "Why do you work so hard
in Frankie's father's garden?"

Nagata looked at him and smiled serenely. "Has Slater-san picked
out a single shrub or turned a single spade of earth here? Has he

contributed the smallest shred of himself to the garden? Oh, yes, certainly it resides on his land. And he said to me, 'Do something with the west corner.' But that was all. No more. He may call this his 'Japanese garden,' and he may show it to all his friends. But Matsuo, there is nothing of him here. This is *my* garden."

"You don't like Slater-san?"

"In truth, I do not *think* of Slater-san. He is wealthy but he is empty inside. Like a hollow shell on the shore. Shake him and nothing falls out. Hold him up to your ear and you will hear only the whisper of the blood rushing through your head."

"But you work for him." Matsuo instantly recognized his error and wished the words back in his mouth, but it was too late. Nagata's face clouded and his voice grew stern.

"I serve only your father, the baron. He and no one else is my master. I use Slater-san as a means of raising you among Americans as your father commanded. Nothing more."

"Forgive my thoughtless words, sensei. Like the Westerners around us, my tongue flies ahead of my thoughts."

"Perhaps you should meditate on that while you weed."

"Weed? But you promised to practice with the *bokken* with me today."

"Your spirit needs honing more than your skills with the wooden sword. I sometimes feel I am failing your father in his command to raise you here yet keep you Japanese." He swept a hand out over the expanse of his work. "Consider my garden. It is like Japanese life. It is ordered, it is clean, it has a design. Each rock, each plant, each tree has its place; each was removed from its nursery or from nature and assumes its proper station in the garden. American life is a weed patch where every member must *find* its place; some spend their entire lives searching and never find their place. In Japan there is no need to look for one's proper station—one is born into it. I was born into mine, you were born into yours. Mine is to be Baron Okumo's samurai retainer; yours is to fill the special role he has planned for you, known only to him.

"The garden tells you all this. Watch the garden as you work here. It can teach you much. It is life, the life you must lead. And there are always surprises." He pointed to the base of the cedar fence. "Look there, for instance. See that bit of green poking between the wooden slats?"

Matsuo scanned the base of the fence until he saw it: A tiny branch had wormed its way between the apparently flush border of two cedar boards and had sprouted a single leaf.

"I see."

"What does it say to you?"

Matsuo would have given two fingers from his left hand to be able to compose a *haiku* on the spot. But the words would not fall into the proper places. Finally, he said, "The tiny plant has persevered where others failed, finding a passage where seemingly there was none, and has won a place in the sun from the land of shadow."

Nagata's face lighted with pleasure, and that in turn warmed Matsuo. Whatever pleased his sensei, pleased him.

"Excellent! You see? Even in the simple fence around a garden, there is courage and there is victory over seemingly insurmountable odds!"

"Can we practice with the bokken now?" Matsuo said.

Nagata laughed from deep in his belly. "Yes! When the Slaters make their Sunday trip to church, we will practice. Now weed and don't mention the bokken again!"

■ ■ ■

The clacking sound drew me around to the rear of the garage.

I hadn't been feeling too good that morning, so Mom and Dad left me behind when they went to church. I felt better after a roll and some juice, so I went out looking for Matsuo. I found him when I found the source of the noise.

They were using wooden swords—lengths of oak the exact size and shape of the big katana of Nagata's daisho. I had always known Matsuo to be quick and agile, but I had never seen him like this. He moved like a tiger, aiming vicious two-handed thrusts and slashes at Nagata with his wooden sword while the older, heavier man, who by all appearances should have been at a disadvantage, kept him at bay with parries and dodges that seemed to require no more than a bend of the wrist or a simple sidestep. Matsuo was soaked with perspiration. Nagata was cool and dry.

Fascinated, I hunkered down in a clump of bushes and watched.

■ ■ ■

Matsuo called on every ounce of speed and agility he had to penetrate Nagata's defense, but to no avail. With an effort, he bottled his frustration, knowing that emotions would only betray his sword. He had to remember what Nagata had taught him—to send his essence along the wooden blade and make himself one with it. *Control the breath, control all thought, control every movement.* He stepped back. Holding his bokken at the ready, its long handle gripped with both hands while its blade was aligned vertically with his right shoulder, he paused to compose himself. Nagata waited for him. Matsuo let himself flow into his sword, making it an extension of his hands. But as he did, a movement at the shaded corner of the garage caught his eye and he looked.

Frankie's face peered out from the bushes.

But that couldn't be! Frankie was at church with his parents! That was why he and Nagata had waited until the big car had gone. They never practiced when anyone was home.

An idea suddenly exploded in Matsuo's brain, a plan that was beautiful in its simplicity, yet it might solve so many problems. As he stood there, contemplating it, he felt a sudden, stinging pain on the left side of his neck.

"Your head rolls serenely downhill," Nagata said, stepping back and wiping imaginary blood from his wooden blade before he thrust it into his belt.

Frankie's face disappeared into the bush as Matsuo rubbed his neck.

"What happened to you?" Nagata said. "You were doing very well. That last was perhaps your best attack yet. And then you let your guard down completely."

Matsuo bowed to Nagata. "I was distracted by a thought," he said.

"You should be far beyond that point!" Nagata said with annoyance. "Too much thought is death in battle! You must *act!* And you must train until the action becomes part of your very nature!"

"I am truly sorry, sensei," Matsuo said. "But it was such a wonderful thought."

Nagata did not ask him the nature of the thought, and Matsuo did not volunteer it. But it had been a truly ingenious thought. It would satisfy giri in the matter of Mick without neglecting the various on to his father and Nagata. And it would help his friend, Frankie, too.

He smiled. Yes, a most wonderful thought.

(From *Mystical Japan* by Francois Fallon):

As we have seen, religion in Japan has virtually nothing to do with ancestor worship, despite that prevailing misconception. They merely recognize their on—their debt or obligation—to what has gone before. There is no Good or Evil in their religion, only the various levels of on. Unlike so many of its Western counterparts, Japanese religion is a joyous, colorful, festive part of everyday life.

There is, however, a notable exception to this rule: The Kakureta Kao—the Order of the Hidden Face.

This mystical sect gained its place in the history of Japan in the sixteenth century during the days of the Nobunaga Shogun-

ate. The Shoguns had wrested the reins of government from the
Emperor and kept Him secluded in Kyoto while they ruled with
an iron fist. After Nobunaga took control of Kyoto and the
Shogunate in 1568, he set about the task of consolidating his
hold by ridding the land of all traces of the Emperor's temporal
power. He accomplished this by destroying not only those who
opposed him, but also those who would not join him. Nobunaga
wanted no challenges from without or within. He began a
program of burning all the Buddhist monasteries in the land. His
armies, however, did not limit themselves to the Buddhists. After
destroying the great Enryakuji Temple of Mount Hiei and slaughtering every living soul within, they attacked every Kakureta Kao
temple in their path as they fanned out north, west, and south of
Kyoto in their sweep of Honshu. It soon became apparent that
the Buddhists were not Nobunaga's real target—it was the
Kakureta Kao!

And with good reason. The order was the most ancient of all,
predating Buddhism and Shintoism. As legend has it, Susanoo,
the Sword God, the direct ancestor of the Emperor, brought the
Hidden Face order into existence in the time of Jimmu, the first
Emperor, and charged it with the mission of protecting the Son of
Heaven, and preserving His power in the world. The various
temples of the Kakureta Kao had been agitating for the Restoration of the Imperial Line and so the Shogun had, in effect,
declared war on the order along with the Buddhists.

Unlike the Buddhists, however, the Hidden Face fought
back. The few fighters of their number battled fiercely, but their
zeal and determination could not overcome the overwhelming
numbers arrayed against them, nor make up for the fact that their
monasteries were not designed to withstand full-scale military
assaults. Nobunaga's armies took a terrible toll, razing each
monastery to the ground after slaughtering any monks who might
have survived the siege.

Finally, only one monastery remained, the oldest, largest,
and best fortified, near Nanao on the thumblike peninsula that
juts off Honshu's west coast into the Sea of Japan. The monks
asked the people of Japan, *daimyo* and peasant alike, to rise up
and restore the Emperor to power in Edo. Their call to arms fell
upon deaf ears. And so, as legend has it, the monks delved into
the cache of ancient lore that was their legacy from the God of
Swords, and found a means to defend themselves.

As the Shogun's armies neared the gates of the monastery,
something happened. Folklore is vague about the exact nature of
the event, but most tales agree that darkness descended and
some sort of mystical wind rose up around the last temple. Some

sources call it The-Wind-That-Bends-Not-The-Trees, others refer
to it as another *Kamikaze,* or "Divine Wind" like the one that
saved Japan by sinking Kubla Khan's invading fleet at the end of
the thirteenth century. But the most commonly accepted name
appears to be *Kuroikaze*—the "Black Wind." The Kuroikaze was
apparently far more devastating than a mere storm of air. The
legends are unclear as to exactly what havoc it wrought, but the
historical records of the Shogunate reveal that less than half the
army returned to Edo alive.

Nobunaga left the Kakureta Kao alone after that and was
eventually slain by his own generals in 1582.

The Hidden Face sect limped through the following centuries, never regaining its power or prominence. It is reduced today
to a single temple, a five-storied pagoda in Tokyo not far from the
Imperial Palace. The members of the Inner Circles of the sect
never leave the temple and no one is allowed inside other than
the select children who are educated there as acolytes. What
goes on within is completely shrouded in mystery.

AUGUST
TOKYO

Under the spell of the drugs, the monk lay on the stained futon and
moaned. Hiroki watched with dry mouth and dripping armpits.
Throughout his childhood and adolescence he had heard rumors of this
room on the top floor of the temple, but this was the first time he had
ever seen it. Its ceiling seemed to stretch into limitless empty black
space above. The darkness around him was relieved only by the four
candles placed at the corners of the futon, and these illuminated only
the fronts of the two dozen or so robed and hooded figures encircling
their fellow monk, some standing, some sitting, some lying on the
floor.

Rare to see so many members of the Inner Circles together in one
room. All were robed uniformly in dark blue. Their silk masks were
the only part of their apparel that distinguished one from the other. But
Hiroki knew many of them by the shapes of their bodies. Those
without hands or feet, or legs or arms were easily recognized. So were
the eyeless ones. The tongueless, earless, and noseless monks were
more difficult. He wondered how he would feel standing here now in

this dark room with these deformed, mutilated holy men if he had not been coming to the temple on an almost daily basis for as long as he could remember.

Hiroki turned his attention to the monk on the futon. This one, a Seer, lay naked but for his mask and fundoshi. He writhed in seeming agony. His scrawny limbs flexed and straightened with spasmodic jerks. As he turned this way and that, the candlelight flickered into the recesses of his empty eye sockets. Suddenly, he stopped and fell limp. Even his breathing stopped. The room was silent as a tomb.

Hiroki glanced at Yajima standing next to him. His fellow acolyte's full face was pale, his lips drawn into a tight line. He searched the hooded figures for the eyes of Shimazu, his sensei, found them through the eyeholes of a red silk mask across from him, and with his own eyes asked a silent, frightened, question. Shimazu's green eyes blinked as he nodded reassuringly. And then Hiroki's attention was drawn to the futon again as the Seer's lungs filled with a great, whistling gasp.

Hiroki backed up half a step as the Seer levered up to a sitting position and stared around the room with those empty sockets. He seemed to be looking elsewhere, elsewhen.

"Death!" he cried. "The Son of the Sun dies with the year! A quiet time follows as a new Emperor, a new Son of Heaven accedes the Throne of the Sun—then war! I see war! I see the Son of Heaven at war with all nations. I see fleets on the sea, fleets in the air, spanning the five continents and the seven seas! All nations feel the sting of Japan's lash! The Son of Heaven is everywhere!" He smiled, showing crooked yellow teeth. "And everywhere victorious!" The smile faded and his voice lowered in volume. "No . . . not everywhere. There is defeat. There come many defeats. I see Tokyo burning once more! The future looks dark. Defeat follows defeat. The Empire's forces are driven back, yet the land remains unsullied! No gaijin foot trods our soil. The Emperor remains untouched! Yet even so, there is no hope!" He sobbed. "All is lost! But wait! When all looks blackest, blackness will save us! The *Kuroikaze*, borne by a noble firstborn, shall return to strike down all who oppose the Imperial Will!" Suddenly he screamed and flung himself backward with both arms shielding eyes he no longer possessed. "The light! The light of the sun! It blinds!"

The Seer fainted, collapsing like an empty husk. Before he could react, Hiroki felt a hand on his shoulder. He and Yajima were guided away from the upper room and the rest of the monks. Shimazu led them down the steps to the tiny classroom on the third level where they had spent much of their acolyteship.

"What does it mean, sensei?" Hiroki said when they were alone. His heart was pounding in time with the whirling of his mind. "I don't understand."

"Always it is the same," the master said, his voice slightly muffled as ever by the embroidered red silk mask he wore. Hiroki had wondered at times if he would recognize the voice if it spoke to him through clear air with no fabric to distort it. He knew, though, that he would never fail to recognize Shimazu's high, thin shoulders and his gaunt, long-fingered hands. "No matter which Seer has the vision, it is always the same."

Hiroki knew better than to ask. He held his tongue, knowing that soon his master would explain all he thought they should know. Finally, he spoke.

"What is your dearest ambition?"

Hiroki didn't hesitate. The answer had been drilled into him since early childhood. He and Yajima answered in unison.

"To die for the Emperor!"

Hiroki paused, unsure whether to speak, but he had to ask. "A 'new Son of Heaven,' sensei?"

"Always you listen carefully." His voice was grave. *"Too* carefully, sometimes. Yes. A new Emperor. The Emperor Taisho will die within the year, and Crown Prince Hirohito will assume the Throne of Heaven."

Hiroki was truly speechless now.

"You two have been privileged tonight. You have been permitted to witness a rite that has been reserved only for the four Inner Circles of the Kakureta Kao. This has been allowed for two reasons. First, because you approach your twenty-first birthdays and have proved yourselves to be admirably discreet and worthy of continued presence in the Order. Second, because the Kakureta Kao has need of your services in the outside world where members such as I can rarely venture."

Shimazu paused for breath and Hiroki had to catch himself from falling as he leaned forward in anticipation of the monk's next words. The Order needed *him?* Ever since he could remember, his father had told him that *he* needed the Order!

"As you heard," the monk finally said, "there will be war. A war we shall win!" Hiroki's puzzled expression must have mirrored Yajima's. Shimazu explained. "You heard it yourself. Initial victories followed by defeats, then the appearance of the Kuroikaze, then the all-pervasive blinding light of the sun, which can only mean the triumph of the Emperor, the God of the Sun, the Son of Heaven."

"Yes!" Hiroki cried. Now he understood! The light at the end of the vision! It could mean nothing else! But—

"When, sensei?" Yajima said. "When?"

Hiroki too hungered for the answer.

"In our lifetimes. We know no more than that. But we know we can trust the visions. Did they not warn us of the *Kanto daishinsai?*"

Hiroki bowed. The vision had certainly been correct about the Great Kanto Earthquake two years ago, and for that he would be eternally grateful. He had been able to warn his family and see them moved to the summer residence on Sagami Bay well before the quake struck on the first of September. The devastation had exceeded his worst imaginings. *Tsunamis* swelled from the seas and swept away the harbor dwellings, toppling even the great *Daibutsu*, the giant bronze statue of the Buddha at Kamakura. And then the fires—the Flowers of Edo—began. Hot coals from hundreds of toppled *hibachi* ignited the tinder wood and paper walls and roofs of the countless houses toppled by the quake. Tokyo ignited like well-aged kindling. *Tatsumaki*—dragon tails of fire—tore through the city like blazing tornadoes, igniting broken gas mains and spilled petroleum, driving people into the rivers and the sea where those who were not drowned were immolated by burning oil floating on the water. When the fires finally were brought under control days later, over one hundred thousand were dead and three-fourths of the city lay in ruins.

"What is your wish, sensei?"

"We have learned through the visions that the Kuroikaze will be crucial to victory in the coming war."

"Which will heap great honor on the Order!" Yajima blurted.

Hiroki saw a crinkling of the skin around Shimazu's green eyes that he had come to interpret as an indulgent smile. He envied Yajima as a recipient of that rare, hidden smile.

"Yes, Yajima. The Order will once again hold the place of honor in the heart of the Son of Heaven that it earned in the days of the Nobunaga Shogunate. *If* . . ."

" 'If,' sensi?" Hiroki said.

Shimazu sighed. "I have decided to trust the two of you with a secret, the gravest secret of the Order. The outside world knows little or nothing of us. Even the Emperors have paid little heed to us during the past century, and would dismiss us entirely if what I am about to tell you was to become public knowledge. I don't want either of you to answer right away. I want you to consider carefully whether you wish to carry the weight of this secret. Until now, only a handful of fully ordained monks above the level of the Fifth Circle have been privileged with this knowledge."

Hiroki closed his eyes and composed his features into an aspect of careful consideration. Of *course* he could be trusted with the secret! It was a burden he craved! He could have told his teacher so immediately, but he wanted to appear properly pensive about the honor he was being offered. But the secret—what could it be? Just before broaching the subject of the secret, Shimazu-san had been discussing the Kuroikaze. Did it concern the Black Winds? Yes! That had to be it!

"I do not want your decision now," Shimazu said. "I will give you both until tomorrow to make up your minds."

Hiroki hid his frustration. *Tomorrow?* He wanted to know now! But Shimazu's slow nod was a sign that they should leave him. They rose, bowed, and left the small teaching room together.

"What do you think the secret could be?" Yajima said as they walked to the central stairway. He was heavyset, bordering on fat, with stubby fingers and the start of a belly. But he was not a jovial sort. Yajima was serious, studious, and intensely devoted to the Order.

"I can't imagine. But it sounds ominous. I'll probably be up all night thinking about it."

"I, too," Yajima said softly.

They bowed as they passed a legless monk dragging himself along the floor by his hands. His eyes blinked at them through the eyeholes in his mask. They made their way carefully down the candle-lit stairway that wound through the core of the square, five-storied pagoda. The stairs were surrounded by rooms and hallways on each floor. There was no electricity in the Kakureta Kao temple; no telephone service, either. The windows were latticed and louvered to admit light and air, and to allow the monks to look out upon the city if they so wished, but they permitted no view of the inside from the city. Everything here was much like it was a thousand years ago when the original structure had been built.

"Do you think learning the secret will delay my ascent into the Fifth Circle?" Yajima said.

Hiroki stared at his friend. They had grown up together in the temple, two students of noble lineage, vying for the honor of Shimazu's approval. But it had been a rivalry without enmity. They were too evenly matched for one to dominate the other, so through the years of petty jealousies and spats and scuffles, a firm bond had developed between them. They rarely saw each other outside the temple, but were almost inseparable within it.

"You're really going on in the Order?"

"I've told you that a hundred times, Hiroki."

"I know, but . . ."

They bowed again as a monk without arms or legs passed in a wheelchair, giving directions to the eyeless monk who pushed him from behind along a second-floor corridor.

"But I just didn't think you really would."

Hiroki shuddered at the thought of moving past the Fourth Circle. That was when they started cutting you up. The students and lay acolytes remained whole, as did the guards and the temple sensei. But the rest submitted themselves to the Order's surgeons. Two procedures were mandatory: castration and the surgical creation of skin folds at the edges of the face to hold the mask in place. Your face was never seen again after that—the mask could be changed at will, but only in the privacy of the monk's personal quarters.

After that, the monk was given some choice as to which of his senses he wished to give up first. If, however, there was a disproportionate number of monks with fused nostrils at that time, he would be instructed to choose another sense for sacrifice. And then it would begin: the incremental whittling away of the body, and with it, the sensory world. And over the years as the perceptions of each of the remaining senses was enhanced and developed to its maximum potential by drugs and rituals, another was removed.

"I yearn for the chance to start on my path toward the Hidden Face, Hiroki. To actually *see* it someday!"

Hiroki nodded but said nothing. After years with the drugs and the rituals, when a monk's natural life was nearing its end, the final contact with the sensory world was severed and the Kakureta Kao—the Hidden Face of the universe and of all reality—was revealed.

Death followed soon after.

Not for me, Hiroki said to himself as they stepped out of the temple into the red splendor of the sunset. It might be truly wonderful to see the Kakureta Kao, but he was thankful that neither his father nor Shimazu had the Inner Circles of the Order in mind for him. Father had placed him here to learn from the Order things that could be learned nowhere else, and to put that knowledge to work in the outside world. Shimazu, too, wished to save him for the outside world, to be the Order's voice on the Imperial Council.

He waved good-bye to Yajima and went out to the bustling streets to look for a taxi or *jinrikisha* home. He was lucky that his father and his sensei seemed to be of one mind as to his future. The only area in which they seemed to disagree was the matter of his marriage to Meiko Mazaki. Shimazu was bitterly opposed to any marriage for him. Hiroki sided with his father here: He wanted Meiko for his wife. And if necessary, he would defy his sensei to have her.

Meiko! He suddenly remembered that he was supposed to meet Father at Viscount Mazaki's summer home on Sagami Bay this evening. Time had flown! He hurried on, spurred by a desire to avoid embarrassing Father by being late and by the heated desire to see her.

Meiko's face appeared before him. Meiko with the flawless skin, the full lips, the perfect cheekbones, the huge dark eyes. To think that in a match arranged for purely political reasons he should be paired with one so utterly lovely. Surely all the gods smiled down on him. Meiko . . . so young and delicate, she dominated his dreams at night and haunted his every waking moment outside the temple during the day.

He broke into a run to find a taxi to the train station.

∎ ∎ ∎

Shimazu took the final sip of the drug the Seers use and put the cup down. He sat cross-legged and waited as the familiar mustard-yellow fog wafted through his mind and colored his thoughts. He waited for enlightenment. It was virtually impossible for one with eyes and without intensive training to see into the future, he knew, but he had tried this many times before and had been rewarded with an occasional vague *impression* of what was to come in the near future.

He tried to encourage enlightenment by concentrating on something from the Seers' visions. They said the Emperor Taisho did not have long to live. He dwelled on that. The Emperor's bizarre behavior was an embarrassment to the Imperial Line. He was mentally deranged. Perhaps it was the will of the gods that he not survive the year, clearing the way for Crown Prince Hirohito to—

Something darted through his mind and disappeared. He emptied his thoughts. It would return if he did not search for it. And then he saw it. The yellow mist parted and he was on the Tokyo docks watching a teenage boy and an aging samurai walk down a gangplank. He looked around. The city was in mourning. The mist closed in and hid the boy from view as Shimazu tried to get another look at him.

He opened his eyes. He had not really needed a second look. He had seen enough of the boy to recognize his resemblance to Hiroki. It was the younger Okumo, entering Tokyo. The signs of mourning around the city could mean only one thing. Matsuo Okumo would be coming home shortly after the Emperor's death.

Shimazu took a deep breath through the silk of his mask. Events in the Order's hundred-year plan were beginning to pick up momentum. The younger Okumo's return was a sign of that.

Shimazu felt a spasm of dread shudder through him. The younger Okumo's return also meant that a momentous decision might soon be at hand. He knew that eventually he must decide which of the Okumo brothers was to die. For the duty of killing one of them had fallen to him many years ago. He knew he would be faithful to that duty.

He only prayed that Hiroki would not be the one.

∎ ∎ ∎

Meiko tried to be attentive to the conversation between her father, Hiroki, and Baron Okumo but her mind wandered. It always turned out like this. The baron would invite her and her parents over to the Okumo residence, or her father would invite the baron and his wife and Hiroki to theirs. The visits had become more frequent this summer since both families had summer residences here on Sagami Bay. But no matter where they met, the routine never varied. The never-mentioned purpose was to allow Hiroki and Meiko to become familiar with each other. But how could she learn about Hiroki when the two fathers drew him to the far side of the garden and entwined him in their incessant talk of politics?

She squirmed slightly in her place on the teak *engawa*. She had tied her *obi* too tightly and it was binding a fold of the new *furisode* kimono against her flank. To distract herself from the discomfort, she looked across the formal garden and down the slope to the bay. With the U-shape of their house's rear blocking off the rest of the slope above and to either side, it was almost as if Sagami Bay belonged to them alone.

She smoothed the apricot fabric of her kimono and traced her finger along the delicate embroidered willow tree branches that swept from the hem up to and over her left shoulder. She counted the birds singing in the branches, and when she was sure she had found them all, she reluctantly tried to turn her attention to the conversation that so intrigued her father, her future father-in-law, and her future husband.

They were talking of America, as usual, a subject that seemed to fascinate her father and the baron. Hiroki was speaking.

". . . the United States will need abject lessons in respect. They treat us like *eta* now. Their immigration laws are a direct slap in the face to the Emperor."

Strong words, Meiko thought. Did Americans really treat Japanese like untouchables?

"On the surface, yes," said the baron. "But the Exclusion Act merely confirmed what we already knew. They have singled us out because of our proven superiority. They *fear* us. If Japan men go to America and buy a farm, they become the best farmers in the land; if they start a factory, they soon produce superior merchandise for less cost. And that is the key to Japan's future: Anything the Americans can do, we can do better! Just as there is an order among individuals, there is an order among nations. And Japan's place is, as we all know, first in that order."

Meiko stifled a sigh as her attention drifted back to the blue of the bay, flecked with the white of sailboats and the wakes of powerboats. Betrothal had seemed so exciting two years ago when she had been only fourteen and Hiroki eighteen. She had never guessed that marriage plans were in the wind when the two families met for the first time and spent a seemingly casual evening together at the home of a mutual acquaintance. She had become suspicious at the second "chance" meeting at the annual chrysanthemum show in Tokyo, and noticed that all the arrangements had been made by go-betweens so that no breaking off of relations in the early stages would threaten the honor of either family. She knew that her father and the baron, both noble members of the Satsuma clan, had been political allies in the past, but were now becoming fast friends as a result of the meetings. It was clear that a link was being forged between the Okumos and the Mazakis. The marriage of Hiroki and Meiko would formalize it.

Meiko studied her future husband. She certainly could not deny that she had been paired with a handsome man. Hiroki's short-cropped hair and chiseled features were pleasing to look at. His smiles were rare, but when one broke through, it brightened his face like a burst of sunshine. He wore a brown *haori* open over a black kimono. She liked the way it accentuated his broad shoulders. But what thrilled her most was the way he looked at her. Most of the time he was properly diffident, showing no undue familiarity. But occasionally she would find him looking at her and would catch an unguarded emotion in his eyes. Meiko knew she was totally unschooled in the ways of men, but she was quite sure she knew desire when she saw it.

The mention of her name made her prick up her ears.

". . . and I think your suggestion that she study in America is a good one," her father was saying to Baron Okumo.

The baron clapped his hands once and nodded vigorously. "I knew you would see my point of view! Most excellent."

"Your arguments are most persuasive," her father said.

Meiko listened with mounting unease. Now she understood the visits of the go-between the past two days. Baron Okumo would never have broached such a subject directly; a go-between was dictated to protect himself and her father from slight. And her father was agreeing! It couldn't be!

"You are most wise to perceive their merits," the baron said. "Especially if your beautiful daughter is to wed Hiroki. If Japan is to ascend to her rightful place among the nations of the world, she will have to deal most often with America during her rise. It is a young, vigorous country that will have to be taught respect for its betters. As we all know, Western ways are strange, and few stranger than America's. When Hiroki comes to occupy an important place on the Imperial Council, a wife familiar with American ways will be of great value to him."

"Yes," her father said. "That is quite clear."

Meiko was sure that neither the baron nor Hiroki was aware of the change in her father's tone, but she noticed it immediately. Her father did not share the baron's enthusiasm for an American education and was only paying lip service to it. But apparently the go-between had made it clear that this was part of the marriage package. This was terrible! The baron must have insisted on it, and no doubt had waived a significant part of the dowry in lieu of it. Whatever the arrangement, she realized with a sinking heart that she was going to America.

The thought of leaving Japan horrified her. She was so happy here in the *Gakushuin*, the Peers' School. To cross the Pacific and live among Americans . . . she was learning English, but the thought of having to speak and listen to it every day, to learn through it . . . she could not do it! She would wither and die in America!

Yet she had to go. The joining of the Mazakis to the old and venerable Okumo house would bring great honor to her father, and she was the link. To even question her father's decision would be unthinkable.

She looked at Hiroki and from the consternation she saw in his face, she knew it was the first he too had heard of it.

"But the marriage!" he said to his father.

"All in good time, my son. Meiko would make you a wonderful bride now, but just think how much more wonderful she will be when she returns from America!" The baron turned to Meiko's father. "I would not ask of you anything that I would not ask of myself. You may not know this, but I sent the younger of my two sons to be raised in America when he was but an infant. *That* is how important I believe America will be to the future of Japan. When Matsuo returns, he will share a place beside Hiroki on the Imperial Council, and together they will lead Japan to her proper place in the world."

Meiko saw a shadow cross Hiroki's face and resentment fill his eyes at the mention of his younger brother. It was gone in an instant, but even in the midst of her own anguish at being sent away from her family to an alien land, Meiko could not help but wonder what enmity there could be between two brothers who did not know each other.

The question was quickly overwhelmed by the mind-numbing prospect of journeying across the Pacific to live and learn in America for four years. She was angry with her father, and furious with the baron and his overbearing demands. Why could she not have some say in her future?

She banished the thought immediately. To question her elders on a matter such as this was unthinkable. She must accept their decisions as if they were her own.

But America!

∎ ∎ ∎

Hiroki passed through the gate to the Yoshiwara district and hurried along its narrow streets. He averted his face from passersby. Had he been in Yotsuya, the *geisha* quarter, he would have looked for familiar faces and greeted them warmly. But here in the red-light district he preferred to be just another passing stranger. He did not want anyone to know of his regular visits to Yokiko, or of his special arrangements with her.

Seeing Meiko invariably raised an urgent need in him. And tonight more so than ever. She had looked so lovely, so desirable, he had wanted to reach out and stroke her cheek, to untie her obi and let the folds of her kimono fall open, to throw himself upon her, to—

He further quickened his pace. He had sent word to Yukiko from his home to make sure that she was free and to prepare herself for him in the usual manner. She knew what to do.

When Hiroki knocked on her door on an ill-lit back street, she opened it immediately. When she saw him she said, "Go away! You're not wanted here!" She tried to close the door on him but Hiroki slammed his shoulder against it and forced his way in.

Yukiko was a big woman, as tall as Hiroki, with large breasts and long-fingered hands. She was dressed like an American flapper tonight —short, bouncy skirt, a fluffy blouse, and a band around her forehead. And black stockings. Excitement expanded within him.

"Get out," she said in a low voice as he closed the door behind him. "I don't want you here!"

Hiroki slapped her across the face, then pushed her across the room. Whenever she resisted him he would hit her again, and again, following her around the tiny room, continually beating her. With each blow his excitement grew. Finally, she was whimpering and begging for him to stop. Panting with exertion and anticipation, he grabbed a handful of her blouse and yanked with all his strength. The flimsy fabric ripped easily. As he pulled the shreds from her, she turned away from him, crossing her arms over her black lace bra. She wailed as he tore the bra from her, exposing her high, full breasts. Then he ripped at the skirt. As she stood trembling before him, clad only in a black garter belt and stockings, the need exploded within him. He grabbed two handfuls of hair and forced her to her knees before him.

As Yukiko began to do what she did best, Hiroki surveyed the torn clothes on the floor. Yukiko always charged him an extra-heavy pillow price for a night like this, but it was worth it. He closed his eyes and dreamed she was Meiko as the pleasure crept through him.

■ ■ ■

"Have you reached your decision, Hiroki Okumo?" Shimazu said.

Hiroki sat alone in his master's quarters. It was a tiny, bare-walled room in the subterranean level of the temple, furnished only with a low bureau with two drawers, a teak chest, and a futon rolled in the corner. Two plain paper lanterns—*chochin*—provided ample illumination, but did nothing to dispel the chilly dampness of the air in the room, nor the musty odor.

Hiroki's eyes burned and his back ached from his night with Yukiko, but his head was clear and he was quiet inside.

"I would be honored with the burden, Shimazu-sensei," he said.

"Very well, then. What I tell you now you must never repeat or discuss with anyone other than Yajima, who has also accepted the burden, or myself. You must never utter the slightest hint of it to any other living soul. Is that clear?"

Hiroki nodded, feeling at once a thrill of exultation in his spine and a twist of fear in his bowels. What could it be that had to be kept so dreadfully secret?

"I shall carry it silently to my grave, sensei."

"Listen carefully, then, and learn. You know well the story of the Siege of the Final Monastery. What you do not know is that the Order was almost eradicated during that siege. The decision to call up the Black Wind was made at the last minute due to the danger to the monastery itself. And even though the Wind devastated our attackers, it appeared that Nobunaga's forces might still carry the day. Seeing this, the Elder Monk, Okamoto, feared that the sacred scrolls containing the directives from Susanoo and the means of calling up the Kuroikaze might fall into the hands of the Shogun. To prevent that, he gathered up the most valuable scrolls and fled into the countryside. He was never seen again."

Hiroki tried to understand what Shimazu was saying to him. "But we won! Nobunaga retreated. The temple was victorious!"

"Yes. We won the battle, but the Shogun was still in power. And worse: We lost the secret of the Black Winds!"

Hiroki sat in mute shock, feeling as if someone had driven a spear through his body and pinned him to the tatami. The entire reputation of the Order rested on the legend of the Kuroikaze and the unspoken knowledge that should the Emperor ever have need of the Black Wind, the Kakureta Kao would be there to call it up for him. But the real truth was that the secret was gone, and it had been lost for centuries!

"That explains it, then!" Hiroki cried.

"Explains what, young Okumo?"

"Forgive me, sensei, I did not mean to speak."

"You have had a revelation. Share it with your teacher that he might learn from you, or learn about you."

Hiroki said, "I have always wondered, sensei, why the Order, if it controlled the Kuroikaze, did not march to Kyoto after defeating the Shogun's army and use the winds to end his rule and restore the Imperial Line."

"You show a clever mind. Yes, now you know why the Shogunate was allowed to endure. The means for ending it were lost to us."

"But the Seers' visions! You said that they all show that the Black Winds will return!"

Shimazu nodded. "The visions show what *can* be, not what *must* be. It is plain to all of us that the Kuroikaze will be crucial to our victory in the coming war, but I do not believe it will drop out of the air into our waiting upturned palms. No, if the Black Winds are to rise again to smite the enemies of the Son of Heaven, we must bend all our efforts to finding the ancient sacred scrolls. And since full members of the Order may not venture out into the world, we must depend on those near to us who can."

Hiroki felt the weight of Shimazu's stare. And then he remembered the Seer's words. "Shimazu-san! Am I the 'noble firstborn' the Seer mentioned?"

"Possibly so. Years ago, when our Seers first began having these visions, we went to many of the nobles and tested their firstborn sons by the *motsu* . . ."

Shimazu's voice trailed off here and he stared at Hiroki in a way that made him uncomfortable. The motsu, the holding, was a rite in which a Seer under the influence of the seeing drugs cradled a child of less than a year of age in his arms and looked into his future. Had mention of the motsu brought back a memory for Shimazu?

"Sensei?"

"Yes-yes." He shook himself. "The Order asked to take certain babes into the temple to be educated as acolytes. Most parents refused, but a few with foresight agreed. Your father was one of them. Yajima's was another. I believe you or Yajima will be the one to restore the power of the Kuroikaze to us."

Awed by the honor his sensei foresaw for him, Hiroki bowed until his forehead touched the floor. "I am not worthy of this trust."

"I was confident the Order could depend on you. And while you and Yajima search for the scrolls in the outer world, the inner members of the Order shall comb all the records we have of the past to help direct your search."

"The vision says we will find it!" Hiroki cried.

"Knowing the future does not clear the path, but sets more thorns upon it instead. We must ask questions in regard to these visions. Have we interpreted them properly? Is the future seen in the visions mutable by our actions or inactions? Can we sit back and do nothing, secure that the outcome of the conflict will favor us? Or must we go on, striving as diligently as we would have had we not the benefit of the Seer's vision? I believe the latter choice must be ours."

As ever, there was great wisdom and insight in his master's words, great power in his conviction. This was why he honored and revered him so.

"Yes, sensei," Hiroki said, but Shimazu was barely listening. His voice rose and his green eyes seemed to glaze over as he talked on.

"Too long have we striven for the chance to go to war for the Emperor. It was in 1850 when we began our Hundred Year Plan by planting the seeds of revolution against the Tokugawa Shogunate. Our seeds bore fruit when the Emperor Meiji took the reins of power and returned the seat of government to Tokyo. Since then it has been a matter of encouraging greater strength within the Empire until we have power enough to challenge the white world in war and defeat it. We were not yet strong enough to enter the Great War of the last decade, but we must be ready for the next one! We must drive the whites out of Asia completely. They are parasites! Lice! Leeches on the body of the Empire! British, French, Dutch, Americans—all sucking the lifeblood from Asia and the Floating Worlds and sending it back to the West! It must stop! All of Asia and the Floating Worlds must be united under the Emperor to drive out the whites! You have walked the streets outside and seen how 'fashionable' it is now to forsake the kimono and wear 'Western-style clothes,' to have a 'Western-style room' in one's home! The whites are slowly, insidiously destroying what is ours by Westernizing Japan. The time is nearing for us to begin 'Nipponizing' the world!"

Hiroki could only bow his agreement. He wanted to jump up and cheer, to embrace his master, but that would not be at all proper. Never had he seen Shimazu so angry, or known him to reveal what must be a white-hot core of rage within. When he straightened up, Shimazu had returned to his placid self.

"Before you leave, Hiroki, I would like to discuss two matters with you."

"Yes, sensei?"

"The first is your brother, Matsuo. Do you expect him from America soon?"

Hiroki clenched his teeth. "Not that I know of, sensei." Matsuo again! His master questioned him regularly about his younger brother. *Why?* "Why do you ask?"

"I wish to meet with him. Make sure you bring him to me when he returns."

Everyone seemed to be interested in Matsuo's return! He was sick of being asked about Matsuo!

"And the other matter, sensei?"

"I wish to discuss your life plan with you."

Hiroki tensed. He knew what was coming. "Yes, sensei?"

"As you know, I heartily encourage you to lead a secular life and take the place on the Imperial Council that your father has planned for you. I feel you will be of greater service to the Emperor and to the Order in that capacity than as a monk progressing through the Inner Circles. But as you also know, I do not feel this is a good time for you to be married. You have two great tasks before you: to take your place in the political structure of the Empire, and to find the Kuroikaze scrolls. Marriage will divert your attention, dilute your resolve, distract you from your purposes. I trust you have come to a decision about your marriage."

Sudden relief flooded through Hiroki as he realized that a decision had indeed been made. Hiroki had not made it himself, but at least it was a decision that would please his master.

"I will not be marrying for years to come—not until Meiko returns from her college education in America."

Hiroki thought he saw a flash of anger in Shimazu's green eyes when there should have been approval. His voice remained neutral, however.

"That is good. It will give you extra time to consider the decision."

"Yes, sensei," Hiroki said, but he thought: *Nothing will change my mind. I will marry Meiko Mazaki no matter what!*

■ ■ ■

Shimazu remained seated in his cross-legged position after Hiroki left. He was furious with Baron Okumo. Shimazu had sent a messenger from the temple to him instructing him to cancel the marriage arrangements. But the baron apparently had other ideas.

Hiroki could *not* be allowed to have a wife, especially one to whom he might become emotionally attached. Had Hiroki been indifferent to his betrothed, Shimazu would not have interfered, but he had sensed the attraction Hiroki harbored for this Meiko Mazaki. Such a union could prove to be a serious distraction in the young man's life.

Especially now. So many divergent threads were weaving together now to form the tapestry of the Empire's future. Dozens of the Empire's leaders in the government, the military, and the *zaibatsu* had received tutelage to varying degrees from the Order, and the number was growing with every year. Many future leaders were being tutored now. The loom was in constant motion. Shimazu had long sensed that Hiroki Okumo would be a central figure in the final pattern. He could not allow his head to be turned by a pretty face.

But the baron had defied the Order. Instead of cancelling the match, he had done what he thought was the next best thing—he had persuaded the girl's father to send her to America for four years of education.

That seemed to be the baron's solution to problems of this sort: Go to America.

Not good enough, Shimazu thought.

This was not the first time the baron had defied the Order. He no doubt saw the sojourn in America as a compromise. But he of all people should be aware that Hiroki's future was not a game, not a political bargaining session. There could be no compromise! Misfortune befell anyone who stood in the way of the Order's mission to bring the Eight Corners of the World under Japan's roof.

Baron Okumo should know that better than anyone. Had he not seen misfortune befall those in the diet and in the various cabinets who stood in the way of Japan's transformation into a first-class military power these past twenty years? He knew it could not be purely accidental that so many of his opponents fell ill or were distracted by illness in their families at times of crucial votes? Or that a cabinet minister hostile to Japan's military growth should die in his bed of a snake bite on the eve of a critical decision involving army funding?

No. Baron Okumo had bargained with his firstborn for such accidents. He was a clever man. He had allowed the infant Hiroki to be brought to the temple for examination. Sensing that the Seer had found the child valuable, he had bargained hard: his permission to allow his son to be trained and educated by the Kakureta Kao in exchange for success in his political endeavors. The pact had been made because the baron shared the Order's outlook. He too wanted Japan to manage its own quarter of the world without Occidental interference.

As long as his aims and the Order's coincided, he would continue to receive its support. Shimazu's long-fingered hands balled into fists. But the ingrate needed a lesson in humility. He needed a reminder as to the wellspring of his current prominence.

The girl would sicken and die before she left for America.

Shimazu rose to his feet and straightened his robe. It was mealtime.

■ ■ ■

The masked, broad-shouldered guard opened the door for Hiroki and he emerged from the cool dank confines of the temple into the steamy air of Tokyo in summer. He was assaulted by the lunchtime clatter of people and vehicles in motion on the street, the smell of exhaust and cooking food in the air, and winced in the brightness of the midday sun.

"Hello, Hiroki."

He looked and saw Yajima sitting on the temple steps.

"Have you been waiting for me?"

"Yes, Hiroki." He came up close and spoke in a hushed, hurried tone. "I know that you have heard the secret now, and I wish to make a pact with you. I don't want our separate searches for That Which We Cannot Name to come between us."

"I don't want to compete with you, Yajima," Hiroki said, and he meant it. He had true affection for his pudgy friend.

"Nor I with you. But I think, for the sake of the Order, we should keep in close contact so that we do not duplicate our efforts."

Hiroki smiled. "An excellent idea. I am with you wholeheartedly."

"I warn you," Yajima said with a smile, "I will be searching as hard as I can. But I still wish you good luck."

"And I wish you the same."

They bowed to each other, then parted. Hiroki walked away thinking that he would have been overwhelmed by the prospect of searching for rolls of paper that had been lost for centuries had he not heard the Seer say they would be found. He swore that *he* would be the one to unearth them! And when he returned them to the Order, his name would be praised throughout the Empire.

And as a smaller but personally important bonus, at last he would hear the end of the incessant talk at home about Matsuo and all the wonderful things he would accomplish when he finally returned from America. He was sick to death of hearing about Matsuo. What about Hiroki and all the years he had spent with the Order to bring honor to the family?

Even his own sensei had inquired about Matsuo's return! Sometimes he thought he hated his younger brother.

DECEMBER ████
SAN FRANCISCO

Mick slammed the baseball bat into the cantaloupes again and again, smashing them to pulp.

Another fine Christmas! (SLAM!) *Dad comes in drunk as a skunk, . . .* (SLAM!) *. . . gets Ma to crying . . .* (SLAM!) *. . . starts beatin' on me and the kids . . .* (SLAM!) *. . . Just another fine fucking Christmas!* (SLAM!)

So much for the cantaloupes.

Mick staggered across the floor. He and the guys had got a bottle of bootleg Christmas cheer from O'Boyle's and had passed it around. Mick had had most of it. One thing had led to another and they wound up in Japtown. And here they were in the store where Chinky-boy worked. "Closed For Christmas" the sign said out front. What kind of shit was that? A heathen Jap closed for Christmas! It was sacrilegious! So they had busted in the back for some fun.

"Here, Mick! Batter up!"

He turned and saw Jerry underhanding an orange toward him. He took a wild home-run swing and missed, spinning around and slipping in the smashed fruit all over the floor. The guys all laughed.

"Try me again!" Mick said, getting into a batter's stance. Jerry tossed another orange and this time Mick connected, spraying everyone with juice, smashed rind, and pulp.

But their laughter was interrupted by a new voice: high-pitched, accented, angry.

"What you do? *Aieee!* What you boy do?"

It was the skinny old Jap who owned the place. The guys began pelting him with fruit. The Jap picked up his broomstick and charged.

They had a good time for a while, dodging him up and down the aisles, dumping bins, tossing fruit and vegetables at him.

"You boy go away!" he kept shouting in his squeaky voice as he chased them in his wooden sandals, swinging his stick. "You boy please go away!"

Vinnie started it. He would see how close he could get to the old Jap without getting hit with the broomstick. Jerry tried it next, then Al. They all got within inches. Mick gave it a go, dancing up to the Jap and sticking his tongue out. But he lost his footing on the slippery floor and the old guy connected with a glancing blow to the head that sent Mick's cap flying. The guys roared.

"Ha! You see?" the old Jap said. "You boy go now, not get hurt!"

Mick reached a hand up to his stinging scalp. It came away bloody. "You dirty son of a bitch!" he screamed. "I'll show you who gets hurt!"

He charged in, swinging the bat. The old Jap tried to protect himself by putting up his skinny arms but Mick just batted them aside, hearing one crack in the process. The old guy cried out in pain and grabbed his forearm. Now the way was clear for Mick to get even and give the old Jap a shot to the head just like he had given Mick. He swung the bat hard. He felt it crunch into the side of the old man's head. The Jap went down like a sack of potatoes.

"Oh, shit!" someone said behind him.

Mick looked down at the Jap. Holy Mother! He wasn't moving or breathing or doing anything!

"Let's get out of here!" another voice said.

"Yeah," Mick said. He was all for that. "But let's hide him somewhere first!"

Now I've done it! he thought. *But he was old, and he didn't have long to go anyway. And he was only a Jap.* He kept telling himself that. *He was only an old Jap.*

■ ■ ■

"Dad! Try to punch me! Go ahead. Try it!"

"Don't be silly."

"C'mon! Don't be afraid. You won't hurt me."

He smiled, then shrugged. "All right. If you insist."

He didn't try to punch me, just give me a shove. I grabbed him by the wrist, spun him around, and had him in an armlock before he knew what happened. I took real pleasure in my father's widened eyes.

"Lucky shot!" he said. "Bet you can't get away with that twice!" He backed away and faced me again.

I laughed. "Try me, big guy!"

It was the day after Christmas and we were alone in the house. Mom was off visiting Aunt Christine and we had just finished snacking on some leftover apple pie. From my position in the dining room, I could see the tree in the living room window and the opened gifts still cluttered beneath it. The late afternoon sun poured through the bay windows, warming the tree and filling the house with the scent of fresh-cut pine.

Instead of swinging at me this time, Dad charged in for a body tackle. I flipped him over my hip and he tumbled to the floor.

"I'm impressed!" he said, standing and brushing off his clothes. He smoothed his moustache with a thumb and forefinger. "Who taught you that?"

"Matsuo," I said, dropping into my usual seat at the table.

"And where'd *he* learn it?"

"From Nagata."

My father nodded. "What else has he been teaching you?"

"How to throw, how to block, how to move. All sorts of swell stuff." I was getting good, but nowhere near as good as Matsuo.

"Is all that so important?"

"It is when you've got a guy like Mick McGarrigle dogging your heels."

"You like Matsuo, don't you."

"He's my best pal, Dad," I said. My daily lessons in jujutsu from Matsuo had brought us closer than ever. He was sharing a secret, an almost magic way of fighting. And I was improving every day. Maybe because I worked so hard at it. I knew that jujutsu could be the equalizer between me and the Micks of the world. But no matter how good I got, I knew Matsuo would always be ten times better. He moved like liquid, like lightning. When we squared off against each other, he always seemed to know what I was going to do before I did it.

Dad sighed. "I don't know, Frankie."

"You don't know *what*, Dad?"

"I don't know if it's such a good idea for you and Matsuo to be so inseparable."

"Because he's Japanese?"

My father's nod set my blood to boiling. I shot to my feet.

"You're just like everybody else!" As I passed him on the way out of the room, he grabbed my arm and stopped me.

"That's not fair, Frankie! Not fair at all! You haven't heard me out!"

I didn't want to hear any more. I felt tears starting in my eyes and I didn't want him to see. But he held me fast and finally I slumped back into my seat.

"Listen to me, Frankie," he said, finding my eyes with his and holding them. "I have nothing against the Japanese. In fact, I *like* the Japanese. But I'm a minority here in California, and I worry that if trouble comes looking for Matsuo because he's Japanese, it just might find you too because you're with him."

"If you like Japanese, how come you never hire any?"

"I'd love to, believe me! Most people don't see them the way I do. They're clean, decent, hardworking people. If I had my way, I'd hire every single one I could find to work in the factory. They don't know anything about precision tool-and-die machining, but I'll bet it wouldn't take them long to learn."

"Then why don't you?" I was interested in his answer, but more than that, this was my father talking to me. He hardly ever talked to me. He was always rushing here and there on business. We almost never got a chance to be together, and now here he was sitting alone with me at the breakfast table talking man-to-man. I almost didn't care now what he said; I just didn't want him to stop.

"It's not that easy, Frankie."

"Sure it is. Someday, when I'm boss at the factory, I'll hire a whole bunch of Japanese and show everybody."

"Not if you want to have a company left."

Something in his voice gave me a chill. "What do you mean?"

"The workers—the white Californians, at least—won't stand for it. They don't want to see Nips hired to take jobs that could go to their brothers and cousins and sons. You'd have a riot on the factory floor every day. Production would fall off, you'd miss deadlines, and your customers would start looking elsewhere for precision steel parts. Soon you'd be out of business."

I could hardly believe my ears. "But you're the boss! You own the place. You can fire anyone who makes trouble!"

Dad's smile was sad as he gave his head a slow shake. "Years ago I might have thought that, too. I worked myself half to death to get that business going. Nobody thought there'd be much demand for precision parts after the war, but I figured there would always be *some* need. So I got together every cent I could beg, borrow, or steal, bought up used machinery at bargain prices, set them up in an old garage, and went looking for customers. Took me a while, but I found them, and I did good work for them, and so I got more customers and more machines and now I've got fat military contracts and own a big factory where I employ a hundred and fifty men in round-the-clock shifts. And what do I have to say about who I hire? *Nothing!*"

"But why not, Dad?"

"If I hire Japs and then have to fire them because of all the dissension their presence will cause, I'll feel like a heel. And it'll prove once and for all that I'm really no longer my own boss, a fact I don't like to face. If on the other hand I fire the white troublemakers, I'll be labeled as someone who favors foreigners over his countrymen. I won't have too many friends after that gets around. And worse, I'll run the risk of getting my car stoned as I drive through the factory gates or maybe even being burned out of this house. At the very least, the old soldiers who make the deals for the Army and the Navy will get wind of it and decide I'm not the sort of man they want to buy from. If that happens, I'm out of business."

I sat there in shock. When I didn't say anything, he smiled and reached over and tousled my hair.

"Sure you still want to take over the factory when you grow up?"

I thought about that for a moment. Then I said, "Yes." I didn't have any friends besides Matsuo anyway. What did I have to lose?

He sighed. "Well, maybe you won't have to worry about that. If some of the stock deals I'm getting into pay off, we'll be so rich that neither you nor I will ever have to even *think* about working for the rest of our days!"

"That would be swell!" I said, smoothing my hair down over my forehead. On impulse, I lifted it up to bare the wine stain. "Doesn't this ever go away?"

Dad lifted his hair to show his own mark. His was a small red crescent just below the hairline, barely visible. The rest was hidden beneath the hair on his scalp. "No. Your grandfather's never went away and neither has mine."

"But mine is so big and ugly!" I pulled the hair back down over it.

"I didn't know it bothered you so much."

"The kids call me Spot."

I saw sympathy and fury weave across his face. "I didn't know."

We sat in silence while I considered how many things my father didn't know about me. Maybe he was thinking the same thing.

Finally he said, "Someday, I'm sure doctors will be able to do something about it. But as for right now . . ."

I forced a smile. "Right now it's the only face I've got!"

He laughed. "Right!" He slapped his palms on the table. "Well! It was a good Christmas, wasn't it?"

"The best! Hope you liked the muffler."

"It's swell."

"You're a hard guy to buy for. You have everything."

A cloud passed over his face. "Not really, Frankie. Not yet. But I'm sure as hell trying!"

I left him there sitting and staring out the window and went to find Matsuo.

■ ■ ■

The late afternoon wind off the San Francisco Bay stung Matsuo's face, making his eyes water. He knew he should have dressed in more than a suit jacket and a scarf, but the cold didn't bother him. He guessed it was the warmth of this Christian holiday called Christmas that insulated him. A wonderful holiday, Christmas, or *Kurisumasu* as the folks in Japantown called it. Such good feelings between people in this season, even the Westerners who would usually scowl or snub a Japan boy had genuine smiles for him these days. Matsuo had adopted Nagata's mixture of Shintoism and Zen Buddhism, but would have gladly traded them for Christianity because of this one holiday.

"Nagata-san!" he called from the ground to the floor above the garage. Frankie stood beside him. "I am leaving now!"

Nagata stuck his head out the door. "It is late, Matsuo," he said in Japanese. "You know I have warned you about being out after dark. It can wait until tomorrow."

"If you will permit, sensei, I would like to collect my pay from Izumi-san today. Frankie is coming with me."

"Very well," Nagata said. "But no dawdling. Return here directly."

Matsuo said, *"Hai,"* and gave a little bow.

"You went too fast for me there," Frankie said as they walked side-by-side toward the trolley stop. "Why are we heading downtown?"

"I have two weeks' pay coming to me. Maybe we can go to a movie tomorrow."

"Swell. If not, we can always practice some throws."

Matsuo had to smile at Frankie. His friend had become totally enthralled with jujutsu. He never seemed to tire of learning new throws or practicing and honing old ones. It had worked quite a change on Frankie. Matsuo had seen a new self-confidence bloom in his friend. He walked with his head high, his back straight, and his shoulders square. He seemed more willing to look people in the eye than before.

Matsuo was amazed at the progress Frankie had made in four short months. He had gone from an awkward, lead-footed novice to an agile, confident fighter—although one who had never been tested. He still had a lot to learn, and every so often Matsuo had to demonstrate to Frankie how far he had to go, but still, he was impressed with his friend's remarkable progress.

The hoped-for confrontation with Mick had not occurred, however. The bully had not returned to school in September. Matsuo had caught glimpses of him and a few of his pals skulking around the downtown area during the past few months, and the talk among the boys in school was that Mick had been trying his hand at petty thievery with some success.

Matsuo had been terribly frustrated at first by Mick's absence. His plan had been to turn Frankie into a fighter and let *him* give Mick a thrashing. It had seemed like a perfect solution. Not only would Frankie satisfy his own giri to his name, but through him, as Frankie's teacher, Matsuo would also satisfy *his* giri without neglecting the various on that constrained him. And in the process, his friend would develop new self-respect. He had considered it a stroke of genius. But his plans had come to naught.

At least they were both being spared further insults. If nothing else, that was something to be thankful for.

"Thinking about Mick?" Frankie said as they stood and shivered at the trolley stop.

"How did you know?"

"Because whenever you think about him you get real quiet and your jaw muscles bulge."

Matsuo rubbed his jaw. Nagata always said he showed too much of his inner face. He must be right.

Frankie said, "If he came up to you right now and started pushing you around, what would you do?"

Matsuo hid a sigh. He knew where this was leading. "I would step aside and let you squash him like a bug."

"I don't know if I could do that!" Frankie said with a laugh. "But I sure could give him one heck of a surprise!" He paused, then said, "Not as big a surprise as you could, though."

Matsuo made no reply in the hope that Frankie would switch to another topic.

He didn't.

"I still can't figure out why you've let Mick push you around all these years. You're the best fighter I've ever seen. You could have mopped the floor with him any time you wanted to."

"I can't mop the floor with anyone. I've told you: Nagata-san forbids me. Shi-no-on."

"But that doesn't make sense, Matsuo. Nagata's an old war-horse. I can't see him allowing his nephew to get pushed around like that."

"I have not lied to you," Matsuo said softly, struggling to hold onto his patience.

Frankie quickly put a hand on his shoulder. "Oh, I didn't mean that. I just . . . I just don't understand. And when I think about all the beatings we took when you could have—"

"It was not my choice but it was my duty. *Wakarimasu ka?*"

"Oh, I understand that perfectly. I just don't understand why Nagata made that rule for you."

"A sensei should not be questioned," Matsuo said, repressing a smile as he remembered all the times he had questioned Nagata's rules.

"If you say so," Frankie said with apparent resignation, but Matsuo sensed the puzzlement in his voice.

The trolley came then, and once they were on it, Frankie said, "I used your Christmas present already."

"Really?" Matsuo said, glad now to be on the happy subject of Christmas. He had given Frankie an ivory *hanko* on Christmas Eve, explaining how to use the little seal and ink pad. "Where?"

Frankie showed him the back of his left hand. There in red ink was the imprint of the hanko, a circle bordered with tiny castles pointing inward toward the ideogram for "friend."

"That's supposed to be used like a signature!"

"I know. But I don't have anything to sign, and I wanted to use it. I sat at my father's desk this morning and filled a couple of sheets of paper with it." He held it up close to his face and inspected it. "I really like it, Matsuo. I think it looks swell. I'm going to start using it on my homework. Everything I hand in will have my hanko on it." He smiled suddenly. "Franko's hanko! I like the sound of that. Pretty soon I won't have to sign my name at all. Mrs. Evans will know it's me just from this."

"It is a poor thing beside your gift to me," Matsuo said. "As soon as spring comes, I'm going to find the proper place for it in the garden."

Matsuo had been moved almost to tears by Frankie's gift. A rock. A special rock, one that Frankie had found nested in the slope by the bay on Thanksgiving Day and had saved for Matsuo. It had a streak of quartz running through its center and green swirls in the stone on either side of the streak. Frankie had said it looked like the stream running through the garden.

The unique and personal nature of the gift had deeply touched Matsuo. The stone had meaning for no one in all of America, in all of the world—except perhaps for Nagata. But it had not been given to Nagata; it had been given to Matsuo, and its specialness had made him ashamed of the little store-bought hanko he had given in return. He wondered how he had come to be honored with a friend as true as Frankie.

Because it was the day after Christmas, the traffic made for a slow trip to Japantown. Matsuo chafed at the snaillike pace of the trolley through the car- and pedestrian-clogged streets. The shadows were lengthening as the sun dropped to the horizon. He had promised Nagata to be home before dark.

Finally, they reached Nihonmachi and jumped from the rear of the car. Together they raced along Geary Street to Izumi's yao-ya, Matsuo in the lead until Frankie overtook him with a surprise burst of speed at the last minute.

And then they both stopped dead. The store was closed. The produce trays in the front were empty. Matsuo tried the door and found it locked.

"What's the matter?" a voice said behind them.

Matsuo looked up and saw Sachi walking down the street in a new gray suit.

"Where's your uncle?"

Sachi shrugged. "I wasn't working today. Must have closed early."

Matsuo wondered about that. Izumi-san loved his profits too much to close on such a busy day. Matsuo peered through the cloudy window into the darkened interior. Nothing moved.

"You think he's all right?"

"Sure," Sachi said. "Look, I've got to get over to my aunt's for dinner. I'll be seeing you." He hurried off.

Matsuo could not shake the feeling that something was wrong.

"Let's go around back," he said to Frankie.

They squeezed through the narrow, garbage-strewn passage to the rear of the building where a rickety wooden stairway curved up to Izumi's rooms over the shop. Matsuo led the way up to another locked door. His persistent knocking was not answered.

"How long has that window been broken?" Frankie said from behind him. He was leaning over the railing on the second-floor landing and staring down at the rear of the store.

Matsuo looked down to where he pointed. His stomach lurched at the sight of the broken pane in the window beside the rear door. Without a word, he raced down the stairs and threw himself against the door. It burst open as soon as he made contact. It hadn't even been latched!

"Izumi-san!" Matsuo called from the doorway, his heart thudding in his throat. "Izumi-san!"

The store was quiet. As quiet as a tomb. The odor of spoiling vegetables filled the closed space of the back room. Matsuo reached up and found the string for the light and pulled it, dreading what he might see. He glanced about, peering into the shadows that shifted and rolled in the light of the swaying bulb. The empty fruit and vegetable crates, which Izumi always insisted that he stack so neatly here, were strewn about in chaos. A few were smashed.

"What *happened* here?" Frankie said, coming up beside him.

"I'm afraid to think," Matsuo said. He saw the old two-box wall telephone nearby with the pad tacked up next to it and the pencil hanging on a string from the mouthpiece. On impulse, he began dialing.

"Who're you calling?" Frankie said.

"Your house." Matsuo was relieved to hear Kimura's voice on the other end. "Oba-san!" he said in Japanese. "Please tell Nagata-san I am down at the yao-ya and something is wrong here. I think there's been a robbery."

Kimura said she would tell him right away. Hoping that nothing worse than a robbery had happened, Matsuo hung up and moved slowly, cautiously through the store, pulling the lights on as he worked his way toward the front. The place was a shambles. All the bins overturned, smashed fruit everywhere, on the floor, the walls, the ceiling.

"Looks like there was a fight," Frankie said.

"Maybe," Matsuo said. "Or maybe somebody just wanted to wreck the place." He hoped that was the answer.

Then he saw Izumi's staff on the floor under a counter. He picked it up and found that he had only half of it. It had been broken in two. Looking further, he found the other piece deeper beneath the counter.

Frankie said, "Oh-oh," and squatted to the floor under one of the lights. "This looks like blood."

Matsuo hurried over. There was a thick brown splatter, half-soaked into the wood. It smeared off toward the left. Matsuo followed it. Despite the chill in the air, he felt sweat begin to run. The brown smears led to a rear corner of the front room of the store where old burlap bags were piled. Something was huddled beneath the pile.

"Izumi-san?" he said.

Feeling sick, he slumped to his knees before the pile and reached out to it. His hand stopped in midair, as if it had come up against an invisible wall. He dreaded what he would find. Every fiber of his being urged him to run away but he had to see, had to know. He pushed his hand forward, gripped a fistful of burlap, and pulled.

He cried out as Izumi's slack, pale face stared up at him with glazed, lifeless eyes.

Frankie's scream sounded over his left shoulder and blended with his own as Frankie scrambled backward across the floor like a terrified spider.

"My God, Matsuo, he's dead!"

Matsuo steeled himself and moved closer, close enough to see the caked mass of dried blood over the side of Izumi's head. He felt sick. He wanted to vomit. But he swallowed the surging bile and moved closer. Matsuo had never seen a dead body before, but he knew that the blood on the floor and on Izumi's scalp was not fresh. He had been dead awhile. Matsuo had seen him on Christmas Eve, had helped him close up early.

Was he murdered yesterday? Christmas Day?

Who? That was the question. Nagata had warned him countless times of the Californians' hatred for Japanese, and he had experienced it in countless ways, but this—*this!*

He felt something in his hand and looked to see the burlap bags that had formed Izumi's shroud. Furious, he hurled them to the floor. Something rolled out from the tangle. He stooped to pick it up.

"What is it, Matsuo?" Frankie said from halfway across the room. He had not budged from there since the body was uncovered.

"A cap." There was a smear of blood along the narrow peak.

Frankie edged forward. "Let's see." He turned the dirty, plaid cloth cap over and over in his hands. "Gee, Matsuo, this looks just like—"

"Mick's," Matsuo said. The fury leaped up in him. He screamed out his hatred and his anguish. In a blind rage, he began kicking and punching at the tables, the produce trays, the empty crates, striking them again and again until they cracked and broke, and then he kept on hitting them, smashing them to kindling.

Damn California! Damn America! Damn Mick McGarrigle and damn the senseless on that had prevented him from breaking McGarrigle's worthless skull all these years!

He kept it up until his knuckles were numb and bloody and his legs ached. Then he slumped to the floor and sobbed.

"You . . . you okay, Matsuo?" Frankie said.

He nodded, unable to speak.

"We'll get the police," Frankie said.

"Don't make me laugh!" Matsuo shouted. "They'll do *nothing!*"

"Yes, they will. Look, we've got the cap and we know whose it is. Half the people in San Francisco must know it's Mick's. It's even got bloodstains on it. We can prove Mick did it!"

"And who will care? Just a lousy old Jap dead and another lousy Jap accusing a white boy. Who will believe me?"

"Well, for one thing, I'll be with you. *I'll* make the charges. I'll tell them *I'm* the one who picked this cap out of the pile on top of the body. You won't be the one making the charges. It will be *me*. I'll be with you all the way."

Matsuo looked at his friend. Frankie stood there with the bloody cap in his hand and it was obvious that he was as angry and as sickened at Izumi's death as Matsuo. Maybe it was possible—maybe with a white boy making the accusation, Mick could be brought to justice. Matsuo still had grave doubts, but with Frankie doing the talking, at least there was a chance.

And if the law wouldn't provide justice, he would have to find a way to kill Mick himself. Giri demanded it.

"Let's go," he said to Frankie.

He replaced the burlap sacks over Izumi's cold, still form and turned out all the lights as they headed for the back door. Matsuo debated for a moment whether or not to lock it, then decided against it. The window next to it was broken anyway. The sun had gone down and it was dark behind the store. They were just starting down the alley when he realized they were not alone.

■ ■ ■

"Where you two guys think you're goin' with my hat?"

At the sound of Mick's voice, I yelped. I sounded like a little girl. And then the sight of those six forms materializing out of the shadows froze my blood. Three came from the alley and the other three from different points behind the store, surrounding us.

I recognized Mick when he stepped up close to me. "I see you found it for me." He snatched it out of my hand. "Thanks, Spot. Someone stole it from me last night when I was a good three sheets to the wind. I didn't even realize it was gone till this morning. We was waitin' till dark to look for it when we seen the lights on."

I opened my mouth to speak, but nothing came out.

"You killed him!" Matsuo said in a low voice. The menace in it snapped Mick's head around, then he turned back to me.

"I don't know what he's talking about. Do you, Spot?"

I couldn't answer.

"You'll pay!" Matsuo said.

Mick looked at me. "I figured he'd say that. Never could count on no Chinky-boy to know what was good for him. But you, Spot. You'll listen. And here's what I want you to do. I want you to turn around and run back to your big house on the hill and forget any of this ever happened, understand?"

My mind raced. We didn't have the cap anymore, but I could still go to the police and tell them about it. At that moment, though, all I wanted in the world was to be out of there and on my way home.

I finally found my voice. "Come on, Matsuo. Let's go."

"Uh-uh," Mick said. "Chinky-boy's stayin' here. We're gonna teach him a few lessons."

"No!" I said and moved toward Matsuo.

I saw it coming. Matsuo had showed me time and time again how to defend myself against that kind of punch, how to grab the opponent's wrist and turn his own strength against him, twisting him around and sending him to the floor with a painful thud. And I had done it countless times, sending Matsuo to the floor as we practiced.

But I could not move. I could do nothing. And Mick rammed his fist into my belly with gut-wrenching force. I fell back and writhed on the ground.

"I guess pallin' around with Chinky-boy here must've affected your hearing, Spot. I said, 'Get!' but you moved the wrong way."

He grabbed my collar and pulled me to my feet. Past his shoulder I could see Matsuo's face in the shadows, silently urging me to use what he had taught me. Somewhere in my brain I knew how to break the hold Mick had on my neck and double him over with pain in the process. But it wouldn't come to me. Fear had a tighter hold on me than Mick. I was a first grade kid again, ready to wet my pants, afraid to strike back for fear that Mick might hurt me again, only worse.

"And I want to get somethin' straight with you before you go, Spot. You weren't here tonight, right? You don't know nothin' about some old Nip getting killed in his shop, right? *Right?*"

I nodded like a marionette. "Right, Mick. Right."

He jerked a thumb over his shoulder at Matsuo. "And you don't know nothin' about him, either. You don't even *know* him, right, Spot?"

Without even thinking, I said, "Right, Mick. Sure."

And then I looked over at Matsuo and saw his face. There was shock there, but what cut through me like a dull saw was the unfathomable hurt in his eyes. He couldn't believe that the lifelong friend who had promised to stand by him had just said he didn't even know him.

I wanted to take the words back but I couldn't. Mick still had a grip on me and I couldn't say a thing on my own.

"Good!" he said, and gave me a shove. "Now get lost!"

I stumbled away along the alley until I reached the street. Then I stopped and turned around. No one was behind me. No one was watching me from the other end. Slowly, stealthily, I slinked back to where I could peer into the area behind the store.

It was dark, but I could see Matsuo's shorter, more compact figure surrounded by the taller whites. I could hear Mick saying something but couldn't make out the words.

Suddenly Matsuo whirled into motion and I saw one of Mick's group double over with a grunt of pain. Then the melee—flying fists and kicking feet. Matsuo hurled one of the whites into another, sending both to the ground. He tried to break free through the opening, but was tackled from behind. He bounded to his feet immediately, but was surrounded and again cut off from escape.

Matsuo wasn't fighting the way I knew he could. He seemed mostly to be defending himself, not attacking. And I knew he could attack. I had seen him come at me in our practices with fists and feet flying, pulling the blows, of course, but devastatingly quick and effective. I saw none of that now. Even in this peril, he was still abiding by his shi-no-on to Nagata!

I could have helped him. I could have charged in and, using little
more than the element of surprise, broken up the circle and given him a
chance to escape. I played the scene over and over in my mind as I
crouched behind my pile of garbage and watched him duck and dodge
and crouch and thrust and parry within the circle of his attackers.
Twice I actually half rose to my feet. But each time I started to go to
him, something held me back. I was anchored with steel cables of fear. I
wanted to move. I wanted to go to his side, but I could not. So I
crouched there and felt the tears streak down my face and the sobs
quake in my chest as I watched Mick and his gang wear Matsuo down.

Then it happened. I saw one of the gang members stoop and lift
something from the ground. I saw a pale blur rise and fall as what
looked like a short length of two-by-four was brought into play. I saw
Matsuo go down from a blow to the back of the head. I cried out in
silence, feeling the pain myself. But still I couldn't move. I stayed
rooted in my safe little garbage burrow and watched as they leapt upon
him like a pack of alley dogs. I saw Matsuo curled into a pitiful little
ball on the ground, trapped between a brick wall and his attackers as
they crowded around him, each angling for the chance to kick him.

And still I did not move!

Then from somewhere behind me came a noise. I froze at the
sound of wooden geta clacking up the alley from the street. From the
corner of my eye I saw Nagata walk swiftly by, his bo tapping the
ground like a walking stick. There was no stealth to his approach as he
stepped up behind the group and shifted his bo to a two-handed grip
near the center. They were too preoccupied to notice him. And then,
moving his staff like a kayak paddler's oar, he waded into them.

Cries of shock and pain filled the alley as Matsuo's attackers were
driven away from him. They tried to re-form and bring Nagata down,
but the big-bellied older man moved like quicksilver among them, his
staff whirling, jabbing, poking, never still, until one of the battered and
bloody youths staggered up the alley toward the street, moaning and
clutching his belly. The others followed, Mick the first among them.

The alleyway was now empty but for Nagata, Matsuo, and me.

Nagata kneeled over Matsuo's still form. I held my breath, praying
that Matsuo would move. And finally, he did. I heard him cry out in
pain as he rolled over onto his back. I saw his legs buckle under him
more than once as he braced himself between Nagata and the wall and
struggled to his feet. Finally, he made it. With Nagata supporting him,
the pair came my way down the alley.

"Word has just come from Japan," Nagata was saying. "The
Emperor Taisho is dead. Your father wants you home."

If Matsuo heard, he gave no indication. They were almost on top
of me now.

I didn't move—not a blink, not a breath. As they passed, I could see the agony in Matsuo's face. His eyes were closed against the pain as he clutched at his right ribs and breathed in short, quick, shallow gasps. And I thought I saw a pain in his face beyond the physical, a pain that reached down to his very soul. The pain I had caused him.

I don't know how long I huddled there in the cold and the garbage. I felt utterly miserable, unspeakably worthless. Finally, I heard a rattle in the debris a few feet away on the other side of the alley. A rat stopped and stared at me before scuttling away into the night.

Then I too crawled away.

■ ■ ■

"They're gone! This is incredible! All three of them *gone!*"

My father stormed through the living quarters above the garage, shouting at the empty rooms.

"They went back to Japan," I said.

"Japan! How do you know?"

"I overheard them talking."

"And you didn't tell me?"

"It was only last night, Dad."

I didn't want to mention last night, didn't want to think about it ever again. I would never have believed I could feel such shame and self-loathing. I was relieved Matsuo was gone, because I knew I could never look him in the eye again. I couldn't even look myself in the eye.

"Didn't he even say good-bye?"

I shook my head, not daring to answer.

"Some friend," my father said. "Well, let's get back to the house. I swear, I'll never understand those people if I live to be a thousand!"

We walked back through the garden, my father grumbling ahead of me while I kept my eyes down on the path, looking at anything but that garden, and thinking about what Nagata had said last night. *"Your father wants you home."* What could that mean? I had always assumed that Matsuo was an orphan.

My father stopped short as we came up to the back door and I bumped into him.

"What the hell is that?" he said.

Sitting on the back doorstep was the stone I had given Matsuo for Christmas.

I couldn't hold it in any longer. I burst out crying.

My father put an arm around my shoulder and I buried my face in his jacket and sobbed like a baby.

"It's okay, Frankie," he said. "I know you liked him, but you'll make other friends. Besides, he took off for the other side of the world without even saying good-bye. What kind of a pal is that? He didn't deserve a friend like you."

The truth of that made me cry even harder.

PART TWO

1 9 2 7
---
1 9 3 2

1 9 2 7

THE YEAR OF THE RABBIT

JANUARY
TOKYO

This is Tokyo?

Matsuo couldn't believe his eyes as he watched through the open window of the touring car. Where were all the beautiful Japanese people in their brightly colored kimonos and even brighter obis who were supposed to fill the streets of Tokyo? All he saw were dull drones: businessmen in drab, Western-style lounge suits and secretaries in tight, short skirts, all trudging along the streets with glum faces.

Seeing them angered Matsuo, temporarily blotting out the dread and anticipation of knowing that he was minutes away from meeting his father and brother for the first time in his memory. He had spent every hour of the slow sail across the Pacific wondering how he would be received. But for the moment, those worries were gone, submerged in an insane urge to leap from the carriage and shout at the pedestrians, to send them scurrying to their homes, not to return until they were properly attired.

And Tokyo itself—where was the magic, the exotic atmosphere? The houses that crowded up to the street were flimsy-looking structures of wood and paper with no foundations and no chimneys and only the narrowest of alleys between; occasionally there was a roof of clay tiles but most seemed to use wooden slats. There was no discernible plan. All seemed to be chaos. There were sushi bars next to kimono shops next to hotels. Where was the neatness, the structure, the order Nagata had described to him in such glowing terms over the years?

"Why the long and troubled face?" said Nagata at his side.

Matsuo hesitated. Dare he say it?

"This is not what I expected, sensei. I thought Tokyo would be . . . different."

"It has changed much," Kimura said from the far side of the car. She did not seem to mind the changes—her face radiated happiness at being back in her homeland.

Nagata nodded vigorously. "That it has. I have read of changes in the newspapers from home, but never realized they were so great. The fire that followed the Great Kanto Earthquake two and a half years ago, that is to blame."

"Ah," said Kimura. "Namazu still shakes his great tail when he is angry, and the earth trembles."

Matsuo searched his memory. *Namazu* . . . he knew that name . . .

Nagata said, "Surely you remember my telling you of the great catfish who swims among the islands of Japan and sometimes causes them to shake."

Of course! "Yes, sensei. I remember now."

"Good," Nagata said. "Some modern people call Namazu a silly superstition, but we know where the truth lies, don't we?"

"But why did Tokyo burn? I thought Namazu caused tsunamis." Matsuo remembered the news in September of 1923 that his family's summer home had narrowly missed destruction by a tidal wave.

"Sometimes, yes," Nagata said. "But this time, Namazu did not merely twitch his tail as he usually does. This time he must have been terribly angry, for he caused the ground to heave and roll like the deck of a ship in a storm. The convulsions of the land caused Tokyo to burn for days. It was three-quarters destroyed before the fire was brought under control. Over one hundred thousand people died. Those who lived escaped only with the clothes on their back and whatever valuables they could carry. Most wear Western clothes now because they lost everything and have no money left to replace their silk kimonos. Western styles are cheaper."

"I see."

Knowing the reason for this drabness gave Matsuo some peace of mind. For a while it had almost seemed that he was back in the Nihonmachi section of San Francisco.

It struck him then that he had grown up in a city recently rebuilt from a great earthquake and fire, and now he was in another one halfway across the world that was in the process of doing the same. Was he destined to dog the trail of disaster?

They passed into the Marunouchi district where there seemed to be little damage. They then came to the moat-encircled Imperial Palace at the center of the Chiyoda-ku district. Matsuo recognized it immediately.

"The Palace! It was not damaged?"

"You don't think Namazu would dare to harm the Son of Heaven?" Nagata said. "If you look now you will see how the great walls just beyond the Imperial moat are composed of huge stones laid one atop the other with no form of cement or grout between them. This makes them better able to withstand the tremors of the earth."

Matsuo wished he could see over those high walls. He knew that behind them lay hundreds of serene acres filled with woods and pools and gardens and pavilions. This was where the Emperor lived and worked and played.

Matsuo had noticed the occupants of a packed streetcar bow as one as the vehicle passed the gates of the Imperial Palace, so he was ready to bow along with Nagata and Kimura as their own car passed. Nagata gave him a small, approving smile.

They went uphill then and turned off the main thoroughfare into a narrow, willow-lined street. Before he knew it, they were parked before a large two-story house with high walls of weathered teak and a black tiled roof. To the left of the entry gate stood a four-foot-high *kodomatsu* of pine, bamboo, and a sprig of plum blossom, the New Year's decoration that was supposed to bring vigor, strength, and long life to all family members. Matsuo hoped he had been included in that wish.

My family. My home.

He drew a tremulous breath and felt the sharp jab of pain by which his ribs reminded him that they were not yet fully healed. And with the pain came the memory of Frankie and how he had run off and left him to face his white attackers alone. The memory of Frankie would be forever linked to pain—in his ribs and in his heart.

But now was the time to push Frankie into the past where he belonged and where he would always stay. Matsuo was home now. Inside, his family awaited him. Here was where he belonged, where he would spend the rest of his life.

As the driver pulled open the gate, the front door to the house opened and a middle-aged man in a dark green kimono embroidered with maple leaves stepped out, followed by a young man all in black. Matsuo recognized them instantly from the many photographs he had received over the years.

"Father!" he cried and broke into a run across the courtyard. Deep in the recesses of his mind a voice sounding very much like Nagata's told him that proper filial piety demanded that he stop and bow before his father but he ignored it. He ran straight ahead, and actually increased his speed in the surge of incredible joy that splashed over him when he saw his father open his arms to him.

And then he was in those arms and they were folding around him. Despite his very best efforts, he burst into tears.

Home at last.

■ ■ ■

Hiroki returned his brother's bow. After that disgraceful display with Father, Matsuo at least had the good manners not to hug him, too.

So, this was the long-lost Matsuo, the little brother from America. He was quite a sight with his bruised face and stiff, splinted spine; he tried to hide it but it was obvious to Hiroki that his younger brother walked with a limp. Even worse, he acted like a country bumpkin, bowing either too low or not bowing low enough. After burning an incense stick before the picture of Mother at the household shrine, he acted like a poorly trained puppy, running from one corner of the room to the next, touching and inspecting everything. Yet the joy in his face and his open adoration of Father was touching in a crude sort of way. Despite his reservations, Hiroki found himself responding to his younger brother's awe and almost serflike deference to him.

And all the while, the notorious Takijiro Nagata stood by the door, watching his protégé like an approving parent.

Eventually, Father went off to a corner of the room with Nagata, leaving Hiroki and Matsuo alone together. Hiroki turned to his brother.

"Do you miss America?"

Matsuo shook his head. Pain flickered across his features. "No. I have no friends there. My life is here."

"But you are going back."

Matsuo bristled visibly. "I am never going back."

His vehemence startled Hiroki. "I think you'd better speak to Father about that."

Matsuo shook his head. "I am *never* going back!"

"Why not? Is that where you got those bruises?"

"He came by those wounds honorably," said Father from behind him. "Nagata-san has just explained the circumstances to me." He leaned forward and placed his hands on Matsuo's shoulders. "He subjected himself to a beating at the hands of hooligans rather than risk exposing his father to public ridicule. I am proud of you, my son. And of Nagata-san, who has done his work well."

As Hiroki watched the old samurai beam and bow, he struggled to hide the resentment that flared within him. He maintained a calm, pleased expression. He could not remember Father ever honoring him so.

"We have an important meeting tomorrow," Father said as he removed his hands from Matsuo's shoulders. He glanced at Nagata and then at Hiroki. "I believe Matsuo has proven himself worthy of attendance."

"I am honored, Father," Matsuo said, bowing.

Hiroki took a deep breath and let it out slowly. It wasn't going to be easy, but he was going to stay calm. Matsuo was a novelty now. Father would be concentrating on him, making a special effort to help the boy feel at home. This was natural and Hiroki would not allow himself to be offended, as long as his younger brother caused him no loss of face. The novelty of Matsuo's presence would wear thin very shortly and Hiroki's natural superiority would manifest itself to all. Until then, he would pay no heed to the extra attentions and privileges lavished on his younger brother. After all, he was a lay acolyte of the Kakureta Kao and was privy to secrets beyond the dreams of everyone else.

He looked over and saw Father and Matsuo deep in animated conversation and felt all his muscles tighten.

No, it was not going to be easy.

■   ■   ■

It will come. I will *belong here.*

But how long until he no longer felt like a visitor? Perhaps it was unreasonable to expect his father and brother to take him into their hearts without getting to know him first. After all, he arrived here a stranger. He was of their own flesh and blood, yet still felt himself to be an outsider.

It will come in time.

He rolled up his futon now and stowed it in the closet. He spied his oak bokken standing in the corner of the closet and took it out. He had not practiced since leaving America. He thrust it through the belt of his kimono, then drew it out in a slashing motion. When he moved now, the pain in his side was bearable, but the ribs did not seem to be healing properly. They remained bent inward on his right flank, forming a fist-sized concavity in the otherwise smooth curve of his chest wall.

The pain reminded him, as it always did, of Frankie. But instead of the anger and gut-aching hurt the memory usually brought, today he missed Frankie.

No! He slashed the wooden sword through the air. He could not miss that betrayer! It was only a little loneliness. And that would pass.

It was Nagata he missed, not Frankie. The man who had risen with him every morning and had structured the minutes and hours of each day for as long as Matsuo could remember had returned to quarters at the rear of this house, tending to Father's affairs, leaving an immense void in Matsuo's life. The world seemed empty without him, as empty as . . .

. . . Japan.

Where was the Japan he had been told about, had spent his days dreaming about? He hadn't found it here in Tokyo. And he hadn't found it on the day trips with his father and brother. He had felt a hint of it in Hayama when he had gazed upon the snow-capped majesty of Mount Fuji, but that was natural beauty. Where was the beauty of the Japanese people, the Japanese culture, Nagata had never stopped telling him about? And where was the sense of honor which flowed from Nagata? Matsuo certainly found no evidence of it in the Tokyo papers, filled as they were with stories of trade wars between the industrial zaibatsu and of political plots and conspiracies and assassinations.

Did the Japan of his dreams exist at all, or was it all some fairy tale concocted by Nagata?

One bright spot though had been yesterday's pilgrimage. At Matsuo's request, Father had taken him to the Shinagawa district to visit the Sengaku-ji Temple. As Matsuo walked through the *Sanmon*—the massive main gate of dark wood—he had felt the weight of the ages upon him. Here, on a snowy December night more than two centuries ago, was where the Forty-seven Ronin had retreated after decapitating Lord Kira. They had satisfied their giri to their dead master. Here was where they chose to satisfy chu. It was within the grounds of the Sengaku-ji that they all committed seppuku.

Matsuo walked reverently among headstones in the temple grave-yard and lit a joss stick to their memory, feeling that here he was at least touching the hem of the Japan Nagata had told him about, the Japan he had expected. Giri lived in the ancient temple. He left the Sengaku-ji reluctantly, but was delighted on the way out to discover that the shoes he had left pointing inward on the steps when he had entered had been turned around while he was inside and left pointing outward to ease his exit.

In the room his father had given him, Matsuo now stood barefoot on the tatami and began a slow *kata,* swinging the oak sword through the air in a ritualized set of movements, testing his flexibility. Yes, there was pain, but it felt good to have the bokken in his hands, to be moving in the familiar patterns again. As he loosened up, he accelerated into a string of the more complex *iai-jutsu* kata, many of which involved leaping up from a crouching position and attacking an imaginary opponent. These were the most demanding, calling for brief slashing barrages interspersed with moments of statuelike stillness.

As Matsuo whirled and slashed at his make-believe enemy, he caught sight of his brother standing in the doorway, watching him. Hiroki's face was set in its usual stern expression, but there was a light in his eyes Matsuo had not seen before. Without a word, he disappeared from the doorway and returned in half a minute with a bokken of his own. He stepped into the room and removed his shirt. Matsuo noticed a dark mark above his right wrist. He looked closer and saw that it was a tattoo of some sort: a black hexagon with a meshwork center.

Oblivious to his brother's stare, Hiroki flexed his muscular arms and shoulders, then bowed to Matsuo and took the ready stance with his bokken. Matsuo returned the bow and held his own wooden sword in the ready position. Then they circled each other.

It took only a few cuts and slashes—all expertly pulled within a fraction of an inch so that only a puff of air touched him—for Matsuo to realize that his brother was an excellent swordsman. Hiroki's movements were quick, graceful, fluid, his style unique, at least to Matsuo. But then, the only style he had ever known was Nagata's.

They wove patterns across the tatamis, Hiroki always on the offensive, Matsuo constantly parrying, dodging, and retreating, hampered by the stiffness in his rib cage and the burning pain there. After a while, he began to get a feel for the rhythm of Hiroki's thrusts, and when he sensed a pause coming, Matsuo stepped forward with a burst of strokes toward his brother's neck and chest, all whispering within a hair's breadth of the skin. Hiroki's eyes hardened as he responded with a blinding flurry of cuts that had Matsuo backpedaling across the room. As Matsuo twisted to avoid a particularly well-aimed thrust, he felt a searing pain lance through his chest wall from his broken ribs. The pain threw him off balance and he fell to the side, ripping through the paper wall of his room and landing in the hall outside.

The pain blinded him for a moment, but when he opened his eyes, he saw Hiroki standing over him, panting, smiling, and holding out his hand to him. Matsuo took it and allowed his brother to help him to his feet. He would have preferred to kneel on the floor and clutch at his ribs, but this was the first time since his arrival that his brother had smiled at him, and he did not wish to demean Hiroki's victory by calling attention to the prior injury. So he clenched his teeth and bowed.

"Nagata-san has taught you well, little brother," Hiroki said, returning the bow.

"I *learned* well and practiced hard." Matsuo saw his brother blink with surprise at his words. He cursed his mouth for allowing the American within him to speak.

"Yes. Well, I suppose that is true," Hiroki said, sounding just the slightest bit unsure of himself.

Matsuo tried to cover his error. "But it is obvious that I was not taught as well as you were by your own sensei." He did not fully believe this. Although his brother was four years older and had that many extra years of training, he felt he might have beaten Hiroki, or at least fought him to a draw, if he had been able to move more freely. "I fear I am a poor samurai."

"'Samurai'? Never call yourself that! You are of noble blood— samurai *serve* you!"

"Yes, my brother." *Will I ever learn?*

"But as for my training, I have had the advantage of having many teachers. Every guard at the temple is adept in the art."

"Temple?"

Hiroki smiled again. "You will learn of that soon enough. But for now, let's go to the *kotatsu* and warm our feet. I wish to speak to you."

Matsuo's spirits lifted at the invitation. Their rooms sat side by side on the second floor overlooking the garden, separated only by a flimsy wall of translucent paper on a walnut frame, but it might as well have been granite block for the effectiveness of the way it divided them. This was the first time his brother had shown a desire to be with him.

They slipped into woolen kimonos as Hiroki led the way to the ground floor and the kotatsu. They seated themselves around the small sunken heater in the floor of a room that overlooked the rear garden. Hiroki took the cushion nearest the window. Matsuo reveled in the warmth that flowed into his feet as he slipped them beneath the coverlet. It was said that warming the feet warmed the whole body, and he believed it.

Hiroki withdrew a packet of cigarettes from a sleeve and offered one to Matsuo who accepted. He knew Father was somewhere in the house and wondered if he would disapprove of his smoking, but for now he wanted to share something with his brother. Hiroki held the match for him, and Matsuo struggled to suppress a cough as he inhaled. The tobacco was strong. They smoked in silence, the two brothers watching each other. Matsuo was fascinated at the way Hiroki held his cigarette between his thumb and forefinger with his palm up.

Eventually Hiroki began questioning him about America. At first he asked about how he had been treated there, but then his questions moved into the area of troop strength and numbers of battleships and destroyers.

"Why do you wish to know, brother?"

"Because someday we will be at war with them," Hiroki said in a low voice.

The certainty in his brother's tone startled Matsuo. "I'm sorry," he said, feeling as if he were letting Hiroki down. "I have no answers for you."

"Then why did Father send you there? You've learned nothing!"

Before Matsuo could frame a reply, he heard his father's voice behind him.

"I did not send your brother to America to be a spy, Hiroki. I sent him there so he would be familiar with the American mind." He turned to Matsuo. "The United States looms large in Japan's future. I plan for you, with your day-to-day knowledge of how Americans think and act, to play an important part in that future."

"But Father," Matsuo said, feeling the room constrict around him, "I know nothing."

"You know more than you think you know," the baron said with a smile. "And you shall know much more."

That had an ominous ring to it but Matsuo pushed all questions aside as his brother spoke.

"If it comes to war, Father, surely the Chinese and the British will pose more of a threat."

"We must learn not to think of war solely in terms of guns and soldiers and ships, but in terms of industry and trade and production. There are many kinds of war, and the hardest fought and most valuable victories will take place in the marketplace between countries." His eyes roamed the room and came to rest on a small five-needle pine *bonsai* on a shelf in the corner. He motioned Hiroki toward the tree. "Bring that over here."

When Hiroki had placed it on the table between them, the baron spoke again.

"Consider this tree as Japan. You will note that it is overdue for repotting and thus quite suitable for what I wish to show you. You will note how its root mass has increased to the point where it is actually lifting the entire tree, mossy base and all, out of its pot. There are three possible futures for this honorable tree: It may have its roots trimmed back and be repotted to reduce its capacity for any sort of substantial growth; or it may be left untended as it is and eventually die, strangled by its own roots; or . . ."

Matsuo leaned forward into the pause. "Yes?"

"Or it may be liberated from the restrictions of its pot to let its pent-up roots find new feeding grounds. Britain has its roots in India and Africa and even in Hong Kong. The United States has the Philippines and Hawaii—and the United States doesn't even *need* roots, having only thirty-one people per square mile as compared to

Japan's four hundred! All of our eighty million live on a group of islands the size of California! The roots of most of the European countries feed off Asia and the Pacific in one way or the other. Why not Japan? Of all countries, *Why not Japan?*"

The fire in his father's eyes awed Matsuo. Here was a man who *believed* in Japan, and would fight for her. All the wonderful things Nagata had said about his father were not only true, but had been understated.

Just then Cho, the head servant, appeared at the door and bowed.

"What is it?" the baron said.

"Toyama-san is here."

The baron strode toward the door. "I have an important guest to see now. But think carefully on what I have said: When Japan spreads its roots, they will become most tightly entangled with America's."

Matsuo turned to his brother after their father was gone. He whispered, "Toyama-san? *The* Toyama-san?"

Hiroki's smile was indulgent. "Yes, little brother, our father has the great and near-great calling on him at all times."

Matsuo stepped to the window and looked out at the garden below. Hiroki rose and hovered over his left shoulder. "That's Toyama?" Matsuo asked his brother.

"Yes."

Even in faraway San Francisco, Matsuo had heard of Mitsuro Toyama. But it was difficult to believe that the thin, mild-looking, bespectacled gentleman strolling through the garden below with his father was the organizer and head of the *Kokuryu-kai,* the Black Dragon Society, the most powerful secret society on the islands of Japan.

"He may be known to the outside world as a supergangster," Hiroki said, "but he is also a superpatriot. Anyone who denies the divinity of the Emperor must soon answer to Toyama-san. He and Father became allies in 1920 when Prince Yamagata was trying to cause a breach between our Emperor—then Crown Prince Hirohito—and his betrothed, Princess Nagako."

Hiroki then launched into a complicated outline of Palace intrigue as the two feuding clans, the Choshus and the Satsumas, schemed to place one of their clan's women as Hirohito's bride-to-be. Through Father's dexterous maneuvering, the Satsumas, the clan to which Matsuo's family belonged, succeeded in making a match between the Crown Prince and Nagako, daughter of Prince Kuniyoshi Kuni, an uncle of Father's and a venerable member of the Satsuma clan. The Choshus were furious and tried bribery, extortion, slander—everything short of assassination to break up the relationship. Toyama-san came to Baron Okumo and offered his assistance.

"Is he a clansman?" Matsuo asked.

"No. He was sent."

"By whom?"

"By the Kakureta Kao," Hiroki said with no little pride.

The Hidden Face? What is that?

"The Order was furious," Hiroki continued, "that the Choshu clan would dare to try to reverse—or even *question*—a decision of the royal family. The Black Dragon Society has members in all levels of Japanese life, from the underworld up through the police to the Palace Guard. But since Toyama-san owes a debt to the Kakureta Kao, the Black Dragons are at the Order's disposal. Needless to say, the path to the wedding between the Emperor-to-be and Princess Nagako was cleared of all obstructions."

Matsuo shook his head slowly in wonder, still watching his father and the infamous Toyama in intimate conversation. "There is so much I have to learn about my family."

"That is true," Hiroki said. He indicated a watercolor on the wall. "See that painting?" Matsuo stood for a closer look. It showed a placid body of water with a gently smoking volcano on the horizon. "Father did it."

Matsuo stared at the painting and felt the tranquillity pour out of the soft blues of the water and the sky. *My father did this?*

He felt Hiroki's hand gently come to rest on his shoulder. "Would you like to learn about your older brother?"

"Oh, yes!" Matsuo said, turning to face Hiroki. "Especially about the temple you mentioned!"

Hiroki's smile faded. "Yes. Of course. Then learn you shall. My sensei at the temple wishes to speak to you. He has many questions about America—and many about you."

Matsuo swallowed and tried to smile. Something about this temple struck an uneasy chord within him.

■ ■ ■

Why Hiroki wanted to take him to the Kakureta Kao temple at night, Matsuo could not guess. What was wrong with the daytime? In the days since Hiroki had told him of the impending audience with the sensei, Shimazu-san, Matsuo had made inquiries of Cho, the chief of the household staff, and read all he could on the sect. What he had learned was intriguing but not comforting. The dark and brooding Hidden Face sect with its stern code of behavior and its masked priests who rarely left the temple and never showed their faces, even to each other, was totally alien to his experience. Its heritage supposedly went back to the time of the Great Jimmu, the first Emperor, which was fitting since it was fanatically devoted to the preservation of the Imperial Line.

Matsuo would have preferred to learn of the Kakureta Kao from afar, but there was no graceful way to decline his brother's invitation.

"You have never seen Tokyo at night, have you?" Hiroki said as they slid into the backseat of the touring car.

Matsuo shook his head. "No." He didn't say that he hadn't liked it much during the day and doubted he would find it any more likable after dark.

"I will show you, then. The Tokyo of the night is an entirely different city from the Tokyo of the day." He gave a rapid-fire set of directions to the driver, and off they went.

"How many districts in San Francisco specialize in nightlife?" Hiroki asked.

Matsuo shrugged. He had heard of the Tenderloin and the red-light district by the waterfront, and assumed there were a few more. "Four or five, maybe."

"Tokyo has more than thirty. We haven't got time for them all, but I'll show you a good sampling."

Matsuo was agape at the seemingly endless array of bars, night-clubs, coffee houses, movie theaters, restaurants, beer halls, and geisha houses that passed outside their car windows. Everywhere lights, lights, lights, flashing and blinking every conceivable color. The tour started at the Ginza in the center of Tokyo with its crowds, its wide, bustling streets, and hundreds of bars and restaurants.

But there was something strange, something wrong, something missing in the crowds of people filling the streets and sidewalks. He couldn't put his finger on it, but something didn't seem right.

But then they were moving again, down to the Tsukiji district near the waterfront where the very rich found the most expensive geishas and restaurants in among the canals; to Kagurasaka filled with military men from the nearby War College; around to Shinagawa, Ueno, and Shimbashi crowded with suburbanites flocking in from the railroad terminal; through Kanda with its bookstores and drunken students; to the geisha quarter, Yotsuya; out to the willow-lined streets of Shibuya, the movie houses of Shinjuku, the open-air cafés of Ikebukuro.

Finally, they passed through a great gate into a very crowded district. Narrow side streets wound away to either side, lined with shoulder-to-shoulder doorways, each with a tiny red light or lantern. A passing street sign read *Gojukken machi,* the Street of Fifty Houses.

"Where are we now?" Matsuo said.

"Yoshiwara—the most famous red-light district in all of the world. Love for sale." His older brother winked at him. "Perhaps I'll bring you down here sometime to sample its pleasures."

Matsuo felt a stirring in his loins. He had seen pictures of lovemaking in the pillow book he had found in Nagata and Kimura's bedroom. *Love for sale.* It had an exciting ring to it. *I've never even held a girl's hand!*

Hiroki tapped the driver on the shoulder. "To the temple."

As they drove through the streets of Yoshiwara with its moving murals of males in search of pleasure, it suddenly struck Matsuo what had been bothering him about the night's tour—no women! Except for prostitutes, bar girls, and an occasional geisha hurrying by in a ricksha, the streets were filled with men only!

"Where are all the women?" he asked.

"Behind the doors, of course."

"No-no. I mean the sisters, wives, and girlfriends of all these men."

Hiroki glanced at him as if he were daft. "Home. Where they belong."

"Don't they go out on the town at night as well?"

"Of course not."

Matsuo looked out the window. The car was weaving along the Ginza again. As it crawled through a particularly thick tangle of cars, rickshas, and pedestrians, he studied the faces of those outside, noting the staggering gaits, the too-bright eyes, the too-loud laughter, the desperation beneath the gaiety. Here was a Japan he never dreamed existed—Japan with its hat off, its collar loosened, and its pants down.

Matsuo didn't like what he saw.

He had witnessed nocturnal squalor and public drunkenness in San Francisco, but that had been balanced by the sight of men and women of all ages out together as couples, arm-in-arm, hand-in-hand. What he saw tonight seemed . . . wrong. These were grown men out on the street, but they were acting like wild schoolboys on a binge. While their mothers and wives and sisters and girlfriends sat home alone. Was that fair?

He hated rating San Francisco in any way over Tokyo, so he sat back in the seat and closed his eyes. He couldn't bear looking at those faces any longer.

■ ■ ■

The temple was a dark, shapeless blot against the sky. A cold wind off Tokyo Bay whistled up the street and knifed through Matsuo's thin coat as he hurried up the steps in Hiroki's wake. Except for the lone torch sputtering near the great iron-braced teak door, the building was completely dark.

"Is anyone here?" he said as he caught up to his brother.

"Of course! The priests *live* here!"

Matsuo resented the tone. Yes, he knew the priests lived here, it was just that it didn't *look* like anyone was here. All of Tokyo was lit up around them, yet this temple could have been a block of solid stone for all the signs of life it exhibited.

Hiroki slammed the giant knocker against the door. Its clank echoed up and down the street. The solid teak of the door was carved with strange murals and ideograms.

The door swung inward smoothly and silently. A tall figure stood just inside. The torchlight flickered off its dark, hooded robe. Matsuo stepped back, frightened. The face was masked. The eyeholes looked black and empty as the night.

Hiroki bowed and the figure spoke.

"Okumo-san." The voice echoed away behind the guard.

"Shimazu-sensei is expecting me."

"And who have you brought?"

"My brother, Matsuo, from America."

The hood turned toward him. "From America."

Matsuo wanted to cringe before those black eyeholes but held firm. He bowed low, trying to show great respect.

"Enter."

As they walked past the guard, Matsuo heard the door clang shut behind them, shutting out the torchlight. For a moment he was lost, disoriented in the blackness. Then, as his eyes adjusted, he saw a long corridor ahead, dimly lit by widely set chochin. His brother was a silhouette in front of him, moving away.

It was cold in here, colder than the January night outside. But Matsuo felt another kind of chill, a cold that crept into his soul. Not evil or malevolent, but an icy calm that only total certainty and unshakable purpose could bring. It seemed to permeate the walls and saturate the air. Didn't Hiroki feel it, too? Or was he part of it?

Matsuo shivered and hurried to catch up.

"Aren't there any electric lights here?" Matsuo said.

He saw Hiroki shake his head in the dimness. "No electricity and no telephones. Little has changed within this temple over the past few hundred years."

After a maze of turns and two downward flights of steps, they came to a small, barely furnished, lantern-lit room where a tall, lean figure with high, narrow shoulders waited. He wore a red mask, and was robed and hooded in dark blue. But most striking were his eyes—dark green and piercing in their intensity. Matsuo had never seen eyes like these. He bowed with his brother and both seated themselves before the priest.

"So, is this the brother who will sit with you one day on the Imperial Council?" Shimazu said. His voice was soft, like sand pouring into still water. Matsuo could see the green eyes flicking back and forth between them behind the red embroidered silk of the mask. He was uncomfortable under their penetrating scrutiny. He looked closely at the mask and noticed with a shock that it was fitted under small flaps of skin along the hairline and in front of the ears. It hung loosely below the chin and jawbone, and puffed out slightly when he spoke.

Above his right wrist Matsuo spotted a black hexagon tattoo with a meshwork center, identical to Hiroki's.

∎ ∎ ∎

Is this the one I will kill? Shimazu thought, relieved and yet strangely tense at being face-to-face with the younger Okumo brother at last.

He was a fine-looking boy, fuller of face than Hiroki, but there was an undeniable family resemblance between them. The boy was a bit cowed by the temple but even as Shimazu watched, he could see Matsuo adjusting.

One of you will have to die, he thought, looking from one to the other. *Which one?*

Having use of the Seers was a boon most times, but it could be a burden at others. Almost twenty years ago at the motsu a Seer had had a vision concerning Hiroki and his yet-to-be-conceived brother. Few currently in the temple knew of it. The vision was more convoluted than most, but it indicated that one of the Okumo brothers would have to be killed.

But it hadn't been clear which one. And when.

Shimazu trusted that in time he would know the who and the when. He prayed it would not be Hiroki. He had watched Hiroki develop from a toddler into a fine young man, devoted to the Emperor and to the Order. It could not be Hiroki who would die. It had to be the other Okumo—Matsuo.

But how to know?

Perhaps a few questions would help indicate the choice.

∎ ∎ ∎

Hiroki's sensei seemed very interested in America. Matsuo found that almost everyone he met in Japan seemed interested in America. But Shimazu's questions were different from Hiroki's. The sensei asked about resources and the nature of the people. Were they warlike or were they peaceful? Would they follow their leaders blindly into battle or would they hesitate and question? Were they hungry for conquest or were they growing fat and happy on what they had?

Matsuo answered as best he could, drawing on what he had learned in his classes and what little he had seen of the huge country. Yet throughout the interrogation he kept asking himself what was so important about America. He wanted no more to do with that country. He wanted to stay here in Japan and forget all about America.

"Do you have any friends in America?" Shimazu asked.

Matsuo felt a catch in his throat. He shook his head.

"If Japan and America were at war, would you hesitate to fight against America?"

"No." Matsuo was utterly sure of that reply.

"What is the best thing you can say about America and Americans?"

Matsuo thought on that one. He remembered the daily slights from strangers, the insults against the Japanese by California officials; he remembered Mick, and Izumi-san's battered head, and Frankie denying him.

Matsuo said, "It is big."

"Very well. What is the *worst* thing you can say about America?"

The words tripped out of his mouth on their own: "Its people do not know giri."

At his side he heard Hiroki's sharp intake of breath and saw Shimazu's eyes widen behind their openings. To not know giri was the greatest insult one man could hurl at another. It said that he was not fit for the company of honorable men, that he should be an outcast. Matsuo realized that he had just placed an entire nation in this category. Well, he had spoken the truth.

Finally, Shimazu nodded with slow approval. "Yes. I think you will make an excellent addition to the Imperial Council."

Normally, Matsuo would have basked in such approbation. Why, he wondered, did Shimazu's approval make him feel so uncomfortable? So . . . unclean?

■ ■ ■

Shimazu meditated a long while after the Okumo brothers had gone. *Which is to die?* He was more confused now than ever. He had been certain that the younger one would arrive full of American ideas and attitudes, that he would be enamored of Occidental ways. Such a boy would have made the choice easy.

But young Matsuo was no soft, decadent American in Japanese skin. He was more like a young samurai ready to lop off heads for the Emperor. The steel within him had been tempered in the furnace of America's racism. He was hard and he was resilient. He would make a fine weapon against the West.

What disturbed him was the developing brotherly bond he sensed between Hiroki and Matsuo. That could prove to be a problem in the future. Hiroki might be so overcome with grief at his brother's death—and Shimazu felt certain it would be Matsuo who would die—that he might not function effectively. Shimazu would have to take measures to divide the brothers should the bond became too strong.

No decision now, though. More time was needed. The elders of the Order had put the matter of choosing which brother would die entirely in his hands. They were not pushing him. And so he would wait, and watch. One slip, one sign that the younger one posed a danger, and Shimazu would snuff him out like a candle.

And with that image in mind, he thought of Hiroki's fiancée. The time had come to do something about her. But he could not allow the elders to know of this plan, this death. He could not let *anyone* know. The slightest suspicion that he was behind the Mazaki girl's death would destroy utterly his relationship with Hiroki.

And she would have to die soon, before she left for America. Even though she would be thousands of miles away during her college years, Hiroki's thoughts would be drawn to her, distracting him from his destiny. Shimazu could not allow that.

He went to the chest in the corner and lifted the lid. In the center was a small case of ebony inlaid with ivory. He opened it and examined the contents. *Doku-ippen:* multiple slivers of wood, each resting in its own groove, each saturated with its own poison. Those in the upper tray were used for instant effect. Those below were subtler, bringing on death of a more lingering sort, but just as inevitable.

Shimazu chose one of the latter variety. There must be no hint of foul play here. Meiko Mazaki's death must appear to be from purely natural causes.

Tomorrow was the *Hatsu-U-Mode* festival. Hiroki had mentioned that the Okumo and Mazaki families would be there.

Shimazu would be there, too.

■ ■ ■

Matsuo caught his first glimpse of her outside the Kameido Tenjin Shrine during the Hatsu-U-Mode festival. He was seated with his father and brother in the special section reserved for noble families. He had been agog at the colorful banners and streamers swirling through the air, and the flower-decked floats rolling through the streets. Here was the Japan he sought, even though the effect was spoiled somewhat by the reality of the surrounding city.

And then he saw her in her cherry blossom–pink kimono with the flying crane embroidery and the pure white obi around her waist, standing slim and straight as she watched the procession with her wide, magnificent eyes. She was perfect. He had never dreamed that someone as lovely as she could exist. It seemed to Matsuo that the gods had created this delicate creature as an affront to all other members of her sex, to make all other women weep with envy.

He saw little of the remainder of the procession. Red elephants in green kimonos would have passed him unnoticed. His eyes were for her alone, and his mind was consumed with devising a means of closing the gap between them.

But before he had formulated a plan, the procession ended. He was ready to do something desperate. And then she was standing and turning his way and walking toward him with her parents close behind and actually smiling in his direction!

Could this be happening? Could this vision possibly find him one tenth—one *hundredth!*—as attractive as he found her? It wasn't possible! This could only happen in a dream!

But Matsuo wasn't dreaming. The vision and her parents stopped before him and bowed. She was even more lovely close up than she had been at long-range. Her eyes . . . he could lose himself in those eyes. Matsuo suddenly realized he was gaping and he hurriedly returned the bow along with his father and brother.

"Count and Countess Mazaki," his father said, "kindly honor me by allowing me to introduce my son, Matsuo, recently returned from America."

Matsuo followed through with the bowing and the amenities, all the while thinking, *That name—Mazaki—why does it sound so familiar?*

Then his father said, "And this is their daughter, Meiko."

Matsuo's stomach lurched and his knees suddenly felt weak. *Meiko Mazaki!* Of course he knew that name. Hiroki had mentioned it so many times! She was his betrothed! His bride-to-be!

"Hello, Matsuo," she said, and her voice was music, a choir of *samisens* playing a divine melody. "It is a long-awaited honor to meet Hiroki's brother."

Matsuo bowed and stammered something as unintelligible to himself as it no doubt was to everybody else. He felt as if he were going to be sick. He wanted to die. Was there no justice in life? Not only was Hiroki allowed to grow up in Japan, but he was betrothed to the most beautiful woman in the world. It wasn't fair!

He looked up and down the street—anywhere but at Meiko. He saw a mendicant monk moving their way through the crowd. He wore an inverted wicker basket over his head. He held the mouthpiece of a flute under the basket but was not playing. A fascinating figure, but Matsuo's eyes were drawn back to Meiko.

■ ■ ■

Shimazu wove his way through the crowd outside the shrine. He could see quite well through the woven wickers of the basket over his head. On those rare occasions when he had to leave the temple, he found it most convenient to pose as a mendicant monk. The inverted wickerwork basket that covered him from the shoulders up allowed him to see but not be seen. He would stop near a crowd, slide his wooden flute up under the basket, and play a few tunes. It amused him to collect a coin or two, and then move on.

He loathed leaving the temple unless absolutely necessary. But this was one of those crucial occasions. The removal of Meiko Mazaki was not something he could entrust to anyone else. No one but he would know the origin of the slow but relentless illness that would sap her strength over the next few weeks, and then take her life.

He continued weaving through the crowd, searching for her, the doku-ippen waiting in a fold in his kimono.

■ ■ ■

So this is Matsuo, Meiko thought as she surreptitiously appraised him. *The Son Who Went To America.*

If the younger Okumo was any example of what life in America produced, she wanted no part of it! He didn't know how to act! She had noticed him staring at her with unabashed vulgarity throughout most of the procession. And he didn't even know how to bow properly. He was like a barbarian who had been taught the motions but none of the sensibilities of good behavior. His every thought could be read in his face, as if someone were painting them there in big bold ideographs.

Father couldn't send her to America—he simply couldn't! What if she returned like Matsuo Okumo?

And yet . . .

She could not deny that there was something endearing about his awkwardness. A certain innocence. A certain vulnerability. She could sense how hard he was trying to please, trying to act properly, and almost against her will, her heart went out to him. He had been exposed to the Western world all his life. It was inevitable that some of its barbarisms would leave their mark.

She spoke briefly to the baron and to Hiroki, who seemed preoccupied. The two families began strolling along the street with the rest of the festivalgoers. She returned her attention to Matsuo.

Certainly he was not unpleasing to look at. He resembled his brother in his muscular build and facial features, but his eyes were softer, less intense, less driven. Right now those eyes were gazing at her. Maybe a few questions would help him compose himself.

"Is it good to be in Japan after all that time in America?" she asked.

His mouth fell open and he glanced left and right as if to assure himself that it was he she was addressing. Finally, he said, "Oh, yes. Very good. Wonderful to be in Japan."

He did not elaborate. Meiko wondered if his was typical of the conversational skill she could expect in America. She tried again.

"How did you like America? Would you want to return?"

Again, he hesitated, but this time she sensed that he was unsure of what to say. Out of the corner of her eye she saw Hiroki lean closer, a concerned look tightening his features.

"It is a very interesting country. Very . . . different from Japan. If my father wishes, I will return there. But I would rather be in Japan than anywhere else in the world."

As he spoke, she thought she saw a wave of pain pass through his eyes, but it was gone as quickly as it had come. She wondered what it could be, then gave a mental shrug. Being raised in a country like America was probably more painful than she could imagine.

Ahead to her left she saw a mendicant monk with a wicker basket over his head. He was moving against the flow of the crowd, angling in her general direction. He held a wooden flute in his one hand as he reached the other into the folds of his worn and tattered kimono. He looked so poor. She wished she had a coin to give him. She turned toward Matsuo again.

"Will you be going to the Peers' School?" she said, trying her English on him.

He made the language switch without dropping a beat. "I start there next week."

His English sounded different from her instructors', all of whom had studied in England.

"Would you help me with the American dialect?"

His face brightened. "I would be honored!"

The adoration that shone from his eyes when he raised his head made her blush. She turned away and was startled to see the basket-headed monk almost beside her.

■ ■ ■

Shimazu had the doku-ippen ready, held firmly between thumb and forefinger, poised to strike. Just a scratch was all that was required. A barely noticeable scrape of the point along the back of her hand as he passed. That was all. Tomorrow she would have a chill. The following day she would begin to run a fever. After that, her days would be numbered.

He was about to step closer for the strike. He would pretend to be jostled by a passerby, would brush against her, bow low in abject apology, then be off. Then he saw the younger Okumo's face as he spoke to her.

He's infatuated! Utterly enthralled by her!

Something stayed Shimazu's hand. He stopped and let them pass on. He had never anticipated such an attraction between Meiko and Matsuo.

This could be useful.

The Mazaki girl could serve to divide the two brothers. A little friction would be good. Not too much; just enough to drive a wedge between them. That would be perfect. He did not want Hiroki to grieve too deeply when Matsuo died.

For now, he would let the Mazaki girl live and wait to see what developed between Matsuo and her. He had time. After all, she was going away to America for four years. She might possibly return equally infatuated with Matsuo Okumo.

Wouldn't that be interesting!

FEBRUARY

This was it! He had found one!

Hiroki's hands trembled as he scanned the ancient ideograms cascading down the yellowed paper. This scroll was of Kakureta Kao origin! Now he knew why he had been forced to learn so many esoteric ideograms during his education in the temple—Shimazu had been preparing him for this moment!

He had come to this temple in Nando because he had learned that its library held many ancient scrolls. Some of those scrolls were rumored to be of Kakureta Kao origin, but no one was sure because it was so difficult to translate the ancient ideograms. So Hiroki had rushed here and had spent every spare hour of the past month sifting through the ancient, decrepit documents to find the one he sought— the one that held the secret to the Kuroikaze.

And this could be it!

Barely able to control his excitement, he began translating bits and pieces. But wait . . . what was this? He leaped ahead in the text. No! It couldn't be!

Suddenly enraged, Hiroki raised the scroll to hurl it against the wall, but forced himself to stop.

Another fruitless search. Another false lead. Another month wasted. He looked at the clutter of ancient scrolls and manuscripts around him and wanted to scatter them across the floor and kick them into dust. That was all they were worth, anyway.

Slowly, he lowered the scroll and replaced it on the table.

No, that wouldn't do at all. This was the fifth temple he had searched since last summer, and if he wanted the cooperation of the various Buddhist sects who maintained them, he had better maintain the utmost propriety. Word would spread quickly that the Okumo-san from the Kakureta Kao was belligerent and destructive. His inquiries after old manuscripts would go unanswered. His requests for time in the temple libraries would be refused.

Not that it would matter if the other scrolls he found were like this one. Oh, it was a Kakureta Kao document, all right—lists of the purchases for an ancient monastery's kitchen. Hardly what he was looking for.

It seemed an impossible task. How could he search all the temples, shrines, and monasteries in Japan? There were thousands of them! He needed a staff of underlings, but he could not employ even one. No one must know that the Order had lost the secret of the Kuroikaze. So how could he ask someone to aid him in the search if he could not tell them what they were looking for?

He had thought of Matsuo but had discarded the notion. The Seer had predicted that someone of noble blood would rediscover the secret of the Black Winds. Matsuo and he shared the same noble blood. He did not want to tempt fate by providing the wrong Okumo with an opportunity to find the scrolls.

He was becoming fond of Matsuo. After all these years as an only child, he found he enjoyed having a brother. Matsuo had the rough edges of an uncut diamond. But it was not Matsuo's fault that he had been raised in America. It was a handicap he was struggling valiantly to overcome. And beneath it all, Hiroki sensed a heart that was firm and true in its devotion to the family and to the Emperor.

Hiroki let out a tired sigh and began shoving the crumbling scrolls back into their respective slots in the storage box. How many temples and shrines were there in Japan? Had anyone ever counted them? Perhaps it was better not to know the total. For as daunting as the task seemed, he would not give up. He would keep on looking. And he would find the secret of the Kuroikaze.

He *had* to find it. The future of Japan depended on it.

He wondered if Yajima was doing any better. He hoped not.

APRIL ████
SAGAMI BAY

Matsuo stood in the cold wet sand, his toes only inches from the waters of the bay.

Spring.

He turned in a slow circle. In the distance, a gentle plume of steam rose into the pale blue sky from the flat, snow-capped top of Fujiyama; at his feet, Sagami Bay stretched away into the Pacific; and up the slope from the shore the cherry and apple trees were blooming with a riot of pinks and white.

Was there a more beautiful place in the world than Japan in the spring? He could not imagine it.

A sudden splash drew his attention to the water again. Father had surfaced and was wading toward shore, holding his net in the water before him.

"Bring the glass jar, Matsuo!"

Matsuo grabbed the quart container from the sand and hurried out into the water to meet his father. It was cold, but easily bearable. He held the jar underwater as Father pushed the contents of his net into it, then held it up in the sunlight. A tentacled, rubbery creature, smaller than his hand, darted in nervous circles within.

"An octopus!"

"Look at its tentacles. See the blue tips? I've never seen anything like it! And neither has the Emperor, I'll wager!"

"The Emperor?"

Father stared at him. "Of course, you don't know. How could you? The Emperor and I have long shared an interest in marine biology. The summer palace is nearby in Hayama and for many years while he was Crown Prince we collected specimens together in these very waters. I may be more than two decades older than he, but I believe he considers me a friend."

While his father toweled off, Matsuo considered this new revelation. Emperor Hirohito—*a friend!* No wonder Father always spoke with such confidence about his two sons becoming Imperial advisors. Matsuo stared out to sea again and wondered at his good fortune to be born into a wealthy, noble family, to have a father who shared a personal interest with the Emperor Himself!

He felt a gentle hand on his shoulder and turned to see that Father was dry now; his jet-black hair, finely streaked with gray, was combed straight back. He was dressed in the old, frayed kimono he used when working in his garden. His dark eyes were bright and gentle.

"What are you thinking, my son?"

"I'm thinking that I never want to leave here," he said, and instantly regretted it. He knew his father planned for him to finish his education in America, and it was his *oya-no-on*—his obligation to his parents—to follow that plan without question. Once again, the American that hid within him like a snail within its shell had spoken through his lips. "But separating myself from this serenity," he quickly added, "will only serve to make it even more beautiful when I return from college in America."

"It will sadden me to see you go," his father said. "But we must be honored that we serve a higher purpose."

"I understand." But he didn't. Not really.

"I want you to travel during those four years. Attend your classes and learn your American business courses well, but whenever you can, travel. See the country. Develop a sense of America and its people. That knowledge may prove to be of immense value to Japan in the future."

"Business courses, Father?"

His father's hand nudged him into a walk along the waterline. They left the speciman jar behind.

"Yes. We will be at war with America at sometime in the future. How near or far in the future I cannot say, but there *will* be war."

"But what good will business courses do in a war?"

Father smiled. "Did I say it would be a shooting war? It may well come to that, I fear. Many of the military believe so, and they are itching for it, especially after the American Immigration Act of three years ago which they find so offensive. And if a military war is necessary for Japan, then so be it. We will fight."

He stopped to pick up a scallop shell, white with deep red stripes. He rinsed it off and handed it to Matsuo. "A beauty, isn't it. Hold it for me."

He began walking again. "But there are ways other than military war for Japan to assume its proper station as leader of all nations. We can dominate the world with trade."

Matsuo's expression must have registered his inner puzzlement, for his father laughed.

"You're not the first to look at me that way, my son, and I'm quite positive you won't be the last. But think: If you make the best products in the world, and you make them faster and finer than anyone else, the monies of the world will flow into your coffers. You will be exacting a tribute from all the other nations without unsheathing a single sword, without firing a single shot."

Matsuo gazed into the bright calm eyes that faced him and suddenly realized the greatness of his father. He remembered the pride in Hiroki's voice when he had spoken of Father that day he had beaten him in the bokken exercise. He had not been able to fully appreciate that pride then. Now he could. Now he could see his father for what he really was: a man of vision, who could not only see the future, but devise ways to shape it.

"Are there many who agree with you?"

He nodded thoughtfully. "A few. At this juncture the country seems to be divided into those who want to turn their backs on the world and return to the samurai days, and those who want to

Westernize Japan until she is indistinguishable from the other industrial nations. Me . . . I'm influenced by the writings of Yoshida Shoin, the man who almost single-handedly sparked the Meiji Restoration. He believed firmly in contact with the West, trade with the West, but not total surrender to the West. He died almost seventy years ago, but his wisdom lives on. We must keep one foot in the past—we must never forget our cultural heritage, for it is the richest in the world. But we must keep the other foot in the present, for that is where we live. And our eyes . . . our eyes must always be looking ahead."

"Everyone speaks of war as the only answer," Matsuo said, thinking of the newspapers and speakers on the radio.

"Not everyone, but very many, it's true. But either way, it will not lessen the importance of the roles you and Hiroki will play. Hiroki, with his education in the Hidden Face temple, will be our foot in our warlike past. I see Hiroki playing a vital part in a shooting war. But you, my son, will be Japan's foot in the present. You will be a general in the *other* war. The one I mentioned before: the economic war. And our enemy in that war will surely be America. That is when you will play your part. If and when that war is declared, you, Matsuo, my son, may well become the most important man in Japan, perhaps in the world."

Matsuo swallowed his dismay. As much as he wanted to please his father, he did not want to be the most important man in Japan. Not if it meant going back to America, even for a day.

DECEMBER ▮▮▮▮
SAN FRANCISCO

"Bet I know what you're thinking, Frankie."

The sound of my father's voice startled me. I hadn't heard him come into the room.

I had been standing at the window, watching a Navy gunboat steam out of the Golden Gate and vanish into the foggy Pacific. It looked cold and rough out there, which was just fine, because that was pretty much in tune with the way I felt. The news on the radio at that moment was fairly grim, too. In preparation for the arrival of 1928 next week, the announcer was recapping the big stories of the past year. Mostly death and destruction: the Lower Mississippi Valley flood, the Sacco and Vanzetti executions, Isadora Duncan's death, Lizzie Borden's death. It seemed to go on and on.

"Not a very good year, was it?" I said to Dad.

"Are you kidding?" he said. "It was a *great* year! Don't listen to those radio guys. They're always down in the mouth. Look at all the good things that went on: Babe Ruth hit sixty homers, that fellow Johnny Weismuller swam the hundred in fifty-one seconds, the Holland Tunnel opened between New Jersey and Manhattan— something I'd like to see happen between here and Oakland so we wouldn't have to depend on that damn ferry—and we've got talking pictures now. Don't tell me you didn't enjoy *The Jazz Singer*. You must have seen it three times!"

I forced a laugh. "You win. It wasn't such a bad year."

"That's the spirit! Now, let me guess what you were thinking about when I came in."

"Bet you can't."

I had been thinking about Matsuo. I hadn't wanted to think about him. I'd thought I'd had him well locked away in a quiet little-used corner of my brain. But too often those memories wanted out and when that happened I didn't have much say. Especially on this day, the day after Christmas. It was a year ago today that I became a spineless turd and deserted my only friend.

I wondered what Matsuo was doing, if he had found a better, truer friend.

"You were thinking about that old engineering scholarship, weren't you?" Dad said, clapping me on the back.

"Yeah. The scholarship."

Let him believe that. Let him believe anything but the truth. He didn't know the truth. Only Matsuo, Mick and his gang, and I knew. Matsuo was gone, and the rest of us weren't talking.

For the thousandth time I wished for a chance to go back and do it differently. But *would* I do it differently? I wasn't sure. And I loathed myself for that uncertainty. Not that it mattered. I'd never get another chance. And I'd never see Matsuo again.

"But you don't *need* a scholarship. If my stock portfolio keeps performing the way it has for the past year, I'll *buy* you a college! Hell! If my stocks don't do anything at *all* next year, I'll still be able to buy you that college!"

My father had become obsessed with the stock market. It was all he talked about, all he seemed to think about. He even had a ticker here in his office at home. The market was a source of endless arguments between my mother and him. She said he was neglecting his own business and borrowing too much to add to his portfolio, and he'd say that thanks to his investments they were now worth millions. I didn't know who was right, but when I heard my mother mention that he had taken out second and third mortgages on the house and on the plant, it made me uneasy. But what did I know? My father had built his company out of nothing, so he had to know a lot more than I did.

I said, "I want that scholarship because it's something that no one can buy for me. I have to *earn* it all by myself."

"Something wrong with my money?" Dad said. "Something wrong with the tool and die business? I thought you said you wanted to run it some day. But if you've changed your mind and now think you're too good for it, just let me know."

"Dad, please . . ." Was he just feeling defensive or was he worried about my going to college? He never had. "You know me better than that. You know I want a chance to run the plant. It's just that . . ."

How could I explain it to him? How could I tell him I needed to do something to make me feel better than someone who scuttled through alleys on his belly?

"I'm waiting," he said.

"All right, Dad. For me, it's not good enough to waltz into that plant and just step into your shoes. You *deserve* the plant—you built it out of nothing. But if I take it over, I want to be able to change things when they need changing. I want to make it the best plant in the world. And to do that, I'll need some training in engineering. And when I've made it the best in the world, then I'll deserve to call it mine!"

"I don't know, Frankie," Dad said, shaking his head. "I don't know if you can handle it. Know-how is only a small part. You've got to go out and meet people, glad-hand them, grease their palms when necessary. I don't know if you're cut out for that. You know, kiddo, your mother and me, we worry about you."

"Worry?" I said. "About me?" I knew they thought I was strange, but I didn't let on.

"Sure! After all, it's your senior year and you should be out with your friends having a good time instead of moping around here or hanging around the plant. Sometimes we wonder if we've failed you somehow."

"Sorry, Dad."

"Don't be sorry. *I'm* the one who should be sorry. I'm sorry you're not enjoying life more. When I was your age I spent every spare minute of every day sweating for a few dimes to keep my brothers and sisters fed. If I'd had the chances you've got now, I'd be out having the time of my life!"

"But I *like* the plant, Dad."

"For God's sake, *why?* What do you want to get yourself involved in that for? Only a sucker would want to give himself an ulcer trying to manage a place like that."

I was shocked. "I . . . I thought you wanted me to take it over someday."

"I did. But I didn't know what I know now. I don't want you to have to spend all your time running around brown-nosing a bunch of military brass to keep the orders coming in when there's money falling out of the air—out of the *air,* Frankie—at the stock exchange."

"I don't understand that stuff, Dad."

"Maybe you'd better learn to understand it, Frankie. Because I don't think you've got the stuff to run the company."

The hurt I felt from those words must have shown on my face, because Dad gave my shoulder a quick squeeze.

"Don't get me wrong, kiddo. I love you. And I think you'd do a great job running the *plant*—but that's a long way from running the company. To run the *company* you've got to get out there and hustle every day for the orders. You've got to have lunch and make pleasant conversation with people you have no respect for, got to invite people to your house that you wouldn't speak more than a few words to on the street. Sometimes you've got to shave points and jimmy balance sheets just to keep your head above water. Frankie, my boy—I don't think that's quite your cup of tea."

"I could learn," I said, knowing he was probably right but too stubborn to admit it to him. "All I need is a chance."

"Okay. You'll get your chance. But in the meantime I want you to learn something else. First thing tomorrow morning when the New York exchanges open, I'll give you some of my stocks to manage. The best way to learn is by doing. You'll have your own little portfolio to manage to help you get to know the ropes."

"But Dad—"

"No buts. I want you to get your feet wet. As soon as you do, you'll see what I mean. You'll learn early what I learned late. I used to work for money, but no more, kiddo. No more! Now I let money work for me!"

Reluctantly I agreed. Mostly to get my father off my back, but also because I was intrigued by what he was saying. Money for nothing. It seemed too good to be true. But what did I know?

But I wasn't giving up on that scholarship. Stocks or not, I was going to try for it.

1 9 2 8

THE YEAR OF THE DRAGON

APRIL ▮
TOKYO

"Nagata-sensei," Matsuo said. "Tell me what to do."

He had performed the tea ceremony with Nagata. And now as Matsuo sipped his tea, he saw Nagata, the man he loved and admired more than any in the world, put his cup on the low table between them, fold his hands over his ample belly, and fix his eyes on Matsuo's.

"Am I such a terrible teacher that you don't know? Am I to hang my head in shame when I go out in public now because my student does not know how to behave?"

Matsuo recognized the overstatement, but realized too that it wasn't far from the truth.

"How can I tell my father that I don't want to go back to America?"

Nagata's face grew stern. "You *cannot* tell him that! It is your father's wish that you finish your education in America. It is your path toward taking your proper station. It is your parental on. Filial piety demands that you follow his wishes!" Nagata lowered his voice. "And because your father plans for you to become an Imperial advisor, one might even say that chu demands that you return to America."

Matsuo stiffened. Chu—the ultimate on—the endless, unrepayable obligation to the Emperor. The discussion was over. To circumvent chu was unthinkable.

"I will go to America," he said, fighting the heaviness within him.

"Of course you will!" Nagata said, slapping his knees and smiling. "Was there ever any doubt?"

Matsuo did not answer. His throat felt locked. He had been in Japan less than a year and a half; only half a year remained here. *So little time!*

Nagata answered for him. "Of course not! And think of it this way: Giri demands that you return to America and clear your name with those who beat you in such a cowardly fashion. It will take all of your cunning to devise a plan whereby you satisfy giri without breaking a law and landing in an American prison."

Matsuo instinctively ran a hand over his right flank where his ribs had been broken. He let his fingers dip into the concavity where the bones had healed improperly.

"Will you help me plan it?"

Nagata shook his head slowly. "I will not be going with you."

The statement so startled Matsuo that he nearly upset the table. "But you must!"

"I too must do the bidding of your father, only for me it is *nushi-no-on*—duty to one's lord. And your father tells me that his estates need my attention. It is from those lands, deeded to your ancestors by the Emperor himself many centuries ago, that your family fortune flows. I am honored by his trust. I must stay."

Alone in America, Matsuo thought. The prospect of crossing the Pacific again was now doubly daunting.

"You are seventeen now," Nagata was saying. "You will be eighteen not too long after you return to America. You will be a man. You will have to learn to live like one."

Matsuo took a deep breath and calmed himself. Yes. He could do that. He would *have* to do that.

"Your hands are quite bruised," he heard Nagata say in an obvious attempt to change the subject.

Matsuo held them up, examining the blue of the fresh bruises and the yellow of the older ones. "I have been studying *te* at the Shotokan *dojo.*"

"Ah! The Okinawan empty-hand defense. I have seen it since our return. Most impressive."

"Shall I show you a kata?"

Matsuo stood and began going through his *shuri-te* movements, kicking and thrusting at the air. He worked on his kata daily for hours, making up for the years of experience the other students in the dojo had on him. He was nearing the top of his class. Soon maybe he would be the best. But his kicks and punches had new force and quickness today. He was losing himself in the routine, imagining Mick McGarrigle as his opponent.

JULY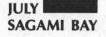
SAGAMI BAY

Matsuo whirled in the air and lashed out at him with a vicious kick. Hiroki drew his head back and closed his eyes against the spray of sand from his brother's foot as it passed within an inch of his jaw.

Although the setting sun was red and low above the hills and the two of them stood within a stone's throw of the bay, the July heat remained insufferable, hanging in the air like wet cotton. The damp sand in a wide circle around them was scuffed and pocked with their footprints, and here and there even an occasional body print. The beach was deserted but for Hiroki and his brother, both clad only in fundoshi, the air silent but for their harsh, rasping breaths as they circled and clashed and parted and circled again.

Hiroki's chest burned from the exertion of the sparring exercise with Matsuo. He knew his younger brother had been studying te, but had never dreamed he had progressed this far in so short a time. His kicks, both high and low, were devastatingly accurate, and his hand strikes were flashing blurs in the humid air.

Had they been engaged in a full contact battle, Hiroki was sure he would have been down by now. He could barely lift his arms and was ready to drop, but he would not allow himself to call a halt. He could not admit defeat at his younger brother's hands.

To his surprise, it was Matsuo who called the halt. Raising his hands, he dropped to the sand and sat there gasping. His chest heaved except at the concavity on the right where the ribs had been broken.

"No more, brother!" he said. "I am too out of breath! You have beaten me again!"

Hiroki flopped across from him. Matsuo had won. They both knew that. Yet his younger brother seemed content merely with the knowledge. He was not requiring an admission of defeat. Hiroki found that almost incomprehensible.

"You have improved immensely, Matsuo," he said. If Matsuo could save face for him, let it never be said that he could not repay in kind. "In fact, I doubt very much that there is another shuri-te-ka in all of the world who has learned as fast as you."

Matsuo bowed his head. "Funikashi-san is a supreme master and teacher. I practice often and have added a personal impetus to my kata."

"And what is that?"

"I fight the American boys who beat me. All of them. At once."

"And do you win?"

Matsuo smiled fiercely and nodded. "Yes. Every time."

"It is said that it is unwise to fight in anger. The mind becomes fogged by its heat."

"The anger is gone," Matsuo said. "All that remains is the need to satisfy giri."

Hiroki understood. He could almost pity the Americans who were Matsuo's target. Almost.

He stretched, feeling the tightness in his muscles seep away. His sweat was cooling and drying. He felt relaxed and close to his brother.

"Speaking of America," he said, "I have a special duty to request of you."

"You need only ask," Matsuo said as he stretched and massaged his own muscles.

"I want you to watch over Meiko during your stay in America."

Matsuo's brow furrowed. "I don't understand. How can I—"

"Meiko will be going to America after the Enthronement. Like you, she is registered in the class of 1932 at the University near San Francisco."

Matsuo looked dumbfounded. "Berkeley?"

"Yes. It is the wish of both fathers. Didn't you know?"

"Know? Of course I didn't know! How can I know something if nobody tells me!" He was suddenly sitting up bo-straight, his eyes wide as the words tumbled from his lips. "Meiko is going to America? To Berkeley?"

"Of course. This has long been in the planning."

"And you *approve?*"

Hiroki settled his gaze on the calm blue line of the horizon and sought a share of its steadfastness. "It is the will of the count. And Father's. I have no say in the matter."

The thought of his Meiko alone in that land of barbarians was almost too much to bear. She would be chaperoned, of course; one of the count's retainers and his wife would go along and maintain a home for her. Her absence for all that time was bad enough, but the realization that it would be another four years before they could be married, before he could touch her, pillow with her . . . He dreamed of wallowing in her innocence for a while before teaching her the special things she had to do to please a man.

"This must be a terrible burden for you to bear," Matsuo said. "But poor Meiko! She must leave Japan and live over *there* for four years! She must feel terrible!"

Hiroki was pierced with a sudden pang of guilt. He had never thought about how the prospect of living in America must be affecting Meiko, only of what it was doing to him.

"But what would you have me do, brother?" Matsuo said.

"Guard her," Hiroki said. "Be the champion of her purity."

"But surely she would never look at a gaijin!"

"Of course not! But she is young and impressionable. I would not want her to return unduly tainted by Western ways."

"Like me?" Matsuo said, and Hiroki saw the pain and defensiveness in his brother's eyes. *Yes, like you,* would have been the honest answer, yet Matsuo had shown himself to be a good and gracious younger brother today by calling the fight to a premature halt. He could certainly be half as gracious.

"Matsuo," he said levelly, "for all the years you spent in America, you show yourself each day to be as much of a Japan man as anyone who was reared here."

Hiroki was surprised and gratified at the sight of the tears that sprang into his brother's eyes before he bowed.

"Katajikenai, my brother. You have made me rich today with those words. I shall stay close by Meiko's side throughout her stay in America. She shall return to you as she left: an honorable Japan woman."

It was Hiroki's turn to bow. When he raised his head, Matsuo was on his feet and running toward the bay. "Look at me!" he shouted. "I'm going to swim back to America!" His last words before he dove headfirst into the water were garbled, but Hiroki thought they sounded like, "Maybe going back won't be so bad after all!"

He didn't know what to make of that.

NOVEMBER
KYOTO

Matsuo was in love.

After almost two years in his homeland, he had finally found the Japan he had been seeking.

Kyoto.

He stood at dawn on the Togetsukyo, the Moon Crossing Bridge, and listened to the Oigawa flowing beneath his feet as he stared out at the misty ancient city where the multifaceted expanse of low tiled roofs was regularly interrupted by jutting temple pagodas. And over the whole scene towered Arashiyama, Storm Mountain.

He had been so overwhelmed by the city that he had been struck dumb during the carriage ride from the station. He had strolled her streets and marveled at her temples and shrines—two thousand of them!—and her beautiful people, all properly kimonoed. He had toured endlessly, soaking up the essences of the city that was the spiritual heart of Japan, the Japan he longed for, the Japan he had dreamed of for so long.

And now it was the morning of the tenth of November, the day of the Enthronement ceremonies, the event that had brought him here.

He was at the Kashiko-Dokoro, the Imperial Sanctuary, with the other guests and dignitaries, Japanese and foreign, when Emperor Hirohito, dressed in a ceremonial robe of white silk damask, arrived with the Empress to inform the Sun Goddess, Amaterasu, of his ascension to the throne. Matsuo was present at the formal enthronement in the afternoon when the Emperor, now in bright orange robes colored like the morning sun, sat on a canopied throne next to his Empress and the air filled with the clamor of drums, gongs, and cymbals. He heard the Emperor declare that he now occupied the throne of Japan and henceforth his reign would be called *Showa*—Enlightened Peace. His heart filled to bursting, Matsuo bowed as low as he could along with the rest of the throng.

The second day of the ceremony was taken up with ritual baths and the ringing of bells throughout the city to summon all the Emperor's ancestors.

On the third day came the rite of *Daijosai*, the Thanksgiving Festival. All foreigners were excluded from this. The Emperor bathed and donned a robe of pure white. After his hands were cleaned by a Shinto priest, he went out to the grounds of the Imperial Palace where two huts had been constructed of raw pine and held together by vines. Barefoot, under an umbrella of woven rushes, he walked along a torch-lit path upon a carpet of rushes which was rolled up after him so that no other might walk upon it. He entered the first hut, the curtains were drawn, and he was left alone within to serve and wait upon the Goddess Amaterasu. Hours later, the Emperor entered the second hut to repeat the ceremony. Finally, with the coming of the dawn, he retired.

Matsuo had not slept at all during the entire three days. Far from tired, he felt exhilarated by the Enthronement. He felt as if the centuries between himself and all his ancestors had been breached and that they had been in silent communion with him throughout the ceremonies. He felt alive, refreshed, renewed. He was ready to face anything.

Even America.

1 9 2 9

THE YEAR OF THE
SNAKE

OCTOBER

It was the last Tuesday in October—a day I'll never forget. I had won
the scholarship and was in my second year at the University of San
Francisco. The engineering courses were going swimmingly. I had no
morning classes on Tuesdays that semester so I was home having coffee
in the kitchen when I heard shouting from Dad's office down the hall.

I looked at Mom. "What's going on?"

She sighed. "Probably your father's made another 'killing' in the
market." She looked tired as she puffed on her cigarette and sipped her
coffee.

"I know you don't like the market," I began—

"Don't like it? I hate it! It's not real!"

"He's making millions."

"Millions on paper, but nothing real. A diamond is a real
investment, gold is real—you can hold them in your hand and know
you really own them. Even this house—" she stopped herself.

"I know it's mortgaged," I said.

"Mortgaged to the hilt! He's borrowed against everything we
own. It's one thing to take a flyer or two in the market, but it's quite
another to risk the roof over our heads!"

I stirred my coffee and said nothing. I had made heavy profits on
the portfolio Dad had given me. Without telling him, I had sold most of
it off two months ago and bought back the mortgages on the house. It
was going to be my Christmas gift to both of them—but really to Mom
because I knew how she had nightmares of being kicked out on the

street. I was tempted to let her in on the secret so she could rest easy, but that would have ruined the Christmas present.

As I passed Dad's office, it sounded as if he were having a violent argument. He slammed down the phone as I peeked in.

His face was ashen. "My God, we're losing everything!"

Fear squeezed my gut. I had never seen my father like this. He was positively frantic, striding from the ticker tape to the window, from the window to his desk, and from there back to the tape, running his hands through his hair as he muttered and shouted curses at the ceiling. He stopped moving only for glances at the ticker tape or for phone calls.

"Dad, what's wrong?"

"The Market! The bottom's dropping out of everything! *Everything!*"

"But didn't you tell me that a drop is just a signal to buy more at bargain prices?"

"A *small* drop, yes, but this is a catastrophe! All my margin accounts are calling. I've got to put up tens of thousands I don't have to cover them!"

"Can't you sell—?"

"Nobody's buying! And I'm already borrowed to the eyeballs! Somebody's got to do something about this, and fast! They should close the Market and let things cool off!" He glanced at the clock on his desk. "My God, it's only ten! Two more hours to go in New York! If it keeps up like this I'll be ruined! Completely ruined!"

"It's not so bad, Dad. I—"

"Don't tell me what's bad!" he screamed, his face turning scarlet. "You have no idea of the magnitude of what's happening!"

With his wild eyes and disheveled hair he looked almost insane then, and it frightened me. I took a step back from him.

"But Dad—!"

"Get out! Get out and leave me alone! I've got to think and I can't do it with you standing there making inane remarks!"

I left him there shaking his fists at the air. I wanted to tell him that we still had the house but guessed that now was not the best time. Maybe tomorrow, when he was more rational.

But tomorrow never came for Dad.

I awoke that night to my mother's screaming and followed the sound to the study where my father sat in his chair at his desk, a bullet hole in his forehead and blood and brains splattered all over the wall behind him.

■ ■ ■

It had been a short service after a brief closed-casket wake, and now I stood at the graveside and cried openly as they lowered him into the ground. Maybe he hadn't been the best father in the world, and maybe he hadn't been around as much as other fathers, but he had always seen the good things in people and in life. He had made his share of mistakes—the worst being his final act—but he had had such vitality and enthusiasm that I forgave him. I missed him terribly.

So I stood there, feeling hollow, beyond shock, beyond any emotion but grief after the ordeal of the past two days. Yet when I looked up at the graveside mourners, I received another shock. Far to the rear, standing next to a tree, was a vaguely familiar form. I wiped my eyes to clear my vision.

It was Matsuo. It had been almost three years. He was taller, broader, his face was different, changed, distorted somehow, but there was no doubt in my mind that it was Matsuo.

As soon as our eyes met, he turned and walked away. I wanted to run after him but I couldn't leave my mother alone at the graveside. So I stood there in silence and watched him disappear into the greenery.

Matsuo was back in America! But where? I knew I had to find him. I had to apologize. I had to explain!

1 9 3 0

THE YEAR OF THE HORSE

JANUARY

I didn't think I'd ever get over not having Dad around, but after a while
the shock and the grief found their niches and our homelife began to
settle into a new pattern. That was when I began to search for Matsuo.
I wandered around Japantown in my spare time but never caught sight
of him. I checked through the registration at the University of San
Francisco but no one named Okumo was listed. I was beginning to
think I had been imagining things.

As a last resort, I decided to try my luck across the bay. There
were a number of Japanese students on the Berkeley campus. I thought
I might talk to some of them and see if they could help me. Trouble
was, I couldn't find any when I wanted to. I asked around the campus as
to where I might find them. The general consensus was, "Who cares."

I gave up. Most likely I had been imagining Matsuo's presence. I'd
been under tremendous stress at the time and my mind had picked
someone out of a simpler, happier time to see.

Sure. That was it. There was no other rational explanation.

Why couldn't I make myself believe it?

On what I had sworn was to be my last day of searching over at
Berkeley, I was sitting in the student cafeteria drinking a cup of coffee
when I had a vision.

A group of girls, obviously just out of class, entered in a bunch,
laughing, giggling, scanning the room to see if any of the Big Men On
Campus were present. Their eyes slid over me like brook water over a

mossy rock. And then someone broke from their group and took a seat at an empty table where she sat alone studying while she sipped and stirred her cup of tea. She was Japanese and wore a white silk kimono embroidered with pink cherry blossoms. Her hair was flawlessly black and straight, and her thick bangs blended perfectly with the rest of the hair that framed her face. And what a face! High cheekbones and dark, almond-shaped eyes, bow lips, and utterly flawless skin.

I could not remember ever seeing a woman half so beautiful. I'm sure that to almost anyone else in the room she stuck out like a sore thumb; but to me she was a swan gliding through a pool filled with toads.

I was mesmerized. I found myself on my feet and moving toward her. I stopped at her table where she sat alone. All the other girls had clustered elsewhere in clucking cliques. Finally, she looked up from her book.

■ ■ ■

Meiko sat and thought of how miserable she was in America.

She missed her mother and father. She missed her friends. She missed Japan. Most of all, she missed feeling that she *belonged*. If one—just *one!*—American girl in all her classes had responded in kind to any of her friendly gestures, her whole outlook might have changed. But it seemed that she was condemned to be "the different one" in this university, condemned to be an outsider by her kimonos and her wooden geta and her difficulties with certain consonants.

The boys who had approached her had been friendly enough at first—warmly lascivious in their approach and angrily cruel in their retreat when they discovered that she was not interested in any relationship that went beyond friendly conversation.

Matsuo Okumo was the only person on this entire barbaric continent who kept her from despair. She had changed her mind about Hiroki's younger brother. He was not an ill-bred bumpkin who did not know proper behavior. She had seen his progress at the Gakushuin where he had learned to act as a true Japanese almost perfectly. She qualified her approval with an "almost" because she had always been able to spot his *faux pas*—but only because she had been watching for them. To any casual observer, Matsuo would have blended in perfectly.

Here in America it was almost the same. He could not hide his pigmentation or facial features, of course, but he managed to blend in extraordinarily well nonetheless. Meiko still found herself bowing at the slightest provocation; Matsuo had dropped immediately the bows that were such a part of daily Japanese life. His walk and even his posture had changed. He now *moved* like an American. And his

English—utterly flawless. He seemed to have not the slightest bit of trouble with the alien consonants that plagued her so.

And so attentive! He saw to it that she wanted for nothing. He toured her through San Francisco and the truly beautiful valleys inland. He had become her safe haven among the barbarians and she found herself looking forward more and more to their times together.

And yet . . . the better she got to know Matsuo and the more she grew to like him, the less she understood him. There were secrets hidden away deep within him in places that he let no one see. But that made him all the more interesting. She felt challenged to penetrate his mystery. And then there were his unpredictable idiosyncrasies— such as his obsession with the American game of pool. Hardly a day would pass when she wanted to talk to him or be with him and he would say that he had to go practice pool. Honestly, at times it was quite—

"Konnichi wa."

Meiko started at the sound of an unfamiliar voice saying a familiar word. She looked up and saw a dark-haired American boy standing across the table from her, holding a tray with two cups and saucers.

"Yes. Hello and good day to you, as well," she said, still off balance from his use of her native tongue. It was the first time since her arrival that an American had spoken a single word of Japanese to her.

"I brought you another tea," he said in surprisingly good Japanese.

"Koohii o nomimasu," she said quickly, telling him that she drank coffee.

His flustered expression and his stammered, "Oh, I'm so sorry, but I thought I saw a tea bag by your cup," convinced her that he had understood her.

"Actually, I hate coffee," she said in English. "I was just testing to see if you really spoke Japanese or had merely memorized a few phrases."

"May I sit here?" he said.

She could tell right then that he was terribly shy, but could not resist testing him again.

"Hito de ippai dewa arimasen," she said.

He told her in near-perfect Japanese that he was well aware that the room was not crowded but that he found this particular table the most appealing.

She laughed. "How can I refuse?"

His name was Frank Slater. He was an engineering major and he was charming. His Japanese was surprisingly good, and since it was obvious that he wanted to try it out on her, she let him. The more he spoke it, the better it got. And gradually his shyness drifted away. She liked him, whoever he was.

"Have you been to Japan?" she asked.

"No. But I'd like to visit someday."

"Then how did you learn to speak my language so well?"

He ran a hand across his face and as his fingers brushed at the hair hanging over his forehead, she caught a glimpse of a purple mark running up from his left eye.

"From a boyhood friend who was Japanese. He and his uncle taught me many things Japanese besides the language. We were the best of friends. Grew up together, in fact. Then I . . . he returned to Japan suddenly three years ago and I haven't seen him since. Or rather, I thought I saw him a couple of weeks ago and I've been searching for him."

"What's his name?" Meiko said. She had a strange feeling about this. "Maybe I know him."

"His name's Matsuo," Frank said. "Matsuo Okumo. Have you heard of him?"

Meiko was startled not only by Frank's mention of Matsuo's name, but by the way Matsuo himself suddenly appeared behind Frank like a ghost out of the night.

"Is that him?" she said, gazing over Frank's head into Matsuo's eyes.

Frank spun around and leapt to his feet. "Matsuo!" he cried. He took an uncertain step forward, then retreated, as if repelled by what he saw. Then he stepped forward again, his arms rising as if to embrace him, but Matsuo turned instead to her and bowed.

"Frankie and I have matters to discuss outside," he said. "Excuse us."

He bowed again, then gripped Frank's upper arm and guided him from the cafeteria.

Meiko sat mute and still. There had been a look in Matsuo's eyes just now that she had never seen before. So cold, so bleak. It chilled her to the marrow. She had never imagined him capable of such dark feelings, but they had been there for all to see.

And Frank Slater seemed to be the cause.

■ ■ ■

It was Matsuo! I'd found him! God, it was good to see him again. Now I could explain everything!

But his face! My God, his nose had been broken and bent to the right. He was still clear-eyed and square-jawed, but that misshapen nose changed his face dramatically! I knew who was responsible for that deformity, and it made me sick!

He had changed in other ways, as well. As he strode ahead of me, I saw again that he had grown taller since we had parted, more sleekly muscular, with broader shoulders. And he moved differently. There had been something vaguely tentative and hesitant about him in the past, but that was gone now. He appeared to be a young man who knew exactly who he was and exactly where he was going.

"Matsuo!" I said as soon as we stepped out into the hall. "I've been looking all over for you! Why didn't you—?"

"Stay away from her," he said coldly as he turned toward me. "She belongs to another."

"Matsuo, I was only talking to her."

He jabbed a finger at me. "Stay away!"

I backed up a step. I had rehearsed this meeting in my mind endlessly for two years. I had worked out a plausible explanation for my cowardice and had structured a convincing plea for understanding and forgiveness.

But just as my courage had deserted me that night after Christmas almost two years ago, so did my carefully rehearsed speech now. His eyes were cold and stony. I looked for anger there, or hatred or pity, anything that might tell me I had a chance of being forgiven. In a desperate search for something to open with, I said,

"Why were you at my father's funeral?"

"To 'pay my respects,' as you say. He was a fair man. He treated me as he did everyone else. I have found that rare in America. I was sorry to learn of his accident."

I felt a now familiar lump forming in my throat. *Accident*. That was how it had been reported in the obituary. Some accident!

"I—I thank you for coming," I said. "But why didn't you wait around after the service? Mom would have liked to see you. And I've been wanting to talk to you. For years."

"There was nothing to say."

"Matsuo . . . about that night, behind Izumi-san's store, I—"

"There is still nothing to say." His voice was flat, toneless.

"You've got to understand! I don't know what happened to me! I panicked!"

"It doesn't matter."

"There's got to be some way I can make it up to you. We were best friends for so many years."

With quick, sharp movements, Matsuo yanked his shirt free of his waistline and pulled it up far enough to bare his right ribs. My stomach turned at the sight of the deep indentation there. I suddenly saw

Matsuo lying on the ground against the fence, and Mick McGarrigle's boot flying in and out, kicking him again and again.

He pulled his shirt down and tucked it back in. "We can never be friends again. And you must never speak to Meiko again."

Still there was no heat of anger or hatred in his voice. I almost wished there had been. I would have much preferred that to the utter contempt I heard. He turned away and left me standing there in the hall.

I leaned against the wall, withering inside. Knowing that the best friend I'd ever had felt that way about me was devastating. Knowing that his feelings were justified made it even worse. But through the haze of pain I heard a name echoing in my mind.

Meiko.

So that was her name. I hadn't even got around to asking her. *Meiko.* It sounded magical. I peered through the square window in the cafeteria door and saw her walking out the far door. Alone. *Meiko.* I wanted to see her again, talk to her again. She had touched something in me. I didn't know what, and I didn't know how, but I had to be with her again. Matsuo could issue all the threats and warnings he wished. It didn't matter. I was going to find her again.

1 9 3 1

THE YEAR OF THE RAM

JUNE

Matsuo played alone. Few of the other fellows who frequented the recreation room cared to test themselves against him anymore. He had started freshman year as the butt of their jokes, a buffoon of sorts, but they had let him play because he was easy pickings when they played for money. That hadn't lasted too long. Now, as a junior, he had won it all back and then some.

Still, he knew he was not ready.

He lined up the shot carefully. It was an important one. He had cleared the table of two racks in a row save for one last ball. He had never before run this many balls without a miss.

His game had begun changing when he began using the *kyo-jutsu* techniques Nagata had taught him with the bow and arrow. He let himself flow into the cue stick, become one with it as he had learned to do with the shaft of an arrow, aligning himself with the cue ball, letting himself slide forward along the green felt, to send the little white sphere rolling toward the black eight ball, to strike it and watch it bounce off the cushion and roll into the corner pocket.

Matsuo straightened and smiled.

Good! But still not good enough.

He opened a window to let in some fresh air. Summer was almost here, and that meant Meiko would be returning to Japan until September. During the summer, California would lose its one bright light. It was just as well that he had spent the last two summers traveling around America, and would do so again this summer for the final time. Berkeley without Meiko would be more than he could bear. He had found that he missed her less when he kept moving.

Meiko . . . he blotted her face from his mind. She belonged to Hiroki. He had to keep reminding himself of that fact. If just for one moment he allowed himself to forget it, there was no telling what he might do. Yet even with his constant reminders, she haunted him night and day. So he had backed away from her, minimized their contact, avoided her whenever he could, watched over her, but from afar.

Frank Slater stayed much closer to her. Despite Matsuo's earlier warnings, Frank had persisted in keeping company with Meiko over the past year and a half. Matsuo had changed his mind and had allowed it to continue unchallenged. He saw no danger in Frank's presence and was amused at the ways the American contrived to "accidentally" run into Meiko all over the campus. There was no future in that relationship. Meiko was a perfectly proper Japan woman who would be returning home in June next year when they both graduated. Frank provided her with the companionship Matsuo could no longer trust himself with.

Matsuo filled the empty hours with his studies and perfecting his pool game. He expended no effort to make any new friends. There were a few guys who seemed blind to his race but he saw no reason to start relationships that had no future. And in the summers, he traveled.

He had begun his trips tentatively, starting with the West Coast and western states in the summer of '29. Last summer he had gone through the Midwest, taking notes all along the way. And next week he would strike out for the industrial Northeast.

Nowhere had he found welcome. These were bad times in America. A great economic depression was ravaging the country, and the sight of a foreign face was met with violence and naked rage at worst; sullen, resentful tolerance at best.

Those were the people. But it was the land that grabbed his attention, held him in thrall. The land.

Since his first trip, he had found the immensity of the country mind numbing. So many resources! Such rich soil! So much room for growth! How could Father's dream of competing industrially with America ever come true? He had been taught since a child that Japan was the nation blessed by the gods; if that was truly so, then the gods themselves must have lived here in America before they blessed Japan. Even in the grips of this terrible depression, he sensed the depth and breadth of America's economic power.

If this was the country Father planned to engage in a trade war, he had his work cut out for him.

Matsuo racked up another set of balls, placed his cue ball, and leaned over the table. He blotted out the chatter from the far end of the room, along with the annoying refrain of "Minnie the Moocher" from the radio standing in the corner.

Maybe tonight he could run the table three times in a row.

He let himself flow into the cue. Lining himself up on the cue ball and the stack, he let himself fly.

For giri!

AUGUST

It felt good to be back in America, Meiko thought as her ship sailed between the two cliffs that formed the Golden Gate.

Until this summer, Meiko had thought such a notion would be inconceivable. But during the eight weeks she had been back in Japan she had found herself grumpy and restive—*bored* even. At first she did not understand it. Her parents doted on her as they had on her past two return trips, and as usual she was the center of every social occasion along the shore of Sagami Bay, the source of knowledge about the giant land across the ocean. Even the baron himself paid a visit to inquire as to how Matsuo was faring in America. And Hiroki had been properly attentive, at least so far as physical presence was concerned. But his mind was preoccupied and he was ever running off to rummage through old temples and shrines.

It should have been a perfect summer, but it was not. Meiko sensed a growing distance between herself and everyone else she had once felt so close to.

She could see Japan itself changing. With each trip home she noticed an increasing number of military uniforms in the stores and on the streets. More this summer than ever before. There was no war on. She found it vaguely disturbing.

And as she and her family discussed the wedding plans for the spring of 1933, she felt none of the happiness she had expected. Where was the excitement, the sense of anticipation, that should come with the approach of the most important day in her life? What was missing? She had moped about, wondering what was wrong with her. And then one day she and her mother had discussed the date she would board ship to return to America, and she had felt her spirits lift.

That was it! She longed to return to San Francisco—*hungered* for it, in fact. And with a rush of feeling, she knew why.

It was not the city itself, which indeed had its beauty, not the lush rolling hills of the countryside around it, not even the company of her one good American friend, Frank Slater, that drew her back.

It was Matsuo.

Meiko could not pinpoint when her feelings for Matsuo had changed. Certainly it had not been overnight. Rather a slow process, instead, progressing from acquaintanceship to friendship to . . . what? Love?

Yes. Love.

She had slowly come to see Matsuo as more than simply Hiroki's younger brother. She sensed his strength, his tenderness, his integrity. She found herself looking forward to his calls at the home where she stayed with one of her father's retainers and his wife, found herself hanging onto his words, waiting for his smiles, hungering for those times when he would hold her arm as they crossed a street.

And she knew Matsuo felt it too. If not love, then at least a strong attraction. She could see it in his eyes, hear it in his voice. Most of all, she could see it in his face when he came in sight of her. All the tension and tautness that living in America caused in him flowed out of his body and his features. That had to be some sort of love.

But what was she to do about it? Less than two years from now she would be wedding Hiroki. But she was doing more than simply marrying Matsuo's brother. She was marrying the Mazaki family to the ancient nobility of the Okumos. The Mazakis were a noble family, too, but their money came from the silk trade rather than from land deeded to them by a past Emperor—like the Okumos. The marriage would bring the Mazakis much closer to the Imperial Line. As Hiroki's wife, she would be cousin-by-marriage to the Empress Nagako, and Meiko's children would be blood cousins to the next Emperor!

Nothing could be allowed to stand in the way of that. The honor of her family was intimately involved here. Her course in life was set.

Meiko wondered what an American girl would think of her situation. They had the freedom to marry whomever they pleased. But they had to wait to be asked and there was always a chance that the one who pleased them would not ask. They might go through life and never be asked. She had always thought the Japanese custom among respectable families of having the family select the spouse and arrange the marriage far superior. That way there was no worry about the future, for the future was guaranteed: She would be a wife and mother and raise a family. And wasn't that the true purpose of marriage? To have children and preserve the continuity of family life? Marriage for love and love alone was silly Western thinking. Just look at all the trouble it caused in America.

And yet . . . Meiko had to admit that now she could see the

American side. She could not approve of it as a universal social custom, for that would lead to chaos, but she could not help fantasizing about marriage to Matsuo. Wouldn't that be wonderful! If only *he* had been the brother to stay home in Japan and Hiroki the one sent to America! Then she would be marrying Matsuo next spring, and she could have love *and* marriage while bringing great honor to her family.

A beautiful fantasy, one she indulged in at every opportunity. But it would never be more than that. She would marry Hiroki and have his children. It would not be so bad. At least she hoped not. But sometimes, when she caught Hiroki staring at her, she saw not love, not even hunger, in his eyes. She sensed a ferocity there that sent a quake through her insides.

Just her imagination, of course. Hiroki was an intense young man who focused all his energies into whatever he did. Their married life would be hectic, but at least Matsuo would be around. At least she would be able to see him and talk to him at family gatherings and when he came to visit his brother or his nephews and nieces.

For now, she would make the most of her last year of maidenhood, reveling in whatever time she could have with him. Which wasn't much. Matsuo had been spending less and less time with her. His calls and visits had been increasingly rare. He seemed to be stepping back from her, disengaging himself from all but the most necessary contact. At first she had been hurt, suspecting that he had found a woman who could give him more than she. But if that was true, why then did his face still change the way it always had when they ran into each other on the campus? And why did his eyes still embrace her as they always had?

She didn't understand. Unless it was because Matsuo was afraid of his own feelings for her and was avoiding her to protect her honor and the honor of both their families.

If that were the case, it only made her love him more.

As her ship neared its mooring, she saw a familiar figure waiting on the dock: Frank Slater. She liked Frank. He was a good friend, a sweet, gentle man. She could not imagine what in the world could have happened between Matsuo and him to cause such enmity.

■　■　■

Meiko's ship arrived ahead of schedule, but I was there when it docked. She was on one of the big Matson liners out of Honolulu. I'd had a letter from her telling me that she had to make the trip in two legs: from Yokohama to Hawaii, and then from Hawaii to San Francisco. Because of the immigration restriction, no Japanese passenger ship found it worthwhile coming here.

The air vibrated with the bass boom of the huge liner's horn as the tugs nosed it into the dock crowded with the families of people returning from Hawaiian vacations. I was up front. I'd been waiting since dawn.

"Frank!" she said when she saw me coming up the gangway. "What a surprise! I never expected you to be waiting!"

She looked absolutely radiant. Her dark eyes sparkled and her smile was so big and bright that I hurt inside. It was wonderful to see her again.

"Couldn't let you carry your bags by yourself, could I?"

"Oh, you're sweet."

She gave me a brief hug and a quick peck on the cheek. A perfectly innocent friendly greeting as far as she was concerned, I'm sure, but the contact, the closeness, the scent of her set my heart to pounding and made me light-headed. I think I actually staggered a little as I picked up her bags.

I didn't understand my feelings toward her. It would have been easy to call it simple infatuation. Certainly I was infatuated, but it went deeper than that.

Was it love? How could it be love? How could I love someone from such an alien culture, who considered my culture barbaric? Who was engaged to be married and would be leaving for the other side of the world in less than a year? How could I love someone like that?

But she was Meiko, and how could I do anything *but* love her?

I had been attracted by her beauty at first, but in the year and a half I had known her, I'd come to see past that. And she had changed in that time. Not her beauty, for if anything she grew more beautiful every year, but I could see monumental changes within her. When I first met her in our sophomore year, she presented me with a mixture of vulnerability and snootiness—although America frightened and awed her, she somehow managed the courage to look down her nose at us. But as time went by, I noticed a gradual softening of her parochial views until she could finally admit to the possibility that there might be other acceptable ways of life outside the social customs of Japan.

She blossomed at Berkeley. Although the country was in economic chaos, the campus provided an oasis for those students who could afford tuition or who had a scholarship, like me. And within that oasis, I could almost see Meiko's mind opening to the myriad possibilities life presented, possibilities she hadn't even known existed, let alone actually considered for herself.

And there, I thought, lay my chance.

Hardly a moment passed that I didn't think about her at least once. Time flew when I was with her and crawled when I wasn't. I wanted her near me always. And so sometime this fall, when I got up the nerve, I would ask her to marry me.

I had to ask. I knew chances were slim that she'd have me, but I'd had encouragement from her during the past year—not from anything she had said or done, actually, but rather from what she *hadn't* said or done.

For instance, she hadn't been talking much about her fiancé. During her sophomore year when we first met, all she could talk about was someone named Hiroki whom her parents had arranged for her to marry. She seemed awfully reticent about exactly who he was, but she was certainly enthusiastic about the match. That had changed. She hardly mentioned him at all toward the end of our junior year. Perhaps a little time in America had taken the blush off the idea of an arranged marriage.

The second encouraging sign was Matsuo's relative absence. A year and a half ago, it had been difficult to find Meiko without Matsuo being somewhere nearby. But as last winter had melted into spring, Matsuo seemed to spend less and less time at her side. Consequently, it became easier and easier for me to spend more time with Meiko. And I took full advantage of whatever opportunities were presented.

We became close. She liked me—I was sure of it. And that was why I thought that maybe—just maybe—I had a chance of persuading her to forget about her coming marriage to this Hiroki fellow and stay here with me in America. She would not have to worry about loss of face or social disgrace for she would be away from all that. We could have a good life together here in America. I had almost a year to convince her of that.

"Did Matsuo send you?" she said as I tried to juggle all four pieces of her luggage.

My stomach gave a little twist. "No. We're still not on the best of terms."

Actually, we hadn't spoken since our sour reunion eighteen months ago. But I had learned through Meiko that Matsuo had given her no details about our past together. I didn't know why he was keeping silent, but I was grateful.

"He is supposed to meet me here at the dock."

I said, "Oh."

I had assumed that she had wanted me to meet her, but as I mentally reviewed her letter, I realized that she had only mentioned the date of her return in passing.

"But I do thank you for coming. Why don't you wait with me. I do wish the two of you could be friends."

So did I, but Matsuo had made it more than clear that we never could be.

"I don't think that would be a good idea," I said. "But I'll bring your bags down to the dock and you can wait there. You must be tired of this ship by now."

"Very tired. Thank you, Frank. You are too kind."

We pushed through the crowd to the street. I left her in a shady spot where a growing number of other passengers were waiting to be picked up. I waved good-bye and made my retreat. But I didn't leave the scene. I found a doorway uphill from her that gave me a clear view of where she sat. I leaned back in the shadows, waiting and watching. If Matsuo didn't show up, I didn't want her to be stranded there.

Matsuo arrived in a cab a few minutes later. He opened the door, stepped out, and before I knew it they were in each other's arms.

My mouth went dry as I watched them. This was not the way she had hugged me—this was a hungry, needful embrace. And then, as quickly as they had come together, they were apart. Even from where I stood I could see by the way they looked away from each other and went about the task of loading her luggage into the cab that they were both acutely embarrassed.

And suddenly, it was all very clear to me why Meiko spoke little of her fiancé and why Matsuo had been limiting his time with her.

With a small lump in my throat and a bigger one in my chest, I left the doorway and walked away.

They were both trapped in a no-win situation and they knew it. I felt sorry for them.

But I felt sorrier for myself.

1 9 3 2

THE YEAR OF THE MONKEY

JUNE

At last, it was time.

Matsuo stood before the mirror in the dorm room he had to himself and inspected the goatee he had been growing since the first of the year. It was patchy, ragged, and ugly—*quite* ugly—but it served its purpose. He put on the horn-rimmed glasses he had recently purchased and considered the result. Even Nagata would have to look closely to recognize him.

But the disguise needed one final touch. He folded a white handkerchief into a narrow band which he tied around his head as a *hachimaki*. Now he was ready for battle. A special kind of battle. One played with a tapered stick and sixteen balls each two and a quarter inches in diameter on a field of green felt enclosed with cushioned bumpers.

A game. But more than a game tonight. More than winning, more than money was at stake tonight.

Matsuo was playing for giri.

He took the ferry across the bay. He blocked out the talk around him which centered on the invasion of the American capital city by thousands of ex-servicemen demanding to cash their bonus certificates.

Things were no more peaceful at home. The Japanese Army had taken over Manchuria last fall and was consolidating its occupation there. And just last month, Prime Minister Inukai had been assassinated in his home before the eyes of his daughter by Army fanatics, all because he had expressed a desire to cut the military budget.

Was Japan as mad as the rest of the world?

Matsuo hated that thought. He leaned forward against the ferry's front railing, drumming his fingers impatiently as he urged the sluggish craft forward through the night toward the lighted tower clock of the Ferry Building on the far side of the water. There was talk of building a huge bridge across the bay, linking Oakland and San Francisco, and another huge suspension bridge across the Golden Gate. He remembered laughing at the idea when he had first heard it proposed, but after visiting New York City last summer and seeing the newly completed Empire State Building thrusting nearly a quarter-mile into the sky, he laughed no longer. If anyone could do it, the Americans could.

Much as he loathed them, he had to admit a grudging admiration for the "can-do" spirit of Americans. Even in the depths of the world's worst depression, they undertook and successfully completed a building taller than anyone had ever dreamed possible. They built to the point where good sense told them to halt, and then kept going, up and up and up. Matsuo had gone to the top. The view from the observation deck had been awe inspiring. And as he had stood there in the wind and looked down at the waterways and the teeming city below, he had thought of Father and his talk of the coming confrontation with America. Japan could beat America in small things; Americans had no appreciation for fine, delicate work. But on a large scale, how could Japan—how could any country—prevail against a people who didn't recognize when enough was enough, who didn't know when to quit?

And what of home? Japan in Manchuria. He knew the province on the mainland would supply desperately needed raw materials for Japan's growing industry, but still the thought of his country at war disturbed him. Surely there were ways Japan could get what it needed without killing people.

After all, he had found a way to settle a grievance without resorting to brute force. Or at least he hoped he had. He would know later tonight.

He brushed away concerns of home. They were for the future. This was now. The ferry was pulling into its San Francisco dock and he wanted no distractions during the conflict ahead.

■   ■   ■

"How much for a birrard table for two hours?" Matsuo said in a thick Japanese accent to the florid-faced man behind the bar at O'Boyle's Pool Emporium. The place had been a tavern before Prohibition, but Matsuo figured that O'Boyle probably sold more liquor now than when it had been legal.

It was early yet on this Wednesday night and there were only a few drinkers lounging around in the smoky dimness. With Repeal a certainty after the presidential election in the coming fall, no one was trying to hide what he was drinking. O'Boyle's had obviously seen better days. Through the grime that covered everything, Matsuo could see the sturdy grain of fine oak paneling on the walls and ceiling, and delicate decorative carving on the support columns. The huge beveled mirrors were as dirty and dingy as the front windows. On an elevated platform at the rear of the room, set off by a low oak railing, sat three billiard tables, each under a bright hanging lamp. No one was using them.

"You mean a pool table?" said the man, whom Matsuo knew to be O'Boyle himself.

Matsuo exaggerated his accent to the point of caricature. "Yes. I wish to pray poo."

O'Boyle looked at him closely. "I can't tell if you're a Chink or a Jap, pal, but either way, you ain't playing in my joint."

"Japanese, and the charge, I believe, is fifty cents per hour?" Matsuo said, placing a silver dollar on the bar top. The charge was a *dime* an hour, he knew, with O'Boyle taking a ten percent cut of whatever money was won.

O'Boyle stared at the hard money for a full minute, then snatched it up. "Okay. Just this once."

Matsuo had already started toward the rear. There was, after all, a depression on.

"But don't use the table on the left!" O'Boyle called after him.

Matsuo went to the wall rack and picked out a cue, then he racked up the balls on the left table.

"Hey!" said O'Boyle, hurrying back. "Can't you understand English, you yellow jerk? I said not that table! It's reserved every Wednesday night!"

Matsuo looked him in the eye through the flat lenses in his glasses. "I *rike* this one." Then he broke the stack.

O'Boyle gave him a nasty smile as he nodded. "Okay, wiseguy. Have it your way. But someone is going to be very unhappy when he finds a Jap using his favorite table."

Matsuo lined up a shot. *I'm counting on that.*

He played for two hours, acquainting himself with the table. Then he heard a voice say,

"Because you're just a stupid Jap who don't know no better, I'll let you off this time."

Matsuo turned and faced the man who had spoken. Mick McGarrigle hadn't changed much. He still had red hair and freckles, still had the same squint, the same arrogant leer. He was beefier across the chest and abdomen, and had a new hat—those were the only differences.

He had brought his own cue stick and was now screwing the two halves together. He was flanked by three cronies.

"My table," he said and jerked his thumb toward the front door. "Get lost."

If a similar confrontation had occurred upon Matsuo's return to America, he would have hurled himself at Mick's throat and killed him. But tonight was different. Matsuo had been planning this moment for years. The anger and rage were there, but he remained cool and controlled behind his disguise.

Matsuo looked him in the eye, waiting for some sign of recognition. None came. Good. His disguise was working. And why not? Between the hachimaki and the goatee, only his eyes and nose were visible; those eyes sat behind glasses and the nose had been broken by Mick during their last encounter.

Matsuo had been watching O'Boyle's for over three years now. The first thing he had done upon returning to America was to scour the seediest areas of San Francisco for Mick. He had found him here in O'Boyle's, on the downhill fringe of the Tenderloin, and for many nights had crouched at the rear window, watching as Mick won match after match against anyone who played him. Players were brought in from other pool halls in other sections of town and pitted against him, but Mick always won. He had a loyal band of followers who always bet with him and were never disappointed. Mick McGarrigle was a hero in O'Boyle's. His life centered around the pool tables here where he was undisputed master.

It was then that Matsuo had decided to learn to play pool.

"Oh?" Matsuo said. "Do you pray birrards?"

"Yeah. I 'pray birrards,' all right," Mick said. This brought a laugh from his companions.

"I wiw surrender to a better prayer," Matsuo said.

"Get lost, Jap," Mick said. "I ain't wasting my time with the likes of you."

Matsuo reached into his pocket and brought out five twenty-dollar gold pieces. "You wish perhaps to prace a wager on a game?"

Mick's eyes fairly bulged at the sight of the gold.

■　■　■

Double eagles!
Mick saw the light gleaming off their shiny surfaces and salivated. Things were tight hustling at the tables, and he figured he would be losing his laborer's job soon, and there wasn't much around to steal these days. A hundred bucks would set him up pretty. And besides, there was talk about the government no longer using gold for money.

Gold coins were starting to disappear. One way or another, he was going to leave here tonight with those double eagles in his pocket.

A crowd began to collect around the table.

"I ain't got that kind of money," Mick said, wondering how he was going to work this.

The Jap said, "Surery you have friends who wiw cover you."

A chorus of excited cries saying they would cover two dollars or five broke from the crowd. Mick was warmed by the response. These were his friends, his fans. He had never let them down. They were with him all the way. He emptied his pockets of whatever cash he had while the O'Boyle's regulars dug deep into their meager funds for the chance to cover the remainder of the bet, supremely confident in their man's ability to beat this upstart Jap.

Within minutes, there was one hundred dollars in paper and coin on Mick's side of the table. The Jap reached over and scooped it up. As he stuffed it all in his jacket pocket, everyone started yelling in protest.

The Jap stared at them through his thick glasses. "The entire group of you does not think you can retrieve this money from one poor Jap should he be the roser?"

They quieted down at that. Mick looked hard at the Jap. Something familiar about him. But they all looked pretty much alike, didn't they?

Mick won the toss for break but that gave the Jap the choice of game. Mick could not believe his luck when the guy picked Chicago. His best game! No one had beaten him at Chicago in two years! The crowd was grinning knowingly and nudging each other. It was all Mick could do to keep from laughing out loud.

This was almost too good to be true!

■   ■   ■

Matsuo knew very well that Chicago was Mick's favorite game. It was also the one Matsuo had been practicing for three years. It required the fifteen balls to be sunk in numerical order. The first player to reach sixty-one points won.

He stood back and watched Mick break. He was an excellent player. That had been evident even from Matsuo's old vantage point at the rear window in the alley. Up close now, Mick's technique was even more impressive. He had excellent control and a surprisingly delicate touch. Matsuo watched with mounting tension as Mick ran his first rack and was progressing confidently through his second when he missed on his twenty-ninth ball.

Matsuo glanced around at the onlookers. There were maybe two dozen of them, mostly men, all in work clothes, relaxed, smoking and drinking and having a good time. And why not? Their man had run twenty-eight balls straight before Matsuo had lifted his cue.

Taking his turn at the table, Matsuo settled down to the game, forgetting about Mick and remembering his kyo-jutsu training, making himself one with the cue stick. After he cleaned the table and ran the next rack, he looked up and noticed that the crowd wasn't quite so noisy or jocular. He glanced at Mick as the balls were being reracked. He was seated on a barstool in the corner with his cue stick across his lap, his face an unreadable mask.

As Matsuo ran his third rack, the crowd became progressively more quiet. Another glance at Mick before he broke the fourth and Matsuo saw that the freckled face was mottled with red; perspiration was beaded along his forehead and upper lip. As Matsuo ran through the fourth rack, he tried to control his excitement, knowing that it would interfere with his game. But he found it hard to resist the mounting exaltation as he saw his score creep closer and closer to the magic total of sixty-one.

Matsuo's score reached sixty. One point to go. Mick was now a sickly pale. Matsuo took aim on the winning ball—number 14. He melted into the cue and called for the corner pocket. But as he thrust the cue stick forward, a heavy boot struck him in the left calf, causing his shot to strike off-center.

Reining in the anger that suddenly raced through him, Matsuo turned and looked at the man who had interfered with his shot. He stood well over six feet and grinned with mock innocence.

"Got a cramp in my leg," he said. The crowd laughed.

"So sorry to hear that," Matsuo said, stepping up close to him. Using *atemi*, he grasped the man's right leg above the knee, striking vital points with his thumb and forefinger. The man howled and dropped to the ground, clutching his leg.

"Ah!" Matsuo said. "Another cramp! So sorry!"

As some of the members of the crowd stepped forward menacingly, Matsuo turned his back and faced Mick.

"Your turn," he said with a bow.

Mick's color was returning to normal. He watched Matsuo with a puzzled expression on his face. After a moment, he shrugged, leaned over the table, and sank the next ball. The crowd cheered as he cleaned the table and the balls were racked again. He ran his score up to forty-eight before he ran into trouble.

Thirteen balls were on the table. Mick needed to sink the 4 for his next point but he was trapped behind the 5 with no shot. He called safe and tapped the cue ball against the 5, leaving Matsuo without a shot.

At least that was the way it looked at first.

But Matsuo didn't want to trade "safe" shots with Mick. He wanted an utterly demoralizing victory. And to achieve that he would have to take risks. He studied the lay of the balls and traced a mental path in his mind. It was possible . . . just possible . . . but it would require the deftest touch imaginable.

He leaned over the table and aimed the cue ball almost 180 degrees away from 4.

He said, "Side pocket."

It looked like an impossible shot, and he hoped that would keep any of Mick's backers from kicking him again. The already quiet room became as silent as a grave. Even the sound of breathing stopped.

Melting into his cue stick more intimately than he had ever done before, becoming one with it, he said a prayer to all his ancestors and let fly at the white ball.

The cue ball banked off the near-end cushion, the side cushion, the far-end cushion, and then rolled toward the 14, losing momentum all the time. Matsuo held his breath as it tapped the ball and sent it rolling. The 4 caromed off the 15 and rolled right up to the lip of the side pocket where it paused, tottered . . .

. . . and rolled in.

Amid a mass exhalation of stale air, someone started to cheer, then caught himself.

I did it! I really did it! Matsuo wanted to shout, to get up on the green felt of the table and do a dance. But he couldn't. He had to remain cool and placid, had to maintain the role of the inscrutable Oriental.

Moving slowly but precisely, Matsuo picked up his jacket and said, "Thank you for a very preasant evening," to the tight-lipped, blanched-faced Mick. He then turned to O'Boyle and handed him a wad of cash. "Drinks for everyone!"

■　■　■

Mick was numb with shock and shame. He had lost! Lost to a Jap! This wasn't happening! He was out of his chair before anyone could laugh or shout or move away from the table.

"Wait a minute, Jap!" he said. "You ain't going anywhere until I get a chance to win back what I lost!"

The crowd watched in silence.

"Gradry." The Jap reached into his pocket, pulled out his original five twenty-dollar gold pieces, and set them in a pile on the felt surface of the pool table. "But I rearry don't want more of your money."

"Don't worry!" Mick flashed a confident sneer for the benefit of the regulars. "You ain't gettin' any!" He turned to the crowd. "All right—who wants a piece of this action?"

The regulars shuffled their feet, looked at each other, at the ground, anywhere but at him, then began to break up and wander back toward the bar. O'Boyle scurried ahead of them with his fistful of money.

"Hey! Where're you goin'?" Mick said to their backs. "He used some cheap Jap tricks to beat me!"

"Maybe you better learn a few of those tricks yourself," somebody muttered.

Their icy rejection was like a gut punch. He took a few steps after them. "I can beat him! You know I can! Cover me and I'll get your money back!"

"Already lost too much," somebody else said.

This can't be! They can't do this to me!

"Wait, fellows . . ."

But they were gone. Only he and the Jap were left in the billiards area, facing each other across the still, silent, green table.

■ ■ ■

Matsuo watched Mick: His face was slack as his gaze flicked from the crowd at the bar, to the pool table, and back to the bar. His reputation was in ruins; his self-respect was shattered; his one pride in life, his skill with a pool cue, had been won away from him in a humiliating defeat.

Matsuo tried to dredge up a mote of pity for him but kept seeing Izumi-san's bloody, broken head. He knew then that no matter how much humiliation he had inflicted on Mick, it was not enough. It would *never* be enough!

In Japan, tonight's defeat might have been cause enough for Mick to consider killing himself. But this was America and Matsuo knew that Mick would never have such grace.

Finally, Mick's gaze came to rest on Matsuo.

"How does it feel?" Matsuo said, dropping his accent and facing Mick squarely. "How do you like being a nobody?"

"Wha?" Mick said dully.

"You let them down, Mick. They put their hard-earned money on you and you lost it. Lost it badly. They'll never trust you again. You're garbage as far as they're concerned."

Mick's face was getting mottled again. "You son of a bitch!" Spittle flecked his lower lip. He reversed his pool stick and charged around the table, swinging the heavy end toward Matsuo's head.

Using his own cue like a bo, Matsuo easily parried the blow, then grabbed Mick's cue and ripped it from his grasp before he could swing again. Mick stared at his empty hands.

Out of the corner of his eye Matsuo noted that they had attracted the attention of the men at the bar. Sensing a fight, they were beginning to drift over.

"You surprise me, Mick," Matsuo said. "I didn't think you had the guts to attack anyone on your own. Your style is more like sneaking up on an old Japanese shopkeeper when his back is turned, or attacking a lone Jap boy in a back alley with a group of your friends and trying to kick him to death."

Mick's jaw dropped as he backed up a step.

"You! I knew there was something wrong about you! They told me you ran back to Japan!"

Matsuo bowed. "Correct. But Chinky-boy is back now."

And then he snapped Mick's pool cue in two.

"Damn your slanty eyes!" Mick screamed. "You're a dead man!"

He pushed through the growing crowd of amused onlookers and rushed behind the bar. Matsuo slipped into his jacket as he saw Mick and O'Boyle arguing and then struggling over something.

Mick ran out from behind the bar with a revolver in his hand. The crowd parted before him. He stopped by the railing and pointed the pistol at Matsuo's head.

The room was deathly silent. Matsuo's mind raced as he looked down the barrel of the gun. He saw Mick cock the hammer, heard the cylinder rachet around, saw Mick's eyes narrow.

"Say good-bye, Jap."

Matsuo dove forward, rolled, and rammed his feet into Mick's belly. The air exploded from Mick in a whoosh, followed immediately by the deafening noise of the shot. The bullet went wild and high, sending the onlookers scurrying for cover. But as he staggered backward, Mick fired again, this time lower. Matsuo felt white-hot pain tear through his shoulder, just to the left of his neck.

He acted instinctively, leaping up through the gun smoke–filled air directly in front of Mick. Without hesitation, he grabbed a handful of red hair, shoved backward, and then rammed his fist into the freckled white of Mick's exposed throat.

The pistol fell from Mick's hand as he dropped to his knees and clutched at his throat. Soft, strangled, gurgling noises wormed from his mouth as he tried to draw air through his crushed larynx. His eyes reddened and bulged as his face darkened toward a dusky blue.

Shouting arose on all sides.

—"He's choking to death!"—"Get a doctor!"—"He's dying!"— "The Jap's killed him!"—"Get him!"—

Matsuo felt himself grabbed from behind by two or three pairs of hands, sending fresh pain lancing through his shoulder. But the pain was blocked by the rage that exploded within him.

Damn these Americans! He was the victim here! *He* had been unarmed and had been wounded by a man with a gun! Anyone with any honor would have been on *his* side! Yet now they were attacking *him!* Just because he was Japanese!

Marshaling all his te skills, he flashed into action. A back kick and two elbow strikes freed him from those holding him, and then he was heading for the door. There were about thirty whites in the room, but though Matsuo's left arm was nearly useless, they couldn't stop him. Those who tried were painfully ignorant of the te style of fighting. Their faces revealed their shocked surprise as well as their pain as they fell like wheat before Matsuo's flying kicks and knife-hand thrusts. In seconds he was out the door and running up the ill-lit street.

But he was not safe yet. A howling mob spewed from the tavern door and followed him uphill.

Matsuo spurred himself on. He had to find a hiding place. He could not fight so many, especially with one arm damaged. He felt wetness in his left palm and glanced down as he passed under a street lamp. His hand was red, with blood dripping down his sleeve from the wound in his shoulder. He knew he couldn't bleed like this for long and stay ahead of that wolf pack. He had to hide!

He picked a dark side street at random and ducked into it. The sidewalk was narrow, the houses pushing their front steps almost to the curb. He saw steps going down under a front staircase to a basement apartment and fairly leaped into the welcoming blackness before his pursuers rounded the corner.

He crouched in the darkest recess and waited. It seemed to take only seconds for the sound of hoarse, angry voices and running feet to approach his hiding place. Matsuo held his breath as they pounded by on the pavement above him. Finally, they were gone.

But not for long, he knew. They would run for maybe a block before figuring out that he must be hiding somewhere behind them. Then they would be back. But he had his plans already set: He would creep up the steps and check for stragglers. If none were about, he would run the other way. He went to stand up—

—and his knees buckled beneath him.

Had he lost that much blood? Looking down, he saw a dark pool by his feet. He fought the panic that clutched at him. If he didn't get away from here, he would be caught and probably strung up by his neck from the nearest lamppost—if he didn't bleed to death first!

He gripped the knob on the door to the basement apartment, praying it would open. But the door held fast—locked.

Desperate, he willed his rubbery legs to straighten. He was halfway to a standing position when the door opened, bathing him in light. He stood there, squinting in the dread illumination, pinned to the wall like some night-crawling insect.

"Get out of here!" It was a woman's voice, but gruff and coarse, like the screech of a rusted hinge.

Matsuo looked up at the bulky form silhouetted in the doorway. The face was totally in shadow.

"Get away from my door!"

"I can't," Matsuo said. And it was true. He knew his legs would not take him up the stairs.

A shotgun appeared, seemingly out of the air. Light glinted along its double-barreled length as it swung forward and pointed at his face.

"Get, or I'll shoot!"

Matsuo could see no way out for him. He looked up to where he guessed the woman's eyes should be.

"Shoot," he said. "It will be a far more honorable death than the one your countrymen have planned for me."

The barrels wavered. "What countrymen?"

"From O'Boyle's."

"You're a Jappo, ain't you? And sweet Jesus, you're bleeding! What did you do to get them riled at you?"

"They'll be here in a few minutes. They can tell you."

"Damn it to hell!" she said. The shotgun disappeared and a pair of strong arms helped Matsuo the rest of the way to his feet and into the apartment. From the doorway he managed to stumble to a chair at the room's only table.

The woman closed the door and leaned the shotgun in the corner next to the door molding. She was faced into the light now and Matsuo could see that she was a portly woman of about sixty years wearing a calico dress with a long apron tied around her neck and waist. Her gray hair was pulled back into a bun. Wire-rimmed glasses sat on her red nose and cheeks.

She came over to him and gasped. "Look at you! Shuck that coat!"

She helped him out of the blood-soaked jacket and the underlying shirts. Then she leaned over his shoulder, adjusting her glasses as she inspected the wound at close range.

She grunted. "Not too bad. A bloody one, but I seen worse." She went into another room and returned with a basin of water. "Who shot you?"

"An old acquaintance," Matsuo said. His breath hissed in and out as she bathed the area with cool water.

"Another Jappo?"

"No. American."

"Why?"

"I beat him at pool."

"Pool? He shot you for that?"

"I made him look very bad."

"And he's out there looking for you so he can finish the job, right?"

"No." Matsuo hesitated, then decided to be honest with this woman. For some reason—perhaps the tender way she was cleaning his wound—he trusted her. "He's dead. I killed him."

Her hands paused in their ministrations, then continued. "All this happen in O'Boyle's?"

"Yes."

She snorted. "Serves you right for frequenting that den of iniquity. Although I must say, I'm surprised they even let someone like you in there."

"That's another part of the problem." Matsuo studied her weathered face as she leaned over him. "May I ask your name?"

"Worth. Betsy Worth. You can call me *Mrs.* Worth." She straightened up. "There! Now it's ready for some stitches."

"Stitches?" Matsuo looked over at his shoulder. Mick's bullet had torn up a triangular flap of flesh as it passed through the meaty area above the left collarbone. Mrs. Worth had cleaned away the blood and pressed the flap back into place, but blood still oozed slowly from beneath the edges. "Are you a nurse?"

"Yes and no," she said, returning with her sewing basket. "Never worked in a hospital or anything like that, but when Mr. Worth and me lived in Colorado, he and his friends used to go hunting for meat nearly every week. Hardly was a time when one of them wouldn't come back hurt or mauled or even accidentally shot by himself or one of the other hunters. I've mended lots of injured men in my time."

She had been threading a curved needle as she spoke. Now she appeared to be ready.

"Okay," she said. "This'll smart a bit."

Matsuo gritted his teeth as she sat down behind him. He felt the needle pierce his skin, felt the thread pull through his flesh, felt the tug as a knot was tied. It hurt, but it was bearable.

Suddenly, he heard voices outside. His heart sank. They had found him. "It's them," he said.

Mrs. Worth must have heard them, too, for she was already helping him to his feet and guiding him toward the back room. Matsuo's head swam and blotches of blackness jittered before his eyes as he moved. She left him leaning against the wall as she hurried back to the table. He had a vague impression of a darkened bedroom behind him.

Fists began hammering on the door to the apartment.

"Hello, in there!" said a voice. "Open up!"

"Coming!" said Mrs. Worth. As she spoke she was gathering up Matsuo's bloody clothes and pulling the chair toward the back room.

She set the chair down beside him in the darkness and dropped the clothes behind it. "Sit and be quiet," she said as she helped Matsuo ease into the chair. Then she closed the door.

Matsuo inched the chair forward and opened the door a crack so he could see into the front room.

"Hold your horses!" Mrs. Worth said as the pounding on the door continued. Matsuo saw her lift the sawed-off shotgun by the barrel with her left hand and hold it behind her ample frame as she opened the door with her right. "What *is* it?" she said, her tone ringing with true annoyance.

She effectively blocked the doorway with her bulk, but Matsuo saw at least half a dozen faces in the stairwell peering into the apartment over and around her.

"There's a killer on the loose," somebody said. "A Jap."

"A killer!" Mrs. Worth said. "And just who did he kill?"

"A friend of ours. Down at O'Boyle's. We know he's been here."

"And how would you know that?"

"Blood. He left a trail of it down the steps and there's a big splotch of it right here outside your door. Where is he?"

"I found him right where you're standing. I told him to git, just like I'm telling you."

"And he left?" The tone was incredulous.

"You don't see him here, do you?"

"No offense, ma'am," said the voice, "but he's pretty dangerous and I don't think he'd run off just on your say-so. Maybe we'd better come in and look around just to be sure he's not forcing you—"

Matsuo saw Mrs. Worth draw the scattergun around to the front of her where it disappeared from view. He could see the men in the stairwell almost stumble over each other as they backed up with widened eyes.

"He found this very persuasive," she said.

Nervous laughter echoed into the apartment. "I'll bet he sure as hell did!" someone said. "Which way did he go?"

"I didn't watch him go. Now, if you gentlemen don't mind, I'll get back to my sewing."

So saying, she closed the door. Matsuo watched her turn the key in the lock and then press her ear against the door. After a while, she straightened up and leaned the shotgun back in its corner.

Matsuo opened the bedroom door all the way as she approached him. He stared into her scowling face in wonder. No words could express his gratitude, but he had to try. "Thank you," he said. "But why—?"

"I know their type. Met plenty of them in Colorado." She helped him back to the kitchen table where he sat in the other chair. "The kind back there used to say the only good Injun was a dead Injun. These fellows are no different. Mr. Worth, however, had different ideas. He thought some of the finest men he ever knew were Injuns."

Matsuo noted the past tense. "Is he . . . ?"

"Passed away a long time ago. Bear got him bad. One of his Injun friends carried him all the way back to our cabin." As if to punish Matsuo for asking her about her late husband, she jabbed the needle into his shoulder for another stitch. "I tried my best to patch him up but he began to fever. He died in my arms. I've always been grateful to that Injun for giving me that last chance to be with him."

"I'm not an Indian," Matsuo said as she knotted the thread.

"You'll do."

■　■　■

She waited with him until dawn. She said anyone looking for him would have given up by then, and probably wouldn't recognize him without his beard, anyway.

"Now remember what I told you," Mrs. Worth said. "Keep that wound clean. Don't let no fluids build up in it. Keep it draining."

She had sutured the flap loosely into place, covered it with a salve and a dry compress, then wrapped the shoulder in a long strip of bed sheet. That done, she had heated up some soup and made him eat it despite his protests of nausea. While he ate she had washed most of the blood out of his coat. As it hung by the stove to dry, she had shaved his goatee, then forced more soup into him.

"And keep changing that dressing today—maybe every two or three hours."

"I will. I will." He rose to his feet. He felt stronger; strong enough to make the walk back to the Oakland ferry. "How can I repay you?" She had already refused the money he had offered her.

"Just get home safe. Don't get yourself into trouble along the way or all my needlework will have been for nothing!"

He looked into her eyes. "There must be something—"

Mrs. Worth reached for the scattergun. "Git!"

Matsuo bowed. "I am indebted. Eternally."

"Git!"

Matsuo got. With a warm glow inside, he climbed the stairs into the milky first light of day. The paper money he had won still crinkled in his pocket but all the twenty-dollar gold double eagles he had brought with him now lay hidden in Mrs. Worth's sugar bowl. She would find them when she had her next cup of tea.

He began walking toward the ferry dock. The pain in his shoulder had subsided to a dull, throbbing ache. The streets were deserted. His jacket was damp but the air was warm and clean and salty.

It was good to be alive. It was *wonderful* to be alive!

And best of all, he and Meiko would set sail for Japan the day after tomorrow, never again, he prayed, to set foot in this thrice-cursed country he hated so. It would be a blessed day when he could bid farewell to a land that produced cowards like Frank Slater and beasts like Mick McGarrigle . . .

. . . and brave, noble people like Mrs. Worth.

He sighed and shook his head as he walked.

Why was nothing ever simple?

PART
THREE

1933

1937

1 9 3 3

THE YEAR OF THE ROOSTER

As I sat waiting to see Commander Foster, I was mentally humming "Stormy Weather." The lyrics were certainly appropriate to the times, especially the "gloom and mis'ry ev'rywhere" part. I had been looking for work for ten months now and had come up empty-handed all around.

Franklin D. Roosevelt was officially President now but I hadn't seen any magic yet. There was still panic in the streets. I remembered the hordes of frightened faces crowded in front of all the locked doors in the financial district last month when he closed all the banks by Presidential order. And now he was taking us off the gold standard. Things were looking pretty black.

"Frankie!" I looked up and saw Commander Foster motioning me toward his office. "Come on in!"

The commander had been one of the few business associates of my father to show up at his funeral. I hated trying to trade on Dad's old contacts, but I was desperate. I was even willing to work for the Navy.

We made polite chitchat for the required interval. He was a gray-haired, jowly, fatherly fellow with an easy smile, but the smile faded when he got down to business.

"I'm afraid the news isn't good, Frankie," he said. "You know I'd help you if I could. I liked your dad—he was an honest man who knew his stuff. You could rely on anything machined in the Slater plant. And because of that, I've gone to bat for you. But Frankie, the Navy's rotten with engineers. There's not enough to do for the ones we already have."

I had expected something like this, but that didn't make it any less disappointing. I guess my face showed it.

"But look," he said, trying to cheer me up. "The government will be starting all sorts of public works programs soon. They'll be building dams and roads and monuments and the like. They'll need engineers."

"But I need something now," I said. "I can't wait until fall or next year." Mom had sold the house and we had moved into a smaller place. We had it free and clear but taxes and living expenses were eating up all our savings. I would have loved an apartment of my own, but that was out of the question.

He shrugged. "All I can offer you is a berth as an ordinary seaman, and I'll have to pull strings even for that."

An ordinary seaman! I didn't even need a high-school education for that! I had an engineering degree and I couldn't use it. I'd be mopping decks. I said nothing.

"If only you had some special talent! Do you play a horn or take shorthand and speak French or German?"

"The only language I speak besides English is Japanese, but I doubt—"

Commander Foster's eyes lit. "Japanese? Do you really? You're not kidding me?"

"I learned it from our gardener as a kid."

"Why didn't you say so! I know someone who's been crying the blues because he can't find enough Navy men who speak Japanese!"

"Why would—?"

"We're keeping a close eye on the Japs these days. They're getting uppity. Marched themselves out of the League of Nations last month saying if we didn't like what they were doing in Manchuria, we could stuff it. Oh, yes. We're watching those monkeys. And Ellis Zacharias, an old classmate of mine from Annapolis, is with the Office of Naval Intelligence now and he's looking for someone just like you. I'll call him today."

He stood up and extended his hand across the table. "Welcome to the United States Navy, Frankie."

MAY ■
TOKYO

Looking back, Meiko would wonder how a day so full of horror could have started so innocently. She remembered riding in the car with her family, all heading out of town for a spring weekend on Sagami Bay. The sun had been shining as they drove toward the train station; the sixty-mile ride south along the coast to their summer home between Odawara and Atami promised to be pleasant and peaceful. She had been thinking about her upcoming wedding.

One week . . . one week and I will be a married woman.

She wondered where the time had gone. It seemed like she had been back in Japan for only a few weeks, and here it was almost a year since she and Matsuo had returned.

She had been so busy with wedding preparations; perhaps that was why time had passed so quickly. She had forced herself into bouts of frenzied activity. It helped blot Matsuo out of her mind. And Matsuo, for his part, had resolutely avoided her, which made it easier for her. For both of them, she knew.

A week from tomorrow she would wed Hiroki. And once she bore his child, the Mazaki family would be forever linked to the noble Okumo line. It was such a signal honor for her to be chosen as the instrument of that linkage, to bring such honor to her family . . .

But she didn't want to be married to Hiroki Okumo. Something about him made her vaguely uneasy. Maybe it was because she wanted his brother!

She shuddered. She was thinking the unthinkable. She had to banish such thoughts from her mind forever!

Yet how things change! Four years ago she had been looking forward to this day with joyful anticipation, aching for its arrival. Now she dreaded it. Matsuo was only part of the reason. She had gone to America and lived there for four years, something beyond the imagining of any Japan woman, and beyond the experience of most Japan men. She had changed.

Hiroki had changed, too. He was still terribly handsome, but as she had come to know him better since her return to Japan, she realized his thoughts and interests were far removed from anything that mattered to her. She had seen hints of the widening gap between them over the years, but now it had become a chasm. All he talked of was politics, every form of politics—national, international, military, Imperial. And he was constantly running off to investigate this temple or that shrine in some remote area of Japan. Becoming a good husband, a man interested in knowing her and being her companion, seemed of no real interest to him.

But it was not her place to complain or object. She glanced up at her father sitting in the front seat next to the driver. The wedding was enormously important to him. It would be a lavish Shinto ceremony with many members of the Imperial Council present. His political influence would balloon after next week.

Politics! Even her father had caught the infection! Probably from
Baron Okumo and Hiroki—the three of them had become fast friends
in recent years. Even this weekend, which was supposed to allow the
family one last brief respite before the whirlwind of last-minute
preparations next week, had been turned into a political maneuver.
Underminister Nitobi was meeting them at the station and accompany-
ing them to Sagami Bay. Meiko didn't fully understand the politics of
the situation, or even what, precisely, Mr. Nitobi was underminister of—neither her father nor her future husband thought she
should bother her head with such things—but she had gathered that
he carried a certain amount of influence in regard to some critical
matter and that his ideas were quite a bit more liberal than those of
the baron, Hiroki, and her father. An "accidental" meeting of
the baron and the underminister was planned for tomorrow evening to see if the baron might persuade him to see things more their
way.

Underminister Nitobi's car pulled up before Tokyo Station just
behind theirs. He was a short, squat little man in a charcoal-gray
business suit and a derby. He sported a pencil-line moustache; his
smiles did not seem to extend beyond his lips. Meiko took an instant
dislike to him and thought her father greeted him with undue courtesy,
being gracious to the point of unctuousness.

Porters came running for the baggage, and they all walked into the
redbrick station as a group. Her father had arranged for a private car,
and so they bypassed the long ticket lines and headed straight for the
platform.

■ ■ ■

It was almost time.

Shimazu stood against a wall and played his wooden flute.
Through the weave of his wicker helmet he watched the crowds of
passengers swirl and eddy across the wide-open floor of Tokyo
Station. He despised this building. It had been built in the shadow of
the Imperial Palace almost twenty years ago during the Meiji period,
but instead of being classical Japanese in design, it had been constructed of red brick and concrete with a slate roof, slavishly modeled
on the great rail station in Amsterdam. Shimazu fervently promised
himself to see to it that this and other Western-inspired abominations
around Tokyo were reduced to rubble after the coming war was over
and the Emperor's reign was secured.

He searched the crowd and found the particular person he was
looking for: a gaunt, nervous young man who paced back and forth
along the length of the platform. Anyone else watching him would

think that he had an important appointment to keep and his train was late. Shimazu knew otherwise. The young man was a student, and a member of the *Shimpeitai*. He was here to kill two people.

Shimazu knew who those two people were—after all, he had been coaching the youth for months, inflaming him, honing his rage, directing its force against those who would stand in the way of the Son of Heaven assuming His proper place as ruler of the world. Those two people would be entering Tokyo Station soon.

Shimazu watched the main entrance and played another tune. He was barely halfway through it when the targets entered the station. But nothing precipitous would happen. At least not until the train pulled into the station.

■ ■ ■

As they waited for the train to arrive, Meiko wandered around the station. She stopped to read one of the posters she had seen plastered on the walls. The nearest one had been affixed to one of the station's stone columns. It read:

SHIMPEITAI

1 The Soldiers of the Gods are ready with Celestial swords to accomplish the Restoration of Showa as their life mission for the glory of the Empire;

2 The Soldiers of the Gods denounce all institutions and activities which are based on liberalism and socialism, and aim to establish a government, an economic policy and a culture which shall be based upon the position of the Emperor; and

3 The Soldiers of the Gods aim at the annihilation of the leaders of the financial groups, the leaders of the political parties, the villains of the Imperial Entourage and their watchdogs who are obstructing the progress of the Empire. They shall thereby establish the Imperial Restoration and proclaim the Imperial Rule throughout the world.

"Ah!" said a voice at Meiko's shoulder. "The Shimpeitai—the Soldiers of the Gods—the Heaven Sent Troops."

It was Underminister Nitobi. He was smiling, but he didn't seem amused. Behind him Meiko could see the station filling with travelers.

"What does it mean?" Meiko asked.

"It means no matter who you are, whether member of the zaibatsu or the major political parties or even the Imperial Court, do not criticize the adventurism of the military or you may fall victim to the 'Celestial swords' of the Shimpeitai."

"But who *are* they?"

"The rank and file are made up mostly of young military officers, fanatically devoted to the Emperor and to *kodo*."

"Ah, yes," Meiko said. "Kodo." Hiroki had spoken of little else since her return. It had originally signified devotion to the will of the Emperor, but had rapidly become a code word for expansionism.

"But I fear the Shimpeitai leaders are less devoted than they claim. Some of them, I fear, would actually like to see the Emperor removed."

Meiko gasped. "I can't believe that!"

"I don't want to believe it either, but I'm afraid it is a fact. Our Emperor is a gentle man. He opposes the militarism which grips this land by the throat. They think that shows weakness, and a willingness to accommodate and even accept domination by the white races. They even whisper that he is *personally* weak, unable to father a son."

Meiko was speechless. Such talk bordered on blasphemy! It was unconscionable!

And yet . . . she had heard grumblings against the Emperor in her *own* house. Hints from her father, Hiroki, and the baron that he was too timid in foreign affairs, a better marine biologist than national leader, and worries about his fathering four daughters and no sons with the Empress Nagako. No member of the Satsumas, of which Nagako was a clanswoman, would rest easy until she had delivered a male heir to the Throne of the Sun. Until that day, the rival Choshu clan would agitate for the Emperor to bed with a concubine—preferably a Choshu virgin—to assure continuity of the Imperial Line, unbroken now for thousands of years.

Yet she knew that no matter what their complaints and dissatisfactions with the Emperor, they would never plot against him personally.

"Why, just this week," Underminister Nitobi was saying, "I sent a long letter to the Diet denouncing the Shimpeitai and the forces behind it." He puffed himself up with pride. "It caused quite a stir, of that I can assure you."

"You aren't afraid?"

She could hear the train approaching from the switching yard. The station was very crowded now, with military uniforms prominent among the travelers.

"Of course not!" he said with a snort, but Meiko caught a trace of uneasiness in his eyes. "And even if I was, I would still speak out. We can't let these fanatics bully us into letting them have their way with whatever of our nation's resources they wish to use. There have to be limits."

Meiko realized that despite his pompous air and his affectations, Underminister Nitobi was quite a courageous man. As he excused himself to rejoin their traveling party, she looked back at the proclamation. The openly threatening tone, the steel-hard, unyielding self-righteousness of the words chilled her. What was happening in the Islands of the Gods?

Meiko heard the train begin to pull into the station. She hurried to join her family and prepare to board.

■ ■ ■

Now! Shimazu thought, mentally urging the student forward. *First Nitobi, then the girl! Now!*

This was the only way to do it at this point. He had been unable to get near the Mazaki girl since her return from America. During the warmer seasons she was out of town at her family's summer home. In less hospitable weather she had been out of reach in either her house or a car. It was too late now for a delicate touch. The wedding was only a week away. Besides, this way served a dual purpose—a meddlesome politician would die along with the girl.

If only a rift had developed during the four years the girl had been away. If only Hiroki were not so determined to marry her. If only the younger Okumo had given in to his feelings and seduced her in America. If only he had persuaded her to marry him and stay there with him, then this risky business would be unnecessary. But Matsuo Okumo had demonstrated his depth of character by resisting the strong feelings Shimazu knew he harbored for his brother's betrothed.

So it is up to me, he thought. Maybe this wasn't necessary. Maybe Hiroki's drive, his singleness of vision would not be diluted by a wife and family. Maybe. Shimazu could not take that chance. He sensed Hiroki's crucial role in the future of the Order. Nothing could be allowed to interfere with that. And so the Mazaki girl had to die here in this Occidental obscenity of a rail station, today, this morning, *now!*

The student had been prepared. He knew what to do. In secret meetings over cups of sake in a room dark as the space behind a blind man's eyes, he had been convinced of the treason implicit in every word and gesture made by Underminister Nitobi, and of the seductive web of treachery woven around the underminister by Viscount Mazaki's American-educated daughter.

The student was convinced that both had to die.

And now, as the train rolled into the station, the student started toward the Mazaki party.

At last!

■ ■ ■

As she stood with her father and the underminister, Meiko saw a young man run out of the crowd to her left. He was shouting something as he ran toward her group but she could not pick out the words. His hand came out of his coat pocket and he waved it about. He was close enough now for Meiko to see that he held a small pistol.

She screamed in terror, and as she did, Underminister Nitobi turned around. The young man cried, *"Tenchu!"* and began firing. The underminister tried to duck and run but could not avoid the bullets. He cried out and spun as he clutched his chest. Bright red blood surged first from his white shirt front, then exploded from his head as his derby flew into the air, then rolled away. He collapsed on the platform. His body shuddered violently, then was still.

"Tenchu!" the young man cried again, brandishing his smoking pistol in the air. Then he turned and pointed it at Meiko's face. She saw the round opening of the muzzle, could almost look down the bore, saw the wild eyes aiming along the barrel. Horrified, she tried to run, but she couldn't move!

Suddenly Meiko felt an impact on her shoulder. She was shoved aside just as the gun fired. But even as she fell, she saw the gunman take aim at her again. The hammer snapped down with a click but there was no shot. The man screamed in frustration and hurled himself headlong in front of the approaching train.

The train station wavered before her as she lay paralyzed on the floor, watching a scarlet pool spread slowly from Underminister Nitobi's body. The air filled with cries of panic and terror. She tore her eyes from the underminister's body and rose to her knees. She turned and gasped.

Someone else was down, further away, near the edge of the platform.

She stumbled forward. *No! No, it can't be!*

That figure on the ground. It looked like—

She stopped as she reached the fallen man. *"Father!"*

There was blood all over his head, dripping down over his right eye. It ran from his nose and his right ear. As she wiped his face with her kimono, he opened his eyes. They were dull and he blinked repeatedly, as if trying to focus them.

"Meiko," he said in a barely audible voice. "Why . . . ?" Then his eyes closed and he said no more. Meiko screamed for a doctor, an ambulance, anyone who could help her father.

■　■　■

Count Mazaki—shot!

Hiroki's mind whirled as he strode through the halls of Tokyo Hospital. He was walking as quickly as he could, but still he could not keep up with Matsuo who was a full two paces ahead of him and pulling away.

How could such a thing happen? Underminister Nitobi would not be missed. He was a stone in the path of Japan's destiny. But Count Mazaki—a man who was not only a staunch political ally, but who was destined to be his father-in-law as well, shot by a gunman crying "Tenchu!"

Punishment of Heaven, indeed! This was disaster!

In his heart, Hiroki knew that he was not free of guilt. After all, hadn't he been a party to the rise of the more violent and headstrong factions in the armed forces? The Kakureta Kao had allied itself with the Black Dragon Society to promote kodo among the military men, especially the young officers. Hiroki had been playing a pivotal part, acting as liaison between the Order and the Black Dragons.

Their plans had been successful beyond their greatest expectations. The army was now straining at its leash, fairly howling to be let loose upon the world to fight for the glory of the Emperor and Japan.

Too successful, perhaps. Count Mazaki might be dead by now.

Up ahead he saw the Mazaki family clustered at the end of the hall. Meiko sat in a chair apart from the others. With her elbows on her knees and her face resting in her hands, she was the picture of dejection. She looked up at their approach and Hiroki saw her expression crumble into naked grief. With a sob she ran forward with her arms outstretched. He stopped to embrace her but she never reached him.

She flung herself into Matsuo's arms and clung to him as if he were the last solid thing in a world that was crumbling to dust.

Hiroki's heart stumbled over a beat. *What is this?* he thought. *Could it be . . . ?*

Hiroki discarded the thought. Since returning from America, Matsuo had been a stranger to Tokyo. Between basic training and studying for his commission in Naval Intelligence, and his growing obsession with learning to fly, he had been away from home far more often than not. And when he was home, he never visited the Mazakis, even when invited.

No, he was sure there could be nothing between his brother and his bride-to-be. She embraced him because he had been closest. That was all. Nothing more.

Yet he could not deny that the sight of his bride-to-be in his brother's arms touched a raw nerve deep within him.

■　■　■

Hiroki is watching!

Matsuo pulled Meiko's arms from around his neck. There was nothing in this world he wanted more than to crush her against him and absorb her quaking sobs. He would stand here all day and hold her and smooth her hair and dry her tears if that was what she needed. But

Hiroki was standing right behind them and he knew he must not allow this embrace to last a moment longer. He pulled away from Meiko and turned her toward his brother. Dazedly, she went to Hiroki.

It was the hardest thing he had ever done.

She leaned against Hiroki now but her eyes were on Matsuo.

"He's not . . . ?" Matsuo did not want to finish the sentence.

Meiko straightened and seemed to gather herself together. "No, he's alive. Just barely. The bullet struck him in the head. He's in surgery now." She began to sob again. "He may die!"

"He'll live," Matsuo told her with a confidence he did not feel. "He is strong and brave. He will live."

"But he lost so much blood!" she said. "And even if he lives, there might be brain damage!"

Matsuo ached to hold her. It was all he could do to keep from reaching out to her. He thrust his hands deep into the pockets of his naval uniform while Hiroki stood there placidly with his hands folded in front of him. Matsuo tried to will his brother to at least put a comforting hand on Meiko's shoulder, but he did not move.

"It's a terrible thing," Hiroki said. "The bullets were obviously meant for Underminister Nitobi, but that does not mitigate the tragedy."

Matsuo could stand it no longer. He took Meiko by the arm and led her back down the hall.

"Let's all sit down."

It was going to be a long, long night.

DECEMBER
TOKYO

Hiroki stood amid the laughing, backslapping celebrants and raised his cup of sake. He said a silent prayer to Heaven, and then downed it in one swallow. All of Tokyo was celebrating. And as soon as the word spread, all of Japan would join in. It had happened only minutes before. The siren on the wall of the Imperial Palace had blasted twice. *Twice!*

Empress Nagako had begun labor last night. And now the baby had been born.

Two blasts meant a boy.

The Emperor had a son! Japan now had an heir to the Throne. And he was a Satsuma! The next Emperor would have the blood of the Satsuma clan in his veins! This indeed was cause for celebration!

He looked around at his fellow celebrants. They had gathered here in their customary private room on the second floor of a restaurant near Sanno Hill. Close by stood Father, speaking to Mitsuro Toyama and his protégé, Koki Hirota, along with other higher-ups in the Kokuryu-kai—the Black Dragon Society. Two special military guests were present today: from the Army there was General Terauchi, and Admiral Nagano from the Navy. The purpose of the gathering was to draw the two service chiefs closer to their circle, to bring them around to a wider view of the Empire's future possibilities as a world power. Hiroki was present ostensibly as the baron's son, but it was no secret that he represented the interests of the Kakureta Kao. Count Mazaki had survived his wound, but was still too infirm to attend.

They had been meeting frequently during the year with other like-minded nobles and statesmen to discuss ways and means of steering Japan to her proper destiny. Their circle of influence was widening steadily, to the point where political observers in the press were referring to them as *Tosei-ha*—the Control Faction.

But all year long, as they had gathered their resources, the specter of the Empress giving birth to another daughter had hung over them like a *dai-katana*. Should a female child be born, the Emperor would be under immense pressure to seek a male heir from a concubine—a woman of the Choshu clan.

Now we can move ahead, Hiroki thought. *Now the world will be ours!*

He waved to Matsuo as he entered the room wearing his navy uniform. He rarely attended these gatherings, but the birth of an heir to the Throne was a special occasion. All reports on Matsuo's progress in the Officers School were wildly enthusiastic. He was a quick learner and the Intelligence Service was avidly courting him. His knowledge of idiomatic American English would prove invaluable in the translation of monitored transmissions between the ships of the American Pacific Fleet. Hiroki was proud of his younger brother.

"Isn't it wonderful?" Matsuo cried, beaming his jubilation.

"It is a sign from Heaven," Hiroki said. "It is a sign to us and to all the world! Our time has come!"

Matsuo's smile broadened as he refused a cup of sake. "Yes. Good times for the Empire!"

The group eventually quieted. Hiroki joined the circle around his father. He noted Matsuo hanging back, an interested listener but not an active participant in the discussion.

"We must now broaden our efforts," Father said. "Not only must we continue working to place the right men in the strategic cabinet posts, but we must begin to undermine the influence of the Kodo faction. They only look north and west! They are like dumb oxen wearing blinders. They see nothing else. They think only of Manchuria and China and Russia in Japan's future. I say why not look south to the Philippines and Malaysia? Why not east? The whole of the Pacific Ocean lies on our doorstep! Countless untapped resources!"

He walked from man to man as he spoke, weaving his spell. Hiroki watched in silent admiration, wishing he could speak half so eloquently. Especially since these were *exactly* the sentiments of the Kakureta Kao.

"Many will say, 'What about Great Britain? What about America?' I say we confront them! The Pacific is *ours!* Our goal should be to make it a Japanese lake!"

Cheers filled the room.

"Hakko-ichi-u!" Hiroki cried and raised his cup of sake.

The others raised their own in response to Shimazu's favorite expression. It meant The Eight Corners of the World Under One Roof. The Tosei-ha was in full agreement as to which country's roof that should be.

"But what *of* America?" Admiral Nagano said after the cups had been drained. "If the Empire confronts her, it will be on the sea. The burden will fall to the Navy. The Navy does not wish to take that confrontation lightly."

Save the Emperor from fainthearted admirals! Hiroki thought, but said nothing.

Father replied with a respectful bow. "A wise and perceptive judgment. But America and Britain are staggering under the worst economic depression in their combined histories. They have never been more vulnerable."

"It might be useful to hear what the honorable baron's American-educated son has to say on the matter," Toyama said.

Father turned to Matsuo and raised his eyebrows. Hiroki saw his brother start as if he had received an electric shock, saw him swallow hard before he spoke. Hiroki suppressed a smile. Matsuo, the Great Authority on America, was obviously unprepared for this.

"Timing will . . ." He swallowed again. "Timing will be all-important in any conflict with the Americans. We know that although their Navy has a sizable number of ships at its disposal, most of them have been deactivated—what the Americans call 'mothballed'—and are rusting at anchor in bays around the country. Because of the huge mothball fleet, they are building few new ships. In another six to eight years those old ships will be hopelessly obsolete as well as rusted beyond repair."

Hiroki watched the assembled leaders of the Tosei-ha smile and nod at each other. He also noted the interest in the eyes of General Terauchi and Admiral Nagano. They liked what they heard. This meeting was working out *very* well. Matsuo's American experience was indeed proving to be an asset.

"But a wise man should never take the United States for granted," Matsuo said, continuing to the subject. "Words, maps, statistics, even photographs cannot convey an accurate conception of the enormous resources in that country. Even the Americans themselves don't realize what they have."

"What good are resources, no matter how boundless, to an inferior race?" Toyama said.

Matsuo bowed. "Yes, Toyama-san, I heartily agree. They are barbarians without our inner strength and resolve, and they do not have a Divine Emperor to inspire them, and they may be weakened by their depression, but . . ." He paused. "I am not sure how to say this. I have no way to prove this, but I have sensed that there are a few Americans—and all it takes is a few—who do not know the meaning of the words, 'It cannot be done.' There is something in America that cultivates this kind of person. I have stood a quarter-mile in the air atop one of their buildings, I have crossed great rivers on their bridges. Give that person enough time and enough resources and he will do the impossible. That is why in any conflict with the Americans we must strike decisively with lightning swiftness, and then settle. We will never survive a protracted war with them."

Hiroki could see that this did not sit well with Toyama or the rest of the Tosei-ha. The Service Chiefs looked concerned, too. And it was plain that Father was embarrassed because of it. He cursed his younger brother for such negative talk in front of these important men.

But then, Matsuo did not have the benefit of the Seer's vision—he did not know that there would be a great war, and that Japan would win. It was up to him to ease the mood—not for Matsuo's sake, but for Father's.

"Ah, but why worry about America now?" Hiroki said into the silence. "We cannot hope to face any country successfully with the present makeup of the cabinet. And we certainly cannot think of turning our eyes east while the Kodo clique controls the young officers."

As he listened to the murmurs of agreement around the room, he was warmed by Father's grateful look. He decided to cap the moment with a final toast.

"To the end of the Kodo clique's power and to the end of short-sighted cabinet members who impede the Destiny of Japan!"

Hiroki glanced across the room at Toyama who bowed almost imperceptibly in his direction. Only days ago, the Black Dragon Society and the Kakureta Kao had initiated a plan that would translate Hiroki's toast into reality.

1 9 3 4

THE YEAR OF THE DOG

OCTOBER
SAGAMI BAY

Meiko sat with Matsuo and watched her father doze in his chair. The poor thing was exhausted. And well he should be after the way she had walked him around the garden today. She too was tired. Her father's left arm and leg were gaining strength steadily but were still very weak and he had to lean heavily on her when he walked. Matsuo had stopped by and had taken the weight of her father for the last circuit of the garden.

She looked at Matsuo. He had knocked on the door one steamy summer day two months ago and said he was here to pay his respects to the count. But Meiko had known from his manner that her father was not the main reason for his visit.

He had been so tentative that day, so hesitant and skittish, like a forest animal ready to bolt at the crack of a twig. Slowly, after weeks of regular visits, he had learned to relax. He would help with her father, then he would sit here at the stone table with her and they would talk softly, never touching, always keeping the table between them. Matsuo was scrupulous about propriety when they were together, but that did not keep the servants from whispering and peeking at them through windows and doorways.

"Wouldn't it be wonderful if all life could be like this?" he said as they sat together in the garden watching evening grow toward night. "So peaceful here now that summer is gone."

She gazed down the slope to where the rising moon glimmered on

146

the bay. Soon it would be too cool to spend much time in the garden. She murmured her agreement.

"The only thing that can compare with it is flying," he said. "Being alone in the air with the clouds and seeing the earth drift by below." He looked at her. "Except that when I fly I am alone."

"Would you take me someday? I would love to fly through a cloud with you."

He suddenly became animated. "Yes! I could bring you to my flight school at Kasumigaura and get permission to use a two-seater! That would be wonderful!"

She loved the excitement in his eyes whenever he spoke of flying. She wondered at the powerful fascination it held for him. Just once, before it was too late, she wanted to share it with him. But she doubted that day would ever come.

"Someday," she said, fighting the urge to reach over and take his hand.

The light faded from his eyes. "Yes. Someday."

"Hiroki came by yesterday," she said. She did not want to change the subject, but knew she had to mention this.

She saw Matsuo stiffen. "Oh?"

"He was inquiring after Father . . . and asking about the wedding."

"I'm not surprised," Matsuo said in a flat voice. "It was supposed to have been eighteen months ago."

"Eighteen months. Yes, he reminded me of that."

"What did you tell him?"

"What I always tell him. What I tell everyone: the truth. I am my father's only daughter. I will stay with my mother to nurse him until he is well or until he is as well as he can be. As long as he keeps trying, *I* will keep trying. I will not give up until *he* gives up."

"You have already worked a small miracle. The doctors said he would never speak again, yet he is talking; they said he would never be on his feet again, but look at what he was able to do today. Your time with him has certainly not been wasted."

"Yet Father wants me to go ahead with the marriage."

She saw Matsuo straighten in his chair. "And . . . ?"

She had bargained with Father. Before the shooting, such a thing would have been unthinkable. But their relationship had changed. She was no longer just his daughter. She had become his nurse and healer and constant companion as well. She could berate him and scold him and tell him what to do when she was working with him. And now . . . she could strike a deal with him. Her temerity amazed her. Probably amazed Father, too.

"I will be married to Hiroki in the spring of 1936. We will decide on a new date for the wedding that winter, no matter how little or how much progress my father has made by then."

"Another eighteen months. Does my brother agree?"

"Yes. I left him no choice."

Meiko had presented the extra year-and-a-half wait to Hiroki as her father's wish. He had appeared frustrated and perhaps a little angry.

"He always has the choice of convincing my father to cancel the marriage arrangement," Matsuo said.

She prayed that he would. How she prayed for that! It would leave her free to marry another someday.

"Do you think it is possible he would do that?" Had Matsuo heard any rumblings of dissatisfaction with her in his home?

"Hiroki has many matters to occupy his mind. They will make the time pass quickly for him. And my father would never cause the count to lose face. To cancel a marriage arrangement while the bride's father is recovering from an assassin's bullet?" Matsuo shook his head slowly and, she knew, sadly. "That would be unthinkable," he said.

Meiko's heart sank. Matsuo was right. Sooner or later, she was destined to be Hiroki Okumo's wife.

There was no hope, no way out. Tears filled her eyes. She willed them away but they ignored her and began to slide down her cheeks. She wished she were one of those American girls she had pitied years ago. Better to have no prospect of marriage than to be this close to the one she loved and yet be forever separated by an impenetrable barrier. Her chest constricted as a sob escaped her.

Matsuo twisted in his seat and looked at her. He half rose, then sat down again. In the dark, she saw his hand slide across the table toward her. It waited there, palm up, open.

She thought about the servants and how they'd talk if they saw them sitting in the dark holding hands.

May the evil kami *take their eyes and tongues!* she thought. She reached out and laid her hand on Matsuo's. She shivered at the contact. Their fingers touched, softly, tentatively at first, then intertwined and locked together.

"Look at the night," Matsuo said after a while, his voice low and thick. "One is allowed only so many perfect, starry nights such as this in a lifetime. They are precious."

Meiko looked into his eyes and knew his pain was as great as hers.

"Yes," she said, biting back another sob. "Yes, they are."

1 9 3 5

THE YEAR OF THE BOAR

MARCH
TOKYO

"Toyama-san and his Black Dragons are doing their part, then?" Shimazu asked.

Hiroki knelt facing his master in Shimazu's quarters in the temple.

"It is going well enough, I suppose," Hiroki said, "but I had hoped that things would move more swiftly."

Lately it seemed that *nothing* was going his way, neither in his personal life, in his public life, nor in his work for the temple. Meiko had become maddeningly obstinate about the wedding. She kept insisting that as long as her father was making progress in his recovery, it was her duty to stay by his side and aid him in every way possible until he was the man he had once been. Hiroki had no argument that would overcome oya-no-on, her duty to her family, and he had to admit that Count Mazaki was making progress, but it was infuriatingly slow. Hiroki wanted Meiko on his futon, thirsted for the time when he could bend her to his needs. He felt the beginnings of arousal. Yes, there would come a time when Meiko would make up for this endless delay.

Shimazu laughed behind his mask. "Ah, Hiroki! Always the impatient one! The ground must be carefully tilled if the seeds we sow are to bear the full, rich harvest we desire. In this case, a stunted harvest will be worse than no harvest at all."

Hiroki bowed his acceptance. Shimazu was right, as always. And as for his work with Toyama and the Black Dragons—

"If only I weren't hampered by the need for discretion," he said. "So many of these young fanatic Army officers are members of the Black Dragon Society and so many are enraged at the Army's passive role, that keeping them stirred up is simple. What is difficult is keeping them stirred up and constrained at the same time."

"Of course. But it would work against our purposes for our involvement to be known. Mark my words: When the explosion comes—and after the next February's elections, it will come with a vengeance—you must be able to wring your hands in dismay and publicly demand with righteous anger that the miscreants be punished."

"I understand."

"It is important that you do. The resultant purge will move the Army more firmly into line with the Order's views, leaving it ready to strike in the proper direction at the proper time."

"Yes. But it is difficult to wait."

"We all wait for things. We here at the temple wait for news of the rediscovery of the Kuroikaze."

Hiroki's muscles tensed. "Has something new been uncovered?"

"Not yet. But I do not fear. The secret of the Black Winds will be unearthed. It has been foreseen. Someone will find it. Yajima is searching especially diligently."

"Yes . . . Yajima." Hiroki caught himself. "I am searching when I can. I wish him well."

"I should hope so. It does not matter who finds the scrolls, only that they be found in time."

Oh, but it *did* matter! *It must be me!* But *how?* He had so many other things to do! He was stretching himself to the breaking point. *Too much to do! Too much!*

But Hiroki knew that more than the scrolls themselves were at stake. They had been reason enough at first for him to scour the cellars and attics and refuse piles of temple after temple and shrine after shrine across the countryside. But he knew there were other benefits for one ready and willing to seize them. The one who unearthed the lost secret of the Kuroikaze would immediately wield enormous new influence within the Order. And influence within the Kakureta Kao could be translated into influence throughout Japan.

During the past few years, Hiroki had come to see that the range of the Order's power and influence was more far-reaching than he had ever imagined. There were men in the Imperial Palace, the armed forces, the highest offices of the government, the press, and all the zaibatsu who either were partly educated in the temple or owed the Order a favor. None of them would forget his debt.

Hiroki had a plan that would test the Order's influence. He did not know how Shimazu would react to it, so he had decided on an oblique approach. And now was as good a time as any to broach it.

"Sensei," he said, carefully, "do you believe the Emperor is receiving all the respect and adulation he is due?"

■ ■ ■

"There can never be enough," Shimazu answered patly. All that can be given is still insufficient." But he thought, *Whence does that question arise?*

He studied Hiroki. He was hiding something. What was he planning that he was keeping secret?

"I realize that," Hiroki said. "But foreigners do not. I hear them snicker when we bow as He passes. And there are academics and intellectuals here in the Emperor's own land writing and lecturing that He is not Divine, that He is a mortal like the rest of us. They say He is a constitutional monarch and nothing more."

Shimazu maintained an impassive expression. He had a vague idea of where Hiroki was leading him. He played along.

"This is nothing new. We have always had doubters among us. They are small voices."

"But they are becoming larger, I fear. And they are dangerous voices, especially now when we are trying to prepare the country for the coming war. We must form a seamless wall behind our Emperor when we challenge the world. There must be no cracks of doubt, no matter how small, to mar that wall."

"Perhaps you are right," Shimazu said, nodding slowly. "What do you have in mind?"

"We must find a way to make it completely unacceptable—*illegal* —to say or write anything that even suggests that the Emperor is less than Divine, or subject to man-made laws. Is there any way the Order can work to bring such laws into being?"

Shimazu noted with amusement that Hiroki was holding his breath as he waited for an answer. After a lengthy pause, Shimazu said, "There are ways."

He watched Hiroki exhale slowly in an attempt to hide his elation. He knew what his pupil had in mind now. Hiroki was borrowing a trick from the Tokugawa Shoguns. They had removed the Emperor from temporal power yet they reinforced his Divine Nature at every opportunity. The idea was elegant in its simplicity: If one deifies the Emperor to a sufficient degree, one can lead His children anywhere in His name.

He was glad to see Hiroki planning so far ahead with such

subtlety. This was what he had groomed him for since he was a child. He was glad his thoughts seemed far from marriage. Let them stay away. As long as no definite wedding date was set, Shimazu would forget about the Mazaki girl and let her go her way. But should a wedding become imminent again . . .

In the meantime, he would advise the Elders of Hiroki's plan, and recommend that they support it. In this case, it might work to the Emperor's advantage.

1 9 3 6

THE YEAR OF THE RAT

FEBRUARY

Matsuo found his brother standing on the eastern edge of Hibiya Park, across from the Imperial Hotel. He was watching a civilian and a young Army captain in conversation perhaps a hundred feet away. On closer scrutiny, Matsuo recognized the civilian as Toyama himself. As Matsuo approached, the two walked away through the park.

"Ah, Matsuo!" Hiroki said with a smile as Matsuo joined him. "A beautiful day, is it not? Such interesting sights."

Matsuo shivered in the cold. Hibiya Park was a dreary place in the winter with its leafless trees and lifeless flower beds. Snow was piled along the edges of the walkway and the heavy air hinted at more to come.

"Look up there, for instance," Hiroki said, pointing to the upper level of the two-story Imperial Hotel across the street.

Matsuo glanced up at the sturdy modern building. Was this why Hiroki had talked him into a "leisurely stroll" on a day as cold and dreary as this? To study the architecture of the Imperial Hotel?

"Where?"

"On the second floor, the third window from the left. See the man there?"

Matsuo squinted through the hazy air. Yes, there was a balding man, either American or European, in a white shirt leaning out the window, craning his neck, peering off to the right toward the Imperial Palace.

"What of him?"

"He thinks he has the perfect perch from which to watch our Emperor as he passes." Hiroki's smile took a malicious twist. "He is about to be disabused of that misconception." He bowed toward the hotel. "Shall we move in for a closer look?"

Puzzled by Hiroki's words and purpose, Matsuo shrugged. "If you wish. I might even suggest that we go into the lobby where it is warmer."

"Are you cold?" Hiroki said with what sounded like genuine surprise. He seemed oblivious to the chill. "Perhaps we should find someplace to have a cup of hot sake after the Emperor passes."

Matsuo hunched his shoulders inside his naval uniform and matched his brother's stride. He glanced at his epaulets and saw moisture condensing on the brass lieutenant's insignia he had so carefully buffed to a high gloss last night.

As he followed his brother toward the hotel, he glanced up again at the window where the Occidental man waited. As he watched, the man turned and cried out with surprise, then he saw pairs of hands drag him from the window. Matsuo grabbed Hiroki's arm and pointed to the now empty window.

Without looking up, his brother said, "I know."

They crossed the street as the Imperial Entourage approached. As they reached the courtyard of the hotel, the front doors flew open. Matsuo watched with alarm as squads of military police hauled Western civilians—some not even fully dressed—out of the hotel and into the cold. They lined them up along the curb, facing the street. Matsuo would have gone over to find out what the matter was but the Entourage was upon them at that moment. He turned toward the street and bowed as the Emperor passed. He noted out of the corner of his eye that the soldiers made the foreigners bow low along with everyone else.

When the Emperor had passed, the soldiers walked off and left the dazed, shaken foreigners standing in the cold, looking at each other in bewilderment. Matsuo finally understood, and it made him uneasy.

He saw Hiroki watching them. His grin was like flint.

"Is that why you brought me out today?" Matsuo said. "To see that display?"

"I wanted to see it for myself." He smiled more warmly at Matsuo. "And I wanted some company. Besides, I thought it would be enlightening for you."

"You approve of that, don't you?" He had a suspicion that Hiroki and the Kakureta Kao were intimately involved in the undisputed frenzy to reinforce the Emperor's Divine Nature that had swept through the government and the military and the press during the past year. But he hesitated to say that aloud in so many words.

"Of course. Don't you approve of giving the Son of Heaven his due respect?"

"My reverence for the Emperor is deep, as you well know. But I am Japanese." Matsuo pointed to the shivering Westerners as they hurried back into the warmth of the Imperial Hotel. "They are not."

"But as you also well know, my brother, it is now forbidden by law to look down upon the Emperor or to stand in any way above him as he passes."

"Laws don't create reverence. It must come from here." He pointed to his heart. "Not from the barrel of a gun."

"Reverence can be learned. And if learned well, it becomes a lifelong habit. The people must not become too comfortable with the Emperor's divinity. It must remain miraculous. The same goes for foreigners. These have been taught a valuable lesson today. One they are unlikely to forget."

"If you were a visitor in Rome, would you care for that sort of treatment every time the Pope passed your hotel?"

Hiroki smiled thinly. "I see no reason for me to ever visit Rome."

Matsuo was discovering a new arrogance in his brother. Or perhaps it had been there all along and only now was it coming out of hiding. He began walking along the street, away from the hotel. Hiroki fell in beside him.

Matsuo said, "Has it occurred to you that all the articles and laws and public demonstrations reinforcing the Divinity of the Emperor during the past year or so are just a little too well timed to be truly spontaneous?"

"Is my brother hinting that there is a faction manipulating the press and the populace?" Hiroki said, arching his eyebrows.

"I don't think it is impossible. Looking at the whole picture, I find that it reeks of orchestration."

"It might not be wise to discuss such a theory so openly. If indeed such diverse and widespread events are orchestrated, one must consider the breadth and reach of the power of the maestros. And beware."

Matsuo studied his brother's bland expression. "I shall."

"Good. And it might also be wise to avoid the Sanno Hill area during the next few days."

"Why?" Matsuo looked toward the rise beyond the Imperial Palace where the new Diet Building was nearing completion. The Diet and the prime minister's residence occupied Sanno Hill. It was the heart of Japan's civil government.

"Something is in the wind," Hiroki said in a flat tone. "Yesterday's elections dealt a blow to the Kodo faction's representation in the diet. I fear they might do something rash. Do not take my words lightly."

Matsuo could read nothing in Hiroki's expression. He knew his brother well enough, however, to sense that he was fairly vibrating with suppressed excitement.

■ ■ ■

Hiroki could barely contain himself. It took a supreme effort of will to remain seated, warming his feet near the sunken kotatsu, while sipping his breakfast tea with his father and brother. He wanted to be up and pacing, burning the nervous energy that tingled through every nerve ending in his body, that set his heart to racing and his palms to sweating.

Something was about to break. The Army's young officers were like caged animals that had been mistreated too long. Under the Order's guidance, Toyama's Black Dragons had fanned the aggressive fervor of the officers to the combustion point. They strained at the leash to be let loose upon China to secure it for the Emperor. The setbacks in the recent election had them frothing at the mouth. They were ready to run wild.

But *when?* This morning? Tonight? Could it be that it had already happened and the news simply had not arrived yet? He couldn't bear this tension.

At least his family was safe. Father would not be going to Sanno Hill today, and he had warned Matsuo yesterday. His brother was home this morning, walking about the room with a heavy, sand-filled ceramic jar dangling from the fingertips of each hand. Matsuo was wearing a gray, half-sleeve kimono which exposed his forearms. Hiroki watched the muscles ripple and bulge as he slowly levered the jars up and down, back and forth. He realized that the strength in his younger brother's hands had to be enormous to manipulate those heavy jars so easily with only his fingertips.

"Are you still so devoted to shuri-te?" he asked, hoping some idle conversation would hasten the passage of time.

"It's no longer shuri-te," Matsuo said. "The Okinowan masters had an enclave last year and agreed to combine the many te disciplines and call them all by one name: *karate.*"

Hiroki was debating whether or not to enroll in a dojo himself when the sudden jangle of the phone made him jump, splattering hot tea on his arm. Cho answered it and called Father to the phone. Hiroki watched his father's face blanch as he listened with the receiver pressed hard against his ear.

"The Army is in revolt!" he cried as he hung up. "Prime Minister Okada has been assassinated and his residence taken over by the rebels! They have dug in and occupy the routes to the Diet. The Imperial Palace is ringed with mutinous troops!"

Hiroki suddenly went cold, despite the warmth from the kotatsu. Why would they ring the palace?

"The Emperor!" Matsuo cried, dropping his jars on the floor. "Have they—?"

"The Emperor is safe . . . for now. No troops have crossed the moat to the palace grounds."

"Are they guarding him or holding him captive?" Hiroki asked.

"That is not clear. But there is more." His voice shook as he spoke. "Murder squads have struck all over Tokyo. General Wanatabe is dead, shot down along with his wife and his servants. Finance Minister Takahashi is also dead. Admiral Suzuki was wounded and Count Makino narrowly escaped with his life. But worst of all, Viscount Saito has been murdered! Only last night—*hours* ago—I had dinner with him and Ambassador Grew at the American Embassy! We watched a silly American movie, *Naughty Marietta*." Father hung his head and covered his eyes. "They shot him thirty-six times!"

Hiroki was alarmed now. The others Father had mentioned were all moderates who questioned and challenged the Army's moves in China and Manchuria. It was logical that the rebel fanatics would attack them. But old Saito-san? A gentle old man, the Lord Keeper of the Privy Seal, at least eighty years of age, dead—to what purpose? What was happening?

"Animals!" Matsuo growled.

"I fear you do the beasts of the field a disservice," Father said. He had regained his composure now.

Hiroki was about to excuse himself when Cho hurried into the room. "Soldiers, my lord!" he said. "At the front door!"

Oh, no! Hiroki thought as terror caught him in an icy grip. *Not here!*

Before he or Father could reply, a young second lieutenant came up behind Cho and pushed him out of the way.

"Baron Okumo?" he said.

"I am he!" Father shouted, stepping forward. "How dare you come into—"

The officer drew his pistol and pointed it at Father, crying, *"Tenchu!"*

Paralyzed with horror, Hiroki stood rooted to the spot. He didn't even see Matsuo move, but suddenly his brother was there, knifing the edge of his hand down onto the officer's gun arm with a *ki-ai* shout. He heard the distinct crack of bone as the gun went off, the bullet tearing through the floor.

Matsuo then became a blur of motion. With a howl of rage, he hammered the officer into the next room, sending him reeling into the enlisted men he had brought with him. Hiroki pushed Cho toward Father. "Take him out back!" he shouted, then followed on his brother's heels. Matsuo needed help.

There were six of them, all armed with old Arisaka rifles, and he could tell from the shocked expressions on the soldiers' faces that they had not expected to run into anything like Matsuo. No sooner had their leader reeled into them than Matsuo was upon them, filling the air with his cries as his fists and feet flew in all directions.

Hiroki made a quick assessment, saw three of the soldiers desperately trying to defend themselves against Matsuo's onslaught, two trying to help their bloodied officer to his feet, and the last one stepping back and aiming his rifle at Matsuo. Hiroki launched himself at that one, knocking him down before he could fire.

Contact with the other man ignited something within him. His fear evaporated into a blood rage. These men were in his home! They wanted to kill his father! He ripped the rifle from the soldier's grip and smashed the butt plate against his head. Once. Then again. He felt something give on the second blow. The man shuddered and lay still.

As he turned, one of the soldiers near the officer raised his rifle toward him. Hiroki lunged, hurling his stolen rifle into the soldier's face, then following it with a kick to the upper belly and a backfist blow to the temple. The soldier went down in a heap.

Looking up he saw that Matsuo had already disposed of one of his opponents and had the other two backpedaling toward the door. The remaining soldier near Hiroki joined them in flight as they all turned and ran.

But they didn't run far. As soon as they were in the open courtyard, they turned in the snow and began firing their rifles. Hiroki and Matsuo crouched inside the door on either side as bullets sang through the house or thudded into the front wall. Hiroki breathed a prayer of thanks to the kami of the house that the builder had chosen thick teak planking for the front.

The firing was wild. The soldiers were discharging their weapons as fast as they could work the bolts.

"I think they're trying to hold us down," Matsuo said. "Watch for someone sneaking around the side."

That was a disturbing thought, but probably accurate. Hiroki glanced around at the side windows, looking for any sign of movement. He hoped Father was safe. The front room was a mess. Blood smeared much of the floor where three soldiers lay still and the young lieutenant groaned through the bloody ruin of his mouth. Hiroki crawled over to where the officer's pistol lay on the floor and retrieved it. He held it up, offering it to Matsuo across the doorway, but his younger brother looked at it with disdain and shook his head.

Still think of yourself as a damn samurai, eh?

He checked the pistol: five shots left. He decided to save them for the unlucky soldier who poked his head in a side window.

The stream of bullets continued for a few minutes more, then stopped suddenly. Hiroki heard a few guttural grunts, and then all was quiet. He watched Matsuo cautiously peek around the door frame, then saw his face break into a wide grin as he leaped to his feet in the doorway and bowed. Hiroki looked out.

There on the front walk stood Nagata, fastidiously cleaning the blood from the long shiny blade of his katana. The snow all around him was bright red. One soldier lay headless to his left, another crouched in the bushes, gripping his wrist as his life spurted out of the stump where his hand had been.

"There were three of them out here," Hiroki said.

Nagata bowed. "I heard a shot and came to investigate. I met him on the side of the house. I left him there."

Hiroki marveled at this stout man of iron in his late sixties. He had vanquished three younger men, the total of whose years probably did not equal his, and appeared to give the deed little more importance than removing some unsightly weeds from the garden.

Nagata flourished and sheathed the katana in one smooth motion. "But why would soldiers attack the house of the baron?"

Hiroki spun and walked back to where the wounded officer lay. "That is what I'm going to find out right now!"

The young lieutenant was dazed and his words were barely intelligible through his broken teeth. Father walked in as Hiroki twisted his broken arm in an effort to get him to talk.

"Why this house? Why assassinate Baron Okumo? *Why?*"

"Captain Ando added his name to the list this morning. He is disloyal to the Imperial Throne. He seeks to make Japan subservient to the United States!"

"How can you say such a thing?" Father said, his hands trembling as he reached for the front of the lieutenant's uniform jacket. "I have spent my life seeking to make Japan the mightiest nation on earth!"

"Captain Ando said you were observed at the American Embassy last night with the traitor Count Saito." He raised his voice. *"Tenchu!* Death to all traitors to the Emperor!"

"I was bargaining for oil and scrap metal!" Father shouted.

"Don't waste your breath, Father," Matsuo said. "He is not worthy of it. You do not owe his type any explanation."

Hiroki motioned to Nagata to drag the lieutenant out as he had the three enlisted men. It was understood that there would be no trial.

He tried to control the trembling within. Part, he knew, was a reaction to the battle, but mostly it arose from fear. If he and Matsuo and Nagata had not been here, if Matsuo had not acted so quickly . . . Father would be dead and it would be entirely his fault.

It wasn't supposed to happen this way. This was not in the plan. Only the foot-dragging, tunnel-visioned politicians were to be eliminated. Not his own father!

He repressed another tremor. Had he started something he could not control?

Father walked slowly into the back room, obviously shaken.

"Father . . . ?" Hiroki said.

"I wish to be alone for a while. To think," Father said.

Feeling rejected but understanding the turmoil that his father must be experiencing, Hiroki stood with Matsuo in the front room for a moment, surveying the carnage. Matsuo spoke first.

"We fight well together, my brother," he said, bowing.

Hiroki returned the bow. "Yes. We defended our home well. But it was you who saved Father's life."

"Only from the first shot. We saved him together."

Hiroki bowed again. He felt very close to Matsuo at this moment. Today's battle had forged a bond between them, one he hoped would never dissolve. Perhaps it never would. But he knew deep in his heart that the course he was setting for his life and his country might test that bond to the limit.

He had gone too far now to turn back, even if he wanted to.

MARCH

Matsuo stared at the front page of the morning edition of *Yomiuri*. The *Ni-ni-roku Jiken,* as the February 26 Mutiny was now being called, was over. The rebellious troops had been arrested and carted off, the tablecloths they had flown as flags from the buildings they had occupied had been taken down, and all seemed quiet in Tokyo. But the entire

Japanese government was reeling from the loss of so many of its elder statesmen.

Matsuo's thoughts were wrenched back to the present by the photograph in the lower right-hand corner of the newspaper's front page. Two young Army officers were pictured. They were identified as Captains Nonaka and Ando, the two who signed the manifesto issued by the mutineers on the day of the rebellion. According to the lieutenant who had tried to kill Father, Ando had been the one who had ordered the killing. And the other one, Nonaka . . . Matsuo had seen him before. Yes, in Hibiya Park, talking to Toyama the day before the rebellion.

"There will be no public trial," Father was saying as he entered the room. He seemed to have recovered from the shock and was back in command.

Hiroki, Toyama, and other members of the Tosei-ha followed him in. General Terauchi and Admiral Nagano were present as well. There had been an almost constant round of meetings at various houses and back rooms since the rebellion.

"What we need now is a plan of action," Toyama said. "What do we do now? Can this tragedy—"

Tragedy! Matsuo thought. *You were behind it!*

"—be turned to the advantage of the Tosei-ha? I realize that may sound callous, but perhaps this is a heaven-sent opportunity." He looked around the room. "Any ideas?"

Suddenly tense, Matsuo focused his attention on the group. He suddenly realized that the future of Japan might well be decided here in this room by this group of men. Hopefully, they would realize the volatility of the Army and act to curb its power. Hiroki spoke up.

"I think we should assess the situation. What we see before us are two gaping voids. I propose that the Kodo elements that have been ripped from the Army be replaced by officers with a broader view of what Japan can accomplish, officers who can see beyond Russia, China, and Manchuria, who are sympathetic to the Tosei-ha."

As nods of agreement came from all the cushions, Matsuo realized with a jolt that this had been planned! Hiroki continued while Matsuo listened with chilled fascination. He was sure Hiroki had cooked up and rehearsed this speech for days, perhaps weeks, yet he was delivering it as if he were making it up as he went along! Matsuo listened with growing horror.

"And as for the government, seven elder statesmen—some called them moderates but I thought of them as dragging anchors—have been assassinated, creating a void in the government. My father has told me that the Emperor has called in Prince Sanjoni to choose a new prime minister. I think we should bend all our efforts toward seeing that men who think like us fill that void, and that a member of Tosei-ha becomes the new prime minister. I believe our esteemed friend and patriot Koki Hirota would make an excellent choice."

Matsuo lifted the newspaper to hide the relief that must have been obvious on his face. A member of the Black Dragon Society as prime minister? They were known the world over as gangsters! It was ludicrous! The Emperor would never approve such a choice.

But at the end of the week, Matsuo heard with astonishment that Hirota had been summoned to the Palace by Prince Sanjoni where he accepted the Emperor's mandate to form a new government. And only two weeks later he learned that General Terauchi had been appointed Minister of War and Admiral Nagano was Minister of Marine.

It was becoming dismayingly clear that the Tosei-ha—the Control Faction—had begun to live up to its name. But Matsuo recalled Hiroki's offhand remark years ago about how the Black Dragon Society answered to the Kakureta Kao. He wondered who ultimately might be controlling the Tosei-ha. With a chill he remembered green eyes peering at him through a silk mask and thought he had his answer.

1 9 3 7

THE YEAR OF THE OX

MARCH

You cannot die, sensei!

Matsuo knelt beside the futon where Nagata lay, breathing heavily. The old samurai was bathed in perspiration and his skin was deathly pale. Matsuo could hear fluid bubbling in his lungs as he breathed. He had been like this since Matsuo's arrival—restless, feverish, unresponsive even when one shouted his name.

Cho had brought him the news and he had rushed here immediately from the Naval Building. Upon his arrival, Kimura had told him that it had begun with chest pain last night. The doctor had come and diagnosed a severe heart attack. Nagata had refused to go to a hospital and had made her swear not to take him if he could no longer decide for himself. He had been like this since dawn.

My sensei is dying.

Aboard the train on his way here, Matsuo had been unable to grasp that simple fact. He had somehow assumed that Nagata was indestructible and would always be there—somewhere—for him to go to when he needed advice, or just someone to talk to. But now that Matsuo was here, now that he saw his old master, he knew. Death was in the air, hovering, waiting. Waiting for Nagata.

Grief tore at him, making him want to cry out his pain. He held it back, for he knew Nagata would want him to be strong for Kimura. Most of all, he felt terror. Terror at the prospect of facing life without Nagata somewhere behind him, guarding the rear. And anguish that the

163

most important man in his life was going to slip away without ever hearing Matsuo tell him what he had meant to him.

"Nagata-sensei," he said softly, gripping the leathery skin of his teacher's hand when Kimura had left the room for a few minutes. "This is Matsuo speaking. I know you cannot hear me, but I must say this to you. I am the son of Baron Okumo, but you will always be my father. You raised me, you taught me, you gave me a part of yourself that I always have with me. I will keep that part of you safe. I will never sully it by forgetting what you have taught me. All that I am and all that I will be, whatever good I do in this world, is because of the part of you that has become mine. As long as *I* live, so will you."

Matsuo gasped as Nagata's eyes opened slowly and fixed on him.

"Don't ever say that," he whispered between gurgling breaths. "Baron is your father . . . owe your life to him . . . talking like an American now!"

Matsuo silently bowed his head, but in his mind he said, *Then so be it. You are the true father of this man.*

Kimura came in and rushed to her husband's side when she saw that his eyes were open. Matsuo backed away to let them be alone. After a while, Kimura beckoned him closer.

"He has a request," she said. Her lips trembled but her eyes were dry. She was proving a worthy samurai wife.

"My daisho . . ." Nagata said in a barely audible voice. ". . . bequeath it to your care."

Matsuo looked over to where the two Masamune blades in their pearl inlaid scabbards rested one above the other on the black lacquered katana-kake. The honor of such a gift left Matsuo weak all over.

"I cannot—"

"You must!" The old samurai suddenly seemed to have found a pocket of strength. His voice grew stronger. "Those blades have magic in them. The destiny of the Empire and beyond is coiled within them. They fought the masked monks hundreds of years ago . . . would have triumphed had not the Black Winds carried the day for the monks. I fear the time will soon come when they will be called upon to drink the blood of the Kakureta Kao again."

That was Hiroki's order. Did he mean—? "I don't understand, Nagata-san."

"The monks wanted you. Still want you, I think. Came to your father and asked to take you into their temple. You were not yet born—not yet conceived! Pressed too hard. Baron was alarmed. Had me bring you to America to keep you from them. Take the daisho and keep it near. It will serve you well."

"I am not worthy!" he said.

Nagata managed a smile as the force drained from his voice. "Way you defended home during Ni-ni-roku Jiken . . . proud to have been your sensei . . . no one more worthy."

And then he closed his eyes and soon his breathing stopped. But a trace of the smile remained on his face.

■   ■   ■

Matsuo lay on his futon that night and turned Nagata's last words over and over in his mind. *They came to your father and asked to take you into their temple before you were born—before you were even conceived.* How could they have known? And what could they have wanted with him? It was a chilling thought.

And what of Father? Had he sent him to the United States to learn American ways, or to hide him from the monks? Which was the truth? Or were both partially true? Was that why he had been forbidden to draw attention to himself in America? Why he had never been allowed to return to Japan even for a visit until he was well into his teens?

Matsuo lifted the two swords of the daisho from the floor beside his futon and cradled them in his arms as he had as a frightened child. He wondered about the nightmares that had plagued him back then. Could those figures crawling toward him have been monks of the Kakureta Kao? He shivered with the memory of his terror. The dream had never recurred since his return to Japan, in 1926. He was glad to be rid of them.

With the swords resting comfortably against him, he drifted off to sleep . . .

. . . and found himself standing in an open field full of armed men under a flawless spring sky. Miles away, on a rise at the far end of a rocky peninsula, sat a huge, squat, three-tiered pagoda. He gazed through the eyeholes of his steel helmet at the hundreds of armored samurai flanking him on either side. They all seemed to be waiting for something. What?

And then some of them were pointing toward the temple. Four horsemen were approaching, bearing a litter between them. It took a long while for them to arrive. When they were close enough for him to make out their features, Matsuo saw that they had none. Each wore a silk mask over his face. They stopped amid the assembled samurai, gently lowered the litter to the ground, then turned and rode back toward the temple.

Matsuo watched them for a moment, then turned his attention to what they had delivered. It appeared to be a basket made of black wicker, no bigger than a small coffin. One of the shogun's officers approached the basket and gingerly lifted the lid. He peered in, then removed his helmet and reached into the basket. He appeared to jostle something within. When he glanced up again, his expression was one of concerned bewilderment. He motioned others closer for a look.

Matsuo stepped forward, curious to see what the Kakureta Kao guards had delivered. But as he neared the basket, he noticed a slight dimming of the light. He looked up and saw a tiny spot of black hovering in the sky, growing bigger by the moment. And the bigger it became, the more rapidly it spread, oozing across the sky like the blackest oil poured on the surface of clear water. It swallowed the sun, casting the whole plain into darkness. A wind began to blow, rising to a cold, dank, sour gale that tore at Matsuo's armor. The horses reared and whinnied, some bolted. Otherwise courageous men bolted, too, running in all directions in wild panic.

Matsuo held his ground in the fading light, fighting the fear and the overwhelming sense of hopelessness that seeped through his pores. Whatever was happening, it was caused by something in that black basket, that wicker coffin. If he could get to it, maybe he could stop this madness.

But the wind blew harder, knocking him off his feet. As he crawled toward the basket, desperate to reach it before the light failed completely and he would be unable to find it, he noticed that the grass all around him was utterly still. He was fighting a wind of hurricane proportions that did not flutter a single blade of grass. But something else was happening to the grass. It was dying, withering, turning brown as he watched.

The wind howled in his ears and tore through his soul as utter blackness engulfed the plain. *There's no hope.* He could not see his hand before his face. He pulled the short wakizashi from its scabbard and forced himself to a kneeling position. *No use.* He positioned the point over his abdomen. *No use at all.* He—

—woke up sweating and trembling. A new dream! Worse than the other! The despair, the hopelessness! He looked down and saw the moonlight through the window gleam from the bare blade of the wakizashi in his hand. Slowly, carefully, he slid it back into his scabbard.

The Black Wind! The Wind-That-Bends-Not-The-Trees! I've seen it! It really happened!

He calmed himself and caressed the daisho. These blades had been there. They had been passed down through the centuries to Nagata, and now to him. Why? What did it mean? Why him?

So many questions, but none more insistent than the one that would plague him all his days until he knew the answer: What had been in that black wicker basket?

JULY
SAGAMI BAY

"Do you think Hiroki has forgotten about me?"

Matsuo stared at Meiko as she sat on the planking next to the centerboard housing. She was in a short, pink kimono that exposed her legs to the knees; she had tied a matching scarf around her head to hold her hair down in the breeze. But there was very little breeze, barely enough to fill the dinghy's single triangular sail and ease it across the still waters of the bay. He leaned back against the transom, his right hand on the rudder handle, instinctively guiding the boat on a broad reach off the easterly breeze coming over the port side.

"You're very beautiful," he said.

Meiko smiled and bowed her head. "That's not what I asked you."

"Yes," he said. "I think he's forgotten about you. For now. Sooner or later, though, he will remember."

Meiko's smile disappeared and she looked away toward the land. Matsuo knew her thoughts. Her father had made a near-complete recovery. Count Mazaki's words were slightly slurred and he still needed a cane when he walked, but on the whole he could hold his own with the other members of the Tosei-ha. Meiko had no further means of delaying the marriage when Hiroki next demanded a wedding date.

I pray that day will never come, he thought.

The frantic schedule of meetings and rallies Hiroki had maintained in the year and a half since the mutiny had apparently kept him too preoccupied and too busy to take time out for a wedding.

He voiced what he hoped was a cheering thought. "Then again, it might be a very long time before the thought of marriage finds room in his mind."

Meiko trailed her hand in the water and said nothing.

Yes, it might very well be a long time before the storm of activity that swirled around his father and brother abated. So much had happened. So much was *still* happening. Koki Hirota's government had lasted barely a year. Prince Konoye was now prime minister but he was unable to rein in the militarists. Even now, in China, Japanese troops were skirmishing with Chiang Kai-shek's garrisons in Wanping and at the Marco Polo Bridge outside Peking.

Matsuo glanced over his shoulder at the coast, now so far behind them. The bathers were barely visible on the shore, and the neighboring Okumo and Mazaki houses were mere blotches on the hillside. Even now, on a beautiful, sunny Sunday afternoon, the Tosei-ha was meeting at the Mazaki house to confer on how to turn the China situation to its advantage.

He turned back to Meiko and drank in the sight of her as she nestled her chin on her arm where it rested on the gunwale and gazed into the shimmering water. She was everything he wanted in life. The Tosei-ha could offer him nothing. All he wanted was right here with him in this little boat.

Let them plot and plan. I'm where I want to be.

■ ■ ■

Hiroki stood at the far end of the garden and gazed down the slope at the calm expanse of Sagami Bay. Father, Toyama, and the other members of the Tosei-ha were behind him at the tables near the house. To his right he could hear the chatter and clatter from the Mazaki kitchen as the servants gossiped and cleaned up after the midday meal. There were lots of sails out there on the bay, tiny white confetti on a field of blue-green. Meiko was down there. Meiko and his brother. They saw a lot of each other, those two. He wondered why that didn't concern him. Perhaps it was because he had watched them when they were together and saw that they acted more like old friends, more like brother and sister, than secretive lovers.

He knew it should have bothered him. His brother and his future wife shared something apart from him, something special that excluded him. Why wasn't he jealous?

Because she was with Matsuo. His brother was an honorable man, totally devoted to his family. He would die rather than bring a breath of scandal to the family. If he could not trust Meiko with Matsuo, then he could trust her with no one.

He sighed. And to be completely honest, perhaps it served his purposes to have Meiko occupied with Matsuo. There was too much happening too fast these days. The headlong pace of events would not screech to a halt and wait for him to get married. A wedding would be such a distraction now.

And yet . . . perhaps he had better bring up the subject with Meiko. Perhaps set a date. Next spring. Maybe things would quiet down by next spring.

He would ask her soon. But not today. Perhaps tomorrow. By next week, for sure.

The chatter of the servants in the kitchen distracted him for a moment. They were gossiping about how the Countess Mazaki's new green kimono had to be returned because she had grown another size since she had been fitted for it. He smiled and shook his head. There were no secrets in a house with too many servants.

Before turning back to the Tosei-ha and the Chinese question, he took one last look at the bay, wondering which sailboat held Meiko and Matsuo.

■ ■ ■

Meiko sensed Matsuo watching her. She watched him in turn, sitting there by the tiller in his loose light blue shirt and his white shorts, like the captain of a battleship.

They had become so close, had seen so much of each other during her father's recovery period, that no one in the Mazaki household, either here at the bay or in Tokyo, seemed to pay much attention to his comings and goings, which were frequent whenever he was released from his duties at Naval Intelligence. He had become a fixture around the house, as unnoticed as the *fusama* and *shoji* that slid back and forth to join and divide the rooms. Meiko was well satisfied with that arrangement.

And yet, as close as they were, there remained that wall between them. A wall of on. They might occasionally hold hands through a chink in that wall, but she knew that Matsuo's on to his brother and his respect for Meiko's on to her father and her family honor prevented him from surrendering to the passion she sensed within him.

"We are alone," he said. Casually, as if he did it every day, he reached out with his foot and stroked one of her bare soles with his great toe. A thrill ran up her leg and spread through her pelvis.

She smiled and pulled her foot away. "No relatives, no nosy servants. Just us. That's nice."

It was dreamlike. On one side she could see the smoking volcano of Mihara, on the other sat the watchful snow-capped peak of Mount Fuji, and all around, the gently rippling water. Nature seemed to be putting on a show especially for them.

Suddenly, Meiko heard laughter from the water. She raised her head and shielded her eyes against the glare. Finally she located the source.

"Look!" she said, pointing to the east. "We're not alone after all."

A small skiff floated at anchor perhaps a hundred yards away. As she watched, two people bobbed to the surface and dropped a number of gray-brown objects over the side into their boat. Then they climbed out of the water. One was male and the other female. They were naked. With little hesitation, they dove into the water again.

She bolted upright. "Oysters! They've found an oyster bed!" She looked at Matsuo. "Let's dive for our own!"

His eyes lit. "A feast!" He turned the boat into the wind, then dropped the little three-tined anchor off the bow.

"Last one to bring up an oyster has to open them!" she cried.

Matsuo glanced at her and grinned. "You haven't a chance of winning!"

"Is that so, Okumo-san?" she said.

Meiko hesitated for a moment. It was customary to dive for oysters in the nude, but she hesitated to bare herself before Matsuo, afraid that it might remove the last few flimsy barriers that kept them apart. She thought about it a moment, then decided she didn't care.

Let the kami of the bay and the boat decide what would happen.

■   ■   ■

Matsuo watched with dry-mouthed fascination as Meiko untied her obi, opened her kimono, and let it drop to the deck. For a moment she stood before him clad only in loose white silk panties. Her breasts were small but firm and full, their nipples erect. He caught a glimpse of her narrow waist, her tiny navel, the curve of her hips, and her skin—her skin was truly flawless. Then with a laugh and a wave she was over the side and into the water with a quick, clean dive.

He stood in the gently rocking boat, gaping at the rising bubbles and widening rings until the luffing sail knocked the boom into his back. He nearly tumbled overboard. He reminded himself that he had seen pearl divers before, doing their work in the nude, but he had never seen, never dreamed, never expected . . .

With trembling hands he stripped down to his fundoshi and dove in after her. As he knifed into the warm water, he caught sight of a pale blur rising to his right. He angled around and kicked back toward the surface.

"Where were you?" Meiko said, laughing and gasping. The water had plastered her hair along the sides of her head. She was more beautiful than ever.

"I just got in," he said as casually as he could. "Find any?"

"Not yet—but I will!" A breath, a graceful surface dive, and she was gone again. Matsuo dove after her.

The deeper he went, the cooler and darker the water became. But he could still see Meiko ahead of him. She reached bottom first and began to hunt over the rocks for oysters. He stroked down to a rock nearby but could not drag his eyes away from her breasts, buoyant and bobbing as she turned this way and that; her silk briefs had become transparent in the water, revealing the dark mound of her pubes. He saw her grab at something, then lunge toward the surface. With bursting lungs and heart, Matsuo followed her up.

■ ■ ■

Meiko held on to the gunwale and waited for Matsuo to appear.

"I found one!" she shouted as he broke the surface. She held up the dark, rough, oblong shell. "I'm first!"

She saw him frown sternly. "Let me see that," he said, swimming to her side. "How do I know it's not just an empty shell."

"It's alive, all right!" she laughed. "And it has a pearl inside, I just know it!"

He clung with one hand to the side of the boat beside her, and as he examined the oyster, his kicking legs brushed against hers, sending a thrill to her very core. She had seen him on the beach before and had noticed his muscular physique. But she had never been this close. She watched the ripple of the muscles under his skin as he turned the shell this way and that. She fought an urge to reach out and feel them move under her hand. When he looked up from the shell she saw his eyes and wondered if her own desire showed as much as his.

She was suddenly afraid. It had been a game of sorts until now—the baring of flesh, the closeness in the water, the not-so-accidental touches—a reckless tempting of fate.

"Let's dive for more!" she said. "There's a whole bed of them down there."

Matsuo didn't move. Neither did she. He dropped the oyster into the water between them. She saw it sink out of sight, twirling like a falling elm seed in spring.

"Meiko."

He put his free hand on her shoulder. His touch was hot; it sent a wave of warmth across her shoulders and down to her submerged breasts. He drew her near. When she felt her nipples brush against his chest, the warmth burst into flame.

She gave into it.

Yielding to the pull of Matsuo's hand on her shoulder, she slipped her arms around his neck, and drew herself closer.

"This is wrong," he said in a hoarse whisper.

Meiko realized that this was their last chance to stop. She said, "I know."

Their bodies pressed together, their lips met, and she forgot about last chances and stopping. She wanted Matsuo, wanted all of him, and knew he wanted her. That was all that mattered now.

■ ■ ■

Matsuo delighted in Meiko's sigh as he ground his lips against hers. He had never felt like this . . . the electric euphoria of her breasts and legs and abdomen pressing against him. He wanted to wrap both arms around Meiko and crush her even more tightly against him, but knew they would sink if he let go of the boat. So he gripped the gunwale with his left hand and caressed her bare back and flanks with his right.

She moaned low in her throat as he squeezed his hand between their bodies and found her breast. From there he slid his fingers down to and then under the waistband of her briefs to the silky mound of her pubes. Electric pulses of pleasure surged through him as Meiko reached down and tugged at his fundoshi, loosening it. He kicked it free while slipping off her briefs.

And then he felt her seal herself against him with her arms around his neck and her legs wrapped tightly around his hips. She stiffened and cried out twice as he gently entered her, and then he turned so he could grip the gunwale with both hands. He glanced at Meiko as she clung between him and the boat, her eyes closed, her head thrown back, her breath hissing through her teeth as she rode him up and down. Matsuo closed his own eyes and let the sun, the water, the sky, and the boat slip away until there was only Meiko and he. He felt the slow explosion building within him. He sensed Meiko stiffening, arching back, her legs tightening around him like a velvet vise. Suddenly she cried out and crushed her lips to his and he exploded within her.

Slowly, the world returned.

■ ■ ■

"Speak to me, Matsuo," she said.

She lay sated and comfortable in the crook of his arm as he steered the boat back toward the land. He had been so quiet since they had climbed back into the boat. Her underpants and his fundoshi were gone, probably on the bottom of the bay, and so they were naked under their clothes. She shivered. The air was warm, but after the heat of their lovemaking, it felt chilly.

What was Matsuo thinking? Did he regret what had happened? She wasn't quite sure of her own feelings. Joy and sadness tangled within her—the joy of knowing that even if she did have to spend the rest of her life with Hiroki, she would have this day to keep and cherish; the sadness of knowing the joy she would be missing all those years.

But Matsuo . . . he lived by such a strict code. Did he share a similar mix of feelings? Or was he filled with guilt? Did he hate her now? Did he feel that he had been seduced into betraying his brother and that she was to blame? If only he would *say* something!

"Did I seduce you?" she asked.

He nodded his head up-and-down gravely.

That's not fair! she wanted to say, but stopped herself. Had that been what she had intended all along by removing her kimono and baring herself to him?

"Do you really believe that?"

He nodded again, but this time he smiled. "Yes, you seduced me. But not today. It was ten years ago last January, at the Hatsu-U-Mode festival."

She nearly melted with relief. Her hand was resting on his abdomen. She moved it down to his shorts. Through the white fabric she felt him swell and harden under her fingers.

It's like magic, she thought, stroking him gently. She had perused her parents' pillow books in secret over the years but had never touched a man before today, and it was all so new. *Just like magic.*

■   ■   ■

Tingling pleasure started at a white-hot center in his groin where Meiko caressed him and spread throughout Matsuo's body. There was only one explanation for how he felt: He had drowned and had been carried off to Heaven. He didn't remember drowning, but only in Heaven could he feel like this.

I should hate myself.

Ever since they had climbed back into the boat, he had waited to be overwhelmed with self-loathing. And why not? He had vowed to love Meiko from afar and be satisfied with that. He had broken that vow. He had betrayed his brother's trust. He had sullied his family honor by deflowering his brother's bride-to-be.

He felt guilty, yes. But he didn't hate himself. He could, perhaps, justify this afternoon in his mind by saying that Hiroki no longer cared about his marriage to Meiko, that he had squandered his right to her by frequenting his prostitutes and their dark services, and by forgoing countless opportunities to set a new date. But to his surprise, Matsuo felt no need to go through moral and ethical gymnastics to save face with himself.

Because he loved Meiko. He loved her more than any woman in the world, and that seemed to be all he needed to know. He trailed his free hand up along Meiko's inner thigh to the slick moisture between her legs. She shuddered and bent her knee to make room for his fingers.

By the time they reached the shore below his family's house, they both were gasping with need. Matsuo beached the boat, pulled it up on the sand, and uncleated the mainsheet. Without waiting to make sure the sail slipped all the way down the mast, he grabbed Meiko's hand and led her up the hill at a run. He did not have to pull her. He led her to the ten-tatami garden cottage that had served as Nagata's quarters when he accompanied the family to Sagami Bay. It had been empty since his death.

He threw open the door and they leaped inside. It was hot and stuffy within but he barely noticed. The door wasn't even closed before she was in his arms and he was kissing her and they were pulling at each other's clothes, the seams of the garments protesting as they were discarded. A breeze swung the door open and as Matsuo reached to push it closed, he thought he saw someone out on the walk, behind the bushes. But he had only a fleeting glimpse before the door swung shut. He heard the latch catch and then he forgot about everything else, for Meiko was hot against him and her lips were searching for his.

■   ■   ■

Hiroki walked to the southeast corner of the garden and looked out on the bay once more. The Tosei-ha members had departed and now the sun was settling down the sky behind him. The beach below was still crowded. He saw a dinghy with sail on the sand. It looked like the family boat, but Meiko and Matsuo were nowhere about.

As he scanned the bay, he noticed a sudden hush in the servants' area to his right. All the chatter had died away, leaving only one male voice speaking. With a start, he recognized it as Cho's. Wondering what the head servant of the Okumo household could be saying that would be of such interest to the Mazaki help, he edged closer to the window.

Feeling as if the ground were heaving under him in an earthquake, he staggered away after hearing only a few sentences. *Matsuo and Meiko . . . naked . . . together!* With rage screaming through him, Hiroki turned and ran down the path toward home. If it was true—and he knew with a sick, certain dread that it was—he would kill Matsuo! All this time pillowing with Meiko while he had not been allowed to touch her! Kill him!

Visions of Matsuo's blurred fists attacking the soldiers who came to kill Father last year swam before his eyes. He stopped. He was sure Matsuo would be too ashamed to defend himself . . . but what if he fought back?

Caution broke through the maelstrom of emotions storming

around him. He fought for control. Even if he killed Matsuo—and Meiko, too—*To feel my fingers around her throat!*—he would only hurt Father more deeply by bringing notoriety as well as disgrace to the family.

He needed Father with him. If he found them now, on his own, he would have to bear the humiliation alone. If Father were there, however, the greater share of humiliation by far would be Matsuo's.

He turned and rushed up to where Father sat with the count.

■　■　■

"Oh, Matsuo," Meiko said as she lay beside him on the wooden plank floor and ran her fingers lightly along his jaw. The second time had been even more wonderful than the first. She felt so at peace with the world. "How can this be wrong?"

"Let's not talk about that," he said. "Let's just lie here and enjoy this while we can. Because very soon we'll have to go to our homes and pretend that nothing has happened."

"That will be the hardest part, won't it?"

She watched him nod solemnly. "It seems almost impossible to do. To see you and be with you and pretend that we're only friends. Can we do it?"

"We have to."

"Forever?"

"I can't imagine being apart from you forever."

"Then what are we going to do?"

Before Matsuo could answer, he heard footsteps outside. He was reaching for their clothes when the door flew open and the bright light of day fell upon them.

■　■　■

It's true!

Hiroki felt the world tilt around him as he and Father stared through the open door at Matsuo and Meiko on the floor of the garden cottage. He saw their nakedness, saw the swell of Meiko's breasts, the dark triangle between her legs, the wet gleam on her thigh, saw the shocked looks on their faces as they tried to cover themselves.

He wanted to shout, wanted to rush in there and throttle them both. Betrayed! Made a fool of by his own brother! Rage crowded the corners of his vision, blind rage and—dare he admit it, even to himself?—lust. The sight of Meiko's naked body had aroused him so suddenly and so powerfully that he didn't know whether he wanted to beat her or rape her. Or both.

He stepped forward but Father put out a restraining arm.

"Get dressed," he said in a calm voice to the two in the cottage.

"We will meet you out here." He closed the door and looked at Hiroki. "I am very sorry for you, my son, but we must remain calm."

"She was to be my wife!" Hiroki said, restraining his voice from a shout. "This is not to be borne!" How could Father stay so calm after what he had just seen?

"The marriage is impossible now, that is certain. But how did you learn—?"

"I overheard Cho telling the Mazaki servants while I was in their garden."

The servants! The servants know! Hiroki screamed to himself. They would be laughing at him. How could he bear this loss of face?

"My heart bleeds for you, Hiroki," Father said. "But none of this can be undone. So we must find the best way to deal with it. Whatever we do, we must not let it distract us from our Greater Purpose. Calm yourself."

Hiroki clenched his jaw and said nothing.

How long has this been going on?

Matsuo and Meiko, his only brother and his bride-to-be—how could they do this to him? How could they betray and humiliate him so? What had he ever done to them to deserve this?

How long have I been a fool? This could not be forgotten. This could not be swept out the door like so much household dust. This could not go unatoned. There had to be payment. The scales would have to be balanced somehow.

Father had told him to be calm. So he calmed himself. He let the heat of his grief and rage cool.

And turn to ice.

∎ ∎ ∎

"What will we *do?*"

Meiko clutched her kimono tightly around her. Despite the heat in the closed room, she felt cold. Matsuo had his shorts back on and was shrugging into his shirt. His face was grim in the dimness.

"We will do what we have to do. We have no choices that I can see. We will step outside and 'face the music,' as the Americans say. Then you will return to your home and I . . ."

She waited but he did not go on. Suddenly she was terrified. "You will *what?*"

"I can no longer live as an honorable man after bringing such disgrace to my family . . ." His voice trailed off again.

"You can't be thinking of . . ." Her lips refused to form the word, seppuku.

He turned his face away.

Meiko crushed both hands over her mouth. The thought of Matsuo cutting open his belly—she felt her gorge rise.

"*No!*"

He rose to his feet. "What else is there for me to do?"

"You can't!" she said, rising in front of him and clasping her arms around him. "You're not a samurai! You don't have to make amends to your daimyo! This is a family matter!"

He led her toward the door.

"Matsuo, speak to me!"

He said nothing. He opened the door and in the stream of light she saw his stony expression. She wanted to scream. Then she saw Hiroki and the baron staring at her with equally stony faces. The weight of their disapproval almost drove her to her knees. She felt vulnerable and dirty, like some loathsome thing that had been dragged out from under a rock to cower before them naked and squinting in the unaccustomed light. The shame and revulsion overcame her and she fled, sobbing as she ran home.

■ ■ ■

Matsuo sensed what Meiko was feeling and longed to run after her. But that would be a luxury, a pleasure he did not deserve. Now he had to face his father and brother. As he bowed low to them, he saw that Father's face was impassive with, yes, a trace of hurt in his eyes, but the true depth of whatever he was feeling was almost perfectly hidden. Hiroki, however, was a different story. Although usually adept at hiding his feelings, Hiroki radiated cold rage. Matsuo knew with a sick feeling that not only had he disgraced himself and his family, but he had poisoned his relationship with his brother forever.

There was only one honorable course open to him.

"If you will wait for me here," he said before either of them could speak, "I will return with the means of rectifying this matter."

Without waiting for a reply, he hurried away to his room. Once there, he went directly to the table where Nagata's daisho rested and lifted both swords from the katana-kake. He held them, one in each hand, and felt the power of their former owner coursing through them.

Help me be strong in this, he prayed to the swords. He shuddered. Did he have the courage? Could he actually do this to himself? Failing would only bring further dishonor upon him.

He ran into Father and Hiroki in the garden just outside the house.

"I *thought* that was your intent!" Father said sternly. "I forbid it!"

"But, Father—"

"Give me those!" he said, holding out his hand.

Didn't he understand? While Matsuo hesitated, his father took a step closer with his hand still outstretched. With a mixture of reluctance and relief, he gave the swords over. But the look of disappointment that flashed across Hiroki's face at that instant hurt him as much as a sword thrust to his belly.

"I will have no more thoughts of seppuku from you," Father said. "This matter does not warrant such drama."

"Father," he said, bowing and cursing the relief that flooded through him, "I have dishonored the family."

"That is true. Your behavior today was shameful. But fortunately it remains a private matter between the two families. And the dishonor is shared equally by both families, for Count Mazaki's daughter is no less culpable than my son."

Matsuo bowed again, speechless with gratitude that Father could find some light in the sea of darkness that had engulfed him.

"We must also take into account the fact that although engaged to your brother, she was not yet your brother's wife. Had she been, your transgression would be truly unforgivable. I hold it as true in my heart that you would have held your brother's wife sacred, and that . . ." He sighed. He seemed to hesitate here and glance at Hiroki. "That it never would have happened if the marriage had not been delayed so long."

Matsuo bowed again, awed by his father's compassion and wisdom, but aware of the pain hidden in his voice.

"But the factors I have mentioned serve only to blunt the dishonor you have done to the family. They in no way mitigate the wound you have inflicted upon your own brother."

Matsuo knew that too well. He could not bring himself to meet his brother's eyes.

■　■　■

Hiroki could hardly believe his ears! What was Father saying? Why was he diluting Matsuo's guilt, intimating that *he* shared part of his brother's shame? He felt as if he were going to explode! The injustice of Father's defense of Matsuo, his all-too-clear attempt to preserve the younger brother's status in the family at the expense of Hiroki's honor and face, only increased the pressure building within. But he could say *nothing!*

Father said, "And there is one more reason—an overwhelming reason—why you must banish all thoughts of seppuku from your head." He paused, then said: "Chu."

Hiroki saw a puzzled look cross Matsuo's face, a look that must have mirrored his own.

"You have a special knowledge that will be of vital importance to the Emperor in the near future. And that future draws nearer every day.

Word has come from Tokyo that tomorrow morning an ultimatum will be presented to the Chinese garrison in Peking to leave the area. If they refuse—and there is no question in my mind that they will—Japan will declare war. Once that happens you can rest assured that Britain and the U.S. will not let it pass unchallenged."

He watched his father lay a gentle hand on Matsuo's shoulder. The gesture felt to Hiroki like a slap in the face. He wanted to shout, *I am the injured party! He is the transgressor! Why this show of tenderness?*

"That is when your American experiences will begin to bear fruit," Father was saying. "Now and in the coming years, the Emperor, through the Imperial Council, will be calling on you more and more. You must not deny him your special knowledge by so ungrateful a gesture as seppuku. Your Emperor needs you. You must be there for him. It is chu!"

Hearing once again about Matsuo's great value to the Emperor made Hiroki want to vomit. All he had heard from his brother so far about the United States were timid words of caution. Is that what Japan could expect from Matsuo Okumo's vaunted American expertise? If so, Japan would be better off if he *did* commit seppuku.

And Hiroki would gladly act as his dear brother's second, standing ready to deliver the beheading stroke after he had slit his belly.

■ ■ ■

Meiko leaned against the outer wall of her house, panting. She fought to catch her breath but it eluded her. She had to compose herself. She could not walk into the house in this state. She had to be calm.

What to do now? The question echoed in her mind endlessly. How to tell Father? How to let him know without reversing the gains he had made with his health? She knew she had to break the news to him before Baron Okumo did. But *how?* How could she make those words come out of her mouth? She could tell Mother. She would swoon, Meiko was sure, but after that, she might be able to help.

But as concerned as she was with her family, her worry for Matsuo swallowed everything else. The look on his face when she had left him—she felt sure he would try seppuku if someone didn't stop him.

Meiko straightened and pushed herself away from the wall, still hot from the sun. She had to know about Matsuo, had to know he was safe and alive before she could even think about anything else.

As she rounded the corner of the house, she saw Kikou crossing the garden. She called her over.

"I have an errand for you," she told the servant girl. "I want you to go to the baron's house and find the younger Okumo-san." Kikou's eyes widened. Meiko would never have sent a servant to find Matsuo in the past, but there was nothing left to hide now. And she had to *know!* "Say nothing to him. Merely see that he is well and then come directly back to me. I will be waiting right here."

The girl hurried off. And Meiko paced.

■ ■ ■

"I hope someday your brother will be able to forgive you," Father was saying. "I do not expect him to be able to do so now, and would not ask him to try. Still, it is my hope that before long the two of you will be able to bury today in your pasts and share a brotherly trust and love again."

Matsuo glanced at Hiroki but saw only cold, steely anger in his face. Without a word, Hiroki turned his back on him and walked toward the house.

"I fear, however," Father said in a low voice as he watched Hiroki go, "that you have inflicted a wound that may never heal." He turned his stern gaze on Matsuo. "You have wounded me as well, my son. I never dreamed you would disappoint me so."

The cut of those words was as painful as anything he could inflict upon himself with the wakizashi.

Cho came running at Father's call. Matsuo watched him hand the swords to the servant, saying, "Return these to their katana-kake." Then he too walked off, leaving Matsuo alone with Cho.

Still clutching the swords, the servant dropped to his knees before Matsuo.

"It is all my fault, Okumo-san," he said with a sob.

"What do you mean by that?" Matsuo asked, angry and disheartened that the servants already knew what had happened.

"I saw you and Miss Mazaki. I whispered it to the other servants. Your brother must have overheard. It is all my fault! I should have my tongue cut out!"

For an instant, Matsuo was ready to agree with him, then saw the tears on the man's face. He clapped his hand gently on a quaking shoulder.

"It is *my* fault, Cho. No one else's."

But Cho did not seem to be listening as he rose and carried the swords back to the house. Matsuo looked up to the clear, blue, perfect sky. It had started out with the promise of a lovely day, and had progressed into an utterly glorious day. Yet now all was tainted. Why? Why did this have to happen?

And Meiko—what terrors must she be going through? He ached

to run to her but fought the urge. He had to stay away, even though they needed each other now more than ever before, if only to give each other comfort. He did not know how long he stood there.

A scream of horror split the air. Matsuo spun around. It seemed to have come from the house, from the north wing. He ran inside and found Kazuko standing in the hall with her hands clasped over her face, her fingers digging into her forehead.

"What's wrong? Did you scream?"

The maid spread her hands and gaped at him. "Okumo-san! You're alive!"

"Of course I'm alive! What made you think—?"

"Kikou screamed and said you were dead! That you had committed seppuku!"

"Kikou? From Count Mazaki's house? What was she doing here?"

"I do not know. I was afraid to look in your room."

A sickening thought suddenly occurred to Matsuo. He brushed by Kazuko and hurried up the hall. Hiroki and Father were coming from the other end. Matsuo turned into his room and stopped abruptly at the entrance.

A man lay facedown on a blood-soaked futon before the mounted daisho. Matsuo had never seen so much blood. Could it all be from one man? Steeling himself against the revulsion that welled up in him, he stepped forward and touched the man's shoulder. Even though he could feel still-warm flesh through the fabric, Matsuo knew the man was dead. He lifted a limp, unexpectedly heavy shoulder. With the short black hair and the loose kimono, it could have been anyone, but Matsuo knew who it was without looking. Even so, he sprang back in horror when he actually saw the face above the slit throat.

"Cho!"

Father and Hiroki rushed into the room then. They turned the body over without ceremony.

"Who has done this?" Father cried.

"He did it himself."

"With *your* daisho?"

Matsuo shook his head sadly. No, Cho would never think to defile those swords with his peasant blood. He pointed to the bloody knife in Cho's lifeless hand. "There's the weapon. And look—he even brought his own futon so he wouldn't sully the floor with his blood."

"But why?" Father said.

Matsuo was too choked with grief to speak, but Hiroki had no such problem.

"He left my brother a message," he said, then strode from the room.

"I forgave him, Father. I told him that."

"But he could not forgive himself!" Father's voice was anything but gentle. "He saw something he should not have seen. Because of it, he could not go on as a member of this household. And since there was no other place for him, he could not go on living."

Then he too turned and left.

Feeling utterly miserable and alone, Matsuo stood with his hands on the swords of the daisho as the weeping servants tended to Cho's body behind him. His whole life seemed to be crumbling before his eyes—a trust broken, a reputation defiled, a betrothal sundered, a good man's life snuffed out. By all the gods, what else would happen before this black day ended?

■ ■ ■

Meiko had heard the scream from the Okumo house and had waited in the lengthening shadows of the garden with her heart thudding madly in her chest. She prayed that it wasn't Matsuo. *It can't be Matsuo! It simply can't be!* But when Kikou stumbled into the garden, gasping, tears streaming down her face, Meiko knew that something terrible had happened. She leaped to her feet to meet the servant girl.

"Kikou, what—?"

"He's dead!" she screamed.

Meiko felt her knees give way and she slumped onto a seat. "You must be mistaken!"

"I saw him! His room was open as I passed and I looked in and saw him on the floor! And the blood! Oh, the blood . . . !"

No! No! No! Feeling as if she had been stabbed through the heart, Meiko forced herself to her feet and staggered away from the sobbing Kikou. She stumbled toward the bay, her mind numb, her feet following the path out of habit.

Matsuo . . . gone. It didn't seem possible. Never to see him again, even from afar, or hear his voice, or his rare laugh. A world without Matsuo was . . . unthinkable. A dark world. A world she had no desire to live in.

The bathers were gone. The beach was in shadow. To her right, the Okumo dinghy nosed into the sand with the rising tide lapping against her stern. On impulse, she pulled the boat into the water and hopped inside. She dropped the rudder and centerboard, then raised the sail. Soon she was underway. The breeze had swung around and was coming off the land. Tears slid down her cheeks as she looked back and bid her home farewell. She knew what she had to do, knew it was best for all concerned. And now that the decision was made, she felt a great sense of peace sweep through her.

She let the sail drag the boom all the way out to starboard, and ran before the wind. Due east. Into the Pacific.

■ ■ ■

Head down, Matsuo plodded along the beach. He needed to be away from the house and had remembered the sailboat, so he had come down to secure it against the tide. It was gone. He looked around in the deepening dusk and saw someone standing at the water's edge not far away. He approached and recognized one of the Mazaki servant girls.

He called to her: "Have you seen our sailboat?"

The girl turned toward him, then took a sudden step backward.

"What's wrong with you?" he said.

She screamed and began to run. Matsuo bolted after her, catching her easily. She wailed with fear as he gripped her arm and halted her flight.

"Stop that!" he shouted. "You know me! I won't hurt you!"

"Okumo-san! You are dead! I saw you!"

Matsuo was nonplussed for a moment, then he remembered the scream earlier when Cho's body was discovered.

"That wasn't me," he told her. *But it should have been.* "That was Cho."

Her hands flew to the sides of her head. "Oh, no! I told her it was you!"

"Who? Meiko?"

"Yes! Oh, please don't be angry!"

Poor Meiko! She would be blaming herself! "Where is she?"

"I saw her take the sailboat."

Fingers of ice clamped around Matsuo's heart. He looked out at the dark, empty expanse of the bay, searching frantically for a patch of white. There was none.

"How long ago?"

"Over an hour. I was waiting for her when you spoke to me." ·

Matsuo spun and ran for the house.

■ ■ ■

Night had fallen. It was time.

Meiko wasn't afraid. Normally, the darkness and the rolling swells of the ocean would have combined to terrify her. Now they only served her purpose. Even the dark leviathan shadows of the freighters that bounced her like a piece of cork in their wakes as they glided past on the crest of high tide could not faze her.

She turned the boat into the gentle breeze, then knelt and said a prayer to the sea to take her quickly. She stood up and began to undress, then stopped. The clothes would weigh her down. As she refastened her obi, she took one last look at the lights that rimmed Sagami Bay and the Izu Peninsula—a brief look, for she knew if she hesitated too long, she would lose her courage. Then she dove overboard. The water was cold. She broke surface, then began to swim further out to sea.

■ ■ ■

She could be anywhere!

Matsuo stood in the cockpit of the borrowed inboard runabout, keeping its engine at full throttle, steering with one hand while he worked the spotlight with the other. His arms and legs were lead weights, the muscles at the back of his neck were knotted with tension. But he could not allow himself a moment's rest.

He knew it would be sheer luck if he found her. Had she run before the wind, straight out to the Pacific, or had she aimed for Oshima? Had she tacked south along the shore of the peninsula, or was she somewhere among the Izu-Sichito—the Seven Izu Islands? Even in full daylight it would be a difficult search. But at night . . .

If only he had some inkling of the direction she had chosen!

He searched on, calling her name, sweeping the dark water with his light, vowing to continue until he was out of gas, and then return at first light.

He fought back the choking fear that he would never find her. He *would* find her! No matter how long it took!

■ ■ ■

So cold. So tired. So weak.

Meiko didn't know how long she had been swimming. It seemed like an eternity. Her arms were so heavy she could barely lift them and her legs dragged her down, kicking fitfully. Her lungs ached and her eyes burned from the salt. Time had lost all meaning. There was only the night and the ocean. For a while the boat had followed her, a vague white form flowing with the current and the easterly breeze. Then she had lost sight of it. How long ago had that been?

From somewhere behind her she heard a crash of splintering wood, but she was too weak to turn and look. Not that she would have been able to see anything in the darkness anyway.

She slipped beneath a swell and swallowed some water. With her last strength she fought to the surface and managed to cough it out. She took a final breath before she went under again. There was no strength left. Her arms floated still and useless above her head, her legs hung below.

Panic stabbed her as she realized she didn't really want to die, that she was afraid to die. She wanted air! She tried to regain the surface but was too weak to do anything to save herself. Her last air bubbled out through her lips and she gulped water. *Air!* But it was too far away.

A roaring filled her ears and the water began to glow around her. She waited for the gods of the sea to take her.

■ ■ ■

Matsuo sat on the beach just south of Atami looking at the remains of the sailboat. A pair of fishermen had found it at dawn and had sculled into shore with what was left of it in tow. The port side was stoved in, the sail torn, the mast broken like a chopstick.

Grief constricted his throat as he visualized the scene in his mind's eye: Meiko aboard the tiny boat, a giant freighter looming out of the dark, its prow catching the boat, cutting it nearly in two, throwing her overboard to drown while the freighter sailed onward, completely oblivious to the death of the person who most brightened Matsuo's world.

He lowered his head into his hands and wept.

TOKYO

Shimazu had never been so frightened. "You didn't hurt him?" he cried. "Tell me he's still alive!"

"Of course he's alive!" Hiroki said. "Why is Matsuo's welfare so important, especially after what he has done?" He was obviously offended.

Shimazu sagged back on his cushion, weak with relief. "I feared you might have done something rash."

"And if I had?" Hiroki's abandonment of his characteristic respectful tone demonstrated the depth of his wounds.

"There must be no bloodshed between you and your brother, is that clear? *Never!*"

Hiroki stiffened. "Why do you say that?"

"Because the future of Japan may well rest on both your shoulders. The Emperor needs you both!"

Hiroki lowered his head and said nothing.

Shimazu longed to tell him of the day thirty years ago when a Seer performed the ancient motsu rite on the children brought to the temple. He held them in his arms and foretold their future as it related to the Order. There had been little of interest until he had cradled Baron

Okumo's firstborn son, Hiroki, and pronounced the words that had electrified all present:

"I see this one and another, a brother. Rejoice! One will raise the Order to the greatest glory of all its days! But beware! One bears the seeds of the Order's destruction! And beware! Should one spill the lifeblood of the other, the Order will be no more!"

Many of the Order present that day had wanted to slay Hiroki and the mother of the unborn child as well, but Shimazu, then but a young monk in the Outer Circles, had spoken out. He had called upon the Order to take up the challenge of the vision, to reach for the greatness it offered. If both children were killed, the threat to the Order would be eliminated, but the Order would also lose its chance to rise "to the greatest glory of all its days." Why couldn't the Order educate both brothers in the temple where they could be closely observed? When one developed signs of being dangerous to the Order, he would be eliminated before he could cause any harm.

There had been much debate among the Elders, but the majority of them sided with the spirit of Shimazu's call to greatness. It was decided to approach Baron Okumo.

The baron had bargained hard. In return for his firstborn he wanted promises of support for his plans to make Japan a world power. Since the baron's ideas were perfectly aligned with the Order's, a deal had been struck. But when the subject of his second son was brought up, the baron became extremely wary. The Elders had been too precipitous—the child had not yet been conceived! The baron gave Hiroki to the Order for education but refused to make any promises regarding his next child.

Shimazu was given the task of overseeing Hiroki's training and all went well until 1910 when the baron's second son was born. Instead of giving the younger brother over to the Order, Baron Okumo had sent him off to America. The Elders had taken this as a sure sign that the younger brother was the dangerous one. Shimazu was not so sure.

One brother must be killed, but which one? The question had haunted Shimazu since the day he had been given charge of the Okumo matter. Did one brother carry the seeds of glory and the other the seeds of destruction, or were they both contained in one? *Spill the lifeblood—* what did that mean? A mere wound, or fratricide? If only the Seers' visions were more precise! Whatever the true meaning, he knew that to be safe there must be no violence between the Okumo brothers.

Yesterday's incident on Sagami Bay had been a close call, yet everything had worked out to perfection! He had long felt it was in the best interests of the Order and the Empire to prevent Hiroki from marrying and to cause a rift between him and his brother. And yesterday, in a matter of hours, the Okumo brothers had become permanently estranged and Hiroki's bride-to-be had become food for the fish of Sagami Bay. Surely the Infinite Face was watching over him!

But did too much animosity remain between the brothers?

He said, "Do you feel you must still satisfy your giri with your brother?"

"My father has forbidden it," Hiroki said, "but—"

"Before you answer fully," Shimazu said, "consider this: The woman who betrayed you is dead; the servant who found them out is dead. Your brother must bear the weight of those two lost lives and endure the shame of his deed whenever he enters his home. Do you not think the scales are balanced?"

Shimazu waited for an answer but Hiroki said nothing.

"I am not asking you to forgive your brother; I ask only that you consider the two lives already spent as payment enough for the face you have lost. Hate your brother, but still find a way to work with him."

Hiroki sighed. "My giri is satisfied. I will not pursue Matsuo any further."

"Excellent! Rejoice! Today is a wonderful day! We move upon China!"

Hiroki smiled, but it was a wan smile, without heart. But that would change. Shimazu was sure of it.

PART
FOUR

1940
━━━
1941

1 9 4 0

THE YEAR OF THE
DRAGON

I decided to take the long way out of Pearl. I had to drive out to the base a few times a week. My office in downtown Honolulu was eight miles to the harbor by the usual route, but if I had the time, I liked to stretch the miles out to ten. On especially beautiful days I could stretch it out to an even dozen. And this was one *hell* of a beautiful day: soft blue sky above, the trades blowing just enough to rustle the algaroba and monkeypod trees and keep you cool. Definitely a day for the twelve-mile route.

I left my cubicle in the District Intelligence Office and headed for my car. I had two jobs for Naval Intelligence these days. Mornings I translated Japanese intercepts for the DIO, and afternoons when there was no field assignment, I did administrative work for ONI out at Pearl. I got into my navy car and followed King Street west—or "ewa" as the natives say. I turned on the car radio and KGBM was playing, appropriately enough, the song everyone was singing, "You Are My Sunshine."

Hard to believe most of Europe was in chains. Czechoslovakia, Albania, Poland, Finland, Norway, the Netherlands, and Belgium—all fallen. And only yesterday the Germans had marched into Paris. To the west the Japanese were pushing deeper and deeper into China, and had taken over Hainan and the Spratly Islands. I was glad America was staying out of it. I didn't want to go to war; didn't know anybody who did. All I wanted was to stay right here on the islands.

I drove past the Punchbowl, the extinct volcanic crater that looms over downtown Honolulu, and continued on out of town to where

King joined Moanalua Road, then followed that north of the salt lake and into Halewa Heights. When I reached the top of my favorite rise, I pulled over, stepped out of the car, lit a cigarette, and gloried in the scenery.

Clouds jammed the peaks of the Koolau Mountains behind me; ahead, the long slope down to the deep blue water of Pearl Harbor was broken by the stacks of the Aiea sugar mill, and out on the green Ewa Plain, stretching beyond Pearl to the Waianae Mountains, white smoke rose from a square of land where a section of sugarcane was being burned prior to harvest.

Two years here and still I felt like a *malihini*. I couldn't get enough of the islands. I had been transferred from the Eleventh Naval District in San Diego in January of 1938, just a few weeks after the Japs sank the U.S.S. *Panay* on the Yangtze River off Nanking. Even though all sorts of official apologies were made and accepted by the diplomats, the Office of Naval Intelligence decided then that it was time to beef up its Japan-watching force in the Pacific. Because I could speak Japanese, I was transferred to Honolulu ONI.

I loved these islands. It wasn't always that way. I hadn't wanted to be two thousand miles from Frisco, but the Depression had been getting worse instead of better, so when the Navy told me to get out here, I didn't see any choice. I got. And I never regretted it. I caught the rhythm of the islands immediately, found myself moving to it naturally, as if I'd been born for it. I sensed it faintly on the day I stepped off the transport in Pearl Harbor's east loch, and knew within a week that I never wanted to leave here. And as time went on, I became determined never to leave.

What was there to go back for? Mom was remarried and happy in her new life. We exchanged an occasional letter and presents at Christmas and on birthdays, but she didn't need me and I didn't need her. California—all of North America, in fact—held nothing for me. Besides, I was in paradise. I loved everything about the islands—the people, the terrain, the trade winds, the special ambiance they called the Aloha Spirit, I loved them all. I even loved the fruit. Frank Slater, the world's greatest melon-hater, *loved* papaya. I spent my time off at Waikiki where I paid one of the beach boys to teach this *haole* to ride the surf, and in a week I was holding my own with the waves off the Kuhio seawall.

I even picked up a working knowledge of island patois, something like pidgin but distinct in its own way. It wasn't easy. With only a dozen or so letters in their alphabet, everything tends to sound alike.

The islands worked a gradual magic on me. Just as my days on the beach burned my skin and caused it to peel away, leaving a new tanned layer beneath, so my time on Oahu caused the old Frank Slater from

California to peel away and be left behind on the sand like so much useless baggage.

I finished my cigarette and drove slowly downhill to Pearl Harbor. At the main gate the marine on duty knew me on sight and waved me past with just a glance at my windshield sticker. I drove up to the intelligence office, a low, white, flat-roofed building just a stone's throw away from CINCPAC HQ. I glanced out at the new battleship moorings along Ford Island, that splotch of green in the middle of Pearl's east loch that sported an airfield and a few hangars; the harbor was quiet today. Few ships in port. I watched the big hammerhead crane by the dry docks swing a refitted tug into the water, then went inside.

Captain Harrison Thornton was grumbling and muttering when I reached the office. I had made lieutenant junior grade, and Harry was my senior officer. He had been assigned to the Fourteenth Naval District last year and had seemed deliriously happy with everything about his Hawaiian post except the paperwork. He was an "old boy" who knew nothing of Naval Intelligence. From what I gathered, almost no one assigned to command the Fourteenth DIO ever did.

Hawaii was a special post. It was considered a preretirement plum for favored senior officers who had kept in touch with friends from their Academy days who were now in High Places. I was sure Harry had thought he had landed a cushy job—until last month. That was when Pearl Harbor had replaced San Diego as the official base of the Pacific Fleet. And that meant a lot more work for the Fourteenth District Intelligence Office. And for Harry Thornton.

"Damn Roosevelt and damn Stark!" he was saying as he rummaged through the pile of papers on his desk. He had a round face and a receding hairline that made his forehead seem to go on forever; thick, bushy eyebrows and thin, almost nonexistent lips. And he was sweating, always sweating. No matter the temperature—and admittedly it was hot today—or the time of day. Even in the early morning when he had just come from home in a fresh uniform, Harry's forehead was always beaded with sweat, his shirt was always wet in the underarms and down the middle of his back. And that ceiling fan was always going round.

"What's the matter?" I asked.

"*Aaah!*" He grimaced with disgust. "We need more help. We can't even keep up with the movements of the ships in and out of the harbor. How are we supposed to coordinate any intelligence?"

"Look at it this way," I told him. "If *we* can't keep it straight, how can the Japs?"

He flashed me a smile, but there was no humor in it. "They've probably got plenty of help. There's a hundred and fifty thou of them on these islands!"

"There!" I said. "That should make you feel lucky. You've only got, what, a hundred ships in the entire fleet, and—"

"One hundred and two, if you please."

"Okay. A hundred and two ships to keep track of. I've got ten times that many Jap agents on Oahu alone!"

"Want to trade?" he said.

I shook my head. I had a lot of drudge work on my end—mainly the translating I had to do every day—but all in all I had it pretty good. I had my own little cubicle in the Honolulu DIO office where I could come and go pretty much as I pleased, as long as I got my translating done. Then I had my paper shuffling out here which was limited mostly to Navy Personnel and contractors who did work for the Navy. Occasionally I did surveillance work, which had its drudge aspects, but at least I was up and moving about. I worked along with the FBI field office over in the Federal Building to keep tabs on the comings and goings at the Japanese Consulate; I also investigated any Japanese locals whose wires home sounded suspicious. I was to report directly to Harry anything that even remotely related to Pearl Harbor and the Pacific Fleet.

"Anything of interest?" Harry asked, shaking out a Camel and offering me one. I took it and lit both with my Zippo, then dropped into a chair.

I shook my head. "You know all the good stuff's Purple."

Harry's thick eyebrows oscillated like Groucho Marx's. "Word has it that Purple is just about broken."

I was out of the chair and leaning over his desk so fast that I startled him. *"Purple? Broken?"* I was whispering, even though there was no one else around to hear me.

"They say Friedman's on the brink."

I sat down again, my mind buzzing. Purple was the most complicated Japanese cipher. All the high-level diplomatic dispatches were encoded with it. God, if we could break Purple . . .

"We'll know everything they're telling each other!" Harry said. "Won't that be nice." There was something malicious about his smile.

"What are you getting at?" I said.

"Think of all the extra translating to be done!"

I laughed. "But at least I'll be translating something worthwhile. Most of what I hear now is empty conversation."

Cracking Purple . . . the possibilities spun through my head for the rest of the day.

When I finished my paper shuffling, I took the shorter, more southerly route back. I listened to Burns and Allen on KGU as I followed the narrow road past Hickam Field, Rogers Airport, and the marshes along Keehi Lagoon. Further toward town, the huge Dole pineapple stood high on its steel legs, challenging the Aloha Tower as tallest structure in Honolulu.

I had two stops to make before returning to my apartment in Kalihi. The first was up on Nuuanu Avenue, in the vicinity of number 1742—the Japanese consulate. I parked in front of a house a few hundred feet up the street and strolled into the yard. The place belonged to a former Navy man and he let us stop by whenever we wanted. I climbed the monkeypod tree in his backyard and picked up the field glasses we kept in a notch there. I watched the backyard of the Japanese consulate for a few minutes. Nothing was going on, so I replaced the glasses and left.

It was all a charade. We had a tap on one of their telephone lines now that got us more information in a week than all the hundreds and hundreds of man-hours we had spent in that tree getting bleary-eyed peering through those glasses. But we were afraid to stop watching them altogether. It was possible the Japs knew we used the tree; if we suddenly stopped, they might get suspicious that we had another source of information. So we took turns making short stops at the tree on Nuuanu Avenue.

On the way home I stopped in at The Bon Marche on North King. I didn't shop there as a rule but I had spotted an ad in the Honolulu *Advertiser* about a sale on shirts. I needed to replace a couple of worn ones.

I passed the counter where a Japanese woman was working and it must have been a full minute before it struck me: *I know her!*

I hurried back and watched her from across the aisle, stunned and speechless. It seemed as impossible as it was improbable. But I knew her.

It was Meiko.

Eight years had passed since I had last seen her but I hadn't forgotten her. I'd find myself thinking about her, visualizing her face at the oddest times. And here she was in Honolulu working as a shop girl.

And as I recognized her, I knew there had been a tragedy. What else could make her end up working as a Honolulu shop girl? Something awful must have happened.

I stepped up to the counter where she was rearranging the nylon stockings under the glass.

"Aloha," I said.

She looked up. "Aloha. Yes, sir. Can I help you?"

Close up, I could see how she had changed. She was still hauntingly beautiful; her hair was as black as the vault of the night and just as glossy as I remembered it. But she had lost weight and she looked drawn. Her almond eyes were still bright and deep, but so much life had gone out of her. A stranger wouldn't notice, but I was no stranger. It seemed as if someone had tapped her and drained off most of her vitality.

"Sir?" she said, looking at me strangely. I guess I had been staring at her. I racked my brain for something infinitely clever to say, some brilliant quip that would bring a smile of instant recognition to her face. I settled for:

"Meiko, it's me, Frank Slater. From college."

She stepped back as if I had just said *boo!* I guess I had changed, too, in those eight years. For one thing, I was wearing a navy uniform; for another, years of carrying and paddling a ten-foot solid redwood surfboard through the waves off Kuhio had filled me out and left me almost as brown as a native. An unexpected benefit of the tan was that it made my Slater Stain almost invisible. I hardly thought about it anymore.

"Oh, Frank!" she said, reaching out to me. "It *is* you!"

I grabbed both her hands and squeezed. If the counter hadn't been between us, I think I would have hugged her.

"But what are you doing here?" we both said at once and laughed. A floor manager strolled by with a sour look on his face. Meiko's smile evaporated.

"Maybe you'd better go. They hired me because a lot of Japanese shop here, but the department manager would love an excuse to get rid of me."

"Can we talk somewhere?" I asked. Suddenly I could feel her withdraw. She didn't move away but I could sense doors and windows slamming shut all around her.

"I have to work," she said in a low voice as her eyes avoided mine. She began realigning the boxes of stockings on the glass countertop.

"What about lunch?"

"They only give me half an hour."

"That's a start—"

"And I brought mine."

"Dinner then."

"I don't know."

"We've got a lot of years to cover."

She finally looked up at me. "All of them bad."

"Sometimes it's good to talk about bad things, especially with an old friend."

She suddenly became interested in those damn stockings again. "I don't deserve any friends."

This was worse than I could have thought. This was not the old Meiko who had loved life and liked herself. This was a different Meiko, defensive, defeated, a stranger. But I wasn't giving up. I had to know if the old Meiko was still in there somewhere. The one who used to sit on the hill overlooking San Francisco Bay and gaze out on the water and smile with such inner peace and tranquillity that you'd have thought she had the world on a string. If she was, how sweet it would be to find her and lead her out if I could.

"Dinner," I said as if it had been decided. "And we'll talk about the weather and nothing more if that's what you want."

She said nothing and I waited. I wasn't going to be put off. Finally she shrugged. "If you wish."

She didn't want to be picked up at her home so I arranged to meet her in front of the store. Seven o'clock sharp. I was already planning what I would wear. I had seen a white tropical worsted suit on sale at The Hub. I'd splurge $27.50 on that and then make reservations at the Royal Hawaiian. This was no routine date. I was going to make this a big night.

I looked at her and wondered if anyone could make Meiko happy again. I had to try. As I left her there, aligning and realigning the nylons, my heart ached for her. What had happened?

■ ■ ■

Tense and jittery, Meiko stood in front of The Bon Marche and waited. She berated herself for letting Frank talk her into dinner, but he had been so persistent. She had tried to cancel out, tried to call him. She found the number of a *Slater, F. X.* in the phone book and called from the phone down the hall from her room, but there had been no answer. That had left her with two choices: Keep the date or simply not show up. Frank didn't know where she lived . . .

. . . But he knew where she worked and he would come by tomorrow to find out why she had broken their date. She could not face that, and she couldn't quit the job. She needed the paltry wage The Bon Marche paid her. There was no choice.

So now she stood in the waning light, dressed in the only good dress she had. She hoped Frank didn't plan to take her anywhere fancy.

As the clock hurried toward seven, she wondered at the vagaries of fate. The one American in the world who knew her well enough to recognize her turning up on this very island.

And yet: Why *didn't* she want to see him? Meiko knew the answer: Because Frank had known her before. He knew the old Meiko, the Meiko who no longer existed, the Meiko she would have to pretend to be tonight. Frank was from the past.

And the past was gone.

Or so she had thought that morning three years ago when she had awakened to bright light and pain, with every muscle fiber in her body afire, every movement a knife thrust of agony.

She was in a hammock in a tiny room. Sunlight streamed through a round window—a porthole. The smell of steamed fish filled the air.

A sweaty, portly man in a stained kimono with a thick Osaka accent leaned over her and told her she was aboard the *Tsuru Maru* and how sorry they were for striking her little boat last night, and how she shouldn't have been out sailing in the dark without at least a lantern. As it was, if he hadn't been on deck having a smoke at that moment and heard the collision, she would have been left behind to drown. It was just by chance that the searchlight found her as she was going down.

The gods had saved her. Why?

The man had said the freighter could not take her back to Japan. She would have to sail with them to their first port of call and make arrangements for a trip back.

Meiko decided that that was the way the gods wanted it. Perhaps they wished her to live but not in Japan. They had sent her away. If that was so, then she would go wherever they wished. Japan offered only disgrace for her. And grief.

The first port of call was Honolulu. And here it was that Meiko had decided to stay.

Meiko did not want Frank to see her dingy little one-room apartment. It was in a run-down tenement off Hotel Street, and so tiny and cluttered, she would have been humiliated to have him call for her there. Yet it was all that she could afford on what she earned, so why should she be embarrassed? None of her acquaintances—and she had no real friends on Oahu, only acquaintances—thought there was anything wrong with her apartment.

Why did I agree to this? she asked herself for the hundredth time. If she hadn't been so shocked to see him standing there on the other side of the counter, she would have been able to think up some excuse that would save him face and allow her the solitude she craved.

She suddenly felt very tired. She didn't want to be the old Meiko tonight—she didn't even know if she *could* be. She just wanted to be left alone in the new life she had made for herself without her family, without Japan . . . and without Matsuo.

Her heart sank when the car pulled in to the curb and Frank jumped out, smiling and holding a hyacinth corsage in his hand. Seven o'clock sharp. Not a minute early, not a minute late.

Meiko had to admit that he looked dashing in his white suit. With little ado, he handed her the corsage, presented his arm to her, and led her to the car.

"Any place in particular you'd like to eat?" he said once they were moving through the traffic.

Alone in my apartment, she thought, but said, "Anywhere you choose will be fine with me, Frank."

"Ever eaten at the Royal Hawaiian?"

"No." And even if she had had the desire to eat there, she never could have afforded it.

"I think you'll like it."

"I don't think I'm dressed properly."

"You're beautiful."

As they drove on in silence, Meiko studied Frank. How he had changed! He seemed bigger physically. His shoulders were broader and the sun had lightened his hair and darkened his skin so that his blue eyes seemed to shine out from his face. She sensed that he had changed within as well. No longer the timid college boy, he was a man now, one who held himself erect and looked the world in the eye as if he were no longer afraid of it.

He parked in front of a huge pink stucco structure with a vaguely caravanserai look and guided her through the lobby to a terrace that led down to the beach. They leaned against the rail and looked out at the surf for a moment, then Frank looked to their left.

"Diamond Head's pretty with the setting sun shining on it, don't you think?"

"Where's Diamond Head?" she said. "I've never seen it."

He gaped at her. "How long have you been here?"

"Three years." *Three interminable years!* "Is something wrong?"

"You mean to tell me you've been here three years and you're still a malihini who hasn't seen Diamond Head?"

"I'm sorry," she said. "Is that wrong?"

"No, not at all," he said quickly. "It's just . . . surprising, that's all." He pointed to the dark brown mountain of volcanic rock towering over the far end of the beach. "That's it."

"It doesn't look like a diamond to me."

"You're right. Looks more like Gibraltar. Actually, it got its name from the calcite crystals sailors found there in the last century and mistook for diamonds."

He led her to the dining room where she learned they had reservations. The room seemed too formal for what she was wearing. She was glad the lighting was low, but she felt awkward until she was safely seated behind a table in one of the booths.

She hesitated when the waiter inquired about cocktails. Frank suggested a mai-tai and ordered a Kirin beer for himself. "In honor of you," he said with a smile.

He made valiant attempts at small talk, rambling on about the islands, about how the biggest and best hotels on Waikiki were owned by someone named Matson who also owned the steamship line that brought the vacationers here from the States. Frank seemed to envy Matson. She noticed a tension in him, as if he were skirting a subject. Meiko tried to hold up her end, but despite her best efforts, the conversation ended with their first drink. Finally, there was silence. It stretched out uncomfortably until Frank said,

"Something happened between you and Matsuo, didn't it?"

The question so startled Meiko that she knocked over her drink. As a wet splotch darkened the pink of the tablecloth to red, she felt panic clutch at her throat. How could he know? How could anyone know? She couldn't breathe! She had to get out where she could get some air!

She struggled out from behind the table and ran across the empty dance floor toward the entrance, and from there toward the beach. The fresh salty night air quelled her gasping, but she ran on, tripping, losing her shoes in the sand as she passed another hotel. Finally she stopped under a huge banyan tree. She leaned against the massive trunk and began to sob.

She heard the soft scuff of shoes on the sand behind her. Frank's voice spoke.

"I'm sorry," he said. "That was stupid. I was desperate for something to say, and desperate to know. I'm sorry."

She turned and saw him standing there with her shoes in his hand.

"But how did you know?"

"I knew how he felt about you, how you felt about him. I could see from your face this morning that something awful has happened in your life." He shrugged his shoulders. "Put all that together with the fact that you're living alone three thousand miles from home, and it can mean only one thing."

"You *knew* he loved me?" Meiko was shocked. "Did he tell you?"

Frank smiled—ruefully, she thought. "No. We didn't talk much. But anyone who saw you together, or heard you talk about him . . ." His voice trailed off.

Were we so transparent? she thought. *Did everybody know?*

"I'm sorry," he said after a long silence. "Let's finish dinner and I promise I won't mention it again."

"I'm not hungry," Meiko said.

Frank exhaled loudly. "I'm glad you said that. I've lost my appetite, too." He pointed to the street that paralleled the beach. "Want to walk?"

"I want to tell you what happened." The words surprised her even as she spoke them.

"You don't have to," Frank said. "It can wait."

"No. It has to be now."

Suddenly she was bursting to unload the burden of what had happened. She had been holding it tight within her for so long, three years that felt like forever, walling it off like a festering sore. And now it screamed for release, as if it had been waiting for the right person to come along, someone who knew Matsuo, someone who might share the pain with her.

They walked along a narrow street lined with stately ironwood trees, he with his hands in his pockets, she with her arms folded tightly across her chest. The story gushed out of her. She felt she was not so much telling it as setting it free.

■   ■   ■

Good Lord! I thought as I held Meiko against me and let her sob. *What she's been through!*

We had circled around and started back on the sand above the surf line when she broke down. I pulled her against me and told her to let it go. She was so small and frail in the circle of my arms, and there seemed to be no end to her tears. I tried to absorb her pain. She had years of unexpressed grief stored up and I would hold her until it was all cried out—even if it took all night.

I tried to avoid the thought of Matsuo killing himself but could not. Seppuku—the horror of jabbing a knife into his belly and ripping it across, then up toward his chest—made my intestines coil with revulsion. But it was so like Matsuo to do something so Japanese. I could almost sense his feeling that he would be ripping the last traces of America out of him with that final act and would thereby go to his beyond as a true Son of Japan.

A useless death. And the worst part of it for me was knowing that he had gone to his grave thinking as he did of me. I had always hoped deep inside that someday I'd get the chance to square myself with Matsuo. That hope was gone now. I held Meiko tighter, trying to release my pain with hers.

I thought about what could have happened to her—she would have drowned out there if that freighter hadn't hit her sailboat! A few yards to the left or right . . .

I pressed Meiko more tightly against me, thinking how the strange turns of life were decided by seconds and minutes, by feet and inches. I'd been in Honolulu two and a half years, Meiko for three; I must have passed The Bon Marche dozens of times during the year she had been working there, yet only today had I stopped in and passed the stocking counter when she was there. If she had been bending down behind the counter or if I had borne left instead of right upon entering the store, I'd have missed her.

Seconds and inches . . .

Meiko pushed herself away and I let her go, reluctantly.

"I'm so sorry," she said, turning away.

"Don't be. You never have to apologize to me." I had a thought. I hesitated, then plunged on. "Did Matsuo ever tell you what happened between us?"

I saw her shake her head in the moonlight. "No."

"Well then I guess it's time for me to do a little soul baring myself." I held my hand out to her, hoping she'd take it. "I'll tell you on the way back to the parking lot."

She placed her hand in mine and suddenly I felt light-headed. Touching her made me realize how deep my emotions ran where Meiko was concerned. I had written them off as youthful infatuation with a girl I could never have, a romanticizing of the unattainable.

Yet here, now, on the Waikiki beach, she no longer seemed an impossible dream.

SEPTEMBER
TOKYO

Hiroki stood in an upper chamber of the Diet Building and surveyed the gathering. Most of the men here would be part of the Imperial Conference, due to begin within the hour. The excitement and anticipation was palpable. Hiroki shared it. This might well be the most important Imperial Conference in the history of the Empire.

"Where is your brother?" Koki Hirota said as he stood next to Hiroki.

"My brother? Matsuo is home. Why do you ask?"

Hirota's face was bland. "I am thinking that it is best for our plans that he not be present at the Imperial Conference. He might voice sentiments similar to those he expressed when the Crown Prince was born."

Hiroki nodded. "Yes. I quite agree."

Matsuo certainly had no place here. Hiroki wondered if he still bore his brother ill will. No. No longer. Such equanimity might not have been possible had Meiko lived on as a constant reminder of the incident; but with her dead, it became a merely unfortunate episode that was to be overlooked and forgotten in the interest of family harmony.

"I am glad too that Admiral Yamamoto will not be attending," Koki was saying.

Hiroki glanced over to where the short, thickset Naval officer in a medal-encrusted uniform stood speaking to a cluster of listeners. "Why is that?"

"He sounds much like your brother."

"Does he?"

He had been ready to do almost anything short of murder to keep Matsuo from attending the Imperial Conference. It would have been highly irregular for him to have been invited, but if Father got it into his head that he wanted Matsuo there, an invitation would have been issued.

Hiroki's fears had proved groundless. Matsuo had no interest in politics. After the incident at the summer house, Matsuo had retreated from the family. For the first year, he had limited his contact to visits for birthdays and an occasional local festival, spending most of his time with Naval Intelligence. He had thrown himself into the work. He had been transferred to Panama for two years to set up a clearing house for intelligence from America, and now he was back. He was gaining quite a reputation as an expert on America. For that reason he might have been invited to the conference if the Tosei-ha had not screened all invitations, weeding out any participants who might speak against the alliance. They wanted no dark clouds of doubt at the conference.

Curious now about Yamamoto, Hiroki sidled closer to the group, trying to make his movement appear to be aimless wandering. As he stopped to listen, a member of the cluster courteously brought him into the conversation.

"Ah, Okumo-san—the admiral was just describing what he sees as the drawbacks of the Tripartite Alliance."

Hiroki knew that after the Imperial Conference today, when the Emperor himself would give approval to Japan's alignment with Germany and Italy, the Tripartite Alliance would be a fact, with only the formal documents to be signed. But he knew that Yamamoto had attended Harvard and had been Naval Attaché in Washington, D.C., for a number of years. He was curious to hear what he had to say. He bowed to the admiral.

"I would be honored to hear the admiral's thoughts."

Yamamoto returned the bow. "As I have been saying, I find many drawbacks, but the two most glaring are these: The pact intimates that Japan has something to gain from alliance with Germany and Italy. I disagree. I find their conduct of the war in Europe despicable. Any association with them taints Japan's honor as a nation."

Hiroki made no reply, although he had to admit that under normal circumstances he would fully agree with Yamamoto's sentiments. But the Tripartite Alliance was a political necessity at the moment. It could be broken later.

"But the most ominous outcome of the alliance is that it means war with the United States."

"Does the admiral feel that Japan should fear war with the United States?"

"I feel Japan should avoid any war she cannot win."

The group's attention was suddenly focused entirely on Hiroki. He did not feel he should leave that statement unanswered.

"The United States is led by a sick, crippled old man who is advised by a cabinet of other sick old men. We have nothing to fear from the likes of them."

Yamamoto shook his head slowly. "It will not be sick old men who build the ships and aircraft they can send after us in an endless stream; it will not be sick old men milling their uniforms and machining their rifles and growing their food; it will not be sick old men marching against us." He straightened his shoulders. "If war must be, I will fight like a thousand devils for Japan. We can give the Americans the fight of their lives . . . for six months. After that they will simply overwhelm us with their material superiority, no matter how bravely we fight."

He bowed and strode away.

As the group broke up, Hiroki watched the admiral leave the room. He realized why Yamamoto had taken his last chance to speak against the alliance. After today, the alliance would carry the approval of the Imperial Will and no voice could be raised against it.

But Koki had been right. Yamamoto did sound like Matsuo. Did it mean something that the two men in Japan most knowledgeable about the United States were the two who seemed to fear war with her most?

It was a disquieting thought and he did not allow himself to dwell on it.

■ ■ ■

Hiroki knelt beside his father in the Imperial Palace. He kept his back rigid, his hands on his knees. He had already bowed so low that his forehead had touched the rough surface of the tatami beneath him. Above him on the dais, seated on an ornately carved throne before a screen of delicately woven gold, was the Emperor himself. Hiroki would never get used to how meek and bookish this Son of Heaven looked with his smooth round face, his sparse moustache, and his owlish eyes behind the thick lenses of his glasses. Arrayed before Him on either side of Hiroki were the highest-ranking officers and politicians in Japan, all on their knees, supplicants before a God.

Hiroki bit down on the inside of his cheek to suppress the tension pounding within him.

An Imperial Conference is a formality, he told himself for the thousandth time. *Just a formality*. The government had made a firm decision to join the German-Italian Axis and transform it into a three-way alliance. By tradition and by the law of the Meiji Constitution, the government had to petition the Emperor's sanction on a national policy of such enormity. The Emperor had no true veto power, however, and had never been known even to attempt such an act. The Emperor's role at an Imperial Conference was to hear the decisions of his advisors and to make no comment. *Just a formality*.

But rumor had it that the Emperor was uneasy about the alliance, and that made Hiroki very anxious. One word, one syllable, one hint of disapproval by so much as the arching of an eyebrow, and the alliance would be off. Months—*years*—of maneuvering by the Tosei-ha and its allies would fall into complete disarray.

And if that happened, Hiroki knew that he would be largely to blame.

After all, hadn't he proposed the idea of saturating the nation with the idea of the Emperor's indisputable Divinity? Hadn't he urged the members of the Tosei-ha to use their influence in the diet to pass laws which made it a punishable offense even to imply otherwise? He had taken the plan from history. The Tokugawa Shoguns had done exactly the same thing: They had bolstered the Emperor's divine status, made him a remote God whose every whim was a mandate to his subjects; and then they had ruled for centuries, doing whatever they pleased in his name.

The country was at that stage now. The Emperor was effectively isolated from his public and the workings of his government. The Tosei-ha could do almost whatever it wished in the name of the Emperor. It was an almost foolproof situation except for a full-dress Imperial Conference such as this. The Emperor's divine status could backfire here if he made an objection known.

Hiroki listened as the last of the cabinet members and service chiefs rose, bowed, and gave his reasons why he thought the Emperor should accept the Tripartite Alliance. He watched the Emperor sit mute and expressionless on his throne. This was the moment. If the Emperor did as he should and let the conference end without comment, the nation's future course would be set. This was the point of no return. Once the Tripartite Alliance was signed, there could be no turning back.

Emperor Hirohito did not move. Instead of rising to signal the end of the Imperial Conference, he sat like a stone carving, his eyes unreadable behind his thick lenses. The conference room fell into utter silence. The rustle of clothing, even the soft susurration of human breath stopped as the Emperor leaned forward a few degrees.

Is he going to speak?

Hiroki broke out in a sweat over his entire body. He could feel the droplets of perspiration collect on his forehead and upper lip.

Why is he waiting?

As the seconds ticked by in the frozen room, Hiroki's heart picked up tempo until he thought it would leap out of his chest.

And then, very suddenly, it was over. Without a word, the Emperor rose to leave. As Hiroki bowed his head to the tatami along with all the others, it took all of his control to suppress a shout of joy.

We've done it! He wanted to run and tell Shimazu. *Nothing can stop us now!*

1 9 4 1

THE YEAR OF THE SNAKE

Meiko watched Frank as he leaned over the side of the boat with his head in a bucket. A glass bottom bucket. He was looking for humpbacks.

"You have to see them!" he had said with unbridled enthusiasm. "They come to the channel every winter to mate. You *have* to see the whales!"

And so here they were in a tiny outboard motorboat off Lahaina, peering into the water.

Actually, she had seen plenty of whales already, gliding up and gracefully breaking the surface to blow spume and take a breath, and then down again in a graceful glide, so monstrously huge, and yet so undeniably gentle. And sometimes anything but gentle when they launched their forty or fifty tons entirely out of the water to land in an explosion of spray and a slap like a cannon shot. They were frightening then.

But Frank was not content to watch them broach from a distance. He wanted to watch them down below, at home, in the depths.

"There's one!" he cried, his voice echoing in the bucket. "A big one!" He slid the bucket toward her along the surface of the water. "Quick! Straight down!"

She looked and in the flickering light filtering down through the

206

crystalline water she saw smaller, rainbow-colored fish in the upper layers—triggers, trumpets, unicorns, tangs, and butterflies—and below them, not one but three humpback whales passing in two different directions directly beneath her.

Where are they going? she wondered. *What are they thinking?* There was a lumbering *wa* about them, a contagious inner peace that Meiko could sense seeping into her soul by small degrees as she watched them.

And then they were gone. But the tranquillity remained. She watched for a while but they did not return.

She slid the bucket back to Frank. "They are beautiful."

He grinned. "I told you you'd love it. Maybe we can see some more."

Meiko watched him put his head back down into the bucket and thought of the many things Frank had helped her see in the past months. The world had been a gray, drab, empty place during the years since Matsuo's death. She had spent those years in a state of emotional anesthesia—a living death, really—with no joy, no pain, no pleasure, no hopes, no plans for the future. She had been sleepwalking through life.

Now she was awake again. There was the salt smell of the water, the sun overhead in a blue sky, and the four islands that surrounded them: the lush green hills of Maui and Lanai on either side, the squat massiveness of Molokai behind, each wearing its white lei of clouds; far to the south sat their poor stunted sister: low, brown, barren Kahoolawe. And all about, these great gentle leviathans leaping and gliding back and forth between the surface and the depths. She had been here for years and had never seen any of this beauty before; now she was feeling what she had thought she would never feel again: peace.

And she owed it all to Frank.

She watched him now, craning his neck into that bucket. A good, kind, gentle man. He had celebrated his thirtieth birthday last summer and yet he still took such boyish pleasure in the wonders of the world. Since their reunion, his quiet love of life had slowly infected her until she too felt alive again. Eight months with Frank now and growing closer all the time, but yet to share that ultimate closeness.

Sitting here in this little boat with him brought back memories of another sunny day in another boat nearly four years ago. Suddenly she saw Matsuo sitting against the transom with his arm draped over the steering arm of the outboard motor. She blinked her eyes and he was gone, but his memory lingered.

Matsuo had been so different—always in motion, always chasing something and never finding it. He had always seemed at odds with the world around him, always fighting for his place in it. Currents of turbulence had seemed to follow him wherever he went. The world was always an exciting place when he was around.

She wondered how she could be attracted to two such opposite poles. Perhaps because the last thing she needed in her life right now was excitement. She needed Frank.

"Good Lord!" he cried as he straightened abruptly. He threw the bucket into the boat and grabbed one of the paddles.

"What's wrong?" Meiko said, alarmed at his frantic motion.

"There's one coming up!" He pointed behind her between strokes. "Right over there!"

Meiko turned and saw nothing but calm water. She kept watching as Frank kept paddling. Suddenly the water directly to her left surged up and fell away as a huge, smooth, glistening gray mass rose to the surface. The globe of an eye bigger than her fist stared impassively in passing. She squealed as the bubbling blowhole appeared and showered the boat with warm, salty spume.

"Touch it!" Frank shouted.

She glanced back and saw him leaning precariously out over the gunwale with his arm stretched to its limit. She looked back at the whale as its flank glided along the surface, paralleling the boat's course in a slow, graceful arc. She too reached out—

—and touched the whale.

Its hide was smooth and slick, surprisingly soft. She let her hand slide along its skin, a gleaming surface that seemed to go on forever. Finally, the whale sank from sight and touch, a tail fin brushing the bottom of the boat as it sounded again, totally oblivious to the touch of the two humans and the puny craft in which they floated.

"We did it!" Frank said breathlessly. He was slumped over the gunwale, staring dazedly at the water. "We actually touched one! I've always wanted to do that! It was like . . . like . . ."

"Like touching a god," Meiko said, staring at her slick palm.

She looked up to find Frank gazing at her in wonder. "Yeah. That's exactly how it was!"

He reached out his hand to her and she took it. The hands that had touched the god joined over the water.

MARCH
TOKYO

To relieve his tension, Matsuo paced back and forth along the length of the spacious office in the Navy Building. The admiral had sent word that he wanted to speak to him about an important matter. He had been attending the annual *Nehan-E*—the ceremony of Nirvana—at the Tofuku-ji in Kyoto. He had been meditating in the *Karasansui*-type garden in the Founder's Hall of the temple, seeking tranquillity in its mixture of greenery and white sand.

He had found himself gravitating more and more to the ancient city since Meiko's death, and had missed it terribly during the years in Panama. Kyoto had become a sanctuary of sorts for him. The agelessness of its countless shrines and temples, and the beauty of its surrounding hills acted as buffers against the growing strife throughout the rest of Japan. He could walk where so many Emperors had walked when Kyoto was the Imperial City, or sit beneath the trees surrounding the five-story pagoda of the To-ji temple, or catch the reflection of the gold-foiled upper levels of the Kinkaku-ji in the placid water that lapped its foundation. He would try to imagine himself living in a less turbulent time.

The only other place where he could find similar peace was high in the air, with Japan spread green, blue, and serene below him.

He found no peace on his futon, that was certain. Especially on nights when he slept with Nagata's daisho within reach. Every so often, the swords would provide him with dreams of Meiko, happy dreams in which she was still alive and walking along an endless shore with someone. He could never see the other, but sensed he was not Japanese. Yet Meiko seemed content. Were these sword-dreams, as he came to call them, visions of the next life? If so, he was glad Meiko was happy.

He heard a door open behind him. Matsuo turned and bowed as Admiral Yamamoto, wearing an unadorned blue wool pea jacket, entered. The admiral returned his bow, then embraced him.

"It has been a long time since Kasumigaura," he said. "Are you still adding to your flight time?"

Matsuo nodded. "Whenever possible. And you?"

"The same, although each passing year affords me less time to escape into the air." He gestured to the chair opposite his desk. "Please, sit down."

As he took his seat, Matsuo scrutinized his old commander, who remained standing. Yamamoto had been in charge of the Navy flight school at Kasumigaura when Matsuo had gone there for training. The admiral had infected him with his vision of air power as an integral part of sea power. Yamamoto had moved on from Kasumigaura to director of the Aeronautical Department of the Navy, and from there to his present position as Commander of the Combined Fleet. Matsuo remembered him as an indefatigable gambler who would think nothing of playing poker, *shogi,* or bridge all night.

But despite the years and all the late nights, he looked little older than when Matsuo had last seen him—his hair was as short and bristly, his jaw as square, his eyes as bright as ever.

"It is the Year of the Snake and next month I will turn fifty-seven years old," he said as he walked to the window and stood gazing out at Tokyo awakening to spring. He paused, then turned and looked Matsuo in the eye. "I fear that by the time I am fifty-eight we will be at war with America."

Matsuo stood silent and stunned. Japan was already at war with China and had annexed portions of the Dutch and French territories in Indochina. Matsuo knew the chest-beating militarists like War Minister Tojo were building toward a wider conflict, perhaps even a challenge to the U.S., but to hear Admiral Yamamoto say it with such conviction was devastating.

"Surely there's some way to avoid that," Matsuo managed to say.

Yamamoto shook his head sadly. "I'm afraid not. From what I remember of our discussions at Kasumigaura, I know your views on war with America are at odds with your brother's. I share your views. We've both seen America from the inside. We both know that Japan cannot survive a war of any duration against it. But the Empire must either expand soon or turn inward forever. If we move into the Philippines, which we must if we expand southward, we run the risk of war with America."

He moved to a map of the Pacific on the wall and pointed to Hawaii. Matsuo noted the stumps of the two fingers he had lost at the battle of Tsushima in the Russo-Japanese War.

"Her fleet has been stationed here for the past nine months—already halfway to Japan. When war is declared"—he swept his right arm westward from Hawaii—"it will move the rest of the way toward us." He swept his left arm eastward from Japan. "The Imperial Navy will rush to meet it." The two arms met in the center of the Western Pacific. "We may or may not win the ensuing battle. I think we will. But even so, our fleet will be severely damaged. And as we work to rebuild, how are we to hold the Philippines, Malaya, the Dutch East Indies, and Singapore without a Navy?"

"I don't know," Matsuo said. "But I do know that the Americans will be rebuilding, too. And faster than we."

Yamamoto nodded curtly. "Exactly! If only I could make the Supreme Command see that!"

"You must!" Matsuo said. "*We* must!"

"No," the admiral said. "I have tried in vain for months. They have decided not to hear what displeases them. So . . ." He took a deep breath. "If we cannot change the way they think on Sanno Hill, we must change the way we meet the U.S. Pacific Fleet. Do you remember how the Japanese Navy opened the war with the Russians in 1904?"

Of course Matsuo knew. Japanese torpedo boats had surprised the Russian fleet off Port Arthur and sank some of its best battleships. It was an historic naval victory. But what did that have to do with—

And then the parallel struck him like a dash of cold water in the face. "You don't mean . . . ?"

Admiral Yamamoto pointed to the area of the Pacific where his arms had met. "We must not meet here. We must meet and defeat them *here.*"

His stubby finger jabbed at Hawaii.

Matsuo shot out of his seat toward the map. The audacity of the plan! It was brilliant! The Americans had moved their fleet from San Diego to Pearl Harbor as an obvious warning to Japan. Hiroki had called the U.S. fleet's presence in the trade lanes *Taiheiyo-no-gan*—a cancer in the Pacific. But Admiral Yamamoto's plan would make use of that very nearness and turn it to Japan's advantage.

"Can it work?" Matsuo said, breathless.

"I don't know. That's why I called you here. We have reams of intelligence concerning Oahu and Pearl Harbor, but none of it specifically geared to planning an attack."

"From the air, of course."

Yamamoto smiled. "Of course. But I need to know if an air attack on the harbor is feasible. That will be your job. I've arranged with Intelligence to relieve you of your present duties and assign you to me. You will report directly to me. And *only* to me."

Matsuo gazed at the map on which the Hawaiian Islands were small splotches of green and brown on a field of blue.

"If we can catch them there with enough ships in port . . ."

"There must be a minimum of four battleships at dock to make the attack worthwhile. Hopefully, we can catch an aircraft carrier there, too. Since we will have to go to war with them eventually, the object of the attack will be to deal a crippling blow at the outset with no damage to us. That will afford us time to consolidate our gains in the Philippines and the East Indies. Within six to nine months after we open hostilities, we should be able to sue for peace on favorable terms. Japan's economic future will be guaranteed and we will have avoided a protracted war with an enemy we cannot defeat."

"You do not intend to hold the Hawaiian Islands?" Matsuo said, still staring at the map. When he heard no reply, he looked up and saw the admiral staring at him, grinning broadly. "Sir?"

"Excellent!" he said, clamping a hand on Matsuo's shoulder. "You are thinking like an admiral! A lightning strike at the harbor and the airports—cripple them and leave them to lick their wounds—might buy us enough time. But if we *occupy* the Hawaiians, we will rob them of a staging area in the Central Pacific, leaving us still more time to consolidate in the South Pacific, and providing us with an extremely valuable bargaining chip when we sit down with them to talk peace: 'Yes, we will return the Hawaiians to you if you will acknowledge our gains in Asia and the South Pacific.'"

"I see only one problem, sir," Matsuo said, hesitantly.

"And what is that? Speak up."

"If I remember my history correctly, in 1904 we broke off diplomatic relations with the Russians and immediately attacked their fleet, *then* we declared war."

Yamamoto nodded. "Yes, that's true. Go on."

"I think that would be a major mistake with the Americans. We must declare war first, then attack immediately. But by all means we *must* declare war first."

"It is the honorable thing to do, I agree," Yamamoto said with narrowed eyes. "But do I sense another, more strategic reason?"

"Yes, sir: the isolationists."

The admiral's eyes widened. "Yes! Yes, of course! You are absolutely right!"

Matsuo knew of few Japanese to whom he could have said that one word and sparked such complete understanding. Only someone who had spent the admiral's years in America would know how its people loathed the thought of a foreign war, and how many of its legislators reflected that sentiment. Those legislators would impede the conduct of any war that smacked of adventurism or where it was thought Americans should mind their own business. Japan had to take advantage of that sentiment.

"From what I have been hearing from America," Matsuo said, "I believe their President Roosevelt wants war. He has tried everything else to bring his country out of its economic depression—war is the only thing left. But I am sure we can count on the isolationist sentiment to impede or greatly slow any rush to declare war on us *as long as they don't feel they have been stabbed in the back*. We must play extremely fair with America. We must declare war first, *then* attack, and attack *only* military targets. If we attack Oahu, we must strictly avoid any direct damage to Honolulu. Anything else, and the isolationists will be clamoring for our heads louder than anybody else."

"An excellent point," Yamamoto said. "I will see that it is an integral part of the plan from the start. And already I see that I was wise in choosing you for this assignment. But before we get to concrete plans," he said, guiding Matsuo toward the door, "we must first have a feasibility study. That will be your job. If the island is too well protected, or the waters around it too well watched, or if they keep most of the fleet at sea, there is no point in attacking Pearl Harbor."

He sobered and stood silent for a moment. His voice was grim as he spoke. "I also chose you because I know you dread war with the United States as much as I. I want you to hold onto that dread and keep it in mind as we make plans I hope we never have to use. Pray that by some miracle we will be diverted from this course."

The enormity of the responsibility he was being given suddenly crashed down on Matsuo. That, and the honor of knowing that Admiral Yamamoto had handpicked him for the task, rendered him momentarily speechless. He bowed and left the office in a daze.

Once outside in the fresh air, he quieted his emotions and decided to get directly to work. But as he hurried toward the Intelligence offices, he could almost sense the wheels of history turning about him.

"What do you know about Pearl Harbor?" he asked Lieutenant Shigeo Mikawa after they had shared some tea and friendly conversation in his office. He knew Shigeo had been concentrating his intelligence efforts on Hawaii.

"Everything," Shigeo said with a grin. He was reed-thin and smoked incessantly, seeming to pride himself on the fact that he could light a cigarette and not remove it once from between his lips until he was done with it. He spoke around one now, squinting against the smoke that drifted up into his eyes. "Absolutely everything. What do you want to know?"

"How about some maps and pictures to start."

"Simple." He pulled open one cabinet drawer after another. "I have topographical maps of Oahu and nautical charts of Pearl Harbor. I have hundreds of pictures of the harbor. Would you prefer color or black-and-white?"

Matsuo was astounded. "Where did you get all this?"

Shigeo passed him the maps. "I had our agents buy these at government offices and at bait and tackle shops. You can keep these. I've got plenty."

"And the photos?"

"Color?"

"Why not?"

Shigeo pulled a large envelope out of the file drawer. "Take your pick. I've got duplicates of almost everything."

Matsuo dumped the contents of the envelope onto Shigeo's desk. He picked up one photo after another. Their colors and focus were perfect. He noticed that some of the best had scalloped edges. He turned one over. It was stamped and carried an address in a residential district of Tokyo. A handwritten message said, "Isn't this lovely!" The printed inscription in the upper-left corner of the card read:

Ford Island: The Pearl in the Harbor.

Matsuo laughed out loud. "A postcard!"

This was going to be easier than he had anticipated.

MARCH ▦
HONOLULU

I awoke to the sound of Meiko sobbing. Tiny sobs, muffled, but each one causing a gentle quake in the bed. We had made love for the first time here in my Kalihi apartment about a month ago and she had been spending the night with increasing frequency ever since. As I rolled over to look at her, she turned away, but I saw the little heaves of her bare shoulders.

I gently pulled her back to face me. Her eyes were red and puffy, her cheeks glistened with tears. I wondered if she might be thinking about Matsuo and a knot formed in my belly. I didn't want her thinking about Matsuo. I wanted her thinking about me.

"Meiko, what's wrong?"

"I'm so happy!" she said and burst into a full-fledged cry.

She clung to me like ivy to a tree.

"If this means you're happy," I said after a while, "what do you do when you're sad?" That managed to raise a tearful smile. "So come on now, tell me what's wrong."

"I'm just happy," she said with a little shrug. "I never thought I'd be happy again." She held me tighter. "But I am."

Meiko could not know how those words made me feel. The past month had meant more to me than any other time in my life. Making love, being together every night and spending every day off together —it was like a dream come true for me. I had never felt this close to a woman before. I wanted it to go on forever. I wanted to make it official.

"Then marry me," I said.

"Oh, Frank . . ." she said, loosening her grip.

I wouldn't let her go. "Uh-uh. You've begged off twice already. Not this time. Say yes or no. And if no, give me a good reason."

"Very well," she said, staring at the ceiling. "You are an American Naval officer; I am Japanese. The United States and Japan are on less than friendly terms and no one seems to expect any improvement in the relationship in the near future. A Japanese wife could be very harmful to your career."

She looked at me and caught me smiling.

"It's not funny!" she said.

"How long did you rehearse that?"

"Never! It's just that I've been . . . thinking about it a lot."

"Oh, you have, have you?" That meant a lot to me. "Well, I've been thinking about it, too. But I've done something about it."

I got out of bed and went to the top drawer of my dresser. Under my socks was the envelope I was looking for. I brought it back to her.

"Remember that little jaunt I had to take to Maui last week? I bought something when I was there."

I handed her the envelope. She pulled out the piece of paper, read it, then looked up at me.

"Is this a deed?"

I nodded. "To a hundred acres of sugarcane on Maui. A descendant of one of the original missionaries is selling off some of his land. I have an option on more."

"Why?"

I settled back on the pillow. "I've been thinking about it for a couple of years now, and I've finally made up my mind: When my present hitch is up, I'm not going to reenlist. I'm going to become a cane farmer."

"But you don't know anything about farming!"

"I'll learn." I ran a finger up her arm, over her shoulder, and down to her breast. *"We'll* learn."

Her eyes were wide. "You're giving up your navy career?"

"Yep. I'm never leaving the islands. I can't imagine living anywhere else. This is paradise. The only thing that will make it less than perfect is not having you with me."

"But Frank—"

"No 'buts'! Your being Japanese won't hurt my navy career because I won't have one. And on Maui you'll probably be better accepted than me."

She was silent. At least she wasn't saying no.

I prodded her: "What do you say? We'll go over there and ignore the rest of the world. Let it all go to hell in a handbasket. We'll have each other and we'll have our farm. Besides cane, we'll grow papaya and pineapples and breadfruit and guava and bananas. We may never be rich, but we'll sure as hell never go hungry."

"We'd be away from everyone, wouldn't we?" she said, gazing off into space.

"Our own little world, where no one will care if you're Japanese or Martian."

She hugged me, then got up and went to where her purse sat on a chair. I watched her slim, naked body as she searched through the purse. Desire rose up in me. She returned to the bed with a bankbook and placed it in my hand.

"What's this?"

"Three hundred dollars. My savings. A small dowry, but I hope you'll accept it."

"Dowry?" Then it hit me. "Does that mean you'll marry me?"

She nodded, smiling, and we embraced. I almost cheered and I almost cried. Now I had *everything*.

"When?"

"Whenever you say," she said. "I have no family to invite."

I thought about that. "If I can get some leave next week, we can get married Friday and honeymoon on our 'plantation.' How's that sound?"

"That sounds wonderful," she said softly, then pressed her slim little body against me. I kissed her and as I drew her closer, the telephone rang. It was Harry Thornton.

"The *Salt Lake City*'s in port," he said, "and its captain was here looking for you."

I was annoyed at being pulled away from Meiko. "So?"

"Captain Zacharias asked for you specifically."

"Zacharias?" I said. "Ellis Zacharias? Is he there?"

"He's over at CINCPAC now, but he's going to stop in here on his way back. He wants to get together with us before he has to ship out. I don't know what he thinks is so damn important, but see if you can get over here by noon."

"I'll be there!"

"What was that about?" Meiko asked as I hung up.

"My old commanding officer when I was in San Diego is in Pearl. I'm going to meet with him later."

"You admire him, don't you," she said, watching me closely.

"I think Ellis Zacharias is the savviest man in Naval Intelligence. But I don't want to talk about him, I want to talk about us. Where were we?"

Meiko slid against me. "We weren't talking."

■ ■ ■

Captain Ellis M. Zacharias, dark-haired, lean-boned, and lean-featured, was sitting in Harry's office puffing on a cigarette when I got there. It was great to see him. I wanted to throw my arms around him but settled instead for a firm handshake.

"You look brown as a beach boy, Frank," he said. "Don't they give you any work to do at this country club?"

"Sure. All officers must go to the beach and swim at least twice a day." He laughed and I said, "C'mon. I'll buy you lunch."

"Sounds good to me."

We strolled over to the Officers Club, the two of us catching up on people we knew during the "old days" in the San Diego District Intelligence Office while Harry tagged along and looked bored. We got ourselves a table and ordered drinks. It was a little early for me, but I ordered a scotch with Zach. Harry had a gin and tonic.

Finally I asked the question that had been plaguing me for months:

"What are you up to with the *Salt Lake City?*"

He looked amused. "What do you mean?"

"Is it secret?" I said. "If it is, I'll shut up. But I've got to say there's something awful strange about the former Chief Intelligence Officer of the Eleventh Naval District commanding a heavy cruiser. Are you on a special intelligence assignment?"

He shook his head. "I'm out of Intelligence. I'm now a cruiser commander. Nothing special. They told me last November they were reassigning me from ONI to the *Salt Lake City,* and so that's where I am. That's it."

I couldn't believe it. Zach had been in Intelligence for a quarter century, had done duty in Japan and spoke the language like a native—the Japanese knew him well, and respected him. Why on earth would ONI isolate him on a cruiser running interference for battleships and carriers just when relationships with Japan were getting hotter and hotter?

"There's got to be more to it. I mean I know you aren't exactly the most popular guy with the Navy Department—"

"Stark doesn't like to hear criticism. Admiral Richardson used to command the Pacific Fleet, but I'm sure you heard his assessment of Pearl Harbor when Stark said the President wanted the fleet moved here."

I nodded. "Called it 'a goddamn mousetrap.'"

"Right. And is Richardson still Fleet Commander? Hell, no. The President told Stark to get someone a little less outspoken. So Kimmel's in and Richardson's out. I'm out, too."

"But that doesn't make any sense at all!"

"Neither does putting the Pacific Fleet in Pearl. I'm in full agreement with Richardson," he said, staring out the window at the harbor. "Pearl *is* a goddamn mousetrap."

"Oh, come now, Captain," Harry said. "It's not so bad. And it puts the fleet right in the thick of things."

Zach looked at him. "That's what I'm afraid of."

I didn't like the sound of that. "What do you mean?"

He turned toward us. "I just brought the *Salt Lake City* through that bottleneck out there. It comes down to less than five hundred yards across and it's so damn shallow I was afraid my keel would drag bottom if I did better than ten knots. A carrier or a big fattie like the *Arizona* would have to *crawl* out of here! You'd need a full spring tide and a good half-day's notice of attack to clear Pearl for action!"

"Come on!" Harry said. "*What* attack?"

Zach's mouth twisted. "I had a nice long chat with Kichisaburo Nomura as he was passing through Frisco last month."

"I know," I said, and was glad I could say it. Nomura was the new Japanese Ambassador to Washington and I had been keeping track of any intercepts that concerned him.

Zach gave me a little salute with his glass. "Still on your toes, Frank. I was real sorry to lose you to the Fourteenth District."

"It's little meetings like that that make me think you're still with Intelligence," I said.

"Nope," he said, shaking his head. "Saw Nomura on my own. We know each other from way back. He says Japan doesn't want war, wants everything nice. He isn't lying, but I'll bet he's been lied to. The guys in power in Tokyo are *hungry*. Just push them a little and it'll mean war."

"You think they'll attack Pearl?" Harry said, sitting up straight and putting his glass down.

"I'm certain of it. If they decide to go to war with us, that's what they'll do. Historically, it's the way they operate. And it makes good sense, too. If they can knock out four or more fatties here, they can then pretty much do what they want in the Philippines and the East Indies. After all, they already outnumber us two to one in the Pacific."

"We'll see them coming," Harry said. "We'll blast them to kingdom come!"

"Will you? I've just been over this with Kimmel, and I'm not so sure. You need constant air reconnaissance in a five-hundred-mile radius for proper warning. Most of those old PBYs on Ford Island are grounded for lack of parts."

"We don't need a five-hundred-mile lead on an attacking fleet to prepare for them!" Harry's tone was becoming downright belligerent.

Zach shook his head slowly. "I'm not talking about a sea battle. War will begin with an air attack on our fleet on a weekend, probably on a Sunday morning, downwind from the north."

"You're really serious, aren't you?" I said. He was making me uneasy.

"I'll put it this way," he said, his expression grim. "If U.S.-Japanese relations deteriorate any further, I'd have a lot of trouble sleeping nights if my ship was berthed here, especially if there were four or more battleships in port with me."

We were all silent and I guess Zach thought he was being too much of a wet blanket. He put down his glass and clapped his hands.

"Well, this is all just back room theorizing. Maybe Nomura will be able to patch things up and we won't have to worry about war. And even if things do deteriorate, at least you've got Purple magic to tip you off to anything big about to happen."

Zach was referring to the intricate little electric machine that had been developed to decrypt the Japanese PA-K2 cipher, known to us as "Purple." You fed cipher gibberish into one end, and clear Japanese or English was printed out the other. To anyone who slaved as I did, decoding and deciphering messages all day, those little machines were, indeed, *magic*.

"Purple magic?" I said. "I wish the hell we did. The only magic we've got is geared to the old Red code."

Zach's face went slack. "God! The Japanese haven't used Red since thirty-seven! You mean to tell me you're practically on top of Japan here and you don't do any Purple deciphering?"

I shook my head. "Nope. We have to depend on summaries from the Navy Department—*when* they get around to sending them to us. I tell you, Zach, it's frustrating as hell."

Harry said nothing.

"Let's order some food," Zach said after a moment. "I don't know what the hell's going on, but it makes me want to get drunk. And I *don't* want to get drunk. Yet. So let's eat."

The three of us studiously avoided the subject of Japan during the meal, but I only picked at my food. I had lost my appetite.

JUNE ■
TOKYO

"Germany has attacked Russia!"

Shimazu heard Hiroki's words and felt his pulse quicken. "You are certain?"

"Absolutely! I had it confirmed before I came!"

This was the beginning! Shimazu could feel events picking up speed, gathering momentum toward war. He had thought something like this was pending as April became May, when the Seers had reported a disturbance in the Face, a sense that something cataclysmic was about to happen. But the disturbance had calmed in early May and nothing else had been reported.

Until now! This was of immense importance! With the Germans attacking her western flank, the Russians would withdraw their forces from the Chinese and Manchurian borders, allowing Japan to reduce her own troop concentrations in those areas.

The lessening of pressure on the Empire's Asian territories left the Order with a long-awaited golden opportunity to make Japan look south . . . and *move* south. Shimazu knew that the men the Order had maneuvered into positions of power would not let the opportunity pass.

"The Supreme Command is responding?"

"Yes. The Chiefs of Service are already moving to call the reservists to colors and begin conscription. They will also be recalling the merchant fleet. All this will take time, of course, but the wheels are already in motion."

Shimazu nodded. "Excellent. There is no time to waste."

That was an understatement. The Chinese adventure was costing Japan twenty-eight thousand gallons of oil per day. Reserves were almost nonexistent. The Empire needed a constant supply of rubber, tin, and iron, as well as oil to hold the Asian possessions.

"It begins now," he told Hiroki. "The French, the Dutch, the British, and the Americans are all around us, stealing our needs from our own table." He spread his arms. "This is *our* part of the world. We want it back—and we will *take* it back!"

JULY
HONOLULU

Meiko didn't understand why Frank was so jumpy. He had been up since before dawn, pacing their apartment like a caged tiger, repeatedly stepping outside and looking up at the sky, then coming back in and pacing again. He would go inside and sit at the table and stare at the papers he had brought home from Pearl. As a rule, he relished the extra sleep he could get on a Saturday morning.

Dawn was just lightening the sky now. Meiko heard the faint sound of a plane's engine and saw Frank's head lift as he heard it too. Without a word, he leaped to the balcony and stared into the empty sky like a madman.

She had asked him earlier if anything was wrong but his answer had been vague. At first she had thought he might have overdone it last night at Captain Thorton's Fourth of July party; after all, Frank's stomach had been bothering him lately, even without the hot dogs, hamburgers, and corn on the cob the captain had served. But when she thought about it, she remembered that Frank had eaten very little last night, and had limited himself to a few beers from the keg.

She was worried about her husband. She had come to care so deeply for Frank. And she was learning to love him. Not that she hadn't loved him on their wedding day—she had, but not as she had loved Matsuo. She doubted she would ever again share that intensity of feeling with anyone else. Was that because of Matsuo himself, or because he had been her first love?

It didn't matter. Matsuo was in the past and gone forever, and she was learning to love Frank more each day.

She got out of bed, wrapped her kimono around her, and joined him on the balcony. He jumped when she slipped her arms around him.

"Won't you tell me what's wrong?"

He turned and looked at her. "Let's take a little ride. I'll try to explain it once we get there."

He acted as if he were guilty of something, and that made Meiko uneasy.

They drove west to a hill overlooking Pearl Harbor. Frank drew her out of the car and walked her up a small rise. They stood by a clump of algaroba trees and Frank put his arm around her shoulders as they looked down on the still-sleeping harbor. The first rays of the sun began to warm her.

"Pearl Harbor is cursed, you know," Frank said in a low voice. "The story goes that the great shark goddess, Kaapuhau, lived in the east loch, that it is a sacred place. They started building Drydock Number One back about the time I was born, and they had nothing but trouble—weird accidents, freak injuries. Then, in 1913, when they were putting the finishing touches on it, the whole thing suddenly burst apart for no known reason, shattering four years' work in minutes. And later when they drained it out again, they found the body of a gigantic shark at the bottom."

Meiko shivered. "What happened after that?"

"They got a big *kahuna* to make the proper sacrifices, and everything went smoothly from then on. But some of the natives still say it's cursed. That the goddess wouldn't have wanted anything built there."

"Is that why you're so tense?"

He laughed, but it sounded strained. "No. It's just that I've been here four years now, and I've never seen so many ships in the harbor."

"But yesterday was the Fourth of July."

"I know—and it's brought most of the Pacific Fleet in for the three-day weekend."

"Frank, I still don't understand. What's wrong with that?"

He sighed, paused, then took a deep breath. He seemed reluctant to speak. "A man I respect very much said to watch out for a Saturday or Sunday morning when there are four or more battleships in port along with a carrier or two. He said if Japan decides to go to war with us, she'll look for that situation and launch a surprise air attack." He pointed at the ship-filled harbor. "Take a look: Most of the Pacific Fleet is asleep down there. Sitting ducks!"

"You don't think Japan is going to attack us, do you?" The thought horrified her.

Frank's arm tightened around her shoulder. "I don't know what to think. There's nothing in the world I want less. But with the way the rest of the world is going to hell, how long can it be before some of the madness touches us here?"

Meiko felt cold all over. "But we're so far away from everything here."

"No," Frank said, shaking his head. "We're right in the middle of it. And something big is brewing. We got word just Wednesday that Japan has ordered two million reservists and draftees to colors. Something's going to happen." He looked heavenward. "But please, God, not here. Not *here!*"

"Why haven't you told me any of this?"

He looked sheepish but said nothing.

Meiko looked up in wonder at her husband and hugged him. "You're worried about me, aren't you? More than anything else, you're worried about me."

"Yes. You, me, *us.* If we go to war, I won't have any choice about re-upping. We won't get to be Maui cane farmers. And if we go to war with Japan . . . God, that'll be so hard on you."

Meiko knew what he was thinking. His concern touched her. "Not as hard as you think. I am barely tolerated by the officers' wives as it is. If they snubbed me completely, it would only be a shade of difference."

"But I'll be doing everything I can to defeat your country. Won't that . . . ?"

With Matsuo dead and her family dishonored because of her, Meiko knew there was nothing in Japan for her. But she didn't want to mention Matsuo now. She searched for another way to reassure Frank.

"Hawaii is my country now," she said finally.

He laughed and that was good to hear after such a grim conversation. "I don't know what I did to deserve you!"

"It must have been something terrible. But truly, I hope you are never sorry you married me, Frank."

He enfolded her in his arms. "Sorry? I can't even imagine that."

She snuggled against him and sensed that he was more relaxed. Yet when she glanced up at his face, she saw that his head was up and he was scanning the horizon.

"Still worrying?"

"Sorry," he said, looking embarrassed at being caught. "I just won't be able to rest easy until this weekend is over and the fleet puts out to sea again. After that, we'll have a long breather—Pearl won't be this crowded again until December."

AUGUST
TOKYO

It was dark on the uppermost floor of the Order's five-story pagoda. The stifling heat and humidity of the Tokyo summer hung in the air and clung to their bodies as the five of them sat cross-legged in a rough circle around the single candle.

"It goes well, then?" said Elder Yonai. He was the most ancient member of the Order, merely a trunk and a head. His limbs had long since been removed at the hips and shoulders. He lay propped up on pillows.

Shimazu waited for Hiroki to answer the Elder. He had brought him here to the Elder Council without warning and knew he was in a state of shock. But Shimazu had wanted the Elders to hear the news from outside firsthand.

Hiroki finally found his voice. "Exceedingly well, Elder. So well, in fact, that I am sure the events of the past few weeks must be the handiwork of the gods themselves."

Elder Ryusaku, who was also a Seer, nodded noncommittally, causing the candlelight to flicker in empty sockets visible through the eyeholes in his mask. "Perhaps. But give us details. What has been the progression of events?"

Hiroki cleared his throat and ticked off the points on his trembling fingers. "Germany attacks Russia. We sign a nonaggression pact with Russia, thus freeing thousands of our troops from the Russian-Manchurian border. We arrange with the Vichy French to move into their Indochina holdings to mine their raw materials. When President Roosevelt hears of this, he insults us by ordering a freeze of all Japanese assets in the United States. The British quickly follow suit. Then the American President goes even further."

"Yes," Shimazu said. "The embargo." Even though it fit so perfectly into the Order's plans, he could not help but feel a flare of resentment.

The long-fingered hands of Kakuichi, the Elder with no voice and no legs, flickered in the air. Yonai translated:

" 'The Empire is cut off completely?' "

"No trade with us except for cotton and food!" Shimazu said.

"And what is the local reaction?" Elder Ryusaku asked.

Hiroki smiled. "If you listen to the wind, you can hear it carrying the angry voices of our people, raised against the United States of America. We had to put extra police in front of the American Embassy to protect it from the raging crowds! They now see that the British and the Americans are trying to strangle us. Without their oil, iron, scrap metal, coal, and all the other raw materials we import from them, Japan will be bankrupt in six months. The British and Americans have left us no choice: We *must* expand southward. Our very survival depends on it!"

All were silent for a moment. Eventually, Elder Yonai spoke in a low voice:

"Perhaps it is the handiwork of the gods we are seeing. But it is not often that the gods move with so little ambiguity. I wonder if this President Roosevelt is not using us as a foil for his own purposes. It is well known that he loathes the Third Reich and its military successes in Europe, and that he would rush to war if only his country would let him. And it is plain to see that it would be to America's great strategic advantage to engage Germany before Britain falls, which it surely must do after Germany takes Moscow and defeats Russia."

His gaze bored into Hiroki.

"Is this President Roosevelt taunting us? Is he trying to provoke us into a rash act before we are fully prepared? Could he want to use Japan, a signer of the Tripartite Act, as a stepping stone to war with Germany?"

Hiroki hesitated, then: "Perhaps that is his plan, Elder. And perhaps his hatred of us plays a part as well. I still burn from his remarks three years ago after we moved into China. Remember? He said we were diseased and should be quarantined."

"Remember?" Shimazu cried, unable to control the fury boiling up in him. "The arrogance of the man! How convenient for this feeble old scion to forget the history of his own nation! It was only a century and a half ago that the United States was a small Caucasian cancer on the east coast of North America. Since then it has spread across the continent, obliterating the native Indians and Mexicans with liquor and disease and bullets. But still it wasn't satisfied! It spread to Alaska and the Aleutians which jut far out into the Pacific. And on to the Hawaiians and Wake and Midway. Then it leaped into our midst in the Philippines, joining the other cancers of the British and Dutch and French. And this Roosevelt now dares to challenge our expansion into China? This man needs a lesson! He needs his nose rubbed in the dirt of his own filthy history!"

Shimazu realized with a start that he was on his feet and shouting.

■ ■ ■

Hiroki sat in mute wonder. He had never seen Shimazu so angry. And in front of the Elders, no less! Hiroki could barely muster the courage to speak. To show such emotion was unthinkable.

Yet he continued to be amazed at his sensei's grasp of the international situation. This seemingly simple monk who never left his temple had his fingers on pulses around the world. Here was another reminder never to underestimate the reach of his sensei.

"If it is war President Roosevelt wants," Elder Ryusaku said in a calm voice after Shimazu had reseated himself, "then war he shall have. But it will be on the Emperor's terms. We will strike when ready, and not a moment sooner!"

And what a strike it will be! Hiroki thought. He had ferreted out some of Yamamoto's still-developing plan to attack Pearl Harbor. It was brilliant! He almost wanted to laugh aloud now as he thought of it. The admiral had been such a fierce opponent of war with the United States that Hiroki had wondered if he could be counted on as Commander of the Combined Fleet. But apparently, once he had accepted the inevitability of the war he did not want, he had become a tiger.

Yes. Everything was perfect!

The limbless Elder Yonai translated Elder Kakuichi's hand signs: "'How is your search for the scrolls progressing?'"

"Very slowly, I'm afraid," Hiroki said, knowing his evasiveness was as transparent as spring water.

Shimazu and the three Elders—even the eyeless Ryusaku—were staring at him, and he felt himself wilt. How was it that he could bend a

nation to his vision and yet still feel like a child when he sat before
these aging, reclusive monks? Sometimes he resented the awe the
Order inspired in him.

"I know you are working hard to assure Japan's future and see that
she fulfills her destiny," Shimazu said gravely, "but you must not
submerge yourself so completely in political activities that you lose
sight of your quest. Remember the vision: In the coming war, Japan
must have the Black Winds."

Hiroki closed his eyes. There weren't enough hours in the day. If
only he was free to have others look for him, if only the loss of the
scrolls did not have to be such a closely guarded secret.

Elder Ryusaku said, "I understand that Yajima has given up
his search of the Kanto plain for the scrolls and turned south. Apparently he has gleaned some information from his efforts that leads him
there. I hope you will shoulder your share of the burden of this
quest. It is important to the Emperor and all of Japan. Do not fail
us."

"I shall not," Hiroki said with a confidence he did not feel, for he
had no idea where he would find the time to do the painstaking searches
the quest required.

He suddenly straightened his back and bowed.

"I shall *not!*"

■   ■   ■

"You look ready to bite someone," Shigeo said as he walked into
Matsuo's cramped, jumbled office at Intelligence headquarters.

"I am losing patience with America," Matsuo growled.

"You?" Shigeo said. "Perhaps we really *are* headed for war."

Matsuo sat and ground his teeth as he thought about the American
embargo.

They want war with us! That is the only explanation!

He was angry. He had been talking down the prospects of war
with the United States to everyone he knew, hoping that would
somehow make a difference. But instead, the events of the past few
weeks had changed the prospects from hopefully unlikely to inevitable.
As it stood now, Japan would either have to accept existence in a
hobbled, crippled, infirm state . . . or go to war.

Which suddenly made his intelligence gathering all the more
crucial.

His mind buzzed with facts and figures, elevations, depressions,
glide paths, and on and on. Commander Fuchida wanted absolute
confirmation that the water around Ford Island where the battleships
and carriers would be moored during an attack was truly only forty-five
feet deep. He was having trouble with the bomber-borne torpedoes—
they were plunging to the bottom and lodging in the mud during

practice runs—and he and Commander Genda were desperate to find a solution. Genda also had to know the thickness of the steel plates on the decks of the battleships so he would be able to devise the proper armor-piercing fittings for the bombs.

Details! Details! They made his head ache!

Shigeo dropped a photo on his desk. "It appears that the watchers are being watched."

Matsuo picked up the photo. "What's this?"

"It was taken out one of the rear windows of our Hawaiian Consulate."

"It's just a bunch of trees."

Shigeo pointed to one of those trees. "Not quite. There's someone in one of those trees."

"Really?"

"Yes. Someone surveys the consulate regularly. This fellow is the most frequent peeper."

Shigeo dropped another photo on the desk. A different lens had been used, clearly revealing the figure of a man in one of the trees studying the consulate through a pair of field glasses. His face was obscured by his hands and the field glasses themselves.

"I wonder who he's with—FBI or ONI?"

"We waited for him to come out from the trees and took this." Shigeo dropped a third photo on the desk. It showed a sandy-haired man of about thirty opening a car door. "He's with ONI. His name is—"

"Frank Slater!" Matsuo cried.

Shigeo was dumbfounded. "How—?"

Matsuo barely heard him. Frank Slater, on Oahu with U.S. Naval Intelligence, was keeping an eye on the Japanese Consulate! It was incredible!

Yet there was a queer sort of logic to it. Frank's father had been involved with the Navy, and Frank knew Japanese—Matsuo had taught him most of it. What more natural place for him to be stationed than Oahu?

"But we only found out about him today! How could you—?"

"Did you actually think you were going to tell me something I didn't already know?" Matsuo said. It never hurt to keep Shigeo slightly off balance. It made him work harder. "What else do you know about him?"

"Well . . . he's been on the island four years, works mostly as a translator, and—oh, yes, he has a Japanese wife."

A Japanese wife, Matsuo thought. *How interesting.*

"Good. Now that you know who he is, what are you going to do about him?"

"For one thing," Shigeo said, "I'm going to inform the consulate to keep its more sensitive contacts out of the backyard on Nuuanu Avenue. For another, I'm going to have some of our people investigate Lieutenant Slater's wife. Maybe we can persuade her to—"

"Stop right there!" Matsuo said. "You'll do nothing of the sort."

Shigeo looked confused. "We do it all the time. It's standard procedure when an American is married to a Japanese."

Matsuo's mind raced. Although time had tempered somewhat his youthful hatred for Frank Slater, he still harbored only contempt for the man. He was a potential enemy and Matsuo should have been willing—even anxious—to do anything necessary to squeeze some intelligence out of him. Anything.

Yet to attempt to subvert Frank's Japanese wife . . .

He shook his head. There had to be limits, even to what he would condone in the name of intelligence. But he couldn't let Shigeo know there was anything personal in the decision.

"It might alert him," Matsuo said. "If he knows we're on to him, he might decide we know about his little treetop surveillance and drop it. But if he keeps it up, we can let him see only those people and activities we want him to see in the backyard of the consulate. And that might work to our advantage."

Shigeo shrugged and nodded. "I suppose so." But he didn't seem convinced.

"Forget Frank Slater's wife," he said emphatically. "Concentrate instead on learning the thickness of the armor plating on the *Arizona*'s deck."

He felt his anger surge up again. If it was war the Americans wanted, it was war they would have—a war like they had never known before.

NOVEMBER
HONOLULU

Zach was back in port, and I could tell he was angry. He had put in a request to CINCPAC headquarters to meet with Saburo Kurusu, Japan's ambassador-at-large and general international troubleshooter, while he was passing through Hawaii, supposedly on a peace mission to the States.

"Kurusu and I go back a ways," he told me as we sat in my cubicle in the downtown DIO building. "I know I could have squeezed something out of him, maybe get a feel for how sincere is this so-called message of peace he's ferrying to Washington."

"They wouldn't okay it?"

He shook his head. "I got orders that kept me on ship doing nothing until he was gone."

I could sense his frustration. It mirrored my own. No one seemed to be taking Naval Intelligence seriously. Since Admiral Turner had taken over War Plans last year, he had bullied all the intelligence services into funneling all their gatherings through his office. ONI was nothing more than a note-keeping operation now. We could gather and translate and pass on, but we could issue no warnings, no alerts. Everything but *everything* had to go through War Plans and then maybe—if Turner saw fit—some of it would be disseminated back to us. Turner had complete control of all service intelligence. No wonder they called him Terrible Turner.

And then just last month, the powers that be had named Rear Admiral Wilkinson as Chief of Naval Intelligence—our fourth chief in a year.

Zach said, "I know Ping—"

"'Ping'?"

"His nickname. He was three years ahead of me at the Academy. A good man. Medal of Honor and all."

"But he's never had a damn thing to do with any sort of intelligence in his entire career!"

"Neither has your Captain Thornton. It seems to be a pattern, doesn't it?"

"A pattern of stupidity!"

Zach leaned forward. "Look. You've got a job to do. You go ahead and do that job as best as you can in spite of what's going on at the top, figuring that somewhere along the line it will make a difference. And above all else, you keep your mouth shut when it comes to criticizing how things are being handled at the top."

"Like you?" I said with a laugh. Everyone in Naval Intelligence knew how outspoken Zach had been about the administration of ONI.

His expression was grim. "No. Not like me. Look where I am: piloting a cruiser."

I said nothing. He had made his point.

"You get Purple magic yet?" he asked.

"No. An eighth machine became available and I pleaded for it, but it went to London."

"London! The Brits already have two!"

"I know."

He shook his head in disgust. "Keep watching the skies, my friend. Watch for an air attack on Pearl. And soon. Tojo became the Japanese premier last month."

"Yeah," I said. "*Kamisori*—'the Razor.' Not a nickname to give one much faith in Kurusu's 'mission of peace,' is it?"

"That's why I wanted a chance to speak to Kurusu. I know Tojo. He's as militaristic and nationalistic as they come. He's not particularly bright, but he's very persuasive. And those he can't persuade, he'll blackmail. He used to command the *Kempeitai,* the Japanese equivalent of the Gestapo, and still has strong ties there. I know for a fact that he's got dossiers on just above everyone in the Japanese government. He became premier without giving up the posts of War Minister and Home Minister. Believe me, he did not come into all that power simply on brains and good looks!"

We laughed about that, then Zach went back to the *Salt Lake City* and I went home to Meiko. My time with her was the only time I could relax and feel real again. Most days my jaw ached from gritting my teeth. After my talk with Zach, I needed to be with her more than ever.

The apartment was empty when I got home so I fiddled with some of the paperwork I'd brought home from Pearl. I knew where Meiko was: walking the Ala Moana beach. She did that a lot. I was pretty sure she was happy being married to me. I did my best to make her happy, but it was so hard to tell with someone like Meiko. She wasn't raised to expect love and happiness in marriage. If it happened—fine. It's a bonus. But it was not the primary purpose of marriage for the Japanese. Preservation of the family and, through the family, the social order— that's what marriage was all about in Japan.

But those walks—I had a feeling she was thinking about *him,* about Matsuo. She never mentioned him but I sensed she wasn't over him yet, that she might never be. I sensed that he had touched a place in her that I hadn't found yet.

But I was searching for it, searching all the time.

TOKYO

Matsuo tossed and rolled on the futon in his apartment. The tension, the excitement, the electric charge of the coming conflict, had made sleep increasingly difficult, almost impossible at times. The very air seemed to crackle with the all-or-nothing sentiments of the premier and his supporters.

Matsuo had taken an instant disliking to General Hideki Tojo. He found the man's personal manner offensive, particularly in his al most slavish imitation of the German fascists. Tojo was considered by many to be a clear thinker and an incisive speaker. Matsuo did not share that opinion, deciding that the general probably earned that reputation because he was much more direct than usual in his pattern of speech, cutting through the typical indirection of Japanese discussion.

But he had to admit the man was effective as a leader. He had infused the country with a war mentality. He had started it in motion and was increasing the momentum. Even Matsuo felt himself caught up in the heady atmosphere, the giddy challenge of risking everything on a national level.

He was even beginning to think there might be a chance of winning. In the hours before dawn when he would lie awake and try to sort out and order the myriad facts he had been accumulating since his first conference with Yamamoto, a small voice would whisper, *This is madness. Madness!* and he would listen to that voice and agree with it. But during the day, the frenetic commotion of his work schedule would drown it out.

All was ready. Commander Genda had solved the problem of the nose-diving torpedoes by fixing simple wooden stabilizers to their fins. Fins had been fitted on armor-piercing shells, readying them for the sixteen-inch armor plate of the battleship decks. The cruise ship, *Taiyo Maru*, had made a test run along the intended course of the carrier fleet, going north and then running east halfway between the Aleutians and Midway, then turning south toward the Hawaiians. Not a single American vessel or plane was sighted during the entire trip.

With the arrival of the carrier *Shokaku* just yesterday, the strike force of carriers, destroyers, cruisers, submarines, and tankers—thirty-two ships in all—was now fully assembled at Tankan Bay in the chilly Kuriles and awaiting the word to go.

There would be no troop ships coming along. Tojo and his War Ministry had vetoed the plan to take and hold the Hawaiians because of the extra manpower it would involve. Matsuo suspected that Japan would regret that decision, but it was out of his hands.

As the sky began to turn the color of the April cherry blossoms on the banks of the Edogawa, Matsuo gave up on sleep. He rolled up his futon, stowed it in the closet, and went outside for the traditional cold morning bath.

When he got to Naval Intelligence, Shigeo was already there. Although Matsuo had said not a word to him of Yamamoto's plan, Shigeo had deduced what was afoot long ago. He had the good manners, however, not to mention his deduction, although his increased enthusiasm for Pearl Harbor intelligence spoke volumes.

He handed Matsuo some recent aerial photographs of Pearl. They were stunning.

"Where did you get these?"

"I had one of our people take a tourist sight-seeing flight in a rental plane out of John Rogers Airport. As you can see, the Pearl anchorage is filling up. Lots of big ships, two of them major carriers—the *Lexington* and the *Enterprise*."

Matsuo studied the top photo. "You're sure of their identity?"

"Confirmed and reconfirmed."

"Battleships?"

"Four in port."

Matsuo shuffled through the photos. The four battleships anchored off Ford Island in the middle of the harbor looked utterly defenseless. Something about that bothered him. Shigeo must have noted his troubled expression.

"Something wrong?" he said as he lit another cigarette.

"I don't know. I have a strange feeling about all this."

"Why? It's perfect!"

"Perhaps it's *too* perfect."

The harbor was so open, the ships so vulnerable, it all gave Matsuo a vague, eerie sense of invitation, as if a giant finger were beckoning behind the photographs.

But that was ridiculous.

He handed the packet back to Shigeo and glanced through the other piles of prints on the desk. There were photos of the Schofield, Wheeler, Hickam, and Ewa airbases, and many of the beaches west of Pearl Harbor and eastward toward Honolulu. He had ordered these in anticipation of the now-scrubbed invasion of the island.

He came upon one that showed a lone woman strolling the sand near the waterline. He laughed and held it up to Shigeo.

"Your photographer has an eye for the women as well as the military installations."

Shigeo grinned. "Sure. Helps maintain the cover of a camera hobbyist."

Matsuo was about to toss the photo back into the pile when something about the woman caught his eye. It was a long shot and her facial features were blurred, but something about the shape of her head, the way she held her shoulders struck a resonance in a corner of his memory. Something familiar about her. The memory dangled just out of reach.

"You like her?" Shigeo said. "She's a pretty one."

"How can you tell? You can't see her face."

"Oh, we've got plenty of other shots of her. She walks that stretch of beach frequently. She's married to an intelligence officer. You said not to approach her, but I felt it wouldn't hurt to build a photo file on her anyway."

The memory was creeping closer . . . almost in sight now . . .

"I don't remember telling you not to approach anyone."

"You most certainly did. Back in August. You were pretty emphatic about it, too: Leave Lieutenant Frank Slater's wife alone."

Mrs. Frank Slater!

And then it came to him. The woman in the photo—she reminded him of Meiko. Frank had known Meiko, had been very obviously attracted to her during their college years. Had he found and married someone who resembled her?

A chill ran up Matsuo's spine. It was an eerie thought.

"What's Mrs. Slater's name?"

Shigeo pulled open a drawer and pulled out a slim file. He flipped through it and pulled out a white card.

"Meiko," he said. "Meiko Slater."

Matsuo felt his legs go soft on him. He quickly pulled a chair around from the side of the desk and dropped into it. He opened his mouth to speak but no sound came forth. Finally he managed a single word.

"Photos."

Shigeo was looking at him strangely as he handed him the file. Matsuo ignored him. Didn't even bother with attempting an explanation. He simply sat there with the file in his hands, trembling inside and out.

"Are you all right? You look like you're going to be sick."

Matsuo could barely hear him. *Could it be her? Could she be alive?*

After a while he calmed himself with the assurance that Frank Slater could not possibly be married to Meiko—*his* Meiko. Still, as he opened the file, he felt his entire body break out in a cold sweat.

He saw the top photo. It was the face of a Japanese woman. Even through the black-and-white graininess he could see the perfect skin and lips, the almond eyes that spoke to his soul. Matsuo held his breath as he flipped through the other photos. They all confirmed the first.

It was Meiko Mazaki.

"She's alive!" he cried, leaping up and throwing the folder of photos into the air. "She's alive!" He was laughing and crying simultaneously as he hugged the astonished Shigeo who must have thought that his superior had gone completely mad.

Meiko was alive. On Oahu. Married to Frank Slater.

He didn't care if she was married to Franklin D. Roosevelt—she was alive! And he didn't care if he had to lie, cheat, falsify reports, or steal a cruiser himself, one way or another Matsuo would find a way to get to Hawaii and bring her back!

DECEMBER 2
TOKYO

Hiroki sat in the high-ceilinged conference room in the Navy Building and listened to the foreign minister with growing irritation.

"I have come to learn that we are planning to commence hostilities against America and Britain this weekend," Minister Togo was saying, "but I have not been told where or exactly when."

Shigenori Togo was being difficult, as usual. It seemed to be his nature. In 1939, as ambassador to Berlin, he had opposed an alliance with Germany and it had been necessary to pull him from that post and send him to Moscow. The pompous little man might be foreign minister, but he had no right to dictate policy to the Supreme Command. He strutted around the meeting room shaking his index finger in the air like a teacher trying to impress some point upon his students. He was especially bold because Premier Tojo was absent.

"We must beg secrecy on that," Army Chief of Staff Sugiyama replied.

"You may beg secrecy on the *where*, but I must know the *when* in order to prepare a formal declaration of war."

Nagano, Navy Chief of Staff, said, "But we are planning a surprise attack."

"Without a formal declaration?" His tone and expression were frankly shocked. "That is contrary to procedures in The Hague Conventions!"

"We need the element of surprise to guarantee our southern objectives."

"At the cost of our national honor?"

He is beginning to sound like Matsuo and Yamamoto, Hiroki thought, but held his tongue for now.

"It is too late," Admiral Nagano said. "The plans are already set in motion."

"Then change the plans. I demand a formal notice of termination of negotiations and declaration of war. And I am quite sure the Emperor will feel the same way should I ask him."

This had gone far enough. Hiroki knew it was time for him to speak. "May I have the honor of offering a comment?" he said.

Foreign Minister Togo nodded. "Of course, Okumo-san. I am

most anxious to hear the thoughts of the Empire's first Minister of Military and Economic Coordination."

Hiroki made a tiny bow. His was a new post with a mandate to see to it that the precious resources in the soon-to-be-conquered territories were put to full use in an efficient, organized manner. It was a sinecure at the moment. His real work would begin with the war.

"The foreign minister is quite correct," he said. "Japan must act in accordance with The Hague Conventions. A formal declaration will be sent to Washington before a single shot is fired."

He noted the shocked faces of the members of the High Command with no little amusement.

"And will you assure me that there will be an adequate interval between the declaration and the attack?" Togo said, obviously suspicious.

"We will adhere to the very letter of The Hague Conventions."

Foreign Minister Togo bowed. "Excellent! Excellent!" He bowed again and left the room—which erupted with confused and angry murmurs as soon as the doors were closed.

"Be calm," Hiroki said.

"I cannot be calm," Nagano cried. "If we follow The Hague Conventions, we must call off the Hawaii raid! We will lose too many aircraft if they are waiting for us!"

"Have any of you read The Hague Conventions?"

They hesitated, then all shook their heads.

"Then allow me to inform you: The Conventions prescribe no minimum time interval. We shall give Washington half an hour's notice. The letter of the law will be satisfied but they will not have time to mobilize a defense."

The members of the High Command smiled and laughed as they clustered around and clapped him on the back. Sake was poured and Hiroki offered the toast that had become his trademark:

"To the day we have tea in Washington!"

HONOLULU

Tuesday started off bad and got steadily worse.

I was already walking on pins and needles—had been since Thanksgiving when the Navy Department issued a war warning, saying that negotiations had broken off and that "an aggressive move by

Japan is expected within the next few days." The trouble was, nobody seemed to think that Pearl would be the object of the "aggressive move." Everyone seemed convinced that Japan would strike south, at the Philippines. Or maybe at Wake. But definitely not at Hawaii. The following day, Admiral Halsey took his flagship, the carrier *Enterprise*, to Wake to beef up defenses there.

CINCPAC's response to the war warning? A Stage One alert. Which meant that security around the base would be tightened against possible enemy sabotage. No more.

I had spent a very bad weekend watching the harbor fill up with more and more ships, watching Battleship Row off Ford Island thicken with heavies. We had eighty-odd ships in port—eight big battleships plus the carrier *Lexington* among them. It was a tempting target. So when Monday morning came, I was relieved that Pearl was still in one piece, but I was exhausted and frazzled, too. Here it was Tuesday and I still hadn't quite recovered from the weekend.

I didn't need bad news, but I began getting it almost immediately.

Pete Jeffries, an ensign from the radio monitoring section, started things on their downhill course by sticking his head into my office and saying,

"Guess what the Japanese Fleet did yesterday?" His tone was anything but ominous; perturbed, mostly.

"What now?"

"They changed all their call signs again."

"*Again?* They did that just a month ago."

"Well, I guess they liked it so much they wanted to do it again." He sighed. "Now we've got to start from scratch figuring out who's talking to who out there."

"Good luck!" I said, and smiled as he waved good-bye. But the smile disappeared as soon as he was gone. It was unheard-of for a navy to change the radio call signals of its warships twice in the space of one month. It required a massive amount of red tape and paperwork, and usually caused a day or two of confusion in the warships' own communications. It was not something a fleet did without sufficient cause and careful consideration. To change the call signals on November 1, and then again on December 1, had to mean something. But what?

I worked through lunch translating deciphered lower-level messages from Japan into English. Garbage—nothing but garbage. Here I was, translating worthless conversations that shouldn't even have been ciphered while the really important stuff—the Purple communiques— were sailing right past us on the airwaves, to be deciphered and translated in Washington, and then trickled down to us here on Oahu when the Washington office saw fit. For eight months now I had been trying to get a Purple magic machine for the Fourteenth District ONI but it was like butting my head against a stone wall. The Washington office kept telling me that it was assessing the situation to see if there was sufficient need for Fourteenth ONI to have Purple magic; every time I called to see what progress had been made, I got the old bureaucratic standby: "We're working on it."

Harry Thornton was no help. His attitude seemed to be that if God had intended for us to have a Purple magic machine, we'd have one. And why fret? The Washington office would let us know if anything important came through. Besides, not having Purple magic meant that much less for Fourteenth ONI to do.

Things got worse after lunch when I went to take my turn monitoring our wiretap into the Japanese consulate. I was relieving Jeff Kaluta. He was there, but he was disassembling all our equipment.

"What's going on?" I asked. "Something wrong with the tap?"

He gave me a disgusted look. "Yeah. We don't have one anymore."

"Oh, hell! How did they catch on?"

"They didn't." He stepped behind me and closed the door to the room. "It was cancelled on our end."

As I stood there in mute shock, he told me the whole story.

A linesman from the Mutual Telephone Company had discreetly reported to ONI and to the FBI that he had come across both our wiretaps into the Japanese consulate on Nuuanu Avenue. He hadn't mentioned anything to the Japanese consulate and he wanted to know what we wanted him to do about them. Bob Shivers over at the FBI office in the Federal Building told him not to touch the FBI line and forget about what he had found.

"But what happened to ours?"

"That asshole Thornton cancelled it!" Kaluta said.

Before I knew exactly where I was going, I was out the door, down to the street, into my car, and headed for Pearl. I took the short route and ignored the scenery. I was in a door-kicking, wall-pounding rage, and I hadn't cooled much by the time I got to Harry's office. But I managed to tuck it out of sight when I walked through the door.

"Yes, Frank?" he said from behind his cluttered desk. "What's on your mind?"

"If I may speak plainly: Why the hell did you cancel our wiretap into the Japanese consulate?"

Thornton's eyebrows rose in surprise. "I should think the reasoning would be obvious. Japanese-American relations are at the rupture point. That linesman is going to talk; word about the tap is going to spread. With all the agents the Japs have on Oahu, how long do you think it'll be before they know they're tapped? That might be all they need to set them off."

My jaw ached. "Sir, if Japanese-American relations are as bad as you say, doesn't that make an inside line on what they're doing more important than ever? *Especially* since we don't have Purple magic?"

"I never approved of that tap, but since it was operating when I arrived, I let it stand. Public knowledge of a wiretap makes us look sneaky. I think we should be above that sort of thing."

"A war warning has been issued. Don't you think—?"

"If the Japs hit anywhere, it won't be here—it'll be to their south. That's the area they want. They won't even come this way—even Wake is too far east for them. Remember: They're after oil and raw materials. There's nothing out here they want."

I went to the window and pointed out to the harbor. "There'll be ninety-six ships sitting out there this weekend—including heavy battleships and a carrier—"

"No carrier," Thronton said. "The *Lexington* weighs anchor for Midway on Thursday."

"Great!" I said. I could hear my voice rising but I couldn't help it. "Just great! We get a war warning and we send the *Big E* and the *Lex*—our extra sources of battle-ready aircraft—off into the Western Pacific!"

"We have aircraft!"

"Sure! But we don't have the recon planes to give us fair warning."

"Have you forgotten the fifty-four brand-new PBY-5's we just got?"

"No. I haven't forgotten them. But they're so new they're still on shakedown flights and we don't have any spare parts. We need *recon!*"

"Halsey's conducting recon all the way to Wake, and Newton will be doing the same when he takes the *Lex* to Midway. We'll have plenty of recon."

"Not to the north where we need it most. You heard Zach— they'll hit us from the north on a weekend."

Thornton laughed. "You and Zacharias! You've both been reading too many Yellow Peril novels! Too many pulp magazines!"

His laughter only infuriated me. He had seen me reading a copy of *Operator #5* a few months ago and wasn't going to let me forget it.

"We aren't in a novel now—this is real life!"

"And real life is going to remain peaceful here on Oahu."

I wanted to scream. *Isn't anybody listening?* But I said nothing. It was no use. There was nothing to do but salute and leave. Thornton was a hopeless case, but he was no worse than anybody else. Everyone seemed to have their heads in the sand. If only someone like Zach were in charge—*then* we'd be ready!

But he wasn't.

And we weren't.

And I felt sick about it. But the worst was yet to come. When I got back to the Honolulu office, I found Pete Jeffries pacing the floor outside the radio room. His expression was grim.

"Still haven't figured out those new call signals yet?"

He glared at me. "You think you're funny?" The malevolence in his voice stopped me cold.

"What's wrong, Pete?"

"You mean you haven't heard?"

"Heard what?"

"We've lost Japanese Carrier Divisions One and Two."

I felt sharp spicules of ice form in my stomach. "What do you mean, 'lost'?"

"*Lost*—as in 'can't find.' They're gone. It's as if the sea swallowed them up. Divisions Three and Four are in the Marshalls and off Formosa. But One and Two . . . shit! We haven't heard a peep out of them in days."

"You mean they could be sitting up north of Kauai right now and you wouldn't know?"

Jeffries looked at me. "With their absolute radio silence and our shitty reconnaissance—yeah! They could be rounding Diamond Head right now and I wouldn't know it!" He laughed. "But don't worry. I'm ninety-five percent sure they're heading into the China Sea to do some dirty work there!"

Don't worry. That was a laugh. I called it a day after that. I didn't want to hear any more. I had an awful feeling that those two "lost" carrier divisions were slipping around to our north and setting up for a strike on Pearl. But I seemed to be the only one in the entire Hawaiian archipelago who was worried about it.

And no one would listen to me.

DECEMBER 3

I made sure to drive by the Japanese consulate on my way to DIO on Wednesday morning. Since we no longer had the phone tap, my little perch in the trees had suddenly graduated from a charade to a vital source of intelligence. What I saw made me glad I'd come.

Smoke was rising from the backyard of the consulate. A group of so-called assistant consuls were standing around a rusty garbage can patiently throwing papers into a roaring fire.

I hurried downtown to my office and put in a call to Bob Shivers at the FBI offices. He confirmed my worst fears.

"Yeah," he said. "They were discussing it on the phone most of last night. They got the word from Tokyo to burn all codebooks except one copy each of type O and type L. How'd you know?"

"Because I just took a look in their backyard. They're following orders."

"Look on the bright side," he said. "It means they'll be using PA-K2 from now on. That's easier to decipher than the J-series. But if you've got an ulcer and you really want to flare it up, check the message Kita got from the foreign ministry yesterday."

"What's it say?"

"Do your own translation. I don't want to influence you."

I hurried to the pile of deciphered messages awaiting translation and flipped through until I found one headed, "Japanese Foreign Ministry to Chief Consul Kita." I started translating. The message was a direct, undisguised espionage request. The most chilling section:

> In view of the present situation, the presence in port of warships, airplane carriers, and cruisers is of utmost importance. Hereafter, to the utmost of your ability, let me know day by day. Wire me in each case whether or not there are any obstruction balloons above Pearl Harbor or if there are any indications that they will be sent up. Also advise me whether the warships are provided with torpedo nets.

"In port." I had never seen the Japanese interested in which ships were *in* port. They had always been more interested in which ships we had cruising around. Why the sudden interest in what ships were anchored in Pearl? Why the interest in the presence of barrage balloons and torpedo nets? Unless . . .

I put in a call to Thornton. He was in a meeting. I sent over a copy of the message with a note stating that Kita and his staff were burning their codebooks and shouldn't we let CINCPAC know? Then I waited for his reply.

It took him until late afternoon to get back to me. His reaction?

"I see no great significance in this information."

No great significance! Japan was burning her codebooks and destroying her own Purple machines all over the world. That, to my mind, was the action of a country readying to go to war with the

world. But if that wasn't enough, her Honolulu consulate was sending out daily reports on the numbers of ships in port at Pearl! *In
port!*

I hurried back to the house and looked for Meiko. I needed to put
this crazy, miserable, rotten day behind me. And the only way I knew to
do that was to sit on that frayed old couch in our tiny living room and
hold her in my arms. Somehow, with her beside me, the world made
some sort of sense. Not a whole hell of a lot, but more than it did
without her.

But she wasn't there. Her bike was gone, which meant she was
over at Ala Moana walking the beach again.

It was a fitting capper on the day.

■ ■ ■

Meiko walked her usual route. Sometimes she thought that if it
weren't for the tides, she could have worn a trench in the sand by now.
She walked the waterline, low tide now, and looked for sea glass. She
had hundreds of pieces at home but she was always looking for more.
Brown and white and green were easy to find, but blue was rare, and
red even rarer. The water was gentle here. Further out, waves crashed
on the coral reefs.

She was walking west, and as she glanced up she saw a man ahead
of her silhouetted against the lowering sun. He looked so odd standing
there fully dressed in a straw fedora, a shirt, and long pants, with his
shod feet in the water and the water lapping at his cuffs. He appeared to
be waiting for someone. He was staring at her.

She ignored him and returned her concentration to the waterline.
Men frequently approached her as she walked the sand, but she had
become adept at making it clear that she wanted no company. Frank, at
least, understood her need to be alone at times and did not press to
accompany her. Thank the gods for Frank! Sometimes she wondered
what she had ever done to deserve him.

She only wished she could do more to ease his burdens. She knew
how he agonized over the growing inevitability of war with Japan, not
for his own sake or even for his country's, but for her. He knew the
agony it would cause her to live among Americans while they were at
war with her homeland—

Meiko stopped herself. She *had* to stop thinking of Japan as home;
Hawaii was home now.

With Matsuo dead and everyone back in Japan undoubtedly
believing her dead, she felt as if she had been cut free of chu and ko and
all the other on of Japanese life. How could she have obligations to
people who believed her dead?

She looked up again and saw that she was closer to the man.

He was still standing there, staring at her. With the sun glaring behind him she could not see his features. Since it was clear that he wasn't going to move, she would have to go around him. She gave him a wide berth, averting her eyes as she passed on his landward side. As she came abreast of him, he removed his hat and turned toward her.

"Meiko?"

His voice was hoarse, but there was something familiar about it. She glanced up and got her first look at his face.

Her knees gave way beneath her. *Matsuo!* She tumbled forward but he caught her. As he supported her before him, she gazed into his face. It couldn't be, but it was! Those same intense eyes, that same broken nose.

"I've been waiting all day for you to come!" he said in a voice thick with emotion, nodding while tears filled his eyes as they filled her own. "Yes! I'm alive, and so are you!"

With a sob of joy Meiko fell into his arms and clung to him as if her very life depended on it.

Matsuo! My Matsuo is back from the dead!

■ ■ ■

I paced back and forth from room to room through the apartment. I picked up the *Advertiser* and skipped the news. I went straight to the funny page. I looked at *Joe Palooka* and *Li'l Abner* but didn't read the words. All I could see was the pictures and they looked like they had been drawn by the same guy. I tried reading my new copy of Raymond Chandler's latest, *Farewell, My Lovely*, but was too tense to concentrate. I listened to "Jack Armstrong" on KGMB, then turned it off. I was on my second scotch and water but the liquor wasn't calming me down. I needed Meiko. Where was she? She usually didn't stay out this long. I began to wonder if something had happened to her. There were some wild drivers on that road to the beach and she had only been on a bicycle.

I was worried and I was looking for something to do, so I decided to take a ride down to Ala Moana and find her.

■ ■ ■

When they had finally stopped their sobbing, and when Meiko had recovered sufficiently from the shock of seeing him alive to trust her legs to bear her weight, they walked back to the banyans that bordered the beach and sat beneath a big one. They told each other their own side of what happened that July day in 1937.

"Poor Cho!" Meiko said when Matsuo had told her whose body Kikou had seen on the floor of his room.

"I felt that way too, at first," Matsuo said. "But no longer. His loose tongue led to our being discovered, and his suicide resulted in driving you away from your family and your homeland."

Meiko was surprised by the bitterness in his tone. She had never heard him speak that way. She looked at him closely for the first time since he had revealed himself—she had been too awed and numb with shock and joy to do any more until now.

Matsuo had changed. He had always had an intensity about him, a driving energy that seemed to propel him through life. But he was incandescent now, as if someone had twisted a knob and turned up the current flowing through him.

"I've come to take you back," he said, holding her hands and looking deep into her eyes. "Back home."

How many times during the years she had thought him dead had she dreamed of this moment? How many times had she fantasized that Matsuo would somehow appear before her alive and well and take her back home? *Home!* A cascade of images splashed before Meiko's eyes—her parents, the house, the green islands of the Inland Sea, shrines, temples, Shinto festivals, *bento* lunches on the streets of Tokyo—

—and then she remembered Frank and gasped. The blinding joy suffusing her suddenly dimmed. She knew in that instant that she faced a terrible choice.

"Matsuo, I'm . . . I'm married."

"I know." She saw sparks in his eyes but his voice was calm. "To Frank Slater. But that doesn't matter now."

"It *does* matter!" she said, feeling a brief flare of anger.

"You married him in the false belief that I was dead. You can't be held to that."

"We married each other in good faith. I made a vow. But it's more than that, Matsuo. He gave my life back to me when I thought there was nothing left. He's been very good *for* me and very good *to* me."

Matsuo watched her, nodding. "I see that. And for that I am indebted to him." He paused, then said, "Do you love him?"

Meiko had been dreading that question, but she had to face it. "I'll never love anyone the way I love you, Matsuo. But yes, I love Frank. In a different way, with a different part of me."

Matsuo looked away. She could see the muscles in his jaw working as he stared out to sea. His voice was bitter when he finally spoke to her.

"What a fool I was! What a dreamer! I thought it would be so easy, like a scene out of a movie. I would reveal myself to you, we would embrace passionately, and then I'd whisk you back to Japan where we would live happily ever after!"

"Matsuo—"

He turned toward her again. "You have to come back with me, Meiko!"

Part of her wanted to forget everything here in Hawaii and run back to Japan with him. But another part called up the vision of a good, kind, decent man sitting and worrying, waiting faithfully for the return of the woman he loved and trusted.

"I can't just leave."

"And I've spent four and a half years mourning you. Now I find you're alive—I can't lose you again, Meiko! I *won't!*"

"I mourned you, too. And I never stopped loving you. And I want to go back with you. But I can't right now."

"You must!"

"Will you think better of me if I desert Frank without a word of explanation? I know what I would think of myself."

That gave him pause.

"Give me time to find a way to tell him."

"There isn't time!" he blurted. "There's less than a week!"

Although the sun was still warm on her skin, Meiko felt an icy blast of cold against her back. "What do you mean?"

He looked away again. "I shouldn't have said that. Forget what you heard."

"You're going to attack the American fleet!" she whispered. "That's it, isn't it? This weekend!"

"Meiko," he said, his eyes wide as he gripped her arm, "you mustn't even think that, let alone repeat it!"

"But Frank expects it!" she said. "He's waiting for it! An air attack from the north on a Saturday or Sunday morning. He thought it might come last weekend. He barely slept the entire time!"

Matsuo's eyes had widened almost to the bulging point as she spoke. "You mean it's a trap?"

"No! No one will listen to him!"

Matsuo seemed relieved, but Meiko felt as if the air had thickened. It was difficult to breathe.

"It's going to happen, isn't it? There's going to be a sneak attack and then war."

"Not a sneak attack. We will declare war first, then attack immediately after."

"But why? *Why?*"

"It has to be," he said, his expression growing fierce. "The Americans have given us no choice!"

Meiko stood up. "There's always a choice. There has to be! You can't—" She gasped as she glanced around the edge of the banyan trunk and saw Frank walking in their direction along the pavement that skirted the beach.

"What's wrong?" Matsuo said, beginning to rise to her side.

"Stay back!" she said, not looking at him and trying not to move her lips. "It's Frank! He mustn't see you!"

"Go to him," Matsuo whispered. "Keep him from coming any closer. I will be right here tomorrow afternoon, waiting to hear your decision."

I don't want to decide! Meiko thought, but she said nothing. Instead, she waved to Frank and ran toward him, biting back a sob when she saw his face brighten at the sight of her, loathing herself for smiling and acting as if nothing were wrong, as if nothing had changed.

But everything had changed.

■   ■   ■

Matsuo waited as long as he could. Finally, when the tension became unbearable, he rose to his knees and peeked around the trunk. He spotted Meiko and Frank about fifty yards down the road. Their backs were to him. They were walking away. As he watched, he saw Frank put an arm over Meiko's shoulders and hug her close.

That simple gesture, the warmth, the intimacy, the possessiveness it implied filled Matsuo with a sudden, blinding rage. He wanted to scream at the top of his lungs and sprint down the road to where they were; he wanted to rip Frank's offending arm from its socket and cast it into the sea. He drove his fist against the trunk and closed his eyes.

Soon the rage passed, leaving him weak. When he looked up again, Meiko and Frank were out of sight. He slumped against the trunk.

What was happening to him? He had never flown into such rages before. It wasn't like him. It was frightening. He had too much to do, too many responsibilities to allow violent emotions to threaten his judgment.

Perhaps that was the problem: too many responsibilities, too many demands coordinating all the intelligence regarding Pearl Harbor. And now, sneaking into Honolulu to meet Meiko, risking his family honor and his commission by fabricating a need to contact this U.S. intelligence officer's wife, saying she possessed sensitive information about the harbor defenses. And then not having the meeting go the way he had hoped . . .

No wonder he felt like a grenade with the pin pulled.

He replaced his hat on his head, rose to his feet, and walked down to the waterline, thinking. What if Meiko decided to stay with Frank? What if she mentioned his slip about the attack on the fleet? That would confirm the suspicions Meiko said Frank already had. And with Meiko's story to back him up, Frank could convince the fleet to scatter throughout the Pacific, making an attack on Pearl Harbor useless.

Matsuo looked out to sea. The Strike Force had already covered more than half the distance to Oahu by now.

What have I done?

■ ■ ■

Meiko lay awake in the bed next to Frank. She had given up even hoping for sleep. She felt as if she were being torn apart. All she could think about was Matsuo—his being alive all these four-odd years, his almost magical appearance here on Oahu, and what she had learned from him today. He had changed so. He'd been more intense, more driven today than she had ever seen him, but she sensed that inside he was still the same old Matsuo.

Yet she didn't want to leave Frank. How could she desert him? He didn't deserve to be hurt like that.

And yet she realized she could not keep herself away from Matsuo now that she knew he was alive. She wanted to be with Matsuo, tonight and every night. She still loved him, had never stopped loving him.

What am I going to do?

The question tortured her. She whimpered softly now with the pain of it.

"You okay?" Frank said from beside her.

"Yes." How long had he been awake? "I just wish I could sleep."

"Something on your mind?" he said, moving closer. "Want to talk about it?"

Please don't be nice, she thought, feeling miserable and unworthy of him. *Please don't be kind and understanding.*

"I—I was thinking about war," she said, and in a way she had been, for Matsuo's slip about an air attack on the fleet had cast a malignant light on his return.

"Aw, don't think about that," he said, slipping his arms around her and hugging her. "That's my job."

"But I don't want anything to happen to you when the war comes."

"Don't worry about me. Guys in my line of intelligence usually get posted behind the lines. We work with radios, not guns."

"But what about this weekend? What if the attack you're expecting actually takes place? Please promise me one thing. No matter what happens, please don't go to the harbor."

"If it's on a Saturday or Sunday morning—and that's when it will happen if it happens at all—I'll be right here with you."

But what if I'm not here? What if I'm gone? Then where will he be? She wanted to tell him what she knew of Japan's plan, but that would mean revealing that Matsuo was alive and here on Oahu. And she couldn't do that. At least not yet.

Maybe not ever.

They lay quietly, side by side in the dark. Soon Frank's breathing became slow and rhythmical as he fell asleep. But for Meiko there was no sleep.

DECEMBER 4

There comes a point when you have to doubt yourself. When everyone thinks you're wrong, maybe you are. When everyone suspects that you're a little bit crazy, maybe you are.

At least you have to wonder.

On Thursday morning I stood on the bulkheading by the Navy Hospital and wondered about myself as I watched Task Force 2, consisting of Pearl's last carrier, the *Lexington,* along with three heavy cruisers and five destroyers, crawl like snails through the narrow channel opposite Waipio Point on their way to Midway. We would have no carrier here until the *Saratoga* pulled in from Puget.

I wished to hell *all* the ships were leaving. Then there would be no reason for anyone to be interested in Pearl. But one glance to my right was all I needed to set my nerves on edge: Eight heavies—the battleships *Pennsylvania, Arizona, West Virginia, California, Maryland, Nevada, Oklahoma,* and *Tennessee*—were lined up two by two along the eastern shore of Ford Island like clay pigeons in a shooting gallery. And more were due in this weekend. We would have more ships in harbor on Saturday and Sunday than at any other time since Fourth of July weekend.

Mentally, I capitulated. I was powerless, so I decided to back off. I had let myself get involved to the point of obsession. Maybe I had lost my perspective. Maybe it was time to just sit back and let the big boys do what they were getting paid for. Maybe Admiral Turner had special reasons for filtering every scrap of intelligence through War Plans and only trickling out what he considered absolutely necessary. Maybe Harry Thornton was privy to what Turner and Stark and all the Navy Department brass were up to and couldn't let me in on it.

All my problems could have been due to the simple fact that I was in an awkward position: Because of my post in translation, I had access to a significant amount of intelligence regarding Japan; I probably knew as much as anyone on Oahu. What I knew had me worried, but I obviously didn't have the whole picture. Those who did have the whole picture did not seem to be worried.

So what was the point in my making myself sick when I didn't know the whole story? It seemed to be affecting my marriage, as well. Meiko was not herself. My fault, I was sure. My obsession with the growing inevitability of a Japanese sneak attack on Pearl must have finally taken its toll on her. She was like a coiled spring this morning, ready to break loose and bounce off the walls at the slightest jolt. She kept starting sentences and never finishing them.

But things were going to change now. I was going to put this sneak attack business out of my head and just go on with my routine daily duties. I was going to get things back to normal again.

■ ■ ■

Meiko tried to melt in the fervor of Matsuo's embrace, but she was too tight, too tense.

She had found him on the beach and told him, "I'll go back with you." Upon hearing those words, he had shouted with joy, wrapped her in his arms, and swung her around. She wanted to share that joy, but could not. Not yet.

She hadn't been able to find a way to leave Frank.

"But not today," she said. "I need more time."

"There isn't much," he said, stepping back and holding her at arm's length. "It has to be now."

She shook her head. "No! I can't! How much time do I have?"

"You must leave here . . ." He paused, his expression grim. "By Saturday night at the very latest."

Meiko felt a wave of nausea ripple through her stomach. She could barely speak. "Then on Sunday morning . . . ?"

Matsuo said nothing at first. He only stared into her eyes. Finally he said, "You have said nothing to Frank? About me? About the attack?"

She could only shake her head.

"Good! For a moment yesterday . . ." He waved a hand in the air. "Never mind. But listen: As long as you will be here a little longer, there is something I want you to do if the opportunity arises."

"Oh, no!" she cried. "You wouldn't ask me! Please don't—"

"It's not as callous as it sounds. I'm not asking you to purposely try to steal or extract information from him, but if the opportunity presents itself—"

"No! How can you ask me to do that?"

"It's not for me! It's for *you!*"

That stunned her. "For me? How?"

He looked away. "I don't want my brother and his type to look upon you as someone slinking back to Japan because of the war—an errant child running home before the storm. I want you to return with your head held high."

Meiko could see the truth in Matsuo's eyes. He *was* thinking of her. He truly cared how her homecoming was perceived. But he was asking her not only to leave Frank, but to betray him as well.

"The attack will be launched no matter what," he went on, seeming to read her mind. "Neither you nor I can change that. But if you can just bring something, any scrap—"

"Frank often brings papers home," she said. "But I don't think they're worth anything. I'll keep watch for anything useful, though." She felt she could safely make that promise, secure in the knowledge that nothing of value would be available to her.

"Good." Matsuo smiled and patted the sand beside him. "Now, sit here and let me tell you of the life we'll have back in Tokyo."

But Meiko barely heard him. An icy hand of guilt and fear had gripped her throat.

"That man," she said, restraining herself from pointing. "The one in the flowered shirt at the water's edge. I'm not sure, but I think this is the third time he has walked by."

Matsuo glanced at him, then away. "You may be right. I haven't been watching. My eyes are only for you when you're near."

Normally those words would have made her blush, but now they swept by her, unnoticed in the wash of her anxiety. What if she were caught with Matsuo? Then she would be responsible not only for disgracing her family four years ago, but disgracing Frank as well.

"I must go."

"Yes," he said in a low voice. "Go. We shouldn't meet here again. I drove through an area called Halewa Heights last night in a car from the consulate. I will go there after sunset tonight and the next three nights and wait until eleven o'clock. You need only to drive or ride your bicycle to a point just above the developed section there and I will find you. But you must come before eleven. After that, it will be too late."

"Too late? Why?"

"No time to explain now. It's best that you don't spend any more time with me here in public." He stood up. "Tonight. Come tonight. *Please.*"

With that, he strode away. Meiko noticed that as Matsuo walked in the general direction of the man in the flowered shirt, the man quickly turned and hurried away.

With tension cramping her muscles and tying her intestines in knots, Meiko headed home.

■　■　■

That night, as Matsuo waited in the consulate car, he stared down at Pearl Harbor spread out far below him. The view from Halewa Heights was perfect. With a simple pair of field glasses, he could see every nook and cranny of the east loch, could almost count the antennae of the battleships lined up in pairs this side of Ford Island. His only regret was that the *Lexington* was gone. He and Yamamoto had hoped to catch one of the Pacific Fleet's three carriers in port; but with eight—*eight!*—heavy battleships as sitting targets, it seemed greedy to ask for more.

Earlier this evening in Honolulu, he had had a long talk with Yoshikawa, one of Naval Intelligence's agents assigned to the Hawaiian consulate as a minor official. They had met in the back room of a seedy bar on Hotel Street. He knew it was a safe room because the bar was owned and run by a Japanese agent. They had talked freely—at least Yoshikawa had. Matsuo mentioned nothing of what he knew of the attack. Only the very highest levels of the government and military knew that Pearl Harbor was to be a target. Consul Kita and his staff knew nothing and Matsuo wanted to keep it that way. If they knew nothing, they could give nothing away, even accidentally, over a tapped phone line.

When Matsuo asked if there had been any mention on the airwaves of Mount Niitaka, Yoshikawa had replied that, yes, an enigmatic message had been received on Tuesday. They had no idea for whom it was intended, but it had read, *"Niitaka yama nobore ichi-ni-rei-ya."*

Matsuo had nodded then, as if the message contained no meaning beyond the words themselves. But now, as he sat here on a dirt road above the skeletons of new houses on the rim of a residential area creeping up the hillside, he gazed at the bulk of the U.S. Pacific Fleet lit up below him in the dark, and heard the words echo in his mind.

Climb Mount Niitaka, 1208.

That was the signal, the go-ahead to the Strike Force from Tokyo: Attack Pearl Harbor, December 8. Matsuo knew that although the force had crossed the international date line, it was still running internally on Tokyo time. And December 8, Tokyo time, would be Sunday in Pearl Harbor.

He checked his watch: 9:00 P.M. In fifty-eight hours, Japan's declaration of war would be delivered to the U.S. Secretary of State in Washington. One hour after that, the bombers of the Strike Force would be attacking those ships below.

Matsuo waited and watched, searching the streets just below for a beautiful Japanese woman on a bicycle until his eyes ached with the strain. He waited until 11:15, and then forced himself to face the obvious.

Meiko wasn't coming tonight.

There was no sense in waiting any longer. The sub that was to pick them up would surface at midnight for ten minutes only. If they weren't there in the inflatable raft Matsuo had in the trunk of the car, it would submerge and return in twenty-four hours.

Reluctantly, Matsuo started the engine and put the car in gear. He hoped Meiko wouldn't wait until the last minute. There were only two nights left.

DECEMBER 6
TOKYO

Hiroki stared around at the tense faces in the War Room. Sugiyama and Nagano, Chiefs of Staff of the Army and Navy, and their Vice Chiefs awaited his words.

They're frightened, he thought. The cold hard reality of what they were about to undertake had seeped through their bluff, confident exteriors. They looked almost ready to back down now. They needed some backbone. They had the advantage of choosing whether or not to fight, of choosing the time and place of battle. But that wasn't enough, it seemed. They wanted even more of an edge.

Hiroki sighed. Perhaps he was being unfair. After all, these men didn't have his advantage. They hadn't listened to the Seer, hadn't heard how the war would be won despite seemingly unconquerable odds. They only knew that they were about to attack one of the world's industrial giants.

"What news do you bring?" Nagano asked.

"I have convinced the foreign minister to delay delivery of the final note another half hour."

The Chief of the Navy waved his fist in the air and shouted *"Banzai!"* The others followed his lead.

The import was clear. With the delegation arriving only half an hour before the attack, and counting on a bare minimum of fifteen minutes to read the declaration, only another scant fifteen minutes remained for the Secretary of State to send a war alert to the Pacific.

Sake was poured, and the Supreme Command awaited Hiroki's toast:

"Tea in Washington!" he said, and they all drank.

■　■　■

"Their cowardice serves our purposes well," Shimazu said after Hiroki had told them of the Supreme Command's jitters. He was well satisfied with the course of events. "The more the Pearl Harbor strike appears to be a sneak attack, the better."

"Why is that, sensei?"

"Consider: The angrier the Americans are, the less likely they will be to agree to an early settlement—something Admiral Yamamoto wants but which we must avoid at all costs. The Order supports this conflict not merely for the Empire's material well-being, but to rid the East of white rule once and for all! There must be no cease-fire until that is accomplished!"

"Perhaps we will be lucky and have a further delay at the Washington end," Hiroki said. "But that seems unlikely. The message will be transmitted in English in our top diplomatic cipher. No translation will be necessary at our embassy."

"I wonder about that code," Shimazu said. "Are you sure it is safe?"

"Absolutely."

Shimazu hoped Hiroki was right. If the Americans intercepted and deciphered the Fourteen Part Message, they would be ready for the Strike Force when it arrived. Japan's plans for a decisive victory could then become a humiliating defeat.

But of course Hiroki was right! The Seers' visions had uniformly predicted stunning victories at the start of the war. And the visions never failed. How had he forgotten that? In the maze of temporal matters that he followed during all his waking hours as he helped guide Japan toward this war, was he losing sight of the spiritual concerns that had first brought him to the Order so many years ago?

Yes, he told himself, regretfully. Yes, I am. But I am doing it for the Son of Heaven, for the Empire, for the honor of the Order. I will put these material matters behind me and seek that spiritual trail again. After the war. After the war is won.

In the meantime, he had had a disturbing vision under the influence of the Seers' drug. In a parting of the yellow mist he had seen Meiko Mazaki returning to Japan. But how could that be? She was dead!

Wasn't she?

OAHU

It was my habit to spend the first Saturday morning of the month at the Pearl office. It was quiet then, the interruptions were rare, and I found it a good time to clean up all the loose ends of paperwork that had accumulated during the preceding month.

The work went quickly. I had managed to get a fairly decent amount of sleep last night, forcibly clearing my mind of any worries about impending disaster for Pearl. And it had worked. I had awakened refreshed and buoyant to find Hawaii still at peace with the world. Meiko was still asleep when I left, but I planned to take her to the Battle of the Bands tonight. She liked American swing music and I figured something like that would help pull her out of the funk she was in.

I checked the wires after lunch. Some *long* messages were going from Tokyo to Washington in Purple. Something was going on. More than ever I wished we had some magic here to decipher it.

I was just finishing up and readying to head back to Honolulu when portly, balding Fred Jansen, Chief Ship's Clerk, hurried past in the hall. He must have spotted me because he stopped short and saluted.

"Sir, is Captain Thornton available today?"

"No, Jansen, he's not." I glanced at the clock: just shy of one. Thornton was probably in his seat at the stadium right now, waiting for the annual Shrine Game to begin. The University of Hawaii was playing Willamette and I doubted there was a man on base who didn't have a bet on the game one way or the other. "Is there a problem?"

"Yes, sir." He held up a foot-long cardboard tube. "I found this lying on top of the safe."

"And?"

"And I think it should be locked up over the weekend but I don't have the combination."

Neither did I. That was limited to the higher-ups in Intelligence such as Commanders Layton and Rochefort, and Captains Mayfield and Thornton.

"Let's see what you've got."

Jansen pulled a large sheet of drafting paper from the tube and spread it out on my desk.

"I didn't feel right leaving this around."

I could see why. It was a map of the harbor with the positions of every single ship penciled in and labeled by name. The torpedo and submarine nets were penciled in, too.

I rolled it up and slipped it back in the tube. "I'll take care of it," I told him.

Obviously relieved to have the matter taken out of his hands, Jansen saluted smartly and hurried out. I intended to see that whoever had left this lying around got hell for it Monday morning. But meantime, what was I going to do with this map?

I could think of only one solution: Bring it home.

I locked up and headed for my car.

■   ■   ■

Meiko concealed her dismay as she stared at the tube Frank had laid on the table.

"Can't you take it back?" she said.

"Honey, I explained that. I couldn't leave it lying around the office."

"But now it's lying around here. What if somebody steals it? Or it gets lost? Or the house burns down?"

Frank laughed good-naturedly. "The first two will never happen, and if, God forbid, the house burns down, well then ONI will just have to draw up another diagram. Look: I'm not even going to hide it." He walked over to the refrigerator and laid the tube on top of it. "There. We'll leave it in plain sight. By tomorrow night, it will be worthless, anyway. It changes day-to-day during the week as the ships go in and out of drydock."

"Then why don't we just burn it?" Her voice sounded shrill in her own ears.

"Meiko, what's wrong?" he said, losing his smile. "I've brought home papers lots of times and it's never bothered you like this. Are you all right?"

"I'm just not feeling well, Frank," she said. And it was true. The presence of the map sickened her. It was like knowing that a snake was coiled somewhere in the house.

He stepped close and put a hand on her forehead. "You getting sick?"

"I don't know. I'll be all right. I'm just so tired all the time."

"Want to call off going to the Battle of the Bands tonight?"

She managed a smile. "If you don't mind. Maybe I'll just go to bed early."

"Sure, hon. Whatever you want. But if you're not better by Monday morning, I'm taking you over to the base hospital and have one of the doctors take a look at you."

"Okay," she said. "Sure. I think I'll go lie down now—maybe take a nap before dinner."

She broke away from him and headed for the bedroom, feeling as if she should be slithering along the floor, leaving a trail of slime behind her.

■ ■ ■

It was eleven o'clock. Meiko checked the phosphorescent glow of the hands on the bedside clock for the dozenth time in the past few minutes.

It has to be now!

She had gone to bed shortly after dinner, complaining again of being tired, and had lain awake ever since while Frank sat in the living room, smoking and listening to the radio. She tossed back and forth under the covers, not knowing what to do, knowing only that she had to leave tonight or never leave at all.

But how? How was she going to leave? She had feigned sleep when Frank had come to bed half an hour ago, and now he was sleeping peacefully beside her. She lay a hand gently on his shoulder.

Poor Frank.

She had tried so desperately these past days to find a way to tell him, but it was hopeless. There was no way, no words that would lessen the pain of her leaving. She would have to sneak off, like a thief in the night.

Thief! Perhaps that was the key! She would steal the harbor diagram and let Frank think that that was why she had left him. Would that make it easier? Would it be less painful for him to think that she had left him for Japan rather than for another man? Meiko doubted it, knowing she was clutching at straws.

She kissed Frank on the cheek and then slowly, carefully, slipped out of bed. On the way out of the room, she grabbed a house kimono off the hook behind the bedroom door and then eased the door closed. She slipped out of her nightgown and into the kimono, then turned the light on. She sat down at the kitchen table and wrote Frank a brief note that she prayed he would understand. She started out knowing exactly what she would say, but as she wrote, the words made less and less sense until she felt the sobs heave in her chest and the tears begin to stream down her cheeks. Finally, she crumpled it up and jotted down the first words that came to her mind. She left it on the table, then took the tube with the map and started for the door.

She stopped with her hand on the knob and looked back toward the bedroom. There had to be more. Frank deserved better than this. The pressure built up inside of her until she felt she would have to scream or explode. Why? Why did it have to be this way? She knew there was no answer. Her course was set now. There could be no turning back.

Loathing herself, Meiko fled the apartment, found her bicycle in the dark, and pedaled at full speed toward Halewa Heights.

■   ■   ■

As soon as I awoke, I knew I was alone. I felt the empty spot beside me on the mattress and knew that Meiko had not merely left the bed, she had left the apartment—it had that unmistakable *empty* feel to it.

I jumped up, calling her name, though I knew I would get no answer. With my heart pounding in my throat, I hurried to the front room. The kitchen lights were still on and the first thing I saw was the note on the table. It took a few moments for my eyes to focus.

> *Dearest Frank—*
> *I have never lied to you, not once since the day we met in The Bon Marche until now. Please do not hate me for what I am doing.*
> *It is chu.*
>
> > *Forgive me.*
> > *Meiko*

Chu? Her obligation to the Emperor? What on earth could—?

And then I glanced at the top of the refrigerator. The tube with the Pearl Harbor diagram was gone.

"Oh, no!" I heard myself say. I felt as if I were crumbling inside. "Oh, God, no!"

Frantic, I ran my hand over the top of the refrigerator and craned my neck to look behind. No tube. No diagram. I looked at the note again. There were two circular spots where the ink had run. They were still damp. Tears? If so, maybe there was hope. She couldn't have written it too long ago. Maybe I could still catch her, still save her from herself and whatever it was she thought chu was demanding of her.

I ran out to the carport. The car was still there but Meiko's bike was gone. There were only two ways she could be headed—the beach or the Japanese consulate. I decided to try Ala Moana first. I didn't know why. Perhaps because Meiko always seemed to gravitate toward the beach. I raced the car through Kalihi, barely pausing at the intersections. But in one of those fraction-of-a-second pauses I saw something. I looked again and it was gone, but instead of continuing on my way to Ala Moana, I idled the car and stared into the night.

It had been far up the street, maybe three-quarters of a mile away, just a flash of movement under a streetlight. It could have been anything—a pedestrian, another car. Or someone riding a bicycle.

I turned and gunned the car. I knew I was wasting time, but there had been something about it, something that drew me that way. I figured it wouldn't take me long to find out what it was, then I could turn around and get out to the beach.

The street ran uphill and merged with Moanaloa Road. As I cruised along, I saw it again, and this time I knew what it was: someone on a bike. I slowed and cut my lights. As I pulled closer, the lights of a car coming the other way plainly showed that the rider was a woman. A long cardboard tube was strapped to her bike's rear fender.

Suddenly it was hard to breathe. Meiko. Where was she going? What did she hope to accomplish by this? I wanted to gun the car ahead of her, cut her off, pull her from the bike, and shake some sense into her.

But I didn't. Instead of flooring the gas pedal, I dropped back. If I stayed half a mile or so behind, matched my speed to hers, and let other cars go by as I hugged the shoulder, I could follow her without her ever guessing. She was obviously going to meet somebody. Somebody who had contacted her and subverted her against me and the country that had adopted her.

I meant to find out who that somebody was.

■   ■   ■

Matsuo paced back and forth in front of the car, smoking and checking his watch incessantly. Where *was* she? Time was so short. Only a few minutes left before he would have to head for the beach. If he missed the rendezvous with the sub, the war would be over for him. Pearl would be attacked tomorrow, and he would be stuck here— maybe imprisoned—for the duration.

If the attack was still on. He had no way of knowing. The agents at the consulate were not monitoring marine signals and did not know what to listen for, anyway. They had no idea Pearl was to be attacked. And radio silence was so strict among the ships of the Strike Force that the sea could have swallowed it up during the night and no one would know. But the force could have been spotted by a reconnaissance flight and, having lost the element of surprise, the raid would be called off and the ships sent back to Tokyo.

None of that would matter to him, though, if he knew he had Meiko back.

He hurled his cigarette butt down and savagely ground it into the dirt until it virtually disintegrated. What was he going to *do!* How could he leave here without Meiko? He knew where she lived. He was tempted to rush into her home and pull her from Frank's bed. But what would that prove? She had to *choose* him over Frank or having her back would mean nothing.

He was about to light another cigarette when he saw Meiko toiling up the hill on her bicycle. She was headed in his general direction but would probably veer to her left to stay on the road. Triumph and elation shot through him, energizing him. He leaped to the car and reached inside the driver's window.

■ ■ ■

Meiko's lungs burned and her legs ached as she forced her bike through the streets of Halewa Heights. It had been a ride of less than five miles but it had been all uphill. The houses were beginning to thin out here. Most of them were dark and quiet, with cars parked here and there along the dark streets. How would she find Matsuo? It seemed impossible.

And then, up ahead in the featureless dark at the end of the street, she saw a pair of car headlamps flash three times. She urged the bike forward, off the pavement and onto a hard-packed dirt surface. Cleared lots and partially built houses flanked her on either side. Her tires slewed in the sandy dirt so she leaped off and pushed the bike forward. Ahead, she saw someone running toward her.

"Meiko!"

The loud whisper was unmistakably Matsuo's. She threw down the bike and ran forward. He took her in his arms and his embrace was like a vise, almost painful in its intensity.

"I thought you weren't coming! I prayed to all the gods that I would not have to leave here alone!"

At least he hadn't asked if she had brought along any useful intelligence. From the way he had acted on Thursday, she had wondered which was more important to him.

"Get me out of here!" she said. *"Please!"*

She wanted to be far away, beyond the point of no return, to a place where, no matter how she felt or what she decided, there could be no turning back.

"Yes," Matsuo said. "Of course. We'll have to rush. We're almost out of time." He tugged her toward the car behind him.

"Wait!" she said. She ran to her bike and pulled the tube free from the string that had secured it. "I brought a layout of the harbor defenses. It should be—"

She saw headlamps, heard the crunch of tires on gravel, and looked up to see a car roaring toward them. As it skidded to a stop a few feet in front of her, she heard the driver's door open. She couldn't see who it was behind the glare, but she felt all the strength drain out of her in a rush when she recognized the voice.

"Meiko!"

■   ■   ■

I slammed the car into neutral and was out and running toward her before the brake took complete hold. I had seen her startled face in the glow from the headlamps as I pulled up, but I had also spotted another car and a shadowy figure behind her. And the sight of that figure, coupled with the knowledge that he was trying to make a traitor out of my wife, disintegrated the last vestiges of caution or restraint.

I charged.

I ran headlong past Meiko and heard her shout my name as I threw myself at her accomplice. I was in a blind rage, ready to tear him in half with my bare hands. I wasn't sure of how big he was there in the dark, but I was sure the wildfire of rage burning through me would more than make up for whatever I might lack in size. I was wrong.

My attack was brought up short by a sledgehammer blow to the side of my neck. Fiery agony lanced down my left arm, and suddenly it seemed to weigh a ton. Before I could even react to the pain, a fist like a battering ram drove into my belly, doubling me over, leaving me open to a crushing blow to the back of my neck.

I went down and stayed down, racked with pain and unable to move. My opponent squatted down beside me.

"Can't I ever be free of you?"

I didn't recognize the voice at first. It spoke softly, in a tone that was neither mocking nor consoling, but it was cold and hard, filled with an anger equal to my own. Then I placed it. Had I been able, I would have screamed out my shock, my grief that I had been such a gullible fool! How could I have allowed myself to be so completely taken in by Meiko's lies? But I was lying on my side, clutching my belly, and trying not to vomit. All I could manage was an agonized grunt.

"Matsuo!"

I could make out his face now in the spilled light from my car's headlamps. He didn't look any older than when I had last seen him at Berkeley. Meiko came up and stood over us.

"Oh, Frank!" she said, sobbing, and I could see tears glistening on her cheeks. "Oh, Frank, I'm so sorry!"

"You're never where you should be, Frank," Matsuo said in that cold, hard tone. "When someone needs you, you're gone. When you should be gone, you show up. And it is especially tragic that you should show up now. Because I can't let you live."

He grabbed my hair, pushed my head back, then readied his fist for a blow to my exposed throat. Meiko screamed and grabbed his arm.

"*No!* You can't!"

"There's no choice! You told me he expected an attack. Now that you've stolen a diagram of the harbor, he'll *know* a raid is planned!"

"We'll take him with us!"

"Impossible! There's barely room in the raft for two of us! There's no other way!"

Meiko shoved herself between the two of us. "I forbid it! If you kill him, you will have to kill me! Because I'll go to the Navy and tell them myself!"

I saw Matsuo's incredulous expression as he stared at her.

I couldn't understand Meiko. She had led me along, set me up, and now she was defending me. I forgot about trying to understand. The time she was buying me was helping. My intestinal spasms had stopped and I was getting more feeling back into my limbs. There was only one thing for me to do. I had to forget about Meiko and forget about getting even with Matsuo. I had to warn the fleet! If I could make it to my car . . .

It had to be now. I pushed myself off the ground, staggered to my feet, and forced myself into a lopsided run toward the car. I heard scuffling feet behind me, heard Meiko shriek, "*No!*" and then I was in the front seat, thanking God I hadn't shut off the engine, and throwing the car into reverse. A cloud of dust spewed up from the spinning tires, blotting Meiko and Matsuo from view and enveloping the car as it slewed backward.

Suddenly Matsuo burst through the cloud and threw himself against my side of the car. Just inches from me, he caught the window post with his hand and managed to get his feet on the running board. I jammed on the brakes, and almost tossed him off as I revved into first gear, but he held on by his fingertips. I started to roll up the window while making a sharp turn to the right, but before I could get it up far enough to dislodge his hand, he regained his balance. I saw him rear back with his free arm and then I heard a deafening smash as the air around me was filled with countless flying shards of glass. He had smashed the window with his bare hand!

I pulled the car into a sharper turn and tried to fight off Matsuo's arm as it snaked in the window and grabbed the steering wheel. I pounded on that arm, I pulled at his fingers, but he had the wheel in a death grip, holding it into the turn to bring me back toward where we started. In a last, desperate move, I yanked on my door handle and threw myself against the door. The move knocked Matsuo off the running board. With his feet and lower legs dragging in the dirt beside the car, he finally lost his grip on the wheel.

Suddenly, Matsuo let go of the car entirely and hurled himself away. I watched him roll in the dirt, then glanced ahead and realized why he had done it—the car was nosing toward a stand of trees. I stood on the brake but there wasn't enough room to stop. The car skidded, started to spin, then slammed broadside against the trees. I was shaken up but still alert and able to move. I pushed my way out of the car and found Matsuo there, standing by the door, staring at me. There was murder in his eyes.

As he drew his fist back, I only had time for one thought: *He's going to kill me.*

Then his fist flashed forward toward my face and the world exploded into a thousand lights.

■　■　■

Meiko nearly lost all control as she watched Matsuo approach with Frank's limp form slung over his shoulders.

He can't be dead! Oh, please, Frank can't be dead!

Matsuo must have read her thoughts. "He's just unconscious," he said.

Meiko heard herself gasp with relief. "What are you going to do with him?"

Matsuo glanced around at the partially completed houses. "I'm not sure, but I have an idea."

He dumped Frank onto the ground and hurried off to one of the lots. As he rummaged through the building supplies, Meiko knelt beside Frank and gently, gingerly began to brush the hair away from his face.

"Poor Frank," she whispered, feeling utterly wretched. "This is all my fault. If I hadn't come into your life, if I'd only refused to marry you, none of this would have happened."

Matsuo suddenly returned. He had a hammer jammed into his belt and things clinked in his pocket. He lifted Frank and slung him over his shoulders again.

"What—what are you going to do?" Meiko asked, afraid of the answer.

Matsuo had already turned away and started walking uphill. "I'm going to find a place to put him where he'll be safely out of touch until morning," he said over his shoulder.

Meiko followed, chilled and baffled by the change in Matsuo. He was like a raging, bloodthirsty animal! What had happened to make him like this? Was it her fault? Could those years of thinking she was dead have had this effect on him? Was she some sort of bad luck charm? Look how she had disgraced her family—look at poor Frank! Did misfortune taint everyone she loved? She didn't know. She didn't even know if she wanted to return to Japan with this new Matsuo.

She followed him into the wooded area uphill from the new

construction, through the trees until they reached a relatively clear area. Only the stars and a half-moon lit the scene as Matsuo lay Frank on the ground next to a tree. What was he going to do?

"Matsuo . . . ?"

"I'll be through in a minute."

She watched as he removed the hammer from his belt, then took something from his pocket. He raised Frank's forearm against the tree, and held the thing from his pocket over it. She stepped closer and saw that it was a heavy, six-inch nail. She screamed out her horror as Matsuo raised the hammer.

■   ■   ■

I awoke to cries of agony—my own.

When my eyes could focus, I saw Matsuo straightening up to stand over me. Behind him stood Meiko, half-turned away, her face buried in her hands, sobbing. My head and upper back were propped against a tree, the rest of me stretched out on the ground. My arm . . .

The pain in my right forearm went far beyond anything I had ever experienced, ever imagined. It shot out of the center of my arm and pulsed back and forth between my shoulder and fingertips like liquid fire. I looked and saw a heavy-duty nail punched through the flesh of my arm two or three inches this side of my wrist and into the thick trunk of an ironwood tree.

I retched, and the movement caused a spasm of pain in the arm, pain even more intense than before. The world swam around me for an instant.

"I'm letting you live," Matsuo said in a voice cold and harsh for all the softness of its whisper. "For her sake. Because she wants it and because she says you've been good to her. I'm allowing it for another reason as well. Look down there," he said, pointing behind him.

Through pain-blurred eyes I could see the lights of the fleet in the east loch.

"I've positioned you here so you'll have a balcony seat at the show tomorrow morning. I don't want you to miss a minute of it. Your country is trying to strangle mine. You've left us only two roads to follow: Either exist on a leash, or go to war. Tomorrow morning you'll see firsthand the choice we have made. You'll watch the destruction of your Pacific Fleet."

The import of what he was saying finally broke through the haze of pain enveloping me. There *was* going to be an attack on the fleet, and it was set for tomorrow!

"The final part of a declaration of war has already been sent to our Washington Embassy. The Ambassador Nomura and Envoy Kurusu have an appointment with Secretary of State Hull at 1:00 P.M. Washington time. They will present him with the declaration, and shortly after that our planes will be over Pearl Harbor."

He paused, as if for effect, then said, "I am taking a chance leaving you here alive. There is always the chance you could tear yourself free of that nail and warn the fleet. But I know you, Frank. Unless someone comes by and frees you—and there is no one within earshot—you will still be right here tomorrow morning."

He gave me one long last look, as if trying to read my face in the moonlight, then turned and strode away. He stopped at Meiko's side and said something to her, but she lurched away and came toward me. Moonlight glistened off her wet cheeks.

"Oh, Frank!" she said as she threw herself on her knees beside me. "I never knew this would happen! Please believe me! I never knew Matsuo was alive! I swear it!"

"We have to hurry, Meiko!" Matsuo said in Japanese. "We are already late!"

"Please understand, Frank! I have no choice in this!"

Matsuo came up behind her, took her by the arm and fairly dragged her to her feet.

"It is chu, Frank!" she cried as he pulled her away down the hill. "It is chu!"

I lay sprawled against the tree and watched them go, catching a last backward glance from Meiko before they disappeared into the dark. I wanted to call to her, say something that would change her mind, bring her back. But my tongue was stuck against the roof of my mouth and I was too racked by pain and grief to do anything more than stare after her like a mute idiot. After all, what could I say to counter the ancient, almost inborn imperatives of her endless debt to the Emperor? I was no match for chu.

Besides, there was another matter that had to take precedence—I had to get free and warn the fleet!

I tried to shift my position on the ground and suddenly found my voice with a cry of agony. The slightest movement, even the most minute rotation on the spindle of the nail resulted in an unnerving blast of pain that caused my vision to shimmer toward black. How would I ever get free? There was surprisingly little bleeding around the nail now, but I knew that would change if I ever did manage to tear my arm free—I'd pass out from the pain and probably bleed myself into a coma while I was unconscious.

And then I realized—I didn't have to get free! Matsuo had said the final part of the declaration of war had been transmitted to the Japanese Embassy in Washington—eight to ten hours before the attack. It would be in Purple, of course, and Washington had three Purple magic machines!

I would have laughed out loud if I hadn't been in such agony. We would have the message deciphered before the Japs, and a copy on the Secretary of State's desk *hours* before the scheduled presentation. The warning would go out to all units in the Pacific, and when the Jap planes arrived over Oahu, they'd find Army interceptor squadrons in the air and a battle-ready fleet ready and waiting for them.

The last laugh would be on Matsuo and his "surprise" attack!

DECEMBER 7

We're late! Matsuo thought as he paddled the raft out from shore. The other officers at Naval Intelligence had warned him about coming here, telling him it was a fool's errand, too full of risks with too many variables waiting to betray him. And they were right. Nothing had gone according to plan.

He wished Meiko would say something. She had been so quiet during the headlong drive down to the beach from Halewa Heights, and now she sat slumped in the front of the raft like someone in a daze.

"Meiko," he said, finally. "Don't you understand? I did what I had to do."

Her voice was like ice, and sharp as a January wind. "I will *never* understand what you did! I have never seen such brutality! And I will never forget what I saw you do! Matsuo . . . how *could* you?"

He had been brutal with Frank, yes, but the situation demanded it. This was not a game. This was war! Couldn't she see that?

Matsuo stopped rowing and checked his watch. Almost 12:15. So late! The sub could have come and gone already! Most likely it had done just that! So here he was, floating in a raft off Oahu, a United States territory which, eight hours from now, would hate and fear all Japanese. With him was a diagram of the harbor that was to be attacked in the morning. And the woman he had loved as long as he could remember now thought of him as some savage beast.

What else could go wrong?

They waited in silence, but still no submarine. At twelve-thirty, he picked up the paddle and prepared to row ashore. His best hope was to get back to the car and drive to some remote part of the island's mountains to await the outcome of the attack and the war. Perhaps they could find a place to hide for a year or so until the war was over, and then return to Japan.

As he lifted the paddle, the sea to port began to boil. Suddenly a conning tower burst up toward the moonlit sky with water cascading off it on all sides. Matsuo held his breath.

Is it mine?

Then the upper hull broke the surface and he saw the miniature sub and the seaplane lashed to its afterdeck. There was no longer any doubt. Relief swept through him like a comforting breeze.

They were safe!

■   ■   ■

Commander Fuchida lifted his gaze from the diagram and stared at Matsuo, his soft brown eyes glowing. His thin lips curled into a smile under his short bush moustache. "This is a most remarkable achievement!"

Matsuo had been received with more than a little reserve aboard the carrier *Agaki,* flagship of the Strike Force. *And rightly so,* he thought. After all, he would have been suspicious, too, of a man and a woman arriving by seaplane and claiming to have a map of the harbor that was the object of an attack known to only a privileged few in all of Japan. Despite the letter he carried from Yamamoto, signed personally and sealed with his hanko, he and the harbor diagram were still received with suspicion by the ships' officers until Fuchida had entered the ward room, embraced him, and introduced him as the finest intelligence officer in all Japan.

Suddenly, he was among friends.

"It is mostly due to the efforts of Meiko Mazaki," Matsuo said. He wished Meiko were here in the ward room to see the reverence with which the pilots treated her contribution to the attack, but she had locked herself in the cabin that had been assigned to her and refused to come out.

"You are sure these positions are accurate?" Fuchida said.

"I cannot speak for the submarine nets," Matsuo said, "but I have seen the ships in the harbor and they are situated exactly as on that map."

"Then there are no aircraft carriers in port?" The commander could not hide his disappointment.

"No. The last one left on Thursday. But there are eight heavy battleships sitting there along the central island, waiting to be sunk."

A murmur ran around the room as the pilots of the vertical and torpedo bombers pressed more closely around the table. Matsuo drew Commander Fuchida aside.

"I'm a little bit worried," Matsuo said.

Fuchida raised his eyebrows. "About what?"

"Our target. Doesn't it strike you as strange? Ninety-six ships in port, eight of them battleships lined up like targets? The fact that the Strike Force has not seen one ship or reconnaissance plane during its entire journey, even this close to the Hawaiians? And now this diagram of the harbor, identifying and locating every single ship in the east loch? Isn't it all just a little too perfect?"

"Perhaps. But I prefer to think of it as American overconfidence. 'Who would dare to attack us?' they say. Hours from now, they will learn."

"I just hope it's not a trap."

Fuchida shook his head. "No trap. And if it is, we will fight our way through it and out of it. We have contingency plans ready in case the surprise element is lost." He bowed. "But I appreciate your concern."

"One more thing," Matsuo said as the commander began to turn away. "I understand one of the fighter pilots is sick."

Fuchida nodded. "An ear infection. He can't be allowed to fly."

"I will take his place."

"I don't know . . ." Fuchida said slowly. "I will have to think about that."

Matsuo knew this was a typically Japanese way of saying no. He pressed the commander.

"If it was a dive bomber, I wouldn't ask. I don't know the first thing about dive bombing. But I am fully trained in the A6M—trained by the admiral himself. I have taken part in the planning of this operation since the admiral conceived it, and I claim the right to take part in its execution."

Fuchida hesitated, and Matsuo's heart sank. He desperately wanted to strike back at America, at Frank Slater for having had Meiko, at all the Mick McGarrigles and Japanese Exclusion Leagues and Alien Land Laws, at the land of a thousand daily slights whose people had treated him like eta, at the land that had forced his country into this desperate act. Then the flight commander's face broke into a smile and it was like the sun pushing from behind a cloud.

"Of course. You have earned it!"

Matsuo bowed low, his exultation lifting him like a wave. He hurried to Meiko's cabin to tell her the good news. He knocked on her door repeatedly but there was no answer. He tried the handle but it was locked from the inside. Either she was sound asleep or feigning it. He suspected the latter. He ached to sit with her and make her understand his actions, but there was no time. Take-off time for his fighter wing was only hours away, and there was so much to do before he was ready.

Matsuo didn't sleep at all. He spent the next two hours being briefed on the flight plan. The assault force would consist of 353 planes attacking in two waves. He would be flying one of the forty-three fighters providing cover for the first wave. Take-off time for the first wave was 6:00 A.M.; the second would take to the air an hour and a quarter later.

As he donned the fresh uniform he had been given, he could hear the roar of the plane engines as the mechanics turned them over and gave them a final tuning on the flight deck above. He was given a special breakfast of *sekihan*—red beans and rice—and a cup of sake for a ceremonial toast. He raised his glass with the others, but only touched it to his lips. Instead of drinking it, he left it as an offering on the *Agaki*'s portable Shinto shrine.

And then it was time to go. He hung the clipboard with his flight plan around his neck and tied a white hachimaki around his head before he donned his flight helmet. On the way down the corridor, he was handed a bento containing rice balls, pickled fruit and fish, chocolate, and caffeine tablets. The box lunch trembled in his hands as he trotted up the stairs. He would need no stimulants to keep him awake this morning. He felt as if he were coming apart with excitement.

He stepped out onto the deck amid the roar of all the idling engines and felt the cut of the salty east wind. The sky was bright as the sun began to peek over the horizon, a sign, a portent—the real-life model of the Japanese flag. The wind was stiff, however, and raised heavy, white-topped swells on the brightening sea. Pearl Harbor was 230 miles south and slightly east of where he stood. He hoped the sky was as clear there.

A deckhand pointed him toward his plane and he ran for it. He used the familiar routine of climbing into the cockpit and preparing for flight to calm the almost unbearable tension mounting within him. He let the thrum and shimmer of the running engine pulse through his body. He loved this plane—a Mitsubishi A6M2 Zero-sen, the best fighter in the world. Not the fastest, not the most powerful, not the most heavily armed, but it could outmaneuver and knock down anything else in the sky.

He checked his instruments, closed his cockpit hood, and waited as the *Agaki* and the other five carriers turned into the wind. He watched the other fighters take off one by one, then it was his turn. He fought a swirl of vertigo as he nosed toward the end of the deck and saw its rhythmic rise and fall above and below the horizon as it fought the swells. He gunned the engine for all it was worth and shot down the deck. He was airborne before he reached the end and then he was climbing at forty-five degrees. A sudden exhilaration swept through him and he began to laugh. He laughed all the way up to the holding level where he circled protectively with the other fighters until all forty-three of them were in the air. Then the bombers began to take off.

■ ■ ■

Matsuo chewed his lip as he watched the endless fluffy white expanse of cloud cover below. The sun was bright and warm here at 15,000 feet as he kept watch over the 140 bombers of various types a mile below. But where was Oahu?

Ninety minutes flying at 180 miles an hour—the Hawaiian archipelago should have been directly below. But who could tell? Lieutenant Commander Itaya was in charge of the fighters, but he and everyone else was following Fuchida's lead. Were they worried, too? Or did they know exactly where they were? Due to the absolute radio silence they were maintaining, Matsuo could only sit back, hope for the best, and follow the leader.

And then, as if by Divine design, the impenetrable clouds broke open and the sandy shore of a lush green island burst into view far below. He had burned the coastal outline of Oahu into his brain and immediately recognized Kahuku Point, its northernmost tip. Right on target!

Matsuo waited for the signal from Fuchida. If he fired his signal gun once, it meant they had the element of surprise on their side; twice meant "surprise lost." Suddenly it came—a single flare. Matsuo saw the dive bombers drop toward sea level, readying to spearhead the assault. He waited for the fighters to begin dividing into assault groups as planned, but Itaya's plane made no move. Had he missed the signal? Then came another flare. Did that mean "surprise lost," or was Fuchida repeating the single flare for the fighters' benefit?

Matsuo felt a twinge of unease. If "surprise lost" was the message, were they blithely gliding into a tiger's den?

Too late to worry now. Itaya was peeling off with his group toward Hickham Field. Matsuo's group leader was dropping down toward the valley between Oahu's two narrow mountain ranges. Matsuo followed. He would know soon enough when they reached their target: Wheeler Field. If the Army P-40 fighters based there were in the air and ready for battle, he would have the answer to his question.

As the seven planes in his group streaked over Schofield Barracks, Matsuo studied the troop quarters below. They looked quiet enough. Just what one would expect on a sleepy Sunday morning.

Maybe it wasn't a trap after all.

Matsuo checked his watch. 7:54. Almost 1:30 P.M. in the American capital. Already Monday in Tokyo. The fourteen-part declaration of war had been delivered by now. Nothing more to do but follow through with the plan of attack.

He looked ahead and saw the triangle of the intersecting runways at Wheeler Field, dead center in the island. There was no turning back now.

Let the war begin!

■ ■ ■

I had lain awake all night and felt the pain in my right arm subside from a white-hot coal to an icy throb that made me feel as if a part of me were dying. All night I had watched the harbor, waiting to see the ships start weighing anchor and moving out to the open sea. But nothing happened. The lights on the big ships remained stationary. All that moved were the running lights on the skiffs and ferries shuttling between shore and the anchored biggies. And after a while, they too became still.

I waited for the dawn, hoping I'd been wrong, that I'd missed the departure of the likes of the *Arizona* and the *Pennsylvania*. But as the sky lightened, I saw that they were all there—all ninety-six of them.

A faint ray of hope came with the sun. Maybe the attack had been called off. Maybe the declaration of war was never sent. As the sky continued to brighten, I figured that had to be it. A last-minute settlement had been reached—

—and then I heard the sound of their planes.

■ ■ ■

Matsuo followed his group leader in a shallow dive toward the Wheeler airstrips. To his surprise, he saw P-40s lined up in neat rows on the apron, their engines quiet, their propellers still. Matsuo experienced a surge of relief.

No trap! They aren't waiting for us! No trap!

He dove toward the dormant aircraft, strafing them with the 20-mm cannon in his wings. He saw the P-40s shudder and crumble under the onslaught of lead. Some exploded as their gas tanks caught fire.

It was over almost as soon as it had begun. *Like target practice!* A few of the planes managed to gain the air and there had been a brief dogfight or two before the survivors streaked off to protect the harbor. Once again, he was assailed by doubt.

Too easy! Too damn easy!

Matsuo's group left the P-40s burning on the ground as they roared south to join the attack on the harbor. Matsuo held back. He circled Wheeler and made one last low pass to check on the damage they had inflicted. He was satisfied that few if any of these planes would ever fly again and was about to turn south toward Pearl Harbor when he heard a metallic *spang* against his fuselage. He looked down and saw a lone American soldier standing on one of the landing strips firing up at him with an automatic pistol.

Matsuo loosed a burst from his 20-mm cannons to frighten the man off. The bullets tore up the paving on either side of him but he stood his ground like a statue, pistol raised, firing round after round at Matsuo's plane. Matsuo veered off and circled the field again, watching as the man calmly ejected a spent clip and loaded a fresh one.

Matsuo came at him again, lower this time, straight at him. Still the man refused to budge. He raised his pistol and began firing again. Matsuo had him in his sights. All he had to do was press the trigger on his stick to fire the 7.7-mm machine guns above the nose and the lone American below would be torn to shreds.

But he held his fire. There was something precious in that man below. His defiant courage spoke to Matsuo, struck a resonant chord within him. He could not kill him like this—from high above with such an immense advantage in fire power.

He veered off and dipped his wings in salute. And he thought, if America had many soldiers like that one below, Japan was in big trouble!

But why weren't there more like him scrambling for their planes? It seemed as if the entire island was asleep. The declaration of war had been delivered. Hadn't anyone been warned?

Puzzled and disturbed, he flew south toward the harbor. It was 8:20. The first wave should have been through with its attack. The second wave would be arriving soon.

He saw the smoke long before he saw the harbor, and decided to veer eastward before inspecting the damage. He wanted to check Halewa Heights first.

■ ■ ■

I sat there on the ground, pinned to the tree like some goddamn insect, and watched the carnage.

The torpedo bombers came in first, swooping in low toward the ships on Battleship Row, dropping their explosive fish, then veering off. Then came the dive bombers, and finally, the high, horizontal bombers. I saw black and gray bursts of antiaircraft fire begin to blossom in the air, but too late—too damn late!

Suddenly the *Arizona* exploded. One moment it was there, bravely weathering the attack, next its whole front end was exploding, shaking the very ground under me as its forward magazine took a direct hit and sent fiery debris a thousand feet into the air. God! The men aboard!

Her crew must have numbered a thousand! How many could have survived that?

Ahead of her, I saw smoke gush from the *Oklahoma* as she began to capsize. And still the attack went on, relentlessly, until the entire harbor was engulfed in smoke. And just when I thought the Japs had to be out of bullets and bombs, another wave appeared to renew the assault.

What was happening? It was all wrong! The declaration of war should have been decoded and the fleet warned hours ago!

It was all my fault. I had known about the attack. I had lain here all night figuring the people with Purple magic would relay the warning. But they hadn't. Someone, somewhere, had screwed up. I could have made the difference! I could have raised the warning but I didn't. Instead, I chose to spare myself the pain of pulling free of that nail. I sat here and wasted all that time waiting for someone else to do it.

In a blind rage—at Japan, at Meiko and Matsuo, but most of all at myself—I tried to yank my arm free of the spike. The volcanic pain that erupted through me made the world dim and waver. As I fell back against the tree trunk and watched the swimming sky, I heard the drone of a single-engine plane above. I looked up. A lone fighter with big red suns on its wings and fuselage came over the trees and circled twice above me.

I didn't have to see the pilot to know who it was.

■ ■ ■

Matsuo looked down on the wooded slope high on Halewa Heights. Frank was still there, fixed to his tree as Matsuo had known he would be. A boy without honor grows into a man without honor. He banked away and flew over Honolulu, noting that it was virtually unscathed by the attack.

Perfect! he thought as he circled around toward the pall of black smoke that marked the east loch of Pearl Harbor. Everything had gone exactly as planned. Only military targets had been hit. He wanted to get a look at the damage to the U.S. Pacific Fleet before he rejoined his group at the rendezvous point.

Matsuo brought his Zero in low from the east, cruising over the oil tanks and then the Naval Hospital before he banked north toward Ford Island. His heart thudded in his chest as he saw the carnage there.

The east loch was in shambles. His attention was immediately drawn to the line of battleships along Ford Island. They had received the brunt of the attack and were barely visible through the roiling, oily smoke. Two of the battleships had already been sunk, and another was on its way down. He saw men scrambling up and down ladders and around the still-operable antiaircraft guns and across the overturned hulls, or swimming frantically through the burning water.

And he saw so many other men who weren't moving at all as they lay on the decks or floated facedown in the harbor.

Even if the attack were called off now it would already be a success. He should have been cheering but he could not find his voice. The snearing, tearing horror of all the death and violence below seeped into his cockpit and engulfed him with its stench. He tried to shake it off, tried to force a sense of triumph and vindication upon himself by calling up visions of Mick McGarrigle's sneering face, but it didn't work. Instead he found himself remembering Mrs. Worth, who had saved him from that mob in San Francisco almost ten years ago, and wondering if she had a son and if he might be trapped on one of those ships down there . . .

. . . and suddenly he was seeing Frank's face as he left him nailed to that tree last night. By all the gods, had he really done that? Had he really taken a spike and driven it through another man's arm? A man he had known since childhood?

Choking back the bile that surged into his throat, he pulled back on the stick and sent the Zero into a steep climb, away from the carnage below, far up to where the air was clean. Soon he was high over the open sea, heading for the rendezvous area twenty miles northwest of Kanea Point. He was low on gas and hoped he would meet a bomber or two there. They had homing devices and Zeros did not. Without them, he would never get back to his carrier.

He found two horizontal bombers circling. He fell in with them and began to follow them north, hoping to escape forever the terrible devastation at Pearl Harbor by leaving it far behind.

But the memory of those burning ships and all those dead men and the others struggling so desperately to stay alive followed him all the way back to the *Agaki.*

■　■　■

The great carrier had been as silent as a floating coffin since the planes had taken off this morning. But now Meiko heard the sound of running feet and excited voices. She opened the door to her cabin and peeked out into the corridor. It was empty. Yet from somewhere above she thought she heard cheering.

She decided to go see what it was. If nothing else, it would get her into the open. Despite the stale air in her quarters and a queasy stomach from the ceaseless roll of the ship, this was the first time she had ventured outside the cabin.

She had heard Matsuo knocking before he had left; she had crouched silently on the other side of the door, wishing him away. She hadn't wanted to see him, not after what he had done to Frank. He wasn't the Matsuo she had left on Sagami Bay—he had become a brutal stranger.

And yet, since the planes had roared off at dawn, she had done nothing but worry about him.

The cheering from the flight deck doubled in volume. It was 10:00 A.M. Could the planes be returning so soon? She hurried up the stairs.

The air on the deck was deliciously fresh and the midmorning sun made her blink and rub her eyes. All around her crewmen were cheering and waving their caps as they pointed to the south. Meiko squinted into the light and saw nothing at first . . .

. . . and then she spotted them. Dark specks above the horizon, coming in fast. They straggled in alone and in small groups, many with sputtering engines starving for gas. As she watched, a Zero's engine died in the air as it waited to land and the pilot had to ditch it in the swells near the carrier. She was relieved to see him jump from the cockpit and swim toward the lifelines that had been quickly thrown overboard. He wasn't Matsuo.

As each plane hit the deck and rolled to a stop, a cheer rang out from the crewmen as they rushed to push it out of the way of the next incoming plane. And as the jubilant pilots jumped out of their cockpits and down to the deck, they were surrounded and quizzed with a hundred questions on their exploits.

But where was Matsuo? She didn't see him among the returning pilots. Her chest constricted. Had he been hurt? Shot down?

She watched a two-seater land—a bomber, she thought—and then a lone fighter came in, its engine coughing and sputtering. As it rolled to a stop, she waited anxiously to see the pilot's face as he sat motionless in the cockpit. Finally he stepped out on the wing and jumped down to the deck. He brushed off the well-wishers who crowded around and moved hurriedly in her general direction.

She saw now that it was Matsuo, but his face was so pale and strained that she barely recognized him. She was sure he didn't see her. As she watched, he went to the railing, leaned over, and vomited. And when he was through, she saw him fold his arms on the railing and press his forehead down against them.

Meiko waited. Eventually, he seemed to sense her presence. He looked up and she saw his tortured eyes.

"Meiko," he said in a rasping voice. "What have we done?" She held out her arms and he almost fell into them. "What have *I* done?"

His arms went around her. His grip was so tight she could barely breathe. But she said nothing. The old Matsuo—*her* Matsuo—was back, and although nothing was ever going to be the same again, everything was going to be all right.

PART
FIVE

1 9 4 2
---
1 9 4 3

1 9 4 2

THE YEAR OF THE
HORSE

JANUARY
TOKYO

Meiko huddled with her parents around the kotatsu. Winter was settling in on Tokyo. It was cold in the house, but the three of them drank tea and laughed as they warmed their feet.

Meiko would not have cared if there had been icicles on her nose. She felt so good being back home. All through the journey, she had feared she might not even be allowed through the door.

She had had no doubt that her mother would welcome her back with open arms. But Father . . . she had been prepared for a cool, even cold reception, or no reception at all, a blank wall.

The tension and longing within her had risen to an almost unbearable level with every passing league as the victorious Strike Force brought her closer and closer to home. Matsuo had been a great help, reassuring her and building up her self-esteem. She had allowed him into her cabin after the mission, and eventually into her bed where they made love again after four and a half years. At first, it hadn't been the same. Despite the warmth, there had been desperation, and the awful specter of Frank Slater spiked to that tree, with the infinite hurt in his eyes. But across the days of their journey, they had been able to renew the bond that had joined them since adolescence.

She had spent her first few days back in Tokyo in Matsuo's apartment while she waited for word as to whether her father would accept her back into his home. She met Matsuo's friend Shigeo whose jubilation over the success of the raid was uncontained.

She need never have worried. Her father folded her in his arms and wept with joy. To him, she had returned from the dead.

Of all the many changes, the biggest had been in her father. He was grayer, he walked with less of a limp and there was less of a droop to the right side of his mouth, but Meiko sensed a real change within. Where he used to talk incessantly of politics, he no longer even mentioned the subject despite the almost hysterical euphoria that was sweeping the country in the wake of the Pearl Harbor attack and the ensuing cluster of victories against British, Dutch, and American forces. Instead, he concentrated on family matters.

With the feeling around the kotatsu so warm and easy, Meiko decided that now was the best time to make her announcement.

"Matsuo and I are going to be married," she said. She saw her mother lower her eyes and her father avert his.

"I expected this," he said.

"I pray you do not oppose it."

"Matsuo is a fine man and a clansman," he said. "Although I must confess that I had hoped to have nothing more to do with the Okumo family, I am glad for you."

Meiko understood. As much as Father wanted to see her married, the baron, Hiroki, and especially Matsuo, were all painful reminders of her indiscretion. He wanted all that behind them. But she was also sure that he was painfully aware that his only daughter was all but unmarriageable now. She had been the wife of an American—she had told him during her first week home. But he could not know how that had changed her. After experiencing the equality and independence of the American wife, how could she ever assume the role of the meek, subservient, three-steps-behind Japanese wife? She was a misfit now, suitable for marriage only to another misfit.

"We will be happy," she said.

"You will have to face Hiroki. It is inevitable—they are brothers."

"I will not see Hiroki unless I wish to," she said with what she hoped was enough bravado to hide her sudden nausea. "Matsuo has promised: If Hiroki must be seen, Matsuo will see him. In fact, they are together now."

■   ■   ■

This is too much to bear! Hiroki thought as he gripped the underside of his desk in his office on Sanno Hill across the street from the Diet Building. He stared at his brother seated across from him. The rage within was like a living thing, fighting to burst from his skin and launch itself at Matsuo.

But he contained it. He did not shout, he did not raise his voice. He barely frowned.

"Isn't it interesting, brother," he said in a voice of icy calm, "that you should 'accidentally' find this woman in Hawaii? Even more interesting that you should bend Imperial Navy transportation and personnel to your personal use to bring her back to Japan."

He noted with satisfaction how Matsuo stiffened at the suggestion of malfeasance. *Ah, my brother, I can still read you like my first ideogram.*

"She had access to invaluable intelligence. She brought it with her."

"So I have heard. You knew her very presence in Japan would be a source of constant insult to me." Matsuo's presence had been a source of irritation and embarrassment through the years but knowing Meiko was dead, food for the scavengers of the sea bottom, had made that bearable. Now . . . "Yet you did not hesitate to bring her back. And as if that were not enough, you now tell me that you intend to marry her. Is there no end to the loss of face I must endure? Must I suffer not only her presence in Tokyo, but her marriage to my brother as well?"

"I'm sorry you feel that way," Matsuo said, "but it changes nothing."

Hiroki felt his control begin to slip. "How am I to endure this stab in the back from my own brother? Certainly I shall never recognize that queen of whores as my sister-in-law!"

Hiroki immediately regretted his words as he saw a change come over his brother's features. Matsuo's normally soft brown eyes turned cold and stony; Hiroki could almost feel them flicking over his body, planning where to strike the killing blow. There was murder in Matsuo's face, and it sent a quake of terror to Hiroki's very core.

"You will never speak of her that way again," he said in a low, flat, menacing tone. "Is that understood? *Never!*" Before Hiroki could answer, Matsuo went on. "And on the subject of stabs in the back, that is what the Americans are calling our attack on Pearl Harbor."

Hiroki was relieved at the sudden change of subject. He leapt upon it. "The delay in delivering the Fourteen Part Message was purely clerical. There was difficulty in preparing a properly legible transcription and, consequently, the message was delivered late. A mistake. Purely unintentional." *But most fortuitous. Truly the gods work with the Order!*

"The world does not know that. The message was delivered while the attack was in progress. Japan is seen as a craven cowardly nation." Matsuo's eyes clouded as he spoke. "We attacked sleeping men who believed they were at peace with the world. We have lost face as a nation. I am ashamed."

"I'm not," Hiroki said, relaxing into the blasé exterior he had cultivated over the years. "It was unfortunate, but it is over and done with. Besides, it allowed us an unprecedented victory: We've dealt a deathblow to their Pacific Fleet at negligible cost to us."

"They're not dead yet. Did you hear that hypocrite, Roosevelt? He called the raid 'unprovoked' when he knows full well that he did everything in his power to push us toward war! Even the isolationists who used to be against him are on his side now! I had hoped that they would obstruct any war legislation, but even they are shouting for Japanese blood!"

"Let them!" Hiroki said with a laugh. "Our Navy is invincible! Nothing can stand before it. In less than a month we have taken Guam, Wake, and Hong Kong. We have a hundred thousand men on the Malay Peninsula. Manila is ours and we have squeezed General MacArthur onto the Bataan peninsula. There we will crush him. In a few weeks we will move on Burma and Borneo. Nothing stands in our way. We control the sea from Africa to Midway!"

"For how long?"

"For as long as we wish!"

"I fear not. The Germans are stalled outside Moscow. Fighting has ceased all along the Eastern Front while they are in winter quarters. Britain gets a reprieve while the Germans bolster their forces in Russia; that in turn allows America to concentrate her energies on her hated enemy in the Pacific: Japan."

"Let them come!" Hiroki said. "Pearl Harbor is but a taste of what we can do to them. If they want a full serving, they have but to ask! We will drive the British and the Dutch and the Americans out of the Orient, and we will keep them out! Forever!"

Matsuo stared at him in silence, slowly shaking his head. "You have no idea of what we are up against here, do you?"

I know how the war will end! Hiroki thought. Japan housed so many fearful types like Matsuo, especially in the diet. If only he could share his knowledge of the Seers' visions. If they all knew what he knew, there would be not a single faint heart in the Empire!

Hiroki saw no point in debating the matter any further. He stood—a signal for Matsuo to leave. "And now I must get back to my scheduled appointments."

"Of course," Matsuo said, rising and bowing. "I've already taken up too much of your valuable time." He left without another word.

Hiroki remained standing at his desk after his brother was gone. He did have appointments, but all he could think of was Meiko and how she had looked the last time he had seen her . . . naked . . . lying next to his brother on the floor of the garden cottage . . .

A wave of desire swept over him. He had put her out of his mind almost completely, had nearly forgotten she had ever existed, and then the shock of hearing she had returned. Why had the gods allowed her to come back? Why was she even *alive?*

Alive . . . how he would love to change that, to beat her senseless, slowly, methodically, to take her and throttle the life from her as he poured himself into her.

And even then, would that be enough?

He shuddered. He had a new girl in Yoshiwara, one who made Yukiko look tame by comparison. There would be blood tonight, to help wash Meiko from his mind.

For there were too many responsibilities on his shoulders, too many crucial decisions waiting to be made, too many people clamoring for his attention to allow a mere woman to occupy his thoughts.

As Minister of Military and Economic Coordination, he knew he held a position unique in the history of Japan. The pressure of the responsibilities was enormous, but the power . . . Hiroki doubted that even the greatest of the Tokugawa shoguns wielded a tenth of the power he now held over the Empire.

The zaibatsu, great and small, were after him daily for permission to set up branches and businesses in the captured territories, and for first crack at Borneo, Burma, Rangoon, and the Philippines when they fell. In consultation with Shimazu, he coordinated their industrial efforts with troop advances and with available labor supplies. They were relentless in their greedy attempts to be first in line to scoop up and exploit the newly conquered resources. They never left him alone. The calls, the messages, the gifts, the invitations to dinner, to geisha houses, the pressure was enormous. So was the responsibility. Securing Japan's prominence in the world was, after all, what the war was all about, and he was at the heart of it. He could not let some pathetic female interfere.

And yet even as he pressed the buzzer to signal his secretary to send in his next scheduled appointment, he saw Meiko again . . . naked . . . lying next to Matsuo . . .

FEBRUARY

Meiko took a token sip of the third cup of sake and put it down. The *baishakunin,* maiden of the shrine, removed the cups. Meiko raised her

head and saw Matsuo gazing at her with glowing eyes. She knew she
was beautiful in her ornate headdress and bright red silk wedding
kimono.

They turned and faced their families. Her mother and father were
there, pleasant-faced but not smiling. She sensed how they were
inhibited by the presence of the grim-faced Baron Okumo. At least
Hiroki was not here. But then, he had not been asked. Shigeo and other
friends from Naval Intelligence were all around, beaming at them.

With the traditional Shinto ceremony now over, the baron
extended them perfunctory good wishes, then departed. As she and
Matsuo walked out under the shrine's vermilion *torii* and slipped into
their chauffeur-driven car, she wondered at how differently things
were progressing. Had this been five years ago and she was marrying
Hiroki, she would be heading toward a large, elaborate marital banquet
with hundreds of friends and relatives, during which she would change
her clothes numerous times to show herself off. Today the traditional
banquet would be limited to family and their few friends in a small
private room in a restaurant in Chiyoda-ku.

Meiko leaned against Matsuo and didn't care. A tribunal had ruled
that her marriage to Frank in Hawaii had no legal standing in Japan and
that she was free to marry whoever would have her. And now they
were man and wife, just as they had always hoped. She closed her eyes
for a moment and floated on the bliss of a cherished dream come true.

"Matsuo," she said after a moment. She had something to tell him.
Now, alone in the back of a chauffeured car, seemed as good a time as
any. "We've never really discussed it, but do you want children soon,
or should we try to wait?"

"I want them as soon as you want to have them," he said with a
smile. "How about you?"

"I don't think I have much choice anymore."

"What do you mean?"

"I mean that some time this summer you will become a father."

She watched his eyes widen and his jaw drop. "You mean
you . . . us . . . we . . . ?"

She nodded, praying he would smile or laugh or take her in his
arms. He did all three.

"Are you sure?" he said as he held her.

"Of course. A mother knows these things."

Mother . . . she was going to be a mother. Such a strange way to
think of herself. She had always pictured herself with children, and
now it was coming to pass. She had never been pregnant before but she
felt *different*. And she had all the signs—the tender breasts, the
morning nausea. No doubt about it: she was pregnant.

"This is wonderful!" he cried. "But when did it happen?"

"Aboard the *Agaki*."

Matsuo beamed. "My son was conceived at sea!"

"What makes you so sure it's a boy!"

"A father knows these things. When does he arrive?"

"Sometime in September."

He hugged her close. "What a sailor he'll be!"

Meiko reveled in his joy but thought, what matter whether the child was conceived on land or on sea or in the air, he would be a symbol of their love, someone to cherish all their lives.

They kissed.

APRIL

Matsuo stared out the window at the blossoming cherry trees dotting the streets and clustering in the parks around Sanno Hill. Like the blue-smocked clerks and government office workers wandering the walkways on their lunch hour, he tried to draw tranquillity from nature's beauty. But try as he might, he failed. With the reports he had been hearing from the field, he wondered if he would ever find true tranquillity again.

He turned from the window and lit another cigarette. He had been waiting here in Hiroki's office for nearly two hours now and his patience was gone. Hiroki had made himself almost inaccessible in the past few months—the only one in all Japan less accessible was the Emperor himself. The meeting with his brother had been scheduled for eleven o'clock and here it was almost one.

He had work to do! There had been a significant increase in radio signals among the ships of the U.S. Pacific Fleet lately. They were planning something. If he had the key to their codes he would know exactly what, but as it was, he could only monitor the level of activity, be watchful, and wait for a break.

Something was going to happen soon, he was sure of it. Yet no matter what it might be, the matter he had to take up with Hiroki had greater long-term importance.

He would wait.

Just then the door opened and Hiroki walked in, dressed as usual in a long black kimono. He barely nodded to Matsuo as he walked to his desk and sat down. He looked older; flecks of gray were appearing in the sleek black of his hair. Matsuo waited for an apology or explanation of his lateness, but Hiroki merely removed his hanko from his pocket and began stamping documents.

Matsuo swallowed his anger. "Our meeting was at eleven."

"My conference with the premier dragged on longer than I had anticipated. What did you want?"

Matsuo stepped over to the desk and leaned on it, placing his hands over the papers on his brother's desk. "I want your attention."

Hiroki's head snapped up and for an instant Matsuo saw anger and, yes, even a flash of hatred in his face, but then it was gone, hidden away behind the perpetual mask.

Hiroki sighed and laid the hanko on his desk. "Very well. You have it. Please be brief. What did you want to see me about?"

"Bataan," Matsuo said.

Hiroki smiled. "Our greatest victory so far. We humiliated the British by taking Singapore. And now, with the fall of Bataan, we have handed the United States the greatest military defeat in its history. The Emperor is very proud of his military forces."

"Is he proud of the way they treated the tens of thousands of prisoners they took?"

Hiroki's smile vanished. "We do not concern the Emperor with such details."

"Complete disregard for the Geneva Conventions is more than just a 'detail'!"

Since his return, Matsuo had heard sporadic reports of brutality against military captives and civilian populations. He had assumed them to be isolated incidents, an unfortunate but unavoidable horror of war. Any war. But after a while he began to sense a pattern in the incidents. He was investigating them in detail when the reports came in from Bataan. They painted a picture of unrelieved brutality.

Nearly seventy thousand American and Filipino prisoners, all of them weak from hunger, many of them racked with malaria and other jungle diseases, forced to march without food or water at bayonet point like a herd of cattle through sixty-five miles of jungle. Those too weak to march were buried, some while they were still alive. Those who couldn't keep up were bayoneted or clubbed to death and left along the way. Only sixty thousand reached the prison camps.

"It's got to stop!" Matsuo said. "How can we hold up our head as a nation if we persist in such atrocities?"

"The prisoners *had* to be marched through the jungle! The railways were totally inadequate. We were prepared for twenty-five thousand prisoners and we were faced with almost three times that number! We thought they would have their own rations but they didn't, and our troops had only enough along to feed themselves! There was no choice!"

"I don't believe that for a minute, and neither do you. There is always a choice. And this is not an isolated incident. You are supplying prisoners of war as slave labor to the zaibatsu in the conquered territories."

Hiroki shot up from his seat. "What concern of yours is that? You are an intelligence officer. You should limit your concern to Naval Intelligence! Besides, how can you have respect for these mewling creatures who surrender so easily? They have no honor! No courage! No pride! No shame! Do you know that after they have surrendered and been impounded, they actually *ask* us to inform their families that they are alive and imprisoned? Do you believe that? A Japanese soldier with the misfortune to be taken prisoner and who could not find the means to kill himself would want his disgrace at being captured hidden from the world!"

This was not the first time Matsuo had run into this sentiment. It had been most prominent when news had come that General MacArthur had fled Corregidor for Australia. Every officer Matsuo knew had heaped ridicule on the general for not standing and dying with his troops. Matsuo had tried to explain MacArthur's reasons but had invariably failed. Now it was so important that he make Hiroki understand.

"They don't think like us," Matsuo said. "When they've fought all they can and they're outnumbered and victory is impossible, they surrender. They see no shame in surrender when it becomes obvious that their objective will be lost whether they fight on and die, or stop fighting."

Hiroki's features reflected his repugnance. "That is obscene! Unthinkable for a Japanese soldier! He knows that he must sell his life dearly, to take as many as possible of the enemy with him before he dies and then save a last bullet for himself. That is *Bushido!*"

"But Westerners know nothing of Bushido. They come from a different set of religions and values. They view life differently from us. We've got to understand them if we are going to live with them after this war."

Hiroki's expression became smug. "I prefer to act from the assumption that they are going to have to learn to live with *us* after the war."

"If this open flouting of conventions continues, the Americans will not brook any talk of peace until, as one officer recently put in an American newspaper, 'The only place Japanese will be spoken is hell!'"

"Such bravado from such a weak-willed race!" Hiroki said with a laugh. "No wonder our troops are scything through them like so much wheat! I am only sorry that we did not go to war with these pitiful Western nations sooner. We should have banished them from the Orient long ago! As for peace terms, *we* will dictate them when the time comes. Mark my words, brother: The day may come when Japanese is spoken not in hell but in Washington!"

Matsuo realized that persuading his brother was hopeless. Hiroki was so convinced of Japanese invincibility that he did not think it mattered how prisoners of war were treated. It was like talking to a block of granite. Yet he had to keep trying.

"Is there no way I can convince you that we should observe the Geneva Conventions?"

"Why should you bother with me?" Hiroki said blandly.

"Because I cannot get in to see the Emperor. Premier Tojo controls all access to Him. Not only are private conversations forbidden, but I have been refused general audiences with him and am blocked from attending Imperial Conferences. So I have come to you. Next to the premier you are probably the most powerful man in all Japan." As he saw Hiroki puff up slightly, he decided to pursue the appeal to his brother's pride. "One might even say, due to your intimate contacts within both the Army and the Navy, and within the major zaibatsu, that your power exceeds Tojo's. That is why I've—"

Matsuo was cut off by a series of deep, booming explosions from outside. As air raid sirens began to wail, he hurried to the window where his brother joined him. He saw nothing at first, then came the staccato bursts of antiaircraft fire and the sound of a plane. Suddenly it roared into view overhead. Matsuo recognized it at once.

"It's American!"

"Impossible!" Hiroki cried, pressing his face against the glass.

"A B-25 bomber!"

As the plane turned south and disappeared from view, he turned his attention to the noontime crowds and watched them wave and cheer, thinking no doubt that the Japanese Air Force was putting on some kind of show. But this was no show. He saw smoke begin to rise from the industrial quarter in the lowlands to the east. The Americans were here. They had penetrated the sacred airspace over the Imperial Palace.

Matsuo had an uneasy feeling that the war was going to be different from now on.

■ ■ ■

Meiko strolled the Ginza at Matsuo's side, her hand in his. Matsuo was quiet, lost in thought. She didn't know what he was thinking, but she knew he had been deeply disturbed by the American bombing raid last week. She tried to break him out of his reverie.

"You'd never know we were attacked, would you?" she said.

He looked at her. "To look at the buildings, no. But look at the faces, Meiko. That's where the damage is."

Meiko looked, and had to admit there had indeed been a subtle change. Since the stunning success of the Pearl Harbor attack, Tokyo and the rest of Japan had been in a state of euphoria. Western dress, while not forbidden by law, was frowned upon and had all but completely disappeared by the beginning of the year. Women and most men wore kimonos; the men who didn't wore a military-style olive drab jacket and a fatiguelike cap. The dress had not changed since the raid, but Matsuo was right. The eyes had changed: Meiko sensed a hint of concern in the euphoria.

"See it?" Matsuo said. "It doesn't matter that the physical damage done was negligible, the raid was a success. The American papers credit it to a man named Doolittle, and they are playing it for maximum propaganda value over there. But what it has done here in Tokyo is show us that we can go on believing in the invincibility of our armed forces if we wish, but we can no longer consider our defenses impregnable. The war was far away until last week."

"Is that what's been on your mind since the raid?"

"That and other things." He sighed. "I think it's time to end the war. We've accomplished all we set out to do—we're secure from Indochina down through the East Indies, across the Philippines and out as far as the Solomons, Wake, and the Marshalls. We have booted America and Europe out of the Orient. It is time to get to the bargaining table."

Meiko's heart leapt. "That would be wonderful! How soon?"

"I don't know," he said, and lowered his voice. "Not soon, I fear. Admiral Yamamoto has argued for it strenuously but the Supreme Command seems intoxicated by its successes. They're talking of taking the rest of New Guinea and then moving on to Australia." He shook his head. "New Guinea, I can see . . . but even in the unlikely even that we take Australia, we haven't the manpower to hold it."

"When will they say 'enough,' Matsuo?"

"Perhaps never. If we bring the war to an end now, we can dictate most of the terms. If we allow it to go on too long, I fear someone else will be dictating the terms."

Meiko wasn't thinking about terms. She had more immediate concerns. She remembered the panic that had engulfed her at the sound of the air raid sirens and the sound of the explosions, the contractions in her swelling womb. The raid had opened her eyes to the frailty of this city.

She looked at the buildings around her and thought of their own home: wood. Everything was made of wood, and old wood at that. Tokyo had been rebuilt in the mid-Twenties after the Great Kanto Quake and its resultant fire. That meant that most of the houses in the city were made of wood that had had two decades to dry out. Tinderbox houses divided into rooms within by paper walls, wooden floors covered with mats of straw and rushes. Dry, seasoned wood was everywhere. Tokyo was a maze of kindling. Everything was flammable. She looked down—even her shoes, her geta, were made of wood. There didn't seem to be anything in Tokyo that would not go up in flames at the touch of a match.

She shivered and leaned closer to Matsuo. "I want this war over. I don't ever want to hear a bomber over this city again."

"Neither do I. And I certainly don't want our child to be born in a war, to grow up in a city that might come under attack at any moment."

. . . our child . . .

Meiko ran her free hand over the swell of her abdomen. She was about four and a half months pregnant. But yesterday the midwife had said she looked nearly six months along. Meiko had nearly fainted. That couldn't be! December had been the first month she had missed her menses—November's flow had been scanty, but it had come. Oh, by all the gods, it mustn't be! It must be *our* child!

She glanced up and saw Matsuo looking at her strangely.

"Is something wrong?" he asked.

"Of course not. Why do you ask?"

"Because," he said with a faint smile, "if you squeeze my hand any tighter, at least two of my fingers will fall off."

She laughed and loosened her grip, but the knot inside her remained as tight as ever.

MAY ▬▬▬▬
HASHIRAJIMA

The map room of the *Yamato* was immense. Matsuo gazed around and tried to calculate the number of tatami it would take to cover the floor, but found it impossible in such darkness. The only light was pooled in the center over the plotting table where the captains and senior officers of the Combined Fleet watched intently as groups of ships were moved around the map of the Central Pacific.

Matsuo watched and waited for Admiral Yamamoto to take him aside. After analyzing the intelligence reports from the battle of the

Coral Sea earlier in the month, Matsuo had asked for an urgent audience. The admiral had invited him down here to his fleet's anchorage south of Hiroshima to meet him aboard his eighty-thousand-ton flagship, the largest battleship in the world.

"Do you see my strategy for Operation MI?" said a voice at his shoulder.

Matsuo turned and bowed to the admiral, then glanced back at the plotting table. "I believe so."

"This will be the decisive battle. An immense battle. I am committing eight aircraft carriers, eleven battleships, twenty-two cruisers, sixty-five destroyers, twenty-one submarines, and hundreds of planes to the action. We will crush the Pacific Fleet at Midway. Let me show you."

He bellied up to the table and pointed north to the Aleutian Islands where they trailed away from Alaska like the vertebrae of a huge spine. "We will make a feint here at U.S. soil—Dutch Harbor—on June 3, drawing their attention north. On June 4, we will begin bombardment of Midway Island. And in the course of taking it, we will wipe out what's left of their Pacific Fleet."

Matsuo stared at the plotting table, awed by the enormity and complexity of the operation: six separate attack forces engaging in interlocking offensives. Timing was critical. The expense was mind-boggling, the risk enormous. All for a two-thousand-square-acre speck of coral in the middle of nowhere called Midway. The deck space of the attacking ships no doubt exceeded the surface area of the entire island.

Yamamoto drew him aside and spoke in a low voice. "This will end the war. From Midway we can cut off the American supply line to Australia and directly threaten Hawaii. After this victory, my status will be such that I am positive I can convince Premier Tojo to seek peace terms with the United States. Without Australia as a staging area for a counteroffensive, and with Hawaii in jeopardy, the Americans will come to the table. The war will be over. Japan will have all she needs to assure her primacy for the next thousand years!"

Matsuo closed his eyes and sent out a prayer. *If only that could be!* He stepped closer to the admiral. "Then it is all the more critical that you listen to what I have to tell you. It could affect the entire outcome of Operation MI."

Yamamoto's eyes narrowed. "Come to my quarters."

He followed the admiral to his cabin where he refused a cup of sake but lit a cigarette instead. They both settled into well-cushioned chairs.

"Speak," the admiral said.

"I believe the Americans have broken our Naval Code."

"Impossible!"

"Exactly my sentiments until our defeat in the Coral Sea two weeks ago."

He saw Yamamoto's head snap up. The press and the radio were full of accolades for the Imperial Navy's "glorious victory" off New Guinea. And in truth, on paper, the battle appeared to be a victory. The Americans had lost the *Lexington* and suffered serious damage to the *Yorktown,* and had come out the decided loser in tonnage sent to the bottom of the Coral Sea. But one simple fact remained: The object of the attack had been to capture Port Moresby which would have led to control of the southern coast of New Guinea, allowing them to threaten northern Australia.

But despite all the damage the Imperial Navy had inflicted, the Americans had stopped them. Port Moresby was still controlled by the entrenched Australians.

Matsuo was sure that Yamamoto was aware of this. A curt, reluctant nod from the admiral confirmed it.

"The Americans were lucky," Yamamoto said.

"A little *too* lucky," Matsuo replied. "In all the hugeness of the Pacific, the fact that they should just happen to concentrate their carrier strength in that particular area at the very moment we are launching an offensive against Port Moresby is more than I care to lay off to mere chance."

"The Naval Code is too complex. I can't believe that they have broken it."

The admiral was right about the complexity. The Naval Code was an intricate, multilayered system employing five-digit codes from one book which referred to Japanese ideograms which were, in turn, added to another five-digit group from a second codebook. The idea that Americans could penetrate such a labyrinthine system seemed unlikely in the extreme, but Matsuo had his reasons for believing it had been breached.

"I think they got their break after Colonel Doolittle's raid on Tokyo," Matsuo said. "Most of the available ships from the Combined Fleet were sent out in pursuit of the carriers that brought the U.S. bombers within striking range. Radio traffic was high between the ships and, as you know, a radio operator's style on the key is like a signature. If the Americans were listening, they may have been able to identify call signals and ships, names and positions, and to work out a decoding formula from that."

Yamamoto shook his close-shaven head. "I still don't believe it possible."

"Nevertheless, it would not hurt to implement the new code before Operation MI."

"There's no time."

Matsuo fought to keep an impassive expression. He had previously recommended that a change in codes be implemented by May 1, but had been told then that there was "no time." The change had been pushed back to June 1, and now he was being told that it would be pushed back again.

"Sir, it might mean the difference between victory and defeat."

"No more so than a delay of even a few days. We know the *Yorktown* is in Pearl Harbor for repairs and we know that two other Pacific Fleet carriers are in the waters off Australia. A delay could allow the *Yorktown* time to return to service and those other two carriers to be repositioned near Midway. Now is the time." He slammed his hand repeatedly on the arm of his chair. "Now! Now! Now! We will take Midway. And after we do, I shall make certain that it is the final battle of this war!"

Matsuo inclined his head in deference to his superior's wishes. He knew Yamamoto's reputation as an audacious gambler who rarely lost when it counted, but in his heart he felt the admiral was courting disaster.

JUNE ■
TOKYO

"A disaster! An unmitigated disaster!"

Shimazu watched as Hiroki vent his pent-up emotions. With clenched teeth and wild eyes, he raged back and forth, waving a tally of damages suffered at the naval battle off Midway.

Shimazu knew the details. The Americans had somehow anticipated the attack and had been ready and waiting around the tiny island. The two U.S. carriers thought to be safely away off the Australian coast had been there waiting, as had the *Yorktown*, miraculously repaired and seaworthy after the terrible damage she had sustained in the Coral Sea only weeks before. This time the *Yorktown* had not escaped—she had been sent to the bottom for good. But that was an empty victory when measured against the losses inflicted on the Combined Fleet by the American submarines and torpedo bombers: four carriers—*Agaki, Hiryu, Kaga,* and *Soryu*—a heavy cruiser, 2,200 seamen, and 234 aircraft lost, and worst of all, Midway island was still controlled by the Americans!

So now it begins, Shimazu thought.

"You seem to have forgotten," he said when Hiroki had quieted down, "that the Seer had predicted losses after the initial victories. You should have been ready for this, should have expected it."

But he could not blame Hiroki for his reaction. The seemingly endless cascade of victories during the first six months of the war had lulled them all into a false sense of security. There had seemed to be no limit to what Japan could accomplish. He too had begun to doubt the bleaker portions of the Seer's vision.

But there could no longer be any doubt.

"There is a bright side to this defeat," Shimazu said. "It will strengthen the Imperial Forces, leaving them more wary, less cocksure." He pointed to the reports in Hiroki's hand. "Leave those here. They will be burned later. It won't do for the public to know about this massive defeat. Our people have become almost blasé about military victories. They are not prepared for a defeat of this magnitude."

"Steps will be taken to soften the blow," Hiroki said.

"The Emperor, especially, must be protected from this news. I believe the best course of action is to play up the successful capture of the two Aleutian islands, Attu and Kiska. I know that expedition was a mere diversionary tactic, but it is now the only positive result of Operation MI. All reports must emphasize that Japan has a foothold on the North American continent and all U.S. citizens tremble with fear."

"Yes!" Hiroki said, brightening for the first time. "That is an excellent approach! I'll instruct the Minister of Information immediately!"

"And how goes the search for the scrolls?"

"I am meeting with Yajima this afternoon on that very subject!"

"Good."

Shimazu smiled inwardly. He knew that Yajima had requested to see Hiroki a number of times since the beginning of the war and had been refused. But that had been before the battle of Midway. Yajima and the search for the secret of the Kuroikaze had suddenly increased in importance in Hiroki's mind. That was indeed good.

Now, if he could only divine the significance of his latest visions with the Seers' drug. The past two times he had been under its influence, the mists had parted to reveal a child, an infant boy. There seemed to be some great importance attached to him, a focus of power. Who was he? And why was he so important?

■　■　■

Hiroki bit back a cry of shock as Yajima entered his office later that afternoon. It had been almost a year since he had seen him and he had changed so drastically. The former characteristic fullness of his face was gone, his round cheeks were now hollow and sunken. His once plump body was thin to the point of emaciation, and over his left eye was a black disk.

They bowed, and as Yajima seated himself in the chair across from the desk, Hiroki noted that the fourth and fifth fingers on each hand were missing.

"Welcome, my old friend," he said through a tight throat. "You've . . . changed."

Yajima's smile was skeletal. "I am drawing nearer to my goal. Yet I must confess that the nearer I get, the more impatient I become. You know how I have longed to move beyond the Fourth Circle in the Order. For sixteen years I have denied myself the honor."

Hiroki was stunned. If Yajima had decided to move up in the Kakureta Kao, he would no longer be able to search for the scrolls. "I'm sure you will bring as much honor to the Order beyond the Fourth Circle as you have within it. When do you join the Fifth Circle?"

"Why, not until we have found the scrolls," he said with a puzzled expression. "Was that not our agreement?"

"Yes!" Hiroki said, bathing in relief. "But your hands . . . your eye . . ."

That skeletal smile again. "Ah! But I can turn a page as well with three fingers as with five, and I can read with one eye as well as with two. And I can walk as well without toes as with!"

Hiroki hadn't noticed Yajima's feet when he came in, and he had no desire to look now.

"I felt," Yajima continued, "that I was cheating the Order. I could not give up one of my senses entirely and continue to search effectively for the Kuroikaze scrolls, but I could forgo *portions* of my senses. This would leave me better prepared to join the Inner Circles after we found the scrolls. I have been fasting, as well." He smiled again, horribly, beatifically. "It is all working out so well."

Hiroki swallowed. "Yes. That is quite evident. But I feel ashamed. I have not been bearing my share of the burden of the search. That is why I called you here. I wish to take a more active part."

"But you have done much already! You have provided me with funds and have opened doors that would have otherwise remained closed to me. And you are so busy with the war and matters of state. Everyone in the Order is proud of you and the honor you bring to us all. What you are doing is so close to the Emperor's heart. I would feel less than worthless, a selfish traitor if I dragged you away from your duties!"

"I assure you, old friend Yajima, that finding the Kuroikaze scrolls *is* a matter of state. Now tell me, how close are we?"

"Very close. I have traced Monk Okamoto as far south as Onomichi."

Onomichi . . . that was indeed far south, on the Inland Sea.

"You don't think he might have hidden the scrolls on one of the islands, do you?"

Hiroki was relieved to see Yajima shake his head slowly. The Inland Sea was dotted with countless little islands. If they had to search each one of those—

"Nor do I think he crossed to Shikoku or Kyushu. The old temple records I found in Onomichi tell of a monk of the Order stopping for a night's rest, and mention that he was so weak and sick that they urged him to stay longer but he pushed on. I feel . . ." Yajima closed his remaining eye as if watching a vision playing against the inside of his lid. "I feel he finally stopped in Hiroshima."

Hiroki wondered if Yajima had tried the Seer's drug—tried it more than once—in his quest for the scrolls.

"Then that is where we will search!"

" 'We'?" Yajima's sunken features lit. "You will come with me?"

"Of course! You have borne this burden alone for too long."

"But your work here for the war—"

"I know." Hiroki sighed with what he hoped was genuine-sounding reluctance. "I will have to return here from time to time, but when I do, my heart will be with you as you search."

Yajima leapt to his feet. "We will find it soon! I know it! And then the Emperor shall have a weapon that will devastate all who oppose His Divine Will!" His voice softened. "And I shall be free to take my place in the Inner Circles of the Order. To start the final road toward the Face."

They agreed to meet in Hiroshima at the end of the week and begin their search of the temples and shrines there. After his old friend left, Hiroki sat and stared at the blank white wall across from his desk.

Yajima, Yajima, he thought. *You poor man. How can you be so anxious to allow yourself to be whittled away?*

The future of Japan was here, in this office, where the spoils of war were being divided between the service chiefs and the industrial giants. And as Hiroki faithfully executed his duties in seeing that the windfall of resources opening up in Indochina and the East Indies was put to proper and efficient use for the good of the Empire, he made sure that a share of those riches came to the Order, if not in outright cash, then in the form of interest in the financial and industrial concerns exploiting the new resources.

He gained, too, but in a less material way. Hiroki did not intend to lapse into obscurity after the war. He would be owed many favors in postwar Japan. He would be independently powerful. He would no longer need the support of the Kakureta Kao. But he had not reached that stage yet. He still needed the Order behind him to maintain his present post.

And to cement that support, he needed to be with Yajima when the scrolls were unearthed.

AUGUST

The pains started low in her back and radiated around to the front. Sporadically at first, then with a definite rhythm.

False labor! Meiko thought in a panic. *It must be! It's not my time yet!*

She had grown so large over the past month, so unwieldy with her big belly and her swollen ankles, yet still she had clung firm to the hope, the belief that this was Matsuo's baby. But with these pains and with the sudden gush of water as her membranes broke, she could deny the reality no longer.

She told Matsuo to get the midwife. The concern on his face was mixed with joy, wonder, and anticipation. She prayed she would see that same joy when this day was over.

The pains continued, becoming stronger, closer together. The midwife, Michiko, arrived. She banished Matsuo from the room, then began to prepare her for labor and birth. She bathed her and then tied two silken cords to her futon. When the pains became worse, strong enough that they might force her to cry out or moan in pain, Meiko grasped one or both and pulled as hard as she could until the contraction passed. For birth was a private affair and not to be publicized.

As the contractions grew and coalesced, the midwife moved the baby's tiny pallet bed to the side of Meiko's futon. She plumped up and straightened the new, freshly stuffed quilt and coverlet Meiko had made herself. Meiko stared at it during a respite from pain, and felt her eyes fill with tears. So tiny. Soon the life inside her would be lying there. How sad and empty she would feel to be separated from the little one who had been kicking and turning so actively within her these past few months, but how good finally to see and touch that little one! She knew she would want to cuddle and clutch the baby to her all through the night, but also knew that a baby must have its own bed. It would be a bad omen for a child to come into the world and not have its own bed.

Pain blurred the thought, and soon the contractions blurred together until finally, with the midwife's prompting, there came a final searing pain she thought would tear her apart, and then it was over. Relieved and almost-empty, she lay gasping and drenched, waiting for that sound, that dear sweet sound that had to come any second.

And then a choking, vibrato wail filled the room.

"Is the baby all right?"

"Yes!" the midwife said. "He's beautiful!"

"Let me see him! Oh, let me see him!"

"Just let me clean him off." Meiko heard the sound of splashing water amid the cries, and then Michiko was kneeling beside her and offering a struggling, towel-wrapped bundle. She saw the jet black hair matted onto the big round head, saw the skinny neck and the tiny fingers clutched under his chin, saw a little ear and tiny nose and gleaming brown eyes as the infant was turned her way . . .

. . . saw the red birthmark flaring up from his left eyebrow toward his hairline.

Meiko wanted to cry out, wanted to push the baby away and hide him from sight, but she could not. He was hers. She loved him instantly and would shower him with all the tenderness and devotion he deserved. He was hers . . . and Frank's.

There were still more contractions and Michiko went to work while Meiko clutched the infant to her. The afterbirth was soon delivered, leaving Meiko with a final, empty feeling.

She sensed movement about her and looked up. Michiko was at the shoji, sliding it back. "It's a boy!" she said.

Matsuo darted into the room, wide-eyed and beaming. He knelt beside her, his hands moving spasmodically in the air as if he wanted to do something with them and didn't know what. He glanced at the bloodstains on the futon, only partially hidden by the coverlet, and his smile vanished.

"Are you all right?"

"I'm fine," she said. *Please don't hate me!*

Matsuo looked at the midwife, who smiled and nodded in agreement, then back at Meiko. His proud grin returned.

"And our boy? Is he as perfect as his mother?" He reached for the baby.

"Matsuo . . ." Meiko began, but didn't know how to finish. She couldn't hide the truth and it would be unforgivable to try even if it were possible. She released the child and held her breath, watching Matsuo's glowing face as he held up the squirming bundle. She saw his face change, darkening like a sunny garden falling under a cloud, saw the smile melt away, the warm loving eyes turn to stone.

"Oh, Matsuo," she said through a sob, feeling as though her heart were tearing in two. "I didn't know! Truly, I didn't!"

With stiff, wooden arms, he handed the baby back to her. She tried to read his face. There was no message in his usually mobile features, frozen now into a mockery of calm. But his eyes! There was grief there, and such pain, such crushing hurt.

Without a word, he turned and left the room.

■ ■ ■

"You may raise him here," he told her the following morning as they sat at the low table and sipped tea.

Thank the gods! Meiko thought as she held the sleeping child in her arms. If Matsuo were a traditional Japan man, he would have banished her from the house. As it was, *he* had left the house.

He had disappeared yesterday and had stayed away all night. Meiko had spent the night alone, crying at times and cursing her fate at others, but all the while staring at the gentle new life lying in its tiny bed next to hers, listening to him breathe, watching him squirm.

With the light of the new day, Matsuo returned, unshaven and bleary-eyed. She tried to catch the odor of sake on him, but there was none. Nor the perfume of another woman. Had he merely wandered the streets all those hours? She hesitated to ask.

"That is very generous of you, Matsuo," she said, searching his face for a clue to his feelings.

"I thought about it all night. The child is blameless. He can live and grow up with us, but I cannot allow him to have my name."

Meiko bowed her head. That was only fair. It was more than fair. "I know how you must—"

"No!" he snapped. "You cannot know how I feel! How could you? I've been by your side every day, watching you swell, feeling a baby I thought was half mine kick and turn under your skin, thinking of names, thinking of his future, wondering how good a father I'd be. Yesterday you gave birth and today you have a son. Yesterday I waited and paced and sweated in the outer room and today I have nothing!"

Meiko could hear the pain in his voice and it cut through to her soul, for she was the cause of it. "I'm sorry. I didn't know. Please believe me."

"How could you not know?"

"The possibility crossed my mind only in the last few months."

"And you said nothing to me?"

"How *could* I? Besides, I didn't believe it was true. I didn't *want* it to be true! If you believe nothing else, believe that!"

He stared at her, his face a mask.

"I was his wife!" she cried. "In all ways! And I loved him as a wife should love a husband."

Matsuo pointed to his temple. "I can accept that here"—he pointed the finger toward his belly—"but not here." He slammed his hand against the floor, startling the baby in her arms. "Am I never to be free of Frank Slater?"

"Neither of us are to be free of him. It came to me as I waited for you to come home: The boy is a sign from the gods that neither of us must ever forget Frank Slater or what we did to him. How we raise this child will somehow mend and heal the damage we did. I am going to name him Nakanaori."

Nakanaori . . . reconciliation. The name had come to her with the first light of day.

"We will never see Frank Slater again," Matsuo said.

"I think we will," Meiko said, and she truly believed it. "I think Nakanaori will bring us back together one day and undo all the wrongs we have done to each other."

Meiko watched Matsuo's eyes unfocus. He seemed to be peering into a place far away and long ago. Was he seeing a frightened boy running from him when he needed his help, or was he seeing a grown man nailed to a tree?

She looked away and took comfort from the baby warm against her.

NOVEMBER
HIROSHIMA

Hiroki leaned over Yajima's shoulder and read once again the fragment they had unearthed as it vibrated in his old friend's trembling, mutilated hands.

> ". . . and he shall thus be deprived during the course of two days of his entire senses: He shall have no feeling on his skin or in his deeper tissues anywhere upon his person, no sensation in his tongue and eyes, nor in his ears, nor in his nostrils. Thus shall he become a focus for the Black Winds. When his sleep ends, the Black Wind will rise and blow until he sleeps again. Woe to the enemies of the Son of Heaven who dare to . . ."

That was all there was to the fragment. Yajima turned to him with a shining eye.

"Do you see, Hiroki? It mentions the Kuroikaze by name!"

Hiroki nodded. His elation was tempered by exhaustion. For months now he had joined Yajima at intervals to sift through the many shrines large and small in Hiroshima and its northern suburbs, following scant clues down blind alleys. When Hiroki was not searching, he was hurrying back north to Tokyo to consult with Shimazu, manage his post, and keep abreast of developments in the war.

And those developments were not good ones. The Americans had invaded the Solomon Islands last month, an archipelago of swampy, disease- and insect-infested coral lumps due east of New Guinea, at the southeast extreme of the Empire. They had established beachheads on Guadalcanal and Tulagi, had even gone so far as to build an airstrip on the small corner they held on Guadalcanal. Despite regular bombings and suicidal frontal assaults by the Japanese infantry, the Americans were holding on and consolidating their positions.

It was only a tiny chink in the Imperial armor, but it made Hiroki more anxious than ever to find the lost scrolls. Against the logic and reason of his everyday dealings with the military, he had come to see the Kuroikaze as the key to the war.

This tiny, ancient Shinto shrine at the base of Mount Futaba with its weathered, crooked torii looked to be just one more dead end. But a torrential rain had begun outside and this had seemed to be as good a place as any to wait out the storm. It had yielded the first hard evidence that their fifteen-year quest would not end in total failure.

"Yes, I see," he said. "But where is the rest?" He and Yajima had combed the rear chamber of this shrine but had found only this long, thin scrap of parchment among its records.

"We shall find the rest if the rest still exists. If this is all that is left, perhaps it is enough."

"But it doesn't tell us how to raise the Kuroikaze."

"I believe it does. It tells us of a man stripped of every last one of his senses, and that he becomes the shoten, the focus of the Black Wind! The surgeons of the Order can easily create such a state!"

Hiroki was almost caught up in Yajima's exhilaration, yet something held him back. "But the members of the Innermost Circle are stripped of their last senses before they are sent to see the Face, are they not?"

"Yes, but this is different. Don't you see how it all fits, Hiroki? The Inner Circles of the Order give up their senses over a period of years, but a Black Wind shoten gives up *all* of his at once! He is abruptly thrust from all contact with the physical world. He can't feel the futon under his back, doesn't know if he is sitting or supine, can't see or hear or smell or taste! He floats in an endless, featureless void. And it must be from that void that he draws the Kuroikaze and sends it against the enemies of the Emperor! Our temple surgeons have the skills to put a man in that state! We can do it, Hiroki! The Black Wind can be ours to command again!"

If only you are right, Yajima! he thought. Then a discomforting thought occurred to him. "It will take a very special sort of man to subject himself to such an ordeal. Who do you . . . ?"

The glow in Yajima's remaining eye provided the answer before Hiroki finished the question.

"I would be honored!" Yajima said. "In fact, Hiroki, I don't think we should search any further today. We should hurry back to the temple and present this remnant of the scrolls to Shimazu immediately! Won't he be proud of us?"

"This will bring enormous honor to our sensei."

"And if I may be so bold as to ask you this favor, my dear friend," Yajima said, bowing low. "Allow me to beg Shimazu for the honor of being the first to become a shoten of the Black Winds."

Hiroki's throat was suddenly too dry for speech. The thought of those knives cutting into this man he had known since childhood, separating him from all his senses . . . he repressed a shudder. He might have tried to dissuade Yajima but knew from the look in his eye that it would be a futile exercise. Yajima *hungered* to offer himself as a sacrificial lamb to the knives of the Order. He pitied him and yet envied him, for he knew what he wanted and was going to achieve it.

"Does this mean . . . ?" Hiroki felt his throat thicken. "Am I to lose my oldest and only friend?"

"Never! Even if I cannot be at your side in the flesh, I will be with you in spirit. And together we shall crush the enemies of the Emperor."

"How can I object, then?" he managed to say. "You have devoted yourself more fully to the search over the years. You should have your wish."

Yajima bowed again. "Hiroki, you are too kind!"

"I also think that you alone should have the honor of presenting the fragment to the temple."

A tear trickled down Yajima's right cheek. "You would permit me that honor?"

"I insist upon it!"

Hiroki did not say that he was reluctant to stand by idle and silent while Yajima offered all that he possessed to the Order.

"Oh, Hiroki! I will be there alone, but I shall not let Shimazu-sensei or the Elders forget for a moment that this fragment would never have been found without you!"

Hiroki thanked him and watched him hurry off. Poor Yajima. Always in such a rush to sacrifice himself. So intent upon the next life that he lost sight of this one.

Not Hiroki. Something told him that there was much more to be learned about the Black Winds, and he would keep searching until he found the remainder. Let Yajima hurl himself upon the altar. Hiroki knew he had too much left to do in this life before he gratefully accepted the next.

1 9 4 3

THE YEAR OF THE RAM

Hiroki returned to the Shinto shrine where they had found the fragment. Desperation was a hammer pounding at his skull. He had been to at least thirty of the major shrines and temples in an ever-widening gyre from this point but had found nothing new. He was losing hope. Either the scrolls were gone forever—rotted to dust or destroyed—or the ancient monk had hidden them too well.

The search was made even more difficult now by the fact that he was searching alone. Yajima had remained in Tokyo at the temple this trip. And there he would remain forever. He would be unable to leave the temple after the Order's surgeons finished their work on him.

Hiroki preferred to be elsewhere while Yajima was being cut off and locked away from the sensory world. He found Tokyo unpleasant in other ways. The Supreme Command had given up on Guadalcanal. Of the forty thousand troops poured onto that jungle island, less than seventeen thousand survived. Far more had succumbed to cholera and other diseases than to American and Australian weaponry, and it was a popular saying around the Imperial War Room that Japan had lost to the jungle, not to the Americans. But Hiroki knew differently. While the workers in the new factories studding the countryside toiled in round-the-clock shifts, they could match but a fraction of the tide of ships and tanks and planes and food surging from America. American soldiers, thousands of miles away from home, with their sturdy clothes and tents and miraculous K-rations, were better housed, clothed, and fed than many Japanese civilians.

Yamamoto's prophetic words before the Imperial Conference on the Tripartite Alliance echoed in his mind: *We can give the Americans the fight of their lives for six months . . . after that they will simply overwhelm us with their material superiority, no matter how bravely we fight.*

Although it was vociferously denied in Tokyo, Hiroki knew that Japan had lost its initiative. His belly rebelled at the thought, but he had forced himself to face it: From now on, it would be a war of attrition until the Kuroikaze could be brought to bear on the enemy. Yajima and many in the Order were sure they had finally regained the secret of the winds. Neither Hiroki nor Shimazu was so sure. The oral tradition of the Kakureta Kao seemed to imply that a chemical potion of some sort had been used to raise the Black Winds. Surgery was never mentioned. Hiroki had failed to convince Yajima to wait a little longer before he went under the knife, but he had never stopped looking for the rest of the scrolls.

He no longer wanted to think about Yajima. Matsuo came to mind. His whore-queen wife had borne a child, but apparently not Matsuo's if reports could be believed. Yet Matsuo let the mother and child remain with him. Truly his brother was a twisted one!

Hiroki set his candle down and peered about the rear chamber of the shrine. It was a tiny room, carved from the natural rock of the mountain against which the shrine had been set. They had pulled everything from the shelves, even looked behind the shelves. There was no place left to look, yet something had drawn him back here. He let his gaze travel over the crockery and utensils littering the floor or upended on the shelves.

Why had he come back? Why did he have this vague sense of foreboding? Had they missed something here? Impossible! They had turned the chamber upside down! They had missed nothing! There was nothing left to—

The candlelight flickered off something smooth and yellow inside one of the urns lying on its side on the floor under a shelf. Hiroki leapt forward, grasped it—and almost dropped it as a gray mouse squeaked and darted out of it. He turned it upside down and shook it: Only dark little droppings fell out. It was empty of further rodents. He held the mouth up to the candle and there it was—old, yellowed paper, curled and crumpled inside. Hiroki's heartbeat picked up its tempo when he recognized the brush strokes of the ideograms. He reached in with two fingers and gently, gingerly, removed the strip.

It was stained with a combination of mouse urine and feces, and gnawed in many places, but there was no mistaking it: He had found another remnant of the scrolls. He began reading the few areas that remained legible and realized that this was from a section immediately preceding the remnant they had discovered last week. He could find no sentence intact and could make no sense of the content. One pair of ideograms showed up repeatedly in the text, however: *kodomo*. Hiroki leaned back, wondering why it appeared so often in conjunction with creating a Black Wind.

Suddenly he cried out and leaped to his feet. He knew! He stood in the tiny stone rear chamber, shaking with horror. He had to contact Yajima! He had to stop him!

Hiroki would have raced for a phone but he knew it would do him no good. There was no telephone in the temple. He ran from the shrine like a man who had seen a ghost. He had to get to Tokyo! Immediately!

TOKYO

The next day's dawn was tinting the sky with a gentle pink when Hiroki's train pulled into Tokyo Station. He hailed a cab and made the driver race to the temple. After he was admitted through the heavy carved doors, he ran through the candle-lit halls to Shimazu's spare quarters and pounded on the door. The monk slid the door open.

"Sensei!" he said without preliminaries. "Yajima—is he . . . ? Have they . . . ?"

Shimazu stepped aside and motioned him into the room. He pointed to a dark corner. "He is here."

Hiroki was suddenly weak with relief. He stepped toward the corner. "Yajima! Thank the gods I arrived in time! I—"

"He can't hear you," Shimazu said.

Hiroki's relief evaporated in a cold blast of remorse. "You mean, the surgery has begun?"

"It is finished."

"Then he is locked away from us forever?"

Shimazu nodded. "Completely and forever. He has no ears to hear our questions and no tongue with which to answer them if he had. He has given us his remaining eye as well as his senses of taste and smell. His spinal cord was severed as high as we dared, cutting off all feeling and control to his body; the nerves to his head and face have been severed as well."

Hiroki felt as if he were shriveling and shrinking inside his skin as he listened to his master's words. He lifted a paper lantern from its hook and brought it closer to the corner. He caught his breath as he saw Yajima.

He was propped up on cushions into a rough semblance of a sitting position. He looked like a limp, tattered doll. He was dressed in a clean, black kimono and his arms and legs were neatly arranged, but Hiroki could tell that there was no power or feeling in those limbs. His right eye was patched now as well as his left. Below them, his face hung loose and expressionless. A thin line of saliva dribbled from a corner of his slack lips.

Suddenly, a low, shapeless moan filled the room. Hiroki leaped back. The hairs on his arms and the back of his neck stood on end.

"I thought you said he could not speak!"

"He cannot. His tongue has been removed but he still breathes. He cannot form words but he can make sounds—sounds he cannot hear."

"Is he in pain?"

Shimazu smiled. "He is beyond pain forever. He does not even know if he is lying or sitting, supine or prone. He dwells now in a state beyond all care, in a void beyond all sensation."

"And has he been able to raise up a Black Wind?" Hiroki said. His voice sounded dead to him. He already knew the answer.

"No," Shimazu said. "Tragically, no." He looked at Hiroki with a puzzled frown. "Why do I sense that you are not surprised at that?"

"Because you are wise and know me well." Hiroki sighed and returned the lamp to its hook. He preferred Yajima in the shadows. "I found another piece of the scrolls just hours ago in Hiroshima."

Shimazu's eyes lit. "More? You've uncovered more?"

"Just a fragment." Hiroki pulled the envelope containing the fragile piece from his kimono and handed it to Shimazu. "But I think it explains why all the surgery on Yajima failed to produce the Kuroikaze."

Shimazu pulled the fragment from the envelope and held it up to the lantern to read it. Then he turned wide eyes toward Hiroki. "Can this be true?"

Hiroki nodded. "I see no other way to interpret it. I—"

He started as Yajima's low, formless wail filled the room again. He stared at the darkened corner. Yajima's mind was alive in there, trapped and utterly isolated within that useless body. Soon he would be completely mad, if not already so.

"*Children?*" Shimazu said, his tone still incredulous.

Hiroki dragged his eyes away from the drooling lump of flesh that his old friend had become. He concentrated on the new fragment, praying the hope and excitement of the promise it offered would wash his pity and grief for Yajima from his mind.

"Yes. The new fragment leaves little doubt that the ancient members of the Order used children to focus the Black Winds."

Shimazu was silent a long time. Finally he said, "Japan is filled with children."

JULY

What's happening to us? Meiko thought as she trudged along the unkempt streets of Tokyo. A year ago there had been no evidence that the country was at war; now it was everywhere. The entire city was scarred and pockmarked. Everywhere she looked, every twenty paces, there were holes and trenches, in the alleys, in the gardens, in vacant lots, along the sidewalks, some up to ten feet long, none more than three feet deep. These were the first and last line of defense for the city's seven million residents against enemy bombings. No bombers had appeared over Tokyo since that single raid in April last year, but who could say it wouldn't happen again tomorrow?

All around her she could see signs of how the war was unraveling the delicate fabric of Japanese life. The countless country folk dragged into the city to work in the factories caused crowding that was almost unbearable. Queues were everywhere: for rice, for tea, for cloth, for train tickets, for bicycle tire patches, for everything. The kimono was fast becoming a relic of a more elegant past. The new, government-approved look for the woman was the *monpei*, a cross between army fatigues and harem pants, tight at the waist and ankles and billowing between.

And the city! Meiko's heart broke for her beloved Tokyo as the army dismantled it by inches for scrap iron. Handrails and lampposts seemed to disappear overnight; grilles were pulled off windows. Boilers, radiators, and pipes were stripped from old buildings, abandoned cars were devoured, skeleton and all.

Meiko wondered what damage was left for American bombers to do that hadn't already been done by her country's own military.

She queued up behind a truck for her regular ration of milk. Usually she sent Nakanaori's nurse out for it, but Sachiko was sick today, so she had come herself. She wondered if she should have brought Naka along instead of leaving him home with Matsuo. Ever since he was thirty days old, when she had been sure that his life was firmly locked into his body and had presented him at the local shrine, mother and son had been virtually inseparable. She double-sashed him to her back—one band under his arms and the other under his rump—and they were off together to wherever she had to go.

She loved her parents, had loved Frank, loved Matsuo, but had never imagined she could ever feel so at one with another human being as she did with Naka. Almost a year old now, he had spent most of his short life literally looking over her shoulder, pressed against her where he could share her warmth and she could feel every breath, every heartbeat, every move he made. She loved that little boy so dearly. More than life itself.

She wished Matsuo could share that love. He avoided Naka. Meiko had feared that his coolness might put the little fellow off, but it only seemed to make Naka gravitate toward him all the more.

Matsuo had not allowed her to refer to him as "Father" in front of the child. But since they lived together, and because he had begun to speak his first words at ten months of age, Naka had to call the man of the house something. Matsuo's proper name was unacceptable, of course; but after much trial and error and endless cajoling, he had finally agreed to allow himself to be called *Oji-san*—"Uncle." Despite the wall of rejection that Matsuo had erected between himself and the child, Naka constantly asked for "Oji-san," saying the name over and over.

Naka was with his "Oji-san" now. She had left the two of them alone together today. She wanted to give Naka a chance to work his little boy magic on Matsuo. Sooner or later Matsuo would have to yield. But now she wondered if that had been such a good idea. Matsuo had been so depressed since Admiral Yamamoto's death.

She worried about Matsuo. He was alienated from his brother, estranged from his father, and he had few friends. He had worshipped the admiral, but now he was gone, too. Matsuo seemed so alone, so out of place. She ached to help him, but there didn't seem to be anything she could do.

An urge to get back home was growing swiftly within her. She feared the frustrations she sensed in Matsuo might break free when there was only he and Naka in the house. Meiko was sure he would never take them out on a child, and yet she knew Naka was at a very trying age. She shuffled her feet impatiently and willed the milk line to move faster, but it still crawled along at a snail's pace.

■   ■   ■

Matsuo knew he was in a black mood. He didn't try to shake it off. He preferred to wallow in it. He liked the state of physical paresis and mental paralysis it offered. It allowed him to sit cross-legged here at the table and sip tea without the slightest twinge of guilt.

What was there to feel guilty about anyway? There were codes to break, ship and troop movements to track, espionage agent reports to be evaluated, but he was here at home doing something much more important! He was playing nurse for Frank Slater's son!

Naka smiled up at him from the floor, then began to crawl away, his pajamaed legs rustling along the tatami. All the gods surely knew how he loathed the child! Why didn't the child loathe him in return? Or, at the very least, fear him? But no. Naka had only smiles for him, and hugged his leg when he could reach it.

Matsuo forced his clenched jaw muscles to relax and took another sip of tea, barely tasting it. Frank Slater's son. He had hoped he would get used to that fact. The shock had worn off, and the disappointment had settled into a bitter lump at the back of his throat, but the sneering irony of it remained a white-hot coal behind his eyes.

Nakanaori Mazaki, the embodiment of that pain, had just pulled himself up to a standing position along the side support of a nearby shoji. He seemed proud of himself. He had a big round face, dark eyes, and unruly black hair that Meiko combed down in bangs over his birthmark. He looked at Matsuo now and grinned.

"Oji-than!" he said with his tongue thrusting over the last syllable. Matsuo only stared at him, wishing the child had never been born.

Naka turned and slowly, carefully made his way along the translucent paper surface of the sliding door. He seemed afraid to walk free, and never stood without support. Probably normal for an eleven-month-old, but Matsuo had his own interpretation.

A timid soul—just like his father.

Matsuo turned his thoughts inward. He knew his mood was directly attributable to Admiral Yamamoto's death. The news had struck him like a mortar blast. The sanest officer in the Imperial armed forces, the best strategic mind in the Orient, perhaps in the world, had been lost to Japan. On April 18, the Mitsubishi bomber that was taking him to Bougainville on a personal inspection tour of the bases in the Solomons had been pounced upon and shot down by seventeen American P-38 fighters. The Supreme Command, in an effort to conceal the importance of their victim from the Americans, withheld release of the information until late May when the admiral's ashes had been brought back to Japan. Matsuo had stood on the dock and wept as the small white box was ceremoniously unloaded from the battleship *Musashi.*

Matsuo, of course, had learned of the tragedy immediately; he had also gathered from the celebratory tone of a few radio messages monitored shortly after the incident, that the Americans were perfectly aware of the identity of the man they had shot down, and in fact had lain in wait for him!

This was more evidence to bolster Matsuo's contention that American intelligence had shattered all of Japan's codes and ciphers, and that a completely new system had to be designed and put into use. But his demands and his pleas were given only lip service: "Yes, you are probably right, and work is progressing on it even as we speak, but now is not the time to disrupt communications."

Matsuo had his suspicions about the incident. He knew the admiral had been terribly frustrated in his attempts to convince the Supreme Command to offer peace and stop the war while Japan still held some advantages. Yamamoto saw the war now as one prolonged battle of attrition, a battle Japan could not possibly win against the likes of America. Certain defeat lay ahead on Japan's present course. Since Yamamoto could not change that course, and could not honorably resign, only one course of action was left open to him.

Although he would never voice it, Matsuo suspected that Yamamoto knew his announcement of an aerial inspection tour would be intercepted and deciphered. Perhaps he had seen death in combat as preferable to watching his beloved Japan ground into the mud by the ever-growing power of the American war machine.

Japan had lost a national treasure and Matsuo had lost a confidant. Whenever the admiral had come to Tokyo, he had called Matsuo and the two of them would have dinner together. They would discuss the progress of the war—or lack of it—in candid terms. Yamamoto was the only high-ranking officer with whom Matsuo felt safe voicing a frank opinion of the conduct of the war, for he knew the admiral shared those views.

Now he was gone, and Matsuo felt more isolated than ever. He had Meiko, of course, but hardly anyone else. Perhaps it was because of her that he had become isolated. For he did not share the Japanese male's casual attitude toward extramarital sex, be it with mistresses or prostitutes. His fellow intelligence officers used to ask him out regularly for a night on the town, but he always refused. Geishas were boring and he could not dredge up any interest in visiting the bordellos.

He had turned them down so many times that they no longer bothered inviting him. Only Shigeo came around regularly, and he—

His thoughts were interrupted by the sound of tearing paper. Matsuo looked up and saw Naka poking his little index finger through the polished paper of the shoji. He dragged it downward, leaving behind a long ragged tear.

Matsuo cursed under his breath. "*No*, Naka! That is bad! Don't do that!"

The child glanced at him over his shoulder, then turned back to the shoji and poked a new hole with his finger. Matsuo's self-control rent with the sound of the tearing paper. He was up and halfway across the floor with his hand raised to strike when Naka turned toward him again. The innocent smile that beamed out from that little round face, so pleased at being able to puncture and rip the paper, stopped Matsuo in his tracks. Naka twisted his body toward Matsuo and held up his arms. "Oji-than!" he said, still smiling.

Matsuo felt his anger cool and dissipate like breath in a January wind. The shoji was fair game for toddlers all over Japan. He had poked his share of holes in Nagata's as a child. He had to control this rage within him. If he didn't come to terms with it soon—

"Oji-than!"

Suddenly Naka was walking toward him—on his own, free, unsupported! His first steps! Why wasn't Meiko here to see? To catch him? And why was he coming toward Matsuo with outstretched arms, weaving and wobbling like a drunken dwarf? He was going to fall and Matsuo didn't want to catch him—didn't want to so much as touch the child. Yet Naka was looking up at him and grinning so proudly—

Then his foot caught on the edge of a tatami and the smile disappeared as he plunged toward the floor. Matsuo dropped to his knees and caught his outstretched hands before he landed. Grasping him only by his fingers, he balanced Naka on his feet again and let him go. Naka immediately fell against him and threw his arms around his neck. He rested his head on Matsuo's shoulder and said, "Oji-than."

With a will of their own, Matsuo's arms went around the child and embraced the little body gingerly, as if fearing to break it. He was amazed at the waves of emotion swirling through him, especially the warm and protective feelings for this tiny boy who was half Frank Slater. They frightened him and he worked to dam them up, to hide them away. He almost succeeded. Then Naka leaned back and looked him in the face; he smiled and patted Matsuo on the shoulder, saying, "Oji-than" once more.

Matsuo could not help himself. He hugged Naka against him. "I'm sorry!" he whispered. "Sorry for hating you! You no more chose your father than I chose mine." He pushed the startled child back and brushed the hair off his forehead, revealing the red birthmark. He smiled at him and Naka smiled back. "Frank Slater's son—you could have done better, but you could have done worse, too."

■ ■ ■

Meiko paused as she reached for the handle on the front door. There was a high-pitched noise coming from within. It sounded like a child's screams! She almost dropped the milk as she ran inside.

Naka lay on the floor of the main room. His face was a bright red and he was screeching . . . with laughter. Meiko stood back and tried to comprehend what she saw. She would have been less surprised to find a traveling Kabuki company set up and performing in her home than the incredible scene being played out before her:

Matsuo was crouched behind the shoji directly to her right. The paper of one of its panels had been completely shredded. He had poked his head all the way through the ruined panel and was grimacing at Naka, sticking his tongue out to the side and twisting his face into bizarre expressions. Naka screeched again, then rolled over and laughed from deep in his belly.

"What is going on here?"

Matsuo's face lit as he looked up. "Meiko! Watch what he can do! You have to see!" He scurried around to Naka's side of the shoji and lifted him to his feet. He pointed him toward Meiko and let go. "Go to your mother!"

Meiko watched in awe as Naka lurched toward her with out-stretched arms. Joy burst free in her as she laughed and gathered him up and held him high in the air. She swung him onto her hip and turned to Matsuo. She could barely speak.

"*You* taught him?"

"Of course not!" Matsuo said, beaming. "He taught himself! And look what else he taught himself!"

He took Naka from her hip and placed him before the shoji, then stood back by her side to watch. Naka ran his hand over the translucent surface, then methodically, decisively, poked his index finger through the paper. He looked up at Meiko and grinned.

Meiko cringed at the tearing sound as he ripped a long gash in the shoji. "Have I gone insane?" she said to Matsuo.

"No," he said, looking into her eyes. She saw a new softness there, one that had been missing even through her pregnancy, missing ever since that fateful day on Sagami Bay six years ago.

"Then have *you?*"

He laughed. "No! I'm saner than I ever was. It's just that I . . ."

He seemed to search for words. "I think I've wasted too much of our time wishing I could change the past. Nagata used to tell me that a wise and happy man is one who reveres the past and learns from it, but never tries to live there. One can only change the present and the future."

Meiko threw her arms around him. "Matsuo, do you know how much I love you?"

"Still?" he said. "You must have started off with an enormous amount if there can be any left after all I've done and said since I found you again on Oahu."

"I have an endless supply for you!"

She kissed him and snuggled in his arms, feeling safe and warm and right as they watched Naka make new holes in the shoji.

Over the sound of tearing paper, she heard Matsuo say softly, "You have a talent for naming children, too."

NOVEMBER

The ether was wearing off.

Hiroki watched as the child's respiratory rate quickened. Only its diaphragm and chest wall moved as it lay on the futon. No other muscles were capable of voluntary movement. He waited for it to cry out, a sure sign that consciousness had returned.

It? Actually, the child was a *he*—a three-year-old *he*—but Hiroki found it easier, more comfortable, to think of these children as things. It was a simple mental accommodation that allowed him to get through the day.

Hiroki felt that somehow there had to be a better way, but until they found it, this would have to do. So many children, so many surgeries . . .

. . . so many failures.

Even the Order's surgeons were beginning to doubt. They never said as much, but after so many years among the masked members of the Kakureta Kao, Hiroki had learned to read movement and posture as most people read facial expressions. And he had begun to detect a certain cynicism in the surgeons.

Who could blame them? After toiling daily on child after child without once producing a Black Wind *shoten*, even the most devoted monk would have to question the validity of the procedures.

But they *had* to succeed! Even as they stood here the Americans were storming through the Gilbert Islands. Makin and Betio had already fallen, and Tarawa would soon join them. Japan's bravest men were being overwhelmed. Nothing could stop the Americans now except maybe the Black Winds, and even that—

A low moan escaped the child, then rose in pitch to an amorphous shriek of terror. It was conscious now. Before the ether had put it to sleep, life had consisted of touch and taste and smell and sight and sound—a sense of corporeal existence. Now it was awakening to an existence devoid of all those things. Now it was aware, but trapped forever in a formless black void, cut off from all its senses, floating in an endless sea of unimaginable terror.

Hiroki shuddered at the anguish in the sound. What that child must be experiencing! What it must—!

Something was happening. Dread clawed its way up Hiroki's spine with icy fingernails. He did not know what had changed exactly, but everything in the room was suddenly different—malevolently different. Was it darker? Yes. The light from the lanterns had dimmed.

"What's happening?" he said.

The surgeons looked at him, confusion showing through the eyeholes of their masks. Shimazu said nothing, but Hiroki could sense the sudden tension in his posture.

And then the light began to fade more quickly. The temperature plummeted as an inky mist congealed out of the air, swallowing the glow from the lamps. The mist began to writhe and undulate in a breeze that seemed to spring from the very walls of the closed room.

As it rose in velocity, he heard Shimazu cry out. "Kuroikaze! The Black Wind is rising!"

"The sedative!" Hiroki shouted, pointing to one of the surgeons. "Give it now!"

The old monk quickly tied a tourniquet around the child's arm and grabbed a prefilled syringe. As the wind continued to rise, Hiroki watched the surgeon's trembling hand plunge the needle into the arm and empty the clear fluid into the vein.

No! He missed the vein!

He saw the skin rise alongside the vein as the sedative infiltrated the subcutaneous tissue. It would take ten minutes at least before it took effect! They would all be dead by then!

Hiroki lost his footing and slipped to the floor as the wind rose to a howl. "The ether! Get the ether and knock him out!"

"It's downstairs!" one of the surgeons cried.

From the corner of his eye he saw Shimazu crawling toward the child, fighting the wind that shrieked in their ears and tore at their clothes. He grabbed the child's foot and pulled it closer to him. Hiroki saw the flash of a steel blade in his master's hand, saw it rise, saw it plunge downward.

The room brightened and the wind faded to a breeze, then disappeared. The monks picked themselves up from where they had been strewn about the room. They laughed and shouted banzais to each other as they clustered around the body of the child. Hiroki held back. He did not want the sight of that bloody little corpse to dampen the exultation flaring within him.

Japan would win! The Seer's predictions were holding true! They had brought back the Black Wind! Now that they had had a taste of success, they would redouble their efforts to produce another shoten. There would be no near-catastrophic laxity next time. Why this one had succeeded after so many failures, he could not say. But they would find out. They would harness the elemental fury of the Kuroikaze and use it to drive the Americans all the way back across the Pacific!

PART
SIX

1944

1 9 4 4

THE YEAR OF THE MONKEY

MARCH ▓▓▓▓▓▓▓▓▓▓▓▓▓▓▓▓
BALAJURO ATOLL, MARSHALL ISLANDS

It was hot in the hut and I was thirsty, so I took a generous pull from my canteen, savoring the burn of the bourbon as it went down.

I needed that.

Knapp and Ahern, the two others with me in the hut, didn't even look up. They used to nudge each other and point to the canteen when we first got here, but they were used to it now. They knew I had been with the HYPO team at the beginning of the war, and that carried a lot of weight. Besides, I did my share, so they let me be.

I was still in intelligence, but hanging on by my fingertips. Things had changed. *I* had changed. On the eve of the war I had been a deeply committed, supercompetent go-getter of an intelligence officer. The world back then was a verdant, sun-dappled forest that teemed with life and the future was a ripe piece of fruit waiting to be plucked and relished. Now . . .

Now life looked to me like a limitless plain, stretching away in all directions, unmarred by hill or tree or anything that rose above shoe level. I was alone on that plain. It didn't matter that there was no place for me to go, because I didn't have the will to move, not the slightest desire to be anywhere. No matter how many people surrounded me, I was alone.

And when I drank, it was usually alone.

I didn't hide it from myself or from others. No excuses, no whining, no blaming fate or anybody else. No gnawing obsession, no driving compulsion. I was a drunk because I wanted to be. And I was very methodical about it: I drank as much as I could whenever I could. The pains told me how badly I was tearing up my guts, but that was okay. If I had been a Jap, I would have committed seppuku after the MPs found me and freed me from that tree overlooking Pearl. But I didn't have the nerve to drag a knife through my guts. So I was committing seppuku my own way. It was lots slower, but the result would be the same.

Gradually, over the past year and a half, I had been shunted away from the center of intelligence work until I was now posted at a listening post on a lonely atoll in the Marshalls. Balajuro wasn't such a bad place if you didn't mind malarial swamps surrounded by jungle so thick and stratified that sunlight never reached the ground, leaving its floor eternally wet. With each step the ground *slurped* rather than crunched underfoot, sending snakes and insects and slimy wet things better left unidentified crawling and slithering away or buzzing into the air that was already so full of insects that you wanted to keep netting over your head whenever you were outside lest you inhale them by the lungful.

I almost wished the Japs had had a defensive force on Balajuro like they'd had on Kwajalein to the north. Admiral Hill had pounded Kwajalein from offshore for three full days, leaving its jungle a smoldering ruin. But he had just waltzed onto Balajuro and claimed it. That was why the jungle around us was alive and kicking, ever challenging us to battle as it doggedly worked to reclaim the little airstrip and the clearing where we were quartered.

I shared the listening post with two other men: Radioman Everett Ahern and Ensign Sam Knapp. Ahern was all of twenty-one, dark, long-boned, and thin as a rail, with traces of his teenage acne still specking his face. Knapp was closer to my age, blond and baby-faced. We had been cooped up out here for a month but we got along well. The work was pretty boring most of the time—monitor, decode, and translate, and pass on a summary of the intercepts—but we knew it was important. The right bit of information could pinpoint a Jap supply convoy or save a thousand lives during an assault.

Since Midway, no one in intelligence took anything for granted.

Funny how things work out in intelligence.

After I got out of the base hospital at Pearl, I joined Rochefort's HYPO unit. We worked like slaves trying to break JN25, the Japanese Navy's prime code. I was feeling pretty rotten about myself and about life in general then. That was when I started doing some serious drinking. But I confined it to my off-hours. When I was with the HYPO team, I gave it one hundred percent. *Better* than one hundred percent. Because I wanted to get back at the Japs. Oh, how I wanted them to pay for what they had done to Pearl. All those ships, all those men. I hated everything and everyone Japanese.

So we sweated and we cursed and we got nowhere for over four months. Then, from a completely unexpected quarter, came a mother lode. From April 18 to April 21, Yamamoto had practically every ship in the Combined Fleet combing the Western Pacific for the carriers that had helped deliver Doolittle's token raid on Tokyo. We figured out the call signals of the ships and, since we knew what they were after, we added a lot of new pages to our paltry JN25 dictionary.

The new insight into the code allowed us to anticipate the Japanese move on New Guinea and stop them in the Coral Sea before they got to Port Moresby. It gave us warning of the assault on Midway. Instead of getting suckered into the trap they were planning for us, we were ready and waiting for them when they arrived. We whipped their asses at Midway and they've been on the defensive ever since. All because of Jimmy Doolittle's one-way flight over Tokyo.

I suddenly realized that Sam was speaking to me. It seemed they had got into that favorite wartime question: Where Were You When They Attacked Pearl Harbor? I gave him a quizzical look and he repeated his question:

"I said, you were right there at Pearl during the attack, weren't you, Frank?"

"Saw the whole thing, from start to finish."

"That where you got hurt?" Ahern asked, nodding toward my scarred-up right arm.

I held it up and looked at the pair of nickel-sized scars, one on top, one on the underside. The docs put me up at the naval hospital on base and did what they could for my arm, keeping the wound open and draining so it healed from the inside. I got away without an infection, but I still couldn't make a tight fist—my ring finger wouldn't flex all the way.

I'd had to answer an awful lot of questions from the security people. It was humiliating as hell, but I told them the truth: A Japanese agent had come to my house and stolen the maps of the harbor. He nailed me to the tree to keep me from following him.

Nobody asked me about my wife and I didn't volunteer anything. I had learned to stop thinking about Meiko. If I had just enough booze in me, it was almost as if she never existed. But what I hadn't learned to forget was the sight of the flames and the smoke and the earth-jolting thuds as those ships blew up on that clear, quiet Sunday morning. I held myself at least partly responsible for every name on the long casualty lists. I couldn't blot those guys out. Not yet, at least.

"Got this not far from the harbor," I told Ahern.

"I was on the other end of the island when they hit," he said. "Manning a radar station."

"Yeah? Where?"

"On Kahuku Point. We were checking our mobile rig against the army's Opana station."

"On Sunday morning? Didn't you pick up anything?"

"You bet we did!" His youthful face became animated. "We were supposed to close up shop at 7:00 A.M., but just as we were about to shut down, we caught this huge blip on the screen about a hundred forty miles north, three degrees east, and coming our way. It looked like a *lot* of planes. We figured it was that squad of B-17s we were expecting, but just to be sure, we checked with Opana and they had it, too."

"Didn't you call it in?" I said, feeling myself tense up.

"Sure! Called it in to ONI and to the plotting center!"

"And nobody did anything?" I could not believe this.

"You got it. They told us, 'Don't worry about it.' So we didn't. But just for practice we followed them until we lost them in the hills, at about 7:40."

"Shit!" I said. "You had them! God, you could have warned the harbor!"

Ahern slumped back in his chair. "I know that now. But we thought they were ours. We reported it and were told to forget about it. What could we do after that?"

"Nothing," I said. "But Jesus! To think we could have had almost an hour's warning—!"

"We could have had more than that," Sam Knapp said.

"From whom?" I asked.

"The Japs themselves. Their Fourteen Part Message."

I waved him off. "The attack was already well under way when those sneaky bastards delivered their lousy declaration of war!"

"Right," Knapp said with a knowing smirk. "When *they* delivered it."

"What's that supposed to mean?"

"It means we had it intercepted, put through Purple magic, and typed up long before they marched into the State Department."

"Bullshit! How the hell do you know?"

"I was assigned the ONI office in D.C. when the Japs attacked. Scuttlebutt was that we'd had the first thirteen parts of the Japs' Fourteen Part Message deciphered since 1900. Heard the same thing from a friend in the army's Far Eastern section over at G-2. They told me it looked bad. Said they didn't know what the fourteenth part would say, but after reading the first thirteen, it didn't matter. The Japs were breaking off relations. It was war."

I was getting interested now. "You mean to tell me all this was deciphered and typed up by seven o'clock Saturday night?"

"That's what they tell me."

"And you just sat on it?"

"Hell no!" Knapp said, his face reddening. "Not me! I learned this later. I hear Commander Kramer took a copy right over to the White House. It was in Roosevelt's hands by 10:00 P.M.!"

I did some fast calculating: 10:00 P.M. Eastern time was almost sixteen hours before the first shot was fired over Oahu. *Sixteen hours!* If we'd had Purple magic at Pearl, we would have had all that time to get the ships dispersed and ready to fight!

"How about the final part?"

"The whole message was transcribed and circulating around the State Department by 7:30 Sunday morning. That's fact, not rumor."

That was 2:00 A.M. at Pearl! Still plenty of time to get the fleet ready for battle!

"Why didn't anybody tell us?" Ahern was saying, his face slack with astonishment. "How come nobody warned us?"

"Because it never happened that way," I said, as much to convince myself as the kid. "It's all hearsay. It's wild bullshit that gets started when bored guys sit around in ward rooms and mess halls, and monitoring stations"—I paused to let that last one sink in—"waiting for something to happen."

"I guess you're right," he said slowly, then grinned. "Sure. Who'd believe ol' FDR'd leave the whole Pacific Fleet sitting in the harbor if he knew the Japs were coming?" He looked over at Knapp. "Right?"

Knapp shrugged. "Only telling you what I heard."

The talk drifted on to other matters, most especially how I was going to spend my week's leave in Hawaii. I smiled, made comments, nodded when appropriate, but my mind wasn't on the conversation or my coming leave. I was thinking about what Matsuo had said to me on Halewa Heights after he nailed me to that tree. *"The final part of a declaration of war has already been sent to our Washington Embassy."* The neat way his words then dovetailed with Knapp's paranoid ramblings now made me more than a little uncomfortable. It opened the gates and let out all the old questions that had plagued me all through 1941: Why weren't we given enough air recon ability? Why didn't the Honolulu DIO have a Purple magic machine? Why were all of Captain Zacharias's warnings ignored? Why had he been stowed out of the way aboard a heavy cruiser? Why were so many ships allowed to sit in port at once amid so many danger signs like the change of call signals twice in the preceding month, the burning of codebooks, the "disappearance" of Carrier Fleets One and Two?

On and on they went until I physically shook them off.

It didn't matter. It was all over and done with. No one would ever know for sure—least of all me—so why lose sleep over unanswerables?

I took a long pull on my canteen.

■ ■ ■

I was supposed to have been airborne by four in the afternoon, but the PBN-1 that was sent to pick me up developed engine trouble on landing. We didn't get into the air until well after sunset.

But I was finally on my way. I was the only passenger on the plane, and before I settled down for a nap, I gave the island one last good look. Balajuro was shrinking behind me, a lopsided ring of tarnished gold and onyx set in dark water streaked with silver moonlight. I wouldn't miss it for the week I'd be away. One island, like one day, seemed pretty much like any other out here in the Western Pacific.

As I turned away from the window, something in the air down below caught my attention and I looked back. A tiny cloud had appeared over the island. It looked innocent enough, hovering there a few hundred feet above the edge of the atoll's coral-rimmed lagoon, but something about it struck me as wrong.

It was black.

There's no such thing as a black cloud. Smoke can be black, but clouds are water vapor and reflect the light around them. On this perfect night, with a near-full moon over the eastern horizon, that cloud should have been silvery white. Clouds can look black from the ground when there's enough of them to block out the sun or moon, but I was above this one and it was black. Intensely black. I looked for signs of a fire below on the island but saw no flames and no trail of smoke leading up to it.

And the cloud was growing.

Even as I watched, I could see it enlarging from within. It looked almost as if there were a hole in the sky and this black substance was being pumped into the air. Its surface heaved and boiled as if racked with some terrible inner turmoil.

Fear rippled along my skin as the temperature in the cabin seemed to plummet. This was more than just a meteorological curiosity. Its blackness was too intense, too *hungry*. It seemed to devour the moonlight around it. Something was terribly wrong down there.

I lost sight of Balajuro and the cloud as the plane angled away toward the east. I jumped up from my seat and hurried to the pilot's cabin. It took a little doing but I convinced him to bank around to the south for one more look. As Balajuro hove into view, I gasped. The cloud was huge now! The entire lagoon was covered and it was spreading over the jungle!

"What the fuck is *that?*" the pilot said.

I reached for his radio. "I don't know. But I'm going to call down and find out!"

I got Ahern on the air. "Yeah!" he said. "Of course we see it! Some freak typhoon! Never seen one come up so fast! You'd better get moving—see if you can outrun it!"

"Ev!" I shouted into the mike. "That's no typhoon! It's only over Balajuro—like it's sitting on the island!"

"What?" I heard him say through a burst of static. "It's blowing like hell down here. You can barely—" More static, then: "—feels so cold, Frank. And there's something funny about this wind. Aw, it's no use—"

And then the speaker filled with static and we lost him.

"What do we do now, sir?" the pilot said.

The question startled me. I realized I was the ranking officer on the plane. Not a position I wanted, but there was nothing I could do about it now.

"Keep circling," I told him. "But keep clear. I don't want to get any closer to that thing than we are now."

"Don't worry about that, sir," he said. I looked at his face and saw my own unease mirrored there. Something about that cloud poked at the most primitive levels of the brain. Every instinct screamed, *stay away!*

"Maybe it'll move on," I said. "Then we'll go down."

But it didn't move on. It continued to spread inexorably over the island, hovering there. I expected to see flashes of lightning or feel the plane buffeted by storm winds, but all was calm. Too calm. The cloud was settling downward as if to smother the peaceful little atoll.

I got on the air to Tarawa and was finally connected to an officer with some authority. His name was Abrams and he was a captain. When I described what was happening, I heard him curse. The air was full of static, but I was sure he said,

"Shit! Another one!"

"Pardon me, sir?"

"Never mind. Just stay the hell away from that cloud!"

"This has happened before?" I said.

He ignored my question and said, "Anybody got a camera on board?"

"I don't know."

"Well, find out. And if so, get some pictures of that thing. I'm sending out some support."

"Support? Support against what?"

"Don't ask questions, Lieutenant. Just stick around till we get there!"

"Captain," I said, "I don't under—"

"Holy shit!" the pilot said.

I looked out at the cloud and felt my knees go weak. It had changed. It was still hugging the island like a starfish over a clam, but as I watched, it suddenly expanded upward, directly upward, stretching past our altitude and on up toward the stars. It was now a vertical column of black, an onyx pillar soaring into space. It seemed to reach up forever, casting a line of shadow far to the west along the moonlit surface of the Pacific.

As we flew through that shadow, it was as if the moon had ceased to exist. I tried to swallow but my mouth was completely dry. This was beyond science and nature. We were watching a nightmare.

And then it was gone.

The blackness thinned and evaporated like mist in the morning sun. One moment it was there, towering over us; ten seconds later it had vanished without a trace.

The pilot and I sat and gaped at the suddenly empty air, and at Balajuro, visible once more in the gleaming, placid surface of the Pacific. It was as if nothing at all had happened.

I grabbed the radio mike and tried to raise Ahern on the island but my call went unanswered.

"Let's get down there!" I said.

The pilot threw me a worried look. "You really think we should, sir? I mean Tarawa's sending backup. Maybe we should wait."

I shared his reluctance, but Knapp and Ahern were down there, and so were lots of others. Their radios were out and they probably needed help.

I pointed to Balajuro. "Down!"

We did two flyovers and saw no signs of life—no lights, no fires, no movement in the darkness below. I was becoming increasingly uneasy. Even if all their power was gone, there should have been someone around to wave a flashlight at the sound of our engines.

"Land this thing," I said. In response, the pilot veered off toward the water. "Where're you going? The landing strip's down there!"

"Yes, sir. But the strip's pitch dark. No telling what I'll run into before we roll to a stop. We're safer on the lagoon."

"Good thinking." The PBN-1 was amphibious; we would be foolish not to take advantage of that.

As the plane skimmed and settled onto the surface of the lagoon, I heard a dull staccato thumping against the lower hull. It slowed in tempo as the plane slowed, and stopped when the plane came to a halt.

"What was that?"

The pilot shrugged. "Sounded like something in the water."

I got a flashlight and opened the hatch while he pulled the

inflatable raft from its compartment. As soon as I leaned my head outside, I knew something horrible had happened on this little island.

"Hold it!" I told the pilot in a hushed voice as he struggled with the raft. "Listen!"

"Listen to what?" He came up beside me. "I don't hear anything."

"That's just it! It's quiet!"

There was the gentle lap of the waves on the coral rim of the lagoon and against the outer shore to windward, but that was all. No insects buzzing, no birds calling, no animals moving through the brush.

"Is that bad?"

"Damn right it's bad! I've been on this rock for a month and can't remember a single second of quiet. But now! God, it's like a tomb!"

I angled my flashlight down at the water. "Christ!" I said.

The pilot followed my stare. "Damn! Look at that!"

The water was loaded with fish—puffers, tangs, small sharks, rays, eels, crabs, squid, jellyfish, and a horde of others I couldn't identify—all floating belly-up on the surface of the lagoon.

"Dead fish!" the pilot said in a low, awed tone. "That's what was hitting against the hull when we landed!"

I had a feeling even the coral and plankton were dead.

"But what killed them? I've seen plenty of big storms before but never seen one leave a fish-kill like this!"

"That was no storm," I said, feeling very cold inside. "Did you see any damage when we flew over the compound? See any fallen trees?"

"It was too dark."

I looked around. The only thing I could see that had changed was the jungle—changed not just in its silence, but in its very shape. I could see it silhouetted in the moonlight and it looked somehow *different*. I couldn't put my finger on it, but I knew it didn't look like the same jungle I had left earlier this evening.

Suddenly there was a sound: a plane. A couple of them. The radio crackled to life and the pilot ran for it.

"It's that Captain Abrams from Tarawa," he said.

I went forward and took the mike.

"I want you off that lagoon and away from Balajuro, Lieutenant," Abrams told me in clipped, official tones.

"Sir, I had friends on the island. They may need help."

His voice softened just a touch. "Believe me, Lieutenant, whoever was on that island is beyond anyone's help now."

I had pretty well figured that out, especially after seeing all the dead fish, but it raised a lump in my throat to hear him put it into words. I hadn't known Knapp and Ahern long, but they had been good men.

"Cruise to about two miles offshore and anchor there for the night," Abrams said.

The pilot grabbed the mike from me. "I'm already overdue at Midway, sir."

"Whatever orders you had are countermanded as of this moment. You are to anchor as instructed. You will both be debriefed immediately. Over."

The pilot looked at me and shrugged. We both knew we had stumbled onto something big and now we couldn't get out.

■   ■   ■

Balajuro was dead.

I had known that last night. I hadn't known just *how* dead.

The Navy Department men who spent half the night debriefing the pilot and me—the pilot's name was Tom Kendall and we were becoming fast friends—aboard their flying boat were oblique as hell when I asked them about it, so I got the idea I'd be seeing something pretty grim in the morning.

I still wasn't prepared for the reality.

The jungle was *brown*. And it drooped. That was why its outline had looked different in the moonlight last night. It was all brown and wilted. The leaves and palm fronds drooped in death. It looked as if the jungle had melted and shrunken overnight.

We coasted our PBN through the dead fish on the surface of the lagoon. Captain Abrams was waiting on the shore. He was dark, whippet lean, and his hands darted around like hummingbirds when he talked. He was standing in a group of about ten. A few were uniformed, but most were in civies.

"The first thing I want you to know," the captain said, returning our salutes as we stepped ashore, "is that everything you saw last night and everything you will see today is top secret. Everything! That clear?"

His New York City accent was even more pronounced in person than it had been over the radio.

"Yes, sir," we said in unison.

"Good. Now, I want to prepare you for what you're about to see. I'll begin to do that by asking you what's wrong with all those fish out there on the lagoon."

"You mean, besides their being dead, sir?"

Captain Abrams' tone was icy. "Obviously."

I thought about that a moment as I watched the tropical sun beating down on all those white fish bellies. Then it hit me:

"No smell!"

"Exactly."

"But dead fish should stink by now."

His voice was low. "Not when all their bacteria are dead, too."

The enormity of what had happened on Balajuro was beginning to sink in.

"This isn't the first time this has happened, is it, sir?" I said.

He gave me a hard look. "No. This is the third. But you and Kendall are the first to actually see anything of it and survive."

"Some new sort of weapon the Japs are trying out?"

He nodded. "We thought at first it was a gas or something along that line, but after hearing what you two saw . . ."

"That was a lot more than poison gas, sir. That was . . ." I didn't know what to say. I wanted to say it was strange, alien, supernatural, something that didn't belong in this world. But that sounded melodramatic and maybe even a little bit crazy. I was glad I wasn't the sole witness. With every passing hour, that towering column of black cloud seemed less real, less *possible*. Without Kendall to back me up, I'd be doubting my own memory by now.

"It was *what*, Lieutenant?" Abrams said.

"It was a catastrophe, sir. An *un*natural catastrophe."

"You've got that right. And it only gets worse."

He motioned us to follow him. The other half of Abrams' team had landed on the airstrip this morning; as we walked along the jeep path through the jungle to join them, I couldn't escape the feeling that I was in a dream. The silence and utter lack of green in the jungle heightened the nightmarish effect. The path was littered with dead insects, birds, and occasionally a rodent or small monkey. Nothing moved in the brown foliage. Even the moss on the tree trunks was dead. It was like a fake jungle, a sterile Tarzan movie set created by a demented, color-blind designer.

The stillness, the lifelessness—it wormed through the skin and into the soul. I might as well have been on the moon. And it was worse in the compound.

The air about the clearing was funereal when we arrived, and with good reason. I watched a crew of medics carrying sheet-covered bodies from the Quonsets and shacks across the tarmac and onto their special transports.

"Everyone?" I said to Abrams as a loaded stretcher was carried by.

"Everyone. We've yet to find even a cockroach alive after one of these wilts."

" 'Wilt'? Is that what it's called?"

"You got a better name for it?"

I looked around at the drooping jungle. I shook my head. "My two friends, Knapp and Ahern. I'd like to—"

"I don't advise you to see them. We'll have them all identified by dog tag."

"I just want to be sure, sir."

I was getting used to the look he gave me.

"Be my guest."

I went over to the radio shack where we had set up our monitoring post. I didn't want to look at any corpses, but I felt I owed it to those two guys. We had worked together and I thought they might have done the same for me if situations were reversed.

There were two sheeted forms on the floor of the shack. Without allowing myself any time to reconsider, I went down on one knee beside the nearest and slipped the sheet off his face.

It was Knapp, but not as I remembered him. His features were basically the same, but his face seemed to have shrunken. His whole body seemed smaller. It was as if the wilt or whatever it was had sucked the very life out of him. There was no pain in his face, no fear in his expression; only a great sadness, an unplumbed hopelessness.

I checked Ahern. He had looked shrunken to begin with. Now his skin looked like it was sticking directly to his bones. And his expression was the same as Knapp's.

"Kind of gives you the creeps, doesn't it?"

I looked up. Abrams was standing in the doorway.

"What do you mean?"

"That look on their faces. They've all got it. Every corpse on every one of the three islands hit by the wilt. They all look like that. I almost wish they'd have that 'look of unimaginable horror' you read about in those cheap pulp chillers."

I didn't tell Abrams that I happened to like those cheap pulp chillers and still read them whenever I could find them. But I had to agree with him. This hopeless, lost look on their faces—in a way, this was worse than horror.

A breathless civilian appeared at the door beside Abrams. "Captain! We've found something! A child!"

"Alive?"

"No, dead. But he's Japanese!"

They took off at a run. I covered up Knapp and Ahern and ran after them.

■   ■   ■

One of the sailors had noticed something dark floating at the rim of the atoll. He had gone over to investigate and found the child floating facedown just under the surface of the fish-filled water. He looked to be about three years old and he was special in a couple of ways. He was Japanese—there were not supposed to be any Japs of any age on Balajuro—and it looked like he was starting to decompose.

No one could explain either fact.

I looked down at the bloated little body. I didn't want to get too close, but I could see some fresh surgical scars on him. He appeared to have been mutilated. Where the hell had he come from?

As I watched, I saw a live crab ride a wavelet in from the open ocean onto the coral and scuttle the rest of the way into the lagoon where a feast awaited him. Death had laid claim to every living thing on Balajuro last night, but already nature was setting the gears in motion to restore the balance of life and death on the atoll. For the first time since the attack on Pearl, I wasn't thinking about my next drink. I wanted some answers—about the wilt, about this Jap kid.

I took Abrams aside. "I want in on this," I said.

"What's that supposed to mean?"

"This wilt thing—you've got a team that's chasing it around. I'm volunteering to be a member."

Another one of those looks from Abrams. "You started the war as Lieutenant-jay-gee and here you are the same rank after almost two and a half years of active duty. What does that say about you?"

I knew it said a whole lot, and none of it good. Promotions came thick and fast during a war. I held my tongue and he went on.

"I talked to two of your former COs last night. They say you're not as reliable as you used to be."

"That's because I've stopped caring what my COs think."

Abrams pursed his lips. "That's not exactly what I'd call an extenuating circumstance."

"Look at it this way," I said with a shrug. I tried to appear casual but I really wanted this. For the first time in a couple of years I was feeling a tug of interest from something other than the bottle. I didn't want to let go. "I'm a guy who's got nothing to lose, but I'm also a guy who's seen a wilt in action and lived to tell about it. How can you go wrong?"

Abrams gave me an appraising look. "You've got a point there. But none of it matters."

"Why not?"

"Because you and Kendall are automatically on the team. Anybody who's even heard the slightest whisper of a rumor about the wilts is on the team. We're keeping a firm lid on this. We don't want *anyone* to know about it."

"You really think this is a Jap weapon?" I couldn't believe anything human had had anything to do with what I'd seen last night.

"It seems to be playing that way. And if it is, we could be facing *big* trouble from here on in. We don't want any scare stories started, so as far as the fighting man and John Q. Public are concerned, there is no such thing as a 'wilt.' Clear?"

"Very clear, sir," I said. "Why don't we have a drink on it?"

MAY

"The Black Winds are an unqualified success!"

Shimazu looked up from the fresh photographs of a devastated atoll and watched Hiroki's face. His features were animated as he described the total desolation of the smaller islands upon which the children had been set. The fires of hope and fervor had been dampened in Hiroki's eyes since the tragic experience with Yajima. It was encouraging to see them blazing high again.

"But we need more shoten!"

"The surgeons are working to exhaustion." His student knew full well how intricate and involved a process it was to create a shoten. "There are many failures."

"*Too* many! For every success, there are ten failures! There must be another way!"

"There is," Shimazu said, catching Hiroki's eyes. "Find the rest of the scrolls."

"I know that, sensei. But they elude me."

The deployment of the Kuroikaze was entirely in Hiroki's hands. Its means and methods had to remain a secret from the Supreme Command and the Emperor. Especially the Emperor. If He ever became aware that mutilated children were the shoten of the Black Wind, he would certainly forbid their use, no matter how badly they were needed. As with so much of the conduct of this war, it was best not to burden the Emperor with unpleasant details.

"I take it that it is not yet time to hold an Imperial Conference?"

Shimazu looked forward to the day when the Kakureta Kao could stand before the Emperor and be hailed as the saviors of Japan. Then they would be elevated to their rightful place as Guardians of the Empire and could begin the task of purifying Japanese life of all taint of Western influence. After being denied their proper glory for the defeat of the Mongol fleet in the twelfth century and after their failure to overthrow the shogunate in the sixteenth, their time had come at last. All the centuries of waiting were ready to bear fruit. The sweet taste of victory and vindication was on his lips.

"No, sensei. Not yet. We first must gain a major victory."

"And when will that be?" *How much longer must I wait?*

"I don't know. I cannot launch an effective Kuroikaze assault without an arsenal of shoten. How can I gain offensive momentum when the surgeons can provide me with but one shoten a month? It is an impossible situation!"

"The Mongol fleet was destroyed by a single Kuroikaze."

"I humbly remind my sensei that this is a different situation. The Kuroikaze are not well suited for the modern style of naval war. They were best in their ancient use, against a massed army or navy. But this war, with its battles shifting from island to island, with the enemy's troops and ships scattered over thousands of square miles of ocean, I need many shoten! Enough to set them up on a whole string of islands, enough to throw the American troops and commanders into a lather of confusion and terror so that I can sneak a shoten into one of their command posts, or into the center of one of their task forces while it sits at anchor! But that is impossible under the present circumstances."

"The scrolls will be found in time," Shimazu said, comfortable in his faith in the Seer's visions. There were other, less comforting visions, however. The nameless child kept reappearing. He had come to suspect that it was Meiko's child. Why was it in his visions? Why did he sense danger from it? "There will be a way."

"But until they are found," Hiroki said, "we shall need more shoten, many more shoten."

"Bring us the children," Shimazu told his pupil, "and we shall give you your shoten."

■ ■ ■

Hiroki hurried back to his office from the temple. Even with no new conquests by the Imperial Forces, his duties as Minister of Military and Economic Coordination filled every minute of the day. When he arrived, he found Matsuo waiting there.

His younger brother was dressed in his navy uniform. He sat in the chair next to the desk, reading a newspaper as he waited. Hiroki thought he looked tired and drawn. They had seen each other rarely during the past year.

"Yes, dear brother," he said with a polite bow. "How may I be of assistance?"

Matsuo stood and returned the bow. "I have learned of the devastation of three small, American-held islands. I have heard that their destruction is somehow linked to the Kakureta Kao. May I ask how?"

Hiroki hid his surprise. How had word leaked out? But Matsuo was in Intelligence, wasn't he? And he was reputed to be very good at his work. Still, it was disconcerting to know that there was a leak. He had been so careful!

The trial runs of the Black Winds had been carried out under the tightest security. Only the Naval Chief of Service knew why a skeleton-crewed submarine had been placed at the Order's disposal. For each mission, Hiroki had personally overseen the loading of the altered child upon the ship. The sedated shoten had been encased in a wicker basket to hide him from the prying eyes of the crew and escorted to his destination by two members of the Order's Outer Circles. Hiroki had wanted to go himself but Shimazu had forbidden it, saying that he was too valuable to the Emperor and the war effort. The shoten was landed and deposited in a hidden spot near the shore. The submarine and the acolytes then quickly retreated. When the sedative wore off, the Black Wind rose. The crew was isolated between missions. Still, rumor had leaked out. He supposed it was inevitable.

"I must swear you to secrecy in the name of the Emperor if I tell you," Hiroki said.

"I swear in the name of the Son of Heaven," Matsuo said with a bow.

"Very well. We have loosed the Kuroikaze upon the Americans."

He watched Matsuo's eyes widen. "The Black Winds? But I thought—"

"You thought they were a folk tale. So many do. But I assure you they are not! Japan and all the world will know how real the Kuroikaze are when we learn again to fully control them."

Matsuo's face reflected his concern. "The Order can't control them?"

Hiroki hurried to explain. "It has been centuries since a Black Wind has been unleashed. There is no one alive who has any experience with them. We are readying a full assault against the Americans soon. It will crush them."

Matsuo looked as if he wanted to believe that, but his voice held little conviction. "That will be wonderful. Maybe it is not too late to salvage something from this war."

"We shall salvage victory!" It irked him that his own brother was losing faith in the war effort.

"We shall see. I am curious as to how these Black Winds are called up. Perhaps if the Order shared the secret with the Navy—"

"It is forbidden! The Kakureta Kao is the guardian and wielder of the Black Wind!"

Matsuo smiled. "Somehow, I knew you'd say that." He glanced around the office. "You have been well?"

"Thank you for your concern, yes."

They talked for a few moments about topics of general interest, each avoiding the subject of the other's personal life. Hiroki was tempted to ask after Meiko's child, to question the mark on his face and ask how closely it resembled the one Matsuo had described on the face of his boyhood friend, Frank Slater. But even though he would have dearly loved to reopen a wound that might have healed by now, he resisted the temptation. He feared his brother.

And besides, this was merely polite conversation between two men who were linked by blood but no longer shared affection or interest. He tried to bring the meeting to a close.

"I'm short of time, brother. If you would be so kind to excuse me?"

"Of course," Matsuo said, rising. "I'm so very sorry. It seems there's a shortage of everything these days. Out on the streets it is the necessities of a civilized existence. In here it is time." He held up his copy of the daily *Yomiuri*. "According to today's paper, there is even a shortage of children in a certain quarter of the city. The same quarter as the Kakureta Kao temple. Children are disappearing from schools, from playgrounds, from their yards, even from their beds. Isn't that strange? Would the Order know anything about that?"

Hiroki felt himself tense inside. *What's Matsuo getting at? Does he suspect something?* He studied his brother's features but could see no suspicion there. Could it really be just an idle question?

"Why do you ask such a question?"

"Just curious. Little seems to pass without the Kakureta Kao's knowledge. I was just wondering if the Order might be able to aid the distressed parents."

"The Order is presently concerned with the Emperor's war," he said stiffly. "That takes precedence over everything else."

"Of course," Matsuo said. "I'll let you get on with your busy schedule."

Hiroki found himself trembling after Matsuo had left. No one must ever know of the children. Anyone who found out could not be allowed to live. Even if it was his own brother.

JULY ■
SAIPAN

The wilts were still baffling the hell out of us. They seemed to occur with complete randomness as to time and place. There had been five of them to date, and so far, only Kendall and myself had ever seen one and lived to tell. The brass was getting worried. They were afraid that if word got out about this Japanese superweapon, about how whole islands were denuded of life by something no one could fight, it might demoralize the war effort.

Unfortunately, we were no closer to an answer now than we were four months ago when Balajuro died. The pressure was on our team and I was spending every sober moment on it. And there seemed to be more of those sober moments. Working on the wilts left less time to think about Meiko and Matsuo. And the less I thought about them, the less I wanted to drink.

I had combed through all the before-and-after intelligence reports in the areas around each of the wilts and had come up with one common denominator. I briefed Abrams on my thoughts.

"Before each of the five wilts we've seen so far," I said, "there's invariably a report of a lone enemy sub in the area."

"You think that's significant?" Abrams said. "We spot lone subs all the time."

"But they're usually on the prowl along the shipping lanes or headed toward an anchorage. These aren't. Before four of the five wilts, a sub was spotted heading directly away from the island in question only hours before the wilt struck. You could explain that behavior nicely if you consider that they might be planting a device to cause the wilt."

"Sounds reasonable," Abrams said. "But what's that do for us?"

"It puts us on the lookout for Nip subs sneaking seaward from islands we hold."

He snorted. "Do you know how many islands we hold now? We expend an awful lot of man-hours watching for subs in critical areas. Do you have any idea what it would cost us in manpower to be on the lookout in *non*critical areas?"

"We only have to watch one island," I said. "This one."

"Saipan? What makes you so sure? So far they've only used the wilt on pancake-flat atolls. This is a big island. It's got hills, mountains. How do we know the wilt will even work here?"

"Can we risk assuming it won't? Besides, I think there's been enough death here already, don't you?"

Abrams nodded. "No argument there."

We were both silent for a moment. The cost of taking Saipan had been horrendous. Fifty thousand lives, we figured—three thousand of them ours, the rest Jap soldiers and civilians. The civilian deaths had been the hardest to take. The women and children had hidden themselves in the caves on the northern tip. When the military defense was snuffed out just eight days ago, they killed themselves by the thousands. Apparently they had been told horror stories of how they would be treated by Americans. I heard battle-hardened marines whisper of seeing mothers with children in their arms throwing themselves off the eight-hundred-foot Morubi Bluffs.

Saipan was the capital of the Marianas, and of tremendous psychological importance to the Japs. They'd held Saipan for almost thirty years; it had been their central relay station for communications throughout the South Pacific for all that time; they called it "the gateway to the south."

I said, "We're on prime real estate. From here on northward you've got the Bonins and the Izus leading right up to Tokyo itself like a trail of stepping stones across a swamp. Not to mention the fact that we're now in B-29 range of the Japanese mainland."

"I'm well aware of that," Abrams said impatiently. "That's why we busted our asses to take this rock. So what?"

"They want it back," I said. "They want it back real bad."

He stared at me. "I think you're onto something there! We'll set up a sub-watch! We'll catch the sub as it's coming in, or if we see it running off, we'll comb that end of the coast to find whatever it is they use before it goes off! We'll—"

"You'll lose a lot of good men that way if the wilt starts before they find it."

"You got a better idea?" he said. He pulled out a cigarette as he tried to stare me down.

"Sure. Send one man in. If you can get a fair idea of where the Nips landed, you can evacuate that end of the island and send in that one guy. Who knows? He may be able to find it in time. If he can't, you've only lost one guy."

"And who's going to volunteer for that?" He struck a match and lit his cigarette.

"Me."

I waited to see what Abrams would do. Would he laugh? Or would he take me seriously. I watched as he held the lighted match and stared at me; held it until it burned his fingers. With a curse, he shook it out and dropped it.

"You? What are you, some kinda nut?"

"I'm the best man for the job. I've seen the wilt in action. I know what to expect. I'll know when it's starting and when to turn tail and run."

"You've seen enough to know that running won't do you a damn bit of good. You must have some kind of death wish or something!"

That wasn't so. I didn't want to die. I never had. But something had changed since the Saturday night before the Pearl Harbor raid. Until then the very thought of dying had terrified me; there had been so many things left to do and see. Now, death was okay. I wouldn't look for it, but if it came it was no big deal. As far as I could see, there wasn't much lying ahead worth getting upset about.

"No death wish," I said. "I've got a safety hatch planned out."

Abrams went for the idea when I explained it to him.

■   ■   ■

The sub was sighted two nights later.

It would have been perfect if we had been able to catch it coming in. We could have captured their wilt device and found out what made it tick. But the sub sneaked in unseen. It was spotted leaving though, making a beeline away from Saipan's northeastern shore at 2332 hours. A pair of destroyers gave chase but lost it.

I was on the beach at 2350. While copters, transports, and jeeps moved all the occupying troops south, I began my search. It would have been easier in daylight. Even then, almost anything could have stayed hidden among the craters and shredded palm trees left in the wake of the hellish preassault bombardment a month ago. It was high tide and the sand above the waterline was still so chewed up by Amphtracs that there was no possibility of picking out old trails from new. So there I stood with my puny little flashlight, looking up at the moonlit slopes of Mount Tapotchau, more than a little daunted by the task before me.

But there was no time to stand there wondering. I ran up to the edge of what was left of the jungle and began the search. I didn't know what I was looking for, but I figured there was a good chance it was metallic, so that was what I concentrated on finding.

I walked in lengthening arcs, moving deeper and deeper into the shattered jungle. Everything smelled of death. It was like a wilt had already struck. There were dead animals and dead humans buried in all that debris. They had died over a month ago and must have provided a feast for scavengers. But even now, when the onshore breeze waned, the unmistakable odor of putrefaction rose up like a ghost. At those times I mouth-breathed and pressed on.

I was quickly coming to the conclusion that I had made a mistake. This was an impossible task for one man, too big even for a platoon. But I pressed on. I was all I had right now and it was too late to turn back.

And then it began.

It started with a prickling chill along the back of my neck. I froze and waited for it to go away. It didn't. It spread across my shoulders and down my back. I spun around but saw nothing at first. Then I noticed a dark spot in the moonlit debris off to my left. It seemed to be moving, growing. I realized it was a shadow and looked up.

There it was—a black cloud, roiling, racked with violent swirlings and eddyings, growing in the air. I ran toward it. I figured the device that was generating it would be directly below. If I could get there in time, maybe I could disable it.

Months ago, I had seen another cloud like this from a plane. From that viewpoint, it had seemed to spread slowly over Balajuro. That had been an illusion. For as I looked up now, I could see the cloud expanding at an incredible rate, swallowing the moon, the stars, all of the sky. Before I had gone a hundred feet, the cloud settled over my end of the island like a canopy and I was engulfed in darkness.

The breeze changed, not only in direction but in quality. It came from the center of that cloud. This was no briny puff of trade winds off the ocean. This air was stale, cold, musty, wet, and sour, like an updraft from a forgotten dungeon of the soul. I rubbed my eyes and coughed as a wave of nausea swept over me.

The breeze grew to a wind, the wind to a gale, tearing at me, roaring in my ears, roaring *through* me. It seemed to moan, a sound of such heartbreaking despair that I felt an involuntary sob rise in my throat. I fought against the tide of the wind for about a dozen feet and then stopped. It was no use. I'd never make it.

As I stopped, I looked around, startled. The wind continued to howl by me, buffet my face, tear at my clothes, but the bombed-out jungle was still and quiet around me. Not a leaf or a frond or a blade of grass so much as dipped in a breeze.

Suddenly I felt very cold, and I wanted to be away from here. Over the past few months I had convinced myself, despite what I had seen over Balajuro, that there was a rational, scientific explanation behind the wilts. Now I knew that wasn't so. There was *nothing* rational here! I had to get off this island. I had to get back to the beach! I turned to run but my legs wouldn't carry me. Suddenly, I couldn't go on.

"It's just no use," I heard myself say.

I felt so tired all of a sudden, enveloped in a fog of exhaustion. The beach was two hundred yards away but it might as well have been twenty thousand leagues. I would never make it. Strange emotions wafted about me and then clung: emptiness, abysmal loneliness, eternal, unfulfilled longing. Everything was hopeless, infinitely hopeless. And shot through it all was a formless, abject fear, a silent howl of terror that resonated in the darkest corners of the soul.

I slumped to my knees. "No use at all."

That sounded familiar. I tugged at the memory until it finally came free: Ahern had said the same thing over the radio while the wilt was hitting Balajuro. Was that part of it? Was this desperate inertia part of the wilt? Before it sucked the life out of you, did it take all hope and will first?

I didn't know what the cloud was doing to the jungle—it was dark and there didn't seem to be much left to kill after the offshore barrage—but I knew what it was doing to me.

I fought to my feet. *So weak!* Just standing upright drained me. I was afraid now—really afraid. I lunged toward the beach at a gait that was some combination of a stagger and a stumble. And all the while the hopelessness kept dragging me down, crying out in my brain with my own voice . . .

. . . it's no use you'll never make it so why even try it's all so futile so hopeless you might as well just lie down and give yourself over to the inevitable without this senseless struggle . . .

But I forced myself on. From somewhere under the dank stifling cloud of depression, a tiny spark of anger urged me on, wordlessly, but no less relentlessly. I clung to it: They weren't going to beat me down again! They weren't going to make me give up! Not this time.

And with the anger came hope. There *was* a chance to escape. I *could* make it. All I had to do was put one foot after the other in the direction of the beach and soon I'd be at the motorized launch anchored just beyond the breakers.

So I kept forcing one foot in front of the other. The wind tried to force me back. No matter which way I turned, the wind always seemed to be in my face, pushing at me, impeding me. But I kept on going. Eventually, I was down on the beach. I lurched into the gentle surf. The water was refreshing. It seemed to clear my head. The violence of the wind seemed somehow diminished here.

Squinting through the darkness, I finally picked out the launch and struck out for it. I was feeling stronger now. And the further I got from shore, the stronger I felt. The boat was soon within reach. I pulled myself over the gunwale and reached for the starter button. As the engine roared to life, I cut the anchor rope, threw the engine into gear, and pointed the prow toward the open sea. As soon as we were moving, I pulled the signal pistol from its compartment and fired a flare into the air.

Only after the bright red glow had lit up the sky did I dare a look back.

The black wilt cloud was still there, darker and more ominous than ever, growing, spreading along the beach in either direction, working its way toward the mountains.

Explosions thundered off to my left. The *Indianapolis,* lying offshore, had let loose with her cannon. As the first shells riddled the near jungle, I could barely make out the orange flashes of the explosions through the blackness. The roar was deafening. And then suddenly the blackness began to thin, to break up, to fade away.

Once again there was moonlight on the beach.

■   ■   ■

We combed the beach and the jungle the next day. We found nothing out of the ordinary except the corpse of a small Japanese child. He had been torn almost beyond recognition by the shelling of the beach. Around him were the remnants of some sort of wicker basket, almost like a tiny coffin.

I recalled the other child's body we had found on Balajuro and wondered if there was a connection, but brushed off the thought.

How could there be?

NOVEMBER
TOKYO

Hiroki savored the quiet and solitude here in the lower level of the temple. There was a timelessness about Shimazu's quarters. They looked the same today as they had over thirty years ago when he first stepped through the door. He took comfort in that stability. For change ruled the city outside the temple. It was a relief to find comfort in anything these days. Simply shutting oneself off from the outside world for a moment or two was a joy. But the events of that world had a way of worming their way into every thought, every action, even here in the depths of the Kakureta Kao temple.

"The war is all but lost," he told Shimazu.

He heard his sensei cluck. "Has the Emperor directed his children to surrender?"

"No, but—"

"Then the war is not lost. Don't you remember the Seer's words?"

Hiroki had repeated them over and over in his mind a hundred times a day for the past year. He did not need to hear them again, but he did not stop Shimazu.

" 'And then, when all looks blackest, blackness will save us: The Kuroikaze, borne by a noble firstborn, shall return full force to strike down all who oppose the Imperial Will.' After the blackness will come the blinding light of the Son of the Sun."

Hiroki wanted so much to believe that! But the disasters of the summer—the fall of Saipan and the rest of the Marianas, the defeats in Burma, the start of American high-level bombings on Japan itself—had resulted in Premier Tojo's forced resignation despite all the efforts of the Order to keep him in power. The fall was proving even worse. The Americans had thrust through the Palaus and into the Philippines in a seemingly unstoppable drive, leaving a mortally wounded Imperial Navy foundering in their wake in the Leyte Gulf.

"I don't see how the situation can become blacker. Our army is outgunned and outmanned on every front; our navy is in ruins, our supply lines are shattered, our best pilots are dead and the ones we have left are now using their planes as bombs."

"Ah, yes," Shimazu said. "The kamikaze. I suspect they are not as effective as expected."

Hiroki still marveled at the numbers of men in their late teens and early twenties volunteering to pilot the suicide planes. They vied, *begged* for the chance. And yet, if one were destined to die in battle for the Emperor, what better way to do so than to steer thousands of pounds of explosive into the deck of an American carrier? It was honorable, graceful, dignified, clean, quick, and glorious. And utterly painless.

"They are *very* effective. They've inflicted terrible damage on many American ships. But not enough to turn the tide of battle in our favor. They will continue to inflict serious damage on the Americans, but—" Hiroki sighed. Once again, it was the same old story. "But there are simply too many American Hellcats flying protection for too many American ships with too many antiaircraft guns firing too many rounds at our limited number of kamikaze planes. We simply cannot stop their advance."

He was reminded of Matsuo's warning before the war: *America will bury us with her resources and her productive capacity.* Little Brother had been right, although Hiroki could never admit that.

"The Supreme Command is calling for wholesale use of the Kuroikaze," Hiroki said. "But the Americans have learned how to protect themselves from the Black Winds. Their radar and sonar are everywhere. They spot our shoten-carrying sub and immediately send battleships to the area. They bombard the coast as soon as the Kuroikaze manifests itself. They flatten the jungle in the area of the growing Black Wind and abort it before it reaches full force by killing the shoten."

It was maddening to have the supreme weapon—albeit in short supply—and yet be thwarted in its use by these barbarians.

"We will slow their momentum by more conventional means, then," Shimazu said, calmly. "They have penetrated only our outer circles of defense, but our inner circles are much denser. We will stop them. It will be as the Seer has spoken."

"They will be on Japanese soil in less than a year!"

Shimazu's voice rose. "Then we shall defeat them *here!* They will have to send a million or more troops ashore. The Black Wind will wreak havoc on their armada before they land just like it did to the Mongol Kublai Khan's seven hundred years ago, and it will be waiting on the beaches to destroy those who should get that far! Will they bombard their own troops on the beaches?"

"We don't have enough shoten for that," Hiroki reminded him.

"We will," Shimazu said, smiling serenely. "We will."

Hiroki wanted to scream and pull at his hair. He wished he could take his master by the shoulders and drag him outside into the real world where he would hear a different story. But he only sat quietly and said,

"Yes, sensei."

PART SEVEN

1945

1 9 4 5

THE YEAR OF THE ROOSTER

MARCH
TOKYO

Meiko lay in the dark in Matsuo's arms. She should have felt safe and secure, but instead she felt like a tightly coiled spring. She closed her eyes and tried to sleep but the sound of the wind surrounded her, enveloped her, penetrated her.

The weather had certainly been freakish lately. Just last Sunday it had snowed, blanketing the threadbare, war-weary city with a flawless coast of pristine white. Yet even then the bombers—*B-san,* as the people called the B-29s—had come, invisible above the snow clouds, dropping their packages of fiery death through the gentle flakes that muffled the sound of their passing, lighting sleeping neighborhoods far away with flames that suffused the snow-thick air with a cherry light.

That had been just five days ago. The snow was gone now, melted away in the nightly heat of the firebomb raids and the glow of today's warm, fresh weather. Spring was making its usual surprise entrance in Tokyo.

But the wind concerned her. It had started as a breeze in the morning, stiffened to a gusty wind by afternoon, and by sunset was a full-force gale, nearing hurricane proportions. She watched it lift and warp the bamboo *sudare* half-raised across the window, listened to it rattle the shoji and fusama, and whistle through the transoms. The folding screen in the front room had blown over so many times tonight that Matsuo had finally left it flat on the floor. Meiko listened beyond the wind, above it, searching for another sound.

But the wind was all she heard. As eleven o'clock approached, she began to relax. Maybe they wouldn't come. A lone B-29 had flown over the city this afternoon on reconnaissance. The Americans knew what the weather was like in Tokyo today. Maybe they wouldn't come this time.

And then the sirens began to wail.

Matsuo bolted upright beside her on the futon. "Oh, no! Not tonight!" He leapt to his feet and ran to the window. "Not *tonight!*"

Meiko followed him. The wind roared against their faces as they looked out toward what was called "the plain side of the city." Their home was slightly more toward "the mountain side" of Tokyo. They left their lights out, as did all their neighbors and everyone else in the city, but kept the radio on, tuned to station NHK.

Nothing happened for a while, but Meiko allowed herself no false hope: The radio said a particularly large air flotilla had been sighted and was heading this way. They waited together. Meiko checked on Naka from time to time, but he was sleeping peacefully, as only a two-and-a-half-year-old knew how. When she came back to Matsuo, she could feel the tension in him as she leaned against his arm. Every muscle fiber in his body seemed to be on alert.

Around midnight, they saw the first firebombs drop through the sky. The leading B-29s marked out the target areas with long-burning incendiaries. They plotted a huge square on the plain side, down in the Tokyo flatlands where the big factories squatted with the countless huts of the workers who toiled within huddled around them like hordes of suckling young.

Soon the second wave arrived, carpet-bombing the marked areas. The B-sans were invisible in the black sky but trailed wakes of flame along the ground like waves behind a boat. Horrified, Meiko watched the wild spread of the fires. Soon all the lowlands were alight. The wind whipped the fire heavenward in vortices of flame. The sky was alive with sparks. The tinderbox city had been ignited and the radiance of its burning lit the underbellies of its attackers miles above in the sky. The smell of burning wood filled the air.

And then the fire began to spread beyond the markers.

"It's coming this way," Matsuo said.

Meiko felt her heart cramp and pause in her chest. "Will it reach us?"

"Look at it. Unless some miracle stops the wind, it will be here in no time."

She thought of Naka sleeping in his bed and fought the panic that creeped in from the shadows. "What'll we do?"

"I'm going outside." His face was grim in the approaching glow from the flatlands. "We have water. Maybe I can save the house."

Maybe! Meiko thought as she hung on the window and watched the approaching fire. *We need more than a maybe!*

■   ■   ■

Matsuo could feel the heat as soon as he stepped outside. The air was alive with sparks. He uncoiled the hose and turned it on. The pressure was pitiful, not enough to water the garden, let alone soak down the roof and walls of the house. He checked the rain barrels at the corners of the house. The snowfalls of the past two weeks had run off the roof with the sudden warm spell, filling the barrels to the rims. He dipped two buckets into the nearest and set them in the backyard, kissing Meiko's worried face as he passed her at the window.

Then he stepped back and surveyed the roof. The curved wooden shingles were ripe for a fire. He pulled out a ladder and climbed up, taking a bucket of water with him. The gusts were hotter and stronger up here. He had to hold onto an eave to keep from being blown off. He turned his back to the wind yet still the smoke stung his eyes and choked him. Larger sparks and bits of flaming wood filled the heated air. He wet his hair to keep it from being singed, then tossed the bucket of water over the shingles and watched the water trickle down to the gutters and back into the rain barrels.

Maybe this will work, he thought. He could keep the roof wet this way without wasting much water. But as he shielded his eyes and risked a glance toward the east, he cried out in alarm.

The fire was almost upon them! It was like a living thing, leaping over huge gaps of the city in its westward trek, lighting spotty fires here and there in its haste to engulf the entire city. Matsuo looked down at his puny bucket, then looked again at the approaching holocaust. It only took a second to decide. He tossed the bucket into the garden and scrambled down the ladder to ground level.

"Meiko!" he cried, rushing into the house. "Get Naka! We're leaving!"

"I have him," she said. He could see the little boy clinging drowsily to her neck. "Can't we save our house?"

The *our* cut him like a knife. They had been here only a few years, but they had been good years. It was a good little house, neat, trim, full of memories. *Their* house. And now they were going to lose it.

"Only the kami of the house can save it now. Nothing a couple of humans can do will make any difference. Grab what you can and we'll run for it."

Besides Meiko and Naka, Matsuo could think of only one valuable he could not leave without. He ran to where Nagata's daisho sat on its katana-kake and thrust the two swords into his belt. Everything else was replaceable.

■ ■ ■

So hot!

Meiko ran beside Matsuo as he carried the crying Naka through the smoke-layered, fire-rimmed streets of Tokyo. At times the very air seemed to burn. She was dressed in a light sleeping kimono and feared it or her wooden geta would burst into flame. Every so often Matsuo would stop at a water barrel and insist that Meiko immerse herself in it, then he would do the same. Finally, he would dip Naka's quilt in the water and wrap him up in it again. Naka didn't like being wet. He cried constantly. She was about to protest the repeated dunking when she saw a woman running down the street ahead of them with a child bundled in a quilt and lashed to her back—the bundle was burning. Meiko wanted to cry out to her but she turned a corner and was lost in a sheet of flame.

Confused crowds clustered at every intersection, knots of lost, terrified faces, unable to choose which direction to run. Matsuo pushed through them. He seemed to know where he wanted to go.

"We've got to keep moving upwind and crosswind!" he shouted above the roar of the flames and the blistering gale.

"Which way is that?" she said. The wind seemed to be coming from all directions. "How can you tell?"

He looked into her eyes, then away. "I'm guessing. Let's hope I'm right."

They passed brave firemen trying to fight the endless blazes with failing water pressure. The air grew hotter. Suddenly, to their right, Meiko saw a pillar of flame swirl and funnel into the air. Then another. Then two more. They hung there, twisting and whirling and stabbing at the city below, drinking up the heat and spewing it back. Tornadoes of fire. She had heard of such things in the fire that followed the Great Kanto Earthquake in 1923. Tatsumaki they were called—dragon tails.

As they crossed an intersection, she saw a tatsumaki lash out at a spot three blocks down a side street, causing a whole block of houses to glow from within like paper lanterns, then burst into flame as they were sucked up into the mad, fiery vortex. Matsuo led them through Asakusa at a run, past the temple to Kwan-yin, the Goddess of Mercy. The park around the temple was ablaze, the great gingko trees burning like giant torches. And from within the burning temple itself, Meiko could hear the screams of the devoted who were trapped there. The fire knew nothing of mercy.

Matsuo led them to the banks of the Sumida River where he pressed her and Naka through the throngs lining the bank. There was fire on the far side as well, burning just as wildly as the district they were fleeing. The whole of the sky was a bright orange, as if the earth had drifted too close to the sun. There were no shadows anywhere.

"What will we do, Matsuo?" she cried. For the first time now, she was afraid they might die.

"Take my hand," he said. Holding Naka against him, he pressed through the crowd and onto a bridge.

"But it's burning over there, too!" she cried.

He stopped in the middle of the span and clutched her to him as he leaned on a support.

"We should be safe here," he said. "This bridge is made of steel. There's nothing on it to burn."

But it could get hot. As the tatsumaki lashed the city with their maelstroms of fire, as the very air around them seemed to burn, filling with smoke and ash and flaming bits of wood and paper, the bridge grew more and more crowded, the steel of the bridge's structure grew hotter and hotter. The heat in the air, the hot steel against her, the press of the crowd—Meiko felt as if she were suffocating.

"Matsuo, I can't breathe! And look at Naka!" The little boy's eyes were rolled back and his head was lolling. "We're going to die here!"

She saw Matsuo glance left and right along the span of the bridge. Even if there were someplace to go, they couldn't budge.

Further up the river, the steel of another bridge was beginning to glow with the heat.

"We have to jump," he said.

She looked down at the dark waters below. In the light of the flames she saw charred debris and—was that a body floating by? She looked back up at Matsuo and the panic she felt must have been clear in her eyes.

"Trust me," he said. "I'll get us through this—all three of us—but you've got to believe in me."

She felt the strength in him, saw the determination to live in his eyes, and took courage from that. He helped her up on the railing and then gently pushed her off before she had time to change her mind. Her mind screamed *Naka!* but her body arched itself into a dive and she hit the water cleanly. She took no time to savor the blessed coolness of the deeper water, but fought her way back to the heated surface. There was a splash just behind her as she gulped air, and then she heard a child's coughing cry.

"He's all right!" Matsuo said out of the dark, and then he was beside her, letting the child clutch her neck.

"Oh, Naka!" she said, struggling to keep the two of them afloat. Matsuo helped by partially supporting them.

"Don't fight the current," he said. "Just follow it downstream."

She struggled, half treading, half swimming, moving along the heated water of the sluggish Sumida. A nightmare journey, drifting past the horribly dead in the water and the dying on the bank. Lacy fingers of steam reached up from the surface of the river around them, catching and holding the red light from the flaming city. It would have been beautiful were it not for the screams and cries that filled the air.

Along the way they were joined by other swimmers, some who lasted, some who fell behind and sank from sight. She reached out for what looked like a charred log floating nearby. She grasped it and it rolled over, revealing an open mouth and teeth at one end. She screamed and kicked away from it. Meiko stopped looking around her. She narrowed her world to Naka and Matsuo and herself and the river. She knew if she let any more of her surroundings dwell in her consciousness she would go mad.

She and Matsuo took turns supporting Naka and gradually the flames and heat were left behind. Eventually she found herself slumped wet and cold—she had thought she would never feel a chill again—on a foul, muddy bank within sight of Tokyo Bay. The water of the Sumida was lower than she had ever remembered it. Had it boiled away in places upstream, or were the canals and channels that fed it clogged with bodies?

Clutching Naka against her, and clutched in turn by Matsuo's encircling arms, Meiko watched the city continue to burn as swollen and charred corpses floated by. And still the B-29s kept coming. Despite the inferno below, wave after wave sauntered unchallenged through the air to drop ever more incendiaries on the agonized city. They finally ran out of bombs and planes at around three in the morning. The wind gradually died and the fire gradually burned itself out.

The all-clear sirens sounded at dawn.

■   ■   ■

Matsuo stood in the remains of his house. He had left Meiko and Naka at the Mazaki home, luckily spared in the uphill Akasaka section. Nothing but a smoldering ruin was left of the home he and Meiko had called their own.

But this was a small loss on the scale of last night's horror. And he knew that scale. As soon as Meiko and Naka were safe at his in-laws', he had hurried to the unscathed Diet Building. Chiyoda-ku, the district encompassing the Imperial Palace and the government offices, had been spared. From the uppermost level of the Diet's sturdy tower he looked down to the plain side of Tokyo. The sight left him weak and sick. Even though he had been surrounded by the fire last night, he had not grasped the full extent of its toll. A haze of smoke still covered the area. Where there had been homes and factories and parks and trees there was nothing but a blackened smudge. Central Tokyo had been leveled. Although he lived here, he had never considered the city home. He felt he belonged most in Kyoto. But seeing Tokyo like this tore the heart out of him. He went down to the streets.

Dazed by the enormity of the devastation, Matsuo walked from the periphery of the fire area toward its center. Nothing was left standing except an occasional steel frame, a rare concrete pillar, small sections of stone wall. Here and there a tree trunk or telephone pole stood black and stark against the white pall of smoke that permeated the air. He passed charred carts and burned-out hulks of cars, and then he began seeing bodies. A few at first, huddled in doorways or in the ditches that were supposed to protect them. The odor of burned flesh grew, competing with, then overcoming, the smell of burned wood. Then there were bodies in the street, more and more of them, blackened, wizened, contorted shapes. Some had been virtually incinerated to ash. Others appeared to be merely charred but, when touched, dissolved into feathery fragments that wafted away on the breeze.

The bodies grew in number as he walked on. They were everywhere, countless thousands of blackened corpses in the streets, sometimes piled so thickly that they choked intersections.

He had heard whispers in the halls of the Diet about the early death count: already a hundred thousand dead or missing and the total was rising hourly. Estimates were that the figure would double when all the reports were in.

Two hundred thousand dead! Almost all of them civilians. Matsuo knew how the Americans felt about the Pearl Harbor attack, but their anger could not justify this sort of atrocity. Only the east loch of the harbor had been hit. Honolulu had been spared. Matsuo had been there and had seen that for himself: Not a single bomb, not a single bullet had been aimed at the city. Only military targets had been struck, only soldiers killed. Granted, they had been sleeping and had had no warning of war, and he deeply regretted that, but the fact remained that they had all been members of America's armed forces. The women and children and workers of Tokyo who had been incinerated last night were not soldiers. Yet the planes had kept coming, dropping their incendiaries hour after hour.

Anger bubbled up in him when he thought of all the crisp, flaking corpses in the street, the bigger ones clutching the smaller ones protectively, futilely.

Isn't it enough that they overwhelm us in battle? Do they want to erase us from the face of the earth as a people, too?

This war had to be stopped!

■　■　■

"We cannot let this go unavenged! We must strike back!"

Shimazu sat silently amid the smell of scorched wood and watched Hiroki fling himself about the room, expending his rage in all directions. The fire had burned itself out in the temple's district, but the temple had not escaped unscathed. The roof had caught and burned through on the east side, spreading to the upper floors where the Seers and the surgeons lived. All three of the Seers and many of the surgeons had perished. His heart was heavy with the tragic loss to the Order. He had known those monks all his life.

Curse these American dogs!

"If only I had enough shoten at my disposal!" Hiroki said. "I'd take them to America myself and place them throughout Los Angeles and let those Americans know what it is to die in their homes and streets!"

"We do not have a safe way to transport shoten the five thousand miles to America." Shimazu wondered idly what would happen if an altered child awoke on a submarine and began to generate the Kuroikaze there. "Nor do we have any to spare, especially with the loss of so many of our surgeons in the fire."

"Why didn't the Seers warn of this?"

Shimazu shrugged. He was so tired. "What is the point of such a question? The Seers are dead. We cannot ask them. So why ask me?"

Hiroki did not respond immediately. He seemed sunk in gloom. He began to mutter, more to himself than to anyone else.

"The temple is damaged, we have no more Seers, and not enough surgeons left to produce the shoten we need. The Americans bomb us at their leisure. We don't have enough petrol to train new pilots properly, so we teach them enough to get themselves airborne and crash their craft into an enemy ship." He looked up with haunted eyes. "We are lost."

"Remember what the Seer said," Shimazu reminded his pupil, but had to admit that even he was having doubts now about the outcome of the war. Iwo Jima was about to fall. Manila had been taken earlier in the month and it was only a matter of time before the last Japanese regiments were obliterated from the Philippines. With few minor exceptions, the inexhaustible American war machine had retaken all of the floating worlds Japan had seized a mere three years ago. And with the Third Reich in its death throes in Europe, it was only a matter of time before the Great Bear of Russia turned its hungry eyes toward Japan. The Emperor was more tightly encircled by the white barbarians than ever before. There had to be a way out!

Shimazu sighed. "It is too bad the Seers never looked backward. Perhaps they could have told us where the scrolls were hidden."

Hiroki jumped up and stared at him. "Look backward! Why didn't we ever think of that? We could have had the scrolls years ago!"

"We tried that. But apparently, once one has looked forward with the Seers' elixir, the past is closed to him."

Shimazu could not remember much experimentation by the Seers in the area of looking backward. The past was considered a matter of record; it was always the future that claimed their interest.

"Has anyone who has never looked forward tried to look into the past?"

"Not that I know of."

"Then we must try!"

"We have no new Seers."

"*I* will take their elixir!" Hiroki cried.

Shimazu studied him intently. Surely Hiroki was the Okumo brother who would bring the glory to the Order.

"But you still have your eyes," Shimazu said. "I will not permit you to give them up."

Relief was evident in Hiroki's face as he replied. "Perhaps I won't see as clearly as a Seer, but surely I will see *something!*"

"You have no training. You won't know how to control your visions. How will you guide them to the point in time you desire? How will you focus it in the proper place? You may be endangering yourself for nothing."

"We have to try. There has to be a way!"

Shimazu shook his head. It seemed hopeless. Hiroki had not a Seer's years of experimentation and experience behind him. He would not know how to obtain anything useful out of—

Shimazu suddenly remembered how the Seers held the new children when they were first brought to the temple. They used contact with the child itself to guide and focus their vision. Perhaps that would work for Hiroki.

"There may be a way," he said.

"Anything!" Hiroki cried. "I'll try anything!"

■ ■ ■

Hiroki drank the steaming elixir in slow, steady swallows. It was bitter and yet there was a thick, cloying sweetness to it that almost gagged him. He forced it down, then waited for the blindfold to be tied over his eyes, blocking out the sight of Shimazu and his quarters. When it was in place, he lay back on the futon and waited.

His skin was damp with fear-sweat. What if the elixir damaged normal vision? Who would know? Until now it had only been used by Seers, and they had their eyes removed long before their first dose of the elixir. He couldn't bear to be blind, to be led around by the hand, to be dependent on others. He would commit seppuku before living like that.

Was there any hope of success? Was he risking his eyesight recklessly?

"Open your hand," he heard Shimazu say.

Hiroki did and felt a scrap of parchmentlike paper pressed against his palm.

"What is that?"

"One of the scroll fragments you found. I want you to hold it while you are in the trance. There is good reason to believe that a relic such as this will guide your vision to the right time and place."

"Aren't you afraid it will be damaged?"

"The ideograms on it have been copied and recopied elsewhere. Its message is preserved."

Hiroki closed his fingers gently around the fragment and tried to relax.

Shimazu said, "Think of something that happened an hour ago. Then something that happened yesterday. Guide your vision backward in time. Point out the direction you wish it to follow, and pray it will lead you the rest of the way."

He lay in silence on the futon, waiting, thinking, concentrating. A glowing yellow fog rose up behind his eyelids but he could see nothing else. Time passed slowly in the formless glow within the blindfold. How long would this take—if it worked at all? Nothing was happening. Even the nausea was gone. He was about to give up, to sit up and remove the blindfold when he saw a faint shadow within the fog.

Hiroki stiffened and waited, not sure if he had really seen it or imagined it. It came again, darker this time, lasting longer.

He wanted to shout to Shimazu but held his tongue, afraid he might disturb the effect he was experiencing. The shadows continued to grow darker, and through breaks in the fog, colors began to appear.

Okamoto! he thought, trying to direct the vision to the ancient caretaker of the scrolls. *Find me Okamoto!*

The colors began to solidify into shapes, more clear-cut images that remained just beyond his grasp, taunting him—

Suddenly he was looking through the eyes of another, walking down a street.

Hiroki felt his arms and legs fly about and slam against the futon for support as vertigo spun him like a top. His body knew it was lying flat yet his eyes were telling him that he was up and walking. It was disturbing, disorienting, and he could not close his eyes to shut out the images because they were already closed. Gradually the seasick feeling passed and he adjusted to looking out at the world through the eyes of another.

His excitement grew as he tried to recognize his surroundings in the fading sunset light and realized that he was in the past. The road was packed dirt, alive with quaintly dressed pedestrians and bouncing, rattling carts drawn by either ox or horse or human. The sixteenth century would have looked like this! Was he behind the eyes of Okamoto himself?

But if so, where was Okamoto?

Hiroki watched carefully, trying to pick out a landmark, a familiar mountain or horizon, but it was getting so dark. Soon, his host lit a lantern and carried it ahead of him to light the way. Finally he stopped his trek and set the lantern down.

They were at the building site of a small structure. A foundation had been started and a deep alcove of sorts had been carved out of the volcanic rock of the hillside it abutted. Hiroki watched as hands took up a shovel and began to dig in the earth of the alcove. He heard and felt nothing, but he sensed weakness, a deadly weariness in the arms wielding the shovel. The bites into the earth were shallow, and the shovelfuls of dirt trembled as they were lifted from the hole. Finally the digging stopped. The hands produced an oblong urn from a sack. Its narrow mouth was sealed. It was placed in the hole and the dirt filled in after it. After that was tamped down, another hole was begun. The arms seemed weaker still and the vision blurred and wavered at times. A second urn was buried and then a third hole was started. But when this hole reached half the depth of the first two, the vision shimmered and went black for a few heartbeats.

Hiroki broke out in a cold sweat all over his body. Something was wrong. Had something gone amiss with the elixir? Was it wearing off? Or was it Okamoto? He remembered Yajima saying he had found evidence that the monk had been ill during his southward trek. Was he dying?

Suddenly the vision returned. It was more blurred than before. He saw the hands struggle with a third urn, saw them push it into the shallow third hole and cover it with a thin layer of earth. Then Okamoto was turning, crawling from the alcove, reaching for the lamp. Again the vision swam and faded to a darkness so absolute that Hiroki knew instinctively that there would be no return to light.

Hiroki tried to lift his hands to remove the blindfold but they wouldn't move. He tried to call Shimazu's name but his tongue was frozen. Terror ripped through him. Was he dying like Okamoto? Was the vision carrying him along into death, too? He struggled to turn, to call out, to move even a finger but he could not! He was falling! Falling through an empty, hungry void that had no end! His mind screamed—

And suddenly he heard his voice screaming. Hands were on him and Shimazu was saying, "What's wrong? Are you all right? What do you see?"

He felt his own hands move, dart to his face, pull off the blindfold. Light! Blessed light! Shimazu hung over him, his impassive green eyes staring down through his mask.

I was dying! I almost went down with Okamoto!

And then he recognized the alcove in the vision. It formed the rear chamber of the shrine where he and Yajima had found the fragments. The scrolls were buried under the floor of the shrine!

"I know where they are!" Hiroki shouted. "I can find the scrolls!"

APRIL

Commander Hiroto, Matsuo's immediate superior, handed him a small cup of green tea, saying,

"We have reason to believe the Americans are nearing completion of an atomic bomb."

The words jolted Matsuo. "I thought they were still years away from success, sir."

Commander Hiroto sipped slowly from his own cup. He was a short, brawny man with very short hair and cheeks so round and full that they seemed to squeeze his eyes closed. He was an old hand at espionage and intelligence. Matsuo liked and respected him. He swallowed and shook his head.

"We all thought that, but word from General Arisue's office—"

"General Arisue—!" Matsuo began but the commander silenced him with an upraised hand.

"I know what you are going to say. But hear me out first."

Matsuo settled back. He knew Major General Seizo Arisue as an unprincipled, supremely ambitious man who used every opportunity available—and as head of Army Intelligence there were many—to line his pockets and further his political ambitions. Anything from that man was suspect.

"Two separate sources in Lisbon—double agents—confirm that the American atomic bomb project, centered in a place called Los Alamos in the State of New Mexico, is in an advanced stage of development. They suspect that a prototype will be ready for testing this summer."

"How does Lisbon know all this?"

"Because an American named David Greenglass, a technician at the Los Alamos site, has been selling blueprints to the Russians. If the Americans can produce a working atomic bomb, Japan is doomed."

Matsuo was unimpressed. "I don't see how an atomic weapon can do any more damage than their firebombs did last month!" The sight of those piles of charred corpses still haunted his dreams every night.

"I disagree. The March incendiary raid used three hundred bombers dropping firebombs for three hours and was helped by gale winds. You remember what Dr. Kakihana said when he was here: One atomic bomb dropped by a single plane could wipe out a medium-sized city."

Matsuo closed his eyes and tried to imagine a single bomb causing the horror of destruction he had witnessed that night. It was inconceivable. But Dr. Hidetake Kakihana from the University of Tokyo was world renowned. He remembered listening to him speak to a select group of intelligence officers at the Naval Club a few years ago. He had said then that an atomic bomb was ten years away for Japan, but maybe less for America, depending on how many expatriate German physicists they had working for them. However, he had thought it would take the Americans at least another five years.

Apparently he had been wrong.

And Matsuo remembered something else Dr. Kakihana had mentioned: radiation. This was something released by an atomic bomb that would cause sickness and lingering death affecting as many or more people than it killed with its immediate blast.

One plane, one bomb, and every city in Japan would have its own tenth of March.

Not on my homeland! I can't let that happen!

"They haven't tested it yet," he said, looking for a bright side. "They may never get a working model."

Commander Hirota leveled his gaze at Matsuo. "Can we rely on that?"

"No. Of course not. Is there any way we can get our own set of blueprints?"

"Obviously not from the Russians. They aren't going to share with us, and it is unlikely that this Greenglass will sell to us—he is probably a communist. We've always relied on the German spy network within the borders of the U.S., but with the Third Reich all but dead, organized German espionage in America has fallen apart. Since we have no reliable agents in place, we are left with one obvious option." He fixed Matsuo with his stare. "Send someone to America."

Matsuo felt a trapdoor opening under his chair. He fought to hide his dismay.

"And that someone is me?"

"Who better?" the commander said. "You grew up there, you've traveled the country, you can speak English just like a native. If anyone can pass for an American, it's you."

"I hate America, sir," Matsuo said, carefully. He was phrasing this as delicately as he could. "I would prefer not to go back there."

"You are the best man for the assignment."

"If you will excuse my boldness, sir, I do feel I can better serve the Emperor here."

"You have been chosen. It is chu."

Matsuo repressed a sigh. *It is always chu.* He rose and bowed. "When do I leave?"

"In four to six weeks. A submarine will be requisitioned and specially fitted to take you to the western shore of the United States."

Four to six weeks!

"Is there enough time to set up contacts and—"

"This is an emergency mission, Okumo-san. A desperate gamble. We will arrange what we can, but while you are there you will be on your own much of the time, deciding what to do on a day-to-day basis."

"'Playing it by ear,' as the Americans say."

Commander Hiroto nodded. "Very apt." He paused, then cleared his throat. "We are counting on you, Okumo-san. We don't expect you to bring back even part of the secret of the bomb, nor do we expect your mission to result in any effective sabotage of the project. It would be truly glorious if you could accomplish either, but I am aware of the severe limitations you will face merely by being Asian.

"Simply put, we need to know how far along the Americans are. We need to know if they've had a successful test. Their success will change the whole complexion of the war—of all wars to come. We need to know because the day may come soon when they threaten our cities with atomic destruction unless we surrender. We must know if that threat is real. Hundreds of thousands of lives may depend on your success, Okumo-san."

Matsuo felt the walls of the room closing in on him. He was willing to do anything for the war effort; if he thought it would truly make a difference in the outcome of the war, he might even go so far as to ram an explosives-loaded Zero into the deck of an American carrier; anything short of returning to America.

"I know how you feel about your days in America," Commander Hiroto said, "and I would not ask you if I knew of some other way."

Matsuo bowed to his superior officer, acknowledging the truth of his words. If Commander Hiroto saw no other way, then he would accept that.

But his heart shriveled at the thought: They were sending him back to America!

■　■　■

"Wonderful news on two fronts," Hiroki said, bowing before Shimazu. "The transcriptions are complete, and President Roosevelt is dead!"

"I am aware of both," Shimazu said. "For a while I was afraid that this country bumpkin named Truman might offer more favorable terms of surrender. That would swing tremendous weight to the side of the defeatists in the diet. Even the military might cave in. But true to the vision, President Truman is as much of a warmonger as his predecessor: He too insists on unconditional surrender."

"The war goes on," Hiroki said. "And with the scrolls transcribed, perhaps we shall begin to change the tide."

He could not hide his elation. Two of the three scrolls were once again in the possession of the Order. The third did not seem to matter.

Although the earth under the floor of the shrine in Hiroshima had been thoroughly excavated, the third was never found. He had to presume that it had been accidentally unearthed sometime during the past few centuries and was now lost for good. He had feared that some vital bit of information might be missing and had barely slept during the days and nights the Order's scholars had labored over the scrolls, transcribing the cascade of ideograms, many of them archaic and no longer in use, into more usable language. But that laborious task was now completed and it was clear that the first two scrolls held all the information needed.

"I asked that the full transcription be brought to you here for your perusal," Hiroki said.

"Yes. Very kind of you, but that will not be necessary."

Hiroki looked questioningly into those green eyes, then smiled and bowed. "Ah, yes, sensei. You, too, have been reading the transcribed pages as they have fallen still wet from the brushes of the scholars."

"No," said Shimazu. "I read the originals the night you brought them back from Hiroshima."

Hiroki hid his annoyance as well as his wonder. Shimazu never failed to amaze him. To translate such an array of ancient ideograms at a glance was an extraordinary feat. To say nothing of it demonstrated a great wa. But Hiroki wished his sensei had at least mentioned it to him. He could have been spared so much anxiety if only Shimazu had deigned to inform him that the scrolls held all they needed to know. But then, of course, he hadn't thought to ask.

"Do you think the third scroll contained anything of great value, sensei?"

"No. I believe the third scroll was very short. I gather from the references in the first two and from the fragments we have that it was merely a summary of the others."

That meant they had all the answers! The scrolls told how to distill an extract—an *ekisu*—that would turn any child into a potential Black Wind shoten! No more arduous, time-consuming surgery. No more useless deaths on the operating table. Just a sip of liquid . . .

"That is most heartening to know," Hiroki said. "I intend to oversee the compounding of the *ekisu* as soon as we can assemble all the ingredients. Some of them are . . . esoteric, to say the least."

"True, but they can be found. We may have to send someone to one of the traditional apothecaries in China for a few ingredients. But that should not take long."

Hiroki thought he had better hurry someone off on that mission. No telling how much longer Japan would control any territory in China.

Shimazu said, "You have, I imagine, noticed the recurrent mention of *zasshu* in the second scroll?"

Hiroki had wondered at the recurrent use of the term. It meant "mongrel." It appeared to have great significance to the authors of the scrolls.

"Yes, although I confess that in my hurried, piecemeal reading of the transcriptions I did not fully grasp its import."

"Perhaps the finer points of the author's prose were not carried through to the transcription."

Hiroki could almost imagine a condescending smile behind the silk mask. He bowed.

"Enlighten me, sensei."

"The strongest, most destructive Black Winds are formed by a zasshu shoten—a child of mixed lineage, with one parent Japanese and the other from one of the lesser races."

"A zasshu shoten! There are many mongrels available among the Koreans! A half-Japanese, half-Korean child will meet the criterion!"

"So will a half-Japanese, half-American child," Shimazu said.

"Well, yes, of course, but—" Suddenly Hiroki was aware of his sensei's eyes boring into his. Was he missing something? And then he remembered: "Meiko's child!"

Shimazu nodded. "Yes. That one would make an excellent zasshu shoten. And there is a certain amount of pleasure to be drawn from the delicious irony of the very Americanness of the child being used as a weapon against the Americans, don't you think?"

"Yes, sensei." He thought he sensed more than irony in Shimazu's desire for this particular child. Why?

But irony, delicious or otherwise, meant nothing to Hiroki at this moment. *Meiko* . . . she had hurt him, shunned him, shamed him. Here was a chance to strike back. Perhaps it would even be necessary for someone to slit her throat during the course of the abduction. His honor would be satisfied then, but it wouldn't be *enough!*

Better for her to live, to be wounded as she had wounded him, to feel the pain of loss as he had, to know what it was like to have someone she thought of as her own snatched from her grasp forever.

But no. This was beneath him. He would not lower himself to take her precious little mongrel child from her merely to exact revenge. He would do it for the war, for Japan, for the Emperor.

It was chu.

"But we must not be hasty," Shimazu said. "We have no need of the child until we have the ekisu. And I would not wish to deepen the rift between you and your brother."

"He would not know who took the child or where it was taken, sensei." Suddenly, obtaining this particular child was very important to Hiroki.

"He is an officer with Naval Intelligence," Shimazu said with a reproving tone. "Some say he is one of the finest intelligence officers in all Japan. Do you think you could hide the child from him for long?"

"Would he even look, sensei? I sense that he suffers the mongrel's presence begrudgingly. He has refused to give it his name."

"He may have grown up in America, but he was raised in the Bushido tradition. Will such a man passively suffer the loss of face inherent in having a child stolen from his wife, from under his roof, from his implicit protection? I think not. He will fight to prevent that."

"He will be defeated. I will see to it."

Shimazu shot to his feet. His anger radiated through his mask and robe like an unbanked fire. "Did you sacrifice your ears to the Order without informing me? Have I not told you a thousand times that there is to be no bloodshed between you and your brother!"

"Yes, sensei," Hiroki said, shaken, bowing meekly. And for the thousandth time, he wondered at Shimazu's fervor in this regard. "But if, as you say, Matsuo will leave no stone unturned in his quest to retrieve the zasshu child, what are we to do?"

"We shall wait. Your brother is leaving Japan on an espionage mission to the United States."

Hiroki was shocked at the news. "I did not know!"

"He only found out recently himself. During his absence, it so happens that we will be moving the temple to another city."

More shocking news! "Where, sensei?"

"I have not decided that yet. Tokyo is coming under increasingly heavy attack. It appears to be only a matter of time before this structure is razed by American incendiary bombs. We need a new city. A number are under consideration. When I decide, I shall tell you. And that is when you may take the child. Your brother will be away and by the time he returns the Order will be well established in its new quarters. The trail will be cold, as they say. There will be nothing to connect the Order to the disappearance. Not even your brother will be able to pick up the scent. *If* he returns at all."

"That is a most excellent plan, sensei," Hiroki said, yearning for

the day when his handpicked squad burst into Meiko's home and pulled
that foul mongrel from her grasp.

Soon, he promised himself. *Very soon.*

MAY

"I have a terrible feeling about this," Meiko whispered as she huddled
in Matsuo's arms.

There are no secrets in a Japanese house, and the knowledge that
only a flimsy wood and paper barrier separated them from her sleeping
parents had made their lovemaking hurried and self-conscious. Tonight she could not find the inner peace it usually brought her, a peace
she needed so desperately.

"What's wrong?" Matsuo said.

"I don't want you to go."

"I don't want to go. You know that. But I must."

"Am I going to lose you?" The thought brought tears to her eyes.
She shuddered and Matsuo held her tighter. "You're going into a huge
country filled with millions and millions of people who will all want to
kill you!"

"And I worry about you and Naka. Even though you are in your
father's house, I will have Shigeo look in on you from time to time to
see if you need anything. Don't worry about me. I'll be back."

Will you? She did not dare give voice to those words, but she could
not help thinking them. That fear had haunted her since yesterday
when Matsuo had told her. In that instant she became convinced that
something awful would happen while he was gone. But it was just an
irrational fear, she told herself over and over. Just a silly fear.

"Naka and I will be waiting here for you. We'll go to the shrine
for you every day to leave rice and an *ema* for your safe return."

She clung to him in the darkness.

Oh, Matsuo, my love, don't let them hurt you!

■　　■　　■

Matsuo sat in the darkness with the daisho propped across his
folded legs, his hands resting gently on the scabbards. He would have to
leave the swords here. It was like leaving a part of himself behind, but
he could not risk losing them in America.

He gripped the scabbards more tightly.

What can you tell me?

He closed his eyes and dozed, praying to the kami of the blades for one last sword-dream before he left Japan.

When the images finally came, he was disturbed by what he saw: Frank and Meiko together again. He did not know where or when, but they were together and he was not present.

The memory of the dream was a leaden weight in his belly as he left for the harbor the next morning.

THE CENTRAL PACIFIC

"Smoke on the horizon!"

Matsuo heard the clatter of feet running on the submarine's wooden walkways and opened his cabin door to see what was happening. He headed toward the bridge.

The I-85 was making its way steadily eastward from Yokohama, running below the surface on battery power during the day, knifing through the Pacific swells with its diesels at night. They now were somewhere between Wake and Midway. Naval Intelligence had wanted a direct run to the United States but headquarters had demanded that the sub be fitted with maximum offensive capacity. Matsuo too wanted as brief a voyage as possible but had to admit that the Chief of Staff's reasoning was sound: With fuel oil so precious in Japan now, the greatest tactical advantage had to be squeezed from every drop.

And so the I-85 cruised eastward at top speed but kept its periscope up in the event that an American supply convoy hove into view. And now it had.

Matsuo watched the four young *kaiten* pilots, not yet out of their teens, cluster around Captain Yanagida, begging to be allowed to enter their craft. The captain considered their pleas, then nodded his agreement. With loud shouts of "Banzai!" they ran aft to their quarters.

The captain looked at Matsuo and shrugged. "The targets are too far off for conventional torpedoes."

Matsuo signaled his understanding with a bow, then returned to his cabin. He knew what was to follow and could not bring himself to watch. The standard afterdeck equipment—reconnaissance plane, catapult, and deck gun—had been removed from the I-85 and replaced with four kaiten torpedoes. The four youths, heads banded with bright hachimaki, would down a cup of sake at the ship's shrine and then each would crawl through a tube from the control tower to his personal kaiten. Once sealed inside, he would cast off, never to be seen again. Each eight-ton craft was a human-guided torpedo, a seagoing kamikaze.

The kaiten almost eliminated the element of chance that plagued conventional torpedoes. Its pilot could steer it toward a convoy, pick out a prime target, and aim for a strike amidships. Evasive maneuvers by the target were useless. The kaiten had a thirty-mile range and would follow the ship wherever it ran until it could detonate its powerful warhead against the hull. The convoy's only hope was to sink the kaiten before it struck.

Matsuo concentrated on what was to come for him. Once in America, he had to locate Koe, his contact. No one in Intelligence knew who Koe was, but he had been transmitting ship movements in and out of San Francisco Bay since June of 1942. His messages, boldly sent in uncoded English until the revised codebook was passed to him via Panama in 1943, had been valuable at first, but were quite useless now, what with the Imperial Navy far more concerned with what American ships were doing nearer to Japan. Yet still he kept transmitting, brilliantly, courageously, defiantly, from the very heart of San Francisco. And still his identity was an enigma. He was known only as Koe—the Voice.

Matsuo heard more "banzais," faintly this time, then a clanking on the deck, then silence. Eventually, the captain came to his cabin.

"We are underway again. And we are lighter so we should make better speed."

Matsuo nodded silently, trying not to think of those four fervent boys piloting thirty-two tons of machine and explosive toward the American convoy, dying for a cause that was already lost: Word had come just as he was boarding the I-85 that Germany had surrendered unconditionally. That meant that all the war resources of the white world would be withdrawn from Europe and brought to bear entirely on Japan. The little cluster of islands no bigger than California now stood alone.

He turned his thoughts to Meiko. Leaving her had been the most difficult thing he had ever done. Here, in this propeller-driven underwater coffin, he felt more alone than ever. He wanted to be home with Meiko beside him. But his home had been reduced to a pile of ashes and his country was being ground into the dirt by the American bombers.

Japan could stand and fight like no other country had fought before, could make America modify its call for unconditional surrender —but not if America had an atomic bomb.

Japan had to know, and the Supreme Command thought he could do it. Why? There was nothing special about him.

Why me?

He closed his eyes and prayed he would get to see Meiko again.

JUNE ███████████
PACIFICA, CALIFORNIA

Matsuo stood poised on the ladder under the conning tower hatch, waiting for the captain's signal as the sub rose toward the surface. They had hovered tense and silent just above the seafloor for the better part of three hours while American surface craft cruised above them. Now the captain was at the periscope, turning it this way and that, scanning the surface as the I-85 continued to rise.

"Now!" he shouted and Matsuo began spinning the hatch wheel. Seawater poured in on him but he fought his way up against it to the air and the dim light above.

Only the upper half of the conning tower had broken the surface. Through the fog and the fading light of dusk, he caught sight of a pale strip of beach a hundred and fifty yards away. In a rush, he pulled his belongings clear of the hatch and slammed it down. He could hear the sailors below tightening the wheel behind him as he caught a swell and began swimming to shore. He was barely a dozen feet away from the tower when it gurgled and sank from view.

Clad only in his fundoshi, Matsuo swam as fast as he could. He needed what little light remained from the day to keep his bearings. Once darkness fell, that bleak deserted shore would be swallowed up by the night and he might spend hours swimming in a circle.

He rode a breaker onto the sand and then hurried across the beach to the shelter of the hills that jutted up into the swirling fog. Quickly he tore open the oilskin-wrapped bundle he had carried in from the submarine. It contained the disguise prescribed by Koe. There were no surprises within. He had already tried everything on and it all fit.

First he pulled on the old shirt and pants, and the old American tie shoes, then smeared a thin coat of pale, Caucasian-toned greasepaint on his face. That was followed by the white wig and full beard, then the dark glasses and hat. He had to admit it was quite an effective ensemble. The shaggy hair and beard masked his features, the dark glasses hid his eyes. With the telescoping white cane to complete the picture, he looked like an old blind man—an old *American* blind man.

Now to head north to San Francisco to meet Koe.

Matsuo approached the city from the south. After a three- or four-mile walk along the sand, he climbed uphill and stepped onto the streets of Parkside. He followed them into Forest Hill. New homes clustered where there had been only woods before. The city had grown since he had left it thirteen years ago. He crossed the Panhandle of Golden Gate Park and entered the Western Addition. He kept to Fell Street, skirting Japantown as he made his way toward Market Street.

Market Street had changed, especially the theaters. Many of his favorite movie houses of old were closed or gone or operating under new names. There were new buildings and new signs and new model cars on the pavement, but the Muni buses still ran back and forth and there was more hustle and bustle than ever. He walked along until he neared the hairpin intersection of Market and California, then cut up to California and started the long, steep climb to the crest of old Nob Hill.

It almost seemed a shame, really. Japanese cities were being reduced to rubble and cinders while San Francisco grew and prospered unscathed. And yet he found the timelessness of Nob Hill somehow reassuring. Something from his past was being preserved.

He looked around. It was all still here, all so familiar, as if he had never left. Everything was just as he remembered it. Grace Cathedral was just as granite-block cold and majestic as ever; the old Union Pacific Club still looked like a stolid, brownstone library; the hotels—the Mark Hopkins, the Stanford Court, the Fairmount—buzzed with activity, booked to capacity, apparently.

Standing here in the fog-diffused light from the street lamps, smelling the brine of the bay, listening to the rasp of the cables under the street, he felt a peculiar fullness growing in his chest, in his throat. He fought it, battered it down. He did not want it, refused to recognize it.

And yet it persisted, growing stronger despite his best efforts to smother it. Finally it threatened to overwhelm him.

It felt like home.

No!

Japan was where he belonged! Kyoto and all she represented was the city that had claimed his heart and that was where he knew he belonged, where he would someday live! Why then did the streets and the buildings and the very air of this city on the shore of hated, accursed America wrap him in her arms like a mother welcoming home a long-lost son?

Helpless before her, Matsuo had no choice but to accept the embrace.

He had come home.

■   ■   ■

After a while, he stumbled down Leavenworth's steep incline through Russian Hill, dimly aware of the lights of Alcatraz growing from the midst of the fog-enshrouded bay as he neared the waterfront.

He was to meet Koe on Jefferson Street. No particular block or intersection, just Jefferson Street. Not very precise, but perhaps that was wise. Anyway, he knew Jefferson wasn't very long, running no more than five or six blocks along the waterfront.

So Matsuo hobbled along the littered sidewalk, trying to look infirm and perhaps blind, shuttling slowly back and forth between the redbrick Del Monte cannery and Powell Street, first one side of the street and then the other, stopping at times to watch the late-coming fishing boats unloading their catches for the day, then continuing on his way. He didn't know how long he walked or how many circuits he made, but he was despairing of ever making his contact when he glanced up Taylor Street and saw his mirror image approaching.

Matsuo stopped walking. He leaned against a building on the corner and pretended to feel about in his shoe as if searching for a pebble. The other white-haired, bearded old man with dark glasses paused in front of him.

"Where y'from, Mac?"

Matsuo gave the prearranged answer. "The floating world."

The other turned and headed back up Taylor. "This way."

Fighting the unfounded fear that he had been betrayed and was being led into a trap, Matsuo followed the man for a number of blocks, around a couple of corners, and then down a narrow alley barely wide enough for two men to walk abreast. The other unlocked a door and Matsuo followed him inside.

"Here we are," the man said, turning on the lamp in a small furnished room.

Matsuo closed the door behind him but kept his hand on the knob. "Yes. Here we are. But *who* are we?"

"Koe." He pulled off his white beard and wig, revealing a face that was pure Japanese. And vaguely familiar.

"Sachi!" Matsuo cried as he recognized him. His face was scarred and he was leaner, harder, much tougher looking than when Matsuo had last seen him almost twenty years ago. He pulled off his own beard and wig. "It's me—Matsuo Okumo!"

Sachi's brow furrowed as he studied Matsuo's features, then recognition dawned. "From Izumi-san's store! My God, it's really you!"

Matsuo began to bow but Sachi leaped forward with a grin and pumped his hand.

"To see a Japanese face after all these years, and find out it's someone I know!"

"It's good to see you, too, to know you're all right," Matsuo said. "But of all the Japanese in America, you're the very last one I would have suspected of being Koe."

Sachi's smile remained but it suddenly looked forced. "Well, just goes to show how you never can tell how things'll work out."

Matsuo's instincts told him to let the matter drop, but he had to know, he had to be sure about Sachi. "But you were the all-American nisei. You never cared about Japan, never even wanted to hear about it. You told me you wanted to forget it ever existed."

"Yeah, well that used to be true," he said, his grin dissolving into a tight-lipped grimace of pain and anger, "until our glorious President Roosevelt decided that the American Constitution didn't exist for me! He signed an executive order: anyone with even one Japanese grandparent was outlawed from the West Coast!"

"They've always hated us here," Matsuo said, remembering Mick McGarrigle and the adults who spawned him.

"Here, yes! But this was done in Washington! We had nowhere to turn. We knew what to expect from swine like Hearst." He laughed harshly. "And did he turn tail and run! Closed up his mansion and fled the coast with his tail between his legs! But it wasn't just the Hearsts who came after us. Even so-called liberals like Walter Lippmann got on the Jap-hating bandwagon. There was not one act of sabotage anywhere along the West Coast but Lippmann said that was because we were all waiting for our chance to do something really devastating. FDR and Walter Lippmann, Champions Of The Little Man!" He spat. "Hypocrites! I did a dance when I heard that rotten old bastard had died!"

He paused, as if controlling himself with difficulty. "They gave us five days to settle our affairs, then we were to be evacuated. We were allowed to take along only what we could carry. So we sold off our cars and possessions and there were plenty of our good California neighbors ready to buy at the bargain prices we had to take. Some even tried to haggle us down further. How my mother cried when she sold her curved glass china cabinet and everything in it."

"I'm sorry, Sachi," Matsuo said. But Sachi was not finished. Matsuo sensed that a long-pent-up rage had finally found a vent.

"They herded us like animals into fairgrounds and racetracks, searched us like criminals, then bundled us off to 'relocation centers.' But everyone knew they were concentration camps. They put us in tar paper shacks in deserts where the sun baked us in the day and the wind froze us at night." He lowered his head and his voice softened. "Yet even there, amid all that ugliness, Japanese gardens created from bleached wood and desert flowers began to appear alongside the shacks."

His eyes flashed as he looked up at Matsuo. "It was a land grab! California farmers have been trying to get us out of farming since the turn of the century and this was their big chance. They gobbled up our farmlands as leases and mortgages expired or went past due because the people who had tilled them for years were locked away in concentration camps."

"How did you manage to stay free?"

"I allowed myself to be rounded up just like everybody else. We figured it had to be a mistake. Our country, our President wouldn't do this to us. But after two months it finally got through my thick skull that this was the way it was going to be. It didn't matter that I was born here, that this was my country just as much as it was Hearst's or Lippmann's or FDR's!"

Tears started in Sachi's eyes but he quickly wiped them away and took a deep breath.

"My country thought I was shit, to be scooped up and thrown in a garbage can. If that was the way they wanted it, that was the way it would be. I decided to escape. Nobody else would come with me—they all thought their dear President Roosevelt would change his mind any day. I tunneled out and became Koe."

He looked away. "I would have fought for America, Matsuo! Died for her! I loved her. I always thought of her as *my* country! But she told me in no uncertain terms that she wasn't."

Matsuo didn't know what to do or say. Sachi was a grown man in his midthirties but at this moment he looked like a broken-hearted little boy. He tried to lighten the mood.

"Well, at least now I know why all your messages were in English."

"Yeah," Sachi said with a hint of a smile. "I never did learn Japanese." He shrugged and seemed to compose himself. "Anyway, FDR's executive order was rescinded back in January. Issei and nisei are free to leave the camps. But a lot of them have no place to go. And many of the ones who did leave have been harassed and brutalized. My mother's still there. She's afraid to come back. So save your disguise, my friend. It's not healthy to be a Jap in San Francisco."

Sachi made coffee for both of them on his hot plate—Matsuo would have preferred tea but Sachi hated it and didn't have any—then very briefly transmitted the prearranged code word to signal that contact had been established. After that, they began taking turns manning the headphones to monitor the shortwave receiver for radio instructions from Panama on whom Matsuo was to contact for information from Los Alamos.

"How have you survived?" Matsuo asked, wincing at the bitterness of the thick, black, unsweetened coffee.

"Begging mostly. I play my old blind man role and pick up loose change that way. It's a good disguise. I've found that healthy people don't really look at you if they think you're damaged in some way, or not entirely whole. Kids will stare but adults allow themselves only a quick glance and then look away."

He pointed to a puckered scar on his cheek. "I do this with model airplane glue. I'll show you how later. Anyway, when I can't beg enough, sometimes I steal—like the hot plate, clothes off a line. One way or another, I get enough to get by. My rent is cheap and I've learned to tolerate hunger."

"I brought American money," Matsuo said, glad to know he wouldn't have to go out on the city streets with a tin cup. "But I meant how you've managed to avoid capture."

Sachi smiled. "Almost didn't a few times. I've got a portable transmitter in a beat-up old suitcase that I carry around to different parts of the city to make my broadcasts—rooftops, church steeples, graveyards, Telegraph Hill, even the Praesidio wall—you name it, I've transmitted from it. Never stayed in one place very long, and I never went to the same place twice in the same year."

"You're a brave man," Matsuo said, meaning it.

Sachi shook his head. "Uh-uh. I'm an *angry* man. Hell hath no fury like a man betrayed by his country."

■ ■ ■

Matsuo dozed, then took a turn on the receiver. When his shift was up, he handed the headphones to Sachi. It was morning and he wanted to stretch his legs. He had crossed the Pacific in a cabin on a submarine and this tiny furnished room seemed hardly bigger.

"Just be careful," Sachi said. "Since you won't be begging, leave the white cane here and use the hickory one by the door. Just remember to move slowly but keep moving. You don't want any attention from the cops."

Matsuo reveled in the air and light as he made his way down to the docks. When had he last seen the sun? As he crossed Jefferson Street, he glanced up to his left and stopped dead in his tracks.

He had seen drawings of it before leaving San Francisco in 1932, and grainy black and white photos of it in newspapers since its completion, but nothing had prepared him for the sight of those monolithic red-orange towers and the ribbon of roadway gracefully spanning the gap between. It had been completely lost in the fog last night, but now the Golden Gate Bridge held him spellbound until a horn blast and a hoarse "Trying to get killed?" from a passing Ford alerted him to the fact that he was standing in the middle of the street. He hurried over to the wharf and leaned against a wooden rail, staring in mindless wonder at the bridge's audacious beauty.

When he finally had his fill, he looked to his far right and saw another new bridge, this one going to Oakland. It looked longer than the Golden Gate, but somehow it was just a bridge. The red-orange one here was a work of art as well as an engineering marvel. He turned around and nearly cried out as he saw a white tower jutting up from the top of Telegraph Hill like a gun barrel. That hadn't been there before!

In a state of mild shock, Matsuo wandered along the Embarcadero. San Francisco had changed so drastically! It hadn't been apparent last night in the dark, but there was no hiding it now. So much *busier!* Before he left, it had been a collection of neighborhoods where everybody seemed to know everybody else. Now it was truly a city. Had the war or the bridges done that?

He came to the Ferry Building. At least that hadn't changed, although he doubted it was one-tenth as busy now as it had been before completion of the Bay Bridge that loomed over it. He set his watch to San Francisco time by the tower clock and headed for Chinatown. That hadn't changed. He passed through Nob Hill again, and began a tentative journey down the slope toward the Western Addition, afraid of what he would find there—or rather, what he wouldn't find.

To all outward appearances, perhaps to someone speeding through in a car, Japantown was unchanged. There were people shopping and walking and lingering in doorways, and the Victorian houses still hung their turrets out over the sidewalks. But even a cursory inspection revealed that there were no Japanese faces along Geary and Octavia and Post streets where in the past Caucasians had been rare. All the signs over the shop doors and in the windows were now in English, but here and there an old painted-over ideogram had bled through. What had been Japantown was still full of the living, but to him it was a ghost town.

Matsuo wandered through the different neighborhoods, seeing change everywhere. Eventually, he found himself in the Tenderloin. On a whim, he found Mrs. Worth's apartment and knocked on her door. He was sure she wouldn't recognize him—after all, thirteen years had passed since she had taken him in and stitched up the wound from Mick McGarrigle's bullet—but he just wanted to see her face once more and know she was all right, or find out if she needed anything.

There was no answer, so he knocked again. A man stuck his head out a window on the floor above. "Can I help you, mister?" His tone was anything but solicitous.

"Yes," Matsuo said. "I believe I know this tenant. Is she in?"

The man's face softened. "Betsy? Gee, fella, I'm sorry—she died last month. Heart, they say. You an old friend of hers?"

Matsuo bit his lip, afraid to trust his voice. *One month!* He had missed her by one month! He could only shake his head as he hurried away.

He walked with his head down, not caring where he was going as long as it was away from that empty apartment. When he looked up, he noticed a familiar facade across the street. The sign on the window glass said "O'Boyle's." He crossed over and looked in the window. It looked pretty much the same, even to the pool tables at the rear of the main room where he had crushed Mick McGarrigle's throat.

Why was it that the good things had changed for the worse and the bad things had remained the same?

The change in time zones was playing tricks on him. He was tired and depressed. He felt alone and vulnerable here. This whole mission seemed like a fool's errand. What did the Supreme Command expect him to accomplish? One man against the mightiest war machine in history. It was utterly hopeless.

He pulled himself together and started the steep climb toward Nob Hill.

But he had to try.

TOKYO

"We have found new housing for the Order until the war is over," Shimazu said.

Hiroki bowed. "Where, sensei?"

"Hiroshima. It appears to be a favored city. Very few bombing attacks. The American incendiary raids are coming so frequently now, even in broad daylight, that it is only a matter of time before this structure burns to the ground. Besides, the scrolls remained safe in Hiroshima for four hundred years. The Elders have taken that as a good sign."

"What of the ekisu for the Kuroikaze? I have everything assembled," Hiroki said. The final ingredient, a rare alkaloid from the root of a plant found only on the Chinese mainland, had come in. All was ready.

"We will begin mixing and distilling the ekisu when we resettle in Hiroshima. The Order will move within the week. You should take the American zasshu from the woman before then."

Hiroki felt a ripple of disquiet. "Matsuo—"

"—will not be a factor," Shimazu said. "I have communicated with the Navy Chief of Service. It is unfortunate, but the Navy cannot spare a submarine to pick up your brother from America."

That was all there was to it: We're moving. Get the child. Your brother is to be stranded in America.

Hiroki bowed again, unsure for an instant how he felt about that last part. He no longer loved Matsuo, and knew that he had gone to America on a fool's mission that could only be used as tinder for the defeatists in the diet. But he was still, after all, his brother.

He straightened. What did Matsuo matter? The war was all that counted.

Hiroki turned his thoughts away from Matsuo to Meiko's mongrel. He knew that on this particular mission he could not sit here in the temple and wait for the temple guards to return with the child. He would have to lead them personally to the Mazaki house and oversee their every move.

A thrill of anticipation coursed through him as he pictured the guards sneaking through the house like shadows and spiriting the child off. But somehow that didn't satisfy him. Better to see them breaking through the walls and tearing the little mongrel from Meiko's arms. She would scream in terror at first and wail in grief at her loss later, and in her soul she would know that it was her own fault for mating with a white.

The vision of such a union flashed before him and he thrust it away, repulsed.

He went to choose the men who would accompany him. He would select them for skill at stealth, but that was not an absolute criterion.

■ ■ ■

Meiko adjusted a light quilt over Naka as he lay sleeping on the futon. The days were warming with the approach of summer, but the nights were still cool. She sat back on her heels and watched him for a moment as she did almost every night. He lay spread-eagle on his back in an open, all-embracing posture that perfectly expressed his innocent acceptance of the world around him. Living with her parents these past few months had not been easy. They knew of Naka's American father and their coolness at first toward the child had not helped. But if Naka noticed their aloof attitude, he had not shown it. He would climb on Mother's lap and hug her and follow Father out into the garden and try to help him dig and weed. Soon they were looking for Naka, taking him everywhere, and now they openly adored him. If only the problems of the world could be solved so easily.

Naka, she thought. *In two months you will be three years old. It seems impossible. Where has the time gone?*

She left him in his peaceful slumber and went to her own futon in her old room. And there her thoughts drifted toward Matsuo and she wondered how he was faring in America. Was he safe? Was he hurt? Was he still free or had he been captured? Would she ever see him again? There was no way of knowing. She hoped he was sleeping as peacefully as Naka. Strange to think that here it was nearing midnight, the day almost done, and over there it was nearing dawn on a new day in San Francisco.

She felt herself slip toward sleep and welcomed it. One more day gone, one less day before Matsuo returned.

■ ■ ■

There was something almost nostalgic about returning here to this house in Akasaka. How many times had he come here with his father during the years he and Meiko had been pledged to each other? How many hours had he sat within, how many meals had he shared here?

He pushed those thoughts from his mind. This was not a social call.

He directed the driver along the willow-lined streets. Akasaka was uphill and west from the Imperial Palace, one of the few areas of Tokyo that had not been extensively damaged by the bombers. The Imperial Palace was another. On a quiet night, when the bombs weren't falling and the smoke from whichever part of the city currently aflame was blowing the other way, one might almost forget the war here.

Hiroki waited while the two guards, Masashige and Tsuneo, adjusted black stocking masks over their already masked faces, then donned his own mask. The only openings were for the eyes. All else was covered by long-sleeved sweaters and loose-fitting pants. Anyone in the household who saw them would be unable to provide a single detail linking them to the Order.

The car was left idling at the curb while he led them around to the east side of the house. He had had the count's residence under surveillance and knew where the child slept. He let Masashige assist Tsuneo and him through the window, then left him stationed outside.

Inside the room, there was enough light from outside to make out the small form of the child sleeping soundly on his futon. All was silent in the house. So far, so good.

Hiroki found himself trembling with tension. Until now, he had kept his distance in these matters, never actually going into a home for a child, preferring to let the guards do that sort of thing while he waited outside. He now fully appreciated the wisdom of that course. He was quite convinced that he had been foolish to give in to the compulsion to come along this time. What if the child woke up and started screaming? So many things could go wrong. What if they were caught? The disgrace, the ignominy . . .

Considering this little adventure from the distance and safety of the temple, he had almost wished for a confrontation. Now all he wanted was to be done with the task and out of here.

He calmed himself. The worst thing now would be undue haste, especially with everything going so smoothly. All they had to do was gag the child, wrap him tightly in his quilt, and hand him out the window. The only sound so far had been the slight rattling of the shrubbery as they had climbed in, but that had drawn no attention. The shoji over the window had slid open with barely a whisper. Their bare feet drew only the faintest rustle from the tatami. But as Tsuneo drew the gag from his pocket, his elbow brushed against the shoji next to him.

They both froze.

■ ■ ■

She was awake. It was dark and she didn't know what time it was, how long she had been sleeping, or even *if* she had been sleeping. But she was awake and alert and strangely tense. Had something roused her? She lay still and listened.

Nothing. All was quiet. She closed her eyes and looked for sleep again. As she drifted back down, she heard a scrape. She drew herself up to a sitting position and listened. It had come from the direction of where Naka was sleeping, just on the other side of the shoji. Was he up? Maybe his bladder was full.

She spotted the shadow as she rose to her feet.

Meiko paused and squinted through the dark. There was just enough moonlight filtering through the trees and into the house to cast faint patterns on the floor and walls. But there, on the shoji that separated her quarters from Naka's, was a very solid-looking shadow. A chill spread over her skin, slowly, like a breeze across pond water. Were her eyes playing tricks on her or was that the silhouette of a man?

Meiko blinked. No, just a—

The shadow moved. And another joined it. She screamed and leaped to her feet. As she ran for Naka's room, she heard an answering wail of alarm and fear from her child. She rounded the fusama on the fly and confronted a dark looming form that blocked her path. Behind it she saw a squirming shape being lifted out the window. She screamed.

"No!"

She ducked under the arm that tried to grab and hold her and lunged toward the window. The dark figure there turned and swung a fist at her. The side of her head exploded with pain. Her knees buckled but still she moved toward the moonlight, toward the window, toward her son. Another blow to the back of her neck drove her to the ground. She tried to rise but all the strength seemed to have gone out of her. She began to cry with what little breath she had left, not with grief but with frustration, because she wanted to get up, wanted to get Naka back, but her limbs would not obey her.

Suddenly, her body was rising, but not of its own power. The dark figure was lifting her by the front of her sleeping kimono, holding her up in the moonlight. She could see no expression on the formless black shadow of the face, and only two glittering points where the eyes would be. But she could sense the fury radiating from the body.

Why does this stranger hate me?

And then his right arm rose, paused, then flashed down.

Another explosion of pain, then blackness.

But before the blackness, she saw a mark above her assailant's right wrist: a hollow hexagon with a meshwork center. She knew that sign.

The mark of the Kakureta Kao.

■ ■ ■

Meiko had vague memories of the rest of the night, of her parents rousing her and raising the alarm that brought the police, of describing the kidnappers and the events of the night over and over, of seeing the growing opacity of the officers' faces as she described the tattoo on her assailant's wrist, of being left alone in the cold gray light of dawn in the empty room with only Naka's rumpled futon for company, of sobbing uncontrollably and asking, *Why? Why?*

As soon as it was light enough, she went out to the streets. Because of the gas rationing there were no cabs to be had, so she walked down to the Ginza where she found a ricksha and told the driver to take her to the Kakureta Kao temple. He looked at her strangely—Meiko was not sure if that was due to her bruised face or her destination—but he knew the way and trotted her there.

She saw the smoke from blocks away, but since fires were the rule rather than the exception in Tokyo these days, she attached no special significance to it until the ricksha turned onto the street of the Kakureta Kao.

The temple was burning.

Meiko ran up to a fireman playing a weak stream of water over the flames. "A bomb?" she said.

The fireman shook his head. "No. Just a fire. Some of the neighbors say they saw the monks setting fire to it themselves before they left."

That had to mean that Naka was somewhere else. "Where did they go?"

"Don't know," the fireman said with a shrug. He was obviously overworked and overtired from fighting American-set fires, and more than a little annoyed to be called out for a fire set by Japanese. "On the way here we passed a big black truck heading south. That might have been them."

Meiko hurried back to the ricksha driver and convinced him to follow the road indicated by the fireman. She had him stop every few blocks to ask about a black truck. Finally they found someone who had seen it. It was still traveling south. The ricksha man took her to the southern city limits but would go no further despite her pleadings and offers of double and triple fare. Too dangerous, he said.

With no other option besides walking, she had him run her back to Akasaka where she pleaded with her father for the family car. He gave in with less of an argument than she had expected, even going so far as to offer to drive her in pursuit of the truck. Meiko talked him out of that. She didn't want to endanger him and leave Mother alone. But Father did bring out all the tins of gasoline he had buried among the rocks at the rear of the garden as a reserve in time of emergency. This, he said, was a true emergency.

And so, dressed in one of her mother's oldest kimonos, Meiko headed south as fast as the road would let her. It was bombed out in many areas and washed out in others, and overall in poor repair. With agonizing slowness, she made her way past Sagami Bay where her family's summer home used to be, where she and Matsuo had first made love, past white-capped, imperturbable Mount Fuji, and down toward Nagoya. She never saw the black truck, but it left an indelible trail. Everyone along the road remembered the passing of such a large nonmilitary vehicle in these times when gas was so tightly controlled. They treated her with great respect, assuming, she guessed, that she was a person of great importance to have the fuel to drive a car. They mentioned a number of similar black trucks traveling the road yesterday, but only one this morning.

For a moment as she approached Nagoya and saw the expanse of razed buildings and charred ruins beyond the city limits, Meiko thought she had come full circle back to Tokyo. There was an instant of elation, for something like that could only happen in a nightmare, which meant that this was all a horrible dream and she would awaken in the morning to hear Naka talking to himself on the other side of the shoji.

But it wasn't Tokyo. It truly was Nagoya. She cried a little, but kept on.

Yes, they had seen the truck not too long ago, still headed south. She rode out of Nagoya with a renewed spirit. She was gaining on them. She could feel it. She only prayed that all this was not for nothing. What if her little Naka was not in the truck? And what was she going to do if and when she caught up to the truck? Meiko didn't know. She only knew she had to do something.

She worked her way down along the coast, then followed the trail inland, passing south of Kyoto in the afternoon, noting with relief that although the factories around it had been bombed into ruin, the ancient heart of the city, the soul of her country's culture, had been spared. The work of the gods? Or did the Americans have other plans for Kyoto? After their merciless bombing of other civilian centers, she could not imagine they had a humanitarian motive.

But the why was not important. What mattered was that something of the Old Japan might survive. Certainly little of modern Japan was left standing. But the greatest toll was in the people. The misery she saw in the faces she passed broke her heart. Was there anyone left in the country who had not lost something or someone? Something precious was dying here. Her land was being reduced to a physical, cultural, and spiritual wasteland.

The car sputtered and died outside Kyoto. Meiko began to cry when she saw the fuel gauge on empty. Her father's gas hoard had carried her 250 miles, but it wasn't far enough.

She couldn't give up now, not when she was this close to catching them. There was only one thing to do. She dried her eyes and began walking. North of Osaka, she was able to catch a ride in a farmer's ox-drawn cart. He took her all the way to what was left of Kobe. The ancient city lay in ruins. She was able to buy a bicycle from an injured man who could no longer ride it. She could make better time along the road than any truck. She could weave in and out of the traffic and skirt the bigger rips and tears in the pavement. Her spirits lifted.

The trail led back to following the coast again, this time along the Inland Sea. As she rode, Meiko was only dimly aware of the timeless beauty of the mists and countless islands passing to her left, a source of inspiration for artists since the dawn of civilization. Father had brought her here many times as a child, telling her that its vistas soothed his spirit.

Maybe someday it will soothe mine, too, she thought. But not now. Not today. Until she had Naka back, no contemplation of still waters would calm the storm in her soul.

On and on southward, through Himeji as darkness fell, then on to Okayama, Kurashiki, Onomichi. Her head buzzed with pain. Her legs ached constantly and at times the cramps in her thighs were so agonizing that she had to stop the bike and walk them out. The dark forced her to slow her pace. She hit more of the holes in the road and every bounce amplified the pain in her head until she thought it would explode. But she kept on, and it was outside Mihara that Meiko found the truck.

If not for the predawn pallor of the eastern sky, she would have missed it. She was almost past the truck when she noticed its dark, canted outline at the side of the road. Meiko approached it carefully, like a doe approaching a sleeping tiger. The rear door to the cargo area hung open.

It was empty.

Meiko wanted to cry then but did not have the strength. All her strength—all her physical as well as emotional resources were dried up. She leaned against the open door and stared dully into its dark interior. Where had they gone? She would never find them now.

Something moved within.

Meiko leaped back as a voice spoke from the echoey darkness.

"Nothing here, so don't waste your time looking."

A wizened old man, dirty, bearded, clad in baggy factory work clothes, crawled to the edge of the cargo door and eased himself down to the ground.

"Did you see them?" Meiko asked.

"I watched them all night as they tried to get it moving again. They thought the problem was with a wheel. I could have told them from the very beginning that it was a broken axle, but they treated me as eta when I first spoke to them, so I said nothing more."

"They left?"

"Finally."

"Where did they go?" She could barely breathe. He had to know!

"I heard them speak of Hiroshima," he said.

Thank the gods! "Were there children? Did you see children?"

His head nodded vigorously in the dim light. "Yes. Three or four. There were adults, too, but they kept their faces turned away from me. I only saw the man who was driving, but I have never seen him before." He looked around. "There was a time, you know—"

"Yes, yes!" Meko said. "Please excuse my rudeness, but I must find these people. Did they get on another truck?"

The old man laughed. "No! An ox cart came and took the people and their possessions away."

"The children, too?"

"Of course. Who would leave children behind in the night?"

"How long ago?"

"Not long. Shortly before you arrived."

Meiko leaped on her bicycle. "A thousand thank-yous," she cried as she began to ride off. "Someday I will repay you."

"Better make it quick!" he said with a laugh. "Not much time left! And about that ox cart. It's most unusual. It's yellow—just like the sun!"

Meiko waved and rode off.

Her front tire went flat an hour later. Meiko did not even pause. She rode on the wobbly rubber until it shredded and fell off. Then she rode on the rim. The racket was terrible and the vibrations from the road even worse. But Naka was ahead. She could sense his nearness, and every minute was precious.

■ ■ ■

Hiroshima astounded Meiko. It was whole. Not a bomb had dropped here. The white walls and black-tiled roofs of its suburbs and even the ring of factories along its periphery remained untouched. It was as if there were no war in Hiroshima.

She'd had no sleep in thirty hours and had traveled four hundred miles—half the length of Honshu—in that time. She moved through a haze of fatigue and anguish as she crossed the Ota River and entered the city on foot. How many miles had she walked? She couldn't say. She had given up her bicycle after the rear tire ripped open and now she trod the streets with bare, bloody feet that felt as if they had swollen to twice their normal size. The hope of dawn had been dashed in the light of day when she saw the crowding of the city and realized that there were two or three hundred thousand people living here. How could she find one small child?

And yet, in her heart, she knew she would find him. And she knew she must get him away from here. She did not know why, for Hiroshima seemed a blessed place, a place favored by the gods and spared by the B-29s. Yet the very fact that it remained untouched by the war's otherwise unchecked destruction made her vaguely uneasy. She sensed a warning there.

But she kept moving, searching, and as she walked she saw that her first impression was only partially correct. True, Hiroshima was untouched by the American bombers, but it was not undamaged. The heavy hand of the war was evident everywhere she looked.

The streets were nearly empty of motorized traffic and, just as she had seen in Tokyo, all available iron and steel that could be safely removed from bridges and lampposts and railings and grilles had been stripped from the city. Rows of houses had been laid waste, dismantled to their foundations, not by bombs or artillery, but by soldiers and adolescents creating firebreaks under orders from the Ministry of the Interior. Perhaps they could halt the wild spread of a fire, but not, Meiko knew, if there was a wind blowing like the one in Tokyo in March.

Everywhere she looked she saw vegetables growing, in backyards and front yards, in narrow alleys, in pots and urns. Anything that could hold a handful of dirt became a miniature garden. Even the roofs—the tiles atop many a house were banked with earth and planted with greens. The people of Hiroshima had taken to heart the Ministry of Agriculture's decree that it was the sacred duty of every citizen to help provide food for the war effort. Meiko wished a few patches of unscorched earth remained in Tokyo. Perhaps there would be fewer starving there.

She came to a bridge and stopped at its center. Which river was she crossing? This city was cut this way and that by branches of the Ota

River, and those branches were spanned by over a thousand bridges. She was confused. The sun was rising high in the sky but she didn't know what time it was. Somewhere someone was heating *suimono* and the delicate odor of the clear broth flooded her mouth with saliva. How she would love a bowl now, along with a shady patch of soft earth where she might sip it slowly and relish every drop.

Meiko closed her eyes and swayed. She was hot, hungry, thirsty, weak, and exhausted. She could no longer feel her feet and she dared not look at them. What was worse, she was lost. She seemed to be in a factory-warehouse district but instead of bustling with workers and activity, only a few people and carts passed to-and-fro.

She wanted to fall down where she stood and weep, but was afraid she would never regain her feet again. Where was Naka? How would she ever find him in a city this size whose streets she didn't know, whose people were all strangers? *How?* She wanted to scream!

And then a spot of yellow moved in a corner of her vision. She snapped her eyes left and saw what appeared to be a bright yellow cart set against the wall of a two-story building three blocks away.

She ran toward it—or tried to run. The best she could do was lift her feet just far enough off the street to keep them from dragging. The fading sign on the wall of the building identified it as a tin factory. Surely no one from the Kakureta Kao would be in such a place, so she dared not hope that this might be the same cart that had taken the passengers from the black truck back on the road. But perhaps the owner knew of other yellow carts and where she might find them. And through them she might find Naka. But first she had to find the owner of this cart.

She stepped up to the door and knocked. When no one answered, she began pounding on it.

■ ■ ■

Hiroki peered through the grimy window to see who was banging so persistently on the side door. At this tight angle, all he could tell was that it was a woman. He looked around for one of the acolytes to answer it but none was in sight. He could not use one of the guards because they were masked and that would give away the secret Shimazu insisted they protect: that the Kakureta Kao order was now centered here in Hiroshima. The Supreme Command knew, as did the city police and the army garrison at Hiroshima Castle. But the public knew nothing and all agreed that a lot of annoying and possibly dangerous curiosity could be avoided if matters were left that way.

Hiroki ground his teeth and went to the door. Since the woman obviously was not going away on her own—ignoring her only seemed to make her pound harder—he would have to chase her off. He yanked open the door and looked at the miserable, bedraggled creature that stood there. A beggar? Most certainly a persistent one.

She looked at him and cried, "Hiroki!"

That voice! Beneath the shock and awe in its tones—*No! It can't be!* He stared at the woman, trying to see past her disordered hair and her grime. It looked like Meiko but her face was disfigured, discolored by more than dirt. He detected fresh swellings and bruises around the eyes—

He leaned against the doorjamb, suddenly weak with the memory of how he had taken out his fury upon her last night.

Did I do this? Oh, by the Face, is this my doing?

"Where's Naka?" she said, her voice rising to a scream. "Where's my son?"

The words brought back his composure in a rush. *How can she know? It isn't possible!* He pulled Meiko inside. She struggled out of his grip but he managed to shut the door behind her.

"I don't know what you could possibly mean," he said in as calm a voice as he could muster.

Meiko's face was livid as she stared at him. Her teeth were bared as if she were about to leap at him. She was a different person. He had never seen her like this, never imagined she could react this way. It excited him.

"Yes, you do! Two people from your temple stole him from his bed last night!"

"How can you say—?"

She bared her right forearm and pointed to a spot a few inches above her wrist. "I saw the mark!"

Hiroki swallowed. Curse that tattoo! "Anyone can copy a tattoo! I want to know how you found me here."

"I followed you and your black truck all the way from Tokyo."

He was astounded. "But how?"

"In a car, on a bicycle, on foot, what does it matter? I found you, now give me my son!"

He looked at her feet and gasped at the dried blood and dirt caked there. Yes, he could truly believe she had followed him from Tokyo under her own power. He marveled at her strength of spirit, her tenacity. All for a wretched little zasshu. What a wife she would have made him!

"Answer me!" she cried. "Where is Naka?"

"I cannot tell you!"

Meiko pounded her fists against his chest. "You can! A man saw children taken off your truck! You can! You—"

Suddenly her eyes rolled back in her head and she collapsed on the floor. Hiroki quickly knelt beside her. She was still breathing but she was unconscious. From the look of her dry, cracked lips and sunken eyes, he guessed that she had collapsed from exhaustion and dehydration. He lifted her into his arms and carried her to his quarters.

■ ■ ■

Meiko awoke with a pounding headache. She was lying on a futon. She sat up and saw she was in a small, candle-lit cubicle.

"Ah! You're awake. I saw you stirring and knew it wouldn't be long."

Hiroki knelt before her holding a bowl of soup piled high with *soba* noodles; a pair of chopsticks lay across the rim. Of their own volition, her hands reached out and took it from him. She ate quickly, efficiently, her hands shaking with hunger. She finished the noodles, then tipped the bowl to her lips and drained the broth. While she was eating, she noticed that her feet were wrapped in bandages. She inspected them now.

"I cleaned them for you," Hiroki said with a faint, almost timid smile.

Meiko found that hard to believe. "You? Personally?"

"Yes. I applied an herb ointment under the bandages."

She could not help but be touched. Yet she was still suspicious. "Why would you do such a thing for me?"

"Oh, Meiko," he sighed and she sensed genuine sorrow in him. "If only our lives had worked out differently. We could have had such a good life together. But that one summer day in 1937 ruined everything."

"I never had a chance to apologize to you for violating your trust." She did not say that she had violated his trust in her heart for years before that August day. "That was inexcusable." *And as inevitable as the rise of the sun.*

Hiroki spoke in a soft voice, as if half in a dream. "If not for that day, we would have walked the same road here in Japan. You would not have had to banish yourself to Hawaii for all those years."

In her mind, Meiko suddenly saw Frank's face and felt a rush of warmth. But the thought of Frank brought another name boiling to the surface. *Naka!*

"Where is my son?" she said, struggling to her feet. How could she have forgotten even for a moment that he was missing? She stood over the startled Hiroki. "I demand that you return him to me!"

"No one demands here!"

That voice! The words were spoken barely above a whisper yet Meiko froze at the sound. Someone had entered the cubicle. A tall, thin, high-shouldered figure stood in the doorway. Pale green eyes with tiny pupils peered at her through the holes in his silk mask.

Hiroki shot to his feet and bowed. "Sensei, this is—"

"I am perfectly aware of who this is," said the soft voice. "What I wish to know is why she is in a place where women are forbidden?"

"She followed the last truck from Tokyo, sensei."

The eyes turned from Hiroki and Meiko felt their full impact as they assessed her up and down. They battered her, bored through her, stripped her of any pretense of bravery, and laid bare her fears. She was naked before this monk.

Finally the eyes released her, yet she remained dumbstruck.

"And why would she do such a thing, Okumo-san?"

He wouldn't speak to her. It was as if she were some sort of animal, or an item of clothing or furniture.

"She is searching for her child. She seems to think he is here."

"Really?" The eyes turned back to her and Meiko saw amused puzzlement in them. "Why would anyone go to all that trouble for some wretched little zasshu?"

The dripping contempt in the monk's voice broke the thrall that had held her mute. All caution, all humility and reverence, burned away in a blast of rage.

"How *dare* you speak of my son that way! I want him back now! Show me to him at once or I will go to the police and—"

"Do not waste your time," the monk said without raising his voice the slightest. "The police have been instructed to keep clear of this building at all costs. They will obey those instructions."

"Then I'll go to—"

"The Army and Navy already know better than to get involved, and your husband is in America."

He seemed to be reading her mind, answering her questions before she asked them! A sense of helplessness all but overwhelmed her. She turned to Hiroki.

"Is this the great Shimazu-san you told me about all those years? This is the man you admire so?"

She saw Hiroki's body stiffen, saw his face go slack at her boldness. She didn't care. Perhaps it was her fatigue, perhaps it was the years of living with Frank, an American, and then with Matsuo, who had never learned to act like a meek, perfectly compliant Japan man, that freed her tongue now. Whatever the reason, she hoped it would bring some sort of response from Hiroki, something to confirm Naka's presence here.

"Do you admire someone who waits until a woman's husband is gone and then steals her child? I am ashamed of you, Hiroki Okumo! Perhaps that day in August was the best thing that ever happened to me!"

"That will be quite enough," said the monk in his quiet tone. His eyes were as cold and hard as emeralds. "I cannot show you your son, but we do have children staying with us. I can let you see them if you wish."

"I wish," Meiko said, wondering what the monk hoped to gain from his offer.

Hiroki said, "Sensei, I don't think—"

"She seeks a child. I will show her many." He turned and walked through the doorway. "Come."

Meiko followed him into a hallway lined with rooms and offices, then down a stairwell. To her shock, she realized she was on the second floor. On the ground level were a few small subdivisions and a wide expanse of dusty, dirty floor where drilling and cutting machines stood still and silent on every side.

"We are turning certain children into weapons," the monk said as he led her to the largest. He stopped at the door, took a lighted candle from its sconce, and handed it to her.

"We have no electricity in this area as yet," he told her. "You will need this. Those within do not."

He held the door open for her and Meiko stepped through.

First, there was the odor—urine and feces. The air was thick with it. Next was the sound. If the human voice could rasp and rustle like a fall wind through dry leaves and yet still convey the miseries of the damned, that would be the sound Meiko heard. She hesitated, fighting an instinctive revulsion, then stepped inside. Her bandaged foot struck something and she held the candle low to reveal a wooden boardwalk, almost like a trellis. She stepped up on it and raised her candle to find the source of the odor, and the sound.

There were bodies on the trellis. Small, wasted, naked bodies. They lay motionless with flaccid limbs and slack faces. Only their chest walls moved with their respirations, otherwise they might have been pieces of sculpture.

"These are our failures," said that sinuous, so-calm voice from the doorway behind her. "We feed them as best we can, keep them as clean as we can. But there will be no more failures. We will soon have a new method—a few sips of an ancient ekisu will allow them to finally become what we intended them to be."

With her heart pounding, Meiko held the candle closer. They had no eyes, none of them, just empty sockets. Their nostrils had been sealed, and in the open mouth of the one nearest her she could see no tongue. And from that open mouth came the hoarse rush of air that would have been a wail of fear or grief or terror or all three if the child had had a voice. That mad, voiceless cry was repeated all across the room.

Feeling as if her blood were congealing in her vessels, Meiko began backing away. She saw the candle fall from her nerveless fingers, but it was like watching someone else's hand. She nearly tripped coming off the boardwalk and her head fell back and slammed against the wall. She slid sideways along the wall until she found the door, and then reeled into the light.

She dropped to her knees and retched. "Beast!"

"They will win the war for the Emperor," said that voice. And for the first time she sensed emotion in it. "No sacrifice is too great to that end. The finest young men in Japan are clamoring, *vying* for the chance to give their lives for the Emperor! How dare you moan for your puny misbegotten child!" He turned. "Okumo-san! Show her to the street! The presence of one with so little regard for chu desecrates this place!"

She barely saw Hiroki's tortured face as he led her to the door. "That won't happen to your son," he whispered. "He'll just have to drink something." His last words to her as she stood out on the street were, "Be strong. It is chu."

Chu! Always chu! That would not work anymore! These monsters had to be stopped! But how? She believed what they had said about the police and the military being no help. Hiroki had often boasted about the Order's far-reaching power and influence. Even the newspapers would be useless—the Ministry of Information controlled everything that was printed. Certainly they would not allow this sort of story to see the light of day.

Only one man in all the world could help her get Naka back—and he was in America! Meiko started walking. She had to find Shigeo. He would know when Matsuo was returning. She had to get word to him!

JULY ▉▉▉▉▉▉
SAN FRANCISCO

Matsuo sat on a bench by the wharf, reading the Sunday *Chronicle*. The sun was barely up and he had the view of the bay all to himself. He lit a Lucky Strike—he could not get used to Luckies in a white pack—and rifled through the pages, hunting for something to grab his interest.

He was tired of waiting. So much time wasted doing nothing—it was driving him mad! And all the news from the Pacific—good for the Americans, bad for Japan. He couldn't bear to read it anymore. He turned to the funny pages. He read *The Captain and the Kids* and *Joe Palooka* first. They were pretty much as he remembered them from his college days here. *Gasoline Alley* had the same look, too, except that Walt was older and fatter. But *The Gumps* were unrecognizable. He liked a few of the new ones, especially *Dick Tracy* with characters like Breathless Mahoney and B.O. Plenty.

He folded the paper and sneaked a finger under the false beard. His real beard was filling in but was maddeningly itchy at times. He scratched for a few seconds, then snatched his finger away from his face.

Someone was watching.

A seedy-looking man leaned on the back of the bench, staring at him. He stood with his hands in the pockets of an old tweed jacket that looked as if it had been used to clean a dock; he wore equally filthy overalls and an undershirt which might have been white once. He sat down, close on Matsuo's right, and kept staring at him.

"That's a fake beard, ain't it?" he said in a low voice, full of wonder.

Without a word, Matsuo stood up and hurried away.

"Hey! I'm talkin' to ya! Whatcha hidin'?"

Matsuo ducked into an alley and sprinted for Sachi's quarters.

"Present for you," Sachi said as Matsuo entered. He indicated a flat package wrapped in brown paper. "Word came right after you left that it was ready. I picked it up while you were gone."

His false papers, no doubt, and maybe some information on Los Alamos. A note inside said that the Navy would be unable to send a sub back for him. The enclosed was the best Panama could do to get him back to Japan.

Damn!

He looked and found the identification papers and orders for one Mariano Cruz, a thirty-four-year-old Filipino galley helper from Baguio, on Luzon. There was an identification card with a grainy black-and-white photo of Cruz. He had a vaguely Oriental cast to his features and was bearded like Matsuo, but there the resemblance stopped. Cruz's face was darker and broader, and his nose flatter. He seemed to have rougher skin, too, although that might have been an effect of the photo.

Sachi examined the contents of the package with him.

"Panama's pretty much on the ball, wouldn't you say?"

"They should be," Matsuo said with no little pride. "I set up that office. We used Panamanian agents throughout the Southwest here where Spanish is almost a second language." He looked at the photo again. "But I'll never pass for him!"

Sachi said, "Don't be surprised. You give that beard a few more weeks, get out in the sun to darken your skin some, and you'll pass. Don't forget, we 'all look alike' to most whites."

Matsuo looked at Sachi to see if he was joking but he seemed serious. He put the photo down and picked up Cruz's orders. They instructed him to report to the galley of the heavy cruiser *Indianapolis* at Hunter's Point Navy Yard on or before 6:00 A.M. on July 16.

"The *Indianapolis?*" Matsuo swallowed hard. "I've got to return to the Pacific on a *U.S. Navy* ship?" How was he going to get away with that? And so soon! The sixteenth was less than two weeks away!

According to the letter with the order, Cruz had been on the payroll via the Panama office for three years.

"Looks like his orders came through in a rush," Sachi said, reading over his shoulder. "Something's up. Maybe there's some sort of emergency out in the Pacific that we don't know about."

Matsuo thought of the Kuroikaze and wondered if the Kakureta Kao had finally managed to turn it into an effective weapon.

"But I don't know any more now than I did when I arrived! This is insane! I can't go back with nothing!"

There was another envelope in the package. Inside was a short note: the Panama intelligence net had learned from a German contact in Los Alamos that the Americans were planning to test a nuclear weapon at a desert site in New Mexico called Alamogordo. The time of the test was 2:00 A.M. on July 16. The same day the *Indianapolis* was leaving!

He shoved the papers at Sachi. "Four hours! How can I get from New Mexico to San Francisco in four hours?"

"You don't have to. Maybe somebody else can be found to witness the test and let me know if it is a success. You can't miss that ship. You might not be able to get papers as good as these again. If you don't board the *Indianapolis* you might have to ride out the rest of the war here with me. Someone else can monitor the test."

"Who?"

Sachi shrugged. "How about me? I can come back here afterward and radio out the information."

"No good," Matsuo said. "How would we know it was really you on this end? And convincing the Supreme Command that the Americans have a working atomic bomb will be difficult enough in person. Trying to do so on the basis of a radio transmission will be impossible. I was sent here to find out if the Americans really have an atomic bomb and what it can do. If I don't return with firsthand information, this whole trip will be a waste. I've *got* to see that test."

"You can't. There's no time! There's no way!"

"I'll find one. You just get the word back home that I'll be returning on the *Indianapolis*. Tell them to make arrangements to pick me up off . . ." He consulted the letter from Panama for the ship's itinerary. It was stopping at Hawaii, then moving on to Tinian in the Marianas. "Tinian. I'll jump ship on Tinian."

"All right," Sachi said reluctantly. "I just hope this code is secure."

"Don't worry. It's secure."

"That's what they said before Midway."

"Overconfidence," Matsuo said, remembering his warnings to Admiral Yamamoto. "There's no evidence that they've broken this code."

"But you don't *know*. The Americans broke our top diplomatic code in 1940 and we didn't have the slightest inkling for years."

Matsuo laughed. "1940? That's impossible!"

Sachi shook his head. "Not impossible—true. I sit here lots of nights with nothing to do, so I listen to the shortwave. I heard a couple of intelligence officers talking about 'Purple magic.' It took me a while, but I finally gathered that 'Purple' was their code name for our top diplomatic code, and 'magic' was a machine that deciphered it. The Americans had been privy to our top-level messages since the fall of '40."

"But that can't be!" Matsuo said. "We sent the final section of the declaration of war to our Washington Embassy a good eight hours or more before we attacked Pearl Harbor. If the Americans had been able to decipher the message, the U.S. Pacific Fleet would have been warned and waiting for us when we arrived over Oahu. The very fact that we caught the fleet sleeping is proof positive that they hadn't broken the code!"

Sachi's expression was troubled. "You've got a point there, but, I don't know . . ." He rubbed his eyes. "Logic is on your side, but the men I heard seemed to take it for granted that the diplomatic code was broken. It was old news for them. They were more concerned with breaking other codes."

Matsuo said nothing. He had to respect Sachi's expertise at espionage. His continued success as an operative in the heart of San Francisco was testament to that. But he could not accept that the diplomatic code had been broken more than a year before the beginning of the war. That would mean that the American government had known the content of the entire Fourteen Part Message eight hours before the attack on Pearl and had not warned the fleet. Their silence would indicate that the American President and his cabinet had purposely placed the fleet in jeopardy . . .

Matsuo remembered his feelings that violent Sunday morning in 1941 as his Zero swooped over the hills of Oahu, the uneasy feeling that everything was too perfect, that they were flying into a trap. He remembered his relief when he had found all the American planes neatly lined up on their runways, waiting to be riddled by his cannon.

Now he wondered if it might not have been a trap after all, a trap of another kind, drawing Japan into war in a manner that would so inflame the American people that they would hurl themselves headlong into the conflict they had steadfastly avoided for years despite a President urging them to take arms.

No, Matsuo thought. He could not imagine an American President so cold-bloodedly sacrificing three thousand sailors, no matter how badly he wanted to fight Germany.

He pushed the nagging questions from his mind. He had more important problems to consider: like how to get from Alamogordo to San Francisco in three hours.

ALBUQUERQUE

"You want *three* pairs?" the lady at the counter said.

"Yes, please," Matsuo said hoarsely in his best old-man voice. "My eyes are very sensitive to light and I don't like to be without extra pairs."

"Okay. That'll be $2.97."

Matsuo handed her three singles and she handed him a brown paper bag containing three pairs of sunglasses. After taking his change, he dropped the glasses into the large shopping bag he carried, then made the long walk down to the sandy field surrounding the municipal airport outside of town. He stretched his legs out on the ground and leaned back against a rock. To passersby he would look like an old codger basking in the sun and watching the little planes take off and land. And in a sense, they would be right: That was exactly what he was doing.

Since arriving by train last week, he had lain here and let the sun darken his skin to bring it closer to Filipino coloring while he studied the activity in and around the airport. Now it was late Monday afternoon and things were quiet. He had studied all the planes, looking for the one he wanted. By yesterday he had made his decision: a Seversky S2—a sleek little speed plane whose owner flew it like a race car, tearing up the sky with flagrant disregard for wartime restrictions on the fuel he burned. He either had close connections with the local rationing board or had managed to document some sort of war-related use for the craft.

Matsuo had called the Seversky Company this morning and had learned some details as to speed and range. It fit his needs perfectly, especially the optional electric ignition, which he knew had been installed in this particular plane—he had seen the owner start it up yesterday without a mechanic to give the prop an initial turn. And best of all, the owner took it up on Saturday and Sunday only. He never showed his face all week.

At five o'clock he watched the mechanics and attendants leave. He checked the pockets of his coat. The tool kit and wire cutters were there. He had the extra sunglasses, a change of clothes, his Filipino identity papers, and a sandwich all in the big bag. He had an American .45 automatic tight in his belt.

The plan was simple: Bypass the ignition switch, start the plane up, and head down the runway before anyone could stop him. Alamogordo was a few degrees east of due south from here. He had state maps of New Mexico, Arizona, Nevada, and California for the trip back to San Francisco, but the most important map now was the topographical of Otero County he had stolen from the Albuquerque Public Library. He had studied it exhaustively until he'd found a suitable spot in the Alamogordo area where he ought to be able to land behind a rise about twenty-five miles from the test site. At least on the map it appeared suitable. He would not know for sure until he got there.

He checked his watch. Timing was everything. He had to get there just before dark so he could use the last light of dusk to land. If he was too early, his plane might be spotted on the ground; if late, he'd never find the site in the dark. The watch again: 5:30. Tension knotted up inside him. Time to go.

He rose to his feet and started across the sandy field toward the tarmac. He approached the sleek little racer in a roundabout way, keeping it between him and the airport buildings. He hopped up on the wing and took a quick look through the glass into the cockpit, then pushed back on the canopy. It wouldn't budge—locked. He had expected that. He would either pry it open or, if that failed, break the glass. He was reaching into his bag for the heavy screwdriver when a voice stopped him.

"Hey! What the hell do you think you're doing?"

Matsuo looked up over the canopy. A mechanic in greasy coveralls and a peaked cap was trotting toward the plane. Another man was coming up behind him. He was chubby with a neat little brush moustache; he wore a brown leather aviator's jacket and had a white silk scarf around his neck. Matsuo recognized him—the owner. What was *he* doing here on a Monday night?

"Just looking," Matsuo said hoarsely. He lowered himself stiffly from the wing.

"He has no right being here!" said the owner in clipped tones. "Call the police and have him arrested for trespassing!"

Matsuo edged his hand toward the pistol in his belt, but saw that the mechanic was unenthusiastic about bringing the police into this.

"Aw, don't do that, mister!" Matsuo said. "I didn't hurt nothin'! I just saw this little beauty buzzing around up in the sky yesterday, doing all those fancy loops and turns, and I just had to promise myself that I'd come out here today and take a closer look at her." He ran his hand along the dark blue fuselage. "Never saw anything so beautiful in my life."

"Yes, well . . ." the owner said. Matsuo heard the voice soften with the swelling of his ego. "That's all well and good, but you were standing on the wing. You could have damaged something."

"Oh, I'd never do that!" Matsuo said. "And I'll never go near it again, I promise. It's just that I always wanted to fly but, well, my eyes kept me grounded. Just let me stay for now and watch you take off and maybe . . . maybe do some of those tight little rolls you did yesterday. Okay?"

The pilot expanded his chest. "Very well. But stay well back when I start up."

"Oh, yes, sir. I will. I will." Clutching his shopping bag Matsuo took one step back and waited while the owner keyed open the canopy and climbed into the cockpit. This wasn't what he had planned, but he had to make the best of it.

There came a high-pitched whine as the propeller made a slow turn, then a cough and a cloud of smoke as the engine roared to life. Matsuo let that cough be his signal. Two steps and a leap brought him up on the wing beside the cockpit. Before the owner could say a word, Matsuo had the muzzle of the pistol pointed in his face.

"Out!" Matsuo shouted over the engine noise. "Out now, or I'll shoot you where you sit!"

The owner's face turned a sickly pale but he didn't seem to be able to move. Matsuo grabbed him by the collar and yanked him out onto the wing with him. The mechanic had been crouching under the plane, ready to pull the wheel chocks; he now came around the tail of the plane and stared at them. Matsuo pointed the pistol his way.

"Over here!"

As the mechanic hesitantly came forward, Matsuo kept the pistol to the owner's head and climbed halfway into the cockpit.

"You pull the chocks when I tell you or I'll blow his head off. And don't think I'm bluffing. I just robbed the First National in town. I shot the guard there for tryin' to be a hero and I'll shoot this guy!"

That must have sounded tough enough—the owner whimpered and the mechanic swallowed hard and nodded. Matsuo held the owner by his long silk scarf and slipped the rest of the way into the cockpit. He glanced over the instrument panel, smiled at the full fuel tank, set his feet on the rudder pedals, released the brakes, then nodded to the mechanic. He allowed fifteen seconds for the chocks to be moved, then eased the throttle forward. The plane began to roll.

He released the owner's scarf and said, "You can go now."

The owner stared at him in shock, looking like a man who had just received a reprieve from death but didn't quite believe it.

"Run!" Matsuo shouted.

The owner jumped off the wing and ran. Matsuo gunned the plane forward toward the runway. He glanced at the wind sock over the tiny control tower and turned away from the wind, praying no one was coming in for a landing. Everything looked clear. He taxied to the end of the runway and turned. This was an unfamiliar plane and he wanted all the pavement he could get. He pushed the throttle halfway forward and the little Seversky roared ahead. He gave it more gas and it fairly leaped into the air. The acceleration, combined with the giddy climb and the relief at being up in the air and on his way at last, made him laugh.

As he hurtled into the sky he glanced down and saw the owner shaking a fist at him. Matsuo waved, banked right, and headed due north.

ALAMOGORDO

There was a storm coming. Lightning flashed, starkly illuminating the desert below. Matsuo lay on a rocky, wind-hewn ridge with three sets of sunglasses lined up one after the other over his eyes and stared expectantly toward the Trinity test site on the broad flat expanse of sand some twenty-five miles away.

He was worried. Twenty-five miles seemed far too great a distance to learn anything of value about the power of the atomic bomb, especially at night through all these tinted lenses. Dr. Kakihana had told him to shield his eyes at all costs, no matter how many miles he was from the test site, but this seemed ludicrous. He knew what the doctor had said about the power of this weapon, but Matsuo could not quite bring himself to believe it. He must have been exaggerating. No single bomb could have the unimaginable destructive power Dr. Kakihana had described. Still, his reputation was such that Matsuo kept the multiple pairs of glasses in place.

2:00 A.M. came and went.

At a quarter after, Matsuo began to wonder. *Did it fail?* Could he allow himself that hope? But what if the test had only been postponed? If it was delayed even an hour, he would have to leave without seeing it or risk missing his ship. The only way to cross the Pacific these days was in an American ship. If he missed the *Indianapolis,* he might not get back to Japan at all.

He pounded his fist against the rock in frustration. Everything had gone perfectly until now. He had stolen the plane, feinted to the north to throw off pursuit before turning south, then managed to land it just before dark on a rutted dirt road crossing the desert floor. He had steered it off into the brush, and made his way up to this ridge where he had a view of the test site. His timing had been flawless. Why couldn't the Americans be as precise? Nothing was happening. Failure or delay? How could he know?

He had to wait. No choice but to give the test as much time as possible. If he returned to Japan not knowing if the atomic bomb was a success, his entire mission would have been futile. And if the test was a success, he had to see for himself!

He was pulling the sandwich from his sack when the flash came. For an instant he thought it was a particularly bright bolt of lightning, but then he realized that no lightning bolt had ever burned so brightly or so steadily. Light like the noonday sun ballooned from the desert floor. Bright, intolerably bright, even through the layers of lenses it drove spikes of pain through his eyes and into his brain as it chased night from the desert. All around the fireball, clouds condensed, rose, expanded, layered out, then burned away one after the other in a succession of instants. The fireball looked purple at first, then green, then blazing yellow as it began to rise, drawing clouds of smoke and debris in a tall column in its wake. It slowed and hovered at maybe eight thousand feet with the dust cloud surging up and spreading out around it to form a huge flattened dome. And in the depths of that dome he could still see the red-and-orange fire flashing and raging. It hung there, looming over the desert like some huge and hideous poison mushroom.

Then came the sound of the explosion, a clap of atomic thunder that struck him like a physical blow. The shock wave followed closely behind, shaking the ground and vibrating one of the pairs of sunglasses off his face.

Matsuo barely noticed their loss. He lay transfixed on the trembling ridge, gaping at the cloud as his numbed mind battled to comprehend what he had seen. Dr. Kakihana had warned him of the bomb's unimaginable potential power, but no words could have prepared him for this. This was the fire of hell unleashed on earth. This was the end of war as the world knew it, the beginning of a new age or the end of all ages.

Matsuo felt his control suddenly evaporate. He scrambled to his feet and ran down the narrow rocky path to the desert, slipping twice and once almost falling off the edge. He had never felt so afraid in all his life, afraid for himself, for Meiko, for Japan, afraid even for the future. Japan had to surrender! He could not let what he had just seen on the desert happen in a Japanese city!

With trembling hands he started the Sev-S2 and coasted along the desert floor and up into the night sky. He had a long leg north-northwest to Goldfield, Nevada, then a shorter hop due west to San Francisco. He stayed low, pushed the throttle to the limit, and shot through the air. No laughter this time. He was shaking. He flew like all the demons of hell were after him while the purple afterimage of the explosion danced in the air ahead.

SAN FRANCISCO

Made it!

Matsuo paused for breath as he recognized the mound where he had left his duffel bag and a change of clothes.

It had been a hellish trip. Landing at the airport without clearance hadn't been so bad—it was predawn and air traffic was virtually nil—but the engine had been running on fumes and he had almost killed himself running the plane off the north end of the field and fleeing on foot through the dark marshes.

Now, after a breathless slog through miles of wetlands between the airport and Hunter's Point, Matsuo could rest for a moment before he became Mariano Cruz.

He froze in his tracks. Someone was waiting on the mound. He huddled in the wet grass for a moment, straining his eyes through the dim, predawn half-light. With relief, he recognized Sachi's old-man-with-the-bad-eyes costume. He was sitting on a suitcase.

"Something wrong?" he asked, hurrying up the mound.

"Tell me first if the test was a success," Sachi said.

Matsuo glanced at him without saying anything more. Apparently his look said enough.

"My God, what did you *see!*"

"The end of the war," Matsuo said. "Their bomb works and it's . . ." How could he describe it? "It's utterly devastating."

He sat down and closed his eyes. He was exhausted. Everything seemed to be coming apart. The unbridled fury of the blast he had witnessed had opened a gash in him, and slowly during the breakneck trip from Alamogordo all hope of a negotiated peace had bled out of him. Japan would have to accept the American terms no matter what they were.

"I figured the test was a success," Sachi said. "The Americans—" He paused and shook his head. "Funny, I used to think of myself as an American."

"Well, start thinking of yourself that way again," Matsuo said, "because right now that's the best thing in the world to be."

"Yeah. Maybe. Anyway, I found out why our Filipino friend's orders were so rushed. The Americans were so confident of the test that they delivered one of the bombs right here to Hunter's Point just two days ago." He smiled slyly at Matsuo. "And it's going out on the *Indianapolis*."

Matsuo stared at Sachi. "You're sure?"

"As sure as I can be of anything in this war. The message came through yesterday. That's why I'm here. You've got to see to it that the *Indianapolis* never delivers that bomb."

"That won't work—" Matsuo began.

"Sure it will. We know its route now, too: It stops at Pearl Harbor, Tinian, and Guam. Tinian has the biggest airstrips in the Marianas, maybe in the world. That's where they launch their planes to bomb Japan. That has to be where they're going to drop off this atomic bomb. But we won't know the ship's exact location at any one time." He patted the suitcase he was using as a seat. "If you can somehow use my trusty radio here to send out a signal, a sub can—"

"You don't understand," Matsuo said. "If the *Indianapolis* is sunk, they'll just send another bomb another way, maybe by air. One way or the other, an atomic bomb will be dropped on Japan unless I can get to the Supreme Command, or maybe even the Emperor, and tell what I saw. Don't you see? I've got to get home to tell them what we're up against. If I can stop the war, I can save Japan from these bombs!"

He thought of Meiko and Naka in an atomic holocaust like the one he had seen in the desert hours ago.

"Sachi, I've got to get back to Japan."

"You've got a chance. A message arrived through Panama while you were away. Someone will meet you in a sampan off the northern tip of Tinian after you arrive there."

That was a relief. "Maybe I'll get home after all."

"'Home,'" he said. "You're lucky you can feel that way about Japan."

"I don't really fit in all that well," Matsuo said. He couldn't bring himself to voice his mixed feelings about America. "I was raised here, too, you know."

"Yeah. But you speak Japanese like a native. I don't." He was silent while Matsuo changed his clothes. Then he said, "So the war's over, then?" His voice sounded strange. Matsuo couldn't see his face.

"It has to be."

"What are you going to do after surrender?"

"Try to get by, I guess. How about you?"

"Don't know. Don't know at all."

"You could come to Japan."

"I don't think so. In Japan, I'd always be an American."

"So stay in America."

"Why? I'll always be a 'lousy Jap' here. Besides, I don't know if I can live here anymore after the way they've treated us. Don't know where I'm gonna go."

Matsuo's heart went out to Sachi. He had an inkling of how he felt: a man without a country. He had some of those feelings, too.

"There must be someplace you can call home."

The sadness in Sachi's voice was almost palpable. "Yeah, maybe. Maybe not. Anyway, we've got to get you back to Japan. That's the main thing. I'm sure they've beefed up security because of the bomb, but you'll get on board." His voice hardened with determination. "I guarantee it."

He took his suitcased radio and hurled it into the marsh. Matsuo wanted to ask him why he was throwing it away, but Sachi jerked his thumb over his shoulder toward Hunter's Point.

"Let's go."

Matsuo followed in silence.

■ ■ ■

Matsuo knew nothing about the usual security at American Navy yards, but it seemed to him that there were an awful lot of guards about. He showed his papers at the main gate and was passed through with a curt, "Better move your ass, Cruz."

As he hurried toward the dock area, he saw the ship. Although nowhere near the tonnage of Admiral Yamamoto's old flagship, *Yamoto*, the *Indianapolis* was still a ship of considerable size. It had a strange shape: There was a dip in the superstructure amidships between the two stacks that gave it an odd, swayback appearance. As he neared, he saw a pair of seaplane catapults in the dip and a crane rising above them. He saw motorized launches on chocks and made a quick tally of the ship's visible weaponry. She was old, but she was big, with big eight-inch turret guns. She had probably stood off to sea and pounded her share of Japanese shore positions during the past three and a half years.

He saw two Marine guards and two men in plain suits flanking the gangplank. With his heart thudding wildly in his chest, he walked past them and stepped on the gangplank.

"Whoa!" said one of the civilians. "Let's see some paper, boy! We're gonna have to take a real close look at the likes of you!"

Matsuo smiled shyly as he pulled out his orders and identification papers. He handed them to the one who had spoken. "Yes, sir." He hoped his accent would pass. He noticed the second civilian staring at him intently.

"Another Pineapple for the kitchen," the first muttered, flipping through the papers.

The second said nothing. He had picked up the identification card.

His eyes were flicking back and forth between the photo and Matsuo's face.

"Just where is Baguio, Cruz?" the second said.

Matsuo was glad he had brushed up on his Philippine geography. "On Luzon, sir."

"How come you aren't there fighting the Japs?"

"Sir, I have been working for the Navy since before the war began. I wasn't there when they invaded."

"Your papers show you've been working the mess in San Diego all through the war. How come you suddenly get to go to the Forward Area now?"

Matsuo was ready for this one. "Sir, I did not want to be on a ship that might be shooting at my homeland. Now that the Philippines are free again, I want to go to the fighting."

"Sounds pretty good to me," the first civilian said, but the second still didn't seem satisfied. A marine with a drawn pistol cut off the next question when he trotted up and leaned over the table. He spoke in a whisper, but Matsuo heard enough to pull his already tense insides into a strangle-knot:

"... *possible Jap spy* ... *don't know how reliable* ..."

Matsuo felt as if he had been shot. How had they have found out? Who could have told them anything? Had Cruz had second thoughts about selling his papers? A thousand questions, none of them answerable. And nowhere to run! He was trapped here!

"... *how'd he get in?* ... *seen going over fence* ... *keep you informed* ..."

To hide his shock, he let his gaze roam the contours of the ship while he fought to slow his heart and calm his nerves.

Over the fence? That could only be—

"You're sweating, Mr. Cruz," said the second civilian. "Is something wrong?"

"No, sir!" Matsuo said quickly. "Very hot, yes?"

Still that intense scrutiny. "I don't think so."

Matsuo glanced past him at a squad of Marines marching along the dock. They were scrutinizing the IDs of everyone they saw. And they were coming this way!

This is it, he thought. *It's all over!* Visions of prison cells and firing squads marched before his eyes.

He stood rooted to the spot, refusing to give himself away. He would wait till the last second. If he couldn't bluff his way out of this, then he would have to act. No trials, no public humiliations, no endless waiting for the blindfold and the bullets. He would see it all settled right here on the dock.

The squad was less than a hundred feet away when a burst of gunfire shattered the stillness. Matsuo was jolted by the noise, as were the men at the table. The marines turned and ran off in the direction of the shots, leaving Matsuo staring after them.

Matsuo took no pleasure in the relief that flooded through him. He had a dreadful feeling about those shots.

■ ■ ■

Matsuo held his breath as another marine came trotting up to the table a few minutes later. His pistol was holstered. He didn't whisper as he spoke to the civilians.

"We got him."

"A Jap?" said the first civilian. "What was he after?"

"We'll never know," said the marine. "He's dead."

Matsuo fought to hold his composure as an invisible band tightened around his throat. So casual: *He's dead.* It had to be Sachi. A friend, a good man, a brave man, one who would have been the most loyal of all Americans if his own country hadn't turned against every principle it was supposed to stand for and betrayed him. *He's dead.* Matsuo now understood the significance of Sachi's hurling his radio into the marshes. With the end of the war, he had seen himself as an orphan, a man without a country. Perhaps he hadn't wanted to live like that. So he'd provided a diversion for Matsuo.

"Cruz? Are you deaf, Cruz?" the first civilian said. He was holding the papers and orders out to him. The second was walking off with the marine. "I said you could board."

Matsuo nodded, not trusting his voice. He hurried up the gangplank and did not look back.

■ ■ ■

Matsuo was given no time to mourn Sachi. He was put to work immediately upon checking in. The galley was in chaos due to a large number of Navy personnel aboard as passengers to Pearl Harbor. The messing facilities were taxed to the limit and all galley hands were working at double time. Matsuo was glad for it. There were three other Filipinos in the galley crew and the hectic pace allowed them only a few moments with him. They greeted him with bursts of Spanish in passing which he managed to understand and answer tersely with a few phrases he remembered from his days in Panama. From his very first hour in the galley, he adopted a surly, sullen attitude that invited no small talk. It seemed to work: For the most part they left him to himself.

Within hours of passing under the Golden Gate Bridge, Matsuo found the atomic bomb. He was on his way back from supplying the wardroom amidships with fresh coffee when he saw it. It wasn't hidden away. It was right there in the open on the hangar deck, a fifteen-foot crate fastened down with steel straps and guarded by four armed marines. He stood among the other crew members and passengers staring at it, and listened. Nobody seemed to know what it was, just that it was supposed to end the war. He heard comments about germ warfare—that seemed to be the accepted explanation—and for that reason, everyone was giving the crate a wide berth. Matsuo had to admire the secrecy under which the Americans had developed their weapon.

When he got back to the galley, he was handed a tray stacked with a double lunch. He was given directions to the flag lieutenant's cabin and told to deliver it there.

Flag lieutenant's cabin? That meant this was a flagship. For whom? Was there an admiral on board, or was the ship returning to the war zone to meet him? He wondered what rank of officer he would find.

Matsuo was startled when a U.S. Army captain opened the door to the cabin. *Army?* He would not allow Matsuo inside to place the tray, insisting on taking it himself and quickly closing the door. Matsuo decided he should learn more about that cabin.

An hour later he returned and knocked on the door again. This time a different Army officer—a major—opened the door.

"You are through with lunch, sir?"

The major nodded. "Yeah. Come on in."

As Matsuo stepped inside, he caught a glimpse of some technical-looking equipment with an array of dials and meters before the other officer threw a sheet over them with an annoyed look. But it was the black cylinder in the middle of the floor that snared his attention. It was eighteen inches long and was fastened down by metal straps welded to the cabin deck and secured with a big padlock.

He pulled his eyes away and went about stacking the dishes and coffee cups. He left as quickly as he could, but the image of that cylinder stayed with him. Professor Kakihana's words came back to him about the bomb needing an isotope of uranium to fuel it. *Uranium-235*, he had called it. What if the equipment in the cabin was to measure radioactivity from the cylinder? What if that cylinder contained U-235? And wasn't the atomic bomb development a U.S. Army project? That would explain Army officers on a Navy vessel.

The more he thought about it, the more Matsuo became convinced that the flag lieutenant's cabin housed the heart of the atomic bomb. He would have to learn more about that particular area of the ship.

He made sure he was available when the dinner tray needed delivering. And the breakfast tray on Tuesday morning. By lunchtime, it was, "Where's Cruz? This tray's gotta go up to officer country." He was sure by then that he could pick the lock and carry off the cylinder if he had enough time. But then, what would he do with it?

He took a cigarette break on the fantail deck that night and watched the Pacific churn luminescent in the cruiser's wake. The stifling humidity of the night had brought the crew and passengers up to the deck in search of a cool breeze. They had dragged cots and mattresses and sleeping bags along. Every hatch and every vent was open. Matsuo was no nautical engineer, but he knew that if a torpedo blew a hole in the hull below the waterline under these conditions, the ship would go down in minutes.

Fortunately, the chances of running into a Japanese submarine in the Eastern Pacific these days were nil. But it gave him a bad feeling about the ship. Death seemed to hover over it. Last night he had awakened from a dream of blood-red water cut by gliding fins and filled with slashing teeth. His imagination was undoubtedly being fueled by the knowledge of the nature of the ship's cargo.

His ears were still ringing from the gunnery practice this afternoon. Those big eight-inch batteries were deafening when they let go. And even after they stopped, the silence was only relative. The whine of the turbines below never slackened. The ship was making good time—*too* good. All four engines were running at top speed and edging her toward thirty knots.

They're in a hurry. And with good reason. The sooner they delivered the atom bomb, the sooner it could be dropped, and the sooner the war would be over. *I'd hurry, too.*

He reached into his pocket and fingered the lengths of wire he had filched from the machine shop. They varied in gauge from eighth-inch copper to hair-fine steel. He had a pair of needle-nose pliers to bend them to order.

All he needed was time alone in the flag lieutenant's cabin.

That time came the next morning when he stopped by the cabin to pick up the breakfast dishes. No one answered his knock on the door. Both officers had been up and dressed when he had delivered breakfast so the odds of someone being asleep inside were slim. Matsuo checked up and down the corridor. Empty. A few bends in the heavy copper wire yielded a makeshift key for the clumsy latch-bolt lock under the door handle. His third try brought a solid click as the bolt slid back. He was about to push the door open when he heard voices coming from the gangway at the near end of the corridor. One of them sounded familiar. Rather than duck into the room, he relocked the door and stood where he was, as if waiting.

"—afraid to say anything in sick bay. Afraid I'd give myself—"

The voice cut off as they saw Matsuo. The two Army officers entered the corridor.

"Sirs!" Matsuo said, feigning surprise. "I have been waiting for you to answer the door!"

"We just had a tour of the ship," one said. He opened the door and let Matsuo in to pick up the dishes. Matsuo hid his bitter disappointment as he eyed the cylinder longingly. He might never get another chance!

When the *Indianapolis* rounded Diamond Head at 8:00 A.M. the next morning, the public address system announced that they had set a new world's record for the 2100 miles between the Farallon lightship and Oahu. The ship charged into the narrow mouth of Pearl Harbor and let off its passengers but none of its crew. While it refueled, Matsuo looked toward Ford Island and got a sad, twisting feeling in his chest when he saw the remains of the *Arizona* still settled on the harbor bottom, covered by rainbow sheets of oil still leaking to the surface from below.

By 5:00 P.M. they were on their way out to sea again, making full head toward Tinian. Without all those extra passengers to feed, the pace in the galley now seemed quiet and sedate. Time should have dragged, but the week's trip across the Central Pacific to the Marianas seemed to fly. Although he was constantly on watch for an opportunity to enter the flag lieutenant's cabin alone, the days were never long enough to provide one, and the nights were each an interminable headlong rush across the dark sea under blackout conditions.

Since the Army officers never left their cabin after lights-out, Matsuo allowed himself to relax at night, to go "off-duty" in a true sense and sit on the deck in the dark with other crew members and listen to them talk. He felt safe out here in the dark. He could let the role of Mariano Cruz slip away and be just another faceless voice in the night. Occasionally, he would throw out a comment when prodded, but mostly he would listen.

They were young, and he found most of them likable. Except when they talked about "Dirty Japs." They had their differences in many areas, but were uniform in their feelings toward Japan. They hated the Dirty Japs and were going to make them pay for Pearl Harbor and for Bataan and for all the lousy treatment they had given American prisoners throughout the war; and yet they were fascinated and awestruck by the suicide charges, kamikaze planes, and kaiten torpedoes that the Dirty Japs hurled against them. Matsuo ached to explain the cultural differences to these youths just as he had explained them to Hiroki, and twice he had caught himself on the verge of speaking. It would be dangerous to expose the slightest hint of sympathetic knowledge regarding the Dirty Japs. He could expect no more understanding from these guys than from his own brother.

In times alone he would sit in the dark and wonder at the path of his life. He felt as if he had been robbed of all say in where it led him, that he had lost control and was now at the mercy of two huge, unseen opposing forces, one setting up obstacles, another helping him overcome them. The threads of his life and of others around him seemed to be drawing toward a common destiny.

And where would that be? Tinian?

He could not forget that last sword-dream, either: Frank and Meiko together again . . . without him.

During the week-long voyage to Tinian, Matsuo perfected an almost foolproof method of eavesdropping on the Army officers. He would stand outside their cabin door with a tray half-loaded with dirty dishes. If he heard one of them approach the door, he would retreat down the corridor. If someone entered the corridor, he would simply walk away from the doorway as if he had just left the room.

The vigil yielded little useful information other than the fact that this was not the only atomic weapon. They referred to this particular bomb as Little Boy, but Matsuo learned that there was another bomb ready, one called Fat Man. Then, on Wednesday night, half a day away from Tinian, the subject of targets for Little Boy came up.

"Well, Tokyo is out," said one of the officers. "The big boys feel the Emperor will be more valuable alive after the war."

Matsuo's spirits rose upon hearing that—at least someone in America had insight into the Japanese mind. But they soon plummeted.

"A number of cities have been saved for the bomb. I don't know which one they'll choose. I think Groves is pushing for Kyoto."

Matsuo reeled away from the door. *Kyoto!* They couldn't! They wouldn't burn out the city that housed the soul of Japan!

But deep inside, Matsuo knew they would indeed. Gladly.

He had to stop Little Boy.

THE MARIANA ISLANDS

The *Indianapolis* reached the Marianas the morning of its tenth day out of San Francisco. Matsuo crowded on deck with the rest of the crew as Tinian hove into view. They were all excited, jostling for position to see if they could spot something on the little island that would give them some clue as to the nature of this superweapon that was supposed to end the war. They saw sheer, rusty brown cliffs rising up from the water, topped by typical tropical vegetation. The island was a rough oblong, five miles by twelve, with no mountains to speak of, but it supported the biggest airfield in the world.

Matsuo glared at the island. This was where the *B-san* squadrons loaded up their bombs and took off on the daily raids that were reducing Japan to rubble. And this was where the atom bombs would be loaded and sent to destroy Kyoto.

There had to be something he could do to delay the arrival of the bomb without getting himself killed. All he needed was enough time to get to Japan. Once there, he would tell the Supreme Command what he had seen and bring the war to a halt! He could save Kyoto and everyone in it! But he was helpless. The U-235 was sitting in a cabin on the deck below him and he couldn't get to it! It was maddening!

A flash of color to his right caught his attention. Army beige. He was momentarily paralyzed by the sight of both Army officers leaning on the rail, peering toward the island as the ship approached Tinian Town harbor, then he was pushing roughly through the other sailors and running belowdecks as fast as his legs would carry him.

The corridor outside the flag lieutenant's cabin was deserted. Matsuo slipped the ready copper wire key into the lock and entered. Once he was sure the cabin was empty, he fairly leaped upon the locked-down cylinder. But before touching it, he studied it, memorizing the exact position of the padlock, the metal straps, everything, even down to the tilt of the steel ring in the cylinder's top. Then he went to work on the padlock.

It was a tough one and he hadn't tried something like this since his boyhood days in San Francisco. Time. He needed time and there was none. And his body wasn't helping, either: tremor in his hands, thumping in his chest, sweat coating his fingertips and making the wire slip instead of turn. Every slip ate time, irreplaceable time. He concentrated on Nagata's teaching: Control the breathing, flow into the wire . . .

Suddenly he felt the twisted wire catch the tumblers. He gave it a sharp turn and almost cheered aloud when the shackle popped out of the padlock case. He flipped the metal straps aside and pulled the cylinder free.

It was heavy—lead heavy. He began unscrewing the end piece, using the ring for leverage. It was a fine thread. Two full turns moved it only a sixteenth of an inch. He kept turning, repeatedly drying the perspiration from his hands. How long did he have? How much luck could he count on?

Finally, the end fell free. Inside was another cylinder about the length and diameter of his forearm. He slid it out and laid it on the floor. He immediately began screwing the outer cylinder lid back into place. He was drenched with sweat now and his hands were slipping all over the slick metallic surface. When the lid was fully tightened, he dried the cylinder with a napkin, slipped it back under the metal stays, turned it just so, and refastened the padlock.

Matsuo stepped back and surveyed his work. Was that how he had found it? It seemed right. He picked up the breakfast tray he had delivered earlier, placed the inner cylinder on it, and covered it with a napkin. One last check to be sure he hadn't left any of his makeshift picks behind, then he was out the door, locking it behind him, and off down the hall carrying the tray before him. All he had to do now was find a hiding place for the inner container, and hope the Army officers would not notice any change in the lead cylinder's weight—nor the missing tray and napkin.

An hour later he was back on deck with the rest of the crew watching as the aviation crane lifted the fifteen-foot crate from the hangar deck. The *Indianapolis* had anchored about half a mile offshore and a bargelike craft had come alongside. Matsuo watched with relief as two seamen brought out the now-empty uranium cylinder suspended by its ring on a pole between them. The two Army officers following behind gave no sign that there was anything wrong.

For the first time since he had boarded the ship, Matsuo allowed himself to believe that he might actually have a chance at pulling this off.

■ ■ ■

Meiko pushed the tiller hard to leeward and ducked under the swinging boom as she brought the little sampan about. As the crude lugsail filled with air, she let out the mainsheet and headed southward along Saipan's west shore on a broad reach. The island's cloud-wreathed mountains reminded her of Maui and a pang of remorse and remembrance undulated through her chest.

Meiko was getting the feel of the boat. She had spent many a summer sailing Sagami Bay, but the sampan was waterlogged, which made it heavy and clumsy, though once it was on a tack, it held true. She was dressed in a faded sarong and there was a tangle of fishing nets in the bow. Should the need arise, she was all set to play the part of an island fishing woman. Hopefully, she would be left alone until after dark. Then she would point the little boat south toward Tinian. She gazed at the low mound of land rising up from the sea. Tinian. Only four miles away. Matsuo was due in today and if all went as she planned, she would meet him there tonight.

This had not been easy to arrange. She had known that Matsuo's friends in Naval Intelligence—and they were many—had been baffled and angered by the Navy's refusal to send a submarine to bring him back to Japan. Meiko was sure Hiroki and the Kakureta Kao were behind the betrayal but she dared not voice her suspicions because there was no way of backing them up. Shigeo and some other of Matsuo's closest friends took up the cause with Naval Intelligence—Matsuo must be saved. After weeks of arguing and cajoling, they finally prevailed upon their superiors to make a try at picking him up at the designated spot. Meiko convinced them to let her go, arguing that a sampan had a better chance of slipping past the American shore patrols if it was piloted by a woman rather than a man.

And so here she was. Naval Intelligence had used one of its last

remaining reconnaissance subs to bring her to the eastern edge of the
Philippine Sea, off Saipan. They had surfaced before dawn this
morning, freed the inverted sampan from its lashings on the afterdeck,
set up the mast, and set her to sail in the dark. She had food and water
for a few days, and a compass and sextant hidden away in the prow.
After she picked up Matsuo off the north end of Tinian, they would sail
to a specific latitude and longitude where the sub would meet them.

Meiko saw a patrol boat speeding along outside the reef line. She
continued her tack and hoped it would hold its own course.

It didn't. It swung toward her and picked up speed. Meiko closed
her eyes and wished it away, but when she opened them again the boat
was closer. It pulled alongside and a sailor signaled to her that she was
going to be boarded. She smiled and nodded as she angled the sampan
into the wind, but her insides were knotted up tight.

"We lookee see, lady," said one of the sailors in pidgin English as
he stepped into her boat. "No hurtee. Just lookee see."

Meiko kept smiling and nodding. "Yes-yes. Lookee-see okay."

"Fishy-fish?" another American said from the boat. He looked
like some sort of officer. "Where fish?"

"Just sail," Meiko said.

That did not seem to sit well with the officer. She should have
foreseen this. She cursed herself for not thinking to bring along some
fresh fish to show.

"Oh-*ho!*" said the sailor on her ship. He was reaching into the
prow. "What have we here?" He brought out the compass and sextant
and held them up. "Not your usual sampan gear."

The officer on the patrol boat drew his pistol but didn't point it at
her.

"Mine! Mine!" Meiko said, trying to hide her panic. "To sail far!"

He shook his head. "I don't buy that, lady. Not one bit."

They took her on board the patrol boat and towed her sampan into
the harbor. She was taken to a Quonset hut and left in a hot, stuffy, bare
room furnished only with a battered table and two chairs, where she
waited all day. They fed her lunch, then dinner. They let her use the
bathroom down the hall. At times she dozed in the chair, resting her
head in her arms on the table. Darkness fell and they lit the single bulb
hanging over the table, yet still she remained confined, alone.

What were they doing? Were they going to hold her forever? She
had to get to Tinian to meet Matsuo! They had to let her go!

Then the door opened and she heard a male voice in the hall. It
sounded like the young officer from the patrol boat.

"—all we've got on her. The instruments are Japanese make, but
that doesn't mean anything. This island has been in Nip hands forever.
Everything left over is Japanese make. We didn't find anything else
worth mentioning on her boat."

"You think there's nothing to her, then?" said another voice. It sounded thick, tired.

"I don't know what to think. Your group ordered the extra patrols. You wanted a search of every single boat we found and you wanted to question anyone the least bit suspicious. I'm just following orders."

"So you are. Wait out here. I should be through in a couple of minutes."

An officer entered and closed the door behind him. He was thin, sallow-complected, with loose bags under his tired eyes. He looked bored. But that boredom vanished when he saw Meiko. He stood statue-still in the center of the room and stared at her with wide blue eyes. Meiko wanted to cry out with anguish as she recognized him.

It was Frank.

TINIAN

Matsuo had spent the day in a state of intense agitation, expecting the Americans to come storming out from the island any minute to search the *Indianapolis* for the missing U-235. But the harbor remained peaceful and quiet as the cruiser refueled through the underwater pipeline from the tank field at the north end. It was just about dark when the refueling was complete and Matsuo knew it was time to leave.

He sneaked forward to the anchor chain locker where he had hidden the inner cylinder of uranium. As he held it in his hands, he wondered, *Can I do this? Can I possibly succeed?* The odds against him were astronomical, yet the one thing that kept him going was the knowledge that, after what he had seen in the New Mexico desert ten days ago, nothing he did could possibly worsen the fate the Americans had planned for his country.

He tied the cylinder to his back with strips of sheet he had torn from his bed, then slipped through the open anchor port and shimmied down the chain. The water was warm as he slipped into it soundlessly. He began a silent breaststroke toward Tinian.

He smiled to himself. Mariano Cruz had jumped ship and disappeared. Matsuo Okumo would emerge onshore with the soul of an atomic bomb strapped to his back.

Soon, if luck and all the gods and all his ancestors were with him, it would be time to cut a bargain with the armed forces of the United States of America.

SAIPAN

It seemed to take forever to find my voice. It was Meiko, really Meiko, sitting there on the other side of the table, looking like she hadn't aged a day since I'd last seen her. She looked as shocked to see me as I was to see her. I managed to make it to a chair and sit down across the table from her. I was shaking like a guy with malaria. Somehow I got a cigarette between my lips and lit it.

"My God, what are you doing here?" I said when I could speak.

She seemed to find her own voice with equal difficulty. "I did not intend to be here and I don't wish to be here. Beyond that, I can say no more." She looked at me with those eyes, those soft, brown, almond-shaped eyes. "Have you been sick, Frank? You don't look well."

Christ, I needed a drink.

If I hadn't known better, I would have thought she was genuinely concerned. "Oh, I'm doing just fine!" I said, letting just a tiny fraction of the pain and grief and bitterness seep through. I wanted to scream, to get up and throw my chair through the window, to take her by the throat and throttle her until her face turned blue. But I sat there and kept my voice calm. "I'm eating well, getting plenty of exercise, and at night, if I'm restless, I lull myself to sleep with thoughts of all the thousands of men my wife helped kill at Pearl Harbor a few years ago."

She seemed to cave in at that. I watched her composure crumble as tears rolled down her cheeks. "Oh, Frank! I'm so sorry for that. But you—"

She didn't fool me. "*Can it!*" I said. "What're you doing here, Meiko? Working on another sneaky way to kill a few more of us? Aren't you satisfied with your score from Pearl?"

Her face suddenly hardened. "And aren't you satisfied with the women and children you incinerated in Tokyo last March? Must you go from city to city slaughtering more and more?"

That hit home. I had talked to a few of the men who'd been on the March 9 run. They told me they could smell the burning human flesh all the way up in their B-29s, thousands of feet over Tokyo, that night. It got so bad some of them puked in the planes.

But I wasn't going to let her sidetrack me like this. I'd had nothing to do with that, but she had been directly involved against Pearl.

"Lieutenant?" said a voice from the door as I was about to speak. I looked and saw Crowley, an ensign from communications poking his head through the door.

"What?" I didn't want to be disturbed now.

"Word's just come from Tinian. There's an emergency of some sort. They want all intelligence personnel over there on the double."

"I'm busy now."

"This is top priority. *All* intelligence. No exceptions. The shuttle leaves in twenty."

"What sort of emergency?"

"They wouldn't say. But it's a big one. Somebody's pretty shook up on Tinian." He smiled. "And Captain Abrams said to tell you that you're riding with him."

Oh, God! I thought. *It's a wilt!*

"When do we leave?"

"Yesterday," he said, and was gone.

Of all times to get called away! I wanted to wring the truth out of Meiko. If she were here on Saipan, I knew Matsuo could not be far away. And more than anything else in the world, I wanted to get my hands on Matsuo Okumo.

But I had no choice. I was the Navy's greatest living authority on the wilts. After a long lull, they had started up again. Most of the recent wilts had been around Okinawa, but that didn't mean they couldn't return to the Marianas.

Reluctantly, I gave Meiko over to the Marines for safekeeping until I got back, then headed for the helipad.

"A wilt?" I whispered to Abrams when we were airborne in the copter.

He shook his head.

"Then what's so big that the Tinian people can't handle it themselves?" I asked in a louder voice. There were half a dozen other intelligence officers aboard with us.

"Glad you asked," he said, pulling a sheet of paper from his breast pocket. "This was hand-delivered to me from Tinian Command half an hour ago." He paused to let the significance of that sink in. It wasn't lost on us: The matter was so sensitive that it wasn't going on the air in any shape or form. Tinian Command didn't even want the rest of the U.S. forces to know it had trouble. I was beginning to get a sense of how big this really was.

"What do they want from us?" someone said.

Abrams scanned the paper. "They want us to find two things: a man and a fifteen-inch metal cylinder. Preferably both, but they'll take either."

He went on to explain what he knew. The cylinder had been shipped to Tinian within another cylinder aboard the *Indianapolis*. It had been off-loaded this morning. It was sometime tonight when Tinian discovered that the inner cylinder was missing. By that time, the

Indianapolis had set sail for Guam. A group from Tinian intelligence took a seaplane out to the cruiser and discovered that a galley helper who had been in the same room with the cylinder numerous times was missing. He was last seen on board in Tinian Town harbor. The Tinian intelligence group was still searching the *Indianapolis* but it was pretty obvious that the galley helper must have jumped ship at the harbor.

"We have a photo of this guy?" I asked.

Abrams shook his head. "No. All we know is that he's a bearded Filipino named Mariano Cruz."

"What's in the cylinder?"

"I don't know. They won't say."

"Swell!" someone said. "We'll be combing thirty square miles of tropical island in the dark looking for a thief with no face who's stolen something we're not allowed to know about! Good luck!"

I leaned back and thought about this. Something had clicked when Abrams said "Filipino." I thought of Meiko being found off Saipan in a boat with a compass and sextant hidden in the prow; I pictured Matsuo with a beard and maybe some darkening pigment on his face. I put the two together and realized that Matsuo had the balls for this kind of stunt.

"He's not a Filipino," I said. "He's a Jap."

They all stared at me.

"You a psychic now, Slater?"

I didn't want to let on that I actually knew the guy posing as Mariano Cruz. They might think it could influence my judgment, and I most definitely did not want to be taken out of this search.

"Call it a hunch," I said. "Just remember what I said when we catch the guy."

TINIAN

Matsuo smiled at the sight of all those Americans running around in mad confusion. He crouched in the lush vegetation and watched them through his field glasses from atop Mount Lasso. Not much of a mountain—less than six hundred feet high, he guessed—but it was dead center on Tinian and gave him an excellent view of the island's activities. He had a clear view of the four parallel runways, each over a mile and a half long, that took up most of the north end of the island.

And now, they had finally discovered that the uranium projectile was missing. He had waited all day for that. If they had not found out on their own, he would have been forced to go down there in the morning and tell them himself.

He had changed his plans. He could not meet his contact off the north end tonight. He had to go about this another way. With security in such a state of alarm now, he doubted he could escape the island anyway.

He watched a helicopter land and disgorge half a dozen Navy officers. As they walked toward one of the buildings, Matsuo began to turn his attention elsewhere, then snapped back to the group. Something about the way one of them walked. He focused his field glasses on that particular officer—

By all the gods, it was Frank! Frank Slater!

Matsuo followed him until he disappeared behind the door of the Quonset hut. He smiled ruefully.

So, old friend, our paths cross once more.

Could all these crossings be pure coincidence? Matsuo sensed more strongly than ever the workings of unseen forces. Was some sort of destiny at work here, nudging him and Frank and perhaps even Meiko along convergent paths toward a common fate? He could only wait and see. Right now he welcomed Frank's presence. He owed him an apology. And he wanted to ask a question that had been nagging him since his last stay in San Francisco.

He settled back and waited for Frank to emerge.

It wasn't a long wait.

■ ■ ■

I headed down Broadway past the central bomb dump.

I usually liked Tinian. It was a unique place. There was still plenty of jungle and even a few sugarcane fields left that hadn't been plowed under to make airstrips. For the most part, though, we had made it over completely since taking it from the Japanese. Whoever had been in charge of the make-over design must have been a New Yorker—one with a sense of humor. He must have seen some resemblance between this oblong island and Manhattan, and he must have been homesick, too, because the island now had Broadway, Eighth Avenue, and West End Avenue running north and south, streets numbered in sequence from 42nd to 125th running east and west, and even a Canal Street and Wall Street far below at the southern end.

But tonight the humor palled. It was 2:00 A.M. and I was beat. There were sailors, Air Force men, and marines—everybody who could be spared—out beating the bushes all over the island. There were even a few scientist types roaming around with little boxes that clicked and buzzed and rattled. The louder the clicking, the more excited they got. I didn't understand it and I was too tired to try. I wanted to call it a night but knew I couldn't. Even though I didn't know exactly what I was looking for, I knew it was damned important. I hadn't realized just how important until we'd had our briefing on arrival. The Big Man himself, General Curtis LeMay, who had just been promoted to Chief of Staff of Strategic Air Forces, had come over personally from his headquarters on Guam. A brigadier general named Groves, wearing the Army Corps of Engineers insignia, had done most of the talking, all about how important this mysterious cylinder was to the war effort, how many thousands of American lives it would save, but it was LeMay's presence that had really lent the briefing weight.

This was *Big!*

I needed a drink and a bed. I had no hope of getting the latter but I was looking for Abrams to see if maybe we could do something about the former.

I was walking south along a relatively deserted stretch near the foot of Mount Lasso's dark rise when I heard a rustle in the bushes to my left. Suddenly someone was walking beside me. I glanced up and knew him instantly.

Without thought, without the slightest hesitation, I launched myself at Matsuo's throat. All I could see was the smoke, the flames, the diving planes, the floating bodies in the burning water at Pearl. Their blood was on his hands. I wanted his on mine. A .45 automatic sat in a holster on my belt, forgotten. I flailed at him madly, wildly. Hoarse screeches rasped in my throat as I pounded my fists against him. The pummeling backed him into the brush. I followed, throwing lefts and rights and even kicking him when I had the chance. He partially deflected some of my more vicious blows, but he allowed most of them to land. I began to realize that he could defend himself far better than he was, that he was taking the punishment willingly, as if he thought he deserved it. As if he wanted it.

That stopped me cold.

We were off Broadway now, in the foliage. I couldn't see Matsuo's face. He was just a darker shadow within other shadows. I was breathing like a guy who had just run the Boston Marathon.

"Hello, Frank," he said in his perfect English. "I'm sorry about what I did to your arm. That was unforgivable."

I wanted to kill him. I started for him again but he shoved me back. Easily.

"Tell me something," he said. "When did you break our diplomatic code?"

"None of your fucking business!"

"What can it matter now? It's of no strategic importance. We don't use that code anymore."

"Then why the hell do you want to know?"

"Because if the answer falls after a certain date, I'll invite you to beat me within an inch of my life. If it falls before that date, I won't let you lay a hand on me."

I wondered what he was getting at. Then I remembered what Sam Knapp had told me on Balajuro on the last day of his life.

"1940," I told him. "Sometime in the late summer or early fall."

I heard a sharp intake of breath. "You're absolutely sure?"

"Of course! We had machines that could decipher Purple—that's what we called it—faster than your own people could."

There was a moment of silence, then Matsuo spoke. His voice was strained. "If that is the case, then don't you dare raise your hand against me again. If you do, I will break your arm." I could tell he meant it. "And don't you ever call the Pearl Harbor raid a 'sneak attack' in my presence! *Ever!*"

"Now just a goddamn minute—!" I began, but he cut me off with a voice like ice.

"The first thirteen segments of the Fourteen Part Message were transmitted to our Washington Embassy more than fifteen hours *before* our first plane appeared over Oahu! They left little doubt that we were breaking off diplomatic relations. The final part, containing the formal break, arrived more than six hours before the attack."

"That's a lie!"

I didn't want to believe it! It couldn't be true! It was just rumor! But it jibed so perfectly with what Sam had said.

"No." His voice was low and sad now. "It's true."

I had known Matsuo long enough to know that he was telling the truth. My stomach turned.

He said, "Why weren't you warned?"

That was the question *I* wanted answered. That and so many others. The questions showered down around me like hail, threatening to drive me to my knees. Pearl was in the area threatened by Japan—why hadn't we been given Purple magic? Why hadn't we been given any way to mount an effective aerial reconnaissance? Why had all those ships—ninety-six of them—been in Pearl at once? It was like waving a red flag at the Japanese. And how come the two truly indispensable ships in the fleet, the big carriers *Lexington* and *Enterprise*, were conveniently ordered out just days before the attack?

"I think your government is just as responsible as mine for the lives lost at Pearl Harbor."

"That's insane!"

"I don't think so. I've given this much thought in the past few weeks. Your confirmation that our diplomatic code was broken over a year before the Pearl Harbor attack has brought everything into focus for me."

"You don't get off the hook so easily, Matsuo!"

"I have no hope of that. You see, I helped plan the attack. But I didn't know that I was playing directly into the hand of your President Roosevelt."

"You expect me to believe that my own President planned the deaths of three thousand sailors in his own Navy? You're out of your mind!"

"I doubt President Roosevelt and his circle ever dreamed so many Americans would die in the attack. With their usual American smugness, they underestimated our leaders, men like Admiral Yamamoto, and our weaponry, like the Zero. They probably expected better resistance from the Army fighter squadrons on Oahu— squadrons we destroyed on the ground. But it doesn't matter what they expected. The fact remains that they made Pearl Harbor an irresistible target. Would American isolationists have cared if we attacked the Philippines or Borneo or Korea or Australia? Would that have rallied them to war? Of course not! FDR needed an attack on Americans! And to that end he purposely left your Pacific Fleet exposed and unwarned. His reasoning was simple: If properly alerted, the fleet would have put to sea and dispersed. If we had come upon an empty harbor we would have turned back. Result: no attack. And no attack meant no way to go to war."

"No! You don't believe that any more than I do!"

"Unfortunately, I do believe it." Suddenly he sounded extremely weary. "We have men like that in my own government."

Christ, it couldn't be true! Yet everything Matsuo was saying fitted so perfectly with all the doubts that had plagued me before and since the Pearl attack. I couldn't fight it anymore.

We were set up!

And I had to wonder—had I personally been set up? I thought about the Harbor diagram that had been locked out of its safe so conveniently on Saturday and given over to the ONI man with the Japanese wife—me. Had someone known that Matsuo and Meiko had been meeting? Had the plans been just one more nudge toward attack, a final cherry on top to make Pearl Harbor an irresistible target?

I wanted to lie down. I wanted a drink—*lots* of drinks. I wanted to weep.

"But that is all in the past," Matsuo said. "What you should know right now is that I have stolen your country's atomic bomb."

It took a moment for my brain to switch to the present.

"Atomic bomb? I've heard rumors, but—"

"It's one of the world's best-kept secrets, but the bomb is real, it exists." His voice sounded mechanical. "It's slated to be dropped on Kyoto. I stole the uranium projectile. There is no bomb without it."

So *that* was what all the excitement was about! An atomic bomb!

I'd just read about one in a science fiction magazine called *Astounding Stories*. It was supposed to be the ultimate weapon. Now I understood what General Groves had said about saving countless thousands of American lives. The Allied invasion of the Japanese mainland was still in the planning stages and probably wouldn't start till November, but I'd seen casualty estimates of up to a million Americans. An atom bomb could change all that.

"Where is it?" I said. It was an automatic question. I didn't expect an answer.

"Hidden."

I knew I was going to have to bring him in, or die trying. I couldn't let an atom bomb fall into Japanese hands. I edged my fingers toward my .45.

"Who is the highest-ranking officer on the island?" he said. "The one in charge of bombing Japan?"

My hand was resting on the pistol stock. All I had to do now was get it out of the holster. I kept my voice as calm as possible. "As of a few hours ago, General LeMay."

"Would you take me to him?"

I laughed with relief and Matsuo must have thought I was a little crazy. "Sure! Let's go!"

This was a meeting I just had to see!

■   ■   ■

General Curtis LeMay stormed around his commandeered Quonset hut office. His elation at my capture of "Mariano Cruz" had quickly turned to raging frustration at Matsuo's flat refusal to give up the uranium projectile. The scientists had come in and got excited over all the noise Matsuo caused in their little clicking machines, which I learned were called Geiger-Müller counters. That appeared to be proof that Matsuo had been in contact with the cylinder.

They were finally shooed out and now there were only five people in the room. Beside Abrams, General LeMay, and myself, there was Major General Groves, a pudgy, middle-aged man who I learned was in charge of the atom bomb project. He sat behind a desk looking tired and nervous, nibbling chocolates. Outside in the hall and all around the building, however, was a ring of white-helmeted MPs.

Matsuo sat impassively in the center of the room, secured to his chair by four pairs of handcuffs, one for each wrist and each ankle. I was taking no chances.

"You think this is a game, mister?" LeMay shouted. He was on the husky side with a full face tending toward jowls; his dark hair was parted high and combed up boyishly in the front; not yet forty, he was already a two-star general, the youngest in the Army Air Force. He was the man who planned and executed the March 9 holocaust of Tokyo and was said to be a brilliant tactician. I got the distinct impression that he might have been the one to say it most often. I never saw him without a cigar. Maybe he thought of it as a parallel to MacArthur's corncob pipe.

Matsuo looked at LeMay impassively as the general continued to work up steam, hauling his bulky frame back and forth in front of Matsuo, his cigar puffing like a locomotive stack.

"You've got no leverage here, mister!" he said with a faint midwest accent. "We're going to find that cylinder with or without your help, but it'll go easier on you if you tell us where you hid it. Otherwise, we'll comb this island inch by inch until we find it!"

"I did not say I hid it on the island," Matsuo said softly.

Groves shot out of his chair. "You mean it's in the ocean?"

"I only said it is hidden," Matsuo replied.

"You know," LeMay said, "we Americans don't believe in torture like you Japs, but I'm going to find somebody around here to give you a dose of your own medicine!"

"Excuse me, sir," I said, sensing that this could get out of hand. "But that won't work."

"Yeah?" he said with naked belligerence. "How do you know?"

"Look at him," I said.

LeMay stared at Matsuo, perhaps truly doing so for the first time. He saw what I saw: implacable determination. Matsuo used the moment perfectly.

"I will give you back the uranium projectile," he said.

LeMay chomped on his cigar. "In return for what?"

"For the end of the war." He waited a few beats in the dead silence of the room, then continued. "That is what you wish to use the atom bomb for, is it not? To end the war. You can still use it for that, but without exploding it."

"Oh, really?" He glanced at Groves. "We're all ears, mister!"

"I will return to Japan and convince the government and the military that they cannot withstand the weapon you have developed. I'll tell them what I saw at Alamogordo and—"

Groves shot from his seat. *"What do you know about Alamogordo?"*

"I was there."

"Impossible!"

Matsuo proceeded to tell the general what he had seen. It sounded like the most frightening science fiction I had ever heard, but as he spoke I watched the color drain from Groves' face and realized with horror that Matsuo wasn't exaggerating.

"Your little scheme won't work, mister!" LeMay said. "We have plenty of atom bombs!"

"You have *one* other," Matsuo said, his face flashing with defiance. "It is called Fat Man, and it is still in the United States."

"My God! My God!" General Groves muttered, rubbing a trembling hand across his eyes. "He knows everything!"

"Well, we'll get Fat Man here and use that!"

Matsuo met LeMay's glare calmly. "After you explain how Little Boy was stolen from right under your nose, do you really think they'll want to trust the only other existing atom bomb to your security again?"

That shut LeMay up. He looked like he was ready to have his own little atomic explosion inside his head, but he fumed in silence. I watched Matsuo. I had to admire him. Part of me still hated his guts, but another part of me responded to his courage, and to what he wanted to do. He said he wanted to end the war without using the atom bomb and I believed him. And he was one *hell* of an intelligence officer!

"Sending you to Japan is out," LeMay said finally. "You'd never come back, then we'd have neither you nor the bomb. Forget it!"

"You have my word," Matsuo said.

"Your word isn't worth a nickel, pal!"

That wasn't true. I knew Matsuo would die rather than break his word. But there was no way I'd ever convince LeMay of that. He'd want insurance. Then inspiration struck.

"I know a way," I said.

■ ■ ■

"Meiko!"

Matsuo tried to leap up when they brought her in, but the chair and the cuffs held him back. His Japanese composure slipped completely, but only for an instant, then it was locked back into place again.

She started toward him but the MPs held her back. "Oh, Matsuo! Have they hurt you?"

The way they looked at each other, the need, the love, the undeniable bond between them, was like a knife in my gut.

"Who *is* this?" LeMay said.

"His wife," I told him.

LeMay's face suddenly relaxed into a satisfied smile. "Well, well! Isn't this cozy!" Then his smile vanished and he whirled on me. "How come you know so much about this guy?"

"He used to be my best friend." After I said that, you could have heard a butterfly's wings flapping across the room. I had already put one foot in it. I decided it was time for the other. "And she used to be my wife."

The cigar dropped out of LeMay's mouth and rolled on the floor. Abrams was staring at me as if I'd grown another head.

I saw Matsuo's eyes leave Meiko for the first time since she had entered the room. He looked at me with a slightly cocked head, then briefly inclined his upper body an inch forward. It was the tiniest of bows, but it was an acknowledgment of the trouble I could be buying myself with those statements, and it was a vote of confidence and of gratitude. He had guessed what I was up to.

It took a while to explain everything, but when I showed them my right arm—Meiko turned away at that point—and how I couldn't make a tight fist, I could see the doubt in their faces begin to fade.

"The whole point of this story is that Meiko is our insurance policy. Matsuo will return for her. He went to Hawaii to bring her back to Japan; she was sailing to Tinian in a sampan to pick him up. They're devoted to each other." *God*, it hurt to say that! "One would never desert the other. He'll be back."

"We've got to risk it!" I heard General Groves whisper to LeMay. "We've *got* to get that bomb back! I can't call Washington and tell them it's been stolen! Christ—!"

"Never!" LeMay said.

Groves glanced at Meiko, Matsuo, and me, then pointed LeMay toward the office door. "Outside."

It seemed to take them forever out there, but when the two generals returned, LeMay's face was dark with anger. He glowered at Groves and seemed to hate us all. He walked over to Matsuo.

"Okay, mister. Listen up: There was a big conference in Potsdam yesterday. President Truman, Attlee, and Chiang Kai-shek signed a proclamation setting out surrender terms for you monkeys. I'll get you back to Tokyo. And I'll give you seventy-two hours to either get your government on the air to accept those terms or get yourself to a pickup point we settle on. If the time limit passes and we don't see or hear from you, I'll get Fat Man here and I'll personally see to it that your wife is tied to it when we drop it on your hometown."

Matsuo returned his glare. "For the record, I grew up in San Francisco."

HIROSHIMA

Shimazu watched Hiroki as they sipped green tea. The brazier smoked between them, obscuring, then revealing his student's face. It was haggard, drawn. These days, during the workweek, Hiroki functioned as a cheerleader of sorts, going from one cabinet office to another, bolstering the courage of the ministers, encouraging the Chiefs of Service to keep fighting, to keep resisting those who wanted the Empire to surrender. A harrowing task, Shimazu knew. One with ever-diminishing returns. At least he could find shelter here at times.

Even as he watched, Hiroki's features were relaxing as he lost himself in thought while sipping tranquillity from the bitter liquid.

"How are plans for the final defense going?"

"Very well, sensei. As per our suggestion, General Anami has put the War Ministry to work distributing ten million bamboo spears to the people. Daily classes in their use have begun. When the Americans come ashore, not only will they have to contend with the Black Winds, but with a populace armed down to the last woman and child. We shall deal the Americans such a blow for setting foot upon our islands that the few who survive will scurry back to their side of the Pacific, never to darken our shores again!"

Shimazu could not resist smiling behind his mask. "I do not think a single American foot will ever get close enough to make those bamboo spears necessary."

In response to Hiroki's puzzled expression, Shimazu reached behind him and brought forward a small carved teak box. He lifted the lid to reveal a vial of clear fluid resting on a bed of deep blue velvet within. Hiroki's eyes widened.

"Is all that ekisu?"

"Yes," Shimazu said. "Four ounces of it!"

Hiroki was on his feet. "Four ounces? We've only been able to distill a few drops at a time until now!"

"The process has been perfected while you were in Tokyo. More is being distilled at this very moment!"

"Then we've done it! We can now begin a true offensive with the Black Winds!"

Shimazu nodded. They knew the ekisu worked. They recently had tested their few meager drops on Okinawa. On each occasion, a child, one of the surgical failures, had been sedated, submarined to the island, given a few drops of the fluid, then left onshore. Each had succeeded in becoming a Black Wind shoten.

"We'll need more children," Hiroki said.

"Perhaps not." Shimazu closed the cover over the vial of ekisu and put the box aside. It was too precious to risk spilling. "I think we can use the little mongrels we keep upstairs most effectively against the U.S. fleets at anchor in the harbors they've taken from us. Consider: A woman rows a boat near a nest of American warships in, say, Manila Bay. Just a mother and her child in a tiny open boat. Certainly nothing for a mighty cruiser or aircraft carrier to fear. She stops rowing and gives a dram of clear fluid to the child. Moments later, a Kuroikaze strikes with full force. And when it has finally passed, Manila Bay is still full of perfectly undamaged craft, just as before the storm. However, they now are death ships, manned by corpses!"

Hiroki's eyes glowed. "Yes! Think of the terror! They will be afraid to board their own ships!"

"But that is only the beginning!" Shimazu said, exhilaration rising in him like a tide. "We will take this war to their own soil! All we need is one dedicated man to go to America with a supply of the ekisu."

"Their cities will suffer like ours! What a perfect use for the Kuroikaze! All their factories, all their planes, all their ships and bombs and cannon will be useless against Black Winds within their own borders!"

Shimazu said, "And the message will be clear: Leave Asia! Leave the Pacific! Return to your families now or you won't have any!"

"Then the Seers were right! We can win this war! We *will* win it!"

"You doubted?" Shimazu said.

Hiroki lowered his eyes. "With all the difficulties we've had, sensei, how could I not?"

Shimazu privately admitted that he, too, had had his moments of doubt. "But now you see how it all follows the vision: We have suffered through our darkest moments, and now we have the means of final victory in our hands!"

Hiroki sighed. "As long as the defeatists in the government do not surrender first."

Shimazu smiled. "Have no fear of that. I have seen a copy of the enemy's terms."

He had been terribly concerned on his first reading of the Potsdam Proclamation because it called for the "unconditional surrender of the Japanese armed forces" without mentioning the civilian government. The implied dichotomy was a very obvious inducement to the diet to cave in. However, upon rereading, he noted to his great relief that the proclamation made no provision for the preservation of the Imperial Line. Without such a guarantee, not even the most craven of the defeatists would consider placing his name upon such a blasphemy.

"It is unacceptable to anyone Japanese," he told Hiroki.

"What of this atomic bomb the Americans are supposed to be developing?"

"A myth!" Shimazu said. "A rumor they themselves have planted in a desperate attempt to save themselves from the task of storming our shores."

"I have learned through our contact in Naval Intelligence that my brother is expected back from America soon," Hiroki said. "I wonder if he has learned anything about this bomb."

Shimazu stiffened. Matsuo returning? This was not good news. It could further complicate an already complex situation. The younger Okumo was more resourceful than Shimazu had suspected. He could not be allowed to live any longer. The way was clear: Matsuo was the Okumo who must die, and the sooner, the better.

"It will not matter," he told Hiroki.

"I thought you said he would be isolated in America until after the war."

"I thought I had arranged for that to be the case. How is he returning?"

"That remains elusive. Either Naval Intelligence is not completely sure at this time, or they are restricting the information to a few select people."

"The route is not important. When he returns, send him to me."

"What if he brings proof of this American superweapon?"

"There can be no proof because there is no weapon! The Americans are still many years away from perfecting such a thing. It was a fool's errand but it worked well to our advantage. No matter what your brother says, the terms of the Potsdam Proclamation are unacceptable. His voice will go unheeded." Shimazu *hoped* that would be the case, but one could never be sure about these things.

"But I am concerned how he will react when he learns about the child and my role in his abduction. My brother is so unpredictable. I fear he will be . . . uncontainable."

"Have no fear. Send him to me." Shimazu could not allow one man to interfere with the Empire's destiny. Especially not now when they were so close to success!

"What if he will not come?"

"You have squads of Kempeitai at your disposal in Tokyo, do you not? Surely they can manage to bring one man to Hiroshima. Once he is here among us, I am sure I can reduce his power as a threat to our plans. Send him to me. I will see to it that he is contained."

Forever!

TOKYO

The rubber raft grated against the sand as Matsuo grounded it on the southwest shore of Tokyo Bay. He leaped out, punctured its rubber flank, then kicked the deflating raft back into the gentle current and watched it drift away into the dark. He was wearing only a white shirt and khaki pants, but already he was sweating. Summer had settled upon Japan with a vengeance.

Is it this easy? he thought as he walked along the deserted sandy shore toward the ruins of Yokohama, once the busiest seaport in Japan. The American submarine had breezed past the darkened Yokosuka lighthouse and into the bay, surfaced long enough to put him off, then submerged again. Was the Japanese Navy now so oil-impoverished that it could no longer mount even rudimentary shore patrols? Luckily the enemy belonged to a different race, otherwise Tokyo would be crawling with American spies.

He thought of Meiko's last words before he had left her. They had been allowed one brief embrace on Tinian. As he held her close she had whispered a Hiroshima address in his ear, then said, "Naka is there." There had been no time for clarification before they were pulled apart.

Somehow he had to get to Hiroshima and find out what she meant. The urgency in her voice left no doubt of how important it was to her. But first he had to stop this war. Father would know how.

He picked up his pace toward Yokohama. It would be dawn soon. He had no time to waste.

■   ■   ■

"Matsuo is home!"

That was the news that greeted Hiroki at the front door. He fought the urge to turn around and flee through the streets of Akasaka. Instead he forced himself to cross the threshold and go to where his father and brother were having tea in the room overlooking the garden.

Matsuo rose and bowed correctly as a younger brother should. Hiroki knew this was for Father's sake. Matsuo's face was deeply troubled. His eyes held a haunted look. Something was wrong, but what? Hiroki searched those eyes for hatred, for anger. He saw neither. Could it be that he had not yet spoken to Meiko? Yes! That had to be the answer! Meiko had vanished since their confrontation at the Hiroshima site. Matsuo had not seen her since his return. He didn't know of Hiroki's part in the child's abduction. Relief flooded through him.

"My son!" Father said as Hiroki joined them. His lined face was drawn and his eyes were feverish. "The Americans have an atomic bomb! Matsuo has seen it!"

Hiroki froze as Matsuo looked at him.

"It's true, Hiroki. I saw the test. We must never allow one of those bombs to fall on Japan."

Hiroki steeled himself. This couldn't be true! "They bomb us every day. This will merely be a bigger bomb."

"You don't understand! The bombs they drop on us now are like firecrackers compared to the atomic bomb!"

Hiroki suddenly realized that Matsuo was afraid! He had never seen his brother show fear of anything. By the Hidden Face, what had he *seen?*

"So what should we do?" Hiroki said with a display of contempt. "Roll over like whipped curs and surrender ourselves to their every whim?"

"Would you prefer to sit here like ants on a hill and allow them to kick at us until our islands are reduced to lifeless rock and our race and our culture are obliterated from the face of the earth?"

"I hardly believe that to be possible." Hiroki was not sure how to react. He did not want to appear too openly scornful. Matsuo was most convincing in his tale of an American atomic bomb, and that made him dangerous. If he ever got the diet's ear, the defeatists there could end the war before the Order had a chance to bring the full fury of the Kuroikaze against the Americans.

"Hiroki . . ." Matsuo seemed to be at a loss for words. He ranged about the room, his slippered feet scuffing on the tatami. "How can I convince you? You've seen what months of bombing raids have done to Tokyo? Imagine all this destruction and more occurring within seconds *from a single bomb!*"

Hiroki swallowed. Was that possible? No! He could not believe it! They had somehow tricked Matsuo. But he wouldn't say that. Better to smile ruefully and try to gain his brother's confidence. That might allow him some say in Matsuo's course of action.

"Seems to me there is little left to destroy here. What more can they do?"

"You don't understand! They have been *saving* cities for these bombs!"

"Saving?"

"Yes! We all know that certain cities on Honshu have been left untouched by the bombing raids. We've been attributing that to luck or oversight. It's neither. The Americans have been preserving entire cities so they could wipe them out with a single bomb! And do you know the target for the first bomb?"

Hiroki's mouth went dry. *Hiroshima?*

Father said, "Where?"

"Kyoto."

Father shot to his feet. "No! It cannot be allowed!"

"That's why I came here, Father," Matsuo said. "You must arrange an audience for me with the prime minister and the cabinet. We've got to convince them!"

Father shook his head. "That I fear will be a waste of time. Too much opposition from the military, and even from the cabinet members already tired of the war. They're afraid to press for peace. They're well aware of the atrocities our troops have perpetrated. Unconditional surrender for them is tantamount to placing themselves in the docket of a war crimes tribunal. They would see Japan reduced to rubble before surrendering!"

Hiroki wanted to cry out in anger—Father sounded like a defeatist!—but he held his tongue.

"There's been enough destruction," Father went on. "I was in favor of this war. All three of us were. But it has gone all wrong. It is time to stop it."

"But if the prime minister can't help," Hiroki said, "who can?" He had to know their plans!

"We'll go straight to the Emperor!"

Hiroki's mind reeled. *The Emperor!* He had never thought of that! A direct appeal from Matsuo describing the devastation of Kyoto and the lives that would be lost would undoubtedly sway the Emperor. His Majesty had been carefully shielded from many of the unpleasant truths of the war. If Matsuo was allowed an audience, the Emperor might very well order a surrender. In fact, Hiroki was certain He would! All that was needed was a single word from the Emperor and the war would stop immediately!

"Hiroki!" Father was saying. "Surely with your influence you can arrange an audience."

"Yes!" he said quickly. His mind raced: This might be his chance to stop them. "Leave it to me. I'm certain I can. That is the only way. Only the Emperor can end hostilities in time." He headed for the telephone in Father's study at the far end of the house. "I will call immediately."

WEDNESDAY, AUGUST 1

Matsuo saw his brother staring at him as he walked out to the car. He checked over his navy dress uniform.

"Is something wrong?"

"Do you think an audience with His Majesty is a proper time for the wearing of ceremonial weapons?"

Matsuo placed his hands over the handles of the katana and wakizashi thrust through his belt. He found the question odd. He had always worn Nagata's daisho with his dress uniform. As far as he was concerned, the swords were an integral part of it. He wondered why Hiroki was asking.

"These swords have served the Emperor throughout their lives. They deserve to be with me now." He looked around. "Father isn't coming?"

Hiroki shook his head. He seemed edgy. "This is an audience for one. I will accompany you as far as what is left of the Imperial Household Ministry. After that, you are on your own. The Emperor will see you in the *Obunko*."

Matsuo nodded. Most of the buildings in the palace grounds had been destroyed by fire in late May when airborne firebrands from another of the endless incendiary raids had wafted over the high stone walls. The Emperor had been safe in His air raid shelter, but when He had addressed His subjects on radio the following day, He had seemed almost pleased to be sharing the hardships of other Tokyo residents. Matsuo was sure the Emperor would want as much as he to prevent an atomic bomb from falling on Japan.

But would He believe him? Would He call for surrender?

Matsuo spent the three and a half miles to the palace trying to quell the rising tension within him. It had taken Hiroki two days to arrange, but finally he had been granted a private audience with the Emperor! The prospect was almost terrifying. Yet he could not let his awe of His Majesty overcome him. He had to be persuasive—more persuasive than he had ever been in his entire life. He had to convince the Emperor to announce an end to the war before dawn tomorrow. That was when his time ran out and the American sub would surface for him outside Hiroshima harbor. He had to be there to meet it. If not, Kyoto would be reduced to a slag heap and Meiko would die. If his audience with the Emperor was successful, the deadline would become meaningless: The war would be over.

It's all on me! he thought. The realization made him almost physically ill. He turned his mind to other things.

He thought of Naka. He had been shocked to learn that he had been kidnapped. Meiko had said nothing of that. Only the address in Hiroshima, and that Naka was there. The torment she must have been through! And alone! But if she knew where he was, why hadn't she told anyone? Matsuo realized there was much running beneath the surface here that he didn't understand, so he had said nothing. He allowed Father to continue to think that the child was missing. What did Hiroki think?

"Where were you when Naka was abducted?"

Hiroki looked at him with bland puzzlement. "Naka? Oh, you mean Meiko's son? I was at the temple that night. Can you imagine the audacity of those bandits, breaking into the count's house that way?"

"There was never a ransom note?"

"No. But someday, they shall be found, and then—"

"Someday very soon," Matsuo said. "When the war is over I shall devote myself to tracking them down. And then they shall pay." He placed a hand on the grip of his katana. "Dearly."

Hiroki looked away. "I shall help you."

Suddenly the car slowed to a stop. The gray stone expanse of the Imperial Palace wall was in sight but armed men were blocking the road just ahead. "Who are they?" Matsuo asked the driver.

Hiroki replied. "They appear to be Kempeitai. I understand that they have been conducting random inspections of vehicles nearing the palace."

"On whose authority?" To Matsuo's mind, the Army's secret police were little more than hoodlums.

"They fear an assassination attempt on His Majesty."

"They surely are not going to stop you and me!"

"It might be best to cooperate," Hiroki said. "They are very concerned for the Emperor."

Matsuo looked at his brother more closely. He was drenched in perspiration.

■ ■ ■

This was the moment Hiroki had dreaded. He had to get Matsuo out of the car so that the Kempeitai members could "arrest" him and hold him for "questioning." In reality, Matsuo would be bound, placed in another car, and taken to Hiroshima where he would be handed over to Shimazu for safekeeping. But there was no telling what Matsuo would do. He was so full of anger. Hiroki could sense it coiled within him, ready to lash out at the slightest provocation. He was like a live grenade with the pin pulled; the slightest jostle would spring the safety lever and he would explode.

The leader of the Kempeitai group leaned down to the driver's window. "What is your destination, please?"

"The Imperial Palace."

He looked back at Hiroki and Matsuo. "Will everyone please step out for inspection."

"I am an officer in the Imperial Navy and I have an audience with the Emperor!" Matsuo said. He tapped the driver on the shoulder. "Drive on."

The Kempeitai leader drew his pistol, an old Taisho 04, and pointed it at the driver. "Everyone out, please."

Hiroki could see that Matsuo was fuming. He tried to calm him. "Resistance will only cause us further delay. Just allow them to go through the motions of searching the car for a bomb. After all, they are doing this to safeguard the Emperor."

Matsuo gave him a strange look, but complied. Hiroki followed him out on the same side.

The leader of the Kempeitai kept his pistol leveled at them both. He took one look at Matsuo, then turned to Hiroki and bowed.

"Okumo-san, I thought you said he would be unarmed."

Hiroki wanted to shrink inside his clothes and hide from the look of astonishment and anger on his brother's face.

"This is prearranged, my brother?"

"The war must go on, Matsuo!" Hiroki said. "You must understand. I can't allow you to bring about surrender. We will win! We

finally have the means to drive the Americans back to their own shores
with the Kuroikaze! We will win!"

"Then they'll bomb us from there, Hiroki! Don't you see? They
can use their atomic bombs to return Japan to its original molten lava
without risking more than a few American lives! It's *over*, Hiroki!"

"I can see why Okumo-san wished to keep you from the
Emperor," the Kempeitai leader said.

"Go with them, Matsuo," Hiroki said softly. "No harm will come
to you."

Matsuo looked around at the five Kempeitai who surrounded him.
His shoulders slumped in resignation. "I guess I have no choice."

"Yes, yes," said the Kempeitai leader. "Come quietly." He
stepped toward Matsuo and reached for the swords in his uniform belt.

Suddenly Matsuo was moving. His katana was unsheathed, its
blade flashing in the morning sun. It rose and fell in an arc and suddenly
there was blood spurting from the Kempeitai leader's throat. Before the
others could respond, someone else was screaming and holding a
spurting arm stump. A Kempeitai managed to level his rifle and get off a
shot, but Matsuo was no longer there when the bullet arrived. It struck
another Kempeitai instead. The rifleman's head suddenly leapt from his
body in a geyser of red.

And then it was over. It hardly seemed to have begun and yet now
there were four Kempeitai on the ground and the fifth was running as
fast as he could toward the remnants of downtown Tokyo. Matsuo
stood among the dead, dying, and wounded like the avenging ghost of a
samurai from some forgotten era. Hiroki saw murder in his eyes as he
stepped forward with his bloody sword leveled.

"Matsuo?" Hiroki felt the door handle digging into his spine as he
pressed himself back against the side of the car. Matsuo wouldn't kill
him, would he? Not his own brother!

"Where was I to be taken, Hiroki?"

"To Hiroshima! To the Kakureta Kao temple! Matsuo, you must
under—"

"There's no temple in Hiroshima."

"Yes, there is. We moved there while you were gone! We—"

"Are there many like you in the Kakureta Kao?"

Hiroki straightened. "If you mean ready to fight on until the final
victory, yes! We will fight to the last man! And the heads of the Army
and Navy are with us! And the Ministry of War! You will not get to the
Emperor! Your cause is hopeless!"

"We'll see about that." Suddenly, his eyes narrowed. "Where in
Hiroshima is the new temple?"

Hiroki shook his head, saying nothing. Matsuo stepped within a
foot of him, began to lift his katana—*"Matsuo!"*

Matsuo pulled on a loose fold of Hiroki's kimono and ran his katana blade along it with the cutting edge up. Hiroki felt his face redden at this deliberate humiliation. The driver turned his back so as not to see.

When Matsuo finally dropped the fabric, his blade was clean. Hiroki's kimono was smeared with blood.

Hiroki said, "I will kill you for this."

Matsuo sheathed his sword. "We will settle this after the war. As for now, I am going to see the Emperor."

"The Emperor!" Hiroki laughed. "You have no appointment for an audience!"

"Then I shall get one now."

"Do you really believe that will be allowed? Are you such a fool as to think we let anyone other than a select few have His Majesty's ear?" Hiroki pointed to the walls of the palace. "We control all access to the Emperor! Your cause is lost!"

As he laughed again, he saw his brother's face harden.

"There has to be a way!"

He shoved Hiroki and the driver away from the car and threw himself behind the wheel. Without another word, he sped off toward the palace.

Hiroki shook his head as he watched him go. He knew Matsuo had not a chance in the world of reaching the Emperor. His little display had not gone unnoticed by the Imperial Guards. They surely had heard the shot, and they doubtlessly had seen Matsuo kill or maim four men. Did his brother really think the Guard would even let him onto the palace grounds, let alone speak to the Emperor?

But just to be sure, Hiroki would contact the Minister of Information and see to it that Matsuo was smeared in all the Tokyo newspapers. He would be labeled a murderer, a traitor, a madman. No one in all Japan would even listen to him, let alone allow him within sight of the Emperor!

■ ■ ■

Matsuo raced toward the main gate to the palace grounds. As he pulled up to the bridge that led across the moat, he saw the Imperial Guard forming a cordon across the ramp. Their rifles were all pointed his way. He slowed to a stop and stepped out of the car.

"I must see the Emperor!"

"The Emperor is seeing no one today," said the Captain of the Guard.

"It's important!" Matsuo said. "A matter of life and death for all Japan! You must let me see him!"

"You must go through the proper channels."

"Please!"

"Leave now or we will arrest you!" said the captain.

Matsuo was suddenly furious. There didn't seem to be anything he could do. Hiroki and his ruling clique had locked the Emperor away from the entire world! He heard only what they wanted Him to hear, saw only what they wanted Him to see. Matsuo pounded a fist on the car top, denting it. He had to get in there!

Without thinking, Matsuo slipped back behind the wheel, threw the car into first gear, and gunned it toward the Imperial Guard. If he could just get past them, just get onto the palace grounds, he could find a place to take shelter and hold them off until the Emperor heard of his plea for an audience. He wouldn't care if he was executed immediately afterward, as long as he could have the Emperor's ear for three minutes.

The Imperial Guard opened fire immediately. Windshield glass shattered around him, cutting his face and hands. He kept his head low and shifted into second as he rammed past them. Suddenly another two dozen of the Guard appeared at the far end of the moat. They, too, opened fire, riddling the car with bullets.

Too many! He would never make it across the moat alive!

Matsuo slewed the car around in a screeching turn. The right fender caught the stone guardrail as he came around. It ripped off with a tortured shriek and then he was jamming the accelerator to the floor and tearing away from the palace. A few shots sang past the car as he fled down the road past Hibiya Park and the ruined Imperial Hotel.

He was bleeding from numerous facial cuts, and one of the bullets had creased his shoulder. He could not stay in Tokyo. The only place he could go now was Hiroshima.

TINIAN

Meiko watched Frank across the table from her. He was smoking in silence, leaning back in the chair with his feet up on the table, blowing smoke rings. He had brought her here twice a day to be "interrogated" since Matsuo had left. He had asked her a few questions the first day, but none since. She had explained how Matsuo had shown up on Oahu the week before the attack, how she had truly thought him dead until that moment. She didn't know if Frank believed her or not.

He talked a lot. Often he talked about the war, how it had affected Americans, and asked her how it had affected Japan and how the Japanese people felt about it. He talked on and on about Pearl Harbor, almost as if he were talking to himself about how ill-prepared the

Pacific Fleet was. "Sitting ducks"—he used the phrase over and over. Meiko was beginning to get the feeling that he blamed his own country for the attack as much as Japan. She didn't understand that.

When he wasn't talking about the war and Pearl Harbor, he would just sit there on the other side of the table and smoke. And in the silence, Meiko's thoughts invariably turned to Naka: Was he all right? Had those masked monsters hurt him?

Thinking of Naka with Frank present brought her to the inevitable.

Meiko sensed that despite her unforgivable betrayal, Frank still harbored some feeling for her. It was deeply buried and she had no desire to resurrect it, but there was something he had a right to know.

"I have a son," she told him.

"That's nice," Frank said.

"He will be three years old next week."

"Good. I'm glad for him." He took a deep puff from his cigarette. Meiko waited for the progression of smoke rings but none came. He suddenly lowered his feet to the floor and began to cough. *"Next week?"*

Meiko nodded, smiling.

"You *bitch!*" he said, his face livid. "You mean you were doing double duty in the rack between me and Matsuo? Why you—"

"He has a birthmark," Meiko said quickly before he could go too far.

Frank stopped. "Birthmark?"

Meiko nodded. She drew her fingers from above her left eye up to her hairline. "It's red."

Frank's face went slack. His trembling fingers leapt to his own birthmark. "Like . . . like this?"

"Almost exactly."

As Frank stared at her, tears began to form in his eyes. "Oh, God, Meiko, tell me you're lying! For once in your life, admit that you're lying!"

Meiko felt her own eyes brim over. She realized now that she loved two men, and had hurt one of them terribly. This one.

"I've never lied to you, Frank. Never."

Like a man in a trance, Frank straightened from his seat and stumbled around the table. He held his arms out to her. She hesitated a moment, then rose to embrace him.

■ ■ ■

A son! My God, I was a father! I had a son! And I was holding Meiko in my arms again. It was almost like we'd never been apart.

"I didn't know whether or not to tell you," she said. "I didn't know if it would bring you joy or more pain." She leaned back and looked at me. "I've caused you enough pain."

I let her go. "That you have," I said. "But this . . ."

"His name is Nakanaori."

I knew the word: reconciliation. *Nakanaori*. It didn't make up for everything, but it did go a long way toward healing wounds I'd thought would fester forever. A son . . .

"We call him Naka."

We? A sudden thought chilled me. "What did Matsuo say? How did he—?"

"He hated all of us at first—you, me, Naka—and refused to give the baby his name."

A burst of vindictive laughter welled up in me. Matsuo thought he had won it all, but Meiko gave birth to *my son!*

"But by the time Naka was one," Meiko was saying, "he came to love him like a son and has raised him as his own. Naka calls him Father. He has been very good to your son, Frank."

The laughter withered away inside. Would I have done that for his son? *Could* I have done that?

"Naka and I would have died in the March firebombing of Tokyo if not for Matsuo."

I shuddered. LeMay's bombers had almost killed my boy!

"But where is he now?"

"In . . . in Hiroshima," she said. "Matsuo is stopping in to see him before he returns." She struck me as oddly hesitant and vague. Then she brightened. "Perhaps he'll bring Naka back with him!"

"Oh, I don't know about that. Meeting a sub at night is risky. I'd hate to think of him taking a chance like that."

But if he did. Oh, God, if he did. To think: my own son. Three years old and I'd be meeting him for the first time! It made my knees go soft. I hadn't been particularly anxious for Matsuo's return. Now I couldn't wait.

Then she told me how the child had got to Hiroshima, and why, and the joy in me damn near died.

THURSDAY, AUGUST 2
HIROSHIMA

Matsuo had watched the building in the Kannonmachi section throughout the late afternoon and into the evening. It was now after midnight and he hesitated on his next move.

Was this the right address? Could Naka really be here in this old factory? He had seen a few men come and go. They had not looked like factory workers, yet there had been nothing remarkable about them either. There had been a delivery of vegetables, but little other activity. Near sunset he had seen two little boys looking out at the city from a second-story window. His field glasses showed that neither was Naka, but now at least he knew there were children inside.

He had to go in there. If Naka was being held prisoner, he had to find him and bring him back to Tinian.

Everything else was set. He had used his officer's uniform and Naval Intelligence standing to requisition a launch from the garrison at Hiroshima Castle. If there was a search out for him, word apparently had not yet reached Hiroshima. He got the launch. Then he had set about finding his way by water to the building in question. It didn't take long. Hiroshima was actually a collection of five fingerlike islands divided by the estuarial branches of the Ota River. Nothing in the city was very far from the water.

He saw a lot of Hiroshima along the way. He liked it. It was a city, yet its black tile roofs and profusion of gardens gave it a provincial look. Although unscarred by the incendiary raids that had leveled so many other cities—was this another of the cities the Americans were "saving" for their atomic bombs?—it was haggard and careworn from the war. But people still bustled along with an air of industry and purpose. And all about the women and older children took time out from school and their daily work to drill with bamboo spears against the day when the Americans charged ashore. He turned his mind from the absurdity of it.

Eventually he was able to tie up the launch within a quarter mile of the old factory.

All he had to do now was find Naka.

By the time his watch had edged onto 1:00 A.M., he knew what he would do. He had been watching the windows. Even at this hour, it was hot and unbearably humid out here on the street. It must have been worse inside. All the windows on the second floor were open. They were of no use to him. But on the ground floor, a few had been left open.

With a flashlight from the launch in his back pocket, Matsuo crept toward the building and hoisted himself atop a stack of wooden crates along the west wall. A quick glance through the window showed a dimly lit interior. A cluttered expanse of concrete floor lay directly below him. He slipped through, lowered himself to the floor, found a dark corner, and waited.

■   ■   ■

Shimazu was suddenly wide awake.

Someone is here. An outsider!

He rose from his futon and fitted his silk mask into the skin folds that secured it to his face. He then went to his chest where he kept his case of doku-ippen. He withdrew a glistening two-inch sliver and held it carefully as he folded his hands inside the sleeves of his kimono. He walked through the dark toward the steps that led down to the first level. He would not raise the alarm that would bring everyone rushing from their futons. No, let them all stay asleep up here. He had a feeling about who this intruder was, and he wished to confront him.

■ ■ ■

Matsuo heard footsteps. Had he made too much noise? No, these were slow and measured, like a sentry's. He saw the single figure walk by. The guard's features were indistinct. Matsuo squinted into the dim light and gasped. There *were* no features! The face was covered with a silk mask! Kakureta Kao!

The guard must have heard his sharp intake of breath for he turned and approached Matsuo's hiding place.

"Who's there?" he said.

Matsuo waited until he was under the open window, looking up at it. Then he sprang. He rammed both hands against the back of the guard's head, driving it against the stone wall. There was a dull thud, a sigh, and then the guard went limp. Matsuo lowered the limp form to the floor and stood over him.

What was the Kakureta Kao doing hidden away here in an old Hiroshima tin factory?

Suddenly the pieces were beginning to fit. Naka's disappearance . . . Hiroki . . . the children disappearing in Tokyo . . . a picture was forming, but of what he could not say just yet.

He began to scout the first floor. In a cubicle that once must have been the factory office, he found crates of written records. All varieties—from ancient scrolls and rolled manuscripts to ledger books. One of the ledgers was open on the desk. He played the flashlight over the pages as he flipped through it. It seemed to be medical in nature, describing surgical procedures. Then he came to a list of patient data and stopped. There were first names followed by age and sex. All of the ages were below five. His pulse quickened. He looked ahead again and read the surgical descriptions more closely. Slowly, he went cold. He read on, skipping from page to page, turning them faster and faster. The latest anesthesia had been employed and aseptic techniques had been rigidly followed to avoid postoperative infection, but each case described the same ghastly procedures—the systematic, step-by-step mutilation of a small child.

"Enlightening, is it not, Okumo-san?"

Matsuo nearly cried out at the sound of the voice behind him. He whirled and shone the flashlight into the speaker's face. Shimazu's unmistakable green eyes did not even blink.

■ ■ ■

He was here! He had come on his own, sneaking in like a thief. How wonderful! After hearing Hiroki's report of the debacle in Tokyo, he had despaired of ever getting close enough to Matsuo Okumo. Yet here he was. Truly the All-Knowing Face was smiling tonight!

Shimazu could have tried to poke the little doku-ippen into the skin of the younger Okumo's neck as he stood leaning over the desk, but had decided against it. Matsuo might have sensed his presence at the last instant and put up a struggle, and in that struggle the poison sliver might have punctured the wrong skin. Besides, he wished to savor the moment. He had held off killing Matsuo for nearly twenty years. Better to let the man become used to his presence, let him assume he is in no immediate danger, and then use the doku-ippen in an unguarded moment.

The younger Okumo recovered quickly from his shock. He picked up a ledger from the desk.

"What are these *atrocities?*"

"Surely you've heard of the Kuroikaze, Okumo-san. And surely you've approved of their use against the Americans. True, they haven't been as effective as we might have wished, but they have caused considerable damage and much consternation among the enemy, and they will prove to be even more valuable in the near future. But there's a price to pay for such a weapon, and you've just seen it."

"Children?" Matsuo said, his face twisted in revulsion. "You mutilate children for the Black Winds?"

Shimazu kept his tone as matter-of-fact as possible. He enjoyed shocking this young pup. "I knew your sentimental reaction would be typical of what we might expect from the rest of the populace, so the nature of the Black Wind shoten was hidden from them. Really, what has age to do with it? Since when is someone too young to sacrifice for the Emperor?"

"Where is Naka?"

"Who, may I ask, is Naka?" Shimazu said, knowing perfectly well who he meant.

"My son!"

"Really? I was given to believe you had no son." He raised a finger as if inspiration had struck. "Unless you mean that miserable little zasshu you kept around your house. Yes, he's here. Hiroki obtained him for us."

"My own brother," Matsuo said.

"And why not? Mongrels make the best shoten, and this child carries none of Hiroki's blood, nor any of yours."

"Has he been mutilated like these?" He held up the ledger with his left hand while his right crept toward the grip of the katana in his belt.

Shimazu saw the murderous expression on the younger Okumo's face and realized with a start that he was looking his own death in the eye, that he might have only a few heartbeats left if he did not give the right answer quickly.

"No, no! That is no longer necessary."

"Take me to him!"

"Of course. He is upstairs." He turned his back on Matsuo and led him out of the old office. As they crossed the factory floor, an idea occurred to him while passing the door to the shoten room. "Would you like to see the shoten?"

"The children?" Matsuo said. He shuddered visibly and shook his head. "No. I don't think so."

"Oh, but you must." As he pushed open the door into the darkened room, Shimazu heard the whisper of steel behind him. He turned to see Matsuo standing ready with his katana.

"This had better not be a trick!"

"No trick, I assure you," Shimazu said, fascinated by the way the light shimmered off the blade. "They have given everything but their lives for the Emperor. They deserve at least passing honor."

He switched on the newly installed light and watched Matsuo cautiously approach the door. Shimazu stayed close beside him. He knew what the younger Okumo's reaction would be: For a moment or two he would be mesmerized with horror. That was when Shimazu would strike. The end would be quick for him—too quick for his gaijinlike arrogance, Shimazu thought. First, paralysis of all the voluntary muscles, followed by the involuntary muscles. He would fall to the floor like a puppet without strings, and while he was staring up at Shimazu, his lungs would cease to fill with air, and his heart would slow to a stop. The brother carrying the seeds of the Order's destruction would be dead at last.

He tightened his grip on the doku-ippen hidden in the sleeve of his kimono and moved closer to Matsuo.

■ ■ ■

Matsuo refused to let the monk get behind him. He might be armed or he might try to lock him in this foul-smelling space. As his eyes adjusted to the light, he heard a breathy, rustling chorus of misery, then he saw the children, sprawled all over the room like limp bags of sand—eyeless sockets, fused nasal passages, open mouths.

And from the corner of his eye he caught a sudden flash of movement. Instinctively he ducked away and swung with the katana.

Shimazu cried out and clutched at his wrist as his right hand tumbled free through the air. Matsuo saw it sail out the door, trailing a crimson stream, a thin brown needle still clutched between its thumb and forefinger. Shimazu sank to his knees. Twin geysers of blood pumped into the air momentarily before he compressed the arteries with his left hand.

"Guards!" he screamed. His voice had lost all its languorous and sinuous qualities. It was now harsh and ragged. *"Guards! Kill him! Kill hiiiiim!"*

Matsuo was tempted to slit his throat to shut him up, but knew it was too late. He hurried out to the middle of the floor. Naka! He had to find Naka! But as he looked around he saw a dozen or more of the Kakureta Kao guards pour from their quarters with drawn katana and charge toward him.

Quickly, he saw his choices. He could stand and fight and probably be killed, or he could run. If he ran, he might survive. But that meant leaving Naka here. He cringed at the thought, but saw no alternative.

I'll be back, Naka! he promised as he turned and ran for the door. *I haven't deserted you. I'll be back!*

Then he was out into the night and running through the streets of the Kannonmachi district toward the water. He jumped into the launch, started it, and roared south toward the Inland Sea.

"I'll be back, Naka!" he shouted to the night, seeing that little round face before him. "By all that's holy and otherwise, I'll be back!"

TOKYO

Hiroki was worried about Father. He seemed so morose. He had barely spoken all day. Hiroki found him kneeling before the household shrine, clutching a picture of Mother.

"You mustn't blame yourself, Father. Matsuo has become slightly . . . mad."

Father looked at him with heavy, world-weary eyes. "Your brother is not mad. He is the sanest of us all."

"But you've heard the reports, you've seen the papers. He killed four men, then tried to attack the Emperor, tried to break through a cordon of the Imperial Guard! He has betrayed us! He has betrayed all Japan!"

Father shook his head. "No, Hiroki. You betrayed Matsuo. And it is you and yours who have betrayed Japan. I am a part of it, too. I am directly involved. Because of you I now have one son whom I cannot see because he is a fugitive, and another whom I cannot believe because he is a liar. Please leave me, Hiroki. I wish to be alone."

Crushed, Hiroki bowed and complied with his father's wishes. He dragged himself to his office on Sanno Hill, but Father's words and anguished expression haunted him there, weighing upon him like a mountain. He could not think, could not concentrate. If only Father understood! Maybe that was the key! Sit down with Father and explain to him the Seer's visions, the ekisu for the Kuroikaze, the plans Shimazu and he had for spreading terror and death throughout the United States. Once he understood all this, he would see that Matsuo was wrong and Hiroki was right. Japan could not surrender.

He hurried home to find the house silent and empty of servants. Alarmed, he ran upstairs to Father's sleeping area and found him lying dead in a pool of blood, his wakizashi protruding from his ruined belly. He had committed seppuku—alone, without a second.

Hiroki cried out his rage and anguish. It was all Matsuo's fault!

FRIDAY, AUGUST 3
TINIAN

I watched Matsuo's eyes as he stood before LeMay and Groves in his wrinkled navy uniform. If anything, they looked more haunted than they had before he left. He seemed to be suffering the tortures of the damned. I had been heartbroken that he hadn't returned with my son. Meiko felt the same. Matsuo, I could tell, was heartbroken by the message he bore.

There would be no surrender. That was all there was to it. I looked at the two generals and was shocked to see the relief on their faces. *Relief!* I realized then that there had been more than the obvious reason behind their reluctance to allow Matsuo to return to Japan. It wasn't that they were afraid he might betray them on his peace mission—they had been afraid he would succeed. They *wanted* to drop that bomb! Ending the war had something to do with it, but dammit, they wanted to see the actual effects of an atomic bomb on a real, live, full-sized city populated with hundreds of thousands of real live people—*Japanese* people!

Kyoto was going to be their test site. And its residents their lab rats.

For the first time in my life, I fully understood the phrase, "cold-blooded."

"All right," LeMay said, yanking the cigar from his mouth.

"We're sorry you failed. But now it's time to live up to your end of the bargain. Where's the projectile?"

"You must agree to two conditions before I tell you."

LeMay flew into a rage, pounding the desk, storming around the office in a tantrum. "No conditions! No conditions whatsoever!" It would have been comical had the man been someone other than U.S. Chief of Staff of Strategic Air Forces.

"Let's hear him out, sir," I said.

"You be quiet!" he shouted. "I don't want to hear another word out of you!" He swung on Matsuo. "And you! You're looking for a firing squad!"

"There must be a pistol nearby," Matsuo said. "Do it now."

"And your wife, too!"

"I'm sure she won't mind."

"Curtis, Curtis," General Groves said, as if placating a spoiled child. "Let's hear the conditions. This may be much ado about nothing." He pointed to Matsuo. "Go ahead."

"First condition," Matsuo said, "is that the target city be changed from Kyoto to Hiroshima."

LeMay slammed his palm down on the desk. "No! Absolutely not!"

I scrutinized Matsuo, trying to figure out what he was up to. There had to be a trick here. And then I saw his tortured eyes and knew there was no trick. Matsuo had just made the most brutally wrenching decision of his life. He knew an atomic bomb was going to be dropped on Japan one way or another. There was nothing he could do to prevent that. If he held out until death on the location of the Little Boy projectile, it would only be a matter of days before Fat Man was flown in. Either way, Japan lost. But for some reason I could not fathom, he was saving one city to condemn another. Why?

"Now wait a minute, Curtis," Groves said to LeMay. "Just wait a minute. Hiroshima has been an alternate target all along. That's no problem." To Matsuo he said, "But give me a good reason to make the change."

"The Black Winds that have left so much destruction in their wakes—"

"Black Winds?" LeMay said.

"The wilts!" I cried. "He means the wilts!"

They were both interested now. "What about these Black Winds?" Groves said.

"The . . . apparatus"—he seemed to stumble over the word— "for causing them is in Hiroshima."

"And why should you want to tell us that?" LeMay said.

"I have my reasons."

"All right, all right!" LeMay said. "What's the second condition?"

"That I be allowed to return to Hiroshima and bring my son out before the bomb drops."

Naka? I had just remembered that Meiko had told me that Naka was in Hiroshima! My son was in the city where Matsuo wanted the atomic bomb dropped!

LeMay stared at him. "Your son? How do we know you won't pull something tricky?"

"You'll still have his wife here as hostage," I said.

"How do I know he won't send some suicide squad here to blow everything up? Or try one of those wilts? And don't tell me that his wife's life will make one goddamn bit of difference! I know better!"

Matsuo said, "A suicide raid would only make sense if Little Boy were the only atomic bomb. Since it's not, the raid would accomplish nothing."

"How do we know you've even got a kid?"

"He does," I said. "A three-year-old boy. In Hiroshima." LeMay glared at me. I glared back. "And to make sure he doesn't 'pull something tricky,' I'll go to Hiroshima with him!"

LeMay and Groves went outside for another whispered conference. This one was nowhere near as long as last week's. When they reentered, LeMay said simply,

"Okay. It's a deal."

Matsuo said, "I have your word as American officers on both points?"

Groves nodded. "You do."

"Yes, yes!" LeMay said impatiently. "You have my word, too. Now, where's the goddamn projectile?"

Matsuo hesitated. He shut his eyes. His lips drew into a thin, tight, wavering line. For a moment I thought he was going to cry. After what seemed to be an interminable pause, he pointed a trembling finger down at the floorboards of the office and spoke in a barely audible voice.

"Right under here."

SATURDAY, AUGUST 4
HIROSHIMA

Hiroki could not bring himself to look at the bandaged stump of Shimazu's truncated forearm.

"I will survive, Hiroki," his master said, his eyes heavily glazed from the medications he was taking. "The loss of a hand is nothing."

The words did not comfort Hiroki. "It is entirely my fault!" he said, kneeling abjectly before him. He felt miserable, physically and emotionally. "If only I had—"

"'If only' is a fruitless pursuit. It leads nowhere, yields nothing."

"My father is dead because of Matsuo."

"Seppuku may be an act of strength or weakness. In your father's case it was because he could not continue on the path he had been treading. He was afraid to see his journey through to its end."

Hiroki experienced a flash of resentment. How dare anyone imply that Father was a coward! But a moment's thought told him that Shimazu was right. Father had been afraid to go on. His seppuku had been an act of retreat.

"But if not for Matsuo, he would still be alive! And you would still have your hand!" He pounded his fists on the floor. "He is a madman! With his swords and his outmoded beliefs—he is like some old samurai!"

"A true samurai would fight to the death," Shimazu said.

"So will Matsuo!" Hiroki said, his rage a hot spike behind his eyes. "Because the next time I see him, I will kill him!"

"*No!*" Shimazu cried.

Hiroki was stunned by his master's intensity. "Wha—?"

"You must not spill your brother's blood! Not even a drop! *Never!*"

There was so much more to this than mere revulsion at fratricide. Shimazu's eyes had lost their dreamy glaze. He seemed terrified.

"You've said this before, sensei, but after what Matsuo has done, I do not understand."

"It will mean the immediate destruction of the Order."

Hiroki wanted to laugh but the intensity of Shimazu's gaze prevented him. "You must explain this, sensei."

Shimazu took a deep breath. "When you were brought into the temple and underwent the motsu, the Seer said there would be two Okumo boys—"

Matsuo would not be born for years! Hiroki thought.

"—and that should one spill the lifeblood of the other, the Order would be no more."

"But how can that be? Why would my killing Matsuo destroy the Order?"

Shimazu shook his head. "I do not understand it myself, but the Seers have never been wrong. They have been difficult to interpret at times, but this was very clear: '*Should one spill the lifeblood of the other, the Order will be no more.*'"

Hiroki turned the phrases over and over in his mind. There did not seem to be any other way to interpret it.

"I accept the Seer's warning," Hiroki said finally. He saw his master visibly relax. "Yet, Matsuo cannot be allowed to live after what he has done."

"I agree," said Shimazu. The glaze was beginning to creep back into his eyes. "But I do not think we have to look for him. I am sure he will come to us. For that reason, I am directing you to find a nearby *ryokan* and stay there until we have dealt with your brother."

"But sensei—!"

"He will return here for that miserable little zasshu he values so much. I have tripled the guard at night and doubled it during the day. They have been instructed not to apprehend him but to kill on sight. If you are here, we run a terrible risk that you will become involved in the struggle. That might mean the end of us. I want you out of harm's way."

Hiroki bowed. "If that is your wish, sensei."

"It is. We will move the mongrels and all members of the Inner Circles to the upper floor. The scrolls and records will be stored there too for safety. The altered shoten will remain on the ground floor, as will the acolytes and all of the guards. We will be ready for your brother when he returns. He will not last long."

Hiroki bowed again. There was a nightmarish quality about all this—he was actually plotting the death of his own brother. He wondered if he had ever truly loved him as a brother. But that didn't matter now. Matsuo had gone mad—murderously so. And his wild stories about an American atomic bomb threatened the very future of the Empire. It was tragic, but he had to be stopped. He had to die.

TINIAN

Abrams and I entered the office right behind General Groves, who threw himself into a chair and wormed a small white paper bag from his pocket. The worry lines that had grown in his face over the past few days were smoothing out now.

"Well?" LeMay said. He was the only other person in the room. He glanced at Abrams and me with thinly veiled annoyance. Our presence was tolerated, I think, because, besides the scientists and the two Army officers who had arrived aboard the *Indianapolis*, we were the only two other people on the island—perhaps in the world—who knew that the U-235 projectile had been stolen.

"It's all there," Groves sighed. He pulled a piece of chocolate out of the bag and popped it into his mouth. "The projectile is intact."

"Good!" LeMay smiled and rubbed his palms together. "Did the okay come through from Washington?"

Groves nodded. "The President signed the order. We can drop an atomic bomb anytime after today, weather permitting."

"Okay! I've had planes waiting to head for Kyoto to scout the weather."

"Kyoto?" I said. "Sir, I thought the target was changed to Hiroshima."

"Nah! I just told the Jap that to make him cough up the uranium!"

"You gave your word!" I said. I felt Abrams nudging me in the ribs to shut up, but I wasn't going to shut up. "Your word as an American officer!"

LeMay looked at me like I was some sort of bug that had just crawled out of the jungle, but I wasn't backing down.

He said, "That was against my will. That Jap had us over a barrel. I'd have promised him anything."

I looked at Groves. "You promised, too, sir. Doesn't the word of an officer in the United States Army mean anything?"

LeMay started toward me. "That'll be just about enough—"

"He's got a point, Curtis," Groves said.

"For Christ sake, Les! That was blackmail!"

"Still, the word of a U.S. officer should stand for *something*, don't you think?" He smiled quickly. "Besides, as I said, Hiroshima has been a prime alternate all along. It doesn't cost us anything to keep our word."

"It's just the principle that I object to."

I opened my mouth to ask what was so unprincipled about keeping your word but Abrams stopped me with a sharp, anticipatory nudge in the ribs.

"When can we leave for Hiroshima?" I said instead.

"I didn't promise *you* anything!" LeMay said. "How come you're so interested in going with the Jap? You got some sort of deal working with him?"

I couldn't tell him that the "son" we were going to try and save was mine and not Matsuo's. "I want to see him get his kid out, that's all," I said.

"I don't trust you, Slater." He chewed on his cigar and stared at me. He knew I wanted to go but he didn't know why. I had the feeling he would anchor me here in the Marianas out of pure spite. "But I'll make a deal with you. You're so big on keeping your word and such, let's do this: You give me your word of honor as an officer that you never breathe a word of what's gone on here since last Thursday, and you can go."

"You have my word," I said. "As long as I live."

"And you, Abrams? I want the same from you."

Abrams hesitated. "I'll have to explain this little trip from Saipan."

"That can be arranged."

"All right," Abrams said. He was a career man. He would now be owed a favor in a Very High Place. "You have my word."

"So when do we leave for Hiroshima, sir?" I asked again.

"Couldn't be too soon for me," LeMay said. "And get this straight. That bomb will be dropped on schedule, whether you and that Jap have made it out of there or not."

I could tell by his expression that he'd shed no tears if we were caught in the blast.

I said, "Yes, sir. When will that be, sir?"

"Monday morning, if the weather's right. Now, why don't you two take a stroll? General Groves and I have something to discuss."

We saluted and left the office. Abrams went to make arrangements for his trip back to Saipan. I stayed in the area of the generals' office. The MPs had been pulled and so I was on my own. I wandered around by the office window to see if I could hear what LeMay wanted to discuss without Abrams and me. I leaned against the outer wall and listened.

". . . well, probably not," I heard LeMay say. "But if it ever gets out, we'll look like grade-A assholes."

"So what should we do?" Groves said, talking with his mouth full.

"I think Slater and Abrams will keep mum, but that Jap . . . he might try to make a name for himself after the war."

"Ask for his promise in exchange for letting him go."

"You'd trust a Jap's word?" There was a long pause. I could almost see LeMay chewing on his cigar. "Hey! What about this! What if we change the time of the Alamogordo test?"

"I don't get you."

"Look: This Jap says he saw the test, drove a stolen plane back to San Francisco, got on board the *Indianapolis*, and stole the uranium. What time was the test?"

"Oh, around two-thirty in the morning. It was scheduled for two but we had a little delay."

"Fine. We'll change the official record to show that it took place at *five*-thirty in the morning! You didn't have a little delay—you had a *big* delay—three and a half hours worth of delay!"

"I'm not following you, Curtis."

"Don't you see? If the test took place at 5:30, he couldn't have made it to Frisco in time to board the *Indianapolis* before she sailed! If he says he did, he'll look like a liar!"

"I don't know. A lot of people saw that test."

"All military or security, or government-employed scientists, right? You can get them to keep the lid on—national security and all that. If the official record says 5:30 A.M., that's what people will believe.

And if you change your records to show that Hiroshima was the prime target all along, that's another mark against him. He'll look like a nut-case!"

I could hear the growing enthusiasm in Groves' voice. "You know, this could work! This could really work!"

"It *will* work! I guarantee it! We just fudge a few figures and no one will be the wiser!"

I walked away, smiling. They were going to all that trouble when all they had to do was ask Matsuo for his promise. That was the best security on earth.

■   ■   ■

Meiko watched Matsuo as he sat and stared out the barred window of the interrogation room. Frank had arranged for them to be alone in here for a while. Two MPs stood guard outside the door. He had been staring this way an hour. Her heart broke for him. It broke for Naka, too, still a prisoner of the Hidden Face. She knew Matsuo would have brought him back if at all possible. She just prayed that her child was all right, prayed that he did not know the danger he was in. She had her own pain but knew Matsuo was suffering a far greater pain of his own.

"Did I do the right thing, Meiko?" he asked her for the twentieth time.

"You did the only thing you could do!"

"I could have died without giving them the uranium."

"But if they have another bomb, what would that have accomplished?"

He sighed wearily. "Nothing. At least this way, I can be sure that the heart of the Kakureta Kao will be destroyed. With them out of the way, perhaps all their puppets in the government and the military will allow a surrender. Perhaps the destruction of Hiroshima by an atomic bomb will prompt the Emperor finally to take matters into his own hands and tell the soldiers to lay down their arms."

"Then *some* good will come of this," Meiko said, trying to bring a ray of light into the gloom that enveloped him. "If you died and they brought the second bomb in and dropped it on Kyoto, the Kakureta Kao would continue unscathed."

"They're so sure of victory!" Matsuo said, slamming his hand on the table. "It's idiotic! They would keep us in the war through a second and third and fourth atomic bomb, waiting for that final victory!"

"So you did the right thing! Either way a city would die! You forced the Americans to choose the one with a cancer at its center!"

Matsuo nodded absently and stared out the window again. After a while he said, "Why did you tell Frank about Naka?"

Meiko tensed inside. "I felt he had a right to know."

"I suppose he did," Matsuo said, nodding.

"I'm sorry," she said. "I know I should have asked you first, but they wouldn't let us talk."

He turned to her and smiled. "That's all right. I didn't want him along at first. I thought he might slow me up, hamper me, but I've changed my mind."

"Won't it be dangerous?"

"Yes, but with two of us going, there's a better chance of getting Naka out. I think it will work out for the best."

He went back to staring out the window for a long time. His voice, when he finally spoke again, had a faraway quality.

"Meiko, did you know that there are almost a third of a million people living in Hiroshima?"

"I know," Meiko said, trying not to think of all the children she had seen playing in the streets of the doomed city. "I know."

SUNDAY, AUGUST 5

We stood on the edge of the tarmac, Matsuo, Meiko, and I, watching as the plane that would take two of us to Iwo Jima warmed up its engines in the red light of a cloud-streaked sunset. A couple of MPs stood a dozen feet behind us. Matsuo cut an odd figure there, dressed in his Japanese Navy officer uniform. I was in civilian clothes.

"You don't have to come," Matsuo said to me.

I said, "Yeah, I do."

"You heard what your general said: If the weather's good, that bomb gets dropped at eight tomorrow morning no matter what."

I shrugged, trying to look brave. "I don't have much else going for me. Besides, that kid deserves a chance. I'd like to get a look at him."

"Suit yourself," Matsuo said. He suddenly pointed toward the fence fifty yards away. "Isn't that General LeMay?"

I looked. The portly frame and chugging cigar were unmistakable. "Yep. That's him."

"I'd like to speak to him before I go."

"I doubt very—"

"Ask him for me, will you?"

I knew it was useless but I went anyway. To my surprise, LeMay agreed. "Sure! Why not?" he laughed. "Just make sure he doesn't have those swords on him!"

Matsuo's daisho had already been loaded on the plane along with my side arms. I had the MPs bring him over. He stood across the wire fence from LeMay and looked at us.

"I would like to speak to the general alone, please."

LeMay nodded hesitantly and waved the MPs and me off a few feet. I saw Matsuo lean toward LeMay and speak a few words. The general stiffened and straightened away from him. Matsuo backed up a step and bowed. I wouldn't have believed what happened next if I hadn't seen it myself: LeMay raised his right hand and touched his fingers to the visor of his cap. It was a halfhearted salute, but a salute nonetheless.

■　■　■

Meiko waited for Matsuo to return to her after talking to the general. Frank and the MPs were a ways behind him. He took her in his arms and crushed her against him. His voice was a tight whisper in her ear.

"Good-bye, Meiko," she heard him say. "I love you. I've always loved you and never anyone else." He leaned back and looked at her, his eyes searching her face as if memorizing every pore. "I just wanted you to know that before I left."

Her heart was suddenly thudding in her chest. "You . . . you sound as if you're not coming back!"

"I may not. It will be dangerous."

"But you must! Promise me you will!"

"If nothing else, I will get Naka back to you."

"Naka is not enough!" *What is he trying to tell me?* "I want you both!"

"If there is a way, we will both be back here Tuesday morning."

"I can't choose between the two of you!" she said, clinging to him. "I can't!"

"The choice is not yours." He kissed her. "I love you." He crushed her against him and kissed her again. His voice broke. "I love you so much!"

And then he was off and walking toward the plane that would carry him and Frank on the first leg of their journey to Hiroshima. Meiko stood between the two MPs and cried and waved until the plane was airborne and had disappeared into the north. Finally they led her away to her makeshift cell near the central bomb dump.

MONDAY, AUGUST 6
HIROSHIMA

It was late. Our motorized inflatable planed out nicely on the smooth surface of the water. It was as if we had all of Hiroshima Bay to ourselves. We cruised in the dark past the airport and up a canal. Matsuo said it was a branch of the Ota River, but it looked like a canal to me. The boat was unmarked—even to the point of painting over the "Evinrude" on the little outboard motor. I stayed hunkered down under a tarp, watching ahead as we passed under countless bridges, some heavy-duty, some little more than footpaths, black ribbons against a starlit sky marred by only a few puffy clouds.

"Perfect weather for a bombing," I said. Matsuo said nothing. I looked at my watch: 3:15. The *Enola Gay* would be overhead in less than five hours. The sub that had brought us was waiting on the bottom out in Hiroshima Bay. It would surface at 6:00. If we missed the rendezvous, it had orders not to wait. And I didn't expect them to linger. There would be plenty of light by then and I couldn't blame them for not wanting to risk getting depth-charged—especially not now at the tail end of the war.

So we had less than three hours to get Naka free and out into the bay for the pickup. Plenty of time. At least I hoped it was. If we were late, we'd have to do whatever we could to get out of range of the atomic bomb. We only had so much gas, and I doubted we could row it.

About six miles upstream, we stopped along a nondescript stretch of bulkhead and tied the boat to the nearest piling. It took us a few minutes to assemble our gear. As Matsuo shoved his swords through his belt, I strapped on a service .45.

"You can't take that," he said.

"The hell I can't." I didn't have any swords and wouldn't have known how to use them anyway.

"Stealth is the way we must go. Shots will bring the police and awaken all the of the Kakureta Kao."

"If you think I'm going in there unarmed," I told him, "you're nuts." From what he had told me about these Hidden Face monks, I wasn't taking any chances.

"You have a bayonet."

"I know." I wasn't sure I could shoot another man. I *knew* I couldn't stab one. "But I'm taking the gun, too."

He sighed. "Last resort, then. Promise?"

"Okay. Life or death."

We stowed the grappling iron and rope in the sack and were ready to go.

"Wait," Matsuo said. He withdrew his wakizashi from its scabbard and began cutting at his uniform.

"What are you doing?"

"Resigning from the Imperial Navy."

As I watched, he methodically stripped his uniform of every

insignia, every button, every ribbon, hurling each into the water as he cut it off. When he finished he was left with a naked blue tunic.

"I am now ronin," he said.

A masterless samurai. I didn't say so, but to my mind, Matsuo had always been masterless. He had never been, had never wanted to be, completely American; and I knew somehow that no matter how hard Matsuo had tried to be a good Japan man, the Emperor had never completely owned his soul. Now he was cutting himself free from everyone.

I wasn't wearing a uniform I could deface, but I said,

"So am I."

He looked at me sharply and I think he understood. After figuring out what I had about the Pearl Harbor attack, I was feeling sort of isolated and masterless myself.

"Let's go," he said.

He led me a few blocks then stopped on a corner and pointed to a two-story, flat-roofed building across the street.

"Naka is in there."

I stared at the old factory. My son was in there. Christ! My *son!*

"Where is he?"

Matsuo pointed. "Second floor, third window from the right."

"How do we get in?"

■   ■   ■

Matsuo led Frank across the street to a heavily shadowed corner at the rear of the tin factory. He removed the grappling hook from his sack. He had covered its steel shaft and each of its three tines with rubber hose and electrical tape to muffle its impact. He uncoiled the rope and began swinging the hook in small arcs.

"What about the door?" Frank whispered in his ear.

"Guards on the first floor." Even if there were no one on the first floor, he would not want to bring Frank in there. He might see the children in the walled-off area. Matsuo could not bear the shame of having Frank witness what his countrymen—only a few, yes, but still Japanese—had done to those poor children.

Frank pointed to the third window. "But you said Naka's over there."

"There might be a guard in the room with him. This window up here opens into an empty room." *I hope.*

Matsuo remembered from his surveillance of the building last week that the rear corner window above had remained dark all night. He hoped the Kakureta Kao had not found a use for it since then.

"I'll climb up, find Naka, and send him down to you on the rope."

Frank glanced up at the window. "You're going in alone?"

"Somebody has to be out here when I lower Naka. He knows me. You might frighten him."

Frank nodded. "Guess you're right. Let's go."

Matsuo began swinging the hook in a circle. When it had built up enough momentum, he let it fly. It sailed up over the edge of the roof and landed with a dull thud. Not much of a noise, but like a crash of thunder to Matsuo. He held his breath and waited, watching the windows and doors, waiting for someone to look out to see what had caused the noise.

He allowed two minutes to pass. When no one came out to investigate, he began to pull gently on the rope, slowly dragging the grappling iron along the roof until he was sure it was firmly snagged on the coping.

"Steady the rope for me," he told Frank, then began to climb. The rubber-soled canvas shoes he had got from the Americans were silent on the factory wall as he hauled himself up hand over hand. He reached the second-floor window and peered inside. Dark and quiet. He eased himself through and waited. He sensed the walls of the room—it was small. And it was empty of life except for him. He leaned out, signaled to Frank, and pulled the rope up through the window. Frank crouched and disappeared into the shadows. With no telltale rope hanging from roof to ground, chance of accidental discovery from the outside was small.

Now, to find Naka.

He turned on his flashlight. The room was filled with books, papers, scrolls, much like the cubicle downstairs. In fact, some of these looked the same. Here was the ledger of surgical procedures he had seen last week. The flashlight beam fell on the front page of *Yomiuri Shimbun*, a Tokyo newspaper. The words "Attack on the Imperial Palace" caught his eye. It told of the treacherous attempt by a Naval Officer named Matsuo Okumo to penetrate the defenses of the Imperial Palace and assassinate the Emperor. It said he had spent his early years in American and was quite possibly in league with the enemies of Japan. A nationwide search was underway to capture him.

Matsuo smiled at his brother's inventiveness. He was about to toss the paper aside when he spotted a familiar face in the lower-left corner of the page: Father. He read with growing horror how Baron Okumo had committed seppuku upon learning of the disgrace brought upon his name by his younger son.

Matsuo dropped the paper and closed his eyes. Was there no end to this? He stilled the quaking in his chest. It seemed somehow obscene to weep for a single man, even if he was your father, when so many tens of thousands would die here in a few hours. Perhaps Father was the lucky one. He would never know the terrible reality of the atomic bomb, never have to see Japan bow down and surrender. He was beyond all that now. Matsuo would mourn him later. First he had to get Naka out of here and safely away, then he would look for his brother.

He turned off his flashlight, opened the door, and peered out into the hall. A single bulb burned in the ceiling by the door to the stairs, otherwise all was dark and empty. No sign of a guard. They were probably all downstairs guarding the first-floor windows.

The stairwell door gave him an idea—a way to buy himself some extra time later. He stepped out into the hall and crept toward it.

■ ■ ■

Shimazu suddenly realized he was awake. He lay on the futon and wondered why. The stump of his arm was throbbing but not terribly. The pain was less each day. He had even cut back on the analgesics. He still took the healing elixirs, though, and smeared on the ointments to prevent infection.

But why was he awake? Was someone here? Had the younger Okumo returned? He could not tell. He tried to expand his senses, to reach out and search through the building for an interloper, but his reach was gone. The medications had dulled his senses. He pressed his ear to the floor. All was quiet below. The guards would have raised an alarm if Matsuo had broken in, or even attempted to.

Still, he rarely awoke before he wished without a reason. He had a feeling that something of enormous importance was about to take place. He folded his legs under himself and sat on the futon, listening.

■ ■ ■

Matsuo found the door he gauged to be opposite the third window. He stuffed the flashlight into his pocket and placed his hand on the grip of his katana. With a single motion, he opened the door, slipped inside, closed it behind him, and stood there in the dark, listening.

Soft sounds . . . children breathing in peaceful slumber. His left hand found the light switch, flipped it. As the low-wattage bulb flared to life, he tensed, ready to strike at whomever had been placed on guard here.

But there were only children. Eight of them dressed in short pants and shirts, rubbing their eyes and squinting in the light. He spotted Naka immediately and went to him.

"Everyone be quiet," Matsuo whispered to the boys as he hugged Naka's little body against him. "I'm just going to take Naka away for a while. The rest of you go back to sleep."

"Can't we come, too?" one of them said.

"These are my friends," Naka told him. He turned to the boys with obvious pride. "This is my father."

They all rose and bowed.

Matsuo returned the bow. "I'm so very sorry, but I can only take Naka." Their faces fell.

Naka looked up at him with his innocent eyes. "Please? Nobody likes it here."

Matsuo stared at their little round faces and pleading eyes as they clustered in a circle about him. *So young!* Three and four years old! He knew he could not leave them behind.

But the risk!

"We are *sneaking* out of here," he told them. "If you make a noise they will catch you and bring you back. So you *must* be quiet. Is that understood?"

The circle of faces nodded gravely.

"Very good. Just do everything I tell you and we'll all be out of here in a few minutes."

He arranged them in a line, each with a hand on the shoulder of the one in front of him, then turned out the light and led them out into the hall. It was only thirty feet to the storeroom door. He prayed to any god who was awake, to the kami of this old factory, that no one would trip.

It was the longest thirty feet of his life, but they made it without a mishap and he sagged with relief when he was able to close the storeroom door. Then he gathered them all by the window. He knotted the rope around Naka's middle, looped the excess between his legs, and tied the end one last time at the small of his back. It wouldn't be a comfortable harness, but it was a short trip and he couldn't fall out of it. He lifted Naka to the windowsill. He saw Frank come out of the shadows below. The child clung to him.

"Don't be afraid. I'll let you down slow. It'll be fun. But tell that man down there that there are more children coming. Can you say it?"

Naka rolled his eyes—his *Of course I can* look—and said, "More children coming."

Matsuo started to lower him, letting the rope slide slowly over the sill. When it went slack, he looked out. Frank had him in his arms and was waving.

■ ■ ■

Was this Naka? Was this my boy? I hefted him in my arms. *Are you my son?* I wanted to say.

"More children coming," he told me in Japanese.

More? We were only supposed to get one! I set him down on his feet and began to untie the rope. Then I realized it would speed things up if I didn't. I slipped the boy out and left the harness intact. It was immediately sucked up along the wall and into the window above. I pulled out my flashlight and shone it in the little guy's face. Bangs covered his forehead. I pushed them back and looked.

There it was: the Slater Stain. This was my boy! *Mine!* Mine and Meiko's! He was unmistakably Japanese, but I swore I could see my mother somewhere in his face. The emotions that tumbled through me at that moment were indescribable. Christ, I wanted to lift him up and hug him till he couldn't breathe, but another child was coming down the wall and I had to catch him. How many were there? We were stretching our luck here but I didn't care. The important one was out and down and standing beside me.

"Here comes Akio," he told me. "Be careful."

We'd only just met and already this three-year-old was giving me orders. I loved it!

One after the other came down. As the rope went up for the seventh time, I asked my son, "How many more?"

"Just Masakazu is left. Then my father will come."

My father. I could tell by the pride and love Naka put into those two words that Matsuo had indeed been a father to my son. What he had done to me in Hawaii no longer mattered. I *owed* him.

I looked up at the window. Where was that last child?

∎ ∎ ∎

Matsuo looked around the room. Had he miscounted? Where was the eighth? He thought he had sent only seven down, but the room was empty. He glanced out the window. Frank stood below, looking up expectantly. Matsuo counted seven little forms around him. He looked back at the door. It was open.

Cursing silently, Matsuo stepped out into the hall. Finding it empty, he hurried down to the children's room. There was the eighth, the smallest of them all, curled up on his futon, sucking his thumb. He whimpered as Matsuo came in.

"I don't want to go! I'm afraid!"

"What's your name?" Matsuo said softly as he knelt beside him. "Masakazu."

"Come with me, Masakazu," Matsuo said as he gently picked him up. The child was trembling. "I'll take you down myself."

But as he carried the child through the door, he began to cry.

∎ ∎ ∎

Shimazu leaped to his feet. There was a child out in the hall! He pulled open his door and stepped out just in time to see an adult figure carrying a child into the storeroom.

"He's here!" he shouted. *"Guards! He's up here!"*

Doors all up and down the hall and around the corner began to open. The confused babble of the monks filled the air.

Shimazu called to them. "He's here! He's in the storeroom! He's taking the child! He's the one! The one who must be killed!"

Where were the guards? They should be up here by now!

He heard muffled pounding from the end of the hall, from the direction of the stairs. He hurried to the stairwell doors. He saw them moving slightly, almost bulging toward him, heard the shouts and grunts of the guards behind them.

And then he saw the problem: An iron bar had been passed through the door handles and twisted into a tight loop. As long as that was in place, the doors were locked shut. Shimazu pulled on the bar, trying to straighten it, but with only one hand to work with, it was useless.

If only I had both hands!

The other Inner Circle monks were handicapped worse than he. They would have to find a way to kill the younger Okumo without the guards.

■   ■   ■

The last child was coming down, screaming bloody murder all the way. He was scared half to death, I knew, but that didn't make me want to shut him up any less. He was howling to wake the dead! I stood under him with my arms raised, ready to catch him as soon as I could. The sooner the better. Good thing, too, because suddenly I heard Matsuo cry out in pain above. The rope lost all its tension and the kid plummeted toward me. He screamed louder than ever but I caught him and muffled him against my shirt.

I looked up. The rest of the rope was trailing out the empty window.

"Matsuo?" I called as loudly as I dared. "Matsuo!"

■   ■   ■

The blaze of pain took Matsuo so completely by surprise that he released the rope and lurched around, clutching at his thigh.

"Die!" said a voice from the floor. "You are the one! You bear the seeds! *Die!*"

Matsuo looked down and saw a bald, legless monk inching closer and raising a bloody dagger for another stab. Matsuo backed away but the monk came after him.

And he was not alone.

Like a foul tide oozing into the room, they came. Their masks were off, the light from the hall gleamed on their naked scalps, mind-numbing hatred leered in the sickly white of their exposed faces. They came, some limbless, some eyeless or noseless or earless. They came, one with no limbs at all worming his way toward Matsuo on his belly with a knife clutched in his bared teeth.

My childhood dream! Only this is real!

He slid along the wall, trying to escape the sight of their wizened, distorted forms, the scuffing shuffle along the floor as they neared. The one with the bloody knife slashed at him and missed. An eyeless monk inched forward with tiny steps, a knife in one hand, his free hand groping before him.

Matsuo was in a corner now. There was nowhere left to go. The old fear had come back, reaching out of his past, paralyzing him with revulsion. He was a child again, alone in the dark, alone against these monsters.

"He is the one!" they said, pushing each other on. "He is the one who bears the seeds! He is the one who dies!"

And then Matsuo's hand brushed against the grip of his katana and he knew he wasn't alone. He was not a terrified child now. He was a man. A samurai. *Ronin!*

The sword seemed to leap into his hand, its Masamune blade whispering out of its scabbard and striking straight down, splitting the nearest monk's head in two. He began hacking his way through the monks. This was not battle, this was methodical butchery. But then he thought of those mutilated children in the cubicle downstairs and put extra strength behind his strokes.

■   ■   ■

Shimazu was lifting the lid on the chest in his room when he heard the sound of splintering wood. It came from out in the hall. He hurried out to look.

The relentless battering of the door by the guards had finally borne fruit: One of the handles had ripped out of the wood. The guards were now pouring into the hallway.

"In there!" he shouted, pointing to the storeroom. "He's in there! Kill him!"

■   ■   ■

Matsuo had killed enough of the monks. As much as he loathed them, he took no satisfaction in butchering them. His own attacks on their already mutilated bodies only sickened him. When he had cleared enough room, he turned and leaped for the window. He could grab the rope and slide down to the ground before anyone was even sure he was gone.

As he reached out the window for the rope, he heard the crash of the stairwell door and Shimazu's shouts. There was no time to escape. He called down to Frank in English:

"We've got trouble! Take them to the boat! I'll hold them off!"

He couldn't see Frank's face in the dark, but he heard him.

"You're not coming?"

"I'll catch up later! Get going!"

He turned toward the clatter behind him. When he saw the doorway full of armed men—well-armed men with all their limbs and senses—charging toward him, he knew he wasn't going to catch up with Frank and the children. He would have liked a chance to say good-bye to Naka, but as long as Frank got him back to Meiko, that was all that really mattered.

Besides, this wasn't such a bad way to go. He could think of worse.

He lifted his katana into the vertical ready position and leaped into the center of the room to meet the charge of the guards.

■   ■   ■

I brought the children to a halt about a block from the tin factory. I had been herding them along when it struck me like a blow that I'd lived through this before—or something just like it. Matsuo alone back there facing a ferocious gang while I headed the other way. Just like when we were kids.

No. Not again. I'd suffered under the weight of that memory for almost twenty years now, wishing I could go back and change things. I'd be damned if I was going to add another such memory to my list of regrets. I couldn't go back to 1926, but tonight I could damn well make sure Matsuo didn't face all those goons alone.

The trouble was time. My watch said 4:10 and the stars were starting to fade into the sky. Our sub would be rising out of the bay in less than an hour.

"Stay here," I said to the kids. "Right here." I took Naka by the shoulders. "You'll be in charge, Naka. Make sure nobody goes anywhere. Understand?"

He nodded. "Is my father coming soon?"

"I'm going to bring him back with me."

He smiled—the first time I'd ever seen his smile. "We'll stay right here and wait."

I ran full tilt back to the factory. Above, the sound of steel upon steel rang from the window, mixed with grunts and cries of pain. I grabbed the rope and began pulling myself up. It had looked easier when Matsuo did it. My feet kept slipping on the surface of the wall, the rope kept sliding through my hands, burning the palms, but I managed to reach the second floor.

I'll never forget what I saw through that window. There must have been half a dozen fundoshi-clad swordsmen slicing, stabbing, and jabbing at a lone man in a bloodied Imperial Navy uniform. Three of their number lay dead or dying on the floor along with the deformed corpses of what looked like bald-headed monks. Blood was every-where. And dancing about, his sword singing through the air as he wove a web of steel between himself and everybody else, was Matsuo. But he was wounded—there was a cut down his right cheek and bloody tears on both sleeves of his tunic—and I could tell they were closing in.

I hesitated only a second, then pulled out my .45 and began firing through the window. Two guards fell with the first three shots. Matsuo took advantage of the surprise to cut down two more; the rest retreated to the doorway where they crouched. I couldn't read any expressions through their masks, but they looked ready to charge again.

I swung my legs over the windowsill and slid into the room.

"Hiroki!" Matsuo shouted. "Where are you, dear brother?"

"He is not here," said a voice from out in the hall.

The guards backed away and parted ranks to let a tall, thin monk through. He stood alone in the doorway. His bandaged, handless arm gave him away as the head monk Matsuo had told me about.

"Where is he, then?"

"That is none of your concern." He stepped into the room and stared at me, then turned to Matsuo. "I knew you wanted to surrender, but I never dreamed you were in direct league with the Americans!"

"That is none of *your* concern," Matsuo said, mimicking him.

"But do you really believe you can get away with this? Even in this deserted district, word of gunfire will reach the police soon enough. And even if you escape this building, all of Hiroshima will soon be looking for you and those children. You will be captured and they will be returned to us. You will have accomplished nothing."

Matsuo waved his sword at the bodies cluttering the floor around him.

"Nothing?"

Matsuo moved without warning, darting forward to pull the monk further into the room and slam the door shut in a single motion. There was immediate pounding on the door.

"Stay out there and Shimazu will live. Open the door even an inch and he will die!"

What was on his mind? I wanted to get out of here. The dead bodies all around us—two of them my doing—these monks, the smell of blood and slit intestines was turning my stomach.

He placed the tip of his bloody katana against the monk's throat. "Sit."

The monk glared at Matsuo. "I am not afraid to die."

"I'm not going to kill you. Sit, or I'll send your left hand to keep the right company."

The monk sat. Matsuo turned to me and pointed to the window.

"Get the boys moving. I'll be right behind you. I want to have a few words with Shimazu-san before I leave."

I nodded and went down the rope.

. . .

Shimazu could barely contain the frenzied rage exploding through him as he sat amid the bloodied bodies of his brothers of the Order and watched Matsuo stuff scrolls and record books into his sack. This traitor! This dog! He kills us, then he steals our secrets! The grief, the anger inside him . . . so intense . . . made him weak. He could barely speak.

"Why are you taking those?"

"Because without them no one will ever believe any of this ever happened."

"It's futile to try to escape. Why not surrender and get it over with?"

Matsuo looked at him. "Would you take me in trade for the lives of the children?"

Shimazu was immediately suspicious. Was he truly offering himself to the Order? *I will personally flay you alive!* he thought, then calmed himself. He must consider this rationally. The Order still needed a few zasshu for its purposes, but it could afford to let these go. There would be others easily available here in Hiroshima. But more than anything, the Order—and he, Shimazu—needed the younger Okumo eliminated. This night he had already done incalculable damage to the Order by laying waste to all the Inner Circles. The frenzy rose in Shimazu again as he realized that it would take a generation or more for the Order to recover from what this one man had done! There could be no question now—Matsuo Okumo truly bore the seeds of the Order's destruction. He was infinitely dangerous. It was worth anything to remove him before he did more damage, worth anything for the opportunity to personally wring the life from him!

"That is an interesting thought," Shimazu said in his calmest voice. "Very well." He held out his hand. "Give me your sword and there shall be no pursuit of the American and the children."

"Oh, no," Matsuo said, shaking his head. "I don't trust you. I will only surrender to my brother."

A trick? Perhaps. Perhaps not.

"Your brother alone?"

He shrugged. "No. He can have Kempeitai or temple guards with him, I don't care. As long as Hiroki is there, I know I'll get a fair hearing."

Yes, Shimazu thought, feeling the angry throb in his empty wrist and smelling the reek of death around him . . . *Fair and just. Justice will be done.*

"I shall send for him."

"That won't be necessary. I will meet him later this morning. Eight o'clock. On the Aioi Bridge."

"Why there?"

"It is a public place." Matsuo smiled knowingly. "Less chance of treachery."

The younger Okumo's caution allayed some of Shimazu's suspicions. This might work.

"Very well. I shall tell him."

"Tell him eight o'clock or not at all. I won't wait long."

"He shall be there."

"Good."

And then he was at the window and out and gone.

Shimazu sat unmoving amid the bodies of his fellow monks and felt his heart grow heavy within him.

I weep for you, my brothers. You began the approach to the Hidden Face but were cut down before you were blessed with the sight of it. I shall avenge you, my brothers. Tomorrow the agonized cries of the one who did this shall comfort you in your sleep. This I promise you!

He rose and stepped over the bodies to reach the door. He had to wake Hiroki at the inn where he was staying and prepare him for this meeting. Nothing would go wrong this time.

■ ■ ■

I stood in the bobbing rubber boat as Matsuo handed the children down to me one by one. They were happy and excited about going for a boat ride. When only Naka was left, he picked him up and cradled him in his arms and spoke softly to him.

"Not much time, Matsuo," I said, looking at the ever-lightening sky. "Let's get moving."

Still holding Naka, he turned and looked down at me.

"We're not coming," he said in English.

"What?" was all I could manage.

"Naka is staying with me."

I stood there, mute with shock. I hadn't expected anything like this. But the shock gave way to anger almost immediately. I ripped the .45 out of my holster.

"Put my son down!" I said. "You're both coming back to the sub!"

Matsuo smiled and handed Naka down to me. "That's what I wanted to hear, Frank. I told him you were taking him to his mother and I'd catch up later."

All my insides suddenly twisted up into tight little knots.

" 'Later'? There *is* no 'later' for this city!"

He nodded. "I know."

"You're staying? You're really staying?" I supposed I should have seen this coming. "You can't mean that!"

"Help Meiko take good care of him. Take good care of Meiko, too. She loved you once. She can love you again."

I wanted to scream at him, but I kept my voice low. "This is crazy! It proves nothing, accomplishes nothing! It's pointless!"

"Perhaps," he said softly. "But I must be here when that bomb is dropped." He jabbed his thumb back over his shoulder toward the houses and factories. "I must be with them."

"They won't know the difference!"

"*I* will."

I tried another tack—*damn the time!*

"Look: You don't even know for sure that LeMay is going to keep his word! He could have the *Enola Gay* and the bomb on their way to Kyoto right now instead of here! I don't trust him and you shouldn't either!"

"I don't," Matsuo said. "That's why I gave him my solemn word that I would be standing on the Aioi Bridge at 8:00 A.M. this morning."

"Ground zero," I said, feeling a lead weight settle in my stomach. The proximity fuse would detonate the bomb eighteen hundred feet over the Aioi Bridge in the heart of Hiroshima.

He smiled. "I don't think he'll be late."

"Matsuo—"

"Keep those books and scrolls we took from the Order. Someday you may want to tell about what happened here. They'll be your only proof." He squatted and reached down. "Good-bye, Frank."

We shook hands. I wanted to say something, but my throat was locked. I wanted to cry.

He said, "Thank you for coming back for me. It gave me a chance to say good-bye to Naka."

"We're all square now?"

"For my part, yes. And you?"

"For my part, too," I said. I wouldn't let go of his hand. "We're friends again?"

He nodded. "Friends."

The words poured out of me. I couldn't let go of him, couldn't let him stay here. "I haven't got any other friends, Matsuo. None at all. And now after all these years I've got back the best and only friend I ever had and I don't want to lose him!"

He said nothing.

"Goddammit, Matsuo, I should pull out my .45 right now and shoot you in the leg and drag you on board and save your goddamn life!"

"A true friend would never keep another friend from doing what he has to do," he said.

I released his hand.

He untied the mooring ropes, waited till I pull-started the motor, then kicked us out into the gentle current. I opened the throttle to full. We were cutting this awfully close, but we were moving downstream. Hopefully that would give us extra speed.

"Wave to your father," I told Naka in Japanese. I felt as if someone were choking me.

Naka waved. We all waved. Matsuo waved back until he was lost in the shadows and the mist clinging to the water.

■　■　■

"I have a very bad feeling about this," Hiroki said as he sat next to Shimazu in the rear of the car.

The sun hung like a bright ball over Hiroshima Bay, warming the city. Despite the shady interior of the car and a lightweight kimono, Hiroki was sweating profusely. It wasn't that hot yet.

"Matsuo is playing some sort of game with us. It's not in his character to give up without a fight. There's a catch here, a trick of some sort."

"Possibly," Shimazu said from behind his mask. "That's why we have brought the Kempeitai along."

Hiroki glanced ahead at the eight members of the military secret police marching before the car. There were eight more behind. They afforded scant comfort to his already jangled nerves. The howl of the air raid siren shortly after seven o'clock this morning while he was breakfasting at the ryokan had ruined his appetite. Fortunately, only the single advance warning blast had sounded; the intermittent wails signaling a definite attack never came. The all-clear had sounded while Hiroki was waiting for Shimazu to meet him at the ryokan.

Shimazu continued. "But I doubt there's a trick here. It was a trade on your brother's part. Himself for the children. I read in his face a sincere desire to surrender to you."

"He will be armed and I will not."

"That is your greatest protection. I was glad you were safely away at the ryokan last night. He was looking for you, I'm sure to engage you in combat and slay you. But no matter how much hatred there might be between you, he will not attack an unarmed man. If there is one thing I know about your brother, it is that."

Hiroki had to agree with his master. Matsuo considered himself a samurai, like Nagata. He would follow the code. Still, after seeing the carnage his brother had wrought upon the Order last night, he felt as if he were about to stand naked before a runaway killing machine.

■　■　■

As Matsuo approached the Aioi Bridge, he spied a patch of wild daisies growing at the northeast corner. He picked one and carried it to the center of the span where he laid it on the railing.

Not long now, he thought.

He had had a bad moment earlier when the air raid siren had gone off. He thought LeMay had jumped the gun. But when the single plane had made two passes back and forth over the city at about thirty thousand feet, then flown off, he knew it was a weather-scout checking to see if the target was visible.

It was visible, all right. A clear, bright, beautiful morning with the city awakening to greet it. He wished Hiroshima was still asleep. It would have made these moments so much easier for him.

But the place was alive and bustling with activity: children going to school, people going to work or to the market, walking, riding bicycles, pushing carts, pulling rickshas, especially here on the Aioi Bridge. The bridge was a T-shaped structure straddling a branch of the Ota River at a crotch where it subdivided into two more channels. It connected three of Hiroshima's five "islands." People passing by glanced at his torn, bloody uniform and looked away. He wondered what they made of him.

As the sun warmed the bridge, Matsuo looked around at the sea of white walls and black-tiled roofs. Two structures dominated the scene. High on a mound, Hiroshima Castle stood dark and imposing inside its moat to the northeast, with Mount Futaba rising behind it. He could hear the sound of the soldiers in the garrison doing their morning calisthenics in its courtyard. Just southeast of where he stood was the domed Industrial Promotion Hall at the water's edge. Someone was opening a row of windows on the second floor. Rising beyond that was the tower of the radio station. To the west a cadre of youths and older men began their day's work clearing the local fire lanes.

Only minutes left to live—all of us.

He felt as much at odds with the world around him as ever, but inside he was strangely at peace. No longer was he warring with the American within. He had at last come to terms with that part of himself. He knew that what he had done in the past week would have been impossible for someone raised as a pure Japan man.

But what have I done? Did I make the right choice?

He looked at the people passing and wanted to weep, wanted to stop each one and apologize for what was about to happen. But he could not apologize to everyone about to die in this city. That was why he was here on the bridge. Not because he wanted to die. He wanted so very much to live. There were so many things he wanted to do, to see, so many things he would miss—Japan and its spirit, the children he would never have, and Meiko. But he had condemned this city and its people. If not for him, the atomic bomb would be flying somewhere else right now and everyone around him here would go on with their lives through the morning and into the afternoon with only the news of some terrible new weapon destroying a faraway city to disturb them. But their morning was going to end as it was just beginning.

Because of me.

He had done it to ensure the extinction of the Kakureta Kao. He had to share the fate of the innocents of Hiroshima. He owed them that much, at least.

And Hiroki had to share that fate as well.

He glanced at his watch. Almost eight o'clock. Where was Hiroki? The bomb would be overhead at any moment.

And then he saw the marching Kempeitai and the car. They stopped at the edge of the bridge. Hiroki got out. Before he closed the door, Matsuo spotted a masked figure in the backseat.

Shimazu, too. Excellent!

■ ■ ■

We waited on the bottom of the Inland Sea about twenty-five miles out of Hiroshima. I spent the time with Naka and the boys. They were awed and thrilled by the sub. I managed to lose myself in their excited smiles until a quarter to eight when we surfaced.

This is it.

Lookouts were posted on the conning tower and movie cameras were set up on the deck pointing due west toward Hiroshima. Nobody on board knew what was supposed to happen. All they had been told was that a new "superweapon" was going to be used on Hiroshima at 8:00 A.M. and they were to record the event from out here.

Only it wasn't going to happen precisely at eight. The *Enola Gay* was running about fifteen minutes late. The first mate handed me a pair of Polaroid welder's goggles and invited me up to see the "big bang." I left the kids with a couple of seamen who had taken to them and went on deck. I couldn't believe any one bomb could yield a blast as powerful as the one Matsuo had described. I wanted to see this for myself. Besides, I felt I owed it to Matsuo.

As I stood on the deck and waited, I wondered how I was going to explain this to Meiko, and wondered what my future with Naka would be. I wanted to get to know him, be a father to him. He'd need one. And despite all that had happened, I wanted to be near Meiko, too. Maybe we could work something out.

The men on the deck grew quiet. The breeze died. Even the usually noisy gulls, wheeling, dipping, and gliding over the sub, became silent. Nature sensed the coming cataclysm. The only sound was the gentle lap of the Inland Sea against the hull, and the laughter of Naka and the boys playing below.

■ ■ ■

Hiroki swallowed hard as he approached Matsuo. He tightened his hands into fists to hide the trembling of his fingers. At least he had sixteen Kempeitai with ready rifles along with him. He had almost failed to recognize his brother among the people thronging across the bridge. Leaning on the railing in his torn, bloody Navy tunic with all its insignia cut off, a smile on his lacerated, blood-smeared face, and a daisho in his belt, he looked deranged.

"I see you've brought company," Matsuo said, bowing with exaggerated respect. "Welcome to my new office."

He's a madman!

"You—you wanted to surrender?"

"Yes, dear brother."

The Kempeitai raised their weapons and Hiroki could not help flinching back as Matsuo reached for his swords. But he left them in their scabbards as he removed them from his belt. He presented the daisho to Hiroki with both hands, holding it horizontally, scabbards first. Hiroki took the swords and quickly tucked them under his arm. He should have felt safe now, but he did not.

He saw Matsuo glance quickly at his watch and frown.

"I am now your prisoner," he said.

"This is not like you," Hiroki said.

Matsuo shrugged and smiled. "It doesn't matter anymore."

"Very well."

He could not understand his brother's attitude. Something was wrong here. He wanted to be away from Matsuo as soon as possible. Hiroki turned to motion the Kempeitai forward. They would escort Matsuo back to the tin factory where the Order would deal with him.

"Wait," Matsuo said. "Let's talk a minute. About Father."

Hiroki stiffened. "What is there to say? He could not face the disgrace you brought upon him."

"*I* brought? Or *you* brought?" Matsuo was not smiling now. "He wanted me to see the Emperor. You betrayed us both!"

That stung. It was not *his* fault Father had committed seppuku—it was Matsuo's! But he kept his face expressionless. He wanted to keep Matsuo calm until the Kempeitai had led him away to a safe distance.

"I suppose I am partially to blame," he said in a mollifying tone. "I have had the advantage of knowing how this war will end since long before it began."

"Oh, really?" Matsuo said. "How did you know that?"

Hiroki saw him glance at his watch again. *Why does he keep doing that? What's he waiting for?*

"The Seers have predicted it."

Matsuo smiled again. "The Seers are wrong!"

"The Seers are *never* wrong! They predicted the initial victories, the ensuing defeats, the return of the Kuroikaze, and then, in our darkest hour, the blazing light from above, bright as the sun—the Emperor ascendant in final victory!"

His brother's eyes widened. " 'Blazing light from above'? 'Bright as the sun'?" He began to laugh, a harsh sound, tinged with hysteria, totally devoid of humor.

"Do not mock what you cannot comprehend!"

"I'm not mocking your Seers—only your interpretation! I congratulate them! They foresaw the atomic bomb!"

He laughed again, derisively. The sound nudged Hiroki past fury into rage. His hand found the grip of the katana Matsuo had handed him.

"Be silent or I'll cut you down where you stand!"

Matsuo grinned and threw his arms wide. "Yes! Go ahead! Do it!"

Hiroki unsheathed the blade half its length.

■ ■ ■

Shimazu started forward in his seat in the rear of the car as he saw the partially bared blade of the sword gleam in the sun at Hiroki's side.

"*No!*" he cried aloud.

The younger Okumo seemed to be taunting Hiroki, daring him to kill him. *It mustn't happen!*

And then suddenly the gleam died as the blade was thrust back into the scabbard.

Shimazu slumped back in the seat, drenched with perspiration. He tapped the driver on the shoulder.

"Get out and tell the Kempeitai I said to take him into custody now. Immediately!"

■ ■ ■

"I . . . can't," Hiroki said as he slammed the sword back into the scabbard.

Matsuo noted that his brother had to force himself to let go of the grip. He realized with a pang that he should have sent Nagata's daisho back with Frank, to save them for Naka. Now the swords would be melted to slag in the coming atomic fire.

He glanced at his watch again: 8:13.

Where is that plane? Isn't it coming?

He had to keep Hiroki here, keep him talking. And he had to keep his rage and loathing under control. That was the hardest part. Visions of those paralyzed, eyeless, tongueless, mutilated children flashed before him, and he felt murder blow through his heart like a blast of arctic wind. His own brother! How could he have been a party to such a thing?

"Why can't you?" he said, blandly. "Brotherly love?"

"I am forbidden—by another vision."

"Really? How interesting. What did this one say?"

"That if either of us killed the other, the Order would be doomed. But enough of this. It's time to go."

Suddenly Matsuo heard the sound of a plane. He looked up and there was a high-flying B-29, a black speck in the blue. A mile behind it was a second plane, and a mile behind that, a third.

Better late than never, as the Americans say.

Matsuo stepped toward his brother. In a single seamless motion he pulled his katana free, leaving its scabbard still clamped under Hiroki's arm, and drew it back over his right shoulder. This was the moment. There was no turning back.

"This is for the children!" he said.

He put all his strength into the stroke, bringing the blade around in a horizontal arc and severing his brother's head cleanly from his body.

As twin geysers of crimson shot from the stump of Hiroki's neck, Matsuo swung his blade in the faces of the astonished Kempeitai and charged toward the car where Shimazu sat. With luck, he would make it that far before—

—all the world turned intolerably white, intolerably hot.

■ ■ ■

Across twenty-five miles, through the shaded thickness of my welder's goggles, I winced at the brightness of the flash. I saw the gigantic rising fireball, heard the rolling thunder that followed, watched the water ripple with the shock wave. I was staggered by the incalculable fury of the weapon. But not so the other men with me. They were whooping, cheering, and dancing about on the deck. I stood there like a Puritan minister at a wild New Year's Eve party, clenching my jaw as I watched the mushroom cloud that held the ashes of my boyhood friend, Matsuo Okumo.

There was nothing left to say, nothing left to do but begin healing the wounds. I tore the goggles off and pushed through the revelers. I went below to be with my son.

Our son.

October 1985–September 1987
San Francisco
Oahu and Maui
The Jersey Shore

BIBLIOGRAPHY

Credit for the accuracy of the facts and figures used in the novel, the descriptions of people, times, and places that no longer exist, belongs to the authors of the following books. *Black Wind* is much richer as a result of their work.

Bauer, Helen, and Sherwin Carlquist. *Japanese Festivals*. Tokyo: Tuttle, 1974.

Benedict, Ruth. *The Chrysanthemum and the Sword*. New York: Meridian, 1967.

Campbell, J. W. *The Atomic Story*. New York: Henry Holt, 1947.

Costello, John. *The Pacific War 1941–1945*. New York: Quill, 1982.

Fuchida, Mitsuo, and Masatake Okumiya. *Midway*. New York: Ballantine Books, 1958.

Guillain, Robert. *I Saw Tokyo Burning*. New York: Doubleday, 1981.

Hershey, John. *Hiroshima*. New York: Bantam, 1948.

Hoehling, A. A. *December 7, 1941: The Day the Admirals Slept Late*. New York: Zebra Books, 1983.

LeMay, Curtis E. *Mission With LeMay*. New York: Doubleday, 1965.

Lord, Walter. *Day of Infamy*. New York: Bantam, 1958.

Mosley, Leonard. *Hirohito*. Englewood Cliffs: Prentice-Hall, 1966.

Prange, Gordon W. *At Dawn We Slept*. New York: McGraw-Hill, 1981.

Reid, Howard, and Michael Croucher. *The Fighting Arts*. New York: Simon & Schuster, 1983.

Sheehan, Ed. *Days of '41*. Honolulu: Pearl Harbor–Honolulu Branch 46 Fleet Reserve, 1976.

Thomas, Gordon, and Max Morgan Witts. *Enola Gay*. New York: Pocket Books, 1978.

Toland, John. *The Rising Sun*. New York: Random House, 1970.

Varley, H. Paul. *Japanese Culture*. Tokyo: Tuttle, 1974.